THE
FIRST LAW

Book Two

Before They
Are Hanged

Also by Joe Abercrombie:

The Blade Itself

THE
FIRST LAW

Book Two

Before They Are hanged

Joe Abercrombie

This edition published 2007
by BCA
by arrangement with Gollancz
An imprint of the Orion Publishing Group

CN 150574

I

Typeset at The Spartan Press Ltd,
Lymington, Hants

Printed in Great Britain by
Clays Ltd, St Ives plc

The Orion Publishing Group's policy is to use papers that
are natural, renewable and recyclable products and made
from wood grown in sustainable forests. The logging and
manufacturing processes are expected to conform to the
environmental regulations of the country of origin.

For the Four Readers
You know who you are

PART I

'We should forgive our enemies,
but not before they are hanged.'

Heinrich Heine

The Great Leveller

Damn mist. It gets in your eyes, so you can't see no more than a few strides ahead. It gets in your ears, so you can't hear nothing, and when you do you can't tell where it's coming from. It gets up your nose, so you can't smell naught but wet and damp. Damn mist. It's a curse on a scout.

They'd crossed the Whiteflow a few days before, out of the North and into Angland, and the Dogman had been nervy all the way. Scouting out strange land, in the midst of a war that weren't really their business. All the lads were jumpy. Aside from Threetrees, none of 'em had ever been out of the North. Except for Grim maybe. He weren't saying where he'd been.

They'd passed a few farms burned out, a village all empty of people. Union buildings, big and square. They'd seen the tracks of horses and men. Lots of tracks, but never the men themselves. Dogman knew Bethod weren't far away, though, his army spread out across the land, looking for towns to burn, food to steal, people to kill. All manner o' mischief. He'd have scouts everywhere. If he caught Dogman or any of the rest, they'd be back to the mud, and not quickly. Bloody cross and heads on spikes and all the rest of it, Dogman didn't wonder.

If the Union caught 'em they'd be dead too, most likely. It was a war, after all, and folk don't think too clearly in a war. Dogman could hardly expect 'em to waste time telling a friendly Northman from an unfriendly one. Life was fraught with dangers, alright. It was enough to make anyone nervy, and he was a nervy sort at the best of times.

So it was easy to see how the mist might have been salt in the cut, so to speak.

All this creeping around in the murk had got him thirsty, so he picked his way through the greasy brush, over to where he could hear the river chattering. He knelt down at the water's edge. Slimy down there, with rot and dead leaves, but Dogman didn't reckon a little slime would make the difference, he was about as dirty as a man could be already. He scooped up water in his hands and drank. There was a breath of wind down there, out beyond the trees, pushing the mist in close one minute, dragging it out the next. That's when the Dogman saw him.

He was lying on his front, legs in the river, top half up on the bank. They stared at each other a while, both fully shocked and amazed. He'd got a long stick coming out of his back. A broken spear. That's when the Dogman realised he was dead.

He spat the water out and crept over, checking careful all around to make sure no one was waiting to give him a blade in the back. The corpse was a man of about two dozen years. Yellow hair, brown blood on his grey lips. He'd got a padded jacket on, bloated up with wet, the kind a man might wear under a coat of mail. A fighting man, then. A straggler maybe, lost his crew and been picked off. A Union man, no doubt, but he didn't look so different to Dogman or to anyone else, now he was dead. One corpse looks much like another.

'The Great Leveller,' Dogman whispered to himself, since he was in a thoughtful frame of mind. That's what the hillmen call him. Death, that is. He levels all differences. Named Men and nobodies, south or north. He catches everyone in the end, and he treats each man the same.

Seemed like this one had been dead no more 'n a couple of days. That meant whoever killed him might still be close, and that got the Dogman worried. The mist seemed full of sounds now. Might've been a hundred Carls, waiting just out of sight. Might've been no more than the river slapping at its banks. Dogman left the corpse lying and slunk off into the trees, ducking from one trunk to another as they loomed up out of the grey.

He nearly stumbled on another body, half buried in a heap of leaves, lying on his back with his arms spread out. He passed one on his knees, a couple of arrows in his side, face in the dirt, arse in the air. There's no dignity in death, and that's a fact. The Dogman was starting to hurry along, too keen to get back to the others, tell them what he'd seen. Too keen to get away from them corpses.

He'd seen plenty, of course, more than his share, but he'd never quite got comfortable around 'em. It's an easy thing to make a man a carcass. He knew a thousand ways to do it. But once you've done it, there's no going back. One minute he's a man, all full up with hopes, and thoughts, and dreams. A man with friends, and family, and a place where he's from. Next minute he's mud. Made the Dogman think on all the scrapes he'd been in, all the battles and the fights he'd been a part of. Made him think he was lucky still to be breathing. Stupid lucky. Made him think his luck might not last.

He was halfway running now. Careless. Blundering about in the mist like an untried boy. Not taking his time, not sniffing the air, not listening out. A Named Man like him, a scout who'd been all over the North, should've known better, but you can't stay sharp all the time. He never saw it coming.

Something knocked him in the side, hard, ditched him right on his face.

4

He scrambled up but someone kicked him down. Dogman fought, but whoever this bastard was he was fearsome strong. Before he knew it he was down on his back in the dirt, and he'd only himself to blame. Himself, and the corpses, and the mist. A hand grabbed him round his neck, started squeezing his windpipe shut.

'Gurgh,' he croaked, fiddling at the hand, thinking his last moment was on him. Thinking all his hopes were turned to mud. The Great Leveller, come for him at last . . .

Then the fingers stopped squeezing.

'Dogman?' said someone in his ear, 'that you?'

'Gurgh.'

The hand let go his throat and he sucked in a breath. Felt himself pulled up by his coat. 'Shit on it, Dogman! I could ha' killed you!' He knew the voice now, well enough. Black Dow, the bastard. Dogman was half annoyed at being throttled near to dying, half stupid-happy at still being alive. He could hear Dow laughing at him. Hard laughter, like a crow calling. 'You alright?'

'I've had warmer greetings,' croaked Dogman, still doing his best to get the air in.

'Count yourself lucky, I could've given you a colder one. Much colder. I took you for one of Bethod's scouts. Thought you was out over yonder, up the valley.'

'As you can see,' he whispered, 'no. Where's the others at?'

'Up on a hill, above this fucking mist. Taking a look around.'

Dogman nodded back the way he'd come. 'There's corpses over there. Loads of 'em.'

'Loads of 'em is it?' asked Dow, as though he didn't think Dogman knew what a load of corpses looked like. 'Hah!'

'Aye, a good few anyway. Union dead, I reckon. Looks like there was a fight here.'

Black Dow laughed again. 'A fight? You reckon?' Dogman wasn't sure what he meant by that.

'Shit,' he said.

They were standing up on the hill, the five of them. The mist had cleared up, but the Dogman almost wished it hadn't. He saw what Dow had been saying now, well enough. The whole valley was full of dead. They were dotted high up on the slopes, wedged between the rocks, stretched out in the gorse. They were scattered out across the grass in the valley bottom like nails spilled from a sack, twisted and broken on the brown dirt road. They were heaped up beside the river, heaped on the banks in a pile. Arms and legs and broken gear sticking up from the last shreds of mist. They were everywhere. Stuck with arrows, stabbed with swords, hacked with axes. Crows called as they hopped from one meal to the next. It was a good day for the crows. It had been a while since Dogman saw a proper battlefield, and it brought back some sour memories. Horrible sour.

'Shit,' he said again. Couldn't think of aught else to say.

'Reckon the Union were marching up this road.' Threetrees was frowning hard. 'Reckon they were hurrying. Trying to catch Bethod unawares.'

'Seems they weren't scouting too careful,' rumbled Tul Duru. 'Seems like it was Bethod caught them out.'

'Maybe it was misty,' said Dogman, 'like today.'

Threetrees shrugged. 'Maybe. It's the time of year for it. Either way they were on the road, in column, tired from a long day's tramp. Bethod came on 'em from here, and from up there, on the ridge. Arrows first, to break 'em up, then the Carls, coming down from the tall ground, screaming and ready to go. The Union broke quick, I reckon.'

'Real quick,' said Dow.

'And then it was a slaughter. Spread out on the road. Trapped against the water. Nowhere much to run to. Men trying to pull their armour off, men trying to swim the river with their armour on. Packing in and climbing one on top o' the other, with arrows falling down all round. Some of 'em might've got as far as those woods down there, but knowing Bethod he'd have had a few horsemen tucked away, ready to lick the plate.'

'Shit,' said Dogman, feeling more than a bit sick. He'd been on the wrong end of a rout himself, and the memory weren't at all a happy one.

'Neat as good stitching,' said Threetrees. 'You got to give Bethod his due, the bastard. He knows his work, none better.'

'This the end of it then, chief?' asked Dogman. 'Bethod won already?'

Threetrees shook his head, nice and slow. 'There's a lot of Southerners out there. An awful lot. Most of 'em live across the sea. They say there's more of 'em down there than you can count. More men than there are trees in the North. Might take 'em a while to get here, but they'll be coming. This is just the beginning.'

The Dogman looked out at the wet valley, at all them dead men, huddled and sprawled and twisted across the ground, no more 'n food for crows. 'Not much of a beginning for them.'

Dow curled his tongue and spat, as noisy as he could. 'Penned up and slaughtered like a bunch o' sheep! You want to die like that, Threetrees? Eh? You want to side with the likes of these? Fucking Union! They don't know anything about war!'

Threetrees nodded. 'Then I reckon we'll have to teach 'em.'

There was a great press round the gate. There were women, gaunt and hungry-looking. There were children, ragged and dirty. There were men, old and young, stooped under heavy packs or clutching gear. Some had mules, or carts they were pushing, loaded up with all kinds of useless looking stuff. Wooden chairs, tin pots, tools for farming. A lot had nothing at all, besides misery. The Dogman reckoned there was plenty of that to go round.

They were choking up the road with their bodies and their rubbish. They were choking up the air with their pleading and their threatening. Dogman could smell the fear, thick as soup in his nose. All running from Bethod.

They were shouldering each other pretty good, some pushing in, some pushed out, here and there one falling in the mud, all desperate for that gate like it was their mother's tit. But as a crowd, they were going nowhere. Dogman could see spear tips glinting over the heads of the press, could hear hard voices shouting. There were soldiers up ahead, keeping everyone out of the city.

Dogman leaned over to Threetrees. 'Looks like they don't want their own kind,' he whispered. 'You reckon they'll want us, chief?'

'They need us, and that's a fact. We'll talk to 'em, and then we'll see, or you got some better notion?'

'Going home and staying out of it?' muttered Dogman under his breath, but he followed Threetrees into the crowd anyway.

The Southerners all gawped as they stepped on through. There was a little girl among 'em, looked at Dogman as he passed with great staring eyes, clutching some old rag to her. Dogman tried a smile but it had been a long time since he'd dealt with aught but hard men and hard metal, and it can't have come out too pleasing. The girl screamed and ran off, and she wasn't the only one scared. The crowd split open, wary and silent when they saw Dogman and Threetrees coming, even though they'd left their weapons back with the others.

They made it through to the gate alright, only having to give the odd shove to one man or another, just to start him moving. Dogman saw the soldiers now, a dozen of 'em, stood in a line across the gate, each one just the same as the one next door. He'd rarely seen such heavy armour as they had on, great plates from head to toe, polished to a blinding shine, helmets over their faces, stock-still like metal pillars. He wondered how you'd fight one, if you had to. He couldn't imagine an arrow doing much, or a sword even, less it got lucky and found a joint.

'You'd need a pickaxe for that, or something.'

'What?' hissed Threetrees.

'Nothing.' It was plain they had some strange ideas about fighting down in the Union. If wars were won by the shinier side, they'd have had Bethod well licked, the Dogman reckoned. Shame they weren't.

Their chief was sat in the midst of them, behind a little table with some scraps of paper on it, and he was the strangest of the lot. He'd got some jacket on, bright red. An odd sort of cloth for a leader to wear, Dogman thought. You'd have picked him out with an arrow easy enough. He was mighty young for the job an' all. Scarcely had a beard on him yet, though he looked proud enough of himself all the same.

There was a big man in a dirty coat arguing with him. Dogman strained to listen, trying to make sense of their Union words. 'I've five children out here,' the farmer was saying, 'and nothing to feed them with. What do you suggest I do?'

An old man got in first. 'I'm a personal friend of the Lord Governor, I demand you admit me to the—'

The lad didn't let either one finish. 'I don't give a damn who your friends are, and I don't care if you have a hundred children! The city of Ostenhorm is full. Lord Marshal Burr has decreed that only two hundred refugees be admitted each day, and we have already reached our limit for this morning. I suggest you come back tomorrow. Early.'

The two men stood there staring. 'Your limit?' growled the farmer.

'But the Lord Governor—'

'Damn you!' screamed the lad, thumping at the table in a fit. 'Only push me further! I'll let you in alright! I'll have you dragged in, and hung as traitors!'

That was enough for those two, they backed off quick. Dogman was starting to think he should do the same, but Threetrees was already making for the table. The boy scowled up at 'em as though they stank worse than a pair of fresh turds. Dogman wouldn't have been so bothered, except he'd washed specially for the occasion. Hadn't been this clean in months. 'What the hell do you want? We've no need of spies or beggars!'

'Good,' said Threetrees, clear and patient. 'We're neither. My name is Rudd Threetrees. This here is the Dogman. We're come to speak to whoever's in charge. We're come to offer our services to your King.'

'Offer your services?' The lad started to smile. Not a friendly smile at all. 'Dogman, you say? What an interesting name. I can't imagine how he came by it.' He had himself a little snigger at that piece of cleverness, and Dogman could hear chuckles from the others. A right set of arseholes, he reckoned, stitched up tight in their fancy clothes and their shiny armour. A right set of arseholes, but there was nothing to be gained by telling 'em so. It was a good thing they'd left Dow behind. He'd most likely have gutted this fool already, and got them all killed.

The lad leaned forward and spoke real slow, as if to children. 'No Northmen are allowed within the city, not without special permission.'

Seemed that Bethod crossing their borders, slaughtering their armies, making war across their lands weren't special enough. Threetrees ploughed on, but the Dogman reckoned he was ploughing in stony ground, alright. 'We're not asking much. Only food and a place to sleep. There's five of us, each one a Named Man, veterans all.'

'His Majesty is more than well supplied with soldiers. We are a little short of mules however. Perhaps you'd care to carry some supplies for us?'

Threetrees was known for his patience, but there was a limit to it, and Dogman reckoned they were awful close. This prick of a boy had no idea what he was stepping on. He weren't a man to be toyed with, Rudd Threetrees. It was a famous name where they came from. A name to put fear in men, or courage, depending where they stood. There was a limit to his patience alright, but they weren't quite at it yet. Luckily for all concerned.

'Mules, eh?' growled Threetrees. 'Mules can kick. Best make sure one don't kick your head off, boy.' And he turned around and stalked off, down the road the way they came, the scared folks shuffling out the way then crowding back in behind, all shouting at once, pleading with the soldiers why they should be the ones to get let in while the others were left out in the cold.

'That weren't quite the welcome we was hoping for,' Dogman muttered. Threetrees said nothing, just marched away in front, head down. 'What now, chief?'

The old boy shot a grim look over his shoulder. 'You know me. You think I'm taking that fucking answer?' Somehow, the Dogman reckoned not.

Best Laid Plans

It was cold in the hall of the Lord Governor of Angland. The high walls were of plain, cold render, the wide floor was of cold stone flags, the gaping fireplace held nothing but cold ashes. The only decoration was a great tapestry hanging at one end, the golden sun of the Union stitched into it, the crossed hammers of Angland in its centre.

Lord Governor Meed was slumped in a hard chair before a huge, bare table, staring at nothing, his right hand slack around the stem of a wine cup. His face was pale and hollow, his robes of state were crumpled and stained, his thin white hair was in disarray. Major West, born and raised in Angland, had often heard Meed spoken of as a strong leader, a great presence, a tireless champion of the province and its people. He looked a shell of a man now, crushed under the weight of his great chain of office, as empty and cold as his yawning fireplace.

The temperature might have been icy, but the mood was cooler still. Lord Marshal Burr stood in the middle of the floor, feet placed wide apart, big hands clasped white-knuckle tight behind his back. Major West stood at his shoulder, stiff as a log, head lowered, wishing that he had not given up his coat. It was colder in here than outside, if anything, and the weather was bitter, even for autumn.

'Will you take wine, Lord Marshal?' murmured Meed, not even looking up. His voice seemed weak and reedy thin in the great space. West fancied he could almost see the old man's breath smoking.

'No, your Grace. I will not.' Burr was frowning. He had been frowning constantly, as far as West could tell, for the last month or two. The man seemed to have no other expressions. He had a frown for hope, a frown for satisfaction, a frown for surprise. This was a frown of the most intense anger. West shifted nervously from one numb foot to the other, trying to get the blood flowing, wishing he was anywhere but here.

'What about you, Major West?' whispered the Lord Governor. 'Will you take wine?' West opened his mouth to decline, but Burr got in first.

'What happened?' he growled, the hard words grating off the cold walls, echoing in the chilly rafters.

'What happened?' The Lord Governor shook himself, turned his sunken eyes slowly towards Burr, as though seeing him for the first time. 'I lost my sons.' He snatched up his cup with a trembling hand and drained it to the dregs.

West saw Marshal Burr's hands clench tighter still behind his back. 'I am sorry for your loss, your Grace, but I was referring to the broader situation. I am talking of Black Well.'

Meed seemed to flinch at the mere mention of the place. 'There was a battle.'

'There was a massacre!' barked Burr. 'What is your explanation? Did you not receive the King's orders? To raise every soldier you could, to man your defences, to await reinforcements? Under no circumstances to risk battle with Bethod!'

'The King's orders?' The Lord Governor's lip curled. 'The Closed Council's orders, do you mean? I received them. I read them. I considered them.'

'And then?'

'I tore them up.'

West could hear the Lord Marshal breathing hard through his nose. 'You tore . . . them up?'

'For a hundred years, I and my family have governed Angland. When we came here there was nothing.' Meed raised his chin proudly as he spoke, puffing out his chest. 'We tamed the wilderness. We cleared the forests, and laid the roads, and built the farms, and the mines, and the towns that have enriched the whole Union!'

The old man's eyes had brightened considerably. He seemed taller, bolder, stronger. 'The people of this land look first to me for protection, before they look across the sea! Was I to allow these Northmen, these barbarians, these animals to raid across my lands with impunity? To undo the great work of my forefathers? To rob, and burn, and rape, and kill as they pleased? To sit behind my walls while they put Angland to the sword? No, Marshal Burr! Not I! I gathered every man, and I armed them, and I sent them to meet the savages in battle, and my three sons went at their head. What else should I have done?'

'Followed your fucking orders!' screamed Burr at the very top of his voice. West started with shock, the thunderous echoes still ringing in his ears.

Meed twitched, then gaped, then his lip began to quiver. Tears welled up in the old man's eyes and his body sagged again. 'I lost my sons,' he whispered, staring down at the cold floor. 'I lost my sons.'

'I pity your sons, and all those others whose lives were wasted, but I do not pity you. You alone brought this upon yourself.' Burr winced, then swallowed and rubbed at his stomach. He walked slowly to the window and looked out over the cold, grey city. 'You have wasted all your strength, and now I must dilute my own to garrison your towns, your fortresses.

Such survivors as there are from Black Well, and such others as are armed and can fight you will transfer to my command. We will need every man.'

'And me?' murmured Meed, 'I daresay those dogs on the Closed Council are howling for my blood?'

'Let them howl. I need you here. Refugees are coming southwards, fleeing from Bethod, or from the fear of him. Have you looked out of your window lately? Ostenhorm is full of them. They crowd around the walls in their thousands, and this is only the beginning. You will see to their well-being, and their evacuation to Midderland. For thirty years your people have looked to you for protection. They have need of you still.'

Burr turned back into the room. 'You will provide Major West with a list of those units still fit for action. As for the refugees, they are in need of food, and clothing, and shelter. Preparations for their evacuation should begin at once.'

'At once,' whispered Meed. 'At once, of course.'

Burr flashed West a quick glance from under his thick eyebrows, took a deep breath then strode for the door. West looked back as he left. The Lord Governor of Angland still sat hunched in his chair in his empty, freezing hall, head in his hands.

'This is Angland,' said West, gesturing at the great map. He turned to look at the assembly. Few of the officers were showing the slightest interest in what he had to say. Hardly a surprise, but it still rankled.

General Kroy was sitting on the right-hand side of the long table, stiff upright and motionless in his chair. He was tall, gaunt, hard, grey hair cropped close to his angular skull, black uniform simple and spotless. His enormous staff were similarly clipped, shaved, polished, as dour as a bevy of mourners. Opposite, on the left, lounged General Poulder, round-faced, ruddy-skinned, possessed of a tremendous set of moustaches. His great collar, stiff with gold thread, came almost to his large, pink ears. His retinue sat their chairs like saddles, crimson uniforms dripping with braid, top buttons carelessly undone, spatters of mud from the road worn like medals.

On Kroy's side of the room, war was all about cleanliness, self-denial, and strict obedience to the rules. On Poulder's it was a matter of flamboyance and carefully organised hair. Each group glared across the table at the other with haughty contempt, as though only they held the secrets of good soldiering, and the other crowd, try as they might, would never be more than a hindrance.

Either were hindrance enough to West's mind, but neither one was half the obstacle that the third lot presented, clustered around the far end of the table. Their leader was none other than the heir to the throne, Crown Prince Ladisla himself. It was not so much a uniform that he was wearing, as a kind of purple dressing gown with epaulettes. Bedwear with a military motif. The lace on his cuffs alone could have made a good-sized tablecloth, and his staff were little less remarkable in their finery. Some of the richest, most handsome, most elegant, most useless young men in the whole Union were sprawled in their chairs around the Prince. If the measure of a man was the size of his hat, these were great men indeed.

West turned back to the map, his throat uncomfortably dry. He knew what he had to say, he needed only to say it, as clearly as possible, and sit down. Never mind that some of the most senior men in the army were behind him. Not to mention the heir to the throne. Men who West knew despised him. Hated him for his high position and his low birth. For the fact that he had earned his place.

'This is Angland,' said West again, in what he hoped was a voice of calm authority. 'The river Cumnur,' and the end of his stick traced the twisting blue line of the river, 'splits the province into two parts. The southern part is much the smaller, but contains the great majority of the population and almost all the significant towns, including the capital, Ostenhorm. The roads here are reasonably good, the country relatively open. As far as we know, the Northmen have yet to set foot across the river.'

West heard a loud yawning behind him, clearly audible even from the far end of the table. He felt a sudden pang of fury and spun round. Prince Ladisla himself appeared, at least, to be listening attentively. The culprit was one of his staff, the young Lord Smund, a man of impeccable lineage and immense fortune, a little over twenty but with all the talents of a precocious ten-year-old. He was slouched in his chair, staring into space, mouth extravagantly gaping.

It was the most West could do to stop himself leaping over and thrashing the man with his stick. 'Am I boring you?' he hissed.

Smund actually seemed surprised to be picked on. He stared left and right, as though West might have been talking to one of his neighbours. 'What, me? No, no, Major West, not in the least. Boring? No! The River Cumnur splits the province in two, and so forth. Thrilling stuff! Thrilling! I do apologise, really. Late night, last night, you see?'

West did not doubt it. A late night spent drinking and showing off with the rest of the Prince's hangers-on, all so that he could waste everyone's time this morning. Kroy's men might be pedantic, and Poulder's arrogant, but at least they were soldiers. The Prince's staff had no skills whatever, as far as West could see, beyond annoying him, of course. At that, they were all expert. He was almost grinding his teeth with frustration as he turned back to the map.

'The northern part of the province is a different matter,' he growled. 'An unwelcoming expanse of dense forests, trackless bogs, and broken hills, sparsely populated. There are mines, logging camps, villages, as well as several penal colonies operated by the Inquisition, but they are widely scattered. There are only two roads even faintly suitable for large bodies of men or supplies, especially given that winter will soon be upon us.' His stick traced the two dotted lines, running north to south through the woods. 'The western road goes close to the mountains, linking the mining communities. The eastern one follows the coast, more or less. They meet at the fortress of Dunbrec on the Whiteflow, the northern border of Angland. That fortress, as we all know, is already in the hands of the enemy.'

West turned away from the map and sat down, trying to breathe slow and steady, squash down his anger and see off the headache which was already starting to pulse behind his eyes.

'Thank you, Major West,' said Burr as he got to his feet to address the assembly. The room rustled and stirred, only now coming awake. The Lord Marshal strode up and down before the map for a moment, collecting his thoughts. Then he tapped at it with his own stick, a spot well to the north of the Cumnur.

'The village of Black Well. An unremarkable settlement, ten miles or so from the coast road. Little more than a huddle of houses, now entirely deserted. It isn't even marked on the map. A place unworthy of anyone's attention. Except, of course, that it is the site of a recent massacre of our troops by the Northmen.'

'Damn fool Anglanders,' someone muttered.

'They should have waited for us,' said Poulder, with a self-satisfied smirk.

'Indeed they should have,' snapped Burr. 'But they were confident, and why not? Several thousand men, well equipped, with cavalry. Many of them were professional soldiers. Not in the same class as the King's Own perhaps, but trained and determined nonetheless. More than a match for these savages, one would have thought.'

'They put up a good fight though,' interrupted Prince Ladisla, 'eh, Marshal Burr?'

Burr glared down the table. 'A good fight is one you win, your Highness. They were slaughtered. Only those with good horses and very good luck escaped. In addition to the regrettable waste of manpower, there is the loss of equipment and supplies. Considerable quantities of each, with which our enemy is now enriched. Most seriously, perhaps, the defeat has caused panic among the population. The roads our army will depend on are clogged with refugees, convinced that Bethod will come upon their farms, their villages, their homes at any moment. An utter disaster, of course. Perhaps the worst suffered by the Union in recent memory. But disasters are not without their lessons.'

The Lord Marshal planted his big hands firmly on the table and leaned forwards. 'This Bethod is careful, clever, and ruthless. He is well supplied with horse, foot, and archers, and has sufficient organisation to use them together. He has excellent scouts and his forces are highly mobile, probably more so than ours, especially in difficult country, such as that we will face in the northern part of the province. He set a trap for the Anglanders and they fell into it. We must not do the same.'

General Kroy gave a snort of joyless laughter. 'So we should fear these barbarians, Lord Marshal? Would that be your advice?'

'What was it that Stolicus wrote, General Kroy? "Never fear your enemy, but always respect him." I suppose that would be my advice, if I gave any.' Burr frowned across the table. 'But I don't give advice. I give orders.'

Kroy twitched with displeasure at the reprimand, but at least he shut up. For the time being. West knew that he wouldn't stay quiet for long. He never did.

'We must be cautious,' continued Burr, now addressing the room at large, 'but we still have the advantage. We have twelve regiments of the King's Own, at least as many men in levies from the noblemen, and a few Anglanders who avoided the carnage at Black Well. Judging from such reports as we have, we outnumber our enemy by five to one, or more. We have the advantage in equipment, in tactics, in organisation. The Northmen, it seems, are not ignorant of this. Despite their successes, they are remaining north of the Cumnur, content to forage and mount the odd raid. They do not seem keen to come across the river and risk an open battle with us.'

'One can hardly blame 'em, the dirty cowards,' chuckled Poulder, to mutterings of agreement from his own staff. 'Probably regretting they ever crossed the border now!'

'Perhaps,' murmured Burr. 'In any case, they are not coming to us, so we must cross the river and hunt them down. The main body of our army will therefore be split into two parts, the left wing under General Kroy, the right under General Poulder.' The two men eyed each other across the table with the deepest hostility. 'We will push up the eastern road from our camps here at Ostenhorm, spread out beyond the river Cumnur, hoping to locate Bethod's army and bring him to a decisive battle.'

'With the greatest respect,' interrupted General Kroy, in a tone that implied he had none, 'would it not be better to send one half of the army up the western road?'

'The west has little to offer aside from iron, the one thing with which the Northmen are already well supplied. The coast road offers richer pickings, and is closer to their own lines of supply and retreat. Besides, I do not wish our forces to be too thinly spread. We are still guessing at Bethod's strength. If we can bring him to battle, I want to be able to concentrate our forces quickly, and overwhelm him.'

'But, Lord Marshal!' Kroy had the air of a man addressing a senile parent who still, alas, retains the management of their own affairs. 'Surely the western road should not be left unguarded?'

'I was coming to that,' growled Burr, turning back to the map. 'A third detachment, under the command of Crown Prince Ladisla, will dig in behind the Cumnur and stand guard on the western road. It will be their job to make sure the Northmen do not slip around us and gain our rear. They will hold there, south of the river, while our main body splits in two and flushes out the enemy.'

'Of course, my Lord Marshal.' Kroy sat back in his chair with a thunderous sigh, as though he had expected no better but had to try anyway, for everyone's sake, while the officers of his staff tutted and clucked their disapproval for the scheme.

'Well, I find it an excellent plan,' announced Poulder warmly. He smirked across the table at Kroy. 'I am entirely in favour, Lord Marshal. I am at your disposal in any way you should think fit. I shall have my men ready to march within ten days.' His staff nodded and hummed their assent.

'Five would be better,' said Burr.

Poulder's plump face twitched his annoyance, but he quickly mastered himself. 'Five it is, Lord Marshal.' But now it was Kroy's turn to look smug.

Crown Prince Ladisla, meanwhile, was squinting at the map, an expression of puzzlement slowly forming on his well-powdered face. 'Lord Marshal Burr,' he began slowly, 'my detachment is to proceed down the western road to the river, correct?'

'Indeed, your Highness.'

'But we are not to pass beyond the river?'

'Indeed not, your Highness.'

'Our role is to be, then,' and he squinted up at Burr with a hurt expression, 'a purely defensive one?'

'Indeed. Purely defensive.'

Ladisla frowned. 'That sounds a meagre task.' His absurd staff shifted in their seats, grumbled their discontent at an assignment so far beneath their talents.

'A meagre task? Pardon me, your Highness, but not so! Angland is a wide and tangled country. The Northmen may elude us, and if they do it is on you that all our hopes will hang. It will be your task to prevent the enemy from crossing the river and threatening our lines of supply, or, worse yet, marching on Ostenhorm itself.' Burr leaned forward, fixing the Prince with his eye, and shook his fist with great authority. 'You will be our rock, your Highness, our pillar, our foundation! You will be the hinge on which the gate will hang, a gate which will swing shut on these invaders, and drive them out of Angland!'

West was impressed. The Prince's assignment was indeed a meagre one, but the Lord Marshal could have made mucking out the latrines sound like noble work. 'Excellent!' exclaimed Ladisla, the feather on his hat thrashing back and forth. 'The hinge, of course! Capital!'

'Unless there are any further questions then, gentlemen, we have a great deal of work to do.' Burr looked round the half-circle of sulky faces. No one spoke. 'Dismissed.'

Kroy's staff and Poulder's exchanged frosty glances as they hurried to be first out of the room. The two great generals themselves jostled each other in the doorway, which was more than wide enough for both of them, neither wanting to turn his back on the other, or to follow behind him. They turned, bristling, once they had pushed their way out into the corridor.

'General Kroy,' sneered Poulder, with a haughty toss of his head.

'General Poulder,' hissed Kroy, tugging his impeccable uniform smooth. Then they stalked off in opposite directions.

As the last of Prince Ladisla's staff ambled out, holding forth to each other noisily about who had the most expensive armour, West got up to leave himself. He had a hundred tasks to be getting on with, and there was nothing to be gained by waiting. Before he got to the door, though, Lord Marshal Burr began to speak.

'So there's our army, eh, West? I swear, I sometimes feel like a father with a set of squabbling sons, and no wife to help me. Poulder, Kroy, and Ladisla.' He shook his head. 'My three commanders! Every man of them seems to think the purpose of this whole business is his personal aggrandisement. There aren't three bigger heads in the whole Union. It's a wonder we can fit them all in one room.' He gave a sudden burp. 'Damn this indigestion!'

West racked his brains for something positive. 'General Poulder seems obedient, at least, sir.'

Burr snorted. 'Seems, yes, but I trust him even less than Kroy, if that's possible. Kroy, at least, is predictable. He can be depended on to frustrate and oppose me at every turn. Poulder can't be depended on at all. He'll smirk, and flatter, and obey to the tiniest detail, until he sees some advantage to himself, and then he'll turn on me with double the ferocity, you'll see. To keep 'em both happy is impossible.' He squinted and swallowed, rubbing at his gut. 'But as long as we can keep them equally unhappy, we've a chance. The one thing to be thankful for is that they hate each other even more than they do me.'

Burr's frown grew deeper. 'They were both ahead of me in the queue for my job. General Poulder is an old friend of the Arch Lector, you know. Kroy is Chief Justice Marovia's cousin. When the post of Lord Marshal became available, the Closed Council couldn't decide between them. In the end they fixed on me as an unhappy compromise. An oaf from the provinces, eh, West? That's what I am to them. An effective oaf to be sure, but an oaf still. I daresay that if Poulder or Kroy died tomorrow, I'd be replaced the next day by the other. It's hard to imagine a more ludicrous situation for a Lord Marshal, until you add in the Crown Prince, that is.'

West almost winced. How to turn that nightmare into an advantage? 'Prince Ladisla is . . . enthusiastic?' he ventured.

'Where would I be without your optimism?' Burr gave a mirthless chuckle. 'Enthusiastic? He's living in a dream! Pandered to, and coddled, and utterly spoiled his whole life! That boy and the real world are entire strangers to one another!'

'Must he have a separate command, sir?'

The Lord Marshal rubbed at his eyes with his thick fingers. 'Unfortunately, he must. The Closed Council have been most specific on that point. They are concerned that the King is in poor health, and that his heir is seen as an utter fool and wastrel by the public. They hope we might win some great victory here, so they can heap the credit on the Prince. Then they'll ship him back to Adua, glowing with the glamour of the battlefield, ready to become the kind of King the peasants love.'

Burr paused for a moment, and looked down at the floor. 'I've done all I can to keep Ladisla out of trouble. I've put him where I think the Northmen aren't, and with any luck won't ever be. But war is anything but a predictable business. Ladisla might actually be called upon to fight. That's why I need someone to look over his shoulder. Someone with experience in the field. Someone as tenacious and hard-working as his joke of a staff are soft and lazy. Someone who might stop the Prince blundering into trouble.' He looked up from under his heavy brows.

West felt a horrible sinking sensation in his guts. 'Me?'

'I'm afraid so. There's no one I'd rather keep, but the Prince has asked for you personally.'

'For me, sir? But I'm no courtier! I'm not even a nobleman!'

Burr snorted. 'Aside from me, Ladisla is probably the one man in this army who doesn't care whose son you are. He's the heir to the throne! Nobleman or beggar, we're all equally far below him.'

'But why me?'

'Because you're a fighter. First through the breach at Ulrioch and all that. You've seen action, and plenty of it. You've a fighter's reputation, West, and the Prince wants one himself. That's why.' Burr fished a letter from his jacket and handed it across. 'Maybe this will help to sweeten the medicine.'

West broke the seal, unfolded the thick paper, scanned the few lines of neat writing. When he had finished, he read it again, just to be sure. He looked up. 'It's a promotion.'

'I know what it is. I arranged it. Maybe they'll take you a little more seriously with an extra star on your jacket, maybe they won't. Either way, you deserve it.'

'Thank you, sir,' said West numbly.

'What, for the worst job in the army?' Burr laughed, and gave him a fatherly clap on the shoulder. 'You'll be missed, and that's a fact. I'm riding out to inspect the first regiment. A commander should show his face, I've always thought. Care to join me, Colonel?'

Snow was falling by the time they rode out through the city gates. White specks blowing on the wind, melting as soon as they touched the road, the trees, the coat of West's horse, the armour of the guards that followed them.

'Snow,' Burr grumbled over his shoulder. 'Snow already. Isn't that a little early in the year?'

'Very early, sir, but it's cold enough.' West took one hand from his reins to pull his coat tighter round his neck. 'Colder than usual, for the end of autumn.'

'It'll be a damn sight colder up north of the Cumnur, I'll be bound.'

'Yes, sir, and it won't be getting any warmer now.'

'Could be a harsh winter, eh, Colonel?'

'Very likely, sir.' Colonel? Colonel West? The words still seemed strange together, even in his own mind. No one could ever have dreamed a commoner's son would go so far. Himself least of all.

'A long, harsh winter,' Burr was musing. 'We need to catch Bethod quickly. Catch him and put a quick end to him, before we all freeze.' He frowned at the trees as they slipped by, frowned up at the flecks of snow eddying around them, frowned over at West. 'Bad roads, bad ground, bad weather. Not the best situation, eh, Colonel?'

'No, sir,' said West glumly, but it was his own situation that was worrying him.

'Come now, it could be worse. You'll be dug in south of the river, nice and warm. Probably won't see a hair of a Northman all winter. And I hear the Prince and his staff eat pretty well. A damn stretch better than blundering around in the snow with Poulder and Kroy for company.'

'Of course, sir.' But West was less than sure.

Burr glanced over his shoulder at the guards, trotting along at a respectful distance. 'You know, when I was a young man, before I was given the dubious honour of commanding the King's army, I used to love to ride. I'd ride for miles, at the gallop. Made me feel . . . alive. Seems like there's no time for it these days. Briefings, and documents, and sitting at tables, that's all I do. Sometimes, you just want to ride, eh, West?'

'Of course, sir, but now would—'

'Yah!' The Lord Marshal dug his spurs in with a will and his horse bolted down the track, mud flicking up from its hooves. West gaped after him for a moment.

'Damn it,' he whispered. The stubborn old fool would most likely get thrown and break his thick neck. Then where would they be? Prince Ladisla would have to take command. West shivered at the prospect, and kicked his own horse into a gallop. What choice did he have?

The trees flashed past on either side, the road flowed by underneath him. His ears filled with the clattering of hooves, the rattling of harness. The wind rushed in his mouth, stung his eyes. The snow flakes came at him, straight on. West snatched a look over his shoulder. The guards were tangled up with each other, horses jostling, lagging far back down the road.

It was the best he could do to keep up and stay in his saddle at the same time. The last time he'd ridden so hard had been years ago, pounding across a dry plain with a wedge of Gurkish cavalry just behind him. He'd hardly been any more scared then. His hands were gripping the reins painfully tight, his heart was hammering with fear and excitement. He realised that he was smiling. Burr had been right. It did make him feel alive.

The Lord Marshal had slowed, and West reined his own horse in as he drew level. He was laughing now, and he could hear Burr chuckling beside him. He hadn't laughed like that in months. Years maybe, he couldn't remember the last time. Then he noticed something out of the corner of his eye.

He felt a sickening jolt, a crushing pain in his chest. His head snapped forward, the reins were ripped from his hands, everything turned upside down. His horse was gone. He was rolling on the ground, over and over.

He tried to get up and the world lurched. Trees and white sky, a horse's kicking legs, dirt flying. He stumbled and pitched into the road, took a mouthful of mud. Someone helped him up, pulling roughly at his coat, dragging him into the woods.

'No,' he gasped, hardly able to breathe for the pain in his chest. There was no reason to go that way.

A black line between the trees. He staggered forward, bent double, tripping over the tails of his coat, crashing through the undergrowth. A rope across the road, pulled tight as they passed. Someone was half dragging him, half carrying him. His head was spinning, all sense of direction lost. A trap. West fumbled for his sword. It took him a moment to realise that his scabbard was empty.

The Northmen. West felt a stab of terror in his gut. The Northmen had him, and Burr too. Assassins, sent by Bethod to kill them. There was a rushing sound somewhere, out beyond the trees. West struggled to make sense of it. The guards, following down the road. If he could only give them a signal somehow . . .

'Over here . . .' he croaked, pitifully hoarse, before a dirty hand clamped itself over his mouth, dragged him down into the wet undergrowth. He struggled as best he could, but there was no strength in him. He could see the guards flashing by through the trees, no more than a dozen strides away, but he was powerless.

He bit the hand, as hard as he could, but it only gripped tighter, squeezing his jaw, crushing his lips. He could taste blood. His own blood maybe, or blood from the hand. The sound of the guards faded into the woods and was gone, and fear pressed in behind it. The hand let go, gave him a parting shove and he tumbled onto his back.

A face swam into view above him. A hard, gaunt, brutish face, black hair hacked short, teeth bared in an animal scowl, cold, flat eyes, brimful of fury. The face turned and spat on the ground. There was no ear on the other side of it. Just a flap of pink scar, and a hole.

Never in his life had West seen such an evil-looking man. The whole set of him was violence itself. He looked strong enough to tear West in half, and more than willing to do it. There was blood running from a wound in his hand. The wound that West's teeth had made. It dripped from his fingertips onto the forest floor. In his other fist he held a length of smooth wood. West's eyes followed it, horrified. There was a heavy, curved blade at the end, polished bright. An axe.

So this was a Northman. Not the kind who rolled drunk in the gutters of Adua. Not the kind who had come to his father's farm to beg for work. The other kind. The kind his mother had scared him with stories of when he was a child. A man whose work, and whose pastime, and whose purpose, was to kill. West looked from that hard blade to those hard eyes and back, numb with horror. He was finished. He would die here in the cold forest, down in the dirt like a dog.

West dragged himself up by one hand, seized by a sudden impulse to run. He looked over his shoulder, but there was no escape that way. A man was moving through the trees towards them. A big man with a thick beard and a sword over his shoulder, carrying a child in his arms. West blinked, trying to get some sense of scale. It was the biggest man he had ever seen, and the child was Lord Marshal Burr. The giant tossed his burden down on the ground like a bundle of sticks. Burr stared up at him, and burped.

West ground his teeth. Riding off like that, the old fool, what had he been thinking? He'd killed them both with his fucking 'sometimes you just want to ride'. Makes you feel alive? Neither one of them would live out the hour.

He had to fight. Now might be his last chance. Even if he had nothing to fight with. Better to die that way than on his knees in the mud. He tried to dig the anger out. There was no end to it, when he didn't want it. Now there was nothing. Just a desperate helplessness that weighed down every limb.

Some hero. Some fighter. It was the most he could do to keep from pissing himself. He could hit a woman alright. He could throttle his sister half to death. The memory of it still made him choke with shame and revulsion, even with his own death staring him in the face. He had thought he would make it right later. Only now there was no later. This was all there was. He felt tears in his eyes.

21

'Sorry,' he muttered to himself. 'I'm sorry.' He closed his eyes and waited for the end.

'No need for sorry, friend, I reckon he's been bitten harder.'

Another Northman had melted out of the woods, crouching down beside West on his haunches. Lank, matted brown hair hung around his lean face. Quick, dark eyes. Clever eyes. He cracked a wicked grin, anything but reassuring. Two rows of hard, yellow, pointed teeth. 'Sit,' he said, accent so thick that West could scarcely understand him. 'Sit and be still is best.'

A fourth man was standing over him and Burr. A great, broad-chested man, his wrists as thick as West's ankles. There were grey hairs in his beard, in his tangled hair. The leader, it seemed, from the way the others made room for him. He looked down at West, slow and thoughtful, as a man might look at an ant, deciding whether or not to squash it under his boot.

'Which of 'em's Burr, do you think?' he rumbled in Northern.

'I'm Burr,' said West. Had to protect the Lord Marshal. Had to. He clambered up without thinking, but he was still dizzy from the fall, and he had to grab hold of a branch to stop himself falling. 'I'm Burr.'

The old warrior looked him up and down, slow and steady. 'You?' He burst into a peal of laughter, deep and menacing as a storm in the distance. 'I like that! That's nice!' He turned to the evil-looking one. 'See? I thought you said they got no guts, these Southerners?'

'It was brains I said they was short on.' The one-eared man glowered down at West the way a hungry cat looks at a bird. 'And I've yet to see otherwise.'

'I think it's this one.' The leader was looking down at Burr. 'You Burr?' he asked in the common tongue.

The Lord Marshal looked at West, then up at the towering Northmen, then he got slowly to his feet. He straightened and brushed down his uniform, like a man preparing to die with dignity. 'I'm Burr, and I'll not entertain you. If you mean to kill us, you should do it now.' West stayed where he was. Dignity hardly seemed worth the effort now. He could almost feel the axe biting into his head already.

But the Northman with the grey in his beard only smiled. 'I can see how you'd make that mistake, and we're sorry if we've frayed your nerves at all, but we're not here to kill you. We're here to help you.' West struggled to make sense of what he was hearing.

Burr was doing the same. 'To help us?'

'There's plenty in the North who hate Bethod. There's plenty who don't kneel willing, and some who don't kneel at all. That's us. We've a feud with that bastard has been a long time brewing, and we mean to settle it, or die in the trying. We can't fight him alone, but we hear you're fighting him, so we reckoned we'd join you.'

'Join us?'

'We came a long way to do it, and from what we seen on the way you could use the help. But when we got here, your people weren't keen to take us.'

'They was somewhat rude,' said the lean one, squatting next to West.

'They was indeed, Dogman, they was indeed. But we ain't men to back off at a little rudeness. That's when I hit on the notion of talking to you, chief to chief, you might say.'

Burr stared over at West. 'They want to fight with us,' he said. West blinked back, still trying to come to terms with the notion that he might live out the day. The one called Dogman was holding out a sword towards him, hilt first, and grinning. It took West a moment to realise it was his own.

'Thanks,' muttered West as he fumbled with the grip.

'No bother.'

'There's five of us,' the leader was saying, 'all Named Men and veterans. We've fought against Bethod, and we've fought with him, all across the North. We know his style, few better. We can scout, we can fight, we can lay surprises, as you see. We'll not shirk any task worth the doing, and any task that hurts Bethod is worth it to us. What do you say?'

'Well . . . er,' murmured Burr, rubbing his chin with his thumb. 'You plainly are a most . . .' and he looked from one hard, dirty, scarred face to the next '. . . useful set of men. How could I resist an offer so graciously made?'

'Then I better make the introductions. This here is the Dogman.'

'That's me,' growled the lean one with the pointy teeth, flashing his worrying grin again. 'Good to meet.' He grabbed hold of West's hand and squeezed it 'til his knuckles clicked.

Threetrees jerked his thumb sideways at the evil one with the axe and the missing ear. 'This friendly fellow's Black Dow. I'd say he gets better with time, but he don't.' Dow turned and spat on the ground again. 'The big lad is Tul Duru. They call him the Thunderhead. Then there's Harding Grim. He's off out there in the trees, keeping your horses off the road. Not to worry though, he'd have nothing to say.'

'And you?'

'Rudd Threetrees. Leader of this little crew, on account of our previous leader having gone back to the mud.'

'Back to the mud, I see.' Burr took a deep breath. 'Well then. You can report to Colonel West. I'm sure that he can find food and quarters for you, not to mention work.'

'Me?' asked West, sword still dangling from his hand.

'Absolutely.' The Lord Marshal had the tiniest smile at the corner of his mouth. 'Our new allies should fit right in with Prince Ladisla's retinue.' West couldn't decide whether to laugh or cry. Just when he had thought his situation could not be any more difficult, he had five primitives to handle.

Threetrees seemed happy enough with the outcome. 'Good,' he said, slowly nodding his approval. 'That's settled then.'

'Settled,' said the Dogman, his evil smile growing wider still.

The one called Black Dow gave West a long, cold stare.

'Fucking Union,' he growled.

Questions

To Sand dan Glokta, Superior of Dagoska, and for his eyes alone.

You will take ship immediately, and assume command of the Inquisition in the city of Dagoska. You will establish what became of your predecessor, Superior Davoust. You will investigate his suspicion that a conspiracy is afoot, perhaps in the city's ruling council itself. You will examine the members of that council, and uproot any and all disloyalty. Punish treason with scant mercy, but ensure that your evidence is sound. We can afford no further blunders.

Gurkish soldiers already crowd to the peninsula, ready to exploit any weakness. The King's regiments are fully committed in Angland, so you can expect little help should the Gurkish attack. You will therefore ensure that the defences of the city are strong, and that provisions are sufficient to withstand any siege. You will keep me informed of your progress in regular letters. Above all, you will ensure that Dagoska does not, under any circumstances, fall into the hands of the Gurkish.

Do not fail me.

Sult
Arch Lector of his Majesty's Inquisition.

Glokta folded the letter carefully and slipped it back into his pocket, checking once again that the King's writ was safe beside it. *Damn thing.* The big document had been weighing heavily in his coat ever since the Arch Lector passed it to him. He pulled it out and turned it over in his hands, the gold leaf on the big red seal glittering in the harsh sunlight. *A single sheet of paper, yet worth more than gold. Priceless. With this, I speak with the King's own voice. I am the most powerful man in Dagoska, greater even than the Lord Governor himself. All must hear me and obey. As long as I can stay alive, that is.*

The voyage had not been a pleasant one. The ship was small and the Circle Sea had been rough on the way over. Glokta's own cabin was tiny, hot and close as an oven. *An oven swaying wildly all day and all night.* If he had not been trying to eat gruel with the bowl slopping crazily around, he had been vomiting back up those small amounts he had actually managed to swallow. But at least below decks there was no chance of his useless leg giving way and dumping him over the side into the sea. *Yes, the voyage has hardly been pleasant.*

But now the voyage was over. The ship was already slipping up to its mooring in amongst the crowded wharves. The sailors were already struggling with the anchor, throwing ropes on to the dock. Now the gangplank was sliding across from ship to dusty shore.

'Right,' said Practical Severard. 'I'm going to get me a drink.'

'Make it a strong one, but see you catch up with me later. We'll have work to do tomorrow. Lots of work.'

Severard nodded, lanky hair swaying around his thin face. 'Oh, I live to serve.' *I'm not sure what you live for, but I doubt it's that.* He sauntered off, whistling tunelessly, clattered across the plank, down the wharf and off between the dusty brown buildings beyond.

Glokta eyed the narrow length of wood with not a little worry, worked his hand around the handle of his cane, tongued at his empty gums, building himself up to stepping on to it. *An act of selfless heroism indeed.* He wondered for a moment whether he would be wiser to crawl across on his stomach. *It would reduce the chance of a watery death, but it would hardly be appropriate, would it? The city's awe-inspiring Superior of the Inquisition, slithering into his new domain on his belly?*

'Need a hand?' Practical Vitari was looking at him sideways, leaning back on the ship's handrail, red hair sticking up off her head like the spines on a thistle. She seemed to have spent the entire journey basking in the open air like a lizard, quite unmoved by the reeling of the ship, enjoying the crushing heat every bit as much as Glokta despised it. It was hard to judge her expression beneath her black Practical's mask. *But it's a good bet she's smiling. No doubt she's already preparing her first report to the Arch Lector: 'The cripple spent most of the voyage below decks, puking. When we arrived at Dagoska he had to be hoisted ashore with the cargo. Already he has become a laughing stock . . .'*

'Of course not!' snapped Glokta, hobbling up onto the plank as though he took his life in his hands every morning. It wobbled alarmingly as he planted his right foot on it, and he became painfully aware of the grey-green water slapping at the slimy stones of the quay a long drop below him. *Body found floating by the docks . . .*

But in the end he was able to shuffle across without incident, dragging his withered leg behind him. He felt an absurd pang of pride when he made it to the dusty stones of the docks and finally stood on dry land again. *Ridiculous. Anyone would think I'd beaten the Gurkish and saved the city already, rather than hobbled three strides.* To add insult to injury, now that he had become used to the constant lurching of the ship, the stillness of land was making his head spin and his stomach roll, and the rotten salt stink of the baking docks was very far from helping. He forced himself to swallow a mouthful of bitter spit, closed his eyes and turned his face towards the cloudless sky.

Hell, but it's hot. Glokta had forgotten how hot the South could be. Late in the year, and still the sun was blazing down, still he was running with sweat under his long black coat. *The garments of the Inquisition may be excellent for instilling terror in a suspect, but I fear they are poorly suited to a hot climate.*

Practical Frost was even worse off. The hulking albino had covered every exposed inch of his milky skin, even down to black gloves and a wide hat. He peered up at the brilliant sky, pink eyes narrowed with suspicion and misery, broad white face beaded with sweat around his black mask.

Vitari peered sidelong at the pair of them. 'You two really should get out more,' she muttered.

A man in Inquisitor's black was waiting at the end of the wharf, sticking close to the shade of a crumbling wall but still sweating generously. A tall, bony man with bulging eyes, his hooked nose red and peeling from sunburn. *The welcoming committee? Judging by its scale, I am scarcely welcome at all.*

'I am Harker, senior Inquisitor in the city.'

'Until I arrived,' snapped Glokta. 'How many others have you?'

The Inquisitor frowned. 'Four Inquisitors and some twenty Practicals.'

'A small complement, to keep a city of this size free of treason.'

Harker's frown grew more surly yet. 'We've always managed.' *Oh, indeed. Apart from mislaying your Superior, of course.* 'This is your first visit to Dagoska?'

'I have spent some time in the South.' *The best days of my life, and the worst.* 'I was in Gurkhul during the war. I saw Ulrioch.' *In ruins after we burned the city.* 'And I was in Shaffa for two years.' *If you count the Emperor's Prisons. Two years in the boiling heat and the crushing darkness. Two years in hell.* 'But I have never been to Dagoska.'

'Huh,' snorted Harker, unimpressed. 'Your quarters are in the Citadel.' He nodded towards the great rock that loomed up over the city. *Of course they are. In the very highest part of the highest building, no doubt.* 'I'll show you the way. Lord Governor Vurms and his council will be keen to meet their new Superior.' He turned with a look of some bitterness. *Feel you should have got the job yourself, eh? I'm delighted to disappoint you.*

Harker set off into the city at a brisk pace, Practical Frost trudging along beside him, heavy shoulders hunched around his thick neck, sticking to every trace of shade as though the sun were shooting tiny darts at him. Vitari zig-zagged across the dusty street as if it was a dance-floor, peering through windows and down narrow side-streets. Glokta shuffled along doggedly behind, his left leg already starting to burn with the effort.

'The cripple shuffled only three strides into the city before he fell on his face, and had to be carried the rest of the way by stretcher, squealing like a half-slaughtered pig and begging for water, while the very citizens he was sent to terrify watched, dumbstruck . . .'

He curled his lips back and dug his remaining teeth into his empty gums, forced himself to keep pace with the others, the handle of his cane cutting into his palm, his spine giving an agonising click with every step.

'This is the Lower City,' grumbled Harker over his shoulder, 'where the native population are housed.'

A giant, boiling, dusty, stinking slum. The buildings were mean and badly maintained: rickety shacks of one storey, leaning piles of half-baked mud bricks. The people were all dark-skinned, poorly dressed, hungry-looking. A bony woman peered out at them from a doorway. An old man with one leg hobbled past on bent crutches. Down a narrow alley ragged children darted between piles of refuse. The air was heavy with the stink of rot and bad sewers. *Or no sewers at all.* Flies buzzed everywhere. Fat, angry flies. *The only creatures prospering here.*

'If I'd known it was such a charming place,' observed Glokta, 'I'd have come sooner. Seems the Dagoskans have done well from joining the Union, eh?'

Harker did not recognise the irony. 'They have indeed. During the short time the Gurkish controlled the city, they took many of the leading citizens as slaves. Now, under the Union, they are truly free to work and live as they please.'

'Truly free, eh?' *So this is what freedom looks like.* Glokta watched a group of sullen natives crowding round a stall poorly stocked with half-rotten fruit and flyblown offal.

'Well, mostly.' Harker frowned. 'The Inquisition had to weed out a few troublemakers when we first arrived. Then, three years ago, the ungrateful swine mounted a rebellion.' *After we gave them the freedom to live like animals in their own city? Shocking.* 'We got the better of them, of course, but they caused no end of damage. After that they were barred from keeping weapons, or entering the Upper City, where most of the whites live. Since then, things have been quiet. It only goes to show that a firm hand is most effective when it comes to dealing with these primitives.'

'They built some impressive defences, for primitives.'

A high wall cut through the city before them, casting a long shadow over the squalid buildings of the slum. There was a wide pit in front, freshly dug and lined with sharpened stakes. A narrow bridge led across to a tall gate, set between looming towers. The heavy doors were open, but a dozen men stood before them: sweating Union soldiers in steel caps and studded leather coats, harsh sun glinting on their swords and spears.

'A well-guarded gate,' mused Vitari. 'Considering that it's inside the city.'

Harker frowned. 'Since the rebellion, natives have only been allowed within the Upper City if they have a permit.'

'And who holds a permit?' asked Glokta.

'Some skilled craftsmen and so forth, still employed by the Guild of Spicers, but mostly servants who work in the Upper City and the Citadel. Many of the Union citizens who live here have native servants, some have several.'

'Surely the natives are citizens of the Union also?'

Harker curled his lip. 'If you say so, Superior, but they can't be trusted, and that's a fact. They don't think like us.'

'Really?' *If they think at all it will be an improvement on this savage.*

'They're all scum, these browns. Gurkish, Dagoskan, all the same. Killers and thieves, the lot of them. Best thing to do is to push them down and keep them down.' Harker scowled out at the baking slum. 'If a thing smells like shit, and is the colour of shit, the chances are it is shit.' He turned and stalked off across the bridge.

'What a charming and enlightened man,' murmured Vitari. *You read my mind.*

It was a different world beyond the gates. Stately domes, elegant towers, mosaics of coloured glass and pillars of white marble shone in the blazing sun. The streets were wide and clean, the residences well maintained. There were even a few thirsty-looking palms in the neat squares. The people here were sleek, well dressed, and white-skinned. *Aside from a great deal of sunburn.* A few dark faces moved among them, keeping well out of the way, eyes on the ground. *Those lucky enough to be allowed to serve? They must be glad that we in the Union would not tolerate such a thing as slavery.*

Over everything Glokta could hear a rattling din, like a battle in the distance. It grew louder as he dragged his aching leg through the Upper City, and reached a furious pitch as they emerged into a wide square, packed from one edge to the other with a bewildering throng. There were people of Midderland, and Gurkhul, and Styria, narrow-eyed natives of Suljuk, yellow-haired citizens of the Old Empire, bearded Northmen even, far from home.

'Merchants,' grunted Harker. *All the merchants in the world, it looks like.* They crowded round stalls laden with produce, great scales for the weighing of materials, blackboards with chalked-in goods and prices. They bellowed, borrowed and bartered in a multitude of different languages, threw up their hands in strange gestures, shoved and tugged and pointed at one another. They sniffed at boxes of spice and sticks of incense, fingered at bolts of cloth and planks of rare wood, squeezed at fruits, bit at coins, peered through eye-glasses at flashing gemstones. Here and there a native porter stumbled through the crowds, stooped double under a massive load.

'The Spicers take a cut of everything,' muttered Harker, shoving impatiently through the chattering press.

'That must be a great deal,' said Vitari under her breath. *A very great deal, I should imagine. Enough to defy the Gurkish. Enough to keep a whole city prisoner. People will kill for much, much less.*

Glokta grimaced and snarled his way across the square, jolted and barged and painfully shoved at every limping step. It was only when they finally emerged from the crowds at the far side that he realised they were standing in the very shadow of a vast and graceful building, rising arch upon arch, dome upon dome, high over the crowds. Delicate spires at each corner soared into the air, slender and frail.

'Magnificent,' muttered Glokta, stretching out his aching back and squinting up, the pure white stone almost painful to look at in the afternoon glare. 'Seeing this, one could almost believe in God.' *If one didn't know better.*

'Huh,' sneered Harker. 'The natives used to pray here in their thousands, poisoning the air with their damn chanting and superstition, until the rebellion was put down, of course.'

'And now?'

'Superior Davoust declared it off limits to them. Like everything else in the Upper City. Now the Spicers use it as an extension to the marketplace, buying and selling and so on.'

'Huh.' *How very appropriate. A temple to the making of money. Our own little religion.*

'I believe some bank uses part of it for their offices, as well.'

'A bank? Which one?'

'The Spicers run that side of things,' snapped Harker impatiently. 'Valint and something, is it?'

'Balk. Valint and Balk.' *So some old acquaintances are here before me, eh? I should have known. Those bastards are everywhere. Everywhere there's money.* He peered round at the swarming marketplace. *And there's a lot of money here.*

The way grew steeper as they began to climb the great rock, the streets built onto shelves cut out from the dry hillside. Glokta laboured on through the heat, stooped over his cane, biting his lip against the pain in his leg, thirsty as a dog and with sweat leaking out through every pore. Harker made no effort to slow as Glokta toiled along behind him. *And I'll be damned if I'm going to ask him to.*

'Above us is the Citadel.' The Inquisitor waved his hand at the mass of sheer-walled buildings, domes and towers clinging to the very top of the brown rock, high above the city. 'It was once the seat of the native King, but now it serves as Dagoska's administrative centre, and accommodates some of the most important citizens. The Spicers' guildhall is inside, and the city's House of Questions.'

'Quite a view,' murmured Vitari.

Glokta turned and shaded his eyes with his hand. Dagoska was spread out before them, almost an island. The Upper City sloped away, neat grids of neat houses with long, straight roads in between, speckled with yellow palms and wide squares. On the far side of its long, curving wall lay the dusty brown jumble of the slums. Looming over them in the distance, shimmering in the haze, Glokta could see the mighty land walls, blocking the one narrow neck of rock that joined the city to the mainland, the blue sea on one side and the blue harbour on the other. *The strongest defences in the world, so they say. I wonder if we shall be putting that proud boast to the test before too long?*

'Superior Glokta?' Harker cleared his throat. 'The Lord Governor and his council will be waiting.'

'They can wait a little longer, then. I am curious to know what progress you have made in investigating the disappearance of Superior Davoust.' *It would be most unfortunate if the new Superior were to suffer the same fate, after all.*

Harker frowned. 'Well . . . some progress. I have no doubt the natives are responsible. They never stop plotting. Despite the measures Davoust took after the rebellion, many of them still refuse to learn their place.'

'I stand amazed.'

'It is all too true, believe me. Three Dagoskan servants were present in the Superior's chambers on the night he disappeared. I have been questioning them.'

'And what have you discovered?'

'Nothing yet, unfortunately. They have proved exceedingly stubborn.'

'Then let us question them together.'

'Together?' Harker licked his lips. 'I wasn't aware that you would want to question them yourself, Superior.'

'Now you are.'

One would have thought it would be cooler, deep within the rock. But it was every bit as hot as outside in the baking streets, without the mercy of the slightest breeze. The corridor was silent, dead, and stuffy as a tomb. Vitari's torch cast flickering shadows into the corners, and the darkness closed in fast behind them.

Harker paused beside an iron-bound door, mopped fat beads of sweat from his face. 'I must warn you, Superior, it was necessary to be quite . . . firm with them. A firm hand is the best thing, you know.'

'Oh, I can be quite firm myself, when the situation demands it. I am not easily shocked.'

'Good, good.' The key turned in the lock, the door swung open, and a foul smell washed out into the corridor. *A blocked latrine and a rotten rubbish heap rolled into one.* The cell beyond was tiny, windowless, the ceiling almost too low to stand. The heat was crushing, the stench was appalling. It reminded Glokta of another cell. Further south, in Shaffa. Deep beneath the Emperor's palace. *A cell in which I gasped away two years, squealing in the blackness, scratching at the walls, crawling in my own filth.* His eye had begun to twitch, and he wiped it carefully with his finger.

One prisoner lay stretched out, his face to the wall, skin black with bruises, both legs broken. Another hung from the ceiling by his wrists, knees brushing the floor, head hanging limp, back whipped raw. Vitari stooped and prodded at one of them with her finger. 'Dead,' she said simply. She crossed to the other. 'And this one. Dead a good while.'

The flickering light fell across a third prisoner. This one was alive. *Just.* She was chained by hands and feet, face hollow with hunger, lips cracked with thirst, clutching filthy, bloodstained rags to her. Her heels scraped at the floor as she tried to push herself further back into the corner, gibbering faintly in Kantic, one hand across her face to ward off the light. *I remember. The only thing worse than the darkness is when the light comes. The questions always come with it.*

Glokta frowned, his twitching eyes moving from the two broken corpses to the cowering girl, his head spinning from the effort, and the heat, and the stink. 'Well this is very cosy. What have they told you?'

Harker had his hand over his nose and mouth as he stepped reluctantly into the cell, Frost looming just over his shoulder. 'Nothing yet, but I—'

'You'll get nothing from these two, now, that's sure. I hope they signed confessions.'

'Well . . . not exactly. Superior Davoust was never that interested in confessions from the browns, we just, you know . . .'

'You couldn't even keep them alive long enough to confess?'

Harker looked sullen. *Like a child unfairly punished by his schoolmaster.* 'There's still the girl,' he snapped.

Glokta looked down at her, licking at the space where his front teeth used to be. *There is no method here. No purpose. Brutality, for it's own sake. I might almost be sickened, had I eaten anything today.* 'How old is she?'

'Fourteen, perhaps, Superior, but I fail to see the relevance.'

'The relevance, Inquisitor Harker, is that conspiracies are rarely led by fourteen-year-old girls.'

'I thought it best to be thorough.'

'Thorough? Did you even ask them any questions?'

'Well, I—'

Glokta's cane cracked Harker cleanly across the face. The sudden movement caused a stab of agony in Glokta's side, and he stumbled on his weak leg and had to grab at Frost's arm for support. The Inquisitor gave a squeal of pain and shock, tumbled against the wall and slid into the filth on the cell floor.

'You're not an Inquisitor!' hissed Glokta, 'you're a fucking butcher!

Look at the state of this place! And you've killed two of our witnesses! What use are they now, fool?' Glokta leaned forward. 'Unless that was your intention, eh? Perhaps Davoust was killed by a jealous underling? An underling who wanted to silence the witnesses, eh, Harker? Perhaps I should start my investigations with the Inquisition itself!'

Practical Frost loomed over Harker as he struggled to get up, and he shrank back down against the wall, blood starting to dribble from his nose. 'No! No, please! It was an accident! I didn't mean to kill them! I just wanted to know what happened!'

'An accident? You're a traitor or an utter incompetent, and I've no use for either one!' He leaned down even lower, ignoring the pain shooting up his back, his lips curling away to show his toothless smile. 'I understand a firm hand is most effective when dealing with primitives, Inquisitor. You will find there are no firmer hands than mine. Not anywhere. Get this worm out of my sight!'

Frost seized hold of Harker by his coat and hauled him bodily through the filth towards the door. 'Wait!' he wailed, clutching at the door frame, 'please! You can't do this!' His cries faded down the corridor.

Vitari had a faint smile around her eyes, as though she had rather enjoyed the scene. 'What about this mess?'

'Get it cleaned up.' Glokta leaned against the wall, his side still pulsing with pain, wiped sweat from his face with a trembling hand. 'Wash it down. Bury these bodies.'

Vitari nodded towards the one survivor. 'What about her?'

'Give her a bath. Clothes. Food. Let her go.'

'Hardly worth giving her a bath if she's going back to the Lower City.'

She has a point there. 'Alright! She was Davoust's servant, she can be mine. Put her back to work!' he shouted over his shoulder, already hobbling for the door. He had to get out. He could hardly breathe in there.

'I am sorry to disappoint you all, but the walls are far from impregnable, not in their present poor condition . . .' The speaker trailed off as Glokta shuffled through the door into the meeting chamber of Dagoska's ruling council.

It was as unlike the cell below as it was possible for a room to be. *It is, in fact, the most beautiful room I ever saw.* Every inch of wall and ceiling was carved in the most minute detail: geometric patterns of frightening intricacy wound round scenes from Kantic legends in life-size, all painted in glittering gold and silver, vivid red and blue. The floor was a mosaic of wondrous complexity, the long table was inlaid with swirls of dark wood and chips of bright ivory, polished to a high sheen. The tall windows offered a spectacular view over the dusty brown expanse of the city, and the sparkling bay beyond.

The woman who rose to greet Glokta as he entered did not seem out of place in the magnificent surroundings. *Not in the slightest.*

'I am Carlot dan Eider,' she said, smiling easily and holding her hands out to him as though to an old friend, 'Magister of the Guild of Spicers.'

Glokta was impressed, he had to admit. *If only by her stomach. Not even the slightest sign of horror. She greets me as though I were not a disfigured, twitching, twisted ruin. She greets me as though I looked as fine as she does.* She wore a long gown in the style of the South: blue silk, trimmed with silver, it shimmered around her in the cool breeze through the high windows. Jewels of daunting value flashed on her fingers, on her wrists, round her throat. Glokta detected a strange scent as she came closer. *Sweet. Like the spice that has made her so very rich, perhaps.* The effect was far from wasted on him. *I am still a man, after all. Just less so than I used to be.*

'I must apologise for my attire, but Kantic garments are so much more comfortable in the heat. I have become quite accustomed to them during my years here.'

Her apologising for her appearance is like a genius apologising for his stupidity. 'Don't mention it.' Glokta bowed as low as he could, given the uselessness of his leg and the sharp pain in his back. 'Superior Glokta, at your service.'

'We are most glad to have you with us. We have all been greatly concerned since the disappearance of your predecessor, Superior Davoust.' *Some of you, I expect, have been less concerned than others.*

'I hope to shed some light on the matter.'

'We all hope that you will.' She took Glokta's elbow with an effortless confidence. 'Please allow me to make the introductions.'

Glokta refused to be moved. 'Thank you, Magister, but I believe I can make my own.' He shuffled across to the table under his own power, such as it was. 'You must be General Vissbruck, charged with the city's defence.' The General was in his middle forties, running slightly to baldness, sweating abundantly in an elaborate uniform, buttoned all the way to the neck in spite of the heat. *I remember you. You were in Gurkhul, in the war. A Major in the King's Own, and well known for being an ass. It seems you have done well, at least, as asses generally do.*

'A pleasure,' said Vissbruck, scarcely even glancing up from his documents.

'It always is, to renew an old acquaintance.'

'We've met?'

'We fought together in Gurkhul.'

'We did?' A spasm of shock ran over Vissbruck's sweaty face. 'You're . . . *that* Glokta?'

'I am indeed, as you say, *that* Glokta.'

The General blinked. 'Er, well, er . . . how have you been?'

'In very great pain, thank you for asking, but I see that you have

34

prospered, and that is a tremendous consolation.' Vissbruck blinked, but Glokta did not give him time to reply. 'And this must be Lord Governor Vurms. A positive honour, your Grace.'

The old man was a caricature of decrepitude, shrunken into his great robes of state like a withered plum in its furry skin. His hands seemed to shiver even in the heat, his head was shiny bald aside from a few white wisps. He squinted up at Glokta through weak and rheumy eyes.

'What did he say?' The Lord Governor stared about him in confusion. 'Who is this man?'

General Vissbruck leaned across, so close his lips almost brushed the old man's ear. 'Superior Glokta, your Grace! The replacement for Davoust!'

'Glokta? Glokta? Where the hell is Davoust anyway?' No one bothered to reply.

'I am Korsten dan Vurms.' The Lord Governor's son spoke his own name as though it was a magic spell, offered his hand to Glokta as though it was a priceless gift. He was blond-haired and handsome, spread out carelessly in his chair, a well-tanned glow of health about him, as lithe and athletic as his father was ancient and wizened. *I despise him already.*

'I understand that you were once quite the swordsman.' Vurms looked Glokta up and down with a mocking smile. 'I fence myself, and there's really no one here to challenge me. Perhaps we might have a bout?' *I'd love to, you little bastard. If I still had my leg I'd give you a bout of the shits before I was done.*

'I did fence but, alas, I had to give it up. Ill health.' Glokta leered back a toothless smile of his own. 'I daresay I could still give you a few pointers, though, if you're keen to improve.' Vurms frowned at that, but Glokta had already moved on. 'You must be Haddish Kahdia.'

The Haddish was a tall, slender man with a long neck and tired eyes. He wore a simple white robe, a plain white turban wound about his head. *He looks no more prosperous than any of the other natives down in the Lower City, and yet there is a certain dignity about him.*

'I am Kahdia, and I have been chosen by the people of Dagoska to speak for them. But I no longer call myself Haddish. A priest without a temple is no priest at all.'

'Must we still hear about the temple?' whined Vurms.

'I am afraid you must, while I sit on this council.' He looked back at Glokta. 'So there is a new Inquisitor in the city? A new devil. A new bringer of death. Your comings and goings are of no interest to me, torturer.'

Glokta smiled. *Confessing his hatred for the Inquisition without even seeing my instruments. But then his people can hardly be expected to have much love for the Union, they're little better than slaves in their own city. Could he be our traitor?*

Or him? General Vissbruck seemed every inch a loyal military man, a man whose sense of duty was too strong, and whose imagination was too weak, for intrigue. *But few men become Generals without looking to their own profit, without oiling the wheels, without keeping some secrets.*

Or him? Korsten dan Vurms was sneering at Glokta as though at a badly-cleaned latrine he had to use. *I've seen his like a thousand times, the arrogant whelp. The Lord Governor's own son, perhaps, but it's plain enough he has no loyalty to anyone beyond himself.*

Or her? Magister Eider was all comely smiles and politeness, but her eyes were hard as diamonds. *Judging me like a merchant judges an ignorant customer. There's more to her than fine manners and a weakness for foreign tailoring. Far more.*

Or him? Even the old Lord Governor seemed suspect now. *Are his eyes and ears as bad as he claims? Or is there a hint of play-acting in his squinting, his demands to know what's going on? Does he already know more than anyone?*

Glokta turned and limped towards the window, leaned against the beautifully carved pillar beside it and peered out at the astonishing view, the evening sun still warm on his face. He could already feel the council members shifting restlessly, keen to be rid of him. *I wonder how long before they order the cripple out of their beautiful room? I do not trust a one of them. Not a one.* He smirked to himself. *Precisely as it should be.*

It was Korsten dan Vurms who lost patience first. 'Superior Glokta,' he snapped. 'We appreciate your thoroughness in presenting yourself here, but I am sure you have urgent business to attend to. We certainly do.'

'Of course.' Glokta hobbled back to the table with exaggerated slowness as if he were leaving the room. Then he slid out a chair and lowered himself into it, wincing at the pain in his leg. 'I will try to keep my comments to a minimum, at least to begin with.'

'What?' said Vissbruck.

'Who is this fellow?' demanded the Lord Governor, craning forwards and squinting with his weak eyes. 'What is going on here?'

His son was more direct. 'What the hell do you think you're doing?' he demanded. 'Are you mad?' Haddish Kahdia began to chuckle softly to himself. At Glokta, or at the rage of the others, it was impossible to say.

'Please, gentlemen, please.' Magister Eider spoke softly, patiently. 'The Superior has only just arrived, and is perhaps ignorant of how we conduct business in Dagoska. You must understand that your predecessor did not attend these meetings. We have been governing this city successfully for several years, and—'

'The Closed Council disagrees.' Glokta held up the King's writ between two fingers. He let the everyone look at it for a moment, making sure they could see the heavy seal of red and gold, then he flicked it across the table.

The others stared over suspiciously as Carlot dan Eider picked up the document, unfolded it and started to read. She frowned, then raised one well-plucked eyebrow. 'It seems that we are the ignorant ones.'

'Let me see that!' Korsten dan Vurms snatched the paper out of her hands and started to read it. 'It can't be,' he muttered. 'It can't be!'

'I'm afraid that it is.' Glokta treated the assembly to his toothless leer. 'Arch Lector Sult is most concerned. He has asked me to look into the disappearance of Superior Davoust, and also to examine the city's defences. To examine them carefully, and to ensure that the Gurkish stay on the other side of them. He has instructed me to use whatever measures I deem necessary.' He gave a significant pause. 'Whatever . . . measures.'

'What is that?' grumbled the Lord Governor. 'I demand to know what is going on!'

Vissbruck had the paper now. 'The King's writ,' he breathed, mopping his sweaty forehead on the back of his sleeve, 'signed by all twelve chairs on the Closed Council. It grants full powers!' He laid it down gently on the inlaid table-top, as though worried it might suddenly burst into flames. 'This is—'

'We all know what it is.' Magister Eider was watching Glokta thoughtfully, one fingertip stroking her smooth cheek. *Like a merchant who suddenly becomes aware that her supposedly ignorant customer has fleeced her, and not the other way around.* 'It seems Superior Glokta will be taking charge.'

'I would hardly say taking charge, but I will be attending all further meetings of this council. You should consider that the first of a very great number of changes.' Glokta gave a comfortable sigh as he settled into his beautiful chair, stretching out his aching leg, resting his aching back. *Almost comfortable.* He glanced across the frowning faces of the city's ruling council. *Except, of course, that one of these charming people is most likely a dangerous traitor. A traitor who has already arranged the disappearance of one Superior, and may very well now be considering the removal of a second . . .*

Glokta cleared his throat. 'Now then, General Vissbruck, what were you saying as I arrived? Something about the walls?'

The Wounds of the Past

'The mistakes of old,' intoned Bayaz with the highest pomposity, 'should be made only once. Any worthwhile education, therefore, must be founded on a sound understanding of history.'

Jezal gave vent to a ragged sigh. Why on earth the old man had undertaken to enlighten him was past his understanding. The towering self-interest, perhaps, of the mildly senile was to blame. In any case, Jezal was unshakable in his determination not to learn a thing.

'. . . yes, history,' the Magus was musing, 'there is a lot of history in Calcis . . .'

Jezal glanced around him, unimpressed in the extreme. If history was nothing more than age, then Calcis, ancient city-port of the Old Empire, was plainly rich with it. If history went further – to grandeur, to glory, to something which stirred the blood – then it was conspicuously absent.

Doubtless the city had been carefully laid out, with wide, straight streets positioned to give the traveller magnificent views. But what might once have been proud civic vistas, the long centuries had reduced to panoramas of decay. Everywhere there were abandoned houses, empty windows and doorways gazing sadly out into the rutted squares. They passed side-streets choked with weeds, with rubble, with rotting timbers. Half the bridges across the sluggish river had collapsed and never been repaired; half the trees in the broad avenues were dead and withered, throttled by ivy.

There was none of the sheer life that crammed Adua, from the docks, to the slums, to the Agriont itself. Jezal's home might have sometimes seemed swarming, squabbling, bursting at the seams with humanity, but, as he watched the few threadbare citizens of Calcis traipsing through their rotting relic of a city, he was in no doubt which atmosphere he preferred.

'. . . you will have many opportunities to improve yourself on this journey of ours, my young friend, and I suggest you take advantage of them. Master Ninefingers in particular, is well worthy of study. I feel you could learn a great deal from him . . .'

Jezal almost gasped with disbelief. 'From that ape?'

'That ape, as you say, is famous throughout the North. The Bloody-Nine, they call him there. A name to fill strong men with fear or courage, depending on which side they stand. A fighter and tactician of deep cunning and matchless experience. Above all, he has learned the trick of saying a great deal less than he knows.' Bayaz glanced across at him. 'The precise opposite of some people I could name.'

Jezal frowned and hunched his shoulders. He could see nothing to be learned from Ninefingers apart, perhaps, from how to eat with one's hands and go days without washing.

'The great forum,' muttered Bayaz, as they passed into a wide, open space. 'The throbbing heart of the city.' Even he sounded disappointed. 'Here the citizens of Calcis would come to buy and sell, to watch spectacles and hear cases at law, to argue philosophy and politics. In the Old Time it would have been crammed shoulder to shoulder here, until late in the evening.'

There was ample space now. The vast paved area could easily have accommodated fifty times the sorry crowd that was gathered there. The grand statues round the edge were stained and broken, their dirty pedestals leaning at all angles. A few desultory stalls were laid out in the centre, crowded together like sheep in cold weather.

'A shadow of its former glory. Still,' and Bayaz pointed out the dishevelled sculptures, 'these are the only occupants that need interest us today.'

'Really, and they are?'

'Emperors of the distant past, my boy, each with a tale to tell.'

Jezal groaned inwardly. He had nothing more than a passing interest in the history of his own country, let alone that of some decaying backwater in the far-flung west of the World. 'There's a lot of them,' he muttered.

'And these are by no means all. The history of the Old Empire stretches back for many centuries.'

'Must be why they call it old.'

'Don't try to be clever with me, Captain Luthar, you have not the equipment. While your forebears in the Union were running around naked, communicating by gestures and worshipping mud, here my master Juvens was guiding the birth of a mighty nation, a nation that in scale and wealth, in knowledge and grandeur, has never been equalled. Adua, Talins, Shaffa, they are but shadows of the wondrous cities that once thrived in the valley of the great river Aos. This is the cradle of civilisation, my young friend.'

Jezal glanced round him at the sorry statues, the rotting trees, the grimy, the forlorn, the faded streets. 'What went wrong?'

'The failure of something great is never a simple matter, but, where there is success and glory, there must also be failure and shame. Where there are both, jealousies must simmer. Envy and pride led by slow degrees to squabbles, then to feuds, then to wars. Two great wars that ended in terrible disasters.' He stepped smartly towards the nearest of the statues. 'But disasters are not without their lessons, my boy.'

Jezal grimaced. He needed more lessons like he needed a dose of the cock-rot, and he in no sense felt himself to be anyone's boy, but the old man was not in the least put off by his reluctance.

'A great ruler must be ruthless,' intoned Bayaz. 'When he perceives a threat against his person or authority, he must move swiftly, and with no space left for regret. For an example, we need look no further than the Emperor Shilla.' He gazed up at the marble above them, its features all but entirely worn away by the weather. 'When he suspected his chamberlain of harbouring pretensions to the throne, he ordered him put to death on the instant, his wife and all his children strangled, his great mansion in Aulcus levelled to the ground.' Bayaz shrugged. 'All without the slightest shred of proof. An excessive and a brutal act, but better to act with too much force than too little. Better to be held in fear, than in contempt. Shilla knew this. There is no place for sentiment in politics, do you see?'

'I see that wherever I turn in life there's always some fucking old dunce trying to give me a lecture.' That was what Jezal thought, but he was not about to say it. The memory of a Practical of the Inquisition bursting apart before his very eyes was still horribly fresh in his mind. The squelching sound of the flesh. The feeling of spots of hot blood pattering across his face. He swallowed and looked down at his shoes.

'I see,' he muttered.

Bayaz' voice droned on. 'Not that a great King need be a tyrant, of course! To gain the love of the common man should always be a ruler's first aim, for it can be won with small gestures, and yet can last a lifetime.'

Jezal was not about to let that pass, however dangerous the old man might be. It was clear that Bayaz had no practical experience in the arena of politics. 'What use is the love of commoners? The nobles have the money, the soldiers, the power.'

Bayaz rolled his eyes at the clouds. 'The words of a child, easily tricked by flim-flam and quick hands. Where does the nobles' money come from, but from taxes on the peasants in the fields? Who are their soldiers, but the sons and husbands of common folk? What gives the lords their power? Only the compliance of their vassals, nothing more. When the peasantry become truly dissatisfied, that power can vanish with terrifying speed. Take the case of the Emperor Dantus.' He gestured up at one of the many statues, one arm broken off at the shoulder, the other holding out a handful of scum in which a rich bloom of moss had taken hold. The loss of his nose, leaving a grimy crater, had left the Emperor Dantus with an expression of eternal embarrassed bewilderment, like a man surprised whilst on the latrine.

'No ruler has ever been more loved by his people,' said Bayaz. 'He greeted every man as his equal, always gave half his revenues to the poor. But the nobles conspired against him, fixed on one of their number to replace him, and threw the Emperor into prison while they seized the throne.'

'Did they really?' grunted Jezal, staring off across the half-empty square.

'But the people would not abandon their beloved monarch. They rose from their homes and rioted, and would not be subdued. Some of the conspirators were dragged from their palaces and hung in the streets, the others were cowed, and returned Dantus to his throne. So you see, my lad, that the love of the people is a ruler's surest shield against danger.'

Jezal sighed. 'Give me the support of the lords every time.'

'Hah. Their love is costly, and fickle as the changing wind. Have you not stood in the Lords' Round, Captain Luthar, while the Open Council is in session?' Jezal frowned. Perhaps there was some grain of truth in the old man's babble. 'Hah. Such is the love of nobles. The best that one can do is to divide them and work on their jealousies, make them compete for small favours, claim the credit for their successes, and most of all ensure that no one of them should grow too powerful, and rise to challenge one's own majesty.'

'Who is this?' One statue stood noticeably higher than the others. An impressive-seeming man in late middle-age with a thick beard and curling hair. His face was handsome but there was a grim set to his mouth, a proud and wrathful wrinkling of his brow. A man not to be fooled with.

'That is my master, Juvens. Not an Emperor, but the first and last adviser to many. He built the Empire, yet he was also the principal in its destruction. A great man, in so many ways, but great men have great faults.' Bayaz turned his worn staff thoughtfully round in his hand. 'One should learn the lessons of history. The mistakes of the past need only be made once.' He paused for a moment. 'Unless there are no other choices.'

Jezal rubbed his eyes and stared across the forum. The Crown Prince Ladisla, perhaps, might have benefited from such a lecture, but Jezal rather doubted it. Was this why he had been torn away from his friends, from his hard-earned chance at glory and advancement? To listen to the dusty musings of some strange, bald wanderer?

He frowned. There were a group of three soldiers moving towards them across the square. At first he watched them, uninterested. Then he realised they were looking right at him and Bayaz, and moving directly towards them. Now he saw another group of three, and another, coming from different directions.

Jezal's throat felt tight. Their armour and weapons, though of an antique design, looked worryingly effective and well-used. Fencing was one thing. Actual fighting, with its possibilities for serious wounding and death, was quite another. It was not cowardice, surely, to feel worried, not with nine armed men very clearly approaching them, and no possible route of escape.

Bayaz had noticed them too. 'A welcome appears to have been prepared.'

The nine closed in, faces hard, weapons firmly gripped. Jezal squared his shoulders and did his best to look fearsome while meeting nobody's eye, and keeping his hands well away from the hilts of his steels. He had no wish whatsoever for someone to get nervous, and stab him on a whim.

'You are Bayaz,' said their leader, a heavy-set man with a grubby red plume on his helmet.

'Is that a question?'

'No. Our master, the Imperial Legate, Salamo Narba, governor of Calcis, invites you to an audience.'

'Does he indeed?' Bayaz glanced around at the party of soldiers, then raised an eyebrow at Jezal. 'I suppose it would be rude of us to refuse, when the Legate has gone to all the trouble of organising an honour guard. Lead the way.'

Say one thing for Logen Ninefingers, say he's in pain. He dragged himself over the broken cobblestones, wincing every time his weight went onto his bad ankle – limping, gasping, waving his arms to keep his balance.

Brother Longfoot grinned over his shoulder at this sorry display. 'How are your injuries progressing, my friend?

'Painfully,' grunted Logen, through gritted teeth.

'And yet, I suspect, you have endured worse.'

'Huh.' The wounds of the past were many. He'd spent most of his life in some amount of pain, healing too slowly from one beating or another. He remembered the first real wound he'd ever taken, a cut down his face that the Shanka had given him. Fifteen years old, lean and smooth-skinned and the girls in the village had still liked to look at him. He touched his thumb to his face and felt the old scar. He remembered his father pressing the bandage to his cheek in the smoky hall, the stinging of it, wanting to shout but biting his lip. A man stays silent.

When he can. Logen remembered lying on his face in a stinking tent with the cold rain drumming on the canvas, biting on a piece of leather to keep from screaming, coughing it out and screaming anyway while they dug in his back for an arrow-head that hadn't come out with the shaft. It had taken them a day of looking to find the bastard thing. Logen winced and wriggled his tingling shoulder blades at that memory. He hadn't been able to talk for a week from all that screaming.

Hadn't been able to talk for more than a week after the duel with Threetrees. Or walk, or eat, or see hardly. Broken jaw, broken cheek, ribs broken past counting. Bones smashed until he was no more than aching, crying, self-pitying goo, mewling like an infant at every movement of his stretcher, fed by an old woman with a spoon and grateful to get it.

There were plenty more memories, all crowding in and cutting at him. The stump of his finger after the battle at Carleon, burning and burning and making him crazy. Waking up sudden after a day out cold, when he got knocked on the head up in the hills. Pissing red after Harding Grim's spear had pricked him through the guts. Logen felt them now on his tattered skin, all of his scars, and he hugged his arms around his aching body.

The wounds of the past were many, alright, but it didn't make the ones he had now hurt any less. The cut in his shoulder nagged at him, sore as a burning coal. He'd seen a man lose an arm from nothing more than a graze he'd got in battle. First they had to take off his hand, then his arm to the elbow, then all the way to the shoulder. Next he got tired, then he started talking stupid, then he stopped breathing. Logen didn't want to go back to the mud that way.

He hopped up to a crumbling stump of wall and leaned against it, painfully shrugged his coat off, fumbled at the buttons of his shirt with one clumsy hand, pulled the pin out of the bandage and peeled the dressing carefully away.

'How does it look?' he asked.

'Like the parent of all scabs,' muttered Longfoot, peering at his shoulder.

'Does it smell alright?'

'You want me to smell you?'

'Just tell me if it stinks.'

The Navigator leaned forwards and sniffed daintily at Logen's shoulder. 'A marked odour of sweat, but that might be your armpit. I fear that my remarkable talents do not encompass medicine. One wound smells much like another to me.' And he pushed the pin back through the bandage.

Logen worked his shirt on. 'You'd know if it was rotten, believe me. Reeks like old graves, and once the rot gets in you there's no getting rid of it but with a blade. Bad way to go.' And he shuddered and pressed his palm gently against his throbbing shoulder.

'Yes, well,' said Longfoot, already striding off down the near-deserted street. 'Lucky for you that we have the woman Maljinn with us. Her talent for conversation is most extremely limited, but when it comes to wounds, well, I saw the whole business and don't object to telling you, she can stitch skin as calm and even as a master cobbler stitches leather. She can indeed! She pulls a needle as nimble and neat as a queen's dressmaker. A useful talent to have in these parts. I would not be the least surprised if we need that talent again before we're done.'

'It's a dangerous journey?' asked Logen, still trying to struggle back into his coat.

'Huh. The North has always been wild and lawless, heavy with bloody feuds and merciless brigands. Every man goes armed to the teeth, and ready to kill at a moment's notice. In Gurkhul foreign travellers stay free only on the whim of the local governor, at risk of being taken as a slave at any moment. Styrian cities sport thugs and cutpurses on every corner, if you can even get through their gates without being robbed by the authorities. The waters of the Thousand Isles are thick with pirates, one for each merchant, it sometimes seems, while in distant Suljuk they fear and despise outsiders, and likely as not will hang you by your feet and cut your throat as soon as give you directions. The Circle of the World is full of dangers, my nine-fingered friend, but if all that is not enough for you, and you yearn for more severe peril, I suggest that you visit the Old Empire.'

Logen got the feeling that Brother Longfoot was enjoying himself. 'That bad?'

'Worse, oh yes, indeed! Especially if, rather than simply visiting, one undertakes to cross the breadth of the country from one side to the other.'

Logen winced. 'And that's the plan?'

'That is, as you put it, the plan. For time out of mind, the Old Empire has been riven by civil strife. Once a single nation with a single Emperor, his laws enforced by a mighty army and a loyal administration, it has dissolved down the years into a boiling soup of petty princedoms, crackpot republics, city states and tiny lordships, until few acknowledge any leader who does not even now hold a sword over their heads. The lines between tax and brigandage, between just war and bloody murder, between rightful claim and fantasy have blurred and vanished. Hardly a year goes by without another power-hungry bandit declaring himself king of the world. I understand there was a time, perhaps fifty years ago, when there were no fewer than sixteen Emperors at one moment.'

'Huh. Fifteen more than you need.'

'Sixteen more, some might say, and not a one of them friendly to travellers. When it comes to getting murdered, the Old Empire presents a victim with quite the dazzling choice. But one need not be killed by men.'

'No?'

'Oh, dear me, no! Nature has also placed many fearsome obstacles in our path, especially given that winter is now coming fast upon us. Westward of Calcis stretches a wide and level plain, open grassland for many hundreds of miles. In the Old Time, perhaps, much of it was settled, cultivated, crossed by straight roads of good stone in every direction. Now the towns mostly lie in silent ruins, the land is storm-drenched wilderness, the roads are trails of broken stones luring the unwary into sucking bogs.'

'Bogs,' muttered Logen, slowly shaking his head.

'And worse beside. The river Aos, greatest of all rivers within the Circle of the World, carves a deep and snaking valley through the midst of this wasteland. We will have to cross it, but there are only two surviving bridges, one at Darmium, which is our best chance, another at Aostum, a hundred miles or more further west. There are fords, but the Aos is mighty, and fast-flowing, and the valley deep and dangerous.' Longfoot clicked his tongue. 'That is before we reach the Broken Mountains.'

'High, are they?'

'Oh, extremely. Very high, and very perilous. Called Broken for their steep cliffs, their jagged ravines, their sudden plunging drops. There are rumoured to be passes, but all the maps, if indeed there ever were any, were lost long ago. Having negotiated the mountains we will take ship—'

'You plan to carry a ship over the mountains?'

'Our employer assures me he can get one on the other side, though how I do not know, for that land is almost utterly unknown. We will sail due west to the island of Shabulyan, which they say rises from the ocean at the very edge of the World.'

'They say?'

'Rumour is all that anyone knows of it. Even amongst the illustrious order of Navigators, I have heard of no man who lays claim to have set foot upon the place, and the brothers of my order are well known for . . . far-fetched claims, shall we say?'

Logen scratched slowly at his face, wishing that he'd asked Bayaz his plans before. 'It all sounds a long way.'

'One could scarcely conceive, in fact, of a destination more remote.'

'What's there?'

Longfoot shrugged. 'You will have to ask our employer. I find routes, not reasons. Follow me please, Master Ninefingers, and I pray you not to dally. We have a great deal to do if we are to pose as merchants.'

'Merchants?'

'That is Bayaz' plan. Merchants often risk the journey west from Calcis to Darmium, even beyond to Aostum. They are large cities still, and largely cut off from the outside world. The profits one can make carrying foreign luxuries to them – spices from Gurkhul, silks from Suljuk, chagga from the North – are astronomical. Why, you can triple your investment in a month, if you survive! Such caravans are a common sight, well armed and well defended, of course.'

'What about these looters and robbers wandering the plain? Aren't merchants just what they're after?'

'Of course,' said Longfoot. 'It must be some other threat that this disguise is intended to defend against. One directed specifically at us.'

'At us? Another threat? We need more?' But Longfoot was already striding out of earshot.

In one part of Calcis at least, the majesty of the past was not entirely faded. The hall into which they were ushered by their guards, or their kidnappers, was glorious indeed.

Two lines of columns, tall as forest trees, marched down either side of the echoing space, carved from polished green stone fretted with glittering veins of silver. High above, the ceiling was painted a rich blue-black, marked with a galaxy of shining stars, constellations picked out by golden lines. A deep pool of dark water filled the space before the door, perfectly still, reflecting everything. Another shadowy hall below. Another shadowy night sky beyond it.

The Imperial Legate lay sprawled out across a couch on a high dais at the far end of the room, a table before him loaded with delicacies. He was a huge man, round-faced and fleshy. Fingers heavy with golden rings snatched up choice morsels and tossed them into his waiting mouth, eyes never leaving his two guests, or his two prisoners, for a moment.

'I am Salamo Narba, Imperial Legate and governor of the city of Calcis.' He worked his mouth, then spat out an olive stone which pinged into a dish. 'You are the one they call the First of the Magi?'

The Magus inclined his bald head. Narba lifted up a goblet, holding the stem between his heavy forefinger and his heavy thumb, took a swig of wine, sloshed it slowly round in his mouth while he watched them, and swallowed. 'Bayaz.'

'The same.'

'Hmm. I mean no offence.' Here the Legate snatched up a tiny fork and speared an oyster from its shell, 'but your presence in this city concerns me. The political situation in the Empire is . . . volatile.' He picked up his goblet. 'Even more so than usual.' Swig, slosh, swallow. 'The last thing that I need is someone . . . upsetting the balance.'

'More volatile than usual?' asked Bayaz. 'I understood that Sabarbus had finally calmed things.'

'Calmed them under his boot, for a while.' The Legate tore a handful of dark grapes from a bunch and leaned back on his cushions, popping them one by one into his gaping mouth. 'But Sabarbus . . . is dead. Poison, they say. His sons, Scario . . . and Goltus . . . squabbled over his legacy . . . then made war on each other. An exceptionally bloody war, even for this exhausted land.' And he spat the pips out onto the table top.

'Goltus held the city of Darmium, in the midst of the great plain. Scario employed his father's greatest general, Cabrian, to take it under siege. Not long ago, after five months of encirclement, starved of provisions, hopeless of relief . . . the city surrendered.' Narba bit into a ripe plum, juice running down his chin.

'So Scario is close to victory, then.'

'Huh.' The Legate wiped his face with the tip of his little finger and tossed the unfinished fruit carelessly onto the table. 'No sooner had Cabrian finally taken the city, pillaged its treasures and given it over to a brutal sack by his soldiers, than he installed himself in the ancient palace and proclaimed himself Emperor.'

'Ah. You seem unmoved.'

'I weep on the inside, but I have seen all this before. Scario, Goltus, and now Cabrian. Three self-appointed Emperors, locked in a deadly struggle, their soldiers ravaging the land, while the few cities who have maintained their independence look on, horrified, and do their best to escape the nightmare unscathed.'

46

Bayaz frowned. 'I mean to travel westward. I must cross the Aos, and Darmium is the closest bridge.'

The Legate shook his head. 'It is said that Cabrian, always eccentric, has lost his reason entirely. That he has murdered his wife and married his own three daughters. That he has declared himself a living god. The city gates are sealed while he scours the city for witches, devils, and traitors. Every day there are new bodies hanging at the public gibbets he has raised on each corner. No one is permitted either to enter or to leave. Such is the news from Darmium.'

Jezal was more than a little relieved to hear Bayaz say, 'it must be Aostum, then.'

'Nobody will be crossing the river at Aostum any longer. Scario, running from his brother's vengeful armies, fled across the bridge and had his engineers bring it down behind him.'

'He destroyed it?'

'He did. A wonder of the Old Time which stood for two thousand years. Nothing remains. To add to your woes, there have been heavy rains and the great river runs swift and high. The fords are impassable. You will not cross the Aos this year, I fear.'

'I must.'

'But you will not. If you wish for my advice, I would leave the Empire to its misery and return from whence you came. Here in Calcis we have always tried to plough a middle furrow, to remain neutral, and firmly aloof from the disasters that have befallen the rest of the land, one hard upon another. Here we still cling to the ways of our forefathers.' He gestured at himself. 'The city is yet governed by an Imperial Legate, as it was in the Old Time, not ruled by some brigand, some petty chieftain, some false Emperor.' He waved a limp hand at the rich hall around them. 'Here, against the odds, we have managed to retain some vestige of the glory of old, and I will not risk that. Your friend Zacharus was here, not but a month ago.'

'Here?'

'He told me that Goltus was the rightful Emperor and demanded that I throw my support behind him. I sent him scurrying away with the same answer I will give to you. We in Calcis are happy as we are. We want no part of your self-serving schemes. Take your meddling and get you gone, Magus. I give you three days to leave the city.'

There was a long, quiet pause as the last echoes of Narba's speech faded. A long, breathless moment, and all the while Bayaz' frown grew harder. A long, expectant silence, but not quite empty. It was full of growing fear.

'Have you confused me with some other man?' growled Bayaz, and Jezal felt an urgent need to shuffle away from him and hide behind one of the beautiful pillars. 'I am the First of the Magi! The first apprentice of great Juvens himself!' His anger was like a great stone pressing on Jezal's chest, squeezing the air from his lungs, crushing the strength from his body. He held up his meaty fist. 'This is the hand that cast down Kanedias! The hand that crowned Harod! *You* dare to give me *threats*? Is this what you call the glory of old? A city shrunken in its crumbling walls like some withered old warrior cowering in the outsize armour of his youth?' Narba shrank behind his silverware and Jezal winced, terrified that the Legate might explode at any moment and shower the room with gore.

'You think I care a damn for your broken piss-pot of a town?' thundered Bayaz. 'You give me three days? I'll be gone in one!' And he turned on his heel and stalked across the polished floor towards the entrance, the ringing echoes of his voice still grating from the shining walls, the glittering ceiling.

Jezal dithered a moment, weak and trembling, then shuffled guiltily away, following the First of the Magi past the Legate's horrified, dumbstruck guards and out into the daylight.

The Condition of the Defences

To Arch Lector Sult, head of his Majesty's Inquisition.

Your Eminence,

I have acquainted the members of Dagoska's ruling council with my mission. You will not be surprised to learn that they are less than delighted at the sudden reduction in their powers. My investigation into the disappearance of Superior Davoust is already underway, and I feel confident that results will not be long in coming. I will be appraising the city's defences as soon as possible, and will take any and all steps necessary to ensure that Dagoska is impregnable.

You will hear from me soon. Until then, I serve and obey.

Sand dan Glokta,
Superior of Dagoska.

The sun pressed down on the crumbling battlements like a great weight. It pressed through Glokta's hat and onto his stooped head. It pressed through Glokta's black coat and onto his twisted shoulders. It threatened to squeeze the water right out of him, squash the life right out of him, crush him to his knees. *A cool autumn morning in charming Dagoska.*

While the sun attacked him from above, the salt wind came at him head on. It swept in off the empty sea and over the bare peninsula, hot and full of choking dust, blasting the land walls of the city and scouring everything with salty grit. It stung at Glokta's sweaty skin, whipped the moisture from his mouth, tickled at his eyes and made them weep stinging tears. *Even the weather wants to be rid of me, it would seem.*

Practical Vitari teetered along the parapet beside him, arms outstretched like a circus performer on the high rope. Glokta frowned up at her, a gangly black shape against the brilliant sky. *She could just as easily walk down here, and stop making a spectacle of herself. But at least this way there is always the chance of her falling off.* The land walls were twenty strides high at the least.

Glokta allowed himself the very slightest smile at the thought of the Arch Lector's favourite Practical slipping, sliding, tumbling from the wall, hands clutching at nothing. *Perhaps a despairing scream as she fell to her death?*

But she didn't fall. *Bitch. Considering her next report to the Arch Lector, no doubt. 'The cripple continues to flounder like a landed fish. He has yet to uncover the slightest trace of Davoust, or any traitor, despite questioning half the city. The one man he has arrested is a member of his own Inquisition . . .'*

Glokta shaded his eyes with his hand and squinted into the blinding sun. The neck of rock that connected Dagoska with the mainland stretched away from him, no more than a few hundred strides across at its narrowest point, the sparkling sea on both sides. The road from the city gates was a brown stripe through the yellow scrub, cutting southwards towards the dry hills on the mainland. A few sorry-looking seabirds squawked and circled over the causeway, but there were no other signs of life.

'Might I borrow your eye-glass, General?'

Vissbruck flicked the eye-glass open and slapped it sulkily into Glokta's outstretched hand. *Plainly he feels he has better things to do than give me a tour of the defences.* The General was breathing heavily, standing stiffly to attention in his impeccable uniform, plump face shining with sweat. *Doing his best to maintain his professional bearing. His bearing is about the only professional thing about this imbecile, but, as the Arch Lector says, we must work with the tools we have.* Glokta raised the brass tube to his eye.

The Gurkish had built a palisade. A tall fence of wooden stakes that fringed the hills, cutting Dagoska off from the mainland. There were tents scattered about the other side, thin plumes of smoke rising from a cooking fire here or there. Glokta could just about make out tiny figures moving, sun glinting on polished metal. *Weapons and armour, and plenty of both.*

'There used to be caravans from the mainland,' Vissbruck murmured. 'Last year there were a hundred of them every day. Then the Emperor's soldiers started to arrive, and there were fewer traders. They finished the fence a couple of months ago. There hasn't been so much as a donkey since. Everything has to come in by ship, now.'

Glokta scanned across the fence, and the camps behind, from the sea on one side to the sea on the other. *Are they simply flexing their muscles, putting on a show of force? Or are they in deadly earnest? The Gurkish love a good show, but they don't mind a good fight either – that's how they've conquered the whole of the South, more or less.* He lowered the eye-glass. 'How many Gurkish, do you think?'

Vissbruck shrugged. 'Impossible to say. At least five thousand, I would guess, but there could be many more, behind those hills. We have no way of knowing.'

Five thousand. At the least. If it's a show, it's a good one. 'How many men have we?'

Vissbruck paused. 'I have around six hundred Union soldiers under my command.'

Around six hundred? Around? You lackwit dunce! When I was a soldier I knew the name of every man in my regiment, and who was best suited to what tasks. 'Six hundred? Is that all?'

'There are mercenaries in the city also, but they cannot be trusted, and frequently cause trouble of their own. In my opinion they are worse than worthless.'

I asked for numbers, not opinions. 'How many mercenaries?'

'Perhaps a thousand, now, perhaps more.'

'Who leads them?'

'Some Styrian. Cosca, he calls himself.'

'Nicomo Cosca?' Vitari was staring down from the parapet, one orange eyebrow raised.

'You know him?'

'You could say that. I thought he was dead, but it seems there's no justice in the world.'

She's right there. Glokta turned to Vissbruck. 'Does this Cosca answer to you?'

'Not exactly. The Spicers pay him, so he answers to Magister Eider. In theory, he's supposed to follow my orders—'

'But he only follows his own?' Glokta could see in the General's face that he was right. *Mercenaries. A double-edged sword, if ever there was one. Keen, as long as you can keep paying, and provided that trustworthiness is not a priority.* 'And Cosca's men outnumber yours two to one.' *It would appear that, as far as the defences of the city are concerned, I am speaking to the wrong man. Perhaps there is one issue, though, on which he can enlighten me.* 'Do you know what became of my predecessor, Superior Davoust?'

General Vissbruck twitched his annoyance. 'I have no idea. That man's movements were of no interest to me.'

'Hmm,' mused Glokta, jamming his hat down tighter onto his head as another gritty gust of wind blew in across the walls. 'The disappearance of the city's Superior of the Inquisition? Of no interest whatsoever?'

'None,' snapped the General. 'We rarely had cause to speak to one another. Davoust was well-known as an abrasive character. As far as I am concerned, the Inquisition has its responsibilities, and I have mine.' *Touchy, touchy. But then everyone is, since I arrived in town. You'd almost think they didn't want me here.*

'You have your responsibilities, eh?' Glokta shuffled to the parapet, lifted his cane and prodded at a corner of crumbling masonry, not far from Vitari's heel. A chunk of stone cracked away and tumbled from the wall into space. A few moments later he heard it clatter into the ditch, far below. He rounded on Vissbruck. 'As commander of the city's defences, would you count the maintenance of the walls as being among your responsibilities?'

Vissbruck bristled. 'I have done everything possible!'

Glokta counted the points off with the fingers of his free hand. 'The land walls are crumbling and poorly manned. The ditch beyond is so choked with dirt it barely exists. The gates have not been replaced in years, and are falling to pieces on their own. If the Gurkish were to attack tomorrow, I do believe we'd be in quite a sorry position.'

'Not for any oversight on my part, I can assure you! With the heat, and the wind, and the salt from the sea, wood and metal rot in no time, and stone fares little better! Do you realise the task?' The General gestured at the great sweep of the towering land walls, curving away to the sea on either side. Even here at the top, the parapet was wide enough to drive a cart down, and they were a lot thicker at the base. 'I have few skilled masons, and precious little materials! What the Closed Council gives me barely pays for the upkeep of the Citadel! Then the money from the Spicers scarcely keeps the walls of the Upper City in good repair—'

Fool! One could almost believe he did not seriously mean to defend the city at all. 'The Citadel cannot be supplied by sea if the rest of Dagoska is in Gurkish hands, am I right?'

Vissbruck blinked. 'Well, no, but—'

'The walls of the Upper City might keep the natives where they are, but they are too long, too low, and too thin to withstand a concerted attack for long, would you agree?'

'Yes, I suppose so, but—'

'So any plan that treats the Citadel, or the Upper City, as our main line of defence is one that only plays for time. Time for help to arrive. Help that, with our army committed hundreds of leagues away in Angland, might take a while appearing.' *Will never appear at all.* 'If the land walls fall the city is doomed.' Glokta tapped the dusty flags underfoot with his cane. 'Here is where we must fight the Gurkish, and here is where we must keep them out. Everything else is an irrelevance.'

'An irrelevance,' Vitari piped to herself as she hopped from one part of the parapet to another.

The General was frowning. 'I can only do as the Lord Governor and his council instruct me. The Lower City has always been regarded as dispensable. I am not responsible for overall policy—'

'I am.' Glokta held Vissbruck's eye for a very long moment. 'From now on all resources will be directed into the repair and strengthening of the land walls. New parapets, new gates, every broken stone must be replaced. I don't want to see a crack an ant could crawl through, let alone a Gurkish army.'

'But who will do the work?'

'The natives built the damn things in the first place, didn't they? There must be skilled men among them. Seek them out and hire them. As for the ditch, I want it down below sea level. If the Gurkish come we can flood it, and make the city into an island.'

'But that could take months!'

'You have two weeks. Perhaps not even that long. Press every idle man into service. Women and children too, if they can hold a spade.'

Vissbruck frowned up at Vitari. 'And what about your people in the Inquisition?'

'Oh, they're too busy asking questions, trying to find out what happened to your last Superior. Or they're watching me, and my quarters, and the gates of the citadel all day and night, trying to make sure that the same thing doesn't happen to your new one. Be a shame, eh, Vissbruck, if I disappeared before the defences were ready?'

'Of course, Superior,' muttered the General. *But without tremendous enthusiasm, I rather think.*

'Everyone else must work, though, including your own soldiers.'

'But you can't expect my men to—'

'I expect every man to do his part. Anyone who doesn't like it can go back to Adua. He can go back and explain his reluctance to the Arch Lector.' Glokta leered his toothless smile at the General. 'There's no one that can't be replaced, General, no one at all.'

There was a great deal of sweat on Vissbruck's pink face, great drops of it. The stiff collar of his uniform was dark with moisture. 'Of course, every man must do his part! Work on the ditch will begin immediately!' He made a weak attempt at a smile. 'I'll find every man, but I'll need money, Superior. If people work they must be paid, even the natives. Then we will need materials, everything has to be brought in by sea—'

'Borrow what you need to get started. Work on credit. Promise everything and give nothing, for now. His Eminence will provide.' *He'd better.* 'I want reports on your progress every morning.'

'Every morning, yes.'

'You have a great deal to do, General. I'd get started.'

Vissbruck paused for a moment, as though unsure whether to salute or not. In the end he simply turned on his heel and stalked off. *The pique of a professional soldier dictated to by a civilian, or something more? Am I upsetting his carefully laid plans? Plans to sell the city to the Gurkish, perhaps?*

Vitari hopped down from the parapet onto the walkway. 'His Eminence will provide? You'd be lucky.'

Glokta frowned at her back as she sauntered away, then he frowned towards the hills on the mainland, then he frowned up at the citadel. *Dangers on every side. Trapped between the Arch Lector and the Gurkish, and with nobody but an unknown traitor for company. It'll be a wonder if I last a day.*

A committed optimist might have called the place a dive. *But it scarcely deserves the name.* A piss-smelling shack with some oddments of furniture, everything stained with ancient sweat and recent spillages. *A kind of cesspit with half the cess removed.* Customers and staff were indistinguishable:

drunken, fly-blown natives stretched out in the heat. Nicomo Cosca, famed soldier of fortune, sprawled in amongst this scene of debauchery, soundly asleep.

He had his driftwood chair rocked back on its rear legs against the grimy wall, one boot up on the table in front of him. It had probably been as fine and flamboyant a boot as one could hope for, once, black Styrian leather with a golden spur and buckles. *No longer.* The upper was sagging and scuffed grey with hard use. The spur was snapped off short, the gilt on the buckles was flaking away and the iron underneath was spotted with brown rust. A circle of pink, blistered skin peered at Glokta through a hole in the sole.

And a boot could scarcely be better fitted to its owner. Cosca's long moustaches, no doubt meant to be waxed out sideways in the fashion of a Styrian dandy, flopped limp and lifeless round his half-open mouth. His neck and jaw were covered in a week's growth, somewhere between beard and stubble, and there was a scabrous, flaking rash peering out above his collar. His greasy hair stuck from his head at all angles, excepting a large bald spot on his crown, angry red with sunburn. Sweat beaded his slack skin, a lazy fly crawled across his puffy face. One bottle lay empty on its side on the table. Another, half-full, was cradled in his lap.

Vitari stared down at this picture of drunken self-neglect, expression of contempt plainly visible despite her mask. 'So it's true then, you are still alive.' *Just barely.*

Cosca prised open one red-rimmed eye, blinked, squinted up, and then slowly began to smile. 'Shylo Vitari, I swear. The world can still surprise me.' He worked his mouth, grimacing, glanced down and saw the bottle in his lap, lifted it and took a long, thirsty pull. Deep swallows, just as if it were water in the bottle. *A practised drunkard, as though there was any doubt. Hardly the man one would choose to entrust the defence of the city to, at first glance.* 'I never expected to see you again. Why don't you take off the mask? It's robbing me of your beauty.'

'Save it for your whores, Cosca. I don't need to catch what you've got.'

The mercenary gave a bubbling sound, half laugh, half cough. 'You still have the manners of a princess,' he wheezed.

'Then this shithouse must be a palace.'

Cosca shrugged. 'It all looks the same if you're drunk enough.'

'You think you'll ever be drunk enough?'

'No. But it's worth trying.' As if to prove the point he sucked another mouthful from the bottle.

Vitari perched herself on the edge of the table. 'So what brings you here? I thought you were busy spreading the cock-rot across Styria.'

'My popularity at home had somewhat dwindled.'

'Found yourself on both sides of a fight once too often, eh?'

'Something like that.'

'But the Dagoskans welcomed you with open arms?'

'I'd rather you welcomed me with open legs, but a man can't get everything he wants. Who's your friend?'

Glokta slid out a rickety chair with one aching foot and eased himself into it, hoping it would bear his weight. *Crashing to the floor in a bundle of broken sticks would hardly send the right message, now, would it?* 'My name is Glokta.' He stretched his sweaty neck out to one side, and then the other. 'Superior Glokta.'

Cosca looked at him for a long time. His eyes were bloodshot, sunken, heavy-lidded. *And yet there is a certain calculation there. Not half as drunk as he pretends, perhaps.* 'The same one who fought in Gurkhul? The Colonel of Horse?'

Glokta felt his eyelid flicker. *You could hardly say the same man, but surprisingly well remembered, nonetheless.* 'I gave up soldiery some years ago. I'm surprised you've heard of me.'

'A fighting man should know his enemies, and a hired man never knows who his next enemy might be. It's worth taking notice of who's who, in military circles. I heard your name mentioned, some time ago, as a man worth taking notice of. Bold and clever, I heard, but reckless. That was the last I heard. And now here you are, in a different line of work. Asking questions.'

'Recklessness didn't work out for me in the end.' Glokta shrugged. 'And a man needs something to do with his time.'

'Of course. Never doubt another's choices, I say. You can't know his reasons. You come here for a drink, Superior? They've nothing but this piss, I'm afraid.' He waved the bottle. 'Or have you questions for me?'

That I have, and plenty of them. 'Do you have any experience with sieges?'

'Experience?' spluttered Cosca, 'Experience, you ask? Hah! Experience is one thing I am not short of—'

'No,' murmured Vitari over her shoulder, 'just discipline and loyalty.'

'Yes, well,' Cosca frowned up at her back, 'that all depends on who you ask. But I was at Etrina, and at Muris. Serious pair of sieges, those. And I besieged Visserine myself for a few months and nearly had it, except that she-devil Mercatto caught me unawares. Came on us with cavalry before dawn, sun behind and all, damned unfriendly trick, the bitch—'

'I heard you were passed out drunk at the time,' muttered Vitari.

'Yes, well . . . Then I held Borletta against Grand Duke Orso for six months—'

Vitari snorted. 'Until he paid you to open the gates.'

Cosca gave a sheepish grin. 'It was an awful lot of money. But he never fought his way in! You'd have to give me that, eh, Shylo?'

'No one needs to fight you, providing they bring their purse.'

The mercenary grinned. 'I am what I am, and never claimed to be anything else.'

'So you've been known to betray an employer?' asked Glokta.

The Styrian paused, the bottle halfway to his mouth. 'I am thoroughly offended, Superior. Nicomo Cosca may be a mercenary, but there are still rules. I could only turn my back on an employer under one condition.'

'Which is?'

Cosca grinned. 'If someone else were to offer me more.'

Ah, the mercenary's code. Some men will do anything for money. Most men will do anything for enough. Perhaps even make a Superior of the Inquisition disappear? 'Do you know what became of my predecessor, Superior Davoust?'

'Ah, the riddle of the invisible torturer!' Cosca scratched thoughtfully at his sweaty beard, picked a little at the rash on his neck and examined the results, wedged under his fingernail. 'Who knows or cares to know? The man was a swine. I hardly knew him and what I knew I didn't like. He had plenty of enemies, and, in case you hadn't noticed, it's a real snake pit down here. If you're asking which one bit him, well . . . isn't that your job? I was busy here. Drinking.'

Not too difficult to believe. 'What would your opinion be of our mutual friend, General Vissbruck?'

Cosca hunched his shoulders and sank a little lower into his chair. 'The man's a child. Playing soldiers. Tinkering with his little castle and his little fence, when the big walls are all that count. Lose those and the game is done, I say.'

'I've been thinking the very same thing.' *Perhaps the defence of the city could be in worse hands, after all.* 'Work has already begun on the land walls, and on the ditch beyond. I hope to flood it.'

Cosca raised an eyebrow. 'Good. Flood it. The Gurkish don't like the water much. Poor sailors. Flood it. Very good.' He tipped his head back and sucked the last drops from the bottle, then he tossed it on the dirty floor, wiped his mouth with his dirty hand, then wiped his hand on the front of his sweat-stained shirt. 'At least someone knows what they're doing. Perhaps when the Gurkish attack, we'll last longer than a few days, eh?' *Providing we aren't betrayed beforehand.*

'You never know, perhaps the Gurkish won't attack.'

'Oh, I hope they do.' Cosca reached under his chair and produced another bottle. There was a glint in his eye as he pulled the cork out with his teeth and spat it across the room. 'I get paid double once the fighting starts.'

It was evening, and a merciful breeze was washing through the audience chamber. Glokta leaned against the wall by the window, watching the shadows stretch out over the city below.

The Lord Governor was keeping him waiting. *Trying to let me know he's still in charge, whatever the Closed Council might say.* But Glokta didn't mind being still for a while. The day had been a tiring one. Slogging round the city in the baking heat, examining the walls, the gates, the troops. Asking questions. *Questions to which no one has satisfactory answers.* His leg was throbbing, his back was aching, his hand was raw from gripping his cane. *But no worse than usual. I am still standing. A good day, all in all.*

The glowing sun was shrouded in lines of orange cloud. Beneath it a long wedge of sea glittered silver in the last light of the day. The land walls had already plunged half the ramshackle buildings of the Lower City into deep gloom, and the shadows of the tall spires of the great temple stretched out across the roofs of the Upper City, creeping up the slopes of the rock towards the citadel. The hills on the mainland were nothing more than a distant suggestion, full of shadows. *And crawling with Gurkish soldiers. Watching us, as we watch them, no doubt. Seeing us dig our ditches, patch our walls, shore up our gates. How long will they be content to watch, I wonder? How long before the sun goes down for us?*

The door opened and Glokta turned his head, wincing as his neck clicked. It was the Lord Governor's son, Korsten dan Vurms. He shut the door behind him and strode purposefully into the room, metal heel tips clicking on the mosaic floor. *Ah, the flower of the Union's young nobility. The sense of honour is almost palpable. Or did someone fart?*

'Superior Glokta! I hope I have not kept you waiting.'

'You have,' said Glokta as he shuffled to the table. 'That is what happens when one comes late to a meeting.'

Vurms frowned slightly. 'Then I apologise,' he said, in the most unapologetic tone imaginable. 'How are you finding our city?'

'Hot and full of steps.' Glokta dumped himself into one of the exquisite chairs. 'Where is the Lord Governor?'

The frown turned down further. 'I am afraid that my father is unwell, and cannot attend. You understand that he is an old man, and needs his rest. I can speak for him however.'

'Can you indeed? And what do the two of you have to say?'

'My father is most concerned about the work that you are undertaking on the defences. I am told that the King's soldiers have been set to digging holes on the peninsula, rather than defending the walls of the Upper City. You realise that you are leaving us at the mercy of the natives!'

Glokta snorted. 'The natives are citizens of the Union, no matter how reluctant. Believe me, they are more inclined to mercy than the Gurkish.' *Of their mercy I have first-hand experience.*

'They are primitives!' sneered Vurms, 'and dangerous to boot! You have not been here long enough to understand the threat they pose to us! You should talk to Harker. He's got the right ideas as far as the natives are concerned.'

'I talked to Harker, and I didn't like his ideas. I suspect he may have been forced to rethink them, in fact, downstairs, in the dark.' *I suspect he is rethinking even now, and as quickly as his pea of a brain will allow.* 'As for your father's worries, he need no longer concern himself with the defence of the city. Since he is an old man, and in need of rest, I have no doubt he will be happy to pass the responsibility to me.'

A spasm of anger passed across Vurms' handsome features. He opened his mouth to hiss some curse, but evidently thought better of it. *As well he should.* He sat back in his chair, rubbing one thumb and one finger thoughtfully together. When he spoke, it was with a friendly smile and a charming softness. *Now comes the wheedling.* 'Superior Glokta, I feel we have got off on the wrong foot—'

'I only have one that works.'

Vurms' smile slipped somewhat, but he forged on. 'It is plain that you hold the cards, for the time being, but my father has many friends back in Midderland. I can be a significant hindrance to you, if I have the mind. A significant hindrance or a great help—'

'I am so glad that you have chosen to cooperate. You can begin by telling me what became of Superior Davoust.'

The smile slipped off entirely. 'How should I know?'

'Everyone knows something.' *And someone knows more than the rest. Is it you, Vurms?*

The Lord Governor's son thought about it for a moment. *Dense, or guilty? Is he trying to think of ways to help me, or ways to cover his tracks?* 'I know the natives hated him. They were forever plotting against us, and Davoust was tireless in his pursuit of the disloyal. I have no doubt he fell victim to one of their schemes. I'd be asking questions down in the Lower City, if I was you.'

'Oh, I am quite confident the answers lie here in the Citadel.'

'Not with me,' snapped Vurms, looking Glokta up and down. 'Believe me when I say, I would be much happier if Davoust was still with us.'

Perhaps, or perhaps not, but we will get no answers today. 'Very well. Tell me about the city's stores.'

'The stores?'

'Food, Korsten, food. I understand that, since the Gurkish closed the land routes, everything must be brought in by sea. Feeding the people is surely one of a governor's most pressing concerns.'

'My father is mindful of his people's needs in any eventuality!' snapped Vurms. 'We have provisions for six months!'

'Six months? For all the inhabitants?'

'Of course.' *Better than I expected. One less thing to worry about, at least, from this vast tangle of worries.* 'Unless you count the natives,' added Vurms, as though it was of no importance.

Glokta paused. 'And what will they eat, if the Gurkish lay siege to the city?'

Vurms shrugged. 'I really hadn't thought about it.'

'Indeed? What will happen, do you suppose, when they begin to starve?'

'Well . . .'

'Chaos is what will happen! We cannot hold the city with four fifths of the population against us!' Glokta sucked at his empty gums in disgust. 'You will go to the merchants, you will secure provisions for six months! For everyone! I want six months' supplies for the rats in the sewers!'

'What am I?' sneered Vurms. 'Your grocery boy?'

'I suppose you're whatever I tell you to be.'

All trace of friendliness had vanished from Vurms' face now. 'I am the son of a Lord Governor! I refuse to be addressed in this manner!' The legs of his chair squealed furiously as he sprang up and made for the door.

'Fine,' murmured Glokta. 'There's a boat that goes to Adua every day. A fast boat, and it takes its cargo straight to the House of Questions. They'll address you differently there, believe me. I could easily arrange a berth for you.'

Vurms stopped in his tracks. 'You wouldn't dare!'

Glokta smiled. His most revolting, leering, gap-toothed smile. 'You'd have to be a bold man to bet your life on what I'd dare. How bold are you?' The young man licked his lips, but he did not meet Glokta's gaze for long. *I thought not. He reminds me of my friend Captain Luthar. All flash and arrogance, but with no kind of character to hang it on. Prick him with a pin, and he sags like a punctured wineskin.*

'Six months' food. Six months for everyone. And see that it's done promptly.' *Grocery boy.*

'Of course,' growled Vurms, still staring grimly at the floor.

'Then we can get started on the water. The wells, the cisterns, the pumps. People will need something to wash all your hard work down with, eh? You will report to me every morning.'

Vurms' fists clenched and unclenched by his sides, his jaw muscles worked with fury. 'Of course,' he managed to splutter.

'Of course. You may go.'

Glokta watched him stalk away. *And I have talked to two out of four. Two of four, and I have made two enemies. I will need allies if I am to succeed here. Without allies, I will not last, regardless of what documents I hold. Without allies I will not keep the Gurkish out, if they decide to try and come in. Worse yet, I still know nothing of Davoust. A Superior of the Inquisition, disappeared into thin air. Let us hope the Arch Lector will be patient.*

Hope. Arch Lector. Patience. Glokta frowned. *Never have three ideas belonged together less.*

The Thing About Trust

The wheel on the cart turned slowly round, and squeaked. It turned round again, and squeaked. Ferro scowled at it. Damn wheel. Damn cart. She shifted her scorn from the cart to its driver.

Damn apprentice. She didn't trust him a finger's breadth. His eyes flickered over to her, lingered an insulting moment, then darted off. As if he knew something about Ferro that she did not know herself. That made her angry. She looked away from him to the first of the horses, and its rider.

Damn Union boy with his stiff back, sitting in his saddle like a King sits on his throne, as though being born with a good-shaped face was an achievement to be endlessly proud of. He was pretty, and neat, and dainty as a princess. Ferro smiled grimly to herself. The princess of the Union, that's what he was. She hated fine-looking people even more than ugly ones. Beauty was never to be trusted.

You would have had to look far and wide to find anyone less beautiful than the big nine-fingered bastard. He sat in his saddle slumped over like some great sack of rice. Slow-moving, scratching, sniffing, chewing like a big cow. Trying to look like he had no killing in him, no mad fury, no devil. She knew better. He nodded to her and she scowled back. He was a devil wearing a cow's skin, and she was not fooled.

Better than that damn Navigator, though. Always talking, always smiling, always laughing. Ferro hated talk, and smiles, and laughter, each one more than the last. Stupid little man with his stupid tales. Underneath all his lies he was plotting, watching, she could feel it.

That left the First of the Magi, and she trusted him least of all. She saw his eyes sliding to the cart. Looking at the sack he'd put the box in. Square, grey, dull, heavy box. He thought no one had seen, but she had. Full of secrets is what he was. Bald bastard, with his thick neck and his wooden pole, acting as if he had done nothing but good in his life, as if he would not know where to begin at making a man explode.

'Damn fucking pinks,' she whispered to herself. She leaned over and spat onto the track, glowered at their five backs as they rode ahead of her. Why had she let Yulwei talk her into this madness? A voyage way off into the cold west where she had no business. She should have been back in the South, fighting the Gurkish.

Making them pay what they owed her.

Cursing the name of Yulwei silently to herself, she followed the others up to the bridge. It looked ancient – pitted stones splattered with stains of lichen, the surface of it rutted deep where a cart's wheels would roll. Thousands of years of carts, rolling back and forward. The stream gurgled under its single arch, bitter cold water, flowing fast. A low hut stood beside the bridge, settled and slumped into the landscape over long years. Some wisps of smoke were snatched from its chimney and out across the land in the cutting wind.

One soldier stood outside, alone. Drew the short straw, maybe. He'd pressed himself against the wall, swathed in a heavy cloak, horse-hair on his helmet whipping back and forth in the gusts, his spear ignored beside him. Bayaz reined his horse in before the bridge and nodded across.

'We're going up onto the plain. Out towards Darmium.'

'Can't advise it. Dangerous up there.'

Bayaz smiled. 'Dangers mean profits.'

'Profits won't stop an arrow, friend.' The soldier looked them up and down, one by one, and sniffed. 'Varied crowd, aren't you?'

'I take good fighters wherever I can find them.'

'Course.' He looked over at Ferro and she scowled back. 'Very tough, I'm sure, but the fact is the plains are deadly, and more than ever now. Some traders are still going up there, but they're not coming back. That madman Cabrian has raiders out there, I reckon, keen for plunder. Scario and Goltus too, they're little better. We keep some shred of law on this side of the stream, but once you're up there, you're on your own. There'll be no help for you if you're caught out on the plain.' He sniffed again. 'No help at all.'

Bayaz nodded grimly. 'We ask for none.' He spurred his horse and it began to trot over the bridge, onto the track on the other side. The others followed behind, Longfoot first, then Luthar, then Ninefingers. Quai shook the reins and the cart clattered across. Ferro brought up the rear.

'No help at all!' the soldier called after her, before he wedged himself back against the rough wall of his hut.

The great plain.

It should have been good land for riding, reassuring land. Ferro could have seen an enemy coming from miles away, but she saw no one. Only the vast carpet of tall grass, waving and thrashing in the wind, stretching away in every direction, to the far, far, horizon. Only the track broke the monotony, a line of shorter, drier grass, pocked with patches of bare black earth, cutting across the plain straight as an arrow flies.

Ferro did not like it, this vast sameness. She frowned as they rode, peering left and right. In the Badlands of Kanta, the barren earth was full of features – broken boulders, withered valleys, dried-up trees casting their clawing shadows, distant creases in the earth full of shade, bright ridges doused in light. In the Badlands of Kanta, the sky above would be empty, still, a bright bowl holding nothing but the blinding sun in the day, the bright stars at night.

Here all was strangely reversed.

The earth was featureless, but the sky was full of movement, full of chaos. Towering clouds loomed over the plain, dark and light swirling together into colossal spirals, sweeping over the grassland with the raking wind, shifting, turning, ripping apart and flooding back together, casting monstrous, flowing shadows onto the cowering earth, threatening to crush the six tiny riders and their tiny cart with a deluge to sink the world. All hanging over Ferro's hunched up shoulders, the wrath of God made real.

This was a strange land, one in which she had no place. She needed reasons to be here, and good ones. 'You, Bayaz!' she shouted, drawing up level with him. 'Where are we going?'

'Huh,' he grunted, frowning out across the waving grass, from nothing, to nothing. 'We are going westwards, across the plain, over the great river Aos, as far as the Broken Mountains.'

'Then?'

She saw the faint lines around his eyes, across the bridge of his nose, grow deeper, watched his lips press together. Annoyance. He did not like her questions. 'Then we go further.'

'How long will it take?'

'All of winter and into spring,' he snapped. 'And then we must come back.' He dug his heels into his horse's flanks and trotted away from her, up the track towards the front of the group.

Ferro was not so easily put off. Not by this shifty old pink. She dug in her own heels and drew up level with him. 'What is the First Law?'

Bayaz looked sharply over at her. 'What do you know about it?'

'Not enough. I heard you and Yulwei talking, through the door.'

'Eavesdropping, eh?'

'You have loud voices and I have good ears.' Ferro shrugged. 'I am not sticking a bucket on my head just to keep your secrets. What is the First Law?'

The lines round Bayaz' forehead grew deeper, the corners of his mouth turned down. Anger. 'A stricture that Euz placed on his sons, the first rule made after the chaos of ancient days. It is forbidden to touch the Other Side direct. Forbidden to communicate with the world below, forbidden to summon demons, forbidden to open gates to hell. Such is the First Law, the guiding principle of all magic.'

'Uh,' snorted Ferro. It meant nothing to her. 'Who is Khalul?'

Bayaz' thick brows drew in together, his frown deepened, his eyes narrowed. 'Is there no end to your questions, woman?' Her questions galled him. That was good. That meant they were the right questions.

'You'll know if I stop asking them. Who is Khalul?'

'Khalul was one of the order of Magi,' growled Bayaz. 'One of my order. The second of Juvens' twelve apprentices. He was always jealous of my place, always thirsty for power. He broke the Second Law to get it. He ate the flesh of men, and persuaded others to do the same. He made of himself a false prophet, tricked the Gurkish into serving him. That is Khalul. Your enemy, and mine.'

'What is the Seed?'

The Magus' face gave a sudden twitch. Fury, and perhaps the slightest trace of fear. Then his face softened. 'What is it?' He smiled at her, and his smile worried her more than all his anger could have. He leaned towards her, close enough that no one else could hear. 'It is the instrument of your vengeance. Of our vengeance. But it is dangerous. Even to speak of it is dangerous. There are those who are always listening. It would be wise for you to shut the door on your questions, before the answers to them burn us all.' He spurred his horse once again, trotting out ahead of the party on his own.

Ferro stayed behind. She had learned enough for now. Learned enough to trust this First of the Magi less than ever.

A hollow in the ground, no more than four strides across. A sink in the soil, ringed by a low wall of damp, dark earth, full of tangled grass roots. That was the best place they had found to camp for the night, and they had been lucky to find it.

It was as big a feature in the landscape as Ferro had seen all day.

The fire that Longfoot had made was burning well now, flames licking bright and hungry at the wood, rustling and flickering out sideways as a gust of wind swept down into the hollow. The five pinks sat clustered around it, hunched and huddled for warmth, light from it bright on their pinched-up faces.

Longfoot was the only one speaking. His talk was all of his own great achievements. How he had been to this place or that. How he knew this thing or that. How he had a remarkable talent for this, or for that. Ferro was sick of it already, and had told him so twice. The first time she thought she had been clear. The second time she had made sure of it. He would not be talking to her of his idiot travels again, but the others still suffered in silence.

There was space for her, down by the fire, but she did not want it. She preferred to sit above them, cross-legged in the grass on the lip of the hollow. It was cold up here in the wind, and she pulled the blanket tighter round her shivering shoulders. A strange and frightening thing, cold. She hated it.

But she preferred cold to company.

And so she sat apart, sullen and silent, and watched the light drain out of the brooding sky, watched the darkness creep into the land. There was just the faintest glow of the sun now, on the distant horizon. A last feeble brightness round the edges of the looming clouds.

The big pink stood up, and looked at her. 'Getting dark,' he said.

'Uh.'

'Guess that's what happens when the sun goes down, eh?'

'Uh.'

He scratched at the side of his thick neck. 'We need to set watches. Could be dangerous out here at night. We'll take it in shifts. I'll go first, then Luthar—'

'I'll watch,' she grunted.

'Don't worry. You can sleep. I'll wake you later.'

'I do not sleep.'

He stared at her. 'What, never?'

'Not often.'

'Maybe that explains her mood,' murmured Longfoot.

Meant to be under his breath, no doubt, but Ferro heard him. 'My mood is my business, fool.'

The Navigator said nothing as he wrapped himself in his blanket and stretched out beside the fire.

'You want to go first?' said Ninefingers, 'then do it, but wake me a couple of hours in. We each should take our turn.'

Slowly, quietly, wincing with the need not to make noise, Ferro stole from the cart. Dry meat. Dry bread. Water flask. Enough to keep her going for days. She shoved it into a canvas bag.

One of the horses snorted and shied as she slipped past and she scowled at it. She could ride. She could ride well, but she wanted nothing to do with horses. Damn fool, big beasts. Smelled bad. They might move quick, but they needed too much food and water. You could see and hear them from miles away. They left great big tracks to follow. Riding a horse made you weak. Rely on a horse and when you need to run, you find you can't any more.

Ferro had learned never to rely on anything except herself.

She slipped the bag over one shoulder, her quiver and her bow over the other. She took one last look at the sleeping shapes of the others, dark mounds clustered round the fire. Luthar had the blanket drawn up under his chin, smooth-skinned, full-lipped face turned towards the glowing embers. Bayaz had his back to her, but she could see the dim light shining off his bald pate, the back of one dark ear, hear the slow rhythm of his breathing. Longfoot had his blanket pulled up over his head, but his bare feet stuck from the other end, thin and bony, tendons standing out like tree roots from the mud. Quai's eyes were open the tiniest chink, firelight shining wet on a slit of eyeball. Made it look like he was watching her, but his chest was moving slowly up and down, mouth hanging slack, sound asleep and dreaming, no doubt.

Ferro frowned. Just four? Where was the big pink? She saw his blanket lying empty on the far side of the fire, dark folds and light folds, but no man inside. Then she heard his voice.

'Going already?'

Behind her. That was a surprise, that he could have crept around her like that, while she was stealing food. He seemed too big, too slow, too noisy to creep up on anyone. She cursed under her breath. She should have known better than to go by the way things seemed.

She turned slowly round to face him and took one step towards the horses. He followed, keeping the distance between them the same. Ferro could see the glowing fire reflected in one corner of each of his eyes, a curve of cratered, stubbly cheek, the vague outline of his bent nose, a few strands of greasy hair floating over his head in the breeze, slightly blacker than the black land behind.

'I don't want to fight you, pink. I've seen you fight.' She had seen him kill five men in a few moments, and even she had been surprised. The memory of the laughter echoing from the walls, his twisted hungry face, half snarl, half smile, covered in blood, and spit, and madness, the ruined corpses strewn on the stones like rags, all this was sharp in her mind. Not that she was frightened, of course, for Ferro Maljinn felt no fear.

But she knew when to be careful.

'I've no wish to fight you either,' he said, 'but if Bayaz finds you gone in the morning, he'll have me chasing you. I've seen you run, and I'd rather fight you than chase you. At least I'd have some chance.'

He was stronger than her, and she knew it. Almost healed now, moving freely. She regretted helping him with that. Helping people was always a mistake. A fight was an awful risk. She might be tougher than others, but she'd no wish to have her face broken into slop like that big man, the Stone Splitter. No wish to be stuck through with a sword, to have her knees smashed, her head ripped half off.

None of that held any appeal.

But he was too close to shoot, and if she ran he'd rouse the others, and they had horses. Fighting would probably wake them anyway, but if she could land a good blow quickly she might get away in the confusion. Hardly perfect, but what choice did she have? She slowly swung the bag off her shoulder and lowered it to the ground, then her bow and her quiver. She put one hand onto the hilt of her sword, fingers brushing the grip in the darkness, and he did the same.

'Alright then, pink. Let's get to it.'

'Might be there's another way.'

She watched him, suspicious, ready for tricks. 'What way?'

'Stay with us. Give it a few days. If you don't change your mind, well, I'll help you pack. You can trust me.' Trust was a word for fools. It was a word people used when they meant to betray you. If he moved forward a finger's width she would sweep the sword out and take his head off. She was ready.

But he did not move forward and he did not move back. He stood there, a big, silent outline in the darkness. She frowned, fingertips still tickling the grip of the curved sword. 'Why should I trust you?'

The big pink shrugged his heavy shoulders. 'Why not? Back in the city, I helped you and you helped me. Without each other, might be we'd both be dead.' It was true, she supposed, he had helped her. Not as much as she had helped him, but still. 'Time comes you got to stick at something, don't you? That's the thing about trust, sooner or later you just got to do it, without good reasons.'

'Why?'

'Otherwise you end up like us, and who wants that?'

'Huh.'

'I'll do you a deal. You watch my back, I'll watch yours.' He tapped his chest slowly with his thumb. 'I'll stick.' He pointed at her. 'You'll stick. What d'you say?'

Ferro thought about it. Running had given her freedom, but little else. It had taken her through years of misery to the very edge of the desert, hemmed in by enemies. She had run from Yulwei and the Eaters had nearly taken her. Where would she run to now, anyway? Would she run across the sea to Kanta? Perhaps the big pink was right. Perhaps the time had come to stop running.

At least until she could get away unnoticed.

She took her hand away from her sword, slowly folded her arms across her chest, and he did the same. They stood there for a long moment, watching one another in the darkness, in the silence. 'Alright, pink,' she growled. 'I will stick, as you say, and we will see. But I make no fucking promises, you understand?'

'I didn't ask for promises. My turn at the watch. You get some rest.'

'I need no rest, I told you that.'

'Suit yourself, but I'm sitting down.'

'Fine.'

The big pink began to lower himself cautiously towards the earth, and she followed him. They sat cross-legged where they had stood, facing each other, the embers of the campfire glowing beside them, casting a faint brightness over the four sleepers, across one side of the pink's lumpy face, casting a faint warmth across hers.

They watched each other.

Allies

To Arch Lector Sult, head of his Majesty's Inquisition.

Your Eminence,

Work is underway on the defences of the city. The famous land walls, though powerful, are in a shameful condition, and I have taken vigorous steps to strengthen them. I have also ordered extra supplies, food, armour, and weapons, essential if the city is to stand a siege of any duration.

Unfortunately, the defences are extensive, and the scale of the task vast. I have begun the work on credit, but credit will only stretch so far. I most humbly entreat that your Eminence will send me funds with which to work. Without money our efforts must cease, and the city will be lost.

The Union forces here are few, and morale is not high. There are mercenaries within the city, and I have ordered that more be recruited, but their loyalty is questionable, particularly if they cannot be paid. I therefore request that more of the King's soldiers might be sent. Even a single company could make a difference.

You will hear from me soon. Until then, I serve and obey.

Sand dan Glokta,
Superior of Dagoska.

'This is the place,' said Glokta.

'Uh,' said Frost.

It was a rough building of one storey, carelessly built from mud bricks, no bigger than a good-sized wood shed. Chinks of light spilled out into the night from around the ill-fitting door and the ill-fitting shutters in the single window. It was much the same as the other huts in the street, if you could call it a street. It hardly looked like the residence of a member of Dagoska's ruling council. *But then Kahdia is the odd man out in many ways.*

The leader of the natives. The priest without a temple. The one with least to lose, perhaps?

The door opened before Glokta even had the chance to knock. Kahdia stood in the doorway, tall and slender in his white robe. 'Why don't you come in?' The Haddish turned, stepped over to the only chair and sat down in it.

'Wait here,' said Glokta.

'Uh.'

The inside of the shed was no more auspicious than the outside. *Clean, and orderly, and poor as hell.* The ceiling was so low that Glokta could only just stand upright, the floor was hard-packed dirt. A straw mattress lay on empty crates at one end of the single room, a small chair beside it. A squat cupboard stood under the window, a few books stacked on top, a guttering candle burning beside them. Apart from a dented bucket for natural functions, that appeared to be the full extent of Kahdia's worldly possessions. *No sign of any hidden corpses of Superiors of the Inquisition, but you never know. A body can be packed away quite neatly, if one cuts it into small enough pieces . . .*

'You should move out of the slums.' Glokta shut the door behind him on creaking hinges, limped to the bed and sat down heavily on the mattress.

'Natives are not permitted within the Upper City, or had you not heard?'

'I'm sure that an exception could be made in your case. You could have chambers in the Citadel. Then I wouldn't have to limp all the way down here to speak to you.'

'Chambers in the Citadel? While my fellows rot down here in the filth? The least a leader can do is to share the burdens of his people. I have little other comfort to give them.' It was sweltering hot down here in the Lower City, but Kahdia did not seem uncomfortable. His gaze was level, his eyes were fixed on Glokta's, dark and cool as deep water. 'Do you disapprove?'

Glokta rubbed at his aching neck. 'Not in the least. Martyrdom suits you, but you'll have to forgive me if I don't join in.' He licked at his empty gums. 'I've made my sacrifices.'

'Perhaps not all of them. Ask your questions.' *Straight to business, then. Nothing to hide? Or nothing to lose?*

'Do you know what became of my predecessor, Superior Davoust?'

'It is my earnest hope that he died in great pain.' Glokta felt his eyebrows lift. *The very last thing I expected – an honest answer. Perhaps the first honest answer that I have received to that question, but hardly one that frees him from suspicion.*

'In great pain, you say?'

'Very great pain. And I will shed no tears if you join him.'

Glokta smiled. 'I don't know that I can think of anyone who will, but

Davoust is the matter in hand. Were your people involved in his disappearance?'

'It is possible. Davoust gave us reasons enough. There are many families missing husbands, fathers, daughters, because of his purges, his tests of loyalty, his making of examples. My people number many thousands, and I cannot watch them all. The one thing I can tell you is that I know nothing of his disappearance. When one devil falls they always send another, and here you are. My people have gained nothing.'

'Except Davoust's silence. Perhaps he discovered that you had made a deal with the Gurkish. Perhaps joining the Union was not all your people hoped for.'

Kahdia snorted. 'You know nothing. No Dagoskan would ever strike a deal with the Gurkish.'

'To an outsider, the two of you seem to have much in common.'

'To an ignorant outsider, we do. We both have dark skin, and we both pray to God, but that is the full extent of the similarity. We Dagoskans have never been a warlike people. We remained here on our peninsula, confident in the strength of our defences, while the Gurkish Empire spread like a cancer across the Kantic continent. We thought their conquests were none of our concern. That was our folly. Emissaries came to our gates, demanding that we kneel before the Gurkish Emperor, and acknowledge that the prophet Khalul speaks with the voice of God. We would do neither, and Khalul swore to destroy us. Now, it seems, he will finally succeed. All of the South will be his dominion.' *And the Arch Lector will not be in the least amused.*

'Who knows? Perhaps God will come to your aid.'

'God favours those who solve their own problems.'

'Perhaps we can solve some problems between us.'

'I have no interest in helping you.'

'Even if you help yourself as well? I have it in mind to issue a decree. The gates of the Upper City will be opened, your people will be allowed to come and go in their own city as they please. The Spicers will be turned out of the Great Temple, and it shall once again be your sacred ground. The Dagoskans will be permitted to carry arms; indeed, we will provide you with weapons from our own armouries. The natives will be treated like full citizens of the Union. They deserve nothing less.'

'So. So.' Kahdia clasped his hands together and sat back in his creaking chair. 'Now, with the Gurkish knocking at the gates, you come to Dagoska, flaunting your little scroll as though it was the word of God, and you choose to do the right thing. You are not like all the others. You are a good man, a fair man, a just man. You expect me to believe this?'

'Honestly? I don't care a shit what you believe, and I care about doing the right thing even less – that's all a matter of who you ask. As for being a good man,' and Glokta curled his lip, 'that ship sailed long ago, and I wasn't even there to wave it off. I'm interested in holding Dagoska. That and nothing else.'

'And you know you cannot hold Dagoska without our help.'

'Neither one of us is a fool, Kahdia. Don't insult me by acting like one. We can bicker with each other until the Gurkish tide sweeps over the land walls, or we can cooperate. You never know, together we might even beat them. Your people will help us dig the ditch, repair the walls, hang the gates. You will provide a thousand men to serve in the defence of the city, to begin with, and more later.'

'Will I? Will I indeed? And if, with our help, the city stands? Will our deal stand with it?'

If the city stands, I will be gone. More than likely, Vurms and the rest will be back in charge, and our deal will be dust. 'If the city stands, you have my word that I will do everything possible.'

'Everything possible. Meaning nothing.' *You get the idea.*

'I need your help, so I'm offering you what I can. I'd offer you more, but I don't have more. You could sulk down here in the slums with the flies for company, and wait for the Emperor to come. Perhaps the great Uthman-ul-Dosht will offer you a better deal.' Glokta looked Kahdia in the eye for a moment. 'But we both know he won't.'

The priest pursed his lips, stroked his beard, then gave a deep sigh. 'They say a man lost in the desert must take such water as he is offered, no matter who it comes from. I accept your deal. Once the temple is empty we will dig your holes, and carry your stone, and wear your swords. Something is better than nothing, and, as you say, perhaps together we can even beat the Gurkish. Miracles do happen.'

'So I've heard,' said Glokta as he shoved on his cane and grunted his way to his feet, shirt sticking to his sweaty back. 'So I've heard.' *But I've never seen one.*

Glokta stretched out on the cushions in his chambers, head back, mouth open, resting his aching body. *The same chambers that were once occupied by my illustrious predecessor, Superior Davoust.* They were a wide, airy, well-furnished set of rooms. Perhaps they once belonged to a Dagoskan Prince, or a scheming vizier, or a dusky concubine, before the natives were thrown out into the dust of the Lower City. *Better by far than my poky shit-hole in the Agriont, except that Superiors of the Inquisition have been known to go missing from these rooms.*

One set of windows faced northward, out towards the sea, on the steepest side of the rock, the other looked over the baking city. Both were equipped with heavy shutters. Outside it was a sheer drop over bare stone to jagged rocks and angry salt water. The door was six fingers thick, studded with iron, fitted with a heavy lock and four great bolts. *Davoust was a cautious man, and with good reason, it would seem. So how could assassins have got in, and having got in, how could they remove the body?*

He felt his mouth curving into a smile. *How will they remove mine, when they come? Already my enemies mount up – the sneering Vurms, the punctilious Vissbruck, the merchants whose profits I threaten, the Practicals who served Harker and Davoust, the natives with good reason to hate anyone who wears black, my old enemies the Gurkish, of course, and all that providing his Eminence does not get anxious at the lack of progress, and decide to have me replaced himself. Will anyone come searching for my twisted corpse, I wonder?*

'Superior.'

Opening his eyes and lifting his head was a great and painful effort. Everything hurt from his exertions of the past few days. His neck clicked like a snapping twig with every movement, his back was stiff and brittle as a mirror, his leg veered between nagging agony and trembling numbness.

Shickel was standing in the doorway, head bowed. The cuts and bruises on her dark face were healed. There was no outward sign of the ordeal she had suffered in the cells below. She never looked him in the eye, though, always at the floor. *Some wounds take time to heal, and others never do. I should know.*

'What is it, Shickel?'

'Magister Eider sends you an invitation to dinner.'

'Does she indeed?'

The girl nodded.

'Send word that I will be honoured to attend.'

Glokta watched her pad out of the room, head bowed, then he sagged back onto his cushions. *If I disappear tomorrow, at least I will have saved one person. Perhaps that means my life has not been a total waste of time. Sand dan Glokta, shield to the helpless. Is it ever too late to be . . . a good man?*

'Please!' squealed Harker. 'Please! I know nothing!' He was bound tightly to his chair, unable to move his body far. *But he makes up for it with his eyes.* They darted back and forth over Glokta's instruments, glittering in the harsh lamplight on the scarred table top. *Oh yes, you understand better than most how this will work. Knowledge is so often the antidote to fear. But not here. Not now.* 'I know nothing!'

'I will be the judge of what you know.' Glokta wiped some sweat from his face. The room was hot as a busy forge and the glowing coals in the brazier were far from helping. 'If a thing smells like a liar, and is the colour of a liar, the chances are it is a liar, would you not agree?'

'Please! We are all on the same side!' *Are we? Are we really?* 'I have told you only the truth!'

'Perhaps, but not as much of it as I need.'

'Please! We are all friends here!'

'Friends? In my experience, a friend is merely an acquaintance who has yet to betray you. Is that what you are, Harker?'

'No!'

Glokta frowned. 'Then you are our enemy?'

'What? No! I just . . . I just . . . I wanted to know what happened! That's all! I didn't mean to . . . please!' *Please, please, please, I tire of hearing it.* 'You have to believe me!'

'The only thing I have to do is get answers.'

'Only ask your questions, Superior, I beg of you! Only give me the opportunity to cooperate!' *Oh indeed, the firm hand does not seem such a fine idea any longer, does it?* 'Ask your questions, I will do my best to answer!'

'Good.' Glokta perched himself on the edge of the table just beside his tightly bound prisoner and looked down at him. 'Excellent.' Harker's hands were tanned deep brown, his face was tanned deep brown, the rest of his body was pale as a white slug with thick patches of dark hair. *Hardly a fetching look. But it could be worse.* 'Answer me this, then. Why is it that men have nipples?'

Harker blinked. He swallowed. He looked up at Frost, but there was no help there. The albino stared back, unblinking, white skin round his mask beaded with sweat, eyes hard as two pink jewels. 'I . . . I am not sure I understand, Superior.'

'Is it not a simple question? Nipples, Harker, on men. What purpose do they serve? Have you not often wondered?'

'I . . . I . . .'

Glokta sighed. 'They chafe and become painful in the wet. They dry out and become painful in the heat. Some women, for reasons I could never fathom, insist on fiddling with them in bed, as though we derive anything but annoyance from having them interfered with.' Glokta reached towards the table, while Harker's wide eyes followed his every movement, and slid his hand slowly around the grips of the pincers. He lifted them up and examined them, the well-sharpened jaws glinting in the bright lamplight. 'A man's nipples,' he murmured, 'are a positive hindrance to him. Do you know? Aside from the unsightly scarring, I don't miss mine in the least.'

He grabbed the tip of Harker's nipple and dragged it roughly towards him. 'Ah!' squawked the one-time Inquisitor, the chair creaking as he tried desperately to twist away. 'No!'

'You think that hurts? Then I doubt you'll enjoy what's coming.' And Glokta slid the open jaws of the pincers around the stretched out flesh and squeezed them tight.

'Ah! Ah! Please! Superior, I beg you!'

'Your begging is worthless to me. What I need from you is answers. What became of Davoust?'

'I swear on my life that I don't know!'

'Not good enough.' Glokta began to squeeze harder, the metal edges starting to bite into the skin.

Harker gave a despairing shriek. 'Wait! I took money! I admit it! I took money!'

'Money?' Glokta let the pressure release a fraction and a drop of blood dripped from the pincers and spattered on Harker's hairy white leg. 'What money?'

'Money Davoust took from the natives! After the rebellion! He had me round up any that I thought might be rich, and he had them hanged along with the rest, and we requisitioned everything they had and split it between us! He kept his share in a chest in his quarters, and when he disappeared . . . I took it!'

'Where is this money now?'

'Gone! I spent it! On women . . . and on wine, and, and, on anything!'

Glokta clicked his tongue. 'Tut, tut.' *Greed and conspiracy, injustice and betrayal, robbery and murder. All the ingredients of a tale to titillate the masses. Saucy, but hardly relevant.* He worked his hand around the pincers. 'It is the Superior himself, not his money, that interests me. Believe me when I say that I grow tired of asking the question. What became of Davoust?'

'I . . . I . . . I don't know!'

True, perhaps. But hardly the answer I need. 'Not good enough.' Glokta squeezed his hand and the metal jaws bit cleanly through flesh and met in the middle with a gentle click. Harker bellowed, and thrashed, and roared in agony, blood bubbling from the red square of flesh where his nipple used to be and running down his pale belly in dark streaks. Glokta winced at a twinge in his neck and stretched his head out until he heard it click. *Strange how, with time, even the most terrible suffering of others can become . . . tedious.*

'Practical Frost, the Inquisitor is bleeding! If you please!'

'I'th thorry.' The iron scraped as Frost dragged it from the brazier, glowing orange. Glokta could feel the heat of it even from where he was sitting. *Ah, hot iron. It keeps no secrets, it tells no lies.*

'No! No! I—' Harker's words dissolved into a bubbling scream as Frost ground the brand into the wound and the room filled slowly with the salty aroma of cooking meat. A smell which, to Glokta's disgust, caused his empty stomach to rumble. *How long is it since I had a good slice of meat?* He wiped a fresh sheen of sweat from his face with his free hand and worked his aching shoulders under his coat.

An ugly business, that we find ourselves in. So why do I do this? The only answer was the soft crunch as Frost slid the iron carefully back into the coals, sending up a dusting of orange sparks. Harker twisted, and whimpered, and shook, his weeping eyes bulging, a strand of smoke still curling up from the blackened flesh on his chest. *An ugly business, of course.*

No doubt he deserves it, but that changes nothing. Probably he has no clue what became of Davoust, but that changes nothing either. The questions must be asked, and exactly as if he did know the answers.

'Why do you insist on defying me, Harker? Could it be . . . that you suppose . . . that once I'm done with your nipples I'll have run out of ideas? Is that what you're thinking? That your nipples are where I'll stop?'

Harker stared at him, bubbles of spit forming and breaking on his lips. Glokta leaned closer. 'Oh, no, no, no. This is only the beginning. This is before the beginning. Time opens up ahead of us in pitiless abundance. Days, and weeks, and months of it, if need be. Do you seriously believe that you can keep your secrets for that long? You belong to me, now. To me, and to this room. This cannot stop until I know what I need to know.' He reached forward and gripped Harker's other nipple between thumb and forefinger. He took up the pincers and opened their bloody jaws. 'How difficult can that be to understand?'

Magister Eider's dining chamber was fabulous to behold. Cloths of silver and crimson, gold and purple, green and blue and vivid yellow, rippled in the gentle breeze from the narrow windows. Screens of filigree marble adorned the walls, great pots as high as a man stood in the corners. Heaps of pristine cushions were tossed about the floor, as though inviting passers-by to sprawl in comfortable decadence. Coloured candles burned in tall glass jars, casting warm light into every corner, filling the air with sweet scent. At one end of the marble hall clear water trickled gently in a star-shaped pool. There was more than a touch of the theatrical about the place. *Like a Queen's boudoir from some Kantic legend.*

Magister Eider, head of the Guild of Spicers, was herself the centrepiece. *The very Queen of merchants.* She sat at the top of the table in a pristine white gown, shimmering silk with just the slightest, fascinating hint of transparency. A small fortune in jewels flashed on every inch of tanned skin, her hair was piled up and held in place with ivory combs, excepting a few strands, curling artfully around her face. It looked very much as if she had been preparing herself all day. *And not a moment was wasted.*

Glokta, hunched in his chair at the opposite end with a bowl of steaming soup before him, felt as if he had shuffled into the pages of a storybook. *A lurid romance, set in the exotic south, with Magister Eider as the heroine, and myself the disgusting, the crippled, the black-hearted villain. How will this fable end, I wonder?* 'So, tell me, Magister, to what do I owe this honour?'

'I understand that you have spoken to the other members of the council. I was surprised, and just a little hurt, that you had not sought an audience with me already.'

'I apologise if you felt left out. It seemed only fitting that I saved the most powerful until last.'

She looked up with an air of injured innocence. *And a most consummately acted one.* 'Powerful? Me? Vurms controls the budget, issues the decrees, Vissbruck commands the troops, holds the defences. Kahdia speaks for the great majority of the populace. I scarcely figure.'

'Come now.' Glokta grinned his toothless grin. 'You are radiant, of course, but I am not quite blinded. Vurms' budget is a pittance compared to what the Spicers make. Kahdia's people have been rendered almost helpless. Through your pickled friend Cosca you command more than twice the troops that Vissbruck does. The only reason the Union is even interested in this thirsty rock is for the trade that your guild controls.'

'Well, I don't like to boast.' The Magister gave an artless shrug. 'But I suppose that I do have some passing influence in the city. You have been asking questions, I see.'

'That's what I do.' Glokta raised his spoon to his mouth, trying his best not to slurp between his remaining teeth. 'This soup is delicious, by the way.' *And, one hopes, not fatal.*

'I thought you might appreciate it. You see, I have been asking questions also.'

The water plopped and tinkled in the pool, the fabric rustled on the walls, the silverware clicked gently against the fine pottery of their bowls. *I would call that first round a draw.* Carlot dan Eider was the first to break the silence.

'I realise, of course, that you have a mission from the Arch Lector himself. A mission of the greatest importance. I see that you are not a man to mince your words, but you might want to tread a little more carefully.'

'I admit my gait is awkward. A war wound, compounded by two years of torture. It's a wonder I got to keep the leg at all.'

She smiled wide, displaying two rows of perfect teeth. 'I am thoroughly tickled, but my colleagues have found you somewhat less entertaining. Vurms and Vissbruck have both taken a decided dislike to you. Highhanded was the phrase they used, I believe, among others I had better not repeat.'

Glokta shrugged. 'I am not here to make friends.' And he drained his glass of a predictably excellent wine.

'But friends can be useful. If nothing else, a friend is one less enemy. Davoust insisted on upsetting everyone, and the results have not been happy.'

'Davoust did not enjoy the support of the Closed Council.'

'True. But no document will stop a knife thrust.'

'Is that a threat?'

Carlot dan Eider laughed. It was an easy, open, friendly laugh. It was hard to believe that anyone who made such a sound could be a traitor, or a threat, or anything other than a perfectly charming host. *And yet I am not entirely convinced.* 'That is advice. Advice born of bitter experience. I would prefer it if you did not disappear quite yet.'

'Really? I had no idea I was such a winning dinner guest.'

'You are terse, confrontational, slightly frightening, and impose severe restrictions on the menu, but the fact is you are more use to me here than . . .' and she waved her hand, 'wherever Davoust went to. Would you care for more wine?'

'Of course.'

She got up from her chair and swept towards him, feet padding on the cool marble like a dancer's. *Bare feet, in the Kantic fashion.* The breeze stirred the flowing garments around her body as she leaned forwards to fill Glokta's glass, wafted her rich scent in his face. *Just the sort of woman my mother would have wanted me to marry – beautiful, clever, and oh so very rich. Just the sort of woman I would have wanted to marry, for that matter, when I was younger. When I was a different man.*

The flickering candlelight shone on her hair, flashed on the jewels around her long neck, glowed through the wine as it sloshed from the neck of the bottle. *Does she try and charm me merely because I hold the writ of the Closed Council? Nothing more than good business, to be on good terms with the powerful? Or does she hope to fool me, and distract me, and lure me away from the unpleasant truth?* Her eyes met his briefly, and she gave a tiny, knowing smile and looked back to his glass. *Am I to be her little urchin boy, dirty face pressed up against the baker's window, mouth watering for the sweetmeats I know I can never afford? I think not.*

'Where did Davoust go to?'

Magister Eider paused for a moment, then carefully set down the bottle. She slid into the nearest chair, put her elbows on the table, her chin on her hands, and held Glokta's eye. 'I suspect that he was killed by a traitor in the city. Probably an agent of the Gurkish. At the risk of telling you what you already know, Davoust suspected there was a conspiracy afoot within the city's ruling council. He confided as much to me shortly before his disappearance.'

Did he indeed? 'A conspiracy within the ruling council?' Glokta shook his head in mock horror. 'Is such a thing possible?'

'Let us be honest with each other, Superior. I want what you want. We in the Guild of Spicers have invested far too much time and money in this city to see it fall to the Gurkish, and you seem to offer a better chance of holding on to it than those idiots Vurms and Vissbruck. If there is a traitor within our walls I want him found.'

'Him . . . or her.'

Magister Eider raised one delicate eyebrow. 'It cannot have escaped your notice that I am the only woman on the council.'

'It has not.' Glokta slurped noisily from his spoon. 'But forgive me if I don't discount you quite yet. It will require more than good soup and pleasant conversation to convince me of anyone's innocence.' *Although it's a damn sight more than anyone else has offered me.*

Magister Eider smiled as she raised her glass. 'Then how can I convince you?'

'Honestly? I need money.'

'Ah, money. It always comes back to that. Getting money out of my Guild is like trying to dig up water in the desert – tiring, dirty, and almost always a waste of time.' *Somewhat like asking questions of Inquisitor Harker.* 'How much were you thinking of?'

'We could begin with, say, a hundred thousand marks.'

Eider did not actually choke on her wine. *More of a gentle gurgle.* She set her glass down carefully, quietly cleared her throat, dabbed at her mouth with the corner of a cloth, then looked up at him, eyebrows raised. 'You very well know that no such amount will be forthcoming.'

'I'll settle for whatever you can give me, for now.'

'We'll see. Are your ambitions limited to a mere hundred thousand marks, or is there anything else I can do for you?'

'Actually there is. I need the merchants out of the Temple.'

Eider rubbed gently at her own temples, as though Glokta's demands were giving her a headache. 'He wants the merchants out,' she murmured.

'It was necessary to secure Kahdia's support. With him against us we cannot hope to hold the city for long.'

'I've been telling those arrogant fools the same thing for years, but stamping on the natives has become quite the popular pastime nonetheless. Very well, when do you want them out?'

'Tomorrow. At the latest.'

'And they call you high-handed?' She shook her head. 'Very well. By tomorrow evening I could well be the most unpopular Magister in living memory, if I still have my post at all, but I'll try and sell it to the Guild.'

Glokta grinned. 'I feel confident that you could sell anything.'

'You're a tough negotiator, Superior. If you ever get tired of asking questions, I have no doubt you've a bright future as a merchant.'

'A merchant? Oh, I'm not that ruthless.' Glokta placed his spoon in the empty bowl and licked at his gums. 'I mean no disrespect, but how does a woman come to head the most powerful Guild in the Union?'

Eider paused, as though wondering whether to answer or not. *Or judging how much truth to tell when she does.* She looked down at her glass, turned the stem slowly round and round. 'My husband was Magister before me. When we married I was twenty-two years old, he was near sixty. My father owed him a great deal of money, and offered my hand as payment for the debt.' *Ah, so we all have our sufferings.* Her lip twisted in a faint scowl. 'My husband always had a good nose for a bargain. His health began to decline soon after we married, and I took a more and more active role in the management of his affairs, and those of the Guild. By the time he died I was Magister in all but name, and my colleagues were sensible enough to formalise the arrangement. The Spicers have always been more concerned for profit than propriety.' Her eyes flicked up to look at Glokta. 'I mean no disrespect, but how does a war hero come to be a torturer?'

It was his turn to pause. *A good question. How did that happen?* 'There are precious few opportunities for cripples.'

Eider nodded slowly, her eyes never leaving Glokta's face. 'That must have been hard. To come back, after all that time in the darkness, and to find that your friends had no use for you. To see in their faces only guilt, and pity, and disgust. To find yourself alone.'

Glokta's eyelid was twitching, and he rubbed at it gently. He had never discussed such things with anyone before. *And now here I am, discussing them with a stranger.* 'There can be no doubt that I'm a tragic figure. I used to be a shit of a man, now I'm a husk of one. Take your pick.'

'I imagine it makes you sick, to be treated that way. Very sick, and very angry.' *If only you knew.* 'It still seems a strange decision, though, for the tortured to turn torturer.'

'On the contrary, nothing could be more natural. In my experience, people do as they are done to. You were sold by your father and bought by your husband, and yet you choose to buy and sell.'

Eider frowned. *Something for her to think about, perhaps?* 'I would have thought your pain would give you empathy.'

'Empathy? What's that?' Glokta winced as he rubbed at his aching leg. 'It's a sad fact, but pain only makes you sorry for yourself.'

Campfire Politics

Logen shifted uncomfortably in his saddle, and squinted up at the few birds circling around over the great flat plain. Damn but his arse hurt. His thighs were sore, his nose was all full of the smell of horse. Couldn't find a comfortable position to put his fruits in. Always squashed, however often he jammed his hand down inside his belt to move 'em. A damn uncomfortable journey this was turning out to be, in all sorts of ways.

He used to talk on the road, back in the North. When he was a boy he'd talked to his father. When he was a young man he'd talked to his friends. When he'd followed Bethod he'd talked to him, all the day long, for they'd been close back then, like brothers almost. Talk took your mind off the blisters on your feet, or the hunger in your belly, or the endless bloody cold, or who'd got killed yesterday.

Logen used to laugh at the Dogman's stories while they slogged through the snow. He used to puzzle over tactics with Threetrees while they rode through the mud. He used to argue with Black Dow while they waded through bogs, and no subject was ever too small. He'd even traded a joke or two with Harding Grim in his time, and there weren't too many who could say that.

He sighed to himself. A long, painful sigh that caught at the back of his throat. Good times, no doubt, but far behind him now, in the sunny valleys of the past. Those boys were all gone back to the mud. All silent, forever. Worse yet, they'd left Logen out in the middle of nowhere with this lot.

The great Jezal dan Luthar wasn't interested in anyone's stories except his own. He sat stiff upright and aloof the whole time, chin held high, displaying his arrogance, and his superiority, and his contempt for everything like a young man might show off his first sword, long before he learned that it was nothing to be proud of.

Bayaz had no interest in tactics. When he spoke at all he barked in single words, in yeses and in nos, frowning out across the endless grass like a man who's made a bad mistake and can't see his way clear of it. His apprentice too seemed changed since they left Adua. Quiet, hard, watchful. Brother

79

Longfoot was away across the plain, scouting out the route. Probably best that way. No one else had any talk at all. The Navigator, Logen had to admit, had far too much.

Ferro rode some distance away from the rest of this friendly gathering, her shoulders hunched, her brows drawn down in a constant scowl, the long scar on her cheek puckered up an angry grey, doing her best to make the others look like a sack of laughs. She leaned forwards, into the wind, pushing at it, as if she hoped to hurt it with her face. More fun to trade jokes with the plague than with her, Logen reckoned.

And that was the merry band. His shoulders slumped. 'How long until we get to the Edge of the World?' he asked Bayaz, without much hope.

'Some way yet,' growled the Magus through barely open teeth.

So Logen rode on, tired, and sore, and bored, and watched those few birds gliding slowly over the endless plain. Nice, big, fat birds. He licked his lips. 'We could do with some meat,' he muttered. Hadn't had fresh meat in a good long time now. Not since they left Calcis. Logen rubbed his stomach. The fatty softness from his time in the city was already tightening. 'Nice bit of meat.'

Ferro frowned over at him, then up at the few birds circling above. She shrugged her bow off her shoulder.

'Hah!' chuckled Logen. 'Good luck.' He watched her slide an arrow smoothly out from her quiver. Futile gesture. Even Harding Grim could never have made that shot, and he was the best man Logen had ever seen with a bow. He watched Ferro nock her shaft to the curved wood, back arched, yellow eyes fixed on the gliding shapes overhead.

'You'll never bag one of those, not in a thousand years of trying.' She pulled back the string. 'Waste of a shaft!' he shouted. 'You've got to be realistic about these things!' Probably the arrow would drop back down and stab him in the face. Or stick his horse through the neck, so it died and fell over and crushed him under it. A fitting end to this nightmare of a journey. A moment later one of the birds tumbled down into the grass, Ferro's arrow stuck right through it.

'No,' he whispered, gawping open-mouthed at her as she bent the bow again. Another arrow sailed up into the grey sky. Another bird flopped to the earth, just beside the first. Logen stared at it, disbelieving. 'No!'

'Don't tell me you haven't seen stranger things,' said Bayaz. 'A man who talks to spirits, who travels with Magi, the most feared man in all the North?'

Logen pulled his horse up and slithered down from the saddle. He walked through the long grass, bent down on wobbly, aching legs and picked up one of the birds. The shaft had stuck it right through the centre of the breast. If Logen had stabbed it with the arrow at a distance of a foot, he could hardly have done it more neatly. 'That's wrong.'

Bayaz grinned down, hands crossed on the saddle before him. 'In ancient days, before history, so the legends say, our world and the Other Side were joined. One world. Demons walked the land, free to do as they pleased. Chaos, beyond dreaming. They bred with humans, and their offspring were half breeds. Part man, part demon. Devil-bloods. Monsters. One among them took the name Euz. He delivered humanity from the tyranny of devils, and the fury of his battle with them shaped the land. He split the world above from the world below, and he sealed the gates between. To prevent such terror ever coming again, he pronounced the First Law. It is forbidden to touch the Other Side direct, or to speak with devils.'

Logen watched the others watch Ferro. Luthar and Quai, both frowning at this uncanny display of archery. She leaned right back in her saddle, bow string drawn as tight as it would go, glittering point of the next shaft held perfectly steady, still managing to nudge her mount this way and that with her heels. Logen could scarcely make a horse do what he wanted with the reins in his hands, but he failed to see what Bayaz' crazy story had to do with it. 'Devils and so on, the First Law.' Logen waved his hand. 'So what?'

'From the start the First Law was filled with contradictions. All magic comes from the Other Side, falling upon the land as the light falls from the sun. Euz himself was part devil, and so were his sons – Juvens, Kanedias, Glustrod – and others beside. Their blood brought them gifts, and curses. Power, and long life, and strength or sight beyond the limits of simple men. Their blood passed on into their children, growing ever thinner, into their children's children, and so on through the long centuries. The gifts skipped one generation, then another, then came but rarely. The devil-blood grew thin, and died out. It is rare indeed now, when our world and the world below have drifted so far apart, to see those gifts made flesh. We truly are privileged to witness it.'

Logen raised his eyebrows. 'Her? Half devil?'

'Much less than half, my friend.' Bayaz chuckled. 'Euz himself was half, and his power threw up the mountains and gouged out the seas. Half could strike a horror and a desire into your blood to stop your heart. Half could blind you to look upon. Not half. No more than a fraction. But in her, there is a trace of the Other Side.'

'The Other Side, eh?' Logen looked down at the dead bird in his hand. 'So if I was to touch her, would I break the First Law?'

Bayaz chuckled. 'Now that is a sharp question. You always surprise me, Master Ninefingers. I wonder what Euz would say to it?' The Magus pursed his lips. 'I think I could find it in myself to forgive you. She however,' and Bayaz nodded his bald head at Ferro, 'would most likely cut your hand off.'

Logen lay on his belly, peering through the tall grass into a gentle valley with a shallow brook in its bottom. There was a huddle of buildings on the side nearest them, or the shells of buildings. No roofs left, nothing but the tumbledown walls, mostly no more than waist high, the fallen stones from them scattered across the valley's slopes, in amongst the waving grass. It could have been a scene out of the North. Lots of villages abandoned there, since the wars. People driven out, dragged out, burned out. Logen had watched it happen, often. He'd joined in more than once. He wasn't proud of it, but he wasn't proud of much from those times. Or any other, come to think of it.

'Not a lot left to live in,' whispered Luthar.

Ferro scowled at him. 'Plenty left to hide behind.'

Evening was coming on, the sun had dropped low on the horizon and filled the broken village up with shadows. There was no sign of anyone down there. No sounds beyond the giggling water, the slow wind slithering through the grass. No sign of anyone, but Ferro was right. No sign didn't necessarily mean no danger.

'You had best go down there and take a look,' murmured Longfoot.

'I best?' Logen glanced sideways at him. 'You're staying here then, eh?'

'I have no talent for fights. You are well aware of that.'

'Huh,' muttered Logen. 'No talent for the sorting of fights, plenty for the finding of 'em though.'

'Finding things is what I do. I'm here to Navigate.'

'Maybe you could find me a decent meal and a bed to sleep in,' snapped Luthar, in his whining Union accent.

Ferro sucked her teeth with disgust. 'Someone's got to go,' she growled, sliding over the lip of the slope on her belly. 'I'll take the left.'

No one else moved. 'Us too,' Logen grunted at Luthar.

'Me?'

'Who else? Three's a good number. Let's go, and let's keep it stealthy.'

Luthar peered through the grass into the valley, licked his lips, rubbed his palms together. Nervous, Logen could tell, nervous but proud at the same time, like an untried boy before a battle, trying to show he's not scared by sticking his chin out. Logen wasn't fooled. He'd seen it all a hundred times before.

'You planning to wait for the morning?' he grunted.

'Just keep your mind on your own shortcomings, Northman,' hissed Luthar as he started to wriggle forward down the slope. 'You've enough of them!' The rowels of his big, shiny spurs rattled loud as he dragged himself over the edge, clumsy and unpractised, his arse sticking up in the air.

Logen grabbed hold of his coat before he got more than a stride. 'You're not leaving those on are you?'

'What?'

'Those fucking spurs! Stealthy I said! You might as well hang a bell off your cock!'

Luthar scowled as he sat up to pull them off.

'Stay down!' hissed Logen, pushing him back into the grass on his back. 'You want to get us killed?'

'Get off me!'

Logen shoved him down again, then stabbed at him with his finger to make sure he got the point. 'I'm not dying over your fucking spurs and that's a fact! If you can't keep quiet you can stay here with the Navigator.' He glowered over at Longfoot. 'Maybe you both can navigate your way into the village once we've made sure it's safe.' He shook his head and crawled down the slope after Ferro.

She was already halfway to the brook, rolling and slithering over the crumbled walls, sneaking across the spaces in between them, keeping low, hand on the grip of her curved sword, quick and silent as the wind over the plain.

Impressive, no doubt, but Logen was nobody's fool when it came to a spot of sneaking. He'd been known for it, when he was younger. Lost count of the number of Shanka, the number of men he'd come up behind. The first you'll hear of the Bloody-Nine is the blood hissing out of your neck, that used to be the rumour. Say one thing for Logen Ninefingers, say that he's stealthy.

He flowed up to the first wall, slid one leg over it, silent as a mouse. He lifted himself up, smooth as butter, keeping quiet, keeping low. His back foot caught on a set of loose stones, dragged them scraping with him. He grabbed at them, fumbled them, knocked over even more with his elbow and they clattered down loud around him. He stumbled onto his weak ankle, twisted it, squawked with pain, fell over and rolled through a patch of thistles.

'Shit,' he grunted, struggling up, one hand clutching at the hilt of his sword, all tangled up with his coat. Good thing he hadn't had it out, or he could've stuck himself through with it. Happened to a friend of his. So busy shouting that he tripped on a tree root and cut a big piece out of his head on his own axe. Back to the mud double time.

He crouched among the fallen stones, waiting for someone to jump him. No one came. Just the wind breathing through the gaps in the old walls, the water chuckling away in the brook. He crept along beside a heap of rough stones, through an old doorway, slithered over a slumping wall, limping and gasping on his bad foot, scarcely making any effort to stay quiet any longer. There was no one there. He'd known it as soon as he fell. No way they could have missed that sorry performance. The Dogman would most likely have been weeping right about now, had he been alive. He waved up at the ridge, and a moment later he saw Longfoot stand up and wave as well.

'No one here,' he muttered to himself.

'Just as well,' hissed Ferro's voice, not more than a stride or two behind.

'You got a new way of scouting, pink. Make so much noise that they come to you.'

'Out of practice,' grunted Logen. 'Still, no harm done. No one here.'

'There was.' She was standing in the shell of one of the ruined buildings, frowning down at the ground. A burned patch in the grass, a few stones set around it. A campfire.

'No more 'n a day or two old,' muttered Logen, poking at the ashes with a finger.

Luthar walked up behind them. 'No one here after all.' He had a smug, sucked-in look on his face, like he'd somehow been right about something all along. Logen didn't see what.

'Lucky for you there isn't, or we might be stitching you together right about now!'

'I'd be stitching the fucking pair of you!' hissed Ferro. 'I ought to stitch your useless pink heads together! You're both as worthless as a bag of sand in the desert! There's tracks over there. Horses, more than one cart.'

'Merchants maybe?' asked Logen, hopefully. He and Ferro looked at each other for a moment. 'Might be better if we stay off the track from now on.'

'Too slow.' Bayaz had made it down into the village now. Quai and Longfoot weren't far behind with the cart and the horses. 'Far too slow. We stick to the track. We'll see anyone coming in good time out here. Plenty of time.'

Luthar didn't look convinced. 'If we see them, they'll see us. What then?'

'Then?' Bayaz raised an eyebrow. 'Then we have the famous Captain Luthar to protect us.' He looked round at the ruined village. 'Running water, and shelter, of a kind. Seems like a good place to camp.'

'Good enough,' muttered Logen, already rooting through the cart for logs to start a fire of their own. 'I'm hungry. What happened to those birds?'

Logen sat, and watched the others eat over the rim of his pot.

Ferro squatted at the very edge of the shifting light from the campfire, hunched over, shadowy face almost stuck right into her bowl, staring around suspiciously and shoving food in with her fingers like she was worried it might be snatched away any moment. Luthar was less enthusiastic. He was nibbling daintily at a wing with his bared front teeth, as though touching it with his lips might poison him, discarded morsels lined up carefully along the side of his platter. Bayaz chewed away with some relish, his beard glistening with gravy. 'It's good,' he muttered around a mouthful. 'You might want to consider cookery as a career, Master Ninefingers, if you should ever grow tired of . . .' he waved his spoon, 'whatever it is you do.'

84

'Huh,' said Logen. In the North everyone took their turn at the fire, and it was reckoned an honour to do it. A good cook was almost as valued as a good fighter. Not here. These were a sorry crowd when it came to minding the pot. Bayaz could just about get his tea boiled, and that was as far as he went. Quai could get a biscuit out of the box on a good day. Logen doubted whether Luthar would even have known which way up the pot went. As for Ferro, she seemed to despise the whole notion of cooking. Logen reckoned she was used to eating her food raw. Perhaps while it was still alive.

In the North, after a hard day on the trail, when the men gathered around the long fires to eat, there was a strict order to who sat where. The chief would go at the top, with his sons and the Named Men of the clan around him. Next came the Carls, in order of fame. Thralls were lucky to get their own small fires further out. Men would always have their place, and only change it when their chief offered, out of respect for some great service they'd done him, or for showing rare good bones in a fight. Sitting out of place could earn you a kicking, or a killing even. Where you sat round the fire was where you stood in life, more or less.

It was different out here on the plains, but Logen could still see a pattern in who sat where, and it was far from a happy one. He and Bayaz were close enough to the fire, but the others were further than comfort would have put them. Drawn close by the wind, and the cold, and the damp night, pushed further out by each other. He glanced over at Luthar, sneering down into his bowl as though it was full of piss. No respect. He glanced over at Ferro, staring yellow knives at him through narrowed eyes. No trust. He shook his head sadly. Without trust and respect the group would fall apart in a fight like walls without mortar.

Still, Logen had won over tougher audiences, in his time. Threetrees, Tul Duru, Black Dow, Harding Grim, he'd fought each one in single combat, and beaten them all. Spared each man's life, and left him bound to follow. Each one had tried their best to kill him, and with good reasons too, but in the end Logen had earned their trust, and their respect, and their friendship even. Small gestures and a lot of time, that was how he'd done it. 'Patience is the chief of virtues,' his father used to say, and 'you won't cross the mountains in a day.' Time might be against them, but there was nothing to be gained by rushing. You have to be realistic about these things.

Logen uncrossed his stiff legs, took hold of the water-skin and got up, walked slowly over to where Ferro was sitting. Her eyes followed him all the way across. She was a strange one, no doubt, and not just the looks of her, though the dead knew her looks were strange enough. She seemed hard and sharp and cold as a new sword, ruthless as any man that Logen could think of. You would have thought she wouldn't throw a log to save a drowning man, but she'd done more than that to save him, and more than once. Out of all of them, she was the one he'd trust first, and furthest. So he squatted down and held the skin out to her, its bulbous shadow flickering and shifting on the rough wall behind her.

She frowned at it for a moment, then frowned up at Logen. Then she snatched it off him and bent back over her pot, half turning her bony shoulders on him. Not a word of thanks, or a gesture even, but he didn't mind. You won't cross the mountains in a day, after all.

He dropped down again beside the fire, watched the flames dancing, casting shifting light across the grim faces of the group. 'Anyone know any stories?' he asked, hopefully.

Quai sucked at his teeth. Luthar curled his lip at Logen across the fire. Ferro gave no sign that she had even heard. Hardly an encouraging start.

'Not any?' No reply. 'Alright then, I know a song or two, if I can remember the words,' he cleared his throat.

'Very well!' cut in Bayaz. 'If it will save us from a song, I know hundreds of stories. What did you have it in mind to hear about? A romance? A comedy? A tale of bravery against the odds?'

'This place,' cut in Luthar. 'The Old Empire. If it was such a great nation, how did it come to this?' He jerked his head over at the crumbling walls, and what they all knew lay beyond. The miles and miles of nothing. 'A wasteland.'

Bayaz sighed. 'I could tell that tale, but we are lucky enough to have a native of the Old Empire with us on our little trip, and a keen student of history to boot. Master Quai?' The apprentice looked up lazily from the fire. 'Would you care to enlighten us? How did the Empire, once the glittering centre of the world, come to this pass?'

'That story is long in the telling,' murmured the apprentice. 'Shall I start from the beginning?'

'Where else should a man ever start?'

Quai shrugged his bony shoulders and began to speak. 'Almighty Euz, vanquisher of demons, closer of gates, father of the World, had four sons, and to each he gave a gift. To his eldest, Juvens, he gave the talent of High Art, the skill to change the world with magic, tempered by knowledge. To his second son, Kanedias, went the gift of making, of shaping stone and metal to his own purposes. To his third son, Bedesh, Euz gave the skill of speaking with spirits, and of making them do his bidding.' Quai gave a wide yawn, smacked his lips and blinked at the fire. 'So were born the three pure disciplines of magic.'

'I thought he had four sons,' grumbled Luthar.

Quai's eyes slid sideways. 'So he did, and therein lies the root of the Empire's destruction. Glustrod was the youngest son. To him should have gone the gift of communing with the Other Side. The secrets of summoning devils from the world below and binding them to one's will. But such things were forbidden by the First Law, and so Euz gave nothing to his youngest son but his blessing, and we all know what those are worth. He taught the other three their share of his secrets and left, ordering his sons to bring order to the world.'

'Order.' Luthar tossed his platter down on the grass beside him and glanced disdainfully round at the shadowy ruins. 'They didn't get far.'

'At first they did. Juvens set about his purpose with a will, and bent all his power and all his wisdom to it. He found a people that pleased him, living beside the Aos, and favoured them with laws and learning, government and science. He gave to them the skills to conquer their neighbours, and made of their chief an Emperor. Son followed father, year followed year, and the nation grew and prospered. The lands of the Empire stretched as far as Isparda in the south, Anconus in the north, the very shores of the Circle Sea to the east, and beyond. Emperor followed Emperor, but always Juvens was there – guiding, advising, shaping all things according to his grand design. All was civilised, all was peaceful, all was content.'

'Almost all,' muttered Bayaz, poking at the guttering fire with a stick.

Quai gave a smirk. 'We have forgotten Glustrod, just as his father did. The ignored son. The shunned son. The cheated son. He begged all three brothers for a share of their secrets, but they were jealous of their gifts, and all three refused him. He looked upon what Juvens had achieved, and was bitter beyond words. He found dark places in the world, and in secret he studied those sciences forbidden by the First Law. He found dark places in the world, and he touched the Other Side. He found dark places, and he spoke in the tongue of devils, and he heard their voices answer him.' Quai's voice dropped down to a whisper. 'And the voices told Glustrod where to dig . . .'

'Very good, Master Quai,' cut in Bayaz, sternly. 'Your grip on the histories seems much improved. Let us not tarry on the details, however. We can leave Glustrod's diggings for another day.'

'Of course,' murmured Quai, his dark eyes glittering in the firelight, his gaunt face full of gloomy hollows. 'You know best, master. Glustrod laid plans. He watched from the shadows. He garnered secrets. He flattered, and he threatened, and he lied. It did not take him long to turn the weak-willed to his purposes, and the strong-willed against each other, for he was cunning, and charming, and fair to look upon. He heard the voices always, now, from the world below. They suggested that he sow discord everywhere, and he listened. They urged him to eat the flesh of men, and steal their power, and he did so. They commanded him to seek out those devil-bloods that remained in our world, spurned, hated, exiled, and make from them an army, and he obeyed.'

Something touched Logen's shoulder from behind and he near jumped in the air. Ferro was standing over him, the water-skin held out in her hand. 'Thanks,' he growled as he took it from her, pretending that his heart wasn't knocking at his ribs. He took a quick swig and banged the stopper in with his palm, then put it down beside him. When he looked up, Ferro hadn't moved. She stood there above him, looking down at the dancing flames. Logen shuffled up a step, making room. Ferro scowled, sucked her teeth, kicked at the ground, then slowly squatted down on her haunches, making sure to leave plenty of space between them. She held her hands out to the fire and bared her shining teeth at it.

'Cold over there.'

Logen nodded. 'These walls don't keep the wind off much.'

'No.' Her eyes swept across the group and found Quai. 'Don't stop for me,' she snapped.

The apprentice grinned. 'Strange and sinister was the host that Glustrod gathered. He waited for Juvens to leave the Empire, then he crept into the capital at Aulcus and set his well-laid schemes in motion. It seemed as if a madness swept the city. Son fought with father, wife with husband, neighbour with neighbour. The Emperor was cut down on the steps of his palace by his own sons and then, maddened with greed and envy, they turned upon each other. Glustrod's twisted army had slithered into the sewers beneath the city and rose up, turning the streets into charnel pits, the squares into slaughter yards. Some among them could take forms, stealing the faces of others.'

Bayaz shook his head. 'Taking forms. A dread and insidious trick.' Logen remembered a woman, in the cold darkness, who had spoken with the voice of his dead wife, and he frowned and hunched his shoulders.

'A dread trick indeed,' said Quai, his sickly grin growing even wider. 'For who can be trusted if one cannot trust one's own eyes, one's own ears, to tell friend from foe? But worse was to come. Glustrod summoned demons from the Other Side, bound them to his will and sent them to destroy those who might resist him.'

'Summoning and sending,' hissed Bayaz. 'Cursed disciplines. Dire risks. Terrible breaches of the First Law.'

'But Glustrod recognised no law beyond his own strength. Soon he sat in the Emperor's throne room upon a pile of skulls, sucking the flesh of men as a baby sucks milk, basking in his awful victory. The Empire descended into chaos, the very slightest taste of the chaos of ancient days, before the coming of Euz, when our world and the world below were one.'

A gust of wind sighed through the chinks in the ancient stonework around them, and Logen shivered and pulled his blanket tight around him. Damn story was making him nervous. Stealing faces, and sending devils, and eating men. But Quai did not stop. 'When he found out what Glustrod had done, Juvens' fury was terrible, and he sought the aid of his brothers. Kanedias would not come. He stayed sealed in his house, tinkering with his machines, caring nothing for the world outside. Juvens and

Bedesh raised an army without him, and they fought a war against their brother.'

'A terrible war,' muttered Bayaz, 'with terrible weapons, and terrible casualties.'

'The fighting spread across the continent from one end to the other, and drew in every petty rivalry, and gave birth to a host of feuds, and crimes, and vengeances, whose consequences still poison the world today. But in the end Juvens was victorious. Glustrod was besieged in Aulcus, his changelings unmasked, his army scattered. Now, in his most desperate moment, the voices from the world below whispered to him a plan. Open a gate to the Other Side, they said. Pick the locks, and crack the seals, and throw wide the doors that your father made. Break the First Law one last time, they said, and let us back into the world, and you will never again be ignored, be shunned, be cheated.'

The First of the Magi nodded slowly to himself. 'But he was cheated once more.'

'Poor fool! The creatures of the Other Side are made of lies. To deal with them is to grasp the most awful peril. Glustrod made ready his rituals, but in his haste he made some small mistake. Only a grain of salt out of place, perhaps, but the results were horrible indeed. The great power that Glustrod had gathered, strong enough to tear a hole in the fabric of the world, was released without form or reason. Glustrod destroyed himself. Aulcus, great and beautiful capital of the Empire, was laid waste, the land around it forever poisoned. No one ventures within miles of the place now. The city is a shattered graveyard. A blasted ruin. A fitting monument to the folly and the pride of Glustrod and his brothers.' The apprentice glanced up at Bayaz. 'Do I speak the truth, master?'

'You do,' murmured the Magus. 'I know. I saw it. A young fool with a full and lustrous head of hair.' He ran a hand over his bald scalp. 'A young fool who was as ignorant of magic, and wisdom, and the ways of power as you are now, Master Quai.'

The apprentice inclined his head. 'I live only to learn.'

'And in that regard, you seem much improved. How did you like that tale, Master Ninefingers?'

Logen puffed out his cheeks. 'I'd been hoping for something with a few more laughs, but I guess I'll take what's offered.'

'A pack of nonsense, if you ask me,' sneered Luthar.

'Huh,' snorted Bayaz. 'How fortunate for us that no one did. Perhaps you ought to get the pots washed, Captain, before it gets too late.'

'Me?'

'One of us caught the food, and one of us cooked it. One of us has entertained the group with a tale. You are the only one among us who has as yet contributed nothing.'

'Apart from you.'

'Oh, I am far too old to be sloshing around in streams at this time of night.' Bayaz' face grew hard. 'A great man must first learn humility. The pots await.'

Luthar opened his mouth to speak, thought better of it, pushed himself angrily up from his place and threw his blanket down in the grass. 'Damn pots,' he cursed as he snatched them up from around the fire and stomped off towards the brook.

Ferro watched him go, a strange expression on her face that might even have been her version of a smile. She looked back at the fire, and licked her lips. Logen pulled the stopper from the water skin and held it out to her.

'Uh,' she grunted, snatched it from his hand, took a quick swallow. While she was wiping her mouth on her sleeve, she glanced sideways at him, and frowned. 'What?'

'Nothing,' he said quickly, looking away and holding up his empty palms. 'Nothing at all.' He was smiling on the inside, though. Small gestures and time. That was how he'd get it done.

Small Crimes

'Cold, eh, Colonel West?'

'Yes, your Highness, winter is nearly upon us.' There had been a kind of snow in the night. A cold, wet sleet that covered everything in icy moisture. Now, in the pale morning, the whole world seemed half-frozen. The hooves of their horses crunched and slurped in the half-frozen mud. Water dripped sadly from the half-frozen trees. West was no exception. His breath smoked from his runny nose. The tips of his ears tingled unpleasantly, numb from the cold.

Prince Ladisla hardly seemed to notice, but then he was swathed in an enormous coat, hat and mittens of shining black fur, no doubt several hundred marks worth of it. He grinned over. 'The men seem good and fit, though, in spite of it all.'

West could scarcely believe his ears. The regiment of the King's Own that had been placed under Ladisla's command seemed happy enough, it was true. Their wide tents were pitched in orderly rows in the middle of the camp, cooking fires in front, horses tethered nearby in good order.

The position of the levies, who made up a good three quarters of their strength, was less happy. Many were shamefully ill-prepared. Men with no training or no weapons, some who were plainly too ill or too old for marching, let alone for battle. Some had little more than the clothes they stood up in, and those were in a woeful state. West had seen men huddled together under trees for warmth, nothing but half a blanket to keep the rain off. It was a disgrace.

'The King's Own are well provided for, but I'm concerned about the situation of some of the levies, your—'

'Yes,' said Ladisla, talking over him precisely as if he had not spoken, 'good and fit! Chomping at the bit! Must be the fire in their bellies keeps 'em warm, eh, West? Can't wait to get at the enemy! Damn shame we have to wait here, kicking our heels behind this damn river!'

West bit his lip. Prince Ladisla's incredible powers of self-deception were becoming more frustrating with every passing day. His Highness had fixed upon the idea of being a great and famous general, with a matchless force of fighting men under his command. Of winning a famous victory, and being celebrated as a hero back in Adua. Rather than exerting a single particle of effort to make it happen, however, he behaved as if it already had, utterly regardless of the truth. Nothing which was distasteful, or displeasing, or at odds with his cock-eyed notions could be permitted to be noticed. Meanwhile, the dandies on his staff, without a month's military experience between them, congratulated him on his fine judgement, slapped each other on the back, and agreed with his every utterance, no matter how ludicrous.

Never to want for anything, or work for anything, or show the tiniest grain of self-discipline in a whole life must give a man a strange outlook on the world, West supposed, and here was the proof, riding along beside him, smiling away as though the care of ten thousand men was a light responsibility. The Crown Prince and the real world, as Lord Marshal Burr had observed, were entire strangers to one another.

'Cold,' Ladisla murmured. 'Not much like the deserts of Gurkhul now, eh, Colonel West?'

'No, your Highness.'

'But some things are the same, eh? I'm speaking of war, West! War in general! The same everywhere! The courage! The honour! The glory! You fought with Colonel Glokta, didn't you?'

'Yes, your Highness, I did.'

'I used to love to hear stories of that man's exploits! One of my heroes, when I was young. Riding round the enemy, harassing his lines of communication, falling on the baggage train and whatnot.' The Prince's riding crop rode around, harassed, and fell on imaginary baggage in the air before him. 'Capital! And I suppose you saw it all?'

'Some of it, your Highness, yes.' He had seen a great deal of saddle-soreness, sunburn, looting, drunkenness, and vainglorious showing-off.

'Colonel Glokta, I swear! We could do with some of that dash here, eh, West? Some of that vim! That vigour! Shame that he's dead.'

West looked up. 'He isn't dead, your Highness.'

'He isn't?'

'He was captured by the Gurkish, and then returned to the Union when the war ended. He . . . er . . . he joined the Inquisition.'

'The Inquisition?' The Prince looked horrified. 'Why on earth would a man give up the soldiering life for that?'

West groped for words, but then thought better of it. 'I cannot imagine, your Highness.'

'Joined the Inquisition! Well, I never.' They rode in silence for a moment. Gradually, the Prince's smile returned. 'But we were talking of the honour of war, were we not?'

West grimaced. 'We were, your Highness.'

'First through the breach at Ulrioch, weren't you? First through the breach, I heard! There's honour for you, eh? There's glory, isn't it?

That must have been quite an experience, eh, Colonel? Quite an experience!'

Struggling through a mass of broken stones and timbers, littered with twisted corpses. Half-blind with the smoke, half-choking on the dust, shrieks and wails and the clashing of metal coming at him from all around, hardly able to breathe for fear. Men pressing in on all sides, groaning, shoving, stumbling, yelling, running with blood and sweat, black with grime and soot, half-seen faces twisted with pain and fury. Devils, in hell.

West remembered screaming 'Forward!', over and over until his throat was raw, even though he had no idea which way forward was. He remembered stabbing someone with his sword, friend or enemy, he did not know, then or now. He remembered falling and cutting his head on a rock, tearing his jacket on a broken timber. Moments, fragments, as if from a story he once heard someone else telling.

West pulled his coat tighter round his chilly shoulders, wishing it was thicker. 'Quite an experience, your Highness.'

'Damn shame that bloody Bethod won't be coming this way!' Prince Ladisla slashed petulantly at the air with his riding crop. 'Little better than damn guard duty! Does Burr take me for a fool, eh, West, does he?'

West took a deep breath. 'I couldn't possibly say, your Highness.'

The Prince's fickle mind had already moved off. 'What about those pets of yours? Those Northmen. The ones with the comical names. What's he called, that dirty fellow? Wolfman, is it?'

'Dogman.'

'Dogman, that's it! Capital!' The Prince chuckled to himself. 'And that other one, biggest damn fellow I ever saw! Excellent! What are they up to?'

'I sent them scouting north of the river, your Highness.' West rather wished he was with them. 'The enemy are probably far away, but if they aren't, we need to know about it.'

'Of course we do. Excellent idea. So that we can prepare to attack!'

A timely withdrawal and a fast messenger to Marshal Burr was more what West had in mind, but there was no point in saying so. Ladisla's whole notion of war was of ordering a glorious charge, then retiring to bed. Strategy and retreat were not words in his vocabulary.

'Yes,' the Prince was muttering to himself, eyes fixed intently on the trees beyond the river. 'Prepare an attack and sweep them back across the border . . .'

The border was a hundred leagues away. West seized his moment. 'Your Highness, if I may, there is a great deal for me to do.'

It was no lie. The camp had been organised, or disorganised, without a thought for convenience or defence. An unruly maze of ramshackle canvas in a great clearing near the river, where the ground was too soft and had soon been turned into a morass of sticky mud by the supply carts. At first there had been no latrines, then they had been dug too shallow and much too close to the camp, not far from where the provisions were being stored. Provisions which, incidentally, had been badly packed, inadequately prepared, and were already close to spoiling, attracting every rat in Angland. If it had not been for the cold, West did not doubt that the camp would already have been riddled with disease.

Prince Ladisla waved his hand. 'Of course, a great deal to do. You can tell me more of your stories tomorrow, eh, West? About Colonel Glokta and so forth. Damn shame he's dead!' he shouted over his shoulder as he cantered off towards his enormous purple tent, high up on the hill above the stink and confusion.

West turned his mount with some relief and urged it down the slope into the camp. He passed men tottering through the half-frozen sludge, shivering, breath steaming, hands wrapped in dirty rags. He passed men sitting in sorry groups before their patched tents, no two dressed the same, as close to meagre fires as they dared, fiddling with cooking pots, playing miserable games of damp cards, drinking and staring into the cold air.

The better-trained levies had gone with Poulder and Kroy to seek out the enemy. Ladisla had been left with the rump: those too weak to march well, too poorly equipped to fight well, too broken even to do nothing with any conviction. Men who might never have left their homes in all their lives, forced to cross the sea to a land they knew nothing of, to fight an enemy they had no quarrel with, for reasons they did not understand.

Some few of them might have felt some trace of patriotic fervour, some swell of manly pride when they left, but by now the hard marching, the bad food and the cold weather had truly worn, starved, and frozen all enthusiasm out of them. Prince Ladisla was scarcely the inspirational leader to put it back, had he even been making the slightest effort to do so.

West looked down at those grim, tired, pinched faces as he rode past, and they stared back, beaten already. All they wanted was to go home, and West could hardly blame them. So did he.

'Colonel West!'

There was a big man grinning over at him, a man with a thick beard, wearing the uniform of an officer in the King's Own. West realised with a start that it was Jalenhorm. He slid down from his saddle and grabbed hold of the big man's hand in both of his. It was good to see him. A firm, honest, trustworthy presence. A reminder of a past life, when West did not move among the great men of the world, and things were an awful lot simpler. 'How are you, Jalenhorm?'

'Alright, thank you, sir. Just taking a turn round the camp, waiting.' The big man cupped his hands and blew into them, rubbed them together. 'Trying to stay warm.'

'That's what war is, in my experience. A great deal of waiting, in unpleasant conditions. A great deal of waiting, with occasional moments of the most extreme terror.'

Jalenhorm gave a dry grin. 'Something to look forward to then. How're things on the Prince's staff?'

West shook his head. 'A competition to see who can be most arrogant, ignorant, and wasteful. How about you? How's the camp life?'

'We're not so badly off. It's some of these levies I feel sorry for. They're not fit to fight. I heard a couple of the older ones died last night from the cold.'

'It happens. Let's just hope they bury them deep, and a good way from the rest of us.' West could see that the big man thought him heartless, but there it was. Few of the casualties in Gurkhul had died in battle. Accidents, illness, little wounds gone bad. You came to expect it. As badly equipped as some of the levies were? They would be burying men every day. 'Nothing you need?'

'There is one thing. My horse dropped a shoe in this mud, and I tried to find someone to fit a new one.' Jalenhorm spread his hands. 'I could be wrong, but I don't think there's a smith in the whole camp.'

West stared at him. 'Not one?'

'I couldn't find any. There are forges, anvils, hammers and all the rest but . . . no one to work them. I spoke to one of the quartermasters. He said General Poulder refused to release any of his smiths, and so did General Kroy, so, well,' and Jalenhorm shrugged his shoulders, 'we don't have any.'

'No one thought to check?'

'Who?'

West felt the familiar headache tugging at the back of his eyes. Arrows need heads, blades need sharpening, armour and saddles and the carts that haul the supplies break, and need to be repaired. An army with no smiths is little better than an army with no weapons. And here they were, out in the frozen country, miles from the nearest settlement. Unless . . .

'We passed a penal colony on the way.'

Jalenhorm squinted as he tried to remember. 'Yes, a foundry, I think. I saw smoke above the trees . . .'

'They would have some skilled metal-workers.'

The big man's eyebrows went up. 'Some criminal metal-workers.'

'I'll take whatever we can get. Today your horse is short a shoe, tomorrow we might have nothing to fight with! Get a dozen men together, and a wagon. We'll leave at once.'

The prison loomed up out of the trees through the cold rain, a fence of great, mossy logs tipped with bent and rusted spikes. A grim-looking place with a grim purpose. West swung from his saddle while Jalenhorm and his men reined up behind him, then squelched across the rutted track to the gate and hammered on the weathered wood with the pommel of his sword.

It took a while, but eventually a small hatch snapped open. A pair of grey eyes frowned at him through the slot. Grey eyes above a black mask. A Practical of the Inquisition.

'My name is Colonel West.'

The eyes regarded him coldly. 'So?'

'I am in the service of Crown Prince Ladisla, and I need to speak to the commandant of this camp.'

'Why?'

West frowned, doing his very best to look impressive with his hair plastered to his scalp and the rain dripping off his chin. 'There is a war on and I do not have time to bandy words with you! I need to speak to the commandant most urgently!'

The eyes narrowed. They looked at West for a while, and then at the dozen bedraggled soldiers behind him. 'Alright,' said the Practical. 'You can come in, but only you. The rest will have to wait.'

The main street was a stretch of churned-up mud between leaning shacks, water trickling from the eaves, spattering into the dirt. There were two men and a woman in the road, wet through, struggling to move a cart laden with stones, up to the axles in mush. All three had heavy chains on their ankles. Ragged, bony, hollow faces, as empty of hope as they were empty of food.

'Get that fucking cart shifted,' the Practical growled at them, and they stooped back to their unenviable task.

West struggled through the muck towards a stone building at the far end of the camp, trying to hop from one dry patch to another, without success. Another dour Practical was standing on the threshold, water running from a stained oilskin over his shoulders, hard eyes following West with a mixture of suspicion and indifference. He and his guide stepped past without a word and into the dim hall beyond, full of the noise of drumming rain. The Practical knocked at an ill-fitting door.

'Come in.'

A small, spare room with grey walls, cold and smelling slightly of damp. A mean fire flickered in the grate, a sagging shelf was stacked with books. A portrait of the King of the Union stared regally down from one wall. A lean man in a black coat sat writing at a cheap desk. He looked at West for a while, then carefully put down his pen and rubbed at the bridge of his nose with an inky thumb and forefinger.

'We have a visitor,' grunted the Practical.

'So I see. I am Inquisitor Lorsen, commandant of our little camp.'

West gave the bony hand the most perfunctory of squeezes. 'Colonel West. I am here with Prince Ladisla's army. We are camped a dozen miles to the north.'

'Of course. How might I be of assistance to his Highness?'

'We are desperately in need of skilled metal-workers. You run a foundry here, correct?'

'A mine, a foundry, and a smithy for the manufacture of farming tools, but I fail to see what—'

'Excellent. I will take a dozen or so men back with me, the most skilled men you have available.'

The commandant frowned. 'Out of the question. The prisoners here are guilty of the most serious crimes. They cannot be released without a signed order from the Arch Lector himself.'

'Then we have a problem, Inquisitor Lorsen. I have ten thousand men with weapons that need sharpening, armour that needs mending, horses that need shoeing. We might be called into action at any moment. I cannot wait for orders from the Arch Lector or anyone else. I must leave with smiths, and there it is.'

'But you must understand that I cannot allow—'

'You fail to realise the gravity of the situation!' barked West, his temper already fraying. 'By all means send a letter to the Arch Lector! I will send a man back to my camp for a company of soldiers! We can see who gets help first!'

The commandant thought about that for a while. 'Very well,' he said eventually, 'follow me.'

Two dirty children stared at West from the porch of one of the shacks as he stepped out of the commandant's building, back into the incessant drizzle.

'You have children here?'

'We have whole families, if they are judged a danger to the state.' Lorsen glanced sideways at him. 'A shame, but holding the Union together has always required harsh measures. I gather from your silence that you disapprove.'

West watched one of the shabby children limping through the muck, doomed, perhaps, to spend their whole life in this place. 'I think it's a crime.'

The commandant shrugged. 'Don't deceive yourself. Everyone is guilty of something, and even the innocent can be a threat. Perhaps it takes small crimes to prevent bigger ones, Colonel West, but it's up to bigger men than us to decide. I only make sure they work hard, don't prey upon each other, and don't escape.'

'You only do your job, eh? A well-trodden way to avoid responsibility.'

'Which of us is it who lives among them, out here in the middle of nowhere? Which of us is it who watches over them, dresses them, feeds them, cleans them, fights the endless, pointless war against their damn lice? Is it you who stops them beating, and raping, and killing each other? You're an officer in the King's Own, eh, Colonel? So you live in Adua? In fine quarters in the Agriont, among the rich and well groomed?' West frowned, and Lorsen chuckled at him. 'Which of us has truly avoided the responsibility, as you put it? My conscience has never been cleaner. Hate us if you like, we're used to it. No one likes to shake hands with the man who empties the latrine pits either, but pits have to be emptied all the same. Otherwise the world fills up with shit. You can have your dozen smiths, but don't try to take the high ground with me. There is no high ground here.'

West didn't like it, but he had to admit the man made a good case, so he set his jaw and struggled on in silence, head down. They squelched towards a long, windowless, stone-built shed, thick smoke roiling up into the misty air from tall chimneys at each corner. The Practical slid back the bolt on the heavy door and heaved it open, and West followed him and Lorsen into the darkness.

The heat was like a slap in the face after the freezing air outside. Acrid smoke stung at West's eyes, nipped at his throat. The din in the narrow space was frightening. Bellows creaked and wheezed, hammers clanged on anvils sending up showers of angry sparks, red hot metal hissed furiously in water barrels. There were men everywhere, packed in tight together, sweating, and groaning, and coughing, hollow faces half lit by the orange glow from the forges. Devils, in hell.

'Stop your work!' roared Lorsen. 'Stop and form up!'

The men slowly set down their tools, lurched and stumbled and rattled forward to form a line while four or five Practicals looked on from the shadows. A shabby, broken, stooping, sorrowful line. A couple of the men had irons on their wrists as well as their ankles. They scarcely looked like the answer to all of West's problems, but he had no choice. This was all there was.

'We have a visitor, from outside. Say your piece, Colonel.'

'My name is Colonel West,' he croaked, voice cracking on the stinging air. 'There are ten thousand soldiers camped a dozen miles down the road, under Crown Prince Ladisla. We have need of smiths.' West cleared his throat, tried to speak louder without coughing his lungs out. 'Who among you can work metals?'

No one spoke. The men stared at their threadbare shoes or their bare feet, with the odd sidelong glance at the glowering Practicals.

'You need not be afraid. Who can work metals?'

'I can, sir.' A man stepped forward from the line, the irons on his ankles rattling. He was lean and sinewy, slightly stooped. As the lamplight fell across his head West found himself wincing. He was disfigured by hideous burns. One side of his face was a mass of livid, slightly melted-looking scars, no eyebrow, scalp patchy with pink bald spots. The other side was little better. The man scarcely had a face at all. 'I can work a forge, and I did some soldiering too, in Gurkhul.'

'Good,' muttered West, doing his best to swallow his horror at the man's appearance. 'Your name?'

'Pike.'

'Are any of these others good with metal, Pike?'

The burned man shuffled and clanked his way down the line, pulling men forward by their shoulders while the commandant looked on, his frown growing deeper with every passing moment.

West licked his dry lips. Hard to believe that in so little time he could have gone from so horribly cold to so horribly hot, but here he was, more uncomfortable than ever. 'I'll need keys to their irons, Inquisitor.'

'There are no keys. The irons are melted shut. They are not intended ever to be removed and I would strongly advise you not to. Many of these prisoners are extremely dangerous, and you should bear in mind that you will be returning them to us as soon as you can make alternative arrangements. The Inquisition is not in the business of early releases.' He stalked off to speak to one of the Practicals.

Pike sidled up, pulling another convict by the elbow. 'Pardon me, sir,' he murmured, growling voice kept low. 'But could you find a place for my daughter?'

West shrugged his shoulders, uncomfortable. He would have liked to take everyone and burn the damn place to the ground, but he was already pushing his luck. 'It's not a good idea, a woman in amongst all those soldiers. Not a good idea at all.'

'A better idea than staying here, sir. I can't leave her on her own. She can help me at the forge. She can swing a hammer herself if it comes to that. She's strong.'

She didn't look strong. She looked skinny and ragged, bony face smeared with soot and grease. West could have taken her for a boy. 'I'm sorry, Pike, but it's no easy ride where we're going.'

She grabbed hold of West's arm as he turned away. 'It's no easy ride here.' Her voice was a surprise. Soft, smooth, educated. 'Cathil is my name. I can work.' West looked down at her, ready to shake his arm free, but her expression reminded him of something. Painless. Fearless. Empty eyes, flat, like a corpse.

Ardee. Blood smeared across her cheek.

West grimaced. The memory was like a wound that wouldn't heal. The heat was unbearable, every part of him was twitching with discomfort, his uniform like sandpaper against his clammy skin. He had to get out of this horrible place.

He looked away, his eyes stinging. 'Her too,' he barked.

Lorsen snorted. 'Are you joking, Colonel?'

'Believe me, I'm not in a joking mood.'

'Skilled men is one thing. I daresay you need them, but I cannot allow you to simply take whatever prisoners catch your eye—'

West turned on him with a snarl, his patience worn right through. 'Her too, I said!'

If the commandant was impressed by West's fury, he didn't show it.

They stood there for a long moment, staring at each other, while the sweat ran down West's face and the blood pounded loud in his temples.

Then Lorsen nodded slowly. 'Her too. Very well. I cannot stop you.' He leaned in a little closer. 'But the Arch Lector will hear about this. He is far away, and it might take time for him to hear, but hear he will.' Even closer yet, almost whispering in West's ear. 'Perhaps one day you will find yourself visiting us again, but this time to stay. Perhaps, in the meantime, you should prepare your little lecture on the rights and wrongs of penal colonies. There'll be plenty of time for it.' Lorsen turned away. 'Now take my prisoners and go. I have a letter to write.'

Rain

Jezal had always found a good storm a thorough amusement. Raindrops lashing at the streets, and walls, and roofs of the Agriont, hissing from the gutters. Something to be smiled out at through the wet window while one sat, warm and dry in one's quarters. Something that took the young ladies in the park by surprise and made them squeal, sticking their dresses excitingly to their clammy skin. Something to be dashed through, laughing with one's friends, as one made one's way from tavern to tavern, before drying out before a roaring fire with a mug of hot spiced wine. Jezal used to enjoy the rain almost as much as the sun.

But that was before.

Out here on the plains, storms were of a different stamp. This was no petulant child's tantrum, best ignored and soon ended. This was a cold and murderous, merciless and grudge-bearing, bitter and relentless fury of a storm, and somehow it made all the difference that the nearest roof, let alone the nearest tavern, was hundreds of miles behind them. The rain came down in sheets, dousing the endless plain and everything on it with icy water. The fat drops stung at Jezal's scalp like sling-stones, nipped at his exposed hands, the tops of his ears, the back of his neck. Water trickled through his hair, through his eyebrows, down his face in rivulets and into his sodden collar. The rain was a grey curtain across the land, obliterating anything more than a hundred strides ahead, although out here of course, there was nothing ahead or anywhere else.

Jezal shivered and clutched the collars of his coat together with one hand. A pointless gesture, he was already soaked to his skin. Damn shopkeeper back in Adua had assured him that this coat was entirely waterproof. It had certainly cost him enough, and he had looked very well in it in the shop, quite the rugged outdoorsman, but the seams had begun to leak almost as soon as the first drops fell. For some hours now he had been every bit as wet as if he had climbed into the bath with his clothes on, and a good deal colder.

His boots were full of icy water, his thighs were chafed ragged against his wet trousers, the waterlogged saddle creaked and squelched with every movement of his unhappy horse. His nose was running, his nostrils and his lips were sore, the very reins were painful in his wet palms. His nipples in particular were two points of agony in a sea of discomfort. The whole business was utterly unbearable.

'When will it end?' he muttered bitterly to himself, hunching his shoulders and looking up beseechingly at the gloomy heavens, the rain pattering on his face, in his mouth, in his eyes. Happiness seemed at that moment to consist of nothing more than a dry shirt. 'Can't you do something?' he moaned at Bayaz.

'Like what?' the Magus snapped back at him, water coursing down his face and dripping from his bedraggled beard. 'You think that I'm enjoying this? Out on the great plain in a bastard of a storm at my age? The skies make no special dispensation for Magi, boy, they piss on everyone the same. I suggest you adjust to it and keep your whining to yourself. A great leader must share the hardships of his followers, of his soldiers, of his subjects. That is how he wins their respect. Great leaders do not complain. Not ever.'

'Fuck them then,' muttered Jezal under his breath. 'And this rain, too!'

'You call this rain?' Ninefingers rode past him, a big smile spread across his ugly lump of a face. Not long after the drops began to come down hard, Jezal had been most surprised to see the Northman shrug off first his battered coat, and then his shirt, roll them up in an oilskin and ride on stripped to the waist, heedless of the water running down his great slab of scarred back, happy as a great hog wallowing in the mud.

Such behaviour had, at first, struck Jezal as another unforgivable display of savagery, and he had only thanked his stars that the primitive had deigned to keep his trousers on, but as the cold rain began to seep through his coat he had become less sure. It would have been impossible for him to be any colder or wetter without his clothes, but at least he would have been free of the endless, horrible chafing of wet cloth. Ninefingers grinned over at him as though he could read his thoughts. 'Nothing but a drizzle. The sun can't always shine. You have to be realistic!'

Jezal ground his teeth. If he was told to be realistic one more time he would stab Ninefingers with his short steel. Damn half-naked brute. It was bad enough that he had to ride, and eat, and sleep within a hundred strides of a cave-dweller like that, but that he had to listen to his fool advice was an insult almost too deep to bear.

'Damn useless primitive,' he muttered to himself.

'If it comes to a fight I reckon you'll be glad to have him along.' Quai was looking sideways at Jezal, swaying back and forth on the seat of his creaking cart, long hair plastered to his gaunt cheeks by the rain, looking more pale and sickly than ever with a sheen of wet on his white skin.

'Who asked your opinion?'

'A man who doesn't want opinions should keep his own mouth shut.' The apprentice nodded his dripping head at Ninefingers' back. 'That there is the Bloody-Nine, the most feared man in the North. He's killed more men than the plague.' Jezal frowned over at the Northman, sitting sloppy in his saddle, thought about it for a moment, and sneered.

'Doesn't scare me any,' he said, as loud as he could without Ninefingers actually hearing him.

Quai snorted. 'I'll bet you've never even drawn a blade in anger.'

'I could start now,' growled Jezal, giving his most threatening frown.

'Very fierce,' chuckled the apprentice, disappointingly unimpressed. 'But if you're asking me who's the useless one here, well, I know who I'd rather have left behind.'

'Why, you—'

Jezal jumped in his saddle as a bright flash lit the sky, and then another, frighteningly close. Fingers of light clawed at the bulging undersides of the clouds, snaked through the darkness overhead. Long thunder rolled out across the gloomy plain, popped and crackled under the wind. By the time it faded the wet cart had already rolled away, robbing Jezal of his chance to retort. 'Damn idiot apprentice,' he murmured, frowning at the back of his head.

At first, when the flashes had come, Jezal had tried to keep his spirits up by imagining his companions struck down by lightning. It would have been oddly appropriate, for instance, had Bayaz been cooked to a cinder by a stroke from the heavens. Jezal soon despaired of any such deliverance, however, even as a fantasy. The lightning would never kill more than one of them in a day, and if one of them had to go, he had slowly begun to hope it might be him. A moment of brilliant illumination, then sweet oblivion. The kindest escape from this nightmare.

A trickle of water ran down Jezal's back, tickling at his raw skin. He longed to scratch it, but he knew that if he did he would only create ten more itches, spread across his shoulder blades and his neck and all the places hardest to reach with a hooked finger. He closed his eyes, and his head slowly drooped under the weight of his desperation until his wet chin hung against his wet chest.

It had been raining the last time he saw her. He remembered it all with a painful clarity. The bruise on her face, the colour of her eyes, the set of her mouth, one side twisted up. Just thinking of it made him have to swallow that familiar lump in his throat. The lump he swallowed twenty times a day. First thing in the morning, when he woke, and last thing at night, as he lay on the hard ground. To be back with Ardee now, safe and warm, seemed like the realisation of all his dreams.

He wondered how long she might wait, as the weeks dragged on, and she received no word. Might she even now be writing daily letters to Angland that he would never receive? Letters expressing her tender feelings. Letters desperately seeking news. Letters begging for replies. Now her worst expectations would all be confirmed. That he was a faithless ass, and a liar, and had forgotten all about her, when nothing could have been further from the truth. He ground his teeth in frustration and despair at the thought, but what could he do? Replies were hard to send from a blighted, blasted, ruined wasteland, even supposing he could have written one in this epic downpour. He inwardly cursed the names of Bayaz and Ninefingers, of Longfoot and Quai. He cursed the Old Empire and he cursed the endless plain. He cursed the whole demented expedition. It was becoming an hourly ritual.

Jezal began to perceive, dimly, that he had until now had rather an easy life. It seemed strange that he had moaned so long and hard about rising early to fence, or about lowering himself to play cards with Lieutenant Brint, or about how his sausages were always a touch overdone of a morning. He should have been laughing, bright-eyed and with a spring in his step, simply to have been out of the rain. He coughed, and sniffed, and wiped at his sore nose with his sore hand. At least with so much water around, no one would notice him weeping.

Only Ferro looked as if she was enjoying herself even less than him, occasionally glaring at the pissing clouds, her face wrinkled up with hatred and horror. Her spiky hair was plastered flat to her skull, her waterlogged clothes hung limp from her scrawny shoulders, water ran down her scarred face and dripped from the end of her sharp nose, the point of her sharp chin. She looked like a mean-tempered cat dunked unexpectedly in a pond, its body suddenly seeming a quarter of the size it had been, stripped of all its air of menace. Perhaps a woman's voice might be the thing to lift him from this state of mind, and Ferro was the nearest thing to a woman within a hundred miles.

He spurred his horse up alongside her, doing his best to smile, and she turned her scowl on him. Jezal found to his discomfort that at close quarters, much of the menace returned. He had forgotten about those eyes. Yellow eyes, sharp as knives, pupils small as pin-pricks, strange and disconcerting. He wished he had never approached her now, but he could hardly go without saying something.

'Bet it doesn't rain much where you come from, eh?'

'Are you going to shut your fucking hole, or do I have to hurt you?'

Jezal cleared his throat, and quietly allowed his mount to drop back away from her. 'Crazy bitch,' he whispered under his breath. Damn her, then, she could keep her misery. *He* wasn't about to start wallowing in self-pity. That wasn't his way at all.

The rain had finally stopped when they came upon the place, but the air was still full of heavy damp, the sky above was still full of strange colours. The evening sun pierced the swirling clouds with pink and orange, casting an eerie glow over the grey plain.

Two empty carts stood upright, another was tipped up on its side, one wheel broken off, a dead horse still tethered to it, lying with its pink tongue lolling out of its mouth, a pair of broken arrows sticking from its bloody side. The corpses were scattered all around in the flattened grass, like dolls discarded by a bad-tempered child. Some had deep wounds, or limbs broken, or arrows poking from their bodies. One had an arm off at the shoulder, a short length of snapped bone sticking out as if from a butcher's joint.

Rubbish was scattered all around them. Broken weapons, splintered wood. A few trunks smashed open, rolls of cloth ripped out and slashed across the wet ground. Burst barrels, shattered boxes, rooted through and looted.

'Merchants,' grunted Ninefingers, looking down. 'Like we're pretending to be. Life's cheap out here alright.'

Ferro curled her lip. 'Where isn't it?'

The wind whipped cold across the plain, cutting clean through Jezal's damp clothes. He had never seen a corpse before, and here were laid out . . . how many? At least a dozen. He started to feel slightly peculiar halfway through counting them.

No one else seemed much moved, though familiarity with violence was hardly surprising among these characters. Ferro was crawling around the bodies, peering down and prodding them with as little emotion as an undertaker. Ninefingers looked as though he had seen far worse, which Jezal did not doubt he had, and done far worse besides. Bayaz and Longfoot both looked mildly troubled, but not much more so than if they had come upon some unknown horse tracks. Quai scarcely even looked interested.

Jezal could have done with a share of their indifference at that moment. He would not have admitted it, but he was feeling more than a little sick. That skin: slack, and still, and waxy pale, beaded with wet from the rain. That clothing: ripped and rifled through, missing boots, or coats, or shirts even. Those wounds. Ragged red lines, blue and black bruises, rips and tears and gaping mouths in flesh.

Jezal turned suddenly in his saddle, looking behind, to the left, to the right, but every view was the same. Nowhere to run to, if he had even known in what direction the nearest settlement lay. In a group of six and yet he felt utterly alone. In a vast, open space, and yet he felt utterly trapped.

One of the corpses seemed to be staring, unnervingly, straight at him. A young man, no more than Jezal's age, with sandy hair and protruding ears. He could have done with a shave, except, of course, that it hardly mattered now. There was a yawning red gash across his belly, his bloody hands lying on either side of it, as though trying to squeeze it shut. His guts glistened wetly inside, all purple-red. Jezal felt his gorge rising. He was already feeling faint from eating too little that morning. Damn sick of dry biscuit, and he could hardly force down the slops the others put together. He turned away from the sickening scene and stared down at the grass, pretending to be searching for important clues while his stomach clenched and heaved.

He gripped his reins as tightly as he could, forcing down the spit as it rushed into his mouth. He was a proud son of the Union, damn it. What was more he was a nobleman, of a distinguished family. What was still more he was a bold officer of the King's Own, and a winner of the Contest. To vomit at the sight of a little gore would be to disgrace himself before this mixture of fools and primitives, and that could under no circumstances be permitted. The honour of his nation was at stake. He glared fixedly at the wet ground, and he clamped his teeth shut, and he ordered his stomach to be still. Gradually, it began to work. He sucked in deep breaths through his nose. Cool, damp, calming air. He was in complete control. He looked back at the others.

Ferro was squatting on the ground with her hand in one of the victim's gaping wounds as far almost as her wrist. 'Cold,' she snapped at Ninefingers, 'been dead since this morning at least.' She pulled her hand out, fingers slimy with gore.

Jezal had belched half his meagre breakfast down his coat before he had time even to slide out of his saddle. He staggered a couple of drunkard's steps, took a gasping breath and retched again. He bent over, hands on his knees, head spinning, spitting bile out onto the grass.

'You alright?'

Jezal glanced up, doing his best to look nonchalant with a long string of bitter drool hanging from his face. 'Something I ate,' he muttered, wiping at his nose and mouth with his trembling hand. A pitiful ruse, he had to admit.

Ninefingers only nodded, though. 'That meat this morning, most likely. I been feeling sick myself.' He gave one of his revolting smiles and offered Jezal a water skin. 'Best keep drinking. Flush it away, uh?'

Jezal sloshed a mouthful of water round his mouth and spat it out, watching Ninefingers walk back to the bodies, and frowning. That had been strange. Coming from another source it might have seemed almost a generous gesture. He took another swig of water, and began to feel better. He made, somewhat unsteadily, for his horse, and clambered back into the saddle.

'Whoever did it was well armed, and in numbers,' Ferro was saying. 'The grass is full of tracks.'

'We should be careful,' said Jezal, hoping to impose himself on the conversation.

Bayaz turned sharply to look at him. 'We should always be careful! That goes without saying! How far are we from Darmium?'

Longfoot squinted up at the sky, then out across the plain. He licked his finger and held it up to the wind. 'Even for a man of my talents, it is hard to be accurate without the stars. Fifty miles or thereabouts.'

'We'll need to turn off the track soon.'

'We are not crossing the river at Darmium?'

'The city is in chaos. Cabrian holds it, and admits no one. We cannot take the risk.'

'Very well. Aostum it is. We will take a wide route round Darmium and off westward. A slightly longer path but—'

'No.'

'No?'

'The bridge at Aostum lies in ruins.'

Longfoot frowned. 'Gone, eh? Truly, God loves to test his faithful. We may have to ford the Aos then—'

'No,' said Bayaz. 'The rains have been heavy and the great river is deep. The fords are all closed to us.'

The Navigator looked puzzled. 'You, of course, are my employer, and as a proud member of the order of Navigators I will always do my utmost to obey, but I am afraid that I can see no other way. If we cannot cross at Darmium, or at Aostum, and we cannot ford the river . . .'

'There is one other bridge.'

'There is?' Longfoot looked baffled for a moment, then his eyes suddenly widened. 'You cannot mean—'

'The bridge at Aulcus still stands.'

Everyone glanced at each other for a moment, frowning. 'I thought you said the place was a ruin,' said Ninefingers.

'A shattered graveyard, I heard,' murmured Ferro.

'I thought you said no one goes within miles of the place.'

'It would hardly have been my first choice, but there are no others. We will join the river and follow the northern bank to Aulcus.' Nobody moved. Longfoot in particular had a look of stunned horror on his face. 'Now!' snapped Bayaz. 'It is plainly not safe to remain here.' And with that he turned his horse away from the corpses. Quai shrugged and flicked his reigns and the cart grumbled off through the grass after the First of the Magi. Longfoot and Ninefingers followed behind, all frowns and foreboding.

Jezal stared at the bodies, still lying where they had found them, their eyes staring accusingly up into the darkening sky. 'Shouldn't we bury them?'

'If you like,' grunted Ferro, springing up into the saddle in one easy motion. 'Maybe you could bury them in puke.'

Bloody Company

Riding, that was what they were doing. That was what they'd been doing for days. Riding, looking for Bethod, with winter coming on. Bog and forest, hill and valley. Rain and sleet, fog and snow. Looking for signs that he was coming their way, and knowing that there wouldn't be any. A lot of wasted time, to the Dogman's mind, but once you've been fool enough to ask for a task, you better do the one you're given.

'Stupid bloody job, this,' snarled Dow, wincing and twitching and fussing with his reins. He'd never been too much of a one for horseback. Liked to keep his feet on the ground and pointed at the enemy. 'Waste of our fucking time. How d'you put up with scouting, Dogman? Stupid bloody job!'

'Someone's got to get it done, don't they? Least I got a horse now.'

'Well I'm right delighted for you!' he sneered. 'You got a horse!'

The Dogman shrugged his shoulders. 'Better than walking.'

'Better than walking, eh?' scoffed Dow. 'That just binds it all up!'

'I got new breeches and all. Not to mention good woollens. The wind don't blow half so cold round my fruits no more.'

That got a chuckle from Tul, but it seemed Dow wasn't in a laughing mood. 'Wind round your fruits? By the fucking dead, boy, is this what we're come to? You forgotten who you are? You was Ninefingers' closest! You came over the mountains with him in the first place! You're in all them songs along with him! You scouted at the head of armies. A thousand men, all following your say-so!'

'That didn't turn out too happy for anyone concerned,' muttered Dogman, but Dow was already laying into Tul.

'And how about you, big man? Tul Duru Thunderhead, strongest bastard in the North. Wrestled bears and won, I heard. Held the pass all alone, while your clan got clean away. A giant, they say, ten feet tall, born under a storm, and with a belly full o' thunder. What about it, giant? The only thunder I've heard you make lately is when you take a shit!'

'What of it?' snarled Tul. 'You any different? Men used to whisper your name, scared to speak it out loud. They'd grip their weapons tight and stick close by the fire if they thought you was within ten leagues! Black Dow, they used to say, quiet and cunning and ruthless as the wolf! He's killed more men than winter, and he's got less pity in him! Who cares a shit now, eh? Times have changed, and you rolled just as far downhill as the rest of us!'

Dow only smiled. 'That's my point, big lad, that's just my point. We used to be something, each one of us. Named Men. Known men. Feared men. I remember my brother telling me that there ain't no better man than Harding Grim with bow nor blade, no better man in all the North. Steadiest damn hand in the whole Circle of the World! How about that, eh, Grim?'

'Uh,' said Grim.

Dow nodded his head. 'Exactly what I'm saying. Now look at us. We ain't so much rolled downhill as fell off a bloody cliff! Running errands for these Southerners? These fucking women in men's trousers? These damn salad-eaters with their big words and their thin little swords?'

Dogman shifted in his saddle, uncomfortable. 'That West knows what he's about.'

'That West!' sneered Dow. 'He knows his arse from his mouth, and in that he's a damn stretch better than the rest, but he's soft as pig fat, and you know it. Got no bones in him at all! None of 'em have! I'd be shocked to my roots if the better part of 'em have ever seen a skirmish. You reckon they'd stand a charge from Bethod's Carls?' He snorted hard laughter to himself. 'Now there's a joke!'

'It can't be denied they're a piss-weak crowd,' muttered Tul, and the Dogman couldn't very well disagree. 'Half of 'em are too hungry to lift a weapon, let alone swing one with some fire, if they could even work out how. All the good ones went north to fight Bethod, leaving us here with the scrapings from the pot.'

'Scrapings from a piss-pot, I'm thinking. What about you, Threetrees?' called Dow. 'The Rock of Uffrith, eh? You were the spike up Bethod's arse for six months, a hero to every right-thinking man in the North! Rudd Threetrees! There's a man carved out of stone! There's a man who never backs down! You want honour? You want dignity? You want to know what a man should be? Look no fucking further! What do you make of all this, eh? Running errands! Checking these bogs for Bethod where we all know he ain't! Work fit for boys and we're lucky to get it, I suppose?'

Threetrees pulled up his horse and turned it slowly round. He sat in his saddle, hunched up, tired looking, and he stared at Dow for a minute. 'Open your ears and listen for once,' he said, ''cause I don't want to be telling you this every mile we go. The world ain't how I'd like it in all kind o' ways. Ninefingers has gone back to the mud. Bethod's made himself King of the Northmen. The Shanka are fixing to come swarming over the mountains. I've walked too far, and fought too long, and heard enough shit from you to fill a lifetime, and all at an age when I should have my feet up with sons to take care o' me. So you can see I got bigger problems than that life hasn't turned out the way you hoped. You can harp on the past all you please, Dow, like some old woman upset cause her tits used to stay up by themselves, or you can shut your fucking hole and help me get on with things.'

He gave each one of 'em a look in the eye, and the Dogman felt a touch shamed for doubting him. 'As for checking for Bethod where he ain't, well, Bethod's never been one to turn up where he's supposed to be. Scouting's the task we've been given, and scouting's the task I mean to get done.' He leaned forward in his saddle. 'So how's this for a fucking formula? Mouth shut. Eyes open.' And he turned and nudged his horse on through the trees.

Dow took a deep breath. 'Fair enough, chief, fair enough. It's just a shame is all. That's what I'm saying. Just a shame.'

'There's three of 'em,' said Dogman. 'Northmen, for certain, but hard to tell their clan. Being as they're down here, I'm guessing they follow Bethod.'

'More 'n likely,' said Tul. 'Seems that's the fashion these days.'

'Just three?' asked Threetrees. 'No reason for Bethod to have three men on their own all the way out here. Must be more nearby.'

'Let's deal with the three,' growled Dow, 'and get to the rest later. I came here to fight.'

'You came here 'cause I dragged you here,' snapped Threetrees. 'You was all for turning back an hour ago.'

'Uh,' said Grim.

'We can get around 'em if we need to.' Dogman pointed through the cold woods. 'They're up on the slope there, in the trees. No trouble to get around 'em.'

Threetrees looked up at the sky, pink and grey through the branches, and shook his head. 'No. We're losing the light, and I wouldn't like leaving 'em behind us in the dark. Since we're here, and since they're here, we'd best deal with 'em. Weapons it is.' He squatted down, talking quiet. 'Here's how we'll do it. Dogman, get round and above, up on that slope there. Take the one on the left when you hear the signal. You follow me? The one on the left. And best not to miss.'

'Aye,' said Dogman, 'on the left.' Not missing more or less went without saying.

'Dow, you slide in quiet and take the middle.'

'The middle,' growled Dow. 'He's done.'

'That leaves one for you, Grim.' Grim nodded without looking up, rubbing at his bow with a rag. 'Nice and clean, boys. I don't want to be putting one o' you in the mud over this. Places, then.'

The Dogman found a good spot up above Bethod's three scouts and watched from behind a tree trunk. Seemed like he'd done this a hundred times, but it never got any easier on the nerves. Probably just as well. It's when it gets easy that a man makes mistakes.

Dogman was watching for him, so he just caught sight of Dow in the fading light, slithering up through the brush, eyes fixed ahead on his task. He was getting close now, real close. Dogman nocked an arrow and took an aim at the one on the left, breathing slow to keep his hands steady. It was then that he realised. Now he was on the other side, the one that had been on the left was on the right. So which one should he shoot?

He cursed to himself, struggling to remember what Threetrees said. Get around and take the one on the left. Worst thing of all would have been to do nothing, so he aimed up at the one on his left and hoped for the best.

He heard Threetrees call from down below, sounding like a bird out in the woods. Dow gathered himself to jump. Dogman let his arrow fly. It thudded into the back of his task just as Grim's arrow stuck him in the front, and Dow seized hold of the middle one and stabbed him from behind. That left one of 'em untouched, and very surprised-looking.

'Shit,' whispered the Dogman.

'Help!' screamed the last of 'em, before Dow jumped on him. They rolled in the leaves, grunting and thrashing. Dow's arm went up and down – once, twice, three times, then he stood up, glaring through the trees and looking mighty annoyed. Dogman was just shrugging his shoulders when he heard a voice just over his shoulder.

'What?'

Dogman froze, cold all over. Another one, out in the bushes, not ten strides away. He reached for an arrow and nocked it, real quiet, then turned slowly round. He saw two of 'em, and they saw him, and his mouth went sour as old beer. They all stared. Dogman aimed at the bigger one and pulled the string right back.

'No!' he shouted. The arrow thudded into his chest and he groaned and stumbled, fell down on his knees. Dogman dropped his bow and made a snatch at his knife, but he hadn't got it drawn before the other one was on him. They went down hard in the brush, and started rolling.

Light, dark, light, dark. Over and over they went, down the slope, kicking and tearing and punching at each other. Dogman's head smacked against something and he was down on his back, wrestling with this bastard. They hissed at each other, not words exactly, sounds like dogs make fighting. The man pulled his hand free and got a blade out from somewhere and Dogman caught his wrist before he could stab it home.

He was pushing down with all his weight, both hands on the knife. Dogman was pushing the other way, both hands on his wrists, hard as he could, but not hard enough. The blade was coming down slowly, down towards Dogman's face. He was staring at it cross-eyed, a tooth of bright metal not a foot from his nose.

'Die, you fucker!' and it came down another inch. The Dogman's shoulders, his arms, his hands were burning, running out of strength. Staring at his face. Stubble on his chin, yellow teeth, pock marks on his bent nose, hair hanging down around it. The point of the blade nudged closer. Dogman was dead, and there was no help for it.

Snick.

And his head wasn't there any more. Blood washed over Dogman's face, hot and sticky and reeking. The corpse went slack and he shoved it away, blood in his eyes, blood up his nose, blood in his mouth. He staggered up, gasping and choking and spitting.

'Alright, Dogman. You're alright.' Tul. Must've come up on them while they were struggling.

'I'm still alive,' Dogman whispered, the way Logen used to when a fight was done. 'Still alive.' By the dead, though, that had been a close thing.

'They ain't got too much in the way of gear,' Dow was saying, poking round the campsite. Cookpot on the fire, weapons and such like, but not much food. Not enough to be all alone out there in the woods.

'Scouts maybe,' said Threetrees. 'Outriders for some bigger band?'

'Reckon they must be,' said Dow.

Threetrees slapped his hand down on the Dogman's shoulder. 'You alright?'

He was still busy trying to rub the blood off his face. 'Aye, I think so.' Bit shaky still, but that would settle. 'Cuts and scrapes, I reckon. Nothing I'll die of.'

'Good, 'cause I can't spare you. Why don't you take a creep up through them trees and have a look-see, while we clear up this mess here? Find who these bastards were scouting for.'

'Right enough,' said the Dogman, sucking in a big breath and blowing it out. 'Right enough.'

'Stupid bloody job, eh, Dow?' whispered Threetrees. 'Work fit for boys and we're lucky to get it? What do you say now?'

'Could be I made a mistake.'

'A big one,' said the Dogman.

There were a hundred fires burning down there on the dark slopes, a hundred fires and more. There were men down there too, it hardly needed saying. Thralls mostly, lightly armed, but plenty of Carls as well. Dogman could see the last light of the day glinting on their spear tips, and their shield-rims, and their mail coats, polished up and ready for a fight, clustered round close to the flapping standards of each clan's chieftain. Lots of standards. Twenty of 'em, or thirty even, at a quick count. The Dogman had never seen more than ten together before.

'Biggest army there's ever been out of the North,' he muttered.

'Aye,' said Threetrees. 'All fighting for Bethod, and not five days' ride from the Southerners.' He pointed down at one of the banners. 'That Littlebone's standard down there?'

'Aye,' growled Dow, and spat into the brush. 'That's his mark alright. I got scores with that bastard.'

'There's a world o' scores down there,' said Threetrees. 'That's Pale-as-Snow's banner, and Whitesides, and Crendel Goring's over by them rocks. That's some bloody company. Them as went over to Bethod near the beginning. All grown fat on it now, I reckon.'

'What about them ones?' asked the Dogman, pointing out at some that he didn't recognise – evil-looking signs, all leather and bones. Looked like hillmen's marks to him, maybe. 'That ain't Crummock-i-Phail's standard, is it?'

'Nah! He'd never have kneeled to Bethod or anyone else. That mad bastard'll still be up there in the mountains somewhere, calling to the moon and all the rest.'

'Less Bethod done for him,' grunted Dow.

Threetrees shook his head. 'Doubt it. Canny bastard, that Crummock. Been holding Bethod off for years, up in the High Places. He knows all the ways, they say.'

'Whose signs are they then?' asked Dogman.

'Don't know, could be some boys from out east, past the Crinna. There's some strange folk out that way. You know any o' them banners, Grim?'

'Aye,' said Grim, but that was all he said.

'Don't hardly matter whose signs they are,' muttered Dow, 'just look at the numbers of 'em. There's half the fucking North down there.'

'And the worst half,' said Dogman. He was looking at Bethod's sign, set up in the middle of the host. A red circle daubed on black hides, an acre of 'em, it looked like, big as a field, mounted on a tall pine trunk, flapping evil in the wind. Huge great thing. 'Wouldn't fancy carrying it,' he muttered.

Dow slithered over and leaned in close. 'Might be that we could sneak in there in the dark,' he whispered. 'Might be we could sneak in and put a blade in Bethod.'

They all looked at each other. It was a terrible risk, but Dogman had no doubts it was worth the trying. Wasn't a one of them hadn't dreamed of sending Bethod back to the mud.

'Put a blade in him, the bastard,' muttered Tul, and he had a smile right across his face.

'Uh,' grunted Grim.

'That's a task worth doing,' hissed Dow. 'That's real work!'

Dogman nodded, looking down at all them fires. 'No doubt.' Noble work. Work for Named Men like them, or like they used to be, maybe. There'd be some songs about that, alright. Dogman's blood was rushing at the thought, skin prickling on his hands, but Threetrees was having none of it.

'No. We can't risk it. We got to go back and tell the Union. Tell 'em they got guests coming. Bad guests, and in numbers.' He tugged at his beard, and Dogman could tell he didn't like it, backing off. None of 'em did, but they knew he was right, even Dow. Chances were they'd never get to Bethod, and if they did they'd never get out.

'We got to go back,' said Dogman.

'Fair enough,' said Dow. 'We go back. Shame though.'

'Aye,' said Threetrees. 'Shame.'

Long Shadows

'**B**y the dead.'

Ferro said nothing, but for the first time since Logen met her, the scowl had slipped off. Her face was slack, mouth hanging slightly open. Luthar, on the other hand, was grinning like a fool.

'You ever see anything like that?' he shouted over the noise, pointing out at it with a trembling hand.

'There is nothing else like that,' said Bayaz.

Logen had to admit that he'd been wondering what all the fuss was about when it came to crossing a river. Some of the bigger ones in the North could be a problem, especially in the wrong season and with a lot of gear to carry. But if there was no bridge, you found a good ford, held your weapons over your head, and sloshed across. Might take a while for your boots to dry out, and you had to keep your eyes well opened for an ambush, but otherwise there was nothing much to fear from a river. Good place to fill your water-skin.

Filling your skin at the Aos would have been a dangerous business, at least without a hundred strides of rope.

Logen had once stood on the cliffs near Uffrith, and watched the waves crash against the rocks far below, the sea stretching away, grey and foaming out of sight. A dizzy, and a humbling, and a worrying place to stand. The feeling at the brink of the great river's canyon was much the same, except that a quarter mile away or so another cliff rose up from the water. The far bank, if you could use the word about a towering rock face.

He shuffled up gingerly to the very edge, prodding at the soft ground with the toes of his boots, and peered over the brink. Not a good idea. The red earth overhung slightly, bound up with white grass roots, and then the jagged rocks dropped away, almost sheer. Where the frothing water slapped against them, far below, it sent great plumes of bright spray into the air, clouds of damp mist that Logen could almost feel on his face. Tufts of long grass clung to the cracks and the ledges, and birds flitted between them, hundreds of small white birds. Logen could just make out their twittering calls over the mighty rumble of the river.

He thought on being dropped into that thundering weight of dark water –

sucked, and whirled, and ripped around like a leaf in the storm. He swallowed, and shuffled cautiously back from the edge, looking around for something to cling on to. He felt tiny, and weightless, as if a strong gust of wind might snatch him away. He could almost feel the water moving through his boots, the surging, rolling, unstoppable power of it, making the very earth tremble.

'So you can see why a bridge might be such a good idea!' shouted Bayaz in his ear.

'How can you even build a bridge across that?'

'At Aostum the river splits in three, and the canyon is much less deep. The Emperor's architects built islands, and made their bridges of many small arches. Even so, it took them twelve years to build. The bridge at Darmium is the work of Kanedias himself, a gift to his brother Juvens when they were yet on good terms. It crosses the river in a single span. How he did it, none now can say.' Bayaz turned for the horses. 'Get the others, we should keep moving!'

Ferro was already walking back from the brink. 'So much rain.' She looked over her shoulder, frowned and shook her head.

'Don't get rivers like that where you come from, eh?'

'Out in the Badlands, water is the most precious thing you can have. Men kill over a bottle of it.'

'That's where you were born? The Badlands?' A strange name for a place, but it sounded about right for her.

'There are no births in the Badlands, pink. Only deaths.'

'Harsh land, eh? Where were you born, then?'

She scowled. 'What do you care?'

'Just trying to be friendly.'

'Friends!' she sneered, brushing past him towards the horses.

'Why? You got so many out here you couldn't use another?'

She stopped, half turned, and looked at him through narrowed eyes. 'My friends don't last, pink.'

'Nor do mine, but I reckon I'll take the risk if you will.'

'Alright,' she said, but there was nothing friendly in her face. 'The Gurkish conquered my home when I was a child, and they took me for a slave. They took all the children.'

'A slave?'

'Yes, fool, a slave! Bought and sold like meat by the butcher! Owned by someone else, and they do as they please with you, like they would with a goat, or a dog, or the dirt in their gardens! That what you want to know, friend?'

Logen frowned. 'We don't have that custom in the North.'

'Ssss,' she hissed, lip curling with scorn. 'Good for fucking you!'

The ruin loomed over them. A forest of shattered pillars, a maze of broken walls, the ground around it strewn with fallen blocks as long as a man was tall. Crumbling windows and empty doorways yawned like wounds. A ragged black outline, chopped out from the flying clouds like a giant row of broken teeth.

'What city was this?' asked Luthar.

'No city,' said Bayaz. 'At the height of the Old Time, at the greatest extent of the Emperor's power, this was his winter palace.'

'All this?' Logen squinted at the sprawling wreck. 'One man's house?'

'And not even the whole year round. Most of the time, the court would stay in Aulcus. In winter, when the cold snows swept down off the mountains, the Emperor would bring his retinue here. An army of guardsmen, of servants, of cooks, of officials, of princes, and children, and wives, making their way across the plain ahead of the cold winds, taking up residence here for three short months in the echoing halls, the beautiful gardens, the gilded chambers.' Bayaz shook his bald head. 'In times long past, before the war, this place glittered like the sea beneath the rising sun.'

Luthar sniffed. 'So Glustrod tore it down, I suppose?'

'No. It was not in that war, but another that it fell, many years later. A war fought by my order, after the death of Juvens, against his eldest brother.'

'Kanedias,' muttered Quai, 'the Master Maker.'

'A war just as bitter, just as brutal, just as merciless as the one before. And even more was lost. Juvens and Kanedias both, in the end.'

'Not a happy family,' muttered Logen.

'No.' Bayaz frowned up at the mighty wreckage. 'With the death of the Maker, the last of the four sons of Euz, the Old Time ended. We are left only with the ruins, and the tombs, and the myths. Little men, kneeling in the long shadows of the past.'

Ferro stood up in her stirrups. 'There are riders,' she barked, staring off at the horizon. 'Forty or more.'

'Where?' snapped Bayaz, shading his eyes. 'I don't see anything.' Nor could Logen. Only the waving grass and the towering clouds.

Longfoot frowned. 'I see no riders, and I am blessed with perfect vision. Why, I have often been told that—'

'You want to wait until you see them,' hissed Ferro, 'or get off the road before they see us?'

'We'll head into the ruins,' snapped Bayaz over his shoulder. 'And wait for them to pass. Malacus! Turn the cart!'

The wreck of the winter palace was full of shadows, and stillness, and decay. The outsize ruins towered around them, all covered with old ivy and wet moss, streaked and crusted with the droppings of bird and bat. The animals had made the place their palace now. Birds sang from a thousand nests, high in the ancient masonry. Spiders had spun great glistening webs in leaning doorways, heavy with sparkling beads of dew. Tiny lizards sunned themselves in patches of light on the fallen blocks, swarming away as they came near. The rattling of the cart over the broken ground, the footfalls and the hoof beats echoed back from the slimy stones. Everywhere, water dripped, and ran, and plopped in hidden pools.

'Take this, pink.' Ferro slapped her sword into Logen's hands.

'Where are you going?'

'You wait down here, and stay out of sight.' She jerked her head upwards. 'I'll watch them from up there.'

As a boy, Logen had never been out of the trees round the village. As a young man he'd spent days in the High Places, testing himself against the mountains. At Heonan in the winter, the hillmen had held the high pass. Even Bethod had thought that there was no way round, but Logen had found a way up the frozen cliff and settled that score. He could see no way up here, though. Not without an hour or two to spare. Cliffs of leaning blocks heavy with dead creeper, crags of tottering stonework slick with moss, seeming to lean and tip as the clouds moved fast above.

'How the hell you planning to get up . . .'

She was already halfway up one of the pillars. She didn't so much climb as swarm like an insect, hand over hand. She paused at the top for a moment, found a footing she liked, then sprang through the air, right over Logen's head, landed on the wall behind and scrambled up onto it, sending a shower of broken mortar down into his face. She squatted on the top and frowned down at him. 'Just try not to make too much noise!' she hissed, then was gone.

'Did you see . . .' muttered Logen, but the others had already moved further into the damp shadows, and he hurried after them, not wanting to be left alone in this overgrown graveyard. Quai had pulled his cart up further on, and was leaning against it beside the restless horses. The First of the Magi was kneeling near him in the weeds, rubbing at the lichen-crusted wall with his palms.

'Look at this,' snapped Bayaz as Logen tried to edge past. 'These carvings here. Masterpieces of the ancient world! Stories, and lessons, and warnings from history.' His thick fingers brushed gently at the scarred stone. 'We might be the first men to look upon these in centuries!'

'Mmm,' muttered Logen, puffing out his cheeks.

'Look here!' Bayaz gestured at the wall. 'Euz gives his gifts to his three oldest sons, while Glustrod looks on from the shadows. The birth of the three pure disciplines of magic. Some craftsmanship, eh?'

'Right.'

'And here,' grunted Bayaz, knocking some weeds away and shuffling along to the next mossy panel, 'Glustrod plans to destroy his brother's work.' He had to tear at a tangle of dead ivy to get at the one beyond. 'He breaks the First Law. He hears voices from the world below, you see? He summons devils and sends them against his enemies. And in this one,' he muttered, tugging at the weight of brown creeper, 'let me see now . . .'

'Glustrod digs,' muttered Quai. 'Who knows? In the next one he might even have found what he's looking for.'

'Hmm,' grumbled the First of the Magi, letting the ivy fall back across the wall. He glowered at his apprentice as he stood up, frowning. 'Perhaps, sometimes, the past is better left covered.'

Logen cleared his throat and edged away, ducked quickly under a leaning archway. The wide space beyond was filled with small, knotty trees, planted in rows, but long overgrown. Great weeds and nettles, brown and sagging rotten from the rain, stood almost waist high around the mossy walls.

'Perhaps I should not say it myself,' came Longfoot's cheerful voice, 'but it must be said! My talent for navigation stands alone! It rises above the skills of every other Navigator as the mountain rises over the deep valley!' Logen winced, but it was Bayaz' anger or Longfoot's bragging, and that was no choice at all.

'I have led us across the great plain to the river Aos, without a deviation of even a mile!' The Navigator beamed at Logen and Luthar, as though expecting an avalanche of praise. 'And without a single dangerous encounter, in a land reckoned among the most dangerous under the sun!' He frowned. 'Perhaps a quarter of our epic journey is now safely behind us. I am not sure that you appreciate the difficulty involved. Across the featureless plain, as autumn turns to winter, and without even the stars to reckon by!' He shook his head. 'Huh. Truly, the pinnacle of achievement is a lonely place.'

He turned away and wandered over to one of the trees. 'The lodgings are a little past their best, but at least the fruit trees are still in working order.' Longfoot plucked a green apple from a low hanging branch and began to shine it on his sleeve. 'Nothing like a fine apple, and from the Emperor's orchard, no less.' He grinned to himself. 'Strange, eh? How the plants outlast the greatest works of men.'

Luthar sat down on a fallen statue nearby, slid the longer of his two swords from its sheath and laid it across his knees. Steel glinted mirror-bright as he turned it over in his lap, frowned at it, licked a finger and scrubbed at some invisible blemish. He pulled out his whetstone, spat on it, and carefully set to work on the long, thin blade. The metal rang gently as the stone moved back and forward. It was soothing, somehow, that sound, that ritual, familiar from a thousand campfires of Logen's past.

'Must you?' asked Brother Longfoot. 'Sharpening, polishing, sharpening, polishing, morning and night, it makes my head hurt. It's not as if you've even made any use of them yet. Probably find when you need them that you've sharpened them away to nothing, eh?' He chuckled at his own joke. 'Where will you be then?'

Luthar didn't even bother to look up. 'Why don't you keep your mind on getting us across this damn plain, and leave the swords to those who know the difference?' Logen grinned to himself. An argument between the two most arrogant men he had ever met was well worth watching, in his opinion.

'Huh,' snorted Longfoot, 'show me someone who knows the difference and I'll happily never mention blades again.' He lifted the apple to his mouth, but before he could bite into it, his hand was empty. Luthar had moved almost too fast to follow, and speared it on the glinting point of his sword. 'Give me that back!'

Luthar stood up. 'Of course,' he tossed it off the end of the blade with a practised flick of his wrist. Before Longfoot's reaching hands could close around it, Luthar had snatched his short sword from its sheath and whipped it blurring through the air. The Navigator was left juggling with the two even halves for a moment before dropping them both in the dirt.

'Damn your showing off!' he snapped.

'We can't all have your modesty,' muttered Luthar. Logen chuckled to himself while Longfoot stomped back over to the tree, staring up into the branches for another apple.

'Nice trick,' he grunted, strolling through the weeds to where Luthar was sitting. 'You're quick with those needles.'

The young man gave a modest shrug. 'It has been remarked upon.'

'Mmm.' Stabbing an apple and stabbing a man were two different things, but quickness was some kind of start. Logen looked down at Ferro's sword, turned it over in his hands, then slid it out from its wooden sheath. It was a strange weapon to his mind, grip and blade both gently curved, thicker at the end than at the hilt, sharpened only down one edge, with scarcely any point on it at all. He swung it in the air a couple of times. Strange weight, more like an axe than a sword.

'Odd-looking thing,' muttered Luthar.

Logen checked the edge with his thumb. Rough-feeling, it dragged at the skin. 'Sharp, though.'

'Don't you ever sharpen yours?'

Logen frowned. He reckoned he must have spent weeks of his life, all told, sharpening the weapons he'd carried. Every night, out on the trail, after the meal, men would sit and work at their gear, steel scraping on metal and stone, flashing in the light of the campfires. Sharpening, cleaning, polishing, tightening. His hair might have been caked with mud, his skin stiff with old sweat, his clothes riddled with lice, but his weapons had always gleamed like the new moon.

He took hold of the cold grip and pulled the sword that Bayaz had given him out of its stained scabbard. It looked a slow and ugly thing compared to Luthar's swords, and to Ferro's too, if it came to that. There was hardly any shine on the heavy grey blade at all. He turned it over in his hand. The single silver letter glinted near the hilt. The mark of Kanedias.

'Don't know why, but it doesn't need sharpening. I tried it to begin with, but all it did was wear down the stone.' Longfoot had hauled himself up into one of the trees, and was slithering along a thick branch towards an apple hanging out of reach near its end.

'If you ask me,' grunted the Navigator, 'the weapons suit their owners to the ground. Captain Luthar – flash and fine-looking but never used in combat. The woman Maljinn – sharp and vicious and worrying to look upon. The Northman Ninefingers – heavy, solid, slow and simple. Hah!' he chuckled, dragging himself slightly further down the limb. 'A most fitting metaphor! Juggling with words has always been but one among my many remarkable—'

Logen grunted as he swung the sword over his head. It bit through the branch where it met the trunk, clean through, almost to the other side. More than far enough that Longfoot's weight ripped through the rest, and brought the whole limb, Navigator and all, crashing down into the weeds below. 'Slow and simple enough for you?'

Luthar spluttered with laughter as he sharpened his short sword, and Logen laughed as well. Laughing with a man was a good step forward. First comes the laughter, then the respect, then the trust.

'God's breath!' shouted Longfoot, scrabbling his way out from under the branch. 'Can a man not eat without disturbance?'

'Sharp enough,' chuckled Luthar. 'No doubt.'

Logen hefted the sword in his hand. 'Yes, this Kanedias knew how to make a weapon, alright.'

'Making weapons is what Kanedias did.' Bayaz had stepped through the crumbling archway and into the overgrown orchard. 'He was the Master Maker, after all. The one that you hold is among the very least of what he made, forged to be used in a war against his brothers.'

'Brothers,' snorted Luthar. 'I know exactly how he felt. There's always something. Usually a woman, in my experience.' He gave his short sword one last stroke with the whetstone. 'And where women are concerned, I always come out on top.'

'Is that so?' Bayaz snorted. 'As it happens, a woman did enter the case, but not in the way you're thinking.'

Luthar gave a sickening grin. 'What other way is there to think about women? If you ask me – gah!' A large clod of bird shit splattered against the shoulder of his coat, throwing specks of black and grey all over his hair, his face, his newly cleaned swords. 'What the . . . ?' He scrambled from his seat and stared up at the wall above him. Ferro was squatting on top, wiping her hand on a spray of ivy. It was hard to tell with the bright sky behind, but Logen wondered if she might not have the trace of a smile on her face.

Luthar certainly wasn't smiling. 'You fucking mad bitch!' he screamed, scraping the white goo from his coat and flinging it at the wall. 'Bunch of bloody savages!' And he shoved angrily past and through the fallen arch.

Laughter was one thing, it seemed, but the respect might be a while coming.

'In case any of you pinks are interested,' called Ferro, 'the riders are gone.'

'Which way?' asked Bayaz.

'Away east, the way we came, riding hard.'

'Looking for us?'

'Who knows? They didn't have signs. But if they are looking, more than likely they will find our trail.'

The Magus frowned. 'Then you'd best get down from there. We need to move,' He thought about it for a moment. 'And try not to throw any more shit!'

And Next . . . My Gold

To Sand dan Glokta, Superior of Dagoska, and for his eyes alone.

I am most troubled to discover that you think yourself short of both men and money.

As far as soldiers are concerned, you must make do with what you have, or what you can procure. As you are already well aware, the great majority of our strength is committed in Angland. Unfortunately, a certain rebellious temper among the peasantry throughout Midderland is more than occupying what remains.

As to the question of funds, I fear that nothing can be spared. You will not ask again. I advise you to squeeze what you can from the Spicers, from the natives, from anyone else who is to hand. Borrow and make do, Glokta. Demonstrate that resourcefulness that made you so famous in the Kantic War.

I trust that you will not disappoint me.

Sult
Arch Lector of his Majesty's Inquisition.

'Matters proceed with the greatest speed, Superior, if I may say so. Since the gates to the Upper City were opened the work-rate of the natives has tripled! The ditch is down below sea level across the entire peninsula, and deepening every day! Only narrow dams hold back the brine at either end, and at your order the entire business is ready to be flooded!' Vissbruck sat back with a happy smile on his plump face. *Quite as if the whole thing had been his idea.*

Below them in the Upper City, the morning chanting was beginning. A strange wailing that drifted from the spires of the Great Temple, out over Dagoska and into every building, even here, in the audience chamber of the Citadel. *Kahdia calls his people to prayer.*

Vurms' lip curled at the sound. 'That time again already? Damn those natives and their bloody superstitions! We should never have let them back into their temple! Damn their bloody chanting, it gives me a headache!'

And it's worth it for that alone. Glokta grinned. 'If it makes Kahdia happy, your headache is something I can live with. Like it or not, we need the natives, and the natives like to chant. Get used to it, is my advice. That or wrap a blanket round your head.'

Vissbruck sat back in his chair and listened while Vurms sulked. 'I have to admit that I find the sound rather soothing, and we cannot deny the effect the Superior's concessions have had on the natives. With their help the land walls are repaired, the gates are replaced, and the scaffolds are already being dismantled. Stone has been acquired for new parapets but, ah, and here is the problem, the masons refuse to work another day without money. My soldiers are on quarter pay, and morale is low. Debt is the problem, Superior.'

'I'll say it is,' muttered Vurms angrily. 'The granaries are close to capacity, and two new wells have been dug in the Lower City, at great expense, but my credit is utterly exhausted. The grain merchants are after my blood!' *A damn sight less keenly than every merchant in the city is after mine, I daresay.* 'I can scarcely show my face any longer for their clamouring. My reputation is in jeopardy, Superior!'

As if I had no larger concerns than the reputation of this dolt. 'How much do we owe?'

Vurms frowned. 'For food, water, and general equipment, no less than a hundred thousand.' *A hundred thousand? The Spicers love making money, but they hate spending it more. Eider will not come up with half so much, if she even chooses to try.*

'What about you, General?'

'The cost of hiring mercenaries, excavating the ditch, of the repairs to the walls, of extra weapons, armour, ammunition . . .' Vissbruck puffed out his cheeks. 'In all, it comes to nearly four hundred thousand marks.'

It was the most Glokta could do to keep from choking on his own tongue. *Half a million? A king's ransom and more besides. I doubt that Sult could provide so much, even if he had the mind, and he does not. Men die all the time over debts a fraction of the size.* 'Work however you can. Promise whatever you want. The money is on its way, I assure you.'

The General was already collecting his notes. 'I am doing all I can, but people are beginning to doubt that they will ever be paid.'

Vurms was more direct. 'No one trusts us any longer. Without money, we can do nothing.'

'Nothing,' growled Severard. Frost slowly shook his head.

Glokta rubbed at his sore eyes. 'A Superior of the Inquisition vanishes without leaving so much as a smear behind. He retires to his chambers at night, the door is locked. In the morning he does not answer. They break down the door and find . . .' *Nothing.* 'The bed has been slept in, but there is no body. Not the slightest sign of a struggle even.'

'Nothing,' muttered Severard.

'What do we know? Davoust suspected a conspiracy within the city, a traitor intending to deliver Dagoska to the Gurkish. He believed a member of the ruling council was involved. It would seem likely that he uncovered the identity of this person, and was somehow silenced.'

'But who?'

We must turn the question on its head. 'If we cannot find our traitor, we must make them come to us. If they work to get the Gurkish in, we need only succeed in keeping them out. Sooner or later, they will show themselves.'

'Rithky,' mumbled Frost. *Risky indeed, especially for Dagoska's latest Superior of the Inquisition, but we have no choices.*

'So we wait?' asked Severard.

'We wait, and we look to our defences. That and we try to find some money. Do you have any cash, Severard?'

'I did have some. I gave it to a girl, down in the slums.'

'Ah. Shame.'

'Not really, she fucks like a madman. I'd thoroughly recommend her, if you're interested.'

Glokta winced as his knee clicked. 'What a thoroughly heart-warming tale, Severard, I never had you down for a romantic. I'd sing a ballad if I wasn't so short of funds.'

'I could ask around. How much are we talking about?'

'Oh, not much. Say, half a million marks?'

One of the Practical's eyebrows went up sharply. He reached into his pocket, dug around for a moment, pulled his hand out and opened it. A few copper coins shone in his palm.

'Twelve bits,' he said. 'Twelve bits is all I can raise.'

'Twelve thousand is all I can raise,' said Magister Eider. *Scarcely a drop in the bucket.* 'My Guild are nervous, business has not been good, the great majority of their assets are bound up in ventures of one kind or another. I have little cash to hand either.'

I daresay you have a good deal more than twelve thousand, but what's the difference? I doubt even you have half a million tucked away. There probably isn't that amount in the whole city. 'One would almost think they didn't like me.'

She snorted. 'Turning them out of the temple? Arming the natives? Then demanding money? It might be fair to say you're not their favourite person.'

'Might it be fair to say they're after my blood?' *And plenty of it, I shouldn't wonder.*

'It might, but for the time being, at least, I think I've managed to convince them that you're a good thing for the city.' She looked levelly at him for a moment. 'You are a good thing, aren't you?'

'If keeping the Gurkish out is your priority.' *That is our priority, isn't it?* 'More money wouldn't hurt, though.'

'More money never hurts, but that's the trouble with merchants. They much prefer making it to spending it, even when it's in their own best interests.' She gave a heavy sigh, rapped her fingernails on the table, looked down at her hand. She seemed to consider a moment, then she began to pull the rings from her fingers. When she had finally got them all off, she tossed them into the box along with the coins.

Glokta frowned. 'A winning gesture, Magister, but I could not possibly—'

'I insist,' she said, unclasping her heavy necklace and dropping it into the box. 'I can always get more, once you've saved the city. In any case, they'll do me no good when the Gurkish rip them from my corpse, will they?' She slipped her heavy bracelets off her wrists, yellow gold, studded with green gemstones. They rattled down amongst the rest. 'Take the jewels, before I change my mind. A man lost in the desert should take such water—'

'As he is offered, regardless of the source. Kahdia told me the very same thing.'

'Kahdia is a clever man.'

'He is. I thank you for your generosity, Magister.' Glokta snapped the lid of the box shut.

'The least I could do.' She got up from her chair and walked to the door, her sandals hissing across the carpet. 'I will speak with you soon.'

'He says he must speak with you now.'

'What was his name, Shickel?'

'Mauthis. A banker.'

One more creditor, come clamouring for his money. Sooner or later I'll have to just arrest the pack of them. That will be the end of my little spending spree, but it will almost be worth it to see the looks on their faces. Glokta gave a hopeless shrug. 'Send him in.'

He was a tall man in his fifties, almost ill-looking in his gauntness, hollow-cheeked and sunken-eyed. There was a stern precision to his movements, a steady coldness to his gaze. *As though he is weighing the value of all he looks at in silver marks, including me.*

'My name is Mauthis.'

'I was informed, but I am afraid that there are no funds available at the present moment.' *Unless you count Severard's twelve bits.* 'Whatever debt the city has with your bank will have to wait. It will not be for much longer, I assure you.' *Just until the sea dries up, the sky falls in, and devils roam the earth.*

Mauthis gave a smile. *If you could call it that. A neat, precise, and utterly joyless curving of the mouth.* 'You misunderstand me, Superior Glokta. I have not come to collect a debt. For seven years, I have had the privilege of acting as the chief representative in Dagoska, of the banking house of Valint and Balk.'

Glokta paused, then tried to sound off-hand. 'Valint and Balk, you say? Your bank financed the Guild of Mercers, I believe.'

'We had some dealings with that guild, before their unfortunate fall from grace.' *I'll say you did. You owned them, from the ground up.* 'But then we have dealings with many guilds, and companies, and other banks, and individuals, great and small. Today I have dealings with you.'

'Dealings of what nature?'

Mauthis turned to the door and snapped his fingers. Two burly natives entered, grunting, sweating, struggling under the weight of a great casket: a box of polished black wood, bound with bands of bright steel, sealed with a heavy lock. They set it down carefully on the fine carpet, wiped sweat from their foreheads, and tramped out the way they came while Glokta frowned after them. *What is this?* Mauthis pulled a key from his pocket and turned it in the lock. He reached forward and lifted the lid of the chest. He moved out of the way, carefully and precisely, so Glokta could see the contents.

'One hundred and fifty thousand marks in silver.'

Glokta blinked. *And so it is.* The coins flashed and glittered in the evening light. Flat, round, silver, five mark pieces. Not a jingling heap, not some barbarian's horde. Neat, even stacks, held in place by wooden dowels. *As neat and even as Mauthis himself.*

The two porters were gasping their way back into the room, carrying between them a second box, slightly smaller than the first. They placed it on the floor and strode out, not so much as glancing at the fortune glittering in plain view beside them.

Mauthis unlocked the second chest with the same key, raised the lid, and stood aside. 'Three hundred and fifty thousand marks in gold.'

Glokta knew his mouth was open, but he could not close it. Bright, clean, gold, glowing yellow. All that wealth seemed almost to give off warmth, like a bonfire. It tugged at him, dragged at him, pulled him forward. He took a hesitant step, in fact, before he stopped himself. Great big, golden, fifty mark pieces. Neat, even stacks, just as before. *Most men would never in their lives see such coins. Few men indeed can ever have seen so many.*

Mauthis reached into his coat and pulled out a flat leather case. He placed it carefully on the table and unfolded it: once, twice, three times.

'One half of one million marks in polished stones.'

There they lay on the soft black leather, on the hard brown table top, burning with all the colours under the sun. Two large handfuls, perhaps, of multi-coloured, glittering gravel. Glokta stared down at them, numb, and sucked at his gums. *Magister Eider's jewels seem suddenly rather quaint.*

'In total, I have been ordered by my superiors to advance to you, Sand dan Glokta, Superior of Dagoska, the sum of precisely one million marks.' He unrolled a heavy paper. 'You will sign here.'

Glokta stared from one chest to another and back. His left eye gave a flurry of twitches. 'Why?'

'To certify that you received the money.'

Glokta almost laughed. 'Not that! Why the money?' He flailed one hand at it all. 'Why all this?'

'It would appear that my employers share your concern that Dagoska should not fall to the Gurkish. More than that I cannot tell you.'

'Cannot, or will not?'

'Cannot. Will not.'

Glokta frowned at the jewels, at the silver, at the gold. His leg was throbbing, dully. *All that I wanted, and far more. But banks do not become banks by giving money away.* 'If this is a loan, what is the interest?'

Mauthis flashed his icy smile again. 'My employers would prefer to call it a contribution to the defence of the city. There is one condition, however.'

'Which is?'

'It may be that in the future, a representative of the banking house of Valint and Balk will come to you requesting . . . favours. It is the most earnest hope of my employers that, if and when that time comes, you will not disappoint them.'

One million marks worth of favours. And I place myself in the power of a most suspect organisation. An organisation whose motives I do not begin to understand. An organisation that, until recently, I was on the point of investigating for high treason. But what are my options? Without money, the city is lost, and I am finished. I needed a miracle, and here it is, sparkling before me. A man lost in the desert must take such water as is offered . . .

Mauthis slid the document across the table. Several blocks of neat writing, and a space, for a name. *For my name. Not at all unlike a paper of confession. And prisoners always sign their confessions. They are only offered when there is no choice.*

Glokta reached for the pen, dipped it in the ink, wrote his name in the space provided.

'That concludes our business.' Mauthis rolled up the document, smoothly and precisely. He slipped it carefully into his coat. 'My colleagues and I are leaving Dagoska this evening.' *A great deal of money to contribute to the cause, but precious little confidence in it.* 'Valint and Balk are closing their offices here, but perhaps we will meet in Adua, once this unfortunate situation with the Gurkish is resolved.' The man gave his mechanical smile one more time. 'Don't spend it all at once.' And he turned on his heel and strode out, leaving Glokta alone with his monumental windfall.

He shuffled over to it, breathing hard, and stared down. There was something obscene about all that money. Something disgusting. Something frightening, almost. He snapped shut the lids of the two chests. He locked them with trembling hands. He shoved the key in his inside pocket. He stroked the metal bindings of the two boxes with his fingertips. His palms were greasy with sweat. *I am rich.*

He picked up a clear, cut stone the size of an acorn, and held it up to the window between finger and thumb. The dim light shone back at him through the many facets, a thousand brilliant sparks of fire – blue, green, red, white. Glokta did not know much about gemstones, but he was reasonably sure that this one was a diamond. *I am very, very rich.*

He looked back at the rest, sparkling on the flat piece of leather. Some of them were small, but many were not. Several were larger than the one he held in his hand. *I am immensely, fabulously wealthy. Imagine what one could do with so much money. Imagine what one could control . . . perhaps, with this much, I can save the city. More walls, more supplies, more equipment, more mercenaries. The Gurkish, thrown back from Dagoska in disarray. The Emperor of Gurkhul, humbled. Who would have thought it? Sand dan Glokta, once more the hero.*

He rolled the shining little pebbles around with a finger-tip, lost in thought. *But so much spending in so little time could raise questions. My faithful servant Practical Vitari would be curious, and she would make my noble master the Arch Lector curious. One day I beg for money, the next I spend it as if it burns? I was forced to borrow, your Eminence. Indeed? How much? No more than a million marks. Indeed? And who would lend such a sum? Why, our old friends at the banking house of Valint and Balk, your Eminence, in return for unspecified favours, which they might call in at any moment. Of course, my loyalty is still beyond question. You understand, don't you? I mean to say, it's only a fortune in jewels. Body found floating by the docks . . .*

He pushed his hand absently through the cold, hard, glittering stones, and they tickled pleasantly at the skin between his fingers. *Pleasant, but perilous. We must still tread carefully. More carefully than ever . . .*

Fear

It was a long way to the edge of the World, of that there could be no doubt. A long, and a lonely, and a nervous way. The sight of the corpses on the plain had worried everyone. The passing riders had made matters worse. The discomforts of the journey had in no way diminished. Jezal was still constantly hungry, usually too cold, often wet through, and would probably be saddle-sore for the rest of his days. Every night he stretched out on the hard and lumpy ground, dozed and dreamed of home, only to wake to the pale morning more tired and aching than when he lay down. His skin crawled, and chafed, and stung with the unfamiliar feeling of dirt, and he was forced to admit that he had begun to smell almost as vile as the others. It was enough, altogether, to make a civilised man run mad, and now, to add to all of this, there was the constant nagging of danger.

From that point of view, the terrain was not on Jezal's side. Hoping to shake off any pursuers, Bayaz had ordered them away from the river a few days earlier. The ancient road wound now through deep scars in the plain, through rocky gullies, through shadowy gorges, alongside chattering streams in deep valleys.

Jezal began to think on the endless, grinding flatness almost with nostalgia. At least out there one did not look at every rock, and shrub, and fold in the ground and wonder whether there was a crowd of blood-thirsty enemies behind it. He had chewed his fingernails almost until the blood ran. Every sound made him bite his tongue and spin around in his saddle, clutching at his steels, staring for a murderer, who turned out to be a bird in a bush. It was not fear, of course, for Jezal dan Luthar, he told himself, would laugh in the face of danger. An ambush, or a battle, or a breathless pursuit across the plain – these things, he imagined, he could have taken in his stride. But this endless waiting, this mindless tension, this merciless rubbing-by of slow minutes was almost more than he could stand.

It might have helped had there been someone with whom he could share his unease, but, as far as companionship went, little had changed. The cart still rolled along the cracked old road while Quai sat grim and silent on top. Bayaz said nothing but for the occasional lecture on the qualities of great leadership, qualities which seemed markedly absent in himself. Longfoot was off scouting out the route, only appearing every day or two to let them know how skilfully he was doing it. Ferro frowned at everything as though it was her personal enemy, and at Jezal most of all, it sometimes seemed, her hands never far from her weapons. She spoke rarely, and then only to Ninefingers, to snarl about ambushes, or covering their tracks better, or the possibilities of being followed.

The Northman himself was something of a puzzle. When Jezal had first laid eyes on him, gawping at the gate of the Agriont, he had seemed less than an animal. Out here in the wild, though, the rules were different. One could not simply walk away from a man one disliked, then do one's best to avoid him, belittle him in company, and insult him behind his back. Out here you were stuck with the companions you had, and, being stuck with him, Jezal had come slowly to realise that Ninefingers was just a man, after all. A stupid, and a thuggish, and a hideously ugly one, no doubt. As far as wit and culture went, he was a cut below the lowliest peasant in the fields of the Union, but Jezal had to admit that out of all the group, the Northman was the one he had come to hate least. He had not the pomposity of Bayaz, the watchfulness of Quai, the boastfulness of Longfoot, or the simple viciousness of Ferro. Jezal would not have been ashamed to ask a farmer his opinion on the raising of crops, or a smith his opinion on the making of armour, however dirty, ugly or low-born they might have been. Why not consult a hardened killer on the subject of violence?

'I understand that you have led men in battle,' Jezal tried as his opening.

The Northman turned his dark, slow eyes on him. 'More than once.'

'And fought in duels.'

'Aye.' He scratched at the ragged scars on his stubbly cheek. 'I didn't come to look like this from a wobbly hand at shaving.'

'If your hand was that wobbly, you would choose, perhaps, to grow a beard.'

Ninefingers chuckled. Jezal was almost used to the sight now. It was still hideous, of course, but smacked more of good-natured ape than crazed murderer. 'I might at that,' he said.

Jezal thought about it a moment. He did not wish to make himself appear weak, but honesty might earn the trust of a simple man. If it worked with dogs, why not with Northmen? 'I myself,' he ventured, 'have never fought in a full-blooded battle.'

'You don't say?'

'No, truly. My friends are in Angland now, fighting against Bethod and his savages.' Ninefingers' eyes swivelled sideways. 'I mean . . . that is to say . . . fighting against Bethod. I would be with them myself, had not Bayaz asked me to come on this . . . venture.'

'Their loss is our gain.'

Jezal looked sharply across. From a subtler source, that might almost have sounded like sarcasm. 'Bethod started this war, of course. A most dishonourable act of unprovoked aggression on his part.'

'You'll get no argument from me on that score. Bethod's got a gift when it comes to starting wars. The only thing he's better at is the finishing of 'em.'

Jezal laughed. 'You can't mean that you think he'll beat the Union?'

'He's beaten worse odds, but you know best. We don't all have your experience.'

The laughter stuttered out in Jezal's throat. He was almost sure that had been irony, and it made him think for a moment. Was Ninefingers looking at him now, and behind that scarred, that plodding, that battered mask thinking, 'what a fool'? Could it be that Bayaz had been right? That there was something to be learned from this Northman after all? There was only one way to find out.

'What's a battle like?' he asked.

'Battles are like men. No two are ever quite the same.'

'How do you mean?'

'Imagine waking up at night to hear a crashing and a shouting, scrambling out of your tent into the snow with your trousers falling down, to see men all around you killing one another. Nothing but moonlight to see by, no clue who're enemies and who're friends, no weapon to fight with.'

'Confusing,' said Jezal.

'No doubt. Or imagine crawling in the mud, between the stomping boots, trying to get away but not knowing where to go, with an arrow in your back and a sword cut across your arse, squealing like a pig and waiting for a spear to stick you through, a spear you won't even see coming.'

'Painful,' agreed Jezal.

'Very. Or imagine standing in a circle of shields no more than ten strides across, all held by men roaring their loudest. There's just you and one other man in there, and that man's won a reputation for being the hardest bastard in the North, and only one of you can leave alive.'

'Hmm,' murmured Jezal.

'That's right. You like the sound of any of those?' Jezal did not, and Ninefingers smiled. 'I didn't think so, and honestly? Nor do I. I've been in all kind of battles, and skirmishes, and fights. Most of them started in chaos, and all of 'em ended in it, and not once did I not come near to shitting myself at some point.'

'You?'

The Northman chuckled. 'Fearlessness is a fool's boast, to my mind. The only men with no fear in them are the dead, or the soon to be dead, maybe. Fear teaches you caution, and respect for your enemy, and to avoid sharp edges used in anger. All good things in their place, believe me. Fear can bring you out alive, and that's the very best anyone can hope for from any fight. Every man who's worth a damn feels fear. It's the use you make of it that counts.'

'Be scared? That's your advice?'

'My advice would be to find a good woman and steer well clear of the whole bloody business, and it's a shame no one told me the same twenty years ago.' He looked sideways at Jezal. 'But if, say, you're stuck out on some great wide plain in the middle of nowhere and can't avoid it, there's three rules I'd take to a fight. First, always do your best to look the coward, the weakling, the fool. Silence is a warrior's best armour, the saying goes. Hard looks and hard words have never won a battle yet, but they've lost a few.'

'Look the fool, eh? I see.' Jezal had built his whole life around trying to appear the cleverest, the strongest, the most noble. It was an intriguing idea, that a man might choose to look like less than he was.

'Second, never take an enemy lightly, however much the dullard he seems. Treat every man like he's twice as clever, twice as strong, twice as fast as you are, and you'll only be pleasantly surprised. Respect costs you nothing, and nothing gets a man killed quicker than confidence.'

'Never underestimate the foe. A wise precaution.' Jezal was beginning to realise that he had underestimated this Northman. He wasn't half the idiot he appeared to be.

'Third, watch your opponent as close as you can, and listen to opinions if you're given them, but once you've got your plan in mind, you fix on it and let nothing sway you. Time comes to act, you strike with no backward glances. Delay is the parent of disaster, my father used to tell me, and believe me, I've seen some disasters.'

'No backward glances,' muttered Jezal, nodding slowly to himself. 'Of course.'

Ninefingers puffed out his pitted cheeks. 'There's no replacement for seeing it, and doing it, but master all that, and you're halfway to beating anyone, I reckon.'

'Halfway? What about the other half?'

The Northman shrugged. 'Luck.'

'I don't like this,' growled Ferro, frowning up at the steep sides of the gorge. Jezal wondered if there was anything in the world she did like.

'You think we're followed?' asked Bayaz. 'You see anyone?'

'How could I see anyone from down here? That's the point!'

'Good ground for an ambush,' muttered Ninefingers. Jezal looked around him, nervously. Broken rocks, bushes, scrubby trees, the ground was full of hiding places.

'Well, this is the route that Longfoot picked for us,' grumbled Bayaz. 'and there's no purpose in hiring a cleaner if you're going to swab the latrines yourself. Where the hell is that damn Navigator anyway? Never around when you want him, only turns up to eat and boast for hours on end! If you knew how much that bastard cost me—'

'Damn it.' Ninefingers pulled his horse up and clambered stiffly down from his saddle. A fallen tree trunk, wood cracked and grey, lay across the gorge, blocking the road.

'I don't like this.' Ferro shrugged her bow from her shoulder.

'Neither do I,' grumbled Ninefingers, taking a step towards the fallen tree. 'But you have to be real—'

'That's far enough!' The voice echoed back and forth around the valley, brash and confident. Quai hauled on the reins and brought the cart to a sudden halt. Jezal looked along the lip of the gorge, his heart thumping in his mouth. He saw the speaker now. A big man dressed in antique leather armour, sitting carelessly on the edge of the drop with one leg dangling, his long hair flapping softly in the breeze. A pleasant and a friendly-looking man, as far as Jezal could tell at this distance, with a wide smile on his face.

'My name is Finnius, a humble servant of the Emperor Cabrian!'

'Cabrian?' shouted Bayaz. 'I heard he'd lost his reason!'

'He's got some interesting ideas.' Finnius shrugged. 'But he's always seen us right. Let me explain matters – we're all around you!' A serious-seeming man with a short sword and shield stepped out from behind the dead tree trunk. Two more appeared, and then three more, creeping out from behind the rocks, behind the bushes, all with serious faces and serious weapons. Jezal licked his lips. He would laugh in the face of danger, of course, but now it came to it nothing seemed at all amusing. He looked over his shoulder. More men had come from behind the rocks they had passed a few moments before, blocking the valley in the other direction.

Ninefingers folded his arms. 'Just once,' he murmured, 'I'd like to take someone else by surprise.'

'There's a couple more of us,' shouted Finnius, 'up here, with me! Good hands with bows, and ready with arrows.' Jezal saw their outlines now against the white sky, the curved shapes of their weapons. 'So you see that you'll be going no further down this road!'

Bayaz spread his palms. 'Perhaps we can come to some arrangement that suits us both! You need only name your price and—'

'Your money's no good to us, old man, and I'm deeply wounded by the assumption! We're soldiers, not thieves! We have orders to find a certain group of people, a group of people wandering out in the middle of nowhere, far from the travelled roads! An old bald bastard with a sickly-looking boy, some stuck-up Union fool, a scarred whore, and an ape of a Northerner! You seen a crowd that might fit that description?'

'If I'm the whore,' shouted Ninefingers, 'who's the Northerner?'

Jezal winced. No jokes, please no jokes, but Finnius only chuckled. 'They didn't tell me you were funny. Reckon that's a bonus. At least until we kill you. Where's the other one, eh? The Navigator?'

'No idea,' growled Bayaz, 'unfortunately. If anyone dies it should be him.'

'Don't take it too hard. We'll catch up with him later.' And Finnius laughed an easy laugh, and the men around them grinned and fingered their weapons. 'So if you'd be good enough to give your arms to those fellows ahead of you, we can get you trussed up and start back towards Darmium before nightfall!'

'And when we get there?'

Finnius gave a happy shrug. 'Not my business. I don't ask questions of the Emperor, and you don't ask questions of me. That way, no one gets skinned alive. Do you take my meaning, old man?'

'Your meaning is hard to miss, but I am afraid that Darmium is quite out of our way.'

'What are you,' called Finnius, 'soft in the head?'

The nearest man stepped forward and grabbed hold of Bayaz' bridle. 'That's enough of that,' he growled.

Jezal felt that horrible sucking in his guts. The air around Bayaz' shoulders trembled, like the hot air above a forge. The foremost of the men frowned, opened his mouth to speak. His face seemed to flatten, then his head broke open and he was suddenly snatched away as though flicked by a giant, unseen finger. He had not even time to scream.

Nor had the four men who stood behind him. Their ruined bodies, the broken remnants of the grey tree trunk, and a great quantity of earth and rocks around them were ripped from the ground and flung through the air to shatter against the rocky wall of the gorge a hundred strides distant with a sound like a house collapsing.

Jezal's mouth hung open. His body froze. It had taken only a terrifying instant. One moment five men had been standing there, the next they were slaughtered meat among a heap of settling debris. Somewhere behind him he heard the hum of a bowstring. There was a cry and a body dropped down into the valley, bounced from the sheer rocks and flopped rag-like, face down in the stream.

'Ride, then!' roared Bayaz, but Jezal could only sit in his saddle and gape. The air around the Magus was still moving, more than ever. The rocks behind him rippled and twisted like the stones on the bed of a stream. The old man frowned, stared down at his hands. 'No . . .' he muttered, turning them over before him.

The brown leaves on the ground were lifting up into air, fluttering as though on a gust of wind. 'No,' said Bayaz, his eyes opening wide. His whole body had begun to shake. Jezal gawped as the loose stones around them rose from the ground, drifting impossibly upwards. Sticks began to snap from the bushes, clods of grass began to tear themselves away from the rocks, his coat rustled and flapped, dragged upwards by some unseen force.

'No!' screamed Bayaz, then his shoulders hunched in a sudden spasm. A tree beside them split apart with a deafening crack and splinters of wood showered out into the whipping air. Someone was shouting but Jezal could scarcely hear them. His horse reared and he had not the wit to hold on. He crashed onto his back on the earth while the whole valley shimmered, trembled, vibrated around him.

Bayaz' head snapped back, rigid, one hand up and clawing at the air. A rock the size of a man's head flew past Jezal's face and burst apart against a boulder. The air was filled with a storm of whipping rubbish, of fragments of wood, and stone, and soil, and broken gear. Jezal's ears were ringing with a terrifying clattering, rattling, howling. He flung himself down on his face, crossed his arms over his head and squeezed his eyes shut.

He thought of his friends. Of West, and Jalenhorm, and Kaspa, of Lieutenant Brint, even. He thought of his family and his home, of his father and his brothers. He thought of Ardee. If he lived to see them again, he would be a better man. He swore it to himself with silent, trembling lips as the unnatural wind ripped the valley apart around him. He would no longer be selfish, no longer be vain, no longer be lazy. He would be a better friend, a better son, a better lover, if only he lived through this. If only he lived through this. If only . . .

He could hear his own terrified breath coming in quick gasps, the blood surging in his head.

The noise had stopped.

Jezal opened his eyes. He lifted his hands from his head and a shower of twigs and soil fell around him. The gorge was full of settling leaves, misty with choking dust. Ninefingers was standing nearby, red blood running down his dirty face from a cut on his forehead. He was walking slowly sideways. He had his sword drawn, hanging down by his leg. Someone was facing him. One of the men that had blocked the way behind them, a tall man with a mop of red hair. Circling each other. Jezal watched, kneeling, mouth wide open. He felt in some small way that he should intervene, but he had not the beginnings of an idea how to do so.

The red-haired man moved suddenly, leaping forwards and swinging his sword over his head. He moved fast, but Ninefingers was faster. He stepped sideways so that the whistling blade missed his face by inches, then he slashed his opponent across the belly as he passed. The man grunted, stumbled a step or two. Ninefingers' heavy sword chopped into the back of his skull with a hollow clicking sound. He tripped over his own feet and pitched onto his face, blood bubbling from the gaping wound in his head. Jezal watched it spread slowly out through the dirt around the corpse. A wide, dark pool, slowly mingling with the dust and the loose soil on the valley floor. No second touch. No best of three.

He became aware of a scuffling, grunting sound, and looked up to see Ninefingers staggering around with another man, a great big man. The two of them were growling and clawing at each other, wrestling over a knife. Jezal gawped at them. When had that happened?

'Stab him!' shouted Ninefingers as the two of them grappled. 'Fucking stab him!' Jezal knelt there, staring up. One hand gripped the hilt of his long steel as though he were hanging off a cliff and this was the last handful of grass, the other hung limp.

There was a gentle thud. The big man grunted. There was an arrow sticking out of his side. Another thud. Two arrows. A third appeared, tightly grouped. He slid slowly out of Ninefingers' grip, onto his knees, coughing and moaning. He crawled towards Jezal, sat back slowly, grimacing and making a strange mewling sound. He lay back in the road, the arrows sticking up into the air like rushes in the shallows of a lake. He was still.

'What about that Finnius bastard?'

'He got away.'

'He'll get others!'

'It was deal with him or deal with that one there.'

'I had that one!'

'Course you did. If you could have held him another year, maybe Luthar might have got round to drawing a blade, eh?'

Strange voices, nothing to do with him. Jezal wobbled slowly up to his feet. His mouth was dry, his knees were weak, his ears were ringing. Bayaz lay in the road on his back a few strides away, his apprentice kneeling beside him. One of the wizard's eyes was closed, the other slightly open, the lid twitching, a slit of white eyeball showing underneath.

'You can let go of that now.' Jezal looked down. His hand was still clenched around the grip of his steel, knuckles white. He willed his fingers to relax and they slowly uncurled, far away. His palm ached from all that gripping. Jezal felt a heavy hand on his shoulder. 'You alright?' Ninefingers' voice.

'Eh?'

'You hurt?'

Jezal stared at himself, turning his hands over stupidly. Dirty, but no blood. 'I don't think so.'

'Good. The horses ran. Who can blame them, right? If I had four legs I'd be halfway back to the sea by now.'

'What?'

'Why don't you catch them?'

'Who made you the leader?'

Ninefingers heavy brows drew in slightly. Jezal became aware that they were standing very close to one another, and that the Northman's hand was still on his shoulder. It was only resting there, but he could feel the strength of it through his coat, and it felt strong enough to twist his arm off. Damn his mouth, it got him in all kinds of trouble. He expected a punch in the face at the very least, if not a fatal wound in his head, but Ninefingers only pursed his lips thoughtfully and began to speak.

'We're a lot different, you and me. Different in all kind of ways. I see you don't have much respect for my kind, or for me in particular, and I don't much blame you. The dead know I got my shortcomings, and I ain't entirely ignorant of 'em. You may think you're a clever man, and I'm a stupid one, and I daresay you're right. There's sure to be a very many things that you know more about than I do. But when it comes to fighting, I'm sorry to say, there's few men with a wider experience than me. No offence, but we both know you're not one of 'em. No one made me the leader, but this is the task that needs doing.' He stepped closer still, his great paw gripping Jezal's shoulder with a fatherly firmness, halfway between reassurance and threat. 'Is that a worry?'

Jezal thought about it for a moment. He was out of his depth, and the events of the past few minutes had demonstrated beyond question just how far. He looked down at the man that Ninefingers had killed only a moment before, and the cleft in the back of his head yawned wide. Perhaps, for the moment, it would be best if he simply did as he was told.

'No worry,' he said.

'Good!' Ninefingers grinned, clapped him on the shoulder and let him go. 'Horses still need catching, and you're the man for the job, I reckon.'

Jezal nodded, and stumbled away to look for them.

One Hundred Words

T here was something peculiar afoot, that was sure. Colonel Glokta tested his limbs, but he appeared unable to move. The sun was blinding bright in his eyes.

'Did we beat the Gurkish?' he asked.

'We certainly did,' said Haddish Kahdia, leaning over into Glokta's field of view. 'With God's help we put them to the sword. Butchered them like cattle.' The old native went back to chewing on the severed hand he held. He'd already got through a couple of fingers.

Glokta raised his arm to take it, but there was nothing there, only a bloody stump, chewed off at the wrist. 'I swear,' murmured the Colonel, 'it's my hand you're eating.'

Kahdia smiled. 'And it is entirely delicious. I do congratulate you.'

'Utterly delicious,' muttered General Vissbruck, taking the hand from Kahdia and sucking a strip of ragged flesh from it. 'Must be all that fencing you did as a young man.' There was blood smeared across his plump, smiling face.

'The fencing, of course,' said Glokta. 'I'm glad you like it,' though the whole business did seem somewhat strange.

'We do, we do!' cried Vurms. He was cupping the remains of Glokta's foot in his hands like a slice of melon, and nibbling at it daintily. 'All four of us are delighted! Tastes like roast pork!'

'Like good cheese!' shouted Vissbruck.

'Like sweet honey!' cooed Kahdia, sprinkling a little salt onto Glokta's midriff.

'Like sweet money,' purred Magister Eider's voice from somewhere down below.

Glokta propped himself up on his elbows. 'Why, what are you doing down there?'

She looked up and grinned at him. 'You took my rings. The least you can do is give me something in return.' Her teeth sank into his right thigh, deep in like tiny daggers, and scooped out a neat ball of flesh. She slurped blood hungrily from the wound, tongue darting out across his skin.

Colonel Glokta raised his eyebrows. 'You're right, of course. Quite right.' It really hurt a great deal less than one would have expected, but sitting upright was rather draining. He fell back onto the sand and lay there, looking up at the blue sky. 'All of you are quite right.'

She had made it up to his hip now. 'Ah,' giggled the Colonel, 'that tickles!' What a pleasure it was, he thought, to be eaten by such a beautiful woman. 'A little to the left,' he murmured, closing his eyes, 'just a little to the left . . .'

Glokta sat up in bed with an agonising jerk, back arched as tight as a full-drawn bow. His left leg trembled under the clammy sheet, wasted muscles knotted hard with searing cramps. He bit down on his lip with his remaining teeth to keep from screaming, snorted heaving gasps through his nose, face screwed up with his furious efforts to control the pain.

Just when it seemed that his leg would rip itself apart, the sinews suddenly relaxed. Glokta collapsed back into his clammy bed and lay there, breathing hard. *Damn these fucking dreams.* Every part of him was aching, every part of him was weak and trembling, wet with cold sweat. He frowned in the darkness. There was a strange sound filling the room. A rushing, hissing sound. *What is that?* Slowly, gingerly, he rolled over and levered himself out of bed, hobbled to the window and stood there, looking out.

It was as though the city beyond his room had vanished. A grey curtain had descended, cutting him off from the world. *Rain.* It spattered against the sill, fat drops bursting into soft spray, throwing a cool mist into the chamber, dampening the carpet beneath the window, the drapes around the opening, soothing Glokta's clammy skin. *Rain.* He had forgotten that such a thing existed.

There was a flash, lightning in the distance. The spires of the Great Temple were cut out black through the hissing murk for an instant, and then the darkness closed back in, joined by a long, angry muttering of distant thunder. Glokta stuck his arm out through the window, felt the water pattering cold against his skin. A strange, unfamiliar feeling.

'I swear,' he murmured to himself.

'The first rains come.' Glokta nearly choked as he spun around, stumbled, clutched at the wet stones around the window for support. It was dark as hell in the room, there was no telling where the voice had come from. *Did I only imagine it? Am I still dreaming?* 'A sublime moment. The world seems to live again.' Glokta's heart froze in his chest. A man's voice, deep and rich. *The voice of the one who took Davoust? Who will soon take me?*

The room was illuminated by another brilliant flash. The speaker sat cross-legged on the carpet. An old black man with long hair. *Between me and the door. No way past, even if I was a considerably better runner than I am.* The light was gone as soon as it arrived, but the image persisted for a moment, burned into Glokta's eyes. Then came the crash of thunder splitting the sky, echoing in the darkness of the wide chamber. *No one would hear my despairing screams for help, even if anyone cared.*

'Who the hell are you?' Glokta's voice was squeaky with shock.

'Yulwei is my name. You need not be alarmed.'

'Not alarmed? Are you fucking joking?'

'If I had a mind to kill you, you would have died in your sleep. I would have left a body, though.'

'Some comfort.' Glokta's mind raced, thinking over the objects within reach. *I might make it as far as the ornamental tea-jar on the table.* He almost laughed. *And do what with it? Offer him tea? Nothing to fight with, even if I was a considerably more effective fighter than I am.* 'How did you get in?'

'I have my ways. The same ways in which I crossed the wide desert, travelled the busy road from Shaffa unobserved, passed through the Gurkish host and into the city.'

'And to think, you could have just knocked.'

'Knocking does not guarantee an entrance.' Glokta's eyes strained against the gloom, but he could see nothing beyond the vague grey outlines of furniture, the arched grey spaces of the other windows. The rain pattered on the sill behind, hissed quietly on the roofs of the city below. Just when he was wondering if his dream was over, the voice came again. 'I have been watching the Gurkish, as I have these many years. That is my allotted task. My penance, for the part I played in the schism that has split my order.'

'Your order?'

'The Order of Magi. I am the fourth of Juvens' twelve apprentices.'

A Magus. I might have known. Like that bald old meddler Bayaz, and I gained nothing but confusion from him. As if there were not enough to worry about with politics and treachery, now we must have myth and superstition to boot. Still, it looks as if I will last out the night, at least.

'A Magus, eh? Forgive me if I don't celebrate. Such dealings as I've had with your order have been a waste of my time, at best.'

'Perhaps I can repair our reputation, then. I bring you information.'

'Free of charge?'

'This time. The Gurkish are moving. Five of their golden standards pass down the peninsula tonight, under cover of the storm. Twenty thousand spears, with great engines of war. Five more standards wait behind the hills, and that is not all. The roads from Shaffa to Ul-Khatif, from Ul-Khatif to Daleppa, from Daleppa to the sea, all are thick with soldiers. The Emperor puts forth all his strength. The whole South moves. Conscripts from Kadir and Dawah, wild riders from Yashtavit, fierce savages from the jungles of Shamir, where men and women fight side by side. They all come northwards. Coming here, to fight for the Emperor.'

'So many, just to take Dagoska?'

'And more besides. The Emperor has built himself a navy. One hundred sail of great ships.'

'The Gurkish are no sailors. The Union controls the seas.'

'The world changes, and you must change with it or be swept aside. This war will not be like the last. Khalul finally sends forth his own soldiers. An army many long years in the making. The gates of the great temple-fortress of Sarkant are opening, high in the barren mountains. I have seen it. Mamun comes forth, thrice-blessed and thrice-cursed, the fruit of the desert, first apprentice of Khalul. Together they broke the Second Law, together they ate the flesh of men. The Hundred Words come behind, Eaters all, disciples of the Prophet, bred for battle and fed over these long years, adepts in the disciplines of arms and of high Art. No peril like it has faced the world since the Old Time, when Juvens fought with Kanedias. Since before that, perhaps, when Glustrod touched the Other Side, and sought to open the gates to the world below.'

And blah, blah, blah. A shame. He had been making surprising sense for a Magus. 'You want to give me information? Keep your bed-time stories and tell me what happened to Davoust.'

'There is an Eater here. I smell it. A dweller in the shadows. One whose only task is to destroy those who oppose the Prophet.' *And myself the first of them?* 'Your predecessor never left these chambers. The Eater took him, to protect the traitor who works within the city.'

Yes. Now we speak my language. 'Who is the traitor?' Glokta's voice sounded shrill, sharp, greedy in his own ear.

'I am no fortune-teller, cripple, and if I could give you the answer, would you believe me? Men must learn at their own pace.'

'Bah!' snapped Glokta. 'You are just like Bayaz. You talk, and talk, and yet you say nothing. Eaters? Nothing but old stories and nonsense!'

'Stories? Did Bayaz not take you within the Maker's House?' Glokta swallowed, his hand clinging trembling tight to the damp stone under the window. 'Yet still you doubt me? You are slow to learn, cripple. Have I not seen the slaves march to Sarkant, dragged from every land the Gurkish conquer? Have I not seen the countless columns, driven up into the mountains? To feed Khalul and his disciples, to swell their power ever further. A crime against God! A breach of the Second Law, written in fire by Euz himself! You doubt me, and perhaps you are wise to doubt me, but at first light you will see the Gurkish have come. You will count five standards, and you will know I spoke the truth.'

'Who is the traitor?' hissed Glokta. 'Tell me, you riddling bastard!' Silence, but for the splashing of rain, the trickling of water, the rustling of wind in the hangings about the window. A stroke of lightning threw sudden light into every corner.

The carpet was empty. Yulwei was gone.

*

The Gurkish host came slowly forward in five enormous blocks, two in front, three behind, covering the whole neck of land from sea to sea. They moved together in perfect formation to the deep thumping of great drums, rank upon rigid rank, the sound of their tramping boots like the distant thunder of the night before. Already, the sun had sucked away all evidence of the rain, and now it flashed mirror-bright on thousands of helmets, thousands of shields, thousands of swords, glittering arrow-heads, coats of armour. A forest of shining spears, moving inexorably forwards. A merciless, tireless, irresistible tide of men.

Union soldiers were scattered around the top of the land walls, squatting behind the parapet, fingering their flatbows, peering out nervously at the advancing host. Glokta could sense their fear. *And who can blame them? We must be outnumbered ten to one already.* There were no drums up here in the wind, no shouted orders, no hurried preparations. Only silence.

'And here they come,' mused Nicomo Cosca, grinning out at the scene. He alone seemed untouched by fear. *He has either an iron nerve or a leaden imagination. Lazing in a drinking-hole or waiting for death all seems to be one to him.* He was standing with one foot up on the parapet, forearms crossed on his knee, half-full bottle dangling from one hand. The mercenary's battle dress was much the same as his drinking gear. The same sagging boots, the same ruined trousers. His one allowance for the dangers of the battlefield was a black breastplate, etched front and back with golden scrollwork. It too had seen better days, the enamel chipped, the rivets stained with rust. *But it must once have been quite the masterpiece.*

'That's a fine piece of armour you have there.'

'What, this?' Cosca looked down at his breastplate. 'In its day, perhaps, but it's seen some hard use over the years. Been left out in the rain more than once. A gift from the Grand Duchess Sefeline of Ospria, in return for defeating the army of Sipani in the five month war. It came with a promise of her eternal friendship.'

'Nice, to have friends.'

'Not really. That very night she tried to have me killed. My victories had made me far too popular with Sefeline's own subjects. She feared I might try to seize power. Poison, in my wine.' Cosca took a long swig from his bottle. 'Killed my favourite mistress. I was forced to flee, with little more than this damn breastplate, and seek employment with the Prince of Sipani. That old bastard didn't pay half so well, but at least I got to lead his army against the Duchess, and have the satisfaction of seeing her poisoned in her turn.' He frowned. 'Made her face turn blue. Bright blue, believe me. Never get too popular, that's my advice.'

Glokta snorted. 'Over-popularity is scarcely my most pressing worry.'

Vissbruck cleared his throat noisily, evidently upset at being ignored. He gestured towards the endless ranks of men advancing down the isthmus.

'Superior, the Gurkish approach.' *Indeed? I had not noticed.* 'Do I have your permission to flood the ditch?'

Oh yes, your moment of glory. 'Very well.'

Vissbruck strutted to the parapet with an air of the greatest self-importance. He slowly raised his arm, then chopped it portentously through the air. Somewhere, out of sight below, whips cracked and teams of mules strained on ropes. The complaining squeal of wood under great pressure reached them on the battlements, then a creaking and a cracking as the dams gave way, and then an angry thundering as the great weight of salt water broke through and surged down the deep ditch from both ends, foaming angry white. Water met water just beneath them, throwing glittering spray into the air as high as the battlements and higher yet. A moment later, and this new ribbon of sea was calm. The ditch had become a channel, the city had become an island.

'The ditch is flooded!' announced General Vissbruck.

'So we see,' said Glokta. 'Congratulations.' *Let us hope the Gurkish have no strong swimmers among them. They certainly have no shortage of men to choose from.*

Five tall poles waved gently above the tramping mass of soldiers, Gurkish symbols glittering upon them in solid gold. *Symbols of battles fought, and battles won.* The standards of five legions, flashing in the merciless sun. *Five legions. Just as the old man told me. Will ships follow, then?* Glokta turned his head and peered out across the Lower City. The long wharves stuck into the bay like the spines of a hedgehog, still busy with ships. *Ships carrying our supplies in, and a last few nervous merchants out.* There were no walls there. Few defences of any kind. *We did not think we needed them. The Union has always ruled the seas. If ships should come . . .*

'Do we still have supplies of wood and stone?'

The General nodded vigorously, all eagerness. *Finally adjusted to the changes in the chain of command, it seems.* 'Abundant supplies, Superior, precisely as your orders specified.'

'I want you to build a wall behind the docks and along the shoreline. As strong, and as high, and as soon as possible. Our defences there are weak. The Gurkish may test them sooner or later.'

The General frowned out at the swarming army of soldiers crawling over the peninsula, looked down towards the calm docks, and back. 'But surely the threat from the landward side is a little more . . . pressing? The Gurkish are poor sailors, and in any case have no fleet worthy of the name—'

'The world changes, General. The world changes.'

'Of course.' Vissbruck turned to speak to his aides.

Glokta shuffled up to the parapet beside Cosca. 'How many Gurkish troops, would you judge?'

The Styrian scratched at the flaky rash on the side of his neck. 'I count five standards. Five of the Emperor's legions, and plenty more besides. Scouts, engineers, irregulars from across the South. How many troops . . .' He squinted up into the sun, lips moving silently as though his head was full of complex sums. 'A fucking lot.' He tipped his head back and sucked the last drops from his bottle, then he smacked his lips, pulled back his arm and hurled it towards the Gurkish. It flashed in the sun for a moment, then shattered against the hard dirt on the other side of the channel. 'Do you see those carts at the back?'

Glokta squinted down his eye-glass. There did indeed seem to be a shadowy column of great wagons behind the mass of soldiery, barely visible in the shimmering haze and the clouds of dust kicked up by the stomping boots. *Soldiers need supplies of course, but then again . . .* Here and there he could see long timbers sticking up like spider's legs. 'Siege engines,' muttered Glokta to himself. *All just as Yulwei said.* 'They are in earnest.'

'Ah, but so are you.' Cosca stood up beside the parapet, started to fiddle with his belt. A moment later, Glokta heard the sound of his piss spattering against the base of the wall, far below. The mercenary grinned over his shoulder, thin hair fluttering in the salt wind. 'Everyone's in lots of earnest. I must speak to Magister Eider. I'd say I'll be getting my battle money soon.'

'I think so.' Glokta slowly lowered his eye-glass. 'And earning it too.'

The Blind Lead the Blind

The First of the Magi lay twisted on his back in the cart, wedged between a water barrel and a sack of horse feed, a coil of rope for his pillow. Logen had never seen him look so old, and thin, and weak. His breath came shallow, his skin was pale and blotchy, drawn tight over his bones and beaded with sweat. From time to time he'd twitch, and squirm, and mutter strange words, his eyelids flickering like a man trapped in a bad dream.

'What happened?'

Quai stared down. 'Whenever you use the Art, you borrow from the Other Side, and what is borrowed has to be repaid. There are risks, even for a master. To seek to change the world with a thought . . . the arrogance of it.' The corners of his mouth twitched up into a smile. 'Borrow too often, perhaps, one time you touch the world below, and leave a piece of yourself behind . . .'

'Behind?' muttered Logen, peering down at the twitching old man. He didn't much like the way Quai was talking. It was no smiling matter, as far as he could see, to be stuck out in the middle of nowhere without a clue where they were going.

'Just think,' whispered the apprentice. 'The First of the Magi himself, helpless as a baby.' He laid his hand gently on Bayaz' chest. 'He clings on to life by a thread. I could reach out now, with this weak hand . . . and kill him.'

Logen frowned. 'Why would you want to do that?'

Quai looked up, and smiled his sickly smile. 'Why would anyone? I was merely saying.' And he snatched his hand away.

'How long will he stay like this?'

The apprentice sat back in the cart and stared up at the sky. 'There's no saying. Maybe hours. Maybe forever.'

'Forever?' Logen ground his teeth. 'Where does that leave us? You have any idea where we're going? Or why? Or what we do when we get there? Should we turn back?'

'No.' Quai's face was sharp as a blade. Sharper than Logen would ever have expected from him. 'We have enemies behind us. To turn back now would be more dangerous than to continue. We carry on.'

Logen winced, and rubbed at his eyes. He felt tired, and sore, and sick. He wished he'd asked Bayaz his plans when he'd had the chance. He wished he'd never left the North, if it came to that. He could have sought out a reckoning with Bethod, and died in a place he knew, at the hands of men that he at least understood.

Logen had no wish to lead. The time was he'd hungered after fame, and glory, and respect, but the winning of them had been costly, and they'd proved to be hollow prizes. Men had put their faith in him, and he'd led them by a painful and a bloody route straight back to the mud. There was no ambition in him any more. He was cursed when it came to making decisions.

He took his hands away and looked around him. Bayaz still lay muttering in his fevered sleep. Quai was gazing carelessly up at the clouds. Luthar was standing with his back to the others, staring down the gorge. Ferro was sitting on a rock, cleaning her bow with a rag, and scowling. Longfoot had reappeared, predictably, just as the danger ended, and was standing not far away, looking pleased with himself. Logen grimaced, and gave a long sigh. There was no help for it. There was no one else.

'Alright, we head for this bridge, at Aulcus, then we see.'

'Not a good idea,' tutted Longfoot, wandering up to the cart and peering in. 'Not a good idea in the least. I warned our employer of that before his . . . mishap. The city is deserted, destroyed, ruined. A blighted, and a broken, and a dangerous place. The bridge may still stand, but according to rumour—'

'Aulcus was the plan, and I reckon we'll stick with it.'

Longfoot carried on as though he hadn't spoken. 'I think, perhaps, that it would be best if we headed back towards Calcis. We are still less than halfway to our ultimate destination, and have ample food and water for the return journey. With some luck—'

'You were paid to go all the way?'

'Well, er, indeed I was, but—'

'Aulcus.'

The Navigator blinked. 'Well, yes, I see that you are decided. Decisiveness, and boldness, and vigour, it would seem, are among your talents, but caution, and wisdom, and experience, if I may say, are among mine, and I am in no doubt whatsoever that—'

'Aulcus,' growled Logen

Longfoot paused with his mouth half open. Then he snapped it shut. 'Very well. We will follow the road back onto the plains, and head westward to the three lakes. Aulcus is at their head, but the journey is still a long and dangerous one, especially with winter well upon us. There should be—'

'Good.' Logen turned away before the Navigator had the chance to say anything more. That was the easy part. He sucked his teeth, and walked over to Ferro.

'Bayaz is . . .' he struggled for the right word. 'Out. We don't know how long for.'

She nodded. 'We going on?'

'Er . . . I reckon . . . that's the plan.'

'Alright.' She got up from her rock and slung the bow over her shoulder. 'Best get moving then.'

Easier than he'd expected. Too easy, perhaps. He wondered if she was thinking of sneaking off again. He was considering it himself, truth be told. 'I don't even know where we're going.'

She snorted. 'I've never known where I was going. You ask me, it's an improvement, you in charge.' She walked off towards the horses. 'I never trusted that bald bastard.'

And that only left Luthar. He was standing with his back to the others, shoulders slumped, thoroughly miserable-looking. Logen could see the muscles on the side of his head working as he stared at the ground.

'You alright?'

Luthar hardly seemed to hear him. 'I wanted to fight. I wanted to, and I knew how to, and I had my hand on my steels.' He slapped angrily at the hilt of one of his swords. 'I was helpless as a fucking baby! Why couldn't I move?'

'That it? By the dead, boy, that happens to some men the first time!'

'It does?'

'More than you'd believe. At least you didn't shit yourself.'

Luthar raised his eyebrows. 'That happens?'

'More than you'd believe.'

'Did you freeze up, the first time?'

Logen frowned. 'No. Killing comes too easy to me. Always has done. Believe me, you're the lucky one.'

'Unless I'm killed for doing nothing.'

'Well,' Logen had to admit, 'there is that.' Luthar's head dropped even lower, and Logen clapped him on the arm. 'But you didn't get killed! Cheer up, boy, you're lucky! You're still alive, aren't you?' He gave a miserable nod. Logen slid his arm round his shoulder and guided him back towards the horses. 'Then you've got the chance to do better next time.'

'Next time?'

'Course. Doing better next time. That's what life is.'

Logen climbed back into the saddle, stiff and sore. Stiff from all the riding, sore from the fight in the gorge. Some bit of rock had cracked him on the back, that and he'd got a good punch on the side of his head. Could have been a lot worse.

He looked round at the others. They were all mounted up, staring at him. Four faces, as different as could be, but all with the same expression, more or less. Waiting for his say. Why did anyone ever think he had the answers? He swallowed, and dug his heels in.

'Let's go.'

Prince Ladisla's Stratagem

'You really should spend less time in here, Colonel West.' Pike set down his hammer for a moment, the orange light from his forge reflecting in his eyes, shining bright on his melted face. 'People will start to talk.'

West cracked a nervous grin. 'It's the only warm place in the whole damn camp.' It was true enough, but a long way from the real reason. It was the only place in the whole damn camp where no one would look for him. Men who were starving, men who were freezing, men who had no water, or no weapon, or no clue what they were doing. Men who'd died of cold or illness and needed burying. Even the dead couldn't manage without West. Everyone needed him, day and night. Everyone except Pike and his daughter, and the rest of the convicts. They alone seemed self-sufficient, and so their forge had become his refuge. A noisy, and a crowded, and a smoky refuge, no doubt, but no less sweet for that. He preferred it immeasurably to being with the Prince and his staff. Here among the criminals it was more . . . honest.

'You're in the way, Colonel. Again.' Cathil shoved past him, a knife-blade glowing orange in the tongs in one gloved hand. She shoved it into the water, frowning, turning it this way and that while steam hissed up around her. West watched her move, quick and practised, beads of moisture on her sinewy arm, the back of her neck, hair dark and spiky with sweat. Hard to believe he'd ever taken her for a boy. She might handle the metal as well as any of the men, but the shape of her face, not to mention her chest, her waist, the curve of her backside, all unmistakably female . . .

She glanced over her shoulder and caught him looking. 'Don't you have an army to run?'

'They'll last ten minutes without me.'

She drew the cold, black blade from the water and tossed it clattering onto the heap beside the whetstone. 'You sure?'

Maybe she was right at that. West took a deep breath, sighed, turned with some reluctance, and ventured out through the door of the shed and into the camp.

The winter air nipped at his cheeks after the heat of the smithy, and he pulled up the collars of his coat, hugged himself as he struggled down the camp's main road. It was deathly quiet out here at night, once he had left the rattling of the forge behind him. He could hear the frozen mud sucking at his boots, his breath rasping in his throat, the faint cursing of some distant soldier, grumbling his way through the darkness. He stopped a moment and looked up, arms folded round himself for warmth. The sky was perfectly clear, the stars prickling bright, spread across the blackness like shining dust.

'Beautiful,' he murmured to himself.

'You get used to it.'

It was Threetrees, picking his way between the tents with the Dogman at his shoulder. His face was in shadow, all dark pits and white angles like a cliff in the moonlight, but West could tell there was some ill news coming. The old Northman could hardly have been described as a figure of fun at the best of times, but now his frown was grim indeed.

'Well met,' said West in the Northern tongue.

'You think? Bethod is inside five days' march of your camp.'

The cold seemed suddenly to cut through West's coat and make him shiver. 'Five days?'

'If he's stayed put since we saw him, and that ain't likely. Bethod was never one for staying put. If he's marching south, he could be three days away. Less even.'

'What are his numbers?'

The Dogman licked his lips, breath smoking round his lean face in the chill air. 'I'd guess at ten thousand, but he might have more behind.'

West felt colder yet. 'Ten thousand? That many?'

'Around ten, aye. Mostly Thralls.'

'Thralls? Light infantry?'

'Light, but not like this rubbish you have here.' Threetrees scowled around at the shabby tents, the badly built camp fires, close to guttering out. 'Bethod's Thralls are lean and bloody from battles and tough as wood from marching. Those bastards can run all day and still fight at the end of it, if it's needed. Bowmen, spearmen, all well-practised.'

'There's no shortage of Carls and all,' muttered the Dogman.

'That there ain't, with strong mail and good blades, and plenty of horses into the bargain. There'll be Named Men too, no doubt. It's the pick of the crop Bethod's brought with him, and some sharp war leaders in amongst 'em. That and some strange folk from out east. Wild men, from beyond the Crinna. Must have left a few boys dotted about up north, for your friends to chase around after, and brought his best fighters south with him, against your weakest.' The old warrior stared grimly round at the slovenly camp from under his thick eyebrows. 'No offence, but I don't give you a shit of a chance if it comes to a battle.'

The worst of all outcomes. West swallowed. 'How fast could such an army move?'

'Fast. Their scouts might be with us day after tomorrow. Main body a day later. If they've come right on, that is, and it's hard to say if they will. Wouldn't put it past Bethod to try and cross the river lower down, come round behind us.'

'Behind us?' They were scarcely equipped for a predictable enemy. 'How could he have known we were here?'

'Bethod always had a gift for guessing out his enemies. Good sense for it. That and he's a lucky bastard. Loves to take chances. Ain't nothing more important in war than a good slice o' luck.'

West looked around him, blinking. Ten thousand battle-hardened Northmen, descending on their ramshackle camp. Lucky, unpredictable Northmen. He imagined trying to turn the ill-disciplined levies, up to their ankles in mud, trying to get them to form a line. It would be a slaughter. Another Black Well in the making. But at least they had a warning. Three days to prepare their defences, or better still, to begin to retreat.

'We must speak to the Prince at once,' he said.

Soft music and warm light washed out into the chill night air as West jerked back the tent flap. He stooped through, reluctantly, with the two Northmen close behind him.

'By the dead . . .' muttered Threetrees, gaping round.

West had forgotten how bizarre the Prince's quarters must appear to a newcomer, especially one who was a stranger to luxury. It was less a tent than a huge hall of purple cloth, ten strides or more in height, hung with Styrian tapestries and floored with Kantic carpets. The furniture would have been more in keeping in a palace than a camp. Huge carved dressers and gilt chests held the Prince's endless wardrobe, enough to clothe an army of dandies. The bed was a gargantuan four-poster, bigger than most tents in the camp on its own. A highly polished table in one corner sagged under the weight of heaped-up delicacies, silver and gold plate twinkling in the candlelight. One could hardly imagine that only a few hundred strides away, men were cramped, and cold, and had not enough to eat.

Crown Prince Ladisla himself sat sprawled in a huge chair of dark wood, a throne, one could have said, upholstered in red silk. An empty glass dangled from one hand, while the other waved back and forth to the music of a quartet of expert musicians, plucking, fiddling, and blowing gently at their shining instruments in the far corner. Around his Highness were four of his staff, impeccably dressed and fashionably bored, among them the young Lord Smund, who had perhaps become, over the past few weeks, West's least favourite person in the entire world.

'It does you great credit,' Smund was braying loudly to the Prince.

'Sharing the hardships of the camp has always been a fine way to win the respect of the common soldier—'

'Ah, Colonel West!' chirped Ladisla, 'and two of his Northern scouts! What a delight! You must take some food!' He made a floppy, drunken gesture towards the table.

'Thank you, your Highness, but I have eaten. I have some news of the greatest—'

'Or some wine! You must all have wine, this is an excellent vintage! Where did that bottle get to?' He fumbled about beneath his chair.

The Dogman had already crossed to the table and was leaning over it, sniffing at the food like . . . a dog. He snatched a large slice of beef from the plate with his dirty fingers, folded it carefully and stuffed it whole into his mouth, while Smund looked on, lip curled with contempt. It would have been embarrassing, under normal circumstances, but West had larger worries.

'Bethod is within five days march of us,' he nearly shouted, 'with the best part of his strength!'

One of the musicians fumbled his bow and hit a screeching, discordant note. Ladisla jerked his head up, nearly sliding from his seat. Even Smund and his companions were pulled from their indolence.

'Five days,' muttered the Prince, his voice hoarse with excitement, 'are you sure?'

'Perhaps no more than three.'

'How many are they?'

'As many as ten thousand, and veterans to a—'

'Excellent!' Ladisla slapped the arm of his chair as if it were a Northman's face. 'We are on equal terms with them!'

West swallowed. 'Perhaps in numbers, your Highness, but not in quality.'

'Come now, Colonel West,' droned Smund. 'One good Union man is worth ten of their kind.' He stared down his nose at Threetrees.

'Black Well proved that notion a fantasy, even if our men were properly fed, trained, and equipped. Aside from the King's Own, they are none of these things! We would be well advised to prepare defences, and make ready to withdraw if we must.'

Smund snorted his contempt for that idea. 'There is nothing more dangerous in war,' he disclaimed airily, 'than too much caution.'

'Except too little!' growled West, the fury already starting to pulse behind his eyes.

But Prince Ladisla cut him off before he had the chance to lose his temper. 'Gentlemen, enough!' He sprang up from his chair, eyes dewy with drunken enthusiasm. 'I have already decided on my strategy! We will cross the river and intercept these savages! They think to surprise us? Hah!' He lashed at the air with his wine glass. 'We will give them a surprise they will not soon forget! Drive them back over the border! Just as Marshal Burr intended!'

'But, your Highness,' stammered West, feeling slightly queasy, 'the Lord Marshal explicitly ordered that we remain behind the river—'

Ladisla flicked his head, as though bothered by a fly. 'The spirit of his orders, Colonel, not the letter! He can hardly complain if we take the fight to our enemy!'

'These men are fucking fools,' rumbled Threetrees, luckily in the Northern tongue.

'What did he say?' inquired the Prince.

'Er . . . he concurs with me that we should hold here, your Highness, and send to Lord Marshal Burr for help.'

'Does he indeed? And I thought these Northmen were all fire and vinegar! Well, Colonel West, you may inform him that I am resolved on an attack, and cannot be moved! We will show this so-called King of the Northmen that he does not hold a monopoly on victory!'

'Good show!' shouted Smund, stamping his foot on the thick carpet. 'Excellent!' The rest of the Prince's staff voiced their ignorant support.

'Kick them back across the border!'

'Teach them a lesson!'

'Excellent! Capital! Is there more wine?'

West clenched his fists with frustration. He had to make one more effort, however embarrassing, however pointless. He dropped to one knee, he clasped his hands together, he fixed the Prince with his eye and gathered every ounce of persuasiveness he possessed. 'Your Highness, I ask you, I entreat you, I beg you to reconsider. The lives of every man in this camp depend on your decision.'

The Prince grinned. 'Such is the weight of command, my friend! I realise your motives are of the best, but I must agree with Lord Smund. Boldness is the best policy in war, and boldness shall be my strategy! It was through boldness that Harod the Great forged the Union, through boldness that King Casamir conquered Angland in the first place! We will get the better of these Northmen yet, you'll see. Give the orders, Colonel! We march at first light!'

West had studied Casamir's campaigns in detail. Boldness had been one tenth of his success, the rest had been meticulous planning, care for his men, attention to every detail. Boldness without the rest was apt to be deadly, but he saw that it was pointless to say so. He would only anger the Prince and lose whatever influence he might still have. He felt like a man watching his own house burn down. Numb, sick, utterly helpless. There was nothing left for him to do but to give the orders, and do his best to see that everything was conducted as well as it could be.

'Of course, your Highness,' he managed to mutter.

'Of course!' The Prince grinned. 'We are all in agreement, then! Capital!

Stop that music!' he shouted at the musicians. 'We need something with more vigour! Something with blood in it!' The quartet switched effortlessly to a jaunty martial theme. West turned, limbs heavy with hopelessness, and trudged out of the tent into the icy night.

Threetrees was hard on his heels. 'By the dead, but I can't work you people out! Where I come from a man earns the right to lead! His men follow because they know his quality, and respect him because he shares their hardships with 'em! Even Bethod won his place!' He strode up and down before the tent, waving his big hands. 'Here you pick the ones who know the least to lead, and fix on the biggest fool o' the whole pack for a commander!'

West could think of nothing to say. He could hardly deny it.

'That prick'll march the lot o' you right into your fucking graves! Back to the mud with you all, but I'm damned if I'll follow, or any of my boys. I'm done paying for other folks' mistakes, and I've lost enough to that bastard Bethod already! Come on, Dogman. This boat o' fools can sink without us!' And he turned and stalked away into the night.

The Dogman shrugged. 'Ain't all bad.' He closed to a conspiratorial distance, reached deep into his pocket and pulled something out. West stared down at an entire poached salmon, no doubt pilfered from the Prince's table. The Northman grinned. 'I got me a fish!' And he followed his chief, leaving West alone on the bitter hillside, Ladisla's martial music floating through the chill air behind him.

Until Sunset

'**O**y.' A rough hand shook Glokta from his sleep. He rolled his head gingerly from the side he had been sleeping on, clenching his teeth at the pain as his neck clicked. *Does death come early in the morning, today?* He opened his eyes a crack. *Ah. Not quite yet, it seems. Perhaps at lunch time.* Vitari stared down at him, spiky hair silhouetted black in the early morning sun streaming through the window.

'Very well, Practical Vitari, if you really can't resist me. You'll have to go on top, though, if you don't mind.'

'Ha ha. The Gurkish ambassador is here.'

'The what?'

'An emissary. From the Emperor himself, I hear.'

Glokta felt a stab of panic. 'Where?'

'Here in the Citadel. Speaking to the ruling council.'

'Shit on it!' snarled Glokta, scrambling out of bed, ignoring the stabbing pain in his leg as he swung his ruined left foot onto the floor. 'Why didn't they call for me?'

Vitari scowled down at him. 'Maybe they preferred to talk to him without you. You think that could be it?'

'How the hell did he get here?'

'He came in by boat, under sign of parley. Vissbruck says he was duty bound to admit him.'

'Duty-bound!' spat Glokta as he struggled to pull his trousers up his numb and trembling leg, 'That fat fucker! How long has he been here?'

'Long enough for him and the council to make some pretty mischief together, if that's their aim.'

'Shit!' Glokta winced as he shrugged his shirt on.

The Gurkish ambassador was, without doubt, a majestic presence.

His nose was prominent and hooked, his eyes burned bright with intelligence, his long, thin beard was neatly brushed. Gold thread in his sweeping white robe and his tall head-dress glittered in the bright sun. He held his body awesomely erect, long neck stretched out, chin held high, so that he looked always down at everything he deigned to look upon. Hugely tall and thin, he made the lofty, magnificent room seem low and shabby. *He could pass for an Emperor himself.*

Glokta was keenly aware of how bent and awkward he must look as he shuffled, grimacing and sweating, into the audience chamber. *The miserable crow faces the magnificent peacock. Still, battles are not always won by the most beautiful. Fortunately for me.*

The long table was surprisingly empty. Only Vissbruck, Eider, and Korsten dan Vurms were in their seats, and none of them looked pleased to see him arrive. *Nor should they, the bastards.*

'No Lord Governor today?' he barked.

'My father is not well,' muttered Vurms.

'Shame you couldn't stay and comfort him in his illness. What about Kahdia?' No one spoke. 'Didn't think he'd take to a meeting with them, eh?' he nodded rudely at the emissary. 'How lucky for everyone that you three have stronger stomachs. I am Superior Glokta and, whatever you might have heard, I am in charge here. I must apologise for my late arrival, but no one told me you were coming.' He looked daggers at Vissbruck, but the general was not interested in meeting his eye. *That's right, you blustering fool. I won't forget this.*

'My name is Shabbed al Islik Burai.' The ambassador spoke the common tongue perfectly, in a voice every bit as powerful, as authoritative, as arrogant as his bearing. 'I come as emissary from the rightful ruler of all the South, mighty Emperor of mighty Gurkhul and all the Kantic lands, Uthman-ul-Dosht, loved, feared, and favoured above all other men within the Circle of the World, anointed by God's right hand, the Prophet Khalul himself.'

'Good for you. I would bow, but I strained my back getting out of bed.'

Islik gave a delicate sneer. 'Truly a warrior's injury. I have come to accept your surrender.'

'Is that so?' Glokta dragged out the nearest chair and sank into it. *I'm damned if I'm going to stand a moment longer, just for the benefit of this towering oaf.* 'I thought it was traditional to make such offers once the fighting is over.'

'If there is to be fighting, it will not last long.' The ambassador swept across the tiles to the window. 'I see five legions, arrayed in battle order upon the peninsula. Twenty thousand spears, and they are but a fraction of what comes. The troops of the Emperor are more numerous than the grains of sand in the desert. To resist us would be as futile as to resist the tide. You all know this.' His eyes swept proudly across the guilty faces of the ruling council and came to rest on Glokta's with a piercing contempt. *The look of a man who believes he has already won. No one could blame him much for thinking so. Perhaps he has.*

'Only fools or madmen would choose to stand against such odds. You pinks have never belonged here. The Emperor offers you the chance to leave the South with your lives. Open the gates to us and you will be spared. You can leave on your little boats and float back to your little island. Let it never be said that Uthman-ul-Dosht is not generous. God fights beside us. Your cause is lost.'

'Oh, I don't know, we held our own in the last war. I'm sure we all remember the fall of Ulrioch. I know I do. The city burned brightly. The temples especially.' Glokta shrugged. 'God must have been elsewhere that day.'

'That day, yes. But there were other battles. I am sure you also remember a certain engagement, at a certain bridge, where a certain young officer fell into our hands.' The emissary smiled. 'God is everywhere.'

Glokta felt his eyelid flickering. *He knows I am not likely to forget.* He remembered his surprise as a Gurkish spear cut into his body. Surprise, and disappointment, and the most intense pain. *Not invulnerable, after all.* He remembered his horse rearing, dumping him from the saddle. The pain growing worse, the surprise turning into fear. Crawling among the boots and the bodies, gasping for air, mouth sour with dust, salty with blood. He remembered the agony as the blades cut into his leg. The fear turning to terror. He remembered how they dragged him, screaming and crying, from that bridge. *That night they began to ask their questions.*

'We won,' said Glokta, but his mouth was dry, his voice was cracked. 'We proved the stronger.'

'That was then. The world changes. Your nation's entanglements in the icy North put you at a most considerable disadvantage. You have managed to break the first rule of warfare. Never fight two enemies at once.'

His reasoning is hard to fault. 'The walls of Dagoska have frustrated you before,' Glokta said, but it did not sound convincing, even to his own ear. *Hardly the words of a winner.* He felt the eyes of Vurms, and Vissbruck, and Eider on him, making his back itch. *Trying to decide who holds the upper hand, and I know who I'd pick in their shoes.*

'Perhaps some of you have more confidence in your walls than others. I will return at sunset for your answer. The Emperor's offer lasts for this one day only, and will never be repeated. He is merciful, but his mercy has limits. You have until sunset.' And he swept from the room.

Glokta waited until the door had clicked shut before he slowly turned his chair around to face the others. 'What in hell was that?' he snarled at Vissbruck.

'Er . . .' The General tugged at his sweaty collar. 'It was incumbent upon me, as a soldier, to admit an unarmed representative of the enemy, in order to hear his terms—'

'Without telling me?'

'We knew you would not want to listen!' snapped Vurms. 'But he speaks the truth! Despite all our hard work, we are greatly outnumbered, and can expect no relief as long as the war drags on in Angland. We are nothing more than a pinprick in the foot of a huge and hostile nation. It might serve us well to negotiate while we still hold a position of some strength. You may depend upon it that we will receive no terms beyond a massacre once the city has fallen!'

True enough, but the Arch Lector is unlikely to agree. Negotiating a surrender was hardly the task for which I was appointed. 'You are unusually quiet, Magister Eider.'

'I am scarcely qualified to speak on the military aspects of such a decision. But as it turns out, his terms are generous. One thing is certain. If we refuse this offer, and the Gurkish do take the city by force, the slaughter will be terrible.' She looked up at Glokta. 'There will be no mercy then.'

All too true. On Gurkish mercy I am the expert. 'So all three of you are for capitulation?' They looked at each other, and said nothing. 'It has not occurred to you that once we surrender, they might not honour your little agreement?'

'It had occurred,' said Vissbruck, 'but they have honoured their agreements before, and surely some hope . . .' and he looked down at the table top, 'is better than none.' *You have more confidence in our enemy than in me, it would seem. Hardly that surprising. My own confidence could be higher.*

Glokta wiped some wet from under his eye. 'I see. Then I suppose I must consider his offer. We will reconvene when our Gurkish friend returns. At sunset.' He rocked his body back and winced as he pushed himself up.

'You'll consider it?' hissed Vitari in his ear as he limped down the hall away from the audience chamber. 'You'll fucking consider it?'

'That's right,' snapped Glokta. 'I make the decisions here.'

'Or you let those worms make them for you!'

'We've each got our jobs. I don't tell you how to write your little reports to the Arch Lector. How I manage those worms is none of your concern.'

'None of my concern?' Vitari snatched hold of Glokta's arm and he tottered on his weak leg. She was stronger than she looked, a lot stronger. 'I told Sult you could handle things!' she snarled in his face. 'If we lose the city, without so much as a fight even, it's both our heads! And my head is my concern, cripple!'

'This is no time to panic,' growled Glokta. 'I don't want to end up floating in the docks any more than you do, but this is a delicate balance. Let them think they might get their way, then no one will make any rash moves. Not until I'm good and ready. Understand me when I say, Practical, that this will be the first and the last time that I explain myself to you. Now take your fucking hand off me.'

Her hand did not let go, rather the fingers tightened, cutting into Glokta's arm as hard as a vice. Her eyes narrowed, furious lines cut into her freckled face at their corners. *Might I have misjudged her? Might she be about to cut my throat?* He almost grinned at the thought. But Severard chose that moment to step out of the shadows further down the dim hall.

'Look at the two of you,' he murmured as he padded towards them. 'It always amazes me, how love blooms in the least likely places, and between the least likely people. A rose, forcing its way through the stony ground.' He pressed his hands to his chest. 'It warms my heart.'

'Have we got him?'

'Of course. Soon as he stepped out of the audience chamber.'

Vitari's hand had gone limp, and Glokta brushed it off and began to shuffle towards the cells. 'Why don't you come with us?' he called over his shoulder, having to stop himself rubbing the bruised flesh on his arm. 'You can put this in your next report to Sult.'

Shabbed al Islik Burai looked considerably less majestic sitting down. Particularly in a scarred, stained chair in one of the close and sweaty cells beneath the Citadel.

'Now isn't this better, to speak on level terms? Quite disconcerting, having you looming over me like that.' Islik sneered and looked away, as though talking to Glokta were a task far beneath him. *A rich man, harassed by beggars in the street, but we'll soon cure him of that illusion.*

'We know we have a traitor within our walls. Within the ruling council itself. Most likely one of those three worthies to whom you were just now giving your little ultimatum. You will tell me who.' No response. 'I am merciful,' exclaimed Glokta, waving his hand airily, as the ambassador himself had done but a few short minutes before, 'but my mercy has limits. Speak.'

'I am here under a flag of parley, on a mission from the Emperor himself! To harm an unarmed emissary would be expressly against the rules of war!'

'Parley? Rules of war?' Glokta chuckled. Severard chuckled. Vitari chuckled. Frost was silent. 'Do they even have those any more? Save that rubbish for children like Vissbruck, that's not the way grown-ups play the game. Who is the traitor?'

'I pity you, cripple! When the city falls—'

Save your pity. You'll need it for yourself. Frost's fist scarcely made any sound as it sank into the ambassador's stomach. His eyes bulged out, his mouth hung open, he coughed a dry cough, somewhere close to vomiting, tried to breathe and coughed again.

'Strange, isn't it,' mused Glokta as he watched him struggle for air. 'Big men, small men, thin men, fat men, clever men, stupid men, they all respond the same to a fist in the guts. One minute you think you're the most powerful man in the world. The next you can't even breathe by yourself. Some kinds of power are nothing but tricks of the mind. Your people taught me that, below your Emperor's palace. There were no rules of war there, I can tell you. You know all about certain engagements, and certain bridges, and certain young officers, so you know that I've been just where you are now. There is one difference, however. I was helpless, but you can stop this unpleasantness at any time. You need only tell me who the traitor is, and you will be spared.'

Islik had got his breath back now. *Though a good deal of his arrogance is gone, one suspects for good.* 'I know nothing of any traitor!'

'Really? Your master the Emperor sends you here to negotiate without all the facts? Unlikely. But if it's true, you really aren't any use to me at all, are you?'

Islik swallowed. 'I know nothing of any traitor.'

'We'll see.'

Frost's big white fist clubbed him in the face. It would have thrown him sideways if the albino's other fist hadn't caught his head before it fell, smashed his nose and knocked him clean over the back of the chair. Frost and Severard dragged him up between them, righted the chair and dumped him gasping into it. Vitari looked on, arms folded.

'All very painful,' said Glokta, 'but pain can be put to one side, if one knows that it will not last long. If it cannot last, say, past sunset. To truly break a man quickly, you have to threaten to deprive him of something. To hurt him in a way that will never heal. I should know.'

'Gah!' squawked the ambassador, thrashing in his chair. Severard wiped his knife on the shoulder of the man's white robe, then tossed his ear onto the table. It lay there, on the wood: a forlorn and bloody half-circle of flesh. Glokta stared at it. *In a baking cell just like this, over the course of long months, the Emperor's servants turned me into this revolting, twisted mockery of a man. One might have hoped that the chance at doing the same to one of them, the chance at cutting out vengeance, pound for pound, would provide some dull flicker of pleasure.* And yet he felt nothing. *Nothing but my own pain.* He winced as he stretched his leg out and felt the knee click, hissed air through his empty gums. *So why do I do this?*

Glokta sighed. 'Next will come a toe. Then a finger, an eye, a hand, your nose, and so on, do you see? It'll be at least an hour before you're missed, and we are quick workers.' Glokta nodded at the severed ear. 'We could have a pile of your flesh a foot high by that time. I'll carve you until you're nothing but a tongue and a bag of guts, if that's what it takes, but I'll know who the traitor is, that I promise you. Well? Do you know anything yet?'

The ambassador stared at him, breathing hard, dark blood running from his magnificent nose, down his chin, dripping from the side of his head. *Speechless with shock, or thinking on his next move? It hardly matters.* 'I grow bored. Start on his hands, Frost.' The albino seized hold of his wrist.

'Wait!' wailed the ambassador, 'God help me, wait! It was Vurms. Korsten dan Vurms, the governor's own son!'

Vurms. Almost too obvious. But then again, the most obvious answers are usually the right ones. That little bastard would sell his own father if he only thought that he could find a buyer—

'And the woman, Eider!'

Glokta frowned. 'Eider? You sure?'

'She planned it! She planned the whole thing!' Glokta sucked slowly at his empty gums. They tasted sour. *An awful sense of disappointment, or an awful sense of having known all along? She was always the only one with the brains, or the guts, or the resources, for treason. A shame. But we know better than to hope for happy endings.*

'Eider and Vurms,' muttered Glokta. 'Vurms and Eider. Our sordid little mystery comes to a close.' He looked up at Frost. 'You know what to do.'

Long Odds

The hill rose out of the grass, a round, even cone like a thing man-made. Strange, this one great mound standing out in the midst of the level plain. Ferro did not trust it.

Weathered stones stood in a rough circle around its top and scattered about the slopes, some up on end, some lying on their sides, the smallest no more than knee high, the biggest twice as tall as a man. Dark, bare stones, standing defiant against the wind. Ancient, cold, angry. Ferro frowned at them.

It felt as though they frowned back.

'What is this place?' asked Ninefingers.

Quai shrugged. 'Old is what this place is, terribly old. Older than the Empire itself. Built before the time of Euz, perhaps, when devils roamed the earth.' He grinned. 'Built by devils, for all I know. Who can say? Some temple to forgotten gods? Some tomb?'

'Our tomb,' whispered Ferro.

'What?'

'Good place to stop,' she said out loud. 'Get a look across the plain.'

Ninefingers frowned up at it. 'Alright. We stop.'

Ferro stood on one of the stones, hands on hips, staring out across the plain through narrowed eyes. The wind tore at the grass and made waves from it, like the waves on the sea. It tore at the great clouds too, twisting them, ripping them open, dragging them through the sky. It lashed at Ferro's face, nipped at her eyes, but she ignored it.

Damn wind, just like always.

Ninefingers stood beside her, squinting into the cold sun. 'Anything out there?'

'We are followed.' They were far away, but she could see them. Tiny dots in the far distance. Tiny riders moving on the ocean of grass.

Ninefingers grimaced. 'You sure?'

'Yes. You surprised?'

'No.' He gave up looking and rubbed at his eyes. 'Bad news is never a surprise. Just a disappointment.'

'I count thirteen.'

'You can count 'em? I can't even see 'em. They coming for us?'

She raised her arms. 'You see anything else out here? Might be that laughing bastard Finnius found some more friends.'

'Shit.' He looked down at the cart, drawn up at the base of the hill. 'We can't outrun them.'

'No.' She curled her lip. 'You could ask the spirits for their opinion.'

'So they could tell us what? That we're fucked?' Silence for a moment. 'Better to wait, and fight them here. Bring the cart up to the top. At least we've got a hill, and a few rocks to hide behind.'

'That's what I was thinking. Gives us some time to prepare the ground.'

'Alright. We'd best get to it.'

The point of the shovel bit into the ground with the sharp scrape of metal on earth. An all too familiar sound. Digging pits and digging graves. What was the difference?

Ferro had dug graves for all kinds of people. Companions, or as close as she had come to companions. Friends, or as close as she had come to friends. A lover or two, if you could call them that. Bandits, killers, slaves. Whoever hated the Gurkish. Whoever hid in the Badlands, for whatever reason.

Spade up and spade down.

When the fighting is over, you dig, if you are still alive. You gather up the bodies in a line. You dig the graves in a row. You dig for your fallen comrades. Your slashed, your punctured, your hacked and your broken comrades. You dig as deep as you can be bothered, you dump them in, you cover them up, they rot away and are forgotten, and you go on, alone. That's the way it's always been.

But here, on this strange hill in the middle of this strange country, there was still time. Still a chance for the comrades to live. That was the difference, and for all her scorn, and her scowls, and her anger, she clung to it as she clung to the spade, desperate tight.

Strange how she never stopped hoping.

'You dig well,' said Ninefingers. She squinted up at him, standing over her at the edge of the pit.

'Lots of practice.' She dug the spade into the earth beside the hole, planted her hands on the sides and jumped out, sat on the edge with her legs hanging down. Her shirt was stuck to her with sweat, her face was running with it. She wiped her forehead with her dirty hand. He handed her the water-skin and she took it from him, pulled the stopper out with her teeth.

'How long do we have?'

She sucked a mouthful out of the skin and worked it round, spat it out. 'Depends how hard they go.' She took another mouthful and swallowed.

'They are going hard now. They keep that up, they could be on us late tonight, or maybe dawn tomorrow.' She handed the skin back.

'Dawn tomorrow.' Ninefingers slowly pushed the stopper back in. 'Thirteen you said, eh?'

'Thirteen.'

'And four of us.'

'Five, if the Navigator comes to help.'

Ninefingers scratched at his jaw. 'Not very likely.'

'That apprentice any use in a fight?'

Ninefingers winced. 'Not much.'

'How about Luthar?'

'I'd be surprised if he's ever thrown a fist in anger, let alone a blade.'

Ferro nodded. 'Thirteen against two, then.'

'Long odds.'

'Very.'

He took a deep breath and stared down into the pit. 'If you had a mind to run, I can't say I'd blame you.'

'Huh,' she snorted. Strange, but she hadn't even thought about it. 'I'll stick. See how it turns out.'

'Alright. Good. Can't say I don't need you.'

The wind rustled in the grass and sighed against the stones. There were things that should be said at a time like this, Ferro guessed, but she did not know what. She had never had much talk in her.

'One thing. If I die, you bury me.' She held her hand out to him. 'Deal?'

He raised an eyebrow at it. 'Done.' It was a long time, she realised, since she touched another person without the purpose of hurting them. It was a strange feeling, his hand gripped in hers, his fingers tight round hers, his palm pressed against hers. Warm. He nodded at her. She nodded at him. Then they let go.

'What if we both die?' he said.

She shrugged. 'Then the crows can pick us clean. After all, what's the difference?'

'Not much,' he muttered, starting off down the slope. 'Not much.'

The Road to Victory

West stood by a clump of stunted trees, in the cutting wind, on the high ground above the river Cumnur, and watched the long column move. More accurately, he watched it not move.

The neat blocks of the King's Own, up at the head of Prince Ladisla's army, marched smartly enough. You could tell them from their armour, glinting in the odd ray of pale sun that broke through the ragged clouds, from the bright uniforms of their officers, from the red and golden standards snapping at the front of each company. They were already across the river, formed up in good order, a stark contrast with the chaos on the other side.

The levies had started eagerly, early that morning, no doubt relieved to be leaving the miserable camp behind, but it hadn't been an hour before a man here or a man there, older than the others, or worse shod, had started to lag, and the column had grown ragged. Men slipped and stumbled in the half-frozen muck, cursing and barging into their neighbours, boots tripping on the boots of the man in front. The battalions had twisted, stretched, turned from neat blocks into shapeless blobs, merged with the units in front and behind, until the column moved in great ripples, one group hurrying forward while the next was still, like the segments of some monstrous, filthy earthworm.

As soon as they reached the bridge they had lost all semblance of order. The ragged companies squeezed into that narrow space, shoving and grunting, tired and bad-tempered. Those waiting behind pressed in tighter and tighter, impatient to be across so they could rest, slowing everything down still further with the weight of their bodies. Then a cart, which had no business being there in any case, had lost a wheel halfway across, and the sluggish flow of men over the bridge had become a trickle. No one seemed to know how to move it, or who to get to fix it, and contented themselves with clambering over it, or slithering around it, and holding up the thousands behind.

Quite a press had built up in the mud on this side of the fast-flowing water. Men barged and grumbled shoulder to shoulder, spears sticking up into the air at all angles, surrounded by shouting officers and an ever increasing detritus of rubbish and discarded gear. Behind them the great snake of shambling men continued its spastic forward movement, feeding ever more soldiers into the confusion before the bridge. There was not the slightest evidence that anyone had even thought about trying to make them stop, let alone succeeded.

All this in column, under no pressure from the enemy, and with a half decent road to march on. West dreaded to imagine trying to manoeuvre them in a battle line, through trees or over broken ground. He jammed his tired eyes shut, rubbed at them with his fingers, but when he opened them the horrifying, hilarious spectacle was still there before him. He hardly knew whether to laugh or cry.

He heard the sound of hooves on the rise behind him. Lieutenant Jalenhorm, big and solid in his saddle. Short on imagination, perhaps, but a fine rider, and a trustworthy man. A good choice for the task that West had in mind.

'Lieutenant Jalenhorm reporting, sir.' The big man turned in his saddle and looked down towards the river. 'Looks like they're having some trouble on the bridge.'

'Doesn't it just. Only the start of our troubles, I fear.'

Jalenhorm grinned down. 'I understand we have the advantage of numbers, and of surprise—'

'As far as numbers go, maybe. Surprise?' West gestured down at the men milling around on the bridge, heard the vague, desperate shouts of their officers. 'This rabble? A blind man would hear us coming from ten miles distance. A blind and a deaf one would probably smell us before we were halfway to battle order. We'll be all day just getting across the river. And that's hardly the worst of our shortcomings. In the area of command, I fear, the gulf between us and our enemy could not possibly be wider. The Prince lives in a dream, and his staff exist only to keep him there, at any price.'

'But surely—'

'The price could be our lives.'

Jalenhorm frowned. 'Come on, West, I hardly want to be going into battle with that thought first on my mind—'

'You won't be going.'

'I won't?'

'You will pick out six good men from your company, with spare mounts. You will ride as hard as possible for Ostenhorm, then north to Lord Marshal Burr's camp.' West reached into his coat and pulled out his letter. 'You will give him this. You will inform him that Bethod is already behind him with the greater part of his strength, and that Prince Ladisla has most ill-advisedly decided to cross the river Cumnur and give the Northmen battle, directly against the Marshal's orders.' West clenched his teeth. 'Bethod will see us coming from miles away. We are handing the choice of the ground to our enemy, so that Prince Ladisla can appear bold. Boldness is the best policy in war, apparently.'

'West, surely it's not that bad?'

'When you reach Marshal Burr, tell him that Prince Ladisla has almost certainly been defeated, quite possibly destroyed, and the road to Ostenhorm left open. He'll know what to do.'

Jalenhorm stared down at the letter, reached out to take it, then paused. 'Colonel, I really wish that you'd send someone else. I should fight—'

'Your fighting cannot possibly make any real difference, Lieutenant, but your carrying this message might. There is no sentiment in this, believe me. I have no more important task than this one, and you are the man I trust to get it done. Do you understand your orders?'

The big man swallowed, then he took the letter, undid a button and slid it carefully down inside his coat. 'Of course, sir. I am honoured to carry it.' He began to turn his horse.

'There is one more thing.' West took a deep breath. 'If I should . . . get myself killed. When this is over, could you carry a message to my sister?'

'Come on, there'll be no need for—'

'I hope to live, believe me, but this is war. Not everyone will. If I don't come back, just tell Ardee . . .' He thought about it for a moment. 'Just tell her I'm sorry. That's all.'

'Of course. But I hope you'll tell her yourself.'

'So do I. Good luck.' West held out his hand.

Jalenhorm reached down and squeezed it in his own. 'And to you.' He spurred his mount down the rise, away from the river. West watched him go for a minute, then he took a deep breath and set off in the other direction, towards the bridge.

Someone had to get that damn column moving again.

Necessary Evils

The sun was half a shimmering golden disc beyond the land walls, throwing orange light into the hallway down which Glokta shuffled, Practical Frost looming at his shoulder. Through the windows as he passed painfully by he could see the buildings of the city casting long shadows up towards the rock. He could almost tell, at each window that he came to, that the shadows were longer and less distinct, the sun was dimmer and colder. Soon it would be gone. *Soon it will be night.*

He paused for a moment before the doors to the audience chamber, catching his breath, letting the ache in his leg subside, licking at his empty gums. 'Give me the bag, then.'

Frost handed him the sack, put one white hand against the doors. 'You reathy?' he mumbled.

Ready as I'll ever be. 'Let's get on with it.'

General Vissbruck was sitting stiff in his well-starched uniform, jowls bulging slightly over his high collar, hands plucking nervously at each other. Korsten dan Vurms was doing his best to look nonchalant, but his darting tongue betrayed his anxiety. Magister Eider was sitting upright, hands clasped on the table before her, face stern. *All business.* A necklace of large rubies glowed with the last embers of the setting sun. *Didn't take her too long to find some more jewels, I see.*

There was one more member of the gathering, and he showed not the slightest sign of nerves. Nicomo Cosca was lounging against the far wall, not far behind his employer, arms crossed over his black breastplate. Glokta noted that he had a sword at his hip, and a long dagger at the other.

'What's he doing here?'

'This concerns everyone in the city,' said Eider calmly. 'It is too important a decision for you to make alone.'

'So he's going to ensure that you get a fair say, eh?' Cosca shrugged and examined his dirty fingernails. 'And what of the writ, signed by all twelve chairs on the Closed Council?'

'Your paper will not save us from the Emperor's vengeance if the Gurkish take the city.'

'I see. So you have it in mind to defy me, to defy the Arch Lector, to defy the King?'

'I have it in mind to hear out the Gurkish emissary, and to consider the facts.'

'Very well,' said Glokta. He stepped forwards and upended the bag. 'Give him your ear.' Islik's head dropped onto the table with a hollow clonking sound. It had no expression to speak of, beyond an awful slackness, eyes open and staring off in different directions, tongue lolling slightly. It rolled awkwardly along the beautiful table top, leaving an uneven curve of bloody smears on the brightly polished wood, and came to rest, face up, just in front of General Vissbruck.

A touch theatrical, perhaps, but dramatic. You'd have to give me that. No one can be left in any doubt as to my level of commitment. Vissbruck gawped down at the bloody head on the table before him, his mouth slowly falling further and further open. He started up from his seat and stumbled back, his chair clattering over on the tiles. He raised a shaking finger to point at Glokta.

'You're mad! You're mad! There'll be no mercy for anyone! Every man, woman, and child in Dagoska! If the city falls now, there's no hope for any of us!'

Glokta smiled his toothless smile. 'Then I suggest that every one of you commits themselves wholeheartedly to ensuring that the city does not fall.' He looked over at Korsten dan Vurms. 'Unless it's already too late for that, eh? Unless you've already sold the city to the Gurkish, and you can't go back!'

Vurms' eyes flickered to the door, to Cosca, to the horrified General Vissbruck, to Frost, hulking ominous in the corner, and finally to Magister Eider, still sitting steely calm and composed. *And our little conspiracy is jerked from the shadows.*

'He knows!' screamed Vurms, shoving back his chair and stumbling up, taking a step towards the windows.

'Clearly he knows.'

'Then do something, damn it!'

'I already have,' said Eider. 'By now, Cosca's men will have seized the land walls, bridged your channel, and opened the gates to the Gurkish. The docks, the Great Temple, and even the Citadel itself, are also in their hands.' There was a faint rattling beyond the door. 'I do believe that I can hear them now, just outside. I am sorry, Superior Glokta, indeed I am. You have done everything his Eminence could have expected, and more, but the Gurkish will already be pouring into the city. You see that further resistance is pointless.'

Glokta looked up at Cosca. 'May I retort?' The Styrian gave a small smile, a stiff bow. 'Most kind. I hate to disappoint you, but the gates are in the hands of Haddish Kahdia, and several of his most committed priests.

He said that he would open them to the Gurkish – what was his phrase – "when God himself commanded it." Do you have a divine visitation planned?' It was plain from Eider's face that she had not. 'As for the Citadel, it has been seized by the Inquisition, for the safety of his Majesty's loyal subjects, of course. Those are my Practicals that you can hear outside. As for Master Cosca's mercenaries—'

'At their posts on the walls, Superior, as ordered!' The Styrian snapped his heels together and gave an impeccable salute. 'They stand ready to repel any assault by the Gurkish.' He grinned down at Eider. 'I do apologise that I must leave your service at such a crucial time, Magister, but you understand that I had a better offer.'

There was a stunned pause. Vissbruck could hardly have looked more flabbergasted if he had been struck by lightning. Vurms stared around, wild-eyed. He took one more step back and Frost took a stride towards him. Magister Eider's face had drained of colour. *And so the chase ends, and the foxes are at bay.*

'You should hardly be surprised.' Glokta settled back comfortably in his chair. 'Nicomo Cosca's disloyalty is a legend throughout the Circle of the World. There's hardly a land under the sun in which he hasn't betrayed an employer.' The Styrian smiled and bowed once more.

'It is your wealth,' muttered Eider, 'not his disloyalty, that surprises me. Where did you get it?'

Glokta grinned. 'The world is full of surprises.'

'You fucking stupid bitch!' screamed Vurms. His steel was only halfway out before Frost's white fist crunched into his jaw and flung him senseless against the wall. Almost at the same moment the doors crashed open and Vitari burst into the room, half a dozen Practicals behind her, weapons at the ready.

'Everything alright?' she asked.

'Actually, we're just finishing up. Take out the rubbish would you, Frost?'

The albino's fingers closed around Vurms' ankle and hauled him bodily across the floor and out of the audience chamber. Eider watched his slack face slide across the tiles, then looked up at Glokta. 'What now?'

'Now the cells.'

'Then?'

'Then we'll see.' He snapped his fingers at the Practicals, jerked his thumb towards the door. Two of them tramped round the table, seized the Queen of merchants by her elbows and bundled her impassively out of the room.

'So,' asked Glokta, looking over at Vissbruck. 'Does anyone else wish to accept the ambassador's offer of surrender?'

The General, who had been standing silently the whole time, snapped his mouth shut, took a deep breath and stood to stiff attention. 'I am a simple soldier. Of course I will obey any order from his Majesty, or his Majesty's chosen representative. If the order is to hold Dagoska to the last man, I will give the last drop of my blood to do it. I assure you that I knew nothing of any plot. I acted rashly, perhaps, but at all times honestly, in what I felt were the best interests of—'

Glokta waved his hand. 'I am convinced. Bored, but convinced.' *I have already lost half the ruling council today. To lose any more might make me look greedy.* 'The Gurkish will no doubt make their assault at first light. You should look to our defences, General.'

Vissbruck closed his eyes, swallowed, wiped some sweat from his forehead. 'You will not regret your faith in me, Superior.'

'I trust that I will not. Go.'

The General hurried from the room, as though worried that Glokta might change his mind, and the rest of the Practicals followed him. Vitari bent and lifted Vurms' fallen chair and slid it carefully back under the table.

'A neat job.' She nodded slowly to herself. 'Very neat. I'm happy to say I was right about you all along.'

Glokta snorted. 'Your approval is worth less to me than you can ever know.'

Her eyes smiled at him above her mask. 'I didn't say that I approved. I just said that it was neat,' and she turned and sauntered out into the hallway.

That only left him and Cosca. The mercenary leaned against the wall, arms folded carelessly across his breastplate, regarding Glokta with a faint smile. He had not moved the whole time.

'You'd do well in Styria, I think. Very . . . ruthless? Is that the word? Anyway,' and he gave a flamboyant shrug, 'I look forward very much to serving with you.' *Until such time as someone offers you more, eh, Cosca?* The mercenary waved a hand at the severed head on the table. 'Would you like me to do something with that?'

'Stick it on the battlements of the land walls, somewhere it can be easily seen. Let the Gurkish understand the strength of our resolve.'

Cosca clicked his tongue. 'Heads on spikes, eh?' He dragged the head off the table by its long beard. 'Never goes out of fashion.'

The doors clicked shut behind him, and Glokta was left alone in the audience chamber. He rubbed at his stiff neck, stretched his stiff leg out beneath the bloody table. *A good day's work, all in all. But the day is over now.* Outside the tall windows, the sun had finally set over Dagoska.

The sky was dark.

Among the Stones

The first traces of dawn were creeping over the plain. A glimmer of light on the undersides of the towering clouds and along the edges of the ancient stones, a muddy flare on the eastern horizon. A sight a man rarely saw, that first grey glow, or one that Jezal had rarely seen anyway. At home he would have been safely in his quarters now, sleeping soundly in a warm bed. None of them had slept last night. They had spent the long, cold hours in silence, sitting in the wind, peering into the dark for shapes out on the plain, and waiting. Waiting for the dawn.

Ninefingers frowned at the rising sun. 'Almost time. Soon they'll be coming.'

'Right,' muttered Jezal numbly.

'Listen to me, now. Stay here, and watch the cart. There's plenty of 'em, and more than likely some will get round the back of us. That's why you're here. You understand?'

Jezal swallowed. His throat was tight with the tension. All he could think about was how unfair it was. How unfair, that he should die so young.

'Alright. Me and her will be round the front of the hill there, in around the stones. Most of 'em will come up that way, I reckon. You get in trouble, you shout for us, but if we don't come, well . . . do what you can. Might be we're busy. Might be we're dead.'

'I'm scared,' said Jezal. He hadn't meant to say it, but it hardly seemed to matter, now.

Ninefingers only nodded, though. 'And me. We're all scared.'

Ferro had a fierce smile on her face as she tightened the straps of her quiver around her chest, pulled the buckle on her sword-belt one notch further, dragged on her archery guard and worked her fingers, twanged at her bow-string, everything neat, and quick, and ready for violence. While she prepared for a fight that would most likely be the death of them all, she looked as Jezal might have done dressing for a night round the taverns of Adua. Yellow eyes shining, excited in the half light, as if she couldn't wait to get started. He had never seen her look happy before. 'She doesn't look scared.' he said.

Ninefingers frowned over at her. 'Well, maybe not her, but she's not an example I'd want to follow.' He watched her for a moment. 'Sometimes, when someone lives in danger for too long, the only time they feel alive is when death's breathing on their shoulder.'

'Right,' muttered Jezal. The sight of the buckle on his own sword-belt, of the grips of his own steels, so proudly polished, made him feel sick now. He swallowed again. Damn it, but his mouth had never been so full of spit.

'Try to think about something else.'

'Like what?'

'Whatever gets you through it. You got family?'

'A father, two brothers. I don't know how much they like me.'

'Shit on them, then. You got children?'

'No.'

'Wife?'

'No.' Jezal grimaced. He had done nothing with his life but play cards and make enemies. No one would miss him.

'A lover then? Don't tell me there ain't a girl waiting.'

'Well, maybe . . .' But he did not doubt that Ardee would already have found someone else. She had never seemed overly sentimental. Perhaps he should have offered to marry her when he had the chance. At least then someone might have wept for him. 'What about you?' he mumbled.

'What? A family?' Ninefingers frowned, rubbing grimly at the stump of his middle finger. 'I did have one. And now I've got another. You don't pick your family, you take what you're given and you make the best of it.' He pointed at Ferro, then at Quai. 'You see her, and him, and you?' He slapped his hand down on Jezal's shoulder. 'That's my family now, and I don't plan on losing a brother today, you understand?'

Jezal nodded slowly. You don't pick your family. You make the best of it. Ugly, stupid, stinking, strange, it hardly seemed to matter now. Ninefingers held out his hand, and Jezal gripped it in his own, as hard as he could.

The Northman grinned. 'Luck then, Jezal.'

'And to you.'

Ferro knelt beside one of the pitted stones, her bow in one hand, an arrow nocked and ready. The wind made patterns in the tall grass on the plain below, whipped at the shorter grass on the slope of the hill, plucked at the flights of the seven arrows stuck into the earth in front of her in a row. Seven arrows was all she had left.

Nothing like enough.

She watched them ride up to the base of the hill. She watched them climb from their horses, staring upwards. She watched them tighten the buckles on their scuffed leather armour, ready their weapons. Spears, swords, shields, a bow or two. She counted them. Thirteen. She had been right.

But that wasn't much of a comfort.

She recognised Finnius, laughing and pointing up at the stones. Bastard. She would shoot him first, if she got the chance, but there was no point risking a shot at this range. They would be coming soon. Crossing the open ground, struggling uphill.

She could shoot them then.

They began to spread out, peering up at the stones over the tops of their shields, their boots rustling in the long grass below. They had not seen her yet. There was one at the front without a shield, pounding up the slope with a fierce grin on his face, a bright sword in each hand.

She drew the string back, unhurried, felt it dig reassuringly into her chin. The arrow took him in the centre of his chest, right through his leather breastplate. He sank to his knees, wincing and gasping. He pushed himself up with one of his swords, took a lurching step. Her second arrow stuck into his body just above the first and he fell to his knees again, dribbled bloody spit onto the hillside, then rolled onto his back.

But there were plenty more, and still coming on. The nearest one was hunched down behind a big shield, pressing slowly up the slope with it held in front of him, trying not to expose a single inch of flesh. Her arrow thudded into the edge of the heavy wood.

'Ssss,' she hissed, snatching another shaft from the earth. She drew back the string again, taking careful aim.

'Argh!' he cried, as the arrow stuck him through his exposed ankle. The shield faltered and wobbled, drifted to the side.

Her next shaft arced through the air and caught him cleanly through the neck, just above the shield rim. Blood bubbled down his skin, his eyes went wide and he toppled backwards, the shield sliding down the slope after him with her wasted arrow sticking from it.

But that one had taken too long, and too many shafts. They were well up the hillside now, halfway to the first stones, zig-zagging left and right. She snatched her last two arrows from the earth and slithered through the grass, up the slope. That was all she could do, for now. Ninefingers would have to look after himself.

Logen waited, his back pressed against the stone, trying to keep his breathing quiet. He watched Ferro crawl further up the hill, away from him.

'Shit,' he muttered. Outnumbered and in trouble, yet again. He had known this would happen from the first moment he took charge. It always did. Well. He'd fought his way out of scrapes before, and he would fight his way out of this one now. Say one thing for Logen Ninefingers, say he's a fighter.

He heard hurrying footsteps in the grass, and breathless grunting. A man labouring up the hill, just to the left of the stone. Logen held his sword by his right side, fingered the hard metal of the grip, clenched his jaws together. He saw the point of the man's spear wobble past, then his shield.

He stepped out with a fighting roar, swinging the sword round in a great wide circle. It chopped deep into the man's shoulder and opened a huge gash across his chest, spraying blood into the air, lifting him off his feet and sending him crashing down the hill, flopping over and over.

'Still alive!' Logen panted as he sprinted away up the slope. A spear whistled past and sank into the turf beside him as he slid in behind the next stone. A poor effort, but they'd have plenty more. He peered round the edge. He saw quick shapes, rushing from rock to rock. He licked his lips and hefted the Maker's sword. There was blood on the dark blade now, blood on the silver letter near the hilt. But there was much more work to do.

He came up the hillside towards her, peering over the top of his shield, ready to block an arrow if it came. No way to get at him from here, he was watching too hard.

She ducked away behind the stone and slipped into the shallow trench she had dug, started crawling. She came up to the far end, just behind another great rock. She edged round behind it and peered out. She could see him, his side to her, creeping up carefully towards the stone where she had been hiding. It seemed that God was feeling generous today.

Towards her, if not towards him.

The shaft buried itself in his side, just above his waist. He stumbled, stared down at it. She pulled out her last arrow and nocked it. He was trying to pull the first one out when the second one stuck him in the middle of his chest. Right through the heart, she guessed, from the way he fell.

The arrows were gone. Ferro tossed her bow away and drew out the Gurkish sword.

It was time to get close.

Logen stepped round one of the stones and found himself looking straight into a face, close enough almost to feel its breath on his cheek. A young face. A good-looking one, with clean skin and a sharp nose, wide open brown eyes. Logen smashed his forehead into it. The head snapped back and the young man stumbled, enough time for Logen to pull his knife from his belt with his left hand. He let go of his sword, grabbed the edge of the man's shield and tore it out of the way. Brown Eyes' head came up again, blood bubbling from his broken nose, snarling as he pulled back his sword arm for a thrust.

Logen grunted as he stabbed the knife into the man's body. Once, twice, three times. Hard, fast, underhand thrusts that half lifted him off his feet. Blood leaked out from the holes in his guts and over Logen's hands. He groaned, dropped his sword, started to slide down the stone, his legs giving way, and Logen watched him go. A choice between killing and dying is no choice at all. You have to be realistic about these things.

The man sat in the grass, holding his bloody stomach. He looked up at Logen.

'Guh,' he grunted. 'Gurruh.'

'What?'

Nothing else. His brown eyes were glassy.

'Come on!' screamed Ferro. 'Come on, you fucking son of a whore!' She squatted on the grass, ready to spring.

He did not speak her language, but he got the gist. His spear arced spinning through the air. Not a bad throw. She moved to the side and it clattered away into the stones.

She laughed at him and he came charging – a big, bald, bull of a man. Fifteen strides away and she could see the grain on the handle of his axe. Twelve strides, and she could see the creases on his snarling face, the lines at the corners of his eyes, across the bridge of his nose. Eight strides, and she could see the scratches on his leather breastplate. Five strides, and he raised his axe high. 'Thaargh!' he squealed as the grass in front of her suddenly collapsed beneath his feet and he pitched flailing into one of the pits, the weapon flying from his hand.

Should have watched where he stepped.

She sprang forward hungrily, swinging the sword without looking. He yelled as the heavy blade bit deep into his shoulder, squealed and gibbered, trying to get away, scrambling at the loose earth. The sword chopped a hole in the top of his head and he gurgled, thrashed, slid down into the bottom of the pit. The grave. His grave.

He did not deserve one, but never mind. She could drag him out later, and let him rot on the hillside.

He was a big bastard, this one. A great, fat giant of a man, half a head taller than Logen. He had a huge club, big as half a tree, but he threw it around easily enough, shouting and roaring like a madman, little eyes rolling with fury in his pudgy face. Logen dodged and tottered between the stones. Not easy, trying to keep one eye on the ground behind him and one on that huge flailing tree limb. Not easy. Something was bound to go wrong.

Logen stumbled on something. The boot of the brown-eyed man he'd killed a minute before. There's justice for you. He righted himself just in time to see the giant's fist crack him in the mouth. He waddled, dizzy, spitting blood. He saw the club swinging at him and he leaped back. Not far enough. The very tip of the great lump of wood clipped Logen's thigh and nearly dragged him off his feet. He staggered against one of the stones, squawking and dribbling and grimacing from the pain, fumbled his sword and nearly stabbed himself with it, snatched it up just in time to tumble back and fall on his back as the club smashed away a great chunk of rock beside him.

The giant lifted his club high over his head, bellowing like a bull. A fearsome move, perhaps, but not a clever one. Logen sat up and stabbed him through his gut, the dark blade sliding right up to the hilt almost, clean through his back. The club dropped from his hands and thudded on the turf behind him, but with some last desperate effort he leaned down, grabbed hold of a fistful of Logen's shirt and hauled him close, roaring and baring his bloody teeth. He started to raise his great ham of a fist.

Logen pulled the knife out of his boot and rammed the blade into the side of the giant's neck. He looked surprised, for just a moment, then blood dribbled from his mouth and down his chin. He let go of Logen's shirt, stumbled back, spun slowly round, bounced off one of the stones and crashed on his face. Seemed that Logen's father had been right. You can never have too many knives.

Ferro heard the bow string, but by then it was too late. She felt the arrow pierce her through the back of her shoulder, and when she looked down she could see the point sticking out the front of her shirt. It made her arm numb. Dark blood leaked out into the dirty cloth. She hissed to herself as she ducked behind one of the stones.

She still had the sword though, and one good arm to use it. She slithered round the rock, the rough surface scraping at her back, listening. She could heard the archer's footfalls in the grass, searching for her, the soft ringing as he drew a blade. She saw him now, his back to her, looking right and left.

She jumped at him with the sword, but he turned in time and caught the blade on his own. They crashed down into the grass together and rolled over in a tangle. He scrambled up, thrashing and screaming, clutching at his bloody face. The arrow sticking from her shoulder had stabbed him through the eye as they struggled on the floor.

Lucky for her.

She sprang forward and the Gurkish sword chopped his foot out from under him. He screamed again, falling onto his side, mangled leg flopping. He was just pushing himself up when the curved blade hacked halfway through his neck from behind. Ferro scrambled through the grass, away from the body, her left arm hanging nearly useless, her right fist gripped tight around the grip of the sword.

Looking for more work.

Finnius moved this way and that, dancing around, light on his feet. He had a big square shield on his left arm, a short, thick sword in the other hand.

He twirled it around as he moved, watery sun flashing on the edge, grinning all the while, long hair flapping round his face in the wind.

Logen was too tired to move much, so he just stood there and caught his breath, the Maker's sword hanging down by his side.

'What happened to your sorcerer?' grinned Finnius. 'No tricks this time, eh?'

'No tricks.'

'Well, you've led us a merry dance, I'll give you that, but we got here in the end.'

'Got where?' Logen looked down at the corpse of the brown-eyed man, sat against the stone beside him. 'If this was what you wanted you could have killed yourselves days ago and saved me the trouble.'

Finnius frowned. 'You'll find I'm made of different stuff from these fools, Northman.'

'We're all made of the same stuff. I don't need to carve another body to find that out.' Logen stretched his neck out, hefted the Maker's sword in his hand. 'But if you're set on showing me your contents, I'll not disappoint you.'

'Alright, then!' Finnius started forward. 'If you're that keen to see hell!'

He came on fast and hard, the shield up in front of him, herding Logen through the stones, jabbing and chopping quick with the sword. Logen stumbled back, short of breath, looking for an opening but not finding one.

The shield barged into his chest and knocked his breath out, pressed him back. He tried to dodge away but he lurched on his weak leg, and the short sword darted out and caught him across the arm. 'Gah!' squawked Logen, staggering against a stone, drops of blood pattering from the cut into the grass.

'One to me!' chuckled Finnius, dancing sideways and waving his sword around.

Logen stood and watched him, breathing hard. The shield was a big one and this smiling bastard used it well. Gave him quite the advantage. He was quick, no doubt. Quicker than Logen, now, with a bad leg, a cut arm and a thick head from a punch in the mouth. Where was the Bloody-Nine when you wanted him? Logen spat on the ground. This fight he'd have to win alone.

He edged back, stooping more and panting harder than he needed to, letting his arm dangle as if it was useless, blood dripping from his limp fingers, blinking and wincing. He edged back past the stones into a space with more room. A nice wide space, where he could get a decent swing. Finnius followed him, shield held up in front. 'That it?' he grinned as he came on. 'Already fading, eh? I can't say I'm not disappointed, I was hoping for a—'

Logen roared, springing suddenly forward and lifting the Maker's sword above his head in both hands. Finnius scrambled back, but not quite far enough. The grey blade tore a chunk from the corner of his shield, sliced clean through and chopped deep into the side of one of the stones with a mighty clang, sending chips of rock spinning. The impact nearly tore the sword from Logen's hands, sent him flailing sideways.

Finnius groaned. Blood was running from a cut on his shoulder, a cut right through his leather armour and into the flesh. The tip of the sword must have gashed him as it passed. Not deep enough to kill, unfortunately, but deep enough to make the point alright.

It was Logen's turn to grin. 'That it?'

They moved at the same moment. The two blades clanged together, but Logen's grip was the stronger. Finnius' sword twittered as it spun from his hand and away down the hillside. He gasped, snatching at his belt for a dagger, but before he could get there Logen was on him, growling and grunting as he chopped mindlessly away at the shield, hacking great scars in the wood and sending splinters flying, driving Finnius stumbling away. One last blow crashed into the shield and he staggered from the force of it, tripped over the corner of a fallen stone poking through the grass and tumbled onto his back. Logen gritted his teeth and swung the Maker's sword down.

It sliced clean through the greave on Finnius' shin and took his foot off just above the ankle, splattering blood into the grass. He dragged himself backwards, started to scramble up, shrieked as he tried to put his weight on his missing foot, dropped onto the stump and sprawled on his back again, coughing and groaning.

'My foot!' he wailed.

'Put it out of your mind,' growled Logen, kicking the dead thing out of his way and stepping forward.

'Wait!' gurgled Finnius, shoving himself back through the grass with his good leg towards one of the standing stones, leaving a bloody trail behind him.

'For what?'

'Just wait!' He dragged himself up the rock, hopped on his remaining foot, cringing away. 'Wait!' he screamed.

Logen's sword caught the inside rim of the shield, tore the straps away from Finnius' limp arm and flung it bouncing down the slope on its chewed-up edge. Finnius gave a desperate wail and pulled out his knife, poised himself on his one good leg to lunge. Logen chopped a great gash in his chest. Blood sprayed out and showered down his breastplate. His eyes bulged, he opened his mouth wide but all that came out was a gentle wheeze. The dagger dropped from his fingers and fell silently into the grass. He slid sideways and dropped onto his face.

Back to the mud with that.

Logen stood, and blinked, and breathed. The cut on his arm was starting to sting like fire, his leg was aching, his breath was coming in ragged gasps. 'Still alive,' he muttered to himself. 'Still alive.' He closed his eyes for a moment.

'Shit,' he gasped. The others. He started to hobble back up the slope towards the summit.

The arrow in her shoulder had made her slow. Her shirt was wet with blood and she was getting thirsty, and stiff, and sluggish. He slid out from behind one of the stones, and before she knew it he was on her.

There was no room to use the sword any longer, so she let it drop. She made a grab for her knife but he caught her by the wrist, and he was strong. He threw her back against the stone and her head cracked against it, made her dizzy for a moment. She could see a muscle trembling under his eye, the black pores on his nose, the fibres standing out on his neck.

She twisted and struggled, but his weight bore down on her. She snarled and spat, but even Ferro's strength was not endless. Her arms trembled, her elbows bent. His hand found her throat, and tightened round it. He muttered something through clenched teeth, squeezing and squeezing. She could not breathe any longer, and the strength was ebbing out of her.

Then, through her half-closed eyes, she saw a hand slither round his face from behind. A big, pale, three-fingered hand, caked with dry blood. A big, pale forearm followed it, and another, from the other side, folding his head tightly. He wriggled, and struggled, but there was no escape. The thick sinews flexed and squirmed under the skin and the pale fingers dug into his face, dragging his head back and to the side, further and further. He let go of Ferro, and she sagged back against the stone, sucking in the air. He scrabbled uselessly at the arms with his fingernails. He made a long, strange hissing sound as his head was twisted relentlessly round.

'Sssss . . .' Crunch.

The arms let go and he crumpled on the floor, head hanging. Ninefingers stood behind. There was dry blood across his face, blood on his hands, blood soaked through his torn clothes. His face was pale and twitchy, streaked with dirt and sweat.

'You alright?'

'About like you,' she croaked. 'Any left?'

He put one hand on the stone beside her and leaned over, spat blood out onto the grass. 'Don't know. Couple, maybe.'

She squinted up at the summit of the hill. 'Up there?'

'Could be.'

She bent and snatched the curved sword up from the grass, started to limp up the slope, using it like a crutch. She heard Ninefingers struggling after her.

*

For some minutes now, Jezal had heard occasional shouting, screaming, and clashing of metal on metal. Everything was vague and distant, filtering to his ears through the blustering wind across the hilltop. He had no clue what was happening beyond the circle of stones at the hill's summit, and he was not sure he wanted to know. He strode up and down, his hands opening and closing, and all the while Quai sat on the cart, looking down at Bayaz, silent and infuriatingly calm.

It was then that he saw it. A man's head, rising up over the brow of the hill between two tall stones. Next came his shoulders, then his chest. Another appeared not far away. A second man. Two killers, advancing up the slope towards him.

One of them had piggy eyes and a heavy jaw. The other was thinner, with a tangled thatch of fair hair. They moved cautiously up onto the summit of the hill until they stood within the circle of stones, examining Jezal, and Quai, and the cart with no particular urgency.

Jezal had never fought two men at once before. He had never fought to the death before either, but he tried not to think about that. This was simply a fencing match. Nothing new. He swallowed, and drew his steels. The metal rang reassuringly as it slid out, the familiar weight in his palms was a small comfort. The two men stared at him and Jezal stared back, trying to remember what Ninefingers had told him.

Try to look weak. That, at least, did not present much difficulty. He did not doubt that he appeared suitably scared. It was the most he could do not to turn and run. He backed slowly away towards the cart, licking his lips with a nervousness that was anything but feigned.

Never take an enemy lightly. He looked them over, these two. Strong-looking men, well equipped. They both wore armour of rigid leather, carried square shields. One had a short sword, the other an axe with a heavy blade. Deadly-looking weapons, well worn. Taking them lightly was hardly his problem. They spread out, moving round to either side of him, and he watched them go.

The time comes to act, you strike with no backward glances. The one on Jezal's left came at him. He saw the man snarl, saw him rear up, saw the great unwieldy backswing. It was an absurdly simple matter for him to step out of the way and let it thud into the turf beside him. On an instinct he thrust with his short steel and buried it in the man's side up to the hilt, between his breastplate and his backplate, just under his bottom rib. Even as Jezal was ripping the blade back he was ducking under the other's axe and whipping his long steel across at neck height. He danced past them and spun around, steels held ready, waiting for the referee's call.

The one he had stabbed staggered a step or two, wheezing and grabbing at his side. The other stood there, swaying, his piggy eyes bulging, his hand clutched to his neck. Blood began to pour out between his fingers from his slit throat. They fell almost at the same time, face down, right next to each other.

Jezal frowned at the blood on his long steel. He frowned at the two corpses he had made. Almost without thinking he had killed two men. He should have felt guilty, but he felt numb. No. He felt proud. He felt exhilarated! He looked up at Quai, watching him calmly from the back of the cart.

'I did it,' he muttered, and the apprentice nodded slowly. 'I did it!' he shouted, waving his bloody short steel in the air.

Quai frowned, and then his eyes went wide. 'Behind you!' he shouted, half jumping up out of his seat. Jezal turned, bringing up his steels, saw something moving out of the very corner of his eye.

There was a mighty crunching and his head exploded with brilliant light.

Then all was darkness.

The Fruits of Boldness

The Northmen stood on the hill, a thin row of dark figures with the white sky behind them. It was still early, and the sun was nothing more than a bright smear among thick clouds. Patches of half-melted snow were scattered cold and dirty in the hollows of the valley sides, a thin layer of mist was still clinging to the valley floor.

West watched that row of black shapes, and frowned. He did not like the flavour of this. Too many for a scouting, or a foraging party, far too few to mount any challenge, and yet they stayed there on the high ground, watching calmly as Ladisla's army continued its interminable, clumsy deployment in the valley beneath them.

The Prince's staff, and a small detachment of his guards, had made their headquarters on a grassy knoll opposite the Northmen's hill. It had seemed a fine, dry spot when the scouts found it early that morning, well below the enemy perhaps, but still high enough to get a good view of the valley. Since then the passage of thousands of sliding boots, squashing hooves, and churning cartwheels, had ground the wet earth to sticky black muck. West's own boots and those of the other men around were caked with it, their uniforms spattered with it. Even Prince Ladisla's pristine whites had acquired a few smears.

A couple of hundred strides ahead, on lower ground, was the centre of the Union battle line. Four battalions of the King's Own infantry formed the backbone, each one a neat block of bright red cloth and dull steel, looking at this distance as though they had been positioned with a giant ruler. In front of them were a few thin ranks of flatbowmen in their leather jerkins and steel caps; behind were the cavalry, dismounted for the time being, the riders looking strangely ungainly in full armour. Spread out to either side were the haphazard shapes of the levy battalions, with their assortment of mismatched equipment, their officers bellowing and waving their arms, trying to get the gaps to close up, the skewed ranks to straighten, like sheepdogs barking at a flock of wayward sheep.

Ten thousand men, perhaps, all told. Every one of them, West knew, was looking up at that thin screen of Northmen, no doubt with the same nervous mixture of fear and excitement, curiosity and anger that he was feeling at his first sight of the enemy.

They hardly seemed too fearsome through his eye-glass. Shaggy-headed men, dressed in ragged hides and furs, gripping primitive looking weapons. Just what the least imaginative members of the Prince's staff might have been expecting. They scarcely looked like any part of the army that Threetrees had described, and West did not like that. There was no way of knowing what was on the far side of that hill, no reason for those men to be there but to distract them, or draw them on. Not everyone shared his doubts, however.

'They mock us!' snapped Smund, squinting up through his own eye-glass. 'We should give them a taste of Union lances! A swift charge and our horsemen will sweep that rabble aside and carry that hill!' He spoke almost as if the carrying of that hill, irrelevant except for the fact that the Northmen were standing on it, would bring the campaign to a swift and glorious conclusion.

West could do nothing but grit his teeth and shake his head, as he had done a hundred times already today. 'They have the high ground,' he explained, taking care to speak slowly and patiently. 'Poor terrain for a charge, and they may have support. Bethod's main body, for all we know, just over the rise.'

'They look like nothing more than scouts,' muttered Ladisla.

'Looks can lie, your Highness, and that hill is worthless. Time is with us. Marshal Burr will be marching to our aid, while Bethod can expect no help. We have no reason to seek a battle now.'

Smund snorted. 'No reason except that this is a war, and the enemy stand before us on Union soil! You are always carping on the poor state of the men's morale, Colonel!' He jabbed his finger up at the hill. 'What could be more damaging to their spirits than to sit idle in the face of the enemy?'

'A sharp and purposeless defeat?' growled West.

It was an unfortunate chance that one of the Northmen chose that moment to loose an arrow down into the valley. A tiny black sliver sailed up into the sky. It came only from a shortbow. Even with the advantage of height the shaft plopped down harmlessly into open ground a hundred strides or more from the front lines. A singularly pointless gesture, but its effect on Prince Ladisla was immediate.

He abandoned his folding field chair and leaped to his feet. 'Damn them!' he cursed, 'they are mocking us! Issue orders!' He strode up and down, shaking his fist. 'Have the cavalry form up for a charge immediately!'

'Your Highness, I urge you to reconsider—'

'Damn it, West!' The heir to the throne hurled his hat down on the muddy ground. 'You oppose me at every turn! Would your friend Colonel Glokta have hesitated with the enemy before him?'

West swallowed. 'Colonel Glokta was captured by the Gurkish, and caused the deaths of every man under his command.' He bent slowly and picked up the hat, offered it respectfully up to the Prince, wondering all the while whether he had just brought his career to an abrupt end.

Ladisla ground his teeth, breathing hard through his nose, snatched the hat out of West's hand. 'I have made my decision! Mine is the burden of command, and mine alone!' He turned back towards the valley. 'Sound the charge!'

West felt suddenly, terribly tired. It seemed he scarcely had the strength to stand as the confident bugle call rang out in the crisp air, as the horsemen struggled into their saddles, eased forward between the blocks of infantry, trotted down the gentle slope, lances up. They broke into a gallop as they crossed the valley floor, half-obscured in a sea of mist, the thunder of their hoofbeats echoing round the valley. A few scattered arrows fell among them, glancing harmlessly from their heavy armour as they streamed forward. They began to lose momentum as they hit the upward slope, their lines breaking as they pushed on over the gorse and the broken ground, but the sight of all that weight of steel and horseflesh had its effect on the Northmen above. Their ragged line began to waver, then to break. They turned tail and fled, some of them tossing away their weapons as they disappeared over the brow of the hill.

'That's the damn recipe!' yelled Lord Smund. 'Drive 'em, damn it! Drive 'em!'

'Ride them down!' laughed Prince Ladisla, tearing off his hat again and waving it in the air. A scattering of cheers floated up from the levies in the valley, over the distant hammering of hooves.

'Drive them,' muttered West, clenching his fists. 'Please.'

The riders crested the ridge and gradually disappeared from view. Silence fell over the valley. A long, strange, unexpected silence. A few crows circled overhead, croaking their harsh calls to one another. West would have given anything for their view of the battlefield. The tension was almost unbearable. He strode back and forth while the long minutes stretched out, and still no sign.

'Taking their time, eh?'

Pike was standing right next to him, his daughter just behind. West winced and looked away. He still found it somehow painful to look at that burned face for long, especially coming on him sudden and unannounced. 'What are you two doing here?'

The convict shrugged his shoulders. 'There's plenty for a smith to do before a battle. Even more after it. Not much while the fighting's happening, though.' He grinned, slabs of burned flesh folding up like leather on one side of his face. 'Thought I'd take a look at Union arms in action. Besides, what safer place could there be than the Prince's headquarters?'

'Don't mind us,' muttered Cathil, a thin smile on her face, 'we'll make sure to keep out of your way.'

West frowned. If that was a reference to his being constantly in their way he was in no mood to enjoy it. There was still no sign of the cavalry.

'Where the hell are they?' snapped Smund.

The Prince took a break from chewing down his fingernails. 'Give 'em time, Lord Smund, give 'em time.'

'Why doesn't this mist dry up?' murmured West. There was enough sunlight breaking through the clouds now, but the mist only seemed to be thickening, creeping up the valley towards the archers. 'Damn mist, it'll work against us.'

'That's them!' yelled one of the Prince's staff, shrill with excitement, finger stretched out rigid towards the crest of the hill.

West raised his eye-glass, breathless, scanned quickly across the green line. He saw the spear-points, stiff, and regular, rising slowly over the brow. He felt a surge of relief. Rarely had he been happier to be proved wrong.

'It's them!' yelled Smund, grinning broadly. 'They're back! What did I tell you? They're . . .' Helmets appeared beneath the spear-points, and then mailed shoulders. West felt the relief seeping away, horror creeping up his throat. An organised body of armoured men, their round shields painted with faces, and animals, and trees, and a hundred other patterns, no two alike. More men appeared over the crest of the hill to either side of them. More mailed figures.

Bethod's Carls.

They halted just beyond the highest point of the hill. A scattering of men came forward from the even ranks, knelt in the short grass.

Ladisla lowered his eye-glass. 'Are those . . . ?'

'Flatbows,' muttered West.

The first volley drifted up, gently almost, a shifting grey cloud of bolts, like a flock of well trained birds. They were silent for a moment, then the angry rattling of the bow strings reached West's ears. The bolts began to drop towards the Union lines. They fell among the King's Own, clattered down onto their heavy shields, their heavy armour. There were some cries, a few gaps appeared in their lines.

The mood in the headquarters had turned, in the space of a minute, from brash confidence, to mute surprise, to stupefied dismay. 'They have flatbows?' someone spluttered. West stared at the archers on the hill through his eye-glass, slowly cranking back their bowstrings, pulling bolts from their quivers, fitting them into position. The range had been well judged. Not only did they have flatbows, but they knew how to use them. West hurried over to Prince Ladisla, who was gaping at a wounded man being carried, head lolling, from between the ranks of the King's Own.

'Your Highness, we must advance and close the distance so that our archers can return fire, or withdraw to higher ground!' Ladisla only stared at him, giving no sign that he had heard, let alone understood. A second volley arced down into the infantry in front of them. This time it fell among the levies, a unit without shields or armour. Holes opened up all across the ragged formation, holes filled by the rising mist, and the whole battalion seemed to groan and waver. Some wounded man began to make a thin, animal screeching, and would not stop. 'Your Highness, do we advance, or withdraw?'

'I . . . we . . .' Ladisla gaped over at Lord Smund, but for once the young nobleman was at a loss for words. He looked even more stupefied than the Prince, if that was possible. Ladisla's lower lip trembled. 'How . . . I . . . Colonel West, what is your opinion?'

The temptation to remind the Crown Prince that his was the burden of command, and his alone, was almost overpowering, but West bit his tongue. Without some sense of purpose, this rag-tag army might swiftly dissolve. Better to do the wrong thing, than nothing at all. He turned to the nearest bugler. 'Sound the retreat!' he roared.

The bugles called the withdrawal: blaring, discordant. Hard to believe they were the same instruments that had so brazenly called the charge just a few short minutes before. The battalions began to edge slowly backwards. Another volley fell among the levies, and another. Their formations were beginning to come apart, men hurrying backwards to escape the murderous fire, stumbling over each other, ranks dissolving into mobs, the air full of shrieks and confusion. West could scarcely tell where the next set of flatbow bolts fell, the mist had risen so high. The Union battalions had become nothing more than wobbling spears and the odd insubstantial helmet above a grey cloud. Even here, high up among the baggage, the mist was curling round West's ankles.

Up on the hill the Carls began to move. They thrust their weapons in the air and clashed them against their painted shields. They gave a great shout, but not the deep roar that West might have expected. Instead, a weird and chilling howl floated over the valley, a keening wail that cut through the rattling and scraping of metal and into the ears of those watching, down below. A mindless, a furious, a primitive sound. A sound made by monsters, not by men.

Prince Ladisla and his staff gawped at one another, and stuttered, and stared, as the Carls began to tramp down the hill, rank upon rank of them, towards the thickening mist in the valley's bottom where the Union troops were still blindly trying to pull back. West shouldered his way through the frozen officers to the bugler.

'Battle lines!'

The lad turned from staring at the advancing Northmen to staring at West, his bugle hanging from his nerveless fingers.

'Lines!' roared a voice from behind. 'Form lines!' It was Pike, bellowing loud enough to match any drill sergeant. The bugler snapped his instrument to his lips and blew lines for all he was worth. Answering calls echoed through the mist, risen up all around them, now. Muffled bugles, muffled shouts.

'Halt and form up!'

'Form lines now, lads!'

'Prepare!'

'Steady!'

A chorus of rattles and clanks came through the murk. Men moving in armour, spears being set, swords drawn, calls from man to man and from unit to unit. Above all, growing steadily louder, the unearthly howling of the Northmen as they began their charge, surging down from the high ground and into the valley. West felt a chill in his own blood, even with a hundred strides of earth and a few thousand armed men between him and the enemy. He could well imagine the fear those in the front lines were feeling now, as the shapes of the Carls began to rise out of the mist before them, screaming their war cries with their weapons held high.

There was no sound that signified the moment of contact. The clattering grew louder and louder, the shouts and the howls were joined by high-pitched cries, low-pitched growls, shrieks of pain or rage mixed into the terrifying din with ever greater frequency. Nobody in the headquarters spoke. Every man, West among them, was peering into the murk, straining with every sense to get some hint of what might be happening just before them in the valley.

'There!' someone shouted. A faint figure was moving through the gloom ahead. All eyes were fixed on it as it took shape before them. A young, breathless, mud-splattered and highly confused lieutenant. 'Where the hell is the headquarters?' he shouted as he stumbled up the slope towards them.

'This is it.'

The man gave West a flamboyant salute. 'Your Highness—'

'I am Ladisla,' snapped the real Prince. The man turned, bewildered, began to salute once more. 'Speak your message, man!'

'Of course, sir, your Highness, Major Bodzin has sent me to tell you that his battalion is heavily engaged, and . . .' he was still gasping for breath, 'he needs reinforcement.'

Ladisla stared at the young man as though he had been speaking in a foreign language. He looked at West. 'Who is Major Bodzin?'

'Commander of the first battalion of the Stariksa levies, your Highness, on our left wing.'

'Left wing, I see . . . er . . .'

A semi-circle of brightly dressed staff officers had congealed around the breathless lieutenant. 'Tell the Major to hold!' shouted one of them.

'Yes!' said Ladisla, 'tell your Major to hold, and to, er, to drive back the enemy. Yes indeed!' He was warming to his role now. 'To drive them back, and to fight to the last man! Tell Major Clodzin that help is on the way. Most definitely . . . on the way!' And the Prince strode off manfully.

The young Lieutenant turned, peered into the murk. 'Which way is my unit?' he muttered.

More figures were already beginning to take form. Running figures, scrambling through the mud, panting for breath. Levies, West saw straight away, broken from the backs of crumbling units as soon as they had made contact with the enemy. As though there had ever been any chance that they would stand for long.

'Cowardly dogs!' cursed Smund at their receding backs. 'Get back here!' He might as well have given orders to the mist. Everyone was running: deserters, adjutants, messengers seeking for help, for direction, for reinforcement. The first wounded too. Some were limping under their own power, or using broken spears for crutches, some were half-carried by comrades. Pike started forward to help a pale fellow with a flatbow bolt sticking from his shoulder. Another casualty was dragged past on a stretcher, muttering to himself. His left arm was off just below the elbow, oozing blood through a tightly bound stretch of dirty cloth.

Ladisla looked greasy pale. 'I have a headache. I must sit down. What has become of my field chair?'

West chewed at his lip. He had no inkling of what to do. Burr had sent him with Ladisla for his experience, but he was every bit as clueless as the Prince. Every plan relied on being able actually to see the enemy, or at any rate one's own positions. He stood there, frozen, as useless and frustrated as a blind man in a fist fight.

'What is happening, damn it!' The Prince's voice cut across the din, shrill and petulant. 'Where did this damn mist come from? I demand to know what is happening! Colonel West! Where is the Colonel? What is going on out there?'

If only he had been able to provide an answer. Men stumbled and darted and charged through the muddy headquarters, apparently at random. Faces loomed up from the mist and were gone, faces full of fear, confusion, determination. Runners with garbled messages or garbled orders, soldiers with bloody wounds or no weapons. Disembodied voices floated on the cold air, speaking over one another, anxious, hurried, panicked, agonised.

'. . . Our regiment has made contact with the enemy, and are falling back, or were falling back, I think . . .'

'My knee! Damn it, my knee!'

'. . . His Highness the Prince? I have an urgent message from . . .'

'Send, er . . . someone! Whoever is available . . . who is available?'

'. . . King's Own are heavily engaged! They request permission to withdraw . . .'

'What happened to the cavalry? Where are the cavalry?'

'. . . devils not men! The Captain's dead and . . .'

'We are falling back!'

'. . . fighting hard on the right wing and in need of support! In desperate need of support . . .'

'Help me! Somebody, please!'

'. . . And then counterattack! We are attacking all across the line . . .'

'Quiet!' West could hear something in the grey gloom. The jingling of a harness. The mist was so dense now that he could see no more than thirty strides, but the sound of trotting hooves drawing closer was unmistakable. His hand closed round the hilt of his sword.

'The cavalry, they've returned!' Lord Smund started eagerly forwards.

'Wait!' hissed West, to no effect. His eyes strained into the grey. He saw the outlines of horsemen, coming steadily through the gloom. The shapes of their armour, of their saddles, of their helmets were those of the King's Own, and yet there was something in the way they rode – slouching, loose. West drew his sword. 'Protect the Prince,' he muttered taking a step towards Ladisla.

'You there!' shouted Lord Smund at the foremost horseman. 'Prepare your men for another—' The rider's sword chopped into his skull with a hollow clicking sound. A spray of blood went up, black in the white mist, and the horsemen broke into a charge, screaming at the tops of their voices. Terrifying, eerie, inhuman sounds. Smund's limp body was flung out of the way by the leading horse, trampled under the flailing hooves of the one beside it. Northmen, now, unmistakably, growing more horrifyingly distinct as they loomed up out of the murk. The foremost of them had a thick beard, long hair streaming out from beneath an ill-fitting Union helmet, yellow teeth bared, eyes of horse and rider both wide with fury. His heavy sword flashed down and hacked one of the Prince's guards between the shoulder blades as he dropped his spear and turned to run.

'Protect the Prince!' screamed West. Then it was chaos. Horses thundered past all around, riders yelled, hacked about them with swords and axes, men ran in all directions, slipped, fell, were cut down where they stood, were trampled where they lay. The heavy air was full of the wind of passing horsemen, flying mud, screams and panic and fear.

West dived out of the way of flailing hooves, sprawled on his face in the muck, slashed uselessly at a passing horse, rolled and spun and gasped at the mist. He had no idea which way he was facing, everything sounded the same, looked the same. 'Protect the Prince!' he shouted again, pointlessly, voice hoarse, drowned out in the din, spinning round and round.

'Over on the left!' someone shrieked. 'Form a line!' There were no lines. There was no left. West stumbled over a body, a hand clutched at his leg and he slashed at it with his sword.

'Ah.' He was on his face. His head hurt terribly. Where was he? Fencing practice, perhaps. Had Luthar knocked him down again? That boy was getting too good for him. He stretched for the grip of his sword, lying trampled in the mud. A hand slithered through grass, far away, fingers stretching. He could hear his own breathing, painfully loud, echoing in his thumping head. Everything was blurred, shifting, mist before his eyes, mist in his eyes. Too late. He could not reach his sword. His head was throbbing. There was mud in his mouth. He rolled over onto his back, slowly, breathing hard, up onto his elbows. He saw a man coming. A Northman, by his shaggy outline. Of course. There was a battle. West watched him walk slowly forward. There was a dark line in his hand. A weapon. Sword, axe, mace, spear, what was the difference? The man took one more unhurried step, planted his boot on West's jacket, and shoved his limp body down into the mud.

Neither of them said anything. No last words. No pithy phrases. No expressions of anger, or remorse, or of victory, or defeat. The Northman raised his weapon.

His body jolted. He lurched forward a step. He blinked and swayed. He half-turned, slowly, stupidly. His head jolted again.

'Got something in . . .' he said, lips fumbling with the words. He felt at the back of his head with his free hand. 'Where's my . . .' He swivelled round, falling sideways, one leg in the air, and crashed onto his side in the muck. Somebody stood behind him. They came close, leaned over. A woman's face. She seemed familiar, somehow.

'You alive?'

Like that, West's mind clicked back into place. He took a great coughing breath, rolled over and grabbed hold of his sword. There were Northmen, Northmen behind their lines! He scrambled to his feet, clawed the blood out of his eyes. They had been tricked! His head was pounding, spinning. Bethod's cavalry, disguised, the Prince's headquarters, overrun! He jerked around, wild-eyed, boot heels slipping in the mud, looking for enemies in the mist, but there was no one. Only him and Cathil. The sound of hooves had faded, the horsemen had passed, at least for now.

He looked down at his steel. The blade was snapped off a few inches from the hilt. Worthless. He let it fall, prised the Northman's dead fingers from his sword and grabbed hold of the hilt, his head thumping all the time. A heavy weapon with a thick, notched blade, but it would serve.

He stared down at the corpse, lying on its side. The man who had been about to kill him. The back of his skull was a caved in mess of red splinters. Cathil had a smith's hammer in her hand. The head was sticky dark with blood and strands of matted hair.

'You killed him.' She had saved his life. They both knew it, so there hardly seemed any point in saying it.

'What do we do now?'

Head for the front lines. That was what the dashing young officer always did in the stories West had read as a boy. March for the sounds of battle. Rally a new unit from stragglers and lead them into the fray, turn the tide of the fighting at the critical moment. Home in time for dinner and medals.

Looking down at the wreckage and the broken corpses the horsemen had left behind, West almost laughed at the idea. It was suddenly too late for heroics, and he knew it. It had been too late for a long time.

The fates of the men down in the valley had been set long ago. When Ladisla chose to cross the river. When Burr set upon his plan. When the Closed Council decided to send the Crown Prince to win a reputation in the North. When the great noblemen of the Union sent beggars instead of soldiers to fight for their King. A hundred different chances, from days, and weeks, and months before, all coming together here, on this worthless stretch of mud. Chances which neither Burr, nor Ladisla, nor West himself could have predicted or done anything to prevent.

He could make no difference now, no one could. The day was lost.

'Protect the Prince,' he muttered.

'What?'

West began to cast around on the ground, rooting through the scattered junk, rolling over bodies with his dirty hands. A messenger stared up at him, the side of his face split open, bloody pulp hanging out. West retched, covered his mouth, crawled on his hands and knees to the next corpse. One of the Prince's staff, still with a look of faint surprise on his features. There was a ragged sword cut through the heavy gold braid of his uniform, reaching all the way down to his belly.

'What the hell are you doing?' Pike's gruff voice. 'There's no time for this!' The convict had got an axe from somewhere. A heavy northern axe, with blood on the edge. Not a good idea, most likely, for a criminal to have a weapon like that, but West had other worries.

'We must find Prince Ladisla!'

'Shit on him!' hissed Cathil, 'let's go!'

West shook off her hand, stumbled to a heap of broken boxes, wiping more blood out of his eye. Somewhere here. Somewhere near here, Ladisla had been standing—

'No, I beg of you, no!' squealed a voice. The heir to the throne of the Union was lying on his back in a hollow in the dirt, half-obscured by the twisted corpse of one of his guards. His eyes were squeezed shut, arms crossed in front of his face, white uniform spotted with red blood, caked with black mud. 'There will be a ransom!' he whimpered, 'a ransom! More than you can imagine' One eye peered out from between his fingers. He grabbed at West's hand. 'Colonel West! Is it you? You're alive!'

There was no time for pleasantries. 'Your Highness, we have to go!'

'Go?' mumbled Ladisla, his face streaked with tear tracks. 'But surely . . . you can't mean . . . have we won?'

West nearly bit his own tongue off. It was bizarre that the task should fall to him, but he had to save the Prince. The vain and useless idiot might not deserve saving but that changed nothing. It was for his own sake that West had to do it, not for Ladisla's. It was his duty, as a subject to save his future King, as a soldier to save his general, as one man to save another. It was all he could do, now. 'You are the heir to the throne and cannot be spared.' West reached down and grabbed the Prince by the elbow.

Ladisla fumbled with his belt. 'I lost my sword somewhere—'

'We have no time!' West hauled him up, fully prepared to carry him if he had to. He struck off through the mist, the two convicts close behind him.

'Are you sure this is the right way?' growled Pike.

'I'm sure.' He was anything but. The mist was thicker than ever. The pounding in his head and the blood trickling into his eye made it hard to concentrate. The sounds of fighting seemed to come from all around: clashing and grating metal, groans and wails and yells of fury, all echoing in the mist and seeming one moment far away, the next terrifyingly near. Shapes loomed and moved and swam, vague and threatening outlines, shadows drifting, just out of sight. A rider seemed to rise out of the mist and West gasped and raised his sword. The clouds swirled. It was only a supply cart, laden down with barrels, mule standing still before it, driver sprawled out beside, with a broken spear sticking from his back.

'This way,' hissed West, scuttling towards it, trying to keep close to the mud. Carts were good. Carts meant the baggage train, the supplies, the food and the surgeons. Carts meant they were heading up out of the valley, away from the front lines at least, if there still were any such things. West thought about it for a moment. Carts were bad. Carts meant plunder. The Northmen would swarm to them like flies to honey, eager for booty. He pointed off into the mist, away from the empty wagons, the broken barrels, the upended boxes, and the others followed him, silent but for their squelching footfalls, their rasping breath.

They slogged on, over open ground, dirty clumps of wet grass, gently rising. The others passed him, one by one, and he waved them on. Their only chance was to keep moving, but every step was harder than the one before. Blood from the cut on his scalp was tickling away under his hair, down the side of his face. The pain in his head was growing worse, not better. He felt weak, sick, horribly dizzy. He clung to the grip of the heavy sword as though it was keeping him up, bent over double, struggling to stay on his feet.

'You alright?' asked Cathil.

'Keep moving!' he managed to grunt at her. He could hear hooves, or thought that he could. Fear kept him going, and fear alone. He could see the others, ahead of him, labouring forwards. Prince Ladisla well in front, Pike next, Cathil just ahead, looking back over her shoulder. There was a group of trees up ahead, he could see them through the thinning mist. He fixed on their ghostly shapes and made for them, his breath rasping in his throat as he floundered up the slope.

He heard Cathil's voice. 'No.' He turned, horror creeping up his throat. He saw the outline of a rider, not far down the slope.

'Make for the trees!' he gasped. She didn't move, so he grabbed her arm and shoved her forwards, fell on his face in the mud as he did it. He rolled over, floundered up, began to stumble away from her, away from the trees, away from safety, sideways across the slope. He watched the Northman take shape as he rode up out of the mist. He had seen West now, was trotting up towards him, his spear lowered.

West carried on creeping sideways, legs burning, lungs burning, using his last grains of strength to lead the rider away. Ladisla was already in the trees. Pike was just sliding into the bushes. Cathil took one last look over her shoulder and followed him. West could go no further. He stopped, crouching on the hillside, too tired even to stand, let alone fight, and watched the Northman come on. The sun had broken through the clouds, was glinting on the blade of his spear. West had no idea what he would do when he arrived. Apart from die.

Then the horseman reared up in his saddle, scrabbled at his side. There were feathers there. Grey feathers, blowing in the wind. He let go a short scream. His scream stopped, and he stared at West. There was an arrowhead sticking out of his neck. He dropped his spear and tumbled slowly backwards out of his saddle. His horse trotted past, curved away up the slope, slowed to a walk, and stopped.

West crouched against the wet ground for a moment, unable to understand how he had escaped death. He tottered towards the trees, each stride a vast undertaking, all his joints floppy as a puppet's. He felt his knees give way and he crashed down into the brush. There were strong fingers plucking at the wound on his scalp, words muttered in Northern. 'Ah,' yelped West, prising his eyes open a crack.

'Stop whining.' The Dogman was staring down at him. 'Just a scrape. You got off light. Came right to me, but you're lucky still. I been known to miss.'

'Lucky,' muttered West. He turned over in the wet bracken and stared across the valley between the tree trunks. The mist was finally starting to clear, slowly revealing a trail of broken carts, of broken gear, of broken bodies. All the ugly detritus of a terrible defeat. Or a terrible victory, if you stood with Bethod. A few hundred strides away he watched a man running desperately towards another stand of trees. A cook maybe, by his clothes. A horseman followed him, spear couched in his arm. He missed at the first pass, caught him on the way back and knocked him to the ground. West should have felt horror as he watched the rider trot up and stab the helpless runner with his spear, but he only felt a guilty gladness. Glad that it wasn't him.

There were other figures, other horsemen, moving on the slopes of the valley. Other bloody little dramas, but West could watch no more. He turned away, slid back down into the welcoming safety of the bushes.

The Dogman was chuckling softly to himself. 'Threetrees'll shit when he sees what I've caught me.' He pointed at the strange, exhausted, mud-spattered group one by one. 'Half-dead Colonel West, girl with a bloody hammer, man with a face like the back end of a cook-pot, and this one here, less I'm deceived, is the boy who had charge o' this fucking disaster. By the dead but fate plays some tricks.' He shook his head slowly, grinning down at West as he lay on his back, gasping like a landed fish.

'Threetrees . . . is going . . . to shit.'

One for Dinner

To Arch Lector Sult, head of his Majesty's Inquisition.

Your Eminence,

I have happy news. The conspiracy is unmasked, and torn up by the roots. Korsten dan Vurms, the son of the Lord Governor, and Carlot dan Eider, the Magister of the Guild of Spicers, were the principals. They will be questioned, and then punished in such a manner that our people will understand the price of treason. It would appear that Davoust fell victim to a Gurkish agent, long hidden within the city. The assassin is still at large, but with the plotters in our power it cannot be long before we catch him.

I have had Lord Governor Vurms placed under close arrest. The treason of the son renders the father unreliable, and he has been a hindrance in the administration of the city in any case. I will send him back to you by the next ship, so that you and your colleagues on the Closed Council may decide his fate. Along with him will come one Inquisitor Harker, responsible for the deaths of two prisoners who might otherwise have rendered us valuable information. I have questioned him, and am fully satisfied he had no part in any plot, but he is nonetheless guilty of incompetence tantamount to treason. I leave his punishment in your hands.

The Gurkish assault came at first light. Picked troops rushed forwards with ready-made bridges and tall ladders, straight across open ground, and were met with a murderous volley from five hundred flatbows ranged along our walls. It was a brave effort, but a rash one, and was repulsed with much slaughter on their side. Only two bold parties made it to our man-made channel, where bridge, ladder, and men were quickly swept away by a fierce current that flows from the sea into the bay at certain times of day, a happy and unforeseen chance of nature.

Gurkish corpses now litter the empty ground between our channel and their lines, and I have ordered our men to fire upon anyone who attempts to offer succour to the wounded. The groans of the dying and the sight of Gurkish bodies rotting in the sun cannot but cause a useful weakening of their morale.

Though the first taste of victory has come to us, in truth, this attack was little more than a first feeling out of our defences. The Gurkish commander but dips his toe in the water, to test the temperature. His next attack, I do not doubt, will be on a different scale altogether. Three mighty catapults, assembled within four hundred strides of our walls, and more than capable of hurling huge stones clean into the Lower City, yet stand silent. Perhaps they hope to take Dagoska intact, but if our resistance holds, this hesitation cannot long continue.

They certainly do not want for men. More Gurkish soldiers pour onto the peninsula every day. The standards of eight legions are now plainly visible above the throng, and we have spotted detachments of savages from every corner of the Kantic continent. A mighty host, perhaps fifty thousand strong or more, is ranged against us. The Gurkish Emperor, Uthman-ul-Dosht, bends all his power against our walls, but we will hold firm.

You will hear from me soon. Until then, I serve and obey.

Sand dan Glokta,
Superior of Dagoska.

Magister Carlot dan Eider, head of the Guild of Spicers, sat in her chair, hands in her lap, and did her best to maintain her dignity. Her skin was pale and oily, there were dark rings under her eyes. Her white garments were stained with the dirt of the cells, her hair had lost its sheen and hung lank and matted across her face. She looked older without her powder and her jewels, but she still seemed beautiful. *More than ever, in a way. The beauty of the candle flame that has almost burned out.*

'You look tired,' she said.

Glokta raised his brows. 'It has been a trying few days. First there was the questioning of your accomplice Vurms, then the small matter of an assault by the Gurkish army camped outside our walls. You appear somewhat fatigued yourself.'

'The floor of my tiny cell is not that comfortable, and then I have my own worries.' She looked up at Severard and Vitari, leaning against the walls on either side of her, arms folded, masked and implacable. 'Am I going to die in this room?'

Undoubtedly. 'That remains to be seen. Vurms has already told us most of what we need to know. You came to him, you offered him money to forge his father's signature on certain documents, to give orders in his father's name to certain guardsmen, to participate, in short, in the betrayal of the city of Dagoska to the enemies of the Union. He has named everyone involved in your scheme. He has signed his confession. His head, in case you were wondering, is decorating the gate beside that of your friend Islik, the Emperor's ambassador.'

'Both together, on the gate,' sang Severard.

'There are only three things he was not able to give me. Your reasons, your signature, and the identity of the Gurkish spy who killed Superior Davoust. I will have those three from you. Now.'

Magister Eider carefully cleared her throat, carefully smoothed the front of her long gown, sat up as proudly as she could. 'I do not believe that you will torture me. You are not Davoust. You have a conscience.'

The corner of Glokta's mouth twitched slightly. *A brave effort. I do applaud you. But how wrong you are.* 'I have a conscience, but it's a feeble, withered shred of a thing. It couldn't protect you or anyone else from a stiff breeze.' Glokta sighed, long and hard. The room was too hot, too bright, his eyes were sore and twitchy and he rubbed at them slowly as he spoke. 'You could not even guess at the things that I have done. Awful, evil, obscene, the telling of them alone could make you puke.' He shrugged. 'They nag at me from time to time, but I tell myself I had good reasons. The years pass, the unimaginable becomes everyday, the hideous becomes tedious, the unbearable becomes routine. I push it all into the dark corners of my mind, and it's incredible the room back there. Amazing what one can live with.'

Glokta glanced up at Severard's eyes, and Vitari's, glittering hard and pitiless. 'But even supposing you were right, can you seriously pretend that my Practicals would have any such compunction? Well, Severard?'

'Any such a what?'

Glokta gave a sad smile. 'You see. He doesn't even know what one is.' He sagged back in his chair. *Tired. Terribly tired.* He seemed to lack even the energy to lift his hands. 'I have already made all manner of allowances for you. Treason is not normally so gently dealt with. You should have seen the beating that Frost gave to your friend Vurms, and we all know that he was the junior partner in this. He was shitting blood throughout his last few miserable hours. No one has laid a finger on you, yet. I have allowed you to keep your clothes, your dignity, your humanity. You have one chance to sign your confession, and to answer my questions. One chance to comply utterly and completely. That is the full measure of my conscience.' Glokta leaned forwards and stabbed at the table with his finger. 'One chance. Then we strip you and start cutting.'

Magister Eider seemed to cave in, all at once. Her shoulders slumped, her head fell, her lip quivered. 'Ask your questions,' she croaked. *A broken woman. Many congratulations, Superior Glokta. But questions must have answers.*

'Vurms told us who was to be paid, and how much. Certain guards. Certain officials of his father's administration. Himself, of course, a tidy sum. One name was strangely absent from the list. Your own. You, and you alone, asked for nothing. The very Queen of merchants, passing on a certain sale? My mind boggles. What did they offer you? Why did you betray your King and country?'

'Why?' echoed Severard.

'Fucking answer him!' screamed Vitari.

Eider cringed away. 'The Union should never have been here in the first place!' she blurted. 'Greed is all it was! Greed, plain and simple! The Spicers were here before the war, when Dagoska was free. They made fortunes, all of them, but they had to pay taxes to the natives, and how they chafed at that! How much better, they thought, if we owned the city ourselves, if we could make our own rules. How much richer we could be. When the chance came they leaped on it, and my husband was at the front of the queue.'

'And so the Spicers came to rule Dagoska. I am waiting for your reasons, Magister Eider.'

'It was a shambles! The merchants had no interest in running a city, and no skill at doing it. The Union administrators, Vurms and his like, were the scrapings from the barrel, men who were only interested in lining their own pockets. We could have worked with the natives, but we chose to exploit them, and when they spoke out against us we called for the Inquisition, and you beat them and tortured them and hung their leaders in the squares of the Upper City, and soon they despised us as much as they had the Gurkish. Seven years, we have been here, and we have done nothing but evil! It has been an orgy of corruption, and brutality, and waste!' *That much is true. I have seen it for myself.*

'And the irony is, we did not even turn a profit! Even at the start, we made less than before the war! The cost of maintaining the walls, of paying for the mercenaries, without the help of the natives it was crippling!' Eider began to laugh, a desperate, sobbing laughter. 'The Guild is nearly bank-rupt, and they brought it on themselves, the idiots! Greed, plain and simple!'

'And then the Gurkish approached you.'

Eider nodded, her lank hair swaying. 'I have many contacts in Gurkhul. Merchants with whom I have dealt over the years. They told me that Uthman's first word as Emperor was a solemn oath to take Dagoska, to erase the stain his father had brought upon his nation, that he would never rest until his oath was fulfilled. They told me there were already Gurkish spies within the city, that they knew our weakness. They told me there might be a way to prevent the carnage, if Dagoska could be delivered to them without a fight.'

'Then why did you delay? You had control of Cosca and his mercen-aries, before Kahdia's people were armed, before the defences were strengthened, before I even arrived. You could have seized the city, if you had wanted. Why did you need that dolt Vurms?'

Carlot dan Eider's eyes were fixed on the floor. 'As long as Union soldiers held the Citadel, and the city gates, taking them would have meant bloodshed. Vurms could give me the city without a fight. My entire purpose, believe it or not, the purpose you have so ably frustrated, was to avoid killing.'

I do believe it. But that means nothing now. 'Go on.'

'I knew that Vurms could be bought. His father has not long to live, and the post is not hereditary. The son might only have this last chance to profit from his father's position. We fixed a price. We set about the preparations. Then Davoust found out.'

'He meant to inform the Arch Lector.'

Eider gave a sharp laugh. 'He had not your commitment to the cause. He wanted what everyone else wanted. Money, and more than I could raise. I told the Gurkish that the plan was finished. I told them why. The next day Davoust was . . . gone.' She took a deep breath. 'And so there was no going back. We were ready to move, shortly after you arrived. All was arranged. And then . . .' she paused.

'Then?'

'Then you began to strengthen the defences, and Vurms got greedy. He felt that our position was suddenly improved. He demanded more. He threatened to tell you of my plans. I had to go back to the Gurkish to get more. It all took time. Finally we were ready to move again, but by then, it was too late. The chance had passed.' She looked up. 'All greed. But for my husband's greed, we would never have come to Dagoska. But for the Spicers' greed, we might have succeeded here. But for Vurms' greed, we might have given it away, and not a drop of blood spilled over this worthless rock.' She sniffed, and looked back at the floor, her voice growing faint. 'But greed is everywhere.'

'So you agreed to surrender the city. You agreed to betray us.'

'Betray who? There would have been no losers! The merchants could have stepped away quietly! The natives would have been no worse off under Gurkish tyranny than they had been under ours! The Union would have lost nothing but a fraction of its pride, and what is that worth besides the lives of thousands?' Eider stretched forward across the table, her voice growing rough, her eyes wide and shining wet with tears. 'Now what will happen? Tell me that. It will be a massacre! A slaughter! Even if you can hold the city, what will be the price? And you cannot hold it. The Emperor has sworn, and will not be denied. The lives of every man, woman and child in Dagoska are forfeit! For what? So that Arch Lector Sult and his like can point at a map, and say this dot or that is ours? How much death will satisfy him? What were my reasons? What are yours? Why do you do this? Why?'

Glokta's left eye was twitching, and he pressed his hand against it. He stared at the woman opposite through the other. A tear ran down her pale cheek and dripped onto the table. *Why do I do this?*

He shrugged. 'What else is there?'

Severard reached down and slid the paper of confession across the table. 'Sign!' he barked.

'Sign,' hissed Vitari, 'sign, bitch!'

Carlot dan Eider's hand was trembling as she reached for the pen. It rattled against the inside of the inkwell, dripped black spots on the table top, scratched against the paper. There was no flush of triumph. *There never is, but we have one more matter to discuss.*

'Where will I find the Gurkish agent?' Glokta's voice was sharp as a cleaver.

'I don't know. I never knew. Whoever it is will come for you now, as they did for Davoust. Perhaps tonight . . .'

'Why have they waited so long?'

'I told them you were no threat. I told them that Sult would only send someone else . . . I told them I could handle you.' *And so you would have, I do not doubt, were it not for the unexpected generosity of Masters Valint and Balk.*

Glokta leaned forward. 'Who is the Gurkish agent?'

Eider's bottom lip was quivering so badly that her teeth were nearly rattling in her head. 'I don't know,' she whispered.

Vitari smashed her hand down on the table. 'Who? Who? Who is it, bitch? Who?'

'I don't know!'

'Liar!' The Practical's chain rattled over Eider's head and snapped taught around her throat. The one-time Queen of merchants was hauled over the back of her chair, legs kicking at the air, hands fumbling at the chain round her neck, and flung face down onto the floor.

'Liar!' The bridge of Vitari's nose was screwed up with rage, red brows drawn in with effort, eyes narrowed to furious slits. Her boot ground into the back of Eider's head, her back arched, the chain cut white into her clenched fists. Severard looked down on this brutal scene with a slight smile around his eyes, tuneless whistling vaguely audible over the choking, hissing, gurgling of Eider's last breaths.

Glokta licked at his empty gums as he watched her thrashing on the cell floor. *She has to die. There are no options. His Eminence demands harsh punishment. His Eminence demands examples made. His Eminence demands scant mercy.* Glokta's eyelid flickered, his face twitched. The room was airless, hot as a forge. He was damp with sweat, thirsty as hell. He could scarcely draw a breath. He felt almost as if he was the one being strangled.

And the irony is that she is right. My victory is a loss for everyone in Dagoska, one way or another. Already the first fruits of my labours are

*groaning their last in the waste ground before the city gates. There will be no
end to the carnage now. Gurkish, Dagoskan, Union, the bodies will pile up
until we're all buried under them, and all my doing. It would be better by far
if her scheme had succeeded. It would be better by far if I had died in the
Emperor's prisons. Better for the Guild of Spicers, better for the people of
Dagoska, better for the Gurkish, for Korsten dan Vurms, for Carlot dan Eider.
Better even for me.*

Eider's kicking had almost stopped. *One more thing to scrape into the
dark corners. One more thing to nag at me when I'm alone. She has to die,
whatever the rights and wrongs of it. She has to die.* Her next breath was a
muffled rattle. The next was a gentle wheeze. *Almost done now. Almost done.*

'Stop!' barked Glokta. *What?*

Severard looked up sharply. 'What?'

Vitari seemed not to have noticed, the chain was as tight as ever.

'Stop, I said!'

'Why?' she hissed.

Why indeed? 'I give you orders,' he barked, 'not fucking reasons!'

Vitari let go the chain, sneering her disgust, and took her boot off the
back of Eider's head. She did not move. Her breathing was shallow, a
rustling scarcely audible. *But she is breathing. The Arch Lector will expect an
explanation, and a good one. What will my explanation be, I wonder?* 'Take
her back to the cells,' he said, leaning on his cane and getting wearily out of
his chair. 'We might still find a use for her.'

Glokta stood by the window, frowned out into the night, and watched the
wrath of God rain down upon Dagoska. The three huge catapults, ranged
far out of bowshot beyond the city walls, had been in action now since the
afternoon. It took perhaps an hour for each one to be loaded and made
ready. He had watched the procedure through his eye-glass.

First the machine would be aligned, the range would be judged. A group
of white robed, bearded engineers would argue with one another, peering
through eye-glasss of their own, holding up swinging plumb-lines, fiddling
with compasses, and papers, and abacuses, making minute adjustments to
the huge bolts that held the catapult in place.

Once they were satisfied, the great arm was bent back into position. A
team of twenty horses, well-whipped and well-lathered, was required to lift
the enormous counterweight, a block of black iron carved in the shape of a
frowning Gurkish face.

Next the huge shot, a barrel not much less than a stride across, was
painstakingly manoeuvred into the waiting scoop by a system of pulleys
and a team of frowning, bellowing, arm-waving labourers. Then men
stepped away, hurried back fearfully. A lone slave was sent slowly forward
with a long pole, a burning wad at its end. He placed it to the barrel.
Flames leaped up, and somewhere a lever was hauled down, the mighty

weight fell, the great arm, long as a pine trunk, cut through the air, and the burning ammunition was flung up towards the clouds. They had been flying up, and roaring down, for hours now, while the sun slowly sank in the west, the sky darkened around them, the hills of the mainland became a black outline in the distance.

Glokta watched as one of the barrels soared, searing bright against the black heavens, the path of it a fizzing line burned into his eye. It seemed to hang over the city for an age, as high almost as the Citadel itself, and then tumbled, crackling from the sky like a meteor, a trail of orange fire blazing behind. It fell to earth in the midst of the Lower City. Liquid flames shot upwards, spurted outwards, pounced hungrily upon the tiny silhouettes of the slum-huts. A few moments later, the thunder-clap of the detonation reached Glokta at his window and made him wince. *Explosive powder. Who could have supposed, when I saw it fizzing on the bench of the Adeptus Chemical, that it might make such an awesome weapon?*

He half-saw, half-imagined, tiny figures rushing here or there, trying to pull the injured from the burning wreckage, trying to save what they could from their ruined dwellings, chains of ash-blackened natives grimly passing buckets from hand to hand, struggling vainly to contain the spreading inferno. *Those with the least always lose the most in war.* There were fires all across the Lower City now. Glowing, shimmering, flickering in the wind off the sea, reflecting orange, yellow, angry red in the black water. Even up here, the air smelled heavy, oily and choking from the smoke. *Down there it must be hell itself. My congratulations once more, Superior Glokta.*

He turned, aware of someone in the doorway. Shickel, her slight shape black in the lamplight.

'I'm alright,' he murmured, looking back to the majestic, the lurid, the awful spectacle outside the window. *After all, you don't get to see a city burn every day.* But his servant did not leave. She took a step forward into the room.

'You should go, Shickel. I'm expecting a visitor, of a sort, and it could be trouble.'

'A visitor, eh?'

Glokta looked up. Her voice sounded different. Deeper, harder. Her face looked different too, one side in shadow, one side lit in flickering orange from the fires outside the window. A strange expression, teeth half-bared, eyes fixed on Glokta and glittering with a hungry intensity as she padded slowly forward. A fearsome expression, almost. *If I was prone to fear . . .* And the wheels clicked into place.

'You?' he breathed.

'Me.'

You? Glokta could not help himself. He let out a burst of involuntary chuckling. 'Harker had you! That idiot stumbled on you by mistake, and I let you go! And I thought I was the hero!' He could not stop laughing. 'There's a lesson for you, eh? Never do a good turn!'

'I don't need lessons from you, cripple.' She took one more step. Not three strides away from him now.

'Wait!' He held up his hand. 'Just tell me one thing!' She paused, one brow raised, questioning. *Just stay there.* 'What happened to Davoust?'

Shickel smiled. Sharp, clean teeth. 'He never left the room.' She stroked her stomach gently. 'He is here.' Glokta forced himself not to look up as the loop of chain descended slowly from the ceiling. 'And now you can join him.' She got half a step forward before the chain hooked her under the chin and jerked up, dragging her off her feet into the air, hissing and spitting, kicking and thrashing.

Severard sprang up from his hiding-place beneath a table, tried to grab hold of Shickel's flailing legs. He yelped as her bare foot cracked into his face, sent him sprawling across the carpet.

'Shit,' gasped Vitari as Shickel wedged her hand under the chain and began to drag her down from the rafters. 'Shit!' They crashed onto the floor together, struggled for a moment, then Vitari flew through the air, a flailing black shadow in the darkness. She wailed as she crashed into a table in the far corner of the room, flopped senseless on the floor. Severard was still groaning, rolling slowly onto his back in a daze, hands clasped to his mask. Glokta and Shickel were left staring at one another. *Me and my Eater. This is unfortunate.*

He backed against the wall as the girl sprang at him, but she only got a step before Frost barrelled into her at full tilt, crashed on top of her onto the carpet. They lay there for a moment, then she slowly rolled on to her knees, slowly fought her way up to standing, all of the hulking Practical's great weight bearing down on her, slowly took a shuffling step towards Glokta.

The albino's arms were wrapped tight round her, straining with every sinew to drag her away, but she kept moving slowly forward, teeth gritted, one thin arm pinned to her thin body while her free hand clawed out furiously towards Glokta's neck.

'Thhhhh!' hissed Frost, the muscles in his heavy forearms bulging, his white face screwed up with effort, his pink eyes starting from his head. Still it was not enough. Glokta was pressed back against the wall, watching fascinated as the hand came closer, and closer still, just inches from his throat. *This is very unfortunate.*

'Fuck you!' screamed Severard. His stick whistled down and cracked into the grasping arm, breaking it clean in half. Glokta could see the bones poking through the ripped and bloody skin, and yet the fingers still twitched, reaching for him. The stick cracked into her face and her head snapped back. Blood sprayed out of her nose, her cheek was cut right open. Still she came on. Frost was gasping with the effort of keeping her other arm pinned as she strained forwards, mouth snarling, teeth bared, ready to bite Glokta's throat out.

Severard threw down his stick and grabbed her round the neck, dragging her head backwards, grunting with the effort, veins pulsing on his forehead. It was a bizarre sight, two men, one of them big and strong as a bull, trying desperately to wrestle a slip of a girl to the ground. Slowly, the two Practicals began to drag her back. Severard had one of her feet off the floor. Frost gave a great bellow, lifted her and with one last effort flung her against the wall.

She scrabbled at the floor, clawing her way up, broken arm flopping. Vitari growled from the shadows, one of Superior Davoust's heavy chairs raised high in the air. It burst apart over Shickel's head with an almighty crash, and then the three Practicals were on her like hounds on a fox, kicking, punching, grunting with rage.

'Enough!' snapped Glokta. 'We still have questions!' He shuffled up beside the panting Practicals and looked down. Shickel was a broken mess, motionless. A pile of rags, and not even a big one. *Much as when I first found her. How could this girl almost have overcome these three?* Her broken arm was stretched out across the carpet, fingers limp and bloody. *Safe to say no threat to anyone, now.*

Then the arm began to move. The bone slid back into the flesh, made a sickening crunching sound as it straightened out. The fingers twitched, jerked, scratched at the floor, began to slide toward Glokta, reaching for his ankle.

'What is she?' gasped Severard, staring down.

'Get the chains,' said Glokta, cautiously stepping back out of the way. 'Quickly!'

Frost dragged two pairs of great irons clanking from a sack, grunting with the effort of lifting them. They were made for the most powerful and dangerous of prisoners, bands of black iron, thick as a sapling trunk, heavy as anvils. He squeezed one pair tight shut around her ankles, the other round her wrists, ratchets scraping into place with a reassuring finality.

Meanwhile Vitari had hauled a great length of rattling chain from the sack and was winding it round and round Shickel's limp body while Severard held her up, dragging it tight, winding it round and round again. Two great padlocks completed the job.

They were snapped shut just in time. Shickel suddenly came alive, began thrashing on the floor. She snarled up at Glokta, straining at the chains. Her nose had already snapped back into place, the cut across her face had already closed. *As though she was never hurt at all. So Yulwei spoke the truth.* The chains rattled as she lunged forward with her teeth, and Glokta had to stumble back out of the way.

'It's persistent,' muttered Vitari, shoving her back against the wall with her boot. 'You'd have to give it that.'

'Fools!' hissed Shickel. 'You cannot resist what comes! God's right hand is falling upon this city, and nothing can save it! All your deaths are already written!' A particularly bright detonation flared across the sky, casting orange light onto the Practicals' masked faces. A moment later the thunder of it echoed around the room. Shickel began to laugh, a crazy, grating cackle. 'The Hundred Words are coming! No chains can bind them, no gates can keep them out! They are coming!'

'Perhaps.' Glokta shrugged. 'But they will come too late for you.'

'I am dead already! My body is nothing but dust! It belongs to the Prophet! Try as you might, you will learn nothing from me!'

Glokta smiled. He could almost feel the warmth of the flames, far below, on his face.

'That sounds like a challenge.'

One of Them

Ardee smiled at him, and Jezal smiled back. He grinned like an idiot. He could not help it. He was so happy to be back where things made sense. Now they need never be parted. He wanted only to tell her how much he loved her. How much he missed her. He opened his mouth but she pressed her finger to his lips. Firmly.

'Shhh.'

She kissed him. Gently at first, then harder.

'Uh,' he said.

Her teeth nipped at his lip. Playful, to begin with.

'Ah,' he said.

They bit harder, and harder still.

'Ow!' he said.

She sucked at his face, her teeth ripping at his skin, scraping on his bones. He tried to scream, but nothing came out. It was dark, his head swam. There was a hideous tugging, an unbearable pulling on his mouth.

'Got it,' said a voice. The agonising pressure released.

'How bad is it?'

'Not as bad as it looks.'

'It looks very bad.'

'Shut up and hold that torch higher.'

'What's that?'

'What?'

'That there, sticking out?'

'His jaw, fool, what do you think it is?'

'I think I'm going to be sick. Healing is not among my remarkable—'

'Shut your fucking hole and hold the torch up! We'll have to push it back in!' Jezal felt something pressing on his face, hard. There was a cracking sound and an unbearable lance of pain stabbed through his jaw and into his neck, like nothing he had ever felt before. He sagged back.

'I'll hold it, you move that.'

'What, this?'

'Don't pull his teeth out!'

'It fell out by itself!'

'Damn fool pink!'

'What's happening?' said Jezal. But all that came out was a kind of gurgle. His head was throbbing, pulsing, splitting with pain.

'He's waking up now!'

'You stitch then, I'll hold him.' There was a pressure round his shoulders, across his chest, folding him tight. His arm hurt. Hurt terribly. He tried to kick but his leg was agony, he couldn't move it.

'You got him?'

'Yes I've got him! Get stitching!'

Something stabbed into his face. He had not thought the pain could grow any worse. How wrong he had been.

'Get off me!' he bellowed, but all he heard was, 'thugh.'

He struggled, tried to wriggle free, but he was folded tight, and it only made his arm hurt more. The pain in his face got worse. His upper lip, his lower lip, his chin, his cheek. He screamed and screamed and screamed, but heard nothing. Only a quiet wheezing. When he thought his head would surely explode, the pain grew suddenly less.

'Done.'

The grip was released and he lay back, floppy as a rag, helpless. Something turned his head. 'That's good stitching. That's real good. Wish you'd been around when I got these. Might still have my looks.'

'What looks, pink?'

'Huh. Best get started on his arm. Then there's the leg to set an' all.'

'Where did you put that shield?'

'No,' groaned Jezal, 'please . . .' Nothing but a click in his throat.

He could see something now, blurry shapes in the half-light. A face loomed towards him, an ugly face. Bent and broken nose, skin torn and crossed with scars. There was a dark face, just behind it, a face with a long, livid line from eyebrow to chin. He closed his eyes. Even the light seemed painful.

'Good stitching.' A hand patted the side of his face. 'You're one of us, now, boy.'

Jezal lay there, his face a mass of agony, and the horror crept slowly through every limb.

'One of us.'

PART II

'He is not fit for battle that has never seen his own
blood flow, who has not heard his teeth crunch under
the blow of an opponent, or felt the full weight of
his adversary upon him.'

Roger of Howden

Heading North

So the Dogman was just lying there on his face, wet to the skin and trying to keep still without freezing solid, looking out across the valley from the trees, and watching Bethod's army marching. He couldn't see that much of them from where he was lying, just a stretch of the track over a ridge, enough to see the Carls tramping by, painted shields bright on their backs, mail glistening with specks of melted snow, spears sticking up high between the tree trunks. Rank after rank of 'em, marching steady.

They were a good way off, but he was taking quite a risk even getting this close. Bethod was just as careful as ever. He'd got men out all around, up on the ridges and the high points, anywhere where he thought someone could get a sight of what he was up to. He'd sent a few scouts south and some others east, hoping to trick anyone was watching, but he hadn't got the Dogman fooled. Not this time. Bethod was heading back the way he'd come. He was heading north.

Dogman breathed in sharp, and gave a long, sad sigh. By the dead, he felt tired. He watched the tiny figures filing past through the pine branches. He'd spent all those years scouting for Bethod, keeping an eye on armies like this one for him, helping him win battles, helping to make him a King, though he'd never dreamed it at the time. In some ways everything had changed. In others it was just the same as ever. Here he was still, face down in the muck with a sore neck from looking up. Ten years older and not a day better off. He could hardly remember what his ambitions used to be, but this hadn't ever been among 'em, he was sure of that. All that wind blown past, all that snow fallen, all that water flowed by. All that fighting, all that marching, all that waste. Logen gone, and Forley gone, and the candle burning down fast on the rest of 'em.

Grim slithered through the frozen scrub beside him, propped himself on his elbows and peered out towards the Carls moving on the road. 'Huh,' he grunted.

'Bethod's moving north,' whispered Dogman.

Grim nodded.

'He's got scouts out all over, but he's heading north, no doubt. We'd best let Threetrees know.'

Another nod.

Dogman lay there in the wet. 'I'm getting tired.'

Grim looked up, lifted an eyebrow.

'All this effort, and for what? Everything the same as ever. Whose side is it we're on now?' Dogman waved his hand over at the men slogging down the road. 'We supposed to fight all this lot? When do we get a rest?'

Grim shrugged his shoulders, squeezed his lips together like he was thinking about it. 'When we're dead?'

And wasn't that the sorry truth.

Took Dogman a while to find the others. They were nowhere near where they should've been by now. Being honest, they weren't far from where they were when he left. Dow was the first one he saw, sat on a big stone with the usual scowl on his face, glaring down into a gully. Dogman came up next to him, saw what he was looking at. The four Southerners, clambering over the rocks, slow and clumsy as new-born calves. Tul and Threetrees were waiting for them at the bottom, looking mighty short on patience.

'Bethod's heading north,' said Dogman.

'Good for him.'

'Not surprised?'

Dow licked his teeth and spat. 'He's beat every clan that dared face him, made himself a King where there wasn't one before, gone to war with the Union and he's giving 'em a kicking. He's turned the world on its head, the bastard. Nothing he does surprises me now.'

'Huh.' Dogman reckoned he was right enough there. 'You lot ain't got far.'

'No we ain't. This is some right fucking baggage you've saddled us with here, and no mistake.' He watched the four of 'em fumbling their way down the gully below, shaking his head like he'd never seen such a waste of flesh. 'Some right fucking baggage.'

'If you're telling me to feel shamed 'cause I saved some lives that day, I don't. What should I have done?' asked Dogman. 'Left 'em to die?'

'That's one idea. We'd be moving twice the speed without 'em, and eating a deal better and all.' He flashed a nasty grin. 'There's only one that I could find a use for.'

Dogman didn't have to ask which one. The girl was at the back. He could hardly see a woman's shape to her, all wrapped up as she was against the cold, but he could guess it was under there, and it made him nervous. Strange thing, having a woman along. Quite the sorry rarity, since they went north over the mountains, all them months ago. Even seeing one seemed like some kind of a guilty treat. Dogman watched her clambering on the rocks, dirty face half turned towards them. Tough-looking girl, he thought. Seemed like she'd had her share of knocks.

'I reckon she'd struggle,' Dow muttered to himself. 'I reckon she'd kick some.'

'Alright, Dow,' snapped Dogman. 'Best calm yourself down, lover. You know how Threetrees feels about all that. You know what happened to his daughter. He'd cut your fucking fruits off if he heard you talking that way.'

'What?' Dow said, all innocence. 'I'm just talking, aren't I? You can't hardly blame me for that. When's the last time any one of us had a woman?'

Dogman frowned. He knew exactly when it was for him. Pretty much the last time he was ever warm. Curled up with Shari in front of the fire, smile on his face wide as the sea. Just before Bethod chucked him and Logen and all the rest of them in chains, then kicked 'em out into exile.

He could still remember that last sight of her, mouth open wide with shock and fright as they dragged him from the blankets, naked and half asleep, squawking like a rooster that knows it's about to get its neck twisted. It had hurt, to be dragged away from her. Not as bad as Scale kicking him in the fruits had hurt, mind you. A painful night, all in all, one he'd never thought to live through. The sting from the kicks had faded with time, but the ache of losing her never had done, quite.

Dogman remembered the smell of her hair, the sound of her laugh, the feel of her back, pressed warm and soft against his belly while she slept. Well-used memories, picked over and worn thin like a favourite shirt. He remembered it like it was last night. He had to make himself stop thinking about it. 'Don't know that my memory goes back that far,' he grunted.

'Nor mine,' said Dow. 'Ain't you getting tired of fucking your hand?' He peered back down the slope and smacked his lips. Had a light in his eyes that Dogman didn't much like the look of. 'Funny, how you don't miss it so bad until you see it right in front of you. It's like holding out the meat to a hungry man, so close he can smell it. Don't tell me you ain't thinking the same thing.'

Dogman frowned at him. 'I don't reckon I'm thinking quite the same as you are. Stick your cock in the snow if you have to. That should keep you cooled off.'

Dow grinned. 'I'll have to stick it in something soon, I can tell you that.'

'Aaargh!' came a wail from down the slope. Dogman started for his bow, staring to see if some of Bethod's scouts had caught them out. It was just the Prince, slipped and fallen on his arse. Dow watched him rolling on his back, face all squashed up with scorn.

'He's some new kind o' useless, that one, eh? All he does is slow us down to half the rate we need, whine louder than a hog giving birth, eat more 'n his share and shit five times a day.' West was helping him up, trying to brush some of the dirt off his coat. Well, not his coat. The coat that West had given him. Dogman still couldn't see why a clever man would do a damn fool thing like that. Not as cold as it was getting now, middle of winter an' all. 'Why the hell would anyone follow that arsehole?' asked Dow, shaking his head.

'They say his father's the King o' the Union his self.'

'What does it matter whose son y'are, if you ain't worth no more than a turd? I wouldn't piss on him if he was burning, the bastard.' Dogman had to nod. Neither would he.

They were all sat in a circle round where the fire would've been, if Threetrees had let them have one. He wouldn't, of course, for all the Southerners' pleading. He wouldn't, no matter how cold it got. Not with Bethod's scouts about. It would have been good as shouting they were there at the tops of their voices. Dogman and the rest were on one side – Threetrees, Dow and Tul, Grim propped on his elbow like none of this had aught to do with him. The Union were opposite.

Pike and the girl were putting a brave enough face on being cold, tired and hungry. There was something to them told the Dogman they were used to it. West looked like he was near the end of his rope, blowing into his cupped hands like they were about to turn black and fall off. Dogman reckoned he should've kept his coat on, rather than give it to the last of the band.

The Prince was sitting in the midst, holding his chin high, trying to look like he wasn't knackered, covered in dirt, and starting to smell as bad as the rest of 'em. Trying to look like he might be able to give orders that someone might listen to. Dogman reckoned he'd made a mistake there. A crew like his chose leaders because of what they'd done, not whose son they were. They chose leaders with some bones to them, and from that point of view they'd sooner have taken a telling from the girl than from this prick.

'It is high time that we discussed our plans,' he was whining. 'Some of us are labouring in the dark.' Dogman could see Threetrees starting to frown already. He didn't like having to drag this idiot along, let alone pretend he cared a shit for his opinion.

It didn't help much that not everyone could make sense of everyone else. Of the Union, only West spoke Northern. Of the Northmen, only Dogman and Threetrees spoke Union. Tul might've caught the sense of what was being said, more or less. Dow weren't even catching that. As for Grim, well, silence means pretty much the same in every tongue.

'What's he saying now?' growled Dow.

'Something about plans, I reckon,' said Tul back to him.

Dow snorted. 'All an arsehole knows about is shit.' Dogman saw West swallowing. He knew what was being said well enough, and he could tell some folk were running short on patience.

The Prince wasn't near so clever, though. 'It would be useful to know how many days you think it will take us to get to Ostenhorm—'

'We're not going south,' said Threetrees in Northern, before his Highness even finished talking.

West stopped blowing into his hands for a moment. 'We're not?'

'We haven't been since we set out.'

'Why?'

'Because Bethod's heading back north.'

'That's a fact,' said Dogman. 'I seen him today.'

'Why would he turn back?' asked West. 'With Ostenhorm undefended?'

Dogman sighed. 'I didn't stick around to ask. Me and Bethod ain't on the best of terms.'

'I'll tell you why,' sneered Dow. 'Bethod ain't interested in your city. Not yet anyhow.'

'He's interested in breaking you up into pieces small enough to chew on,' said Tul.

Dogman nodded. 'Like that one you was with, that he just finished spitting out the bones of.'

'Excuse me,' snapped the Prince, no idea what was being said, 'but it might help if we continued in the common tongue—'

Threetrees ignored him and carried on in Northern. 'He's going to pull your army into little bits. Then he's going to squash 'em one by one. You think he's going south, so he hopes your Marshal Burr will send some men south. He'll catch 'em napping on his way back north, and if they're few enough he'll cut 'em to pieces like he did those others.'

'Then,' rumbled Tul, 'when all your pretty soldiers are stuck back in the mud or run back across the water . . .'

'He'll crack the towns open like nuts in winter, no rush, and his Carls will make free with the contents.' Dow sucked his teeth, staring across at the girl. Staring like a mean dog might stare at a side of bacon. She stared right back, which was much to her credit, the Dogman thought. He doubted he'd have had the bones to do the same in her position.

'Bethod's going north and we'll be following.' Threetrees said it in a way that made it clear it weren't a matter for discussion. 'Keep an eye on him, hope to move fast and keep ahead, so that if your friend Burr comes blundering through these woods, we can warn him where Bethod's at before he stumbles on him like a blind man falling down a fucking well.'

The Prince slapped angry at the ground. 'I demand to know what is being said!'

'That Bethod is heading north with his army,' hissed West at him through gritted teeth. 'And that they intend to follow him.'

'This is intolerable!' snapped the fool, tugging at his filthy cuffs. 'That course of action puts us all in danger! Please inform them that we will be setting out southwards without delay!'

'That's settled, then.' They all turned to see who spoke, and got quite the shock. Grim, talking Union as smooth and even as the Prince himself. 'You're going south. We're going north. I need to piss.' And he got up and wandered off into the dark. Dogman stared after him, mouth open. Why did he need to learn someone else's language when he never spoke more than two words together in his own?

'Very well!' squawked the Prince, shrill and panicky. 'I should have expected no better!'

'Your Highness!' hissed West at him. 'We need them! We won't make it to Ostenhorm or anywhere else without their help!'

The girl's eyes slid sideways. 'Do you even know which way south is?' Dogman stifled a chuckle, but the Prince weren't laughing.

'We should head south!' he snarled, dirty face twitching with anger.

Threetrees snorted. 'The baggage don't get a vote, boy, even supposing this was a voting band, which it ain't.' He was finally speaking Union, but Dogman didn't reckon the Prince would be too happy to know what was being said. 'You had your chance to give the orders, and look where it's got you. Not to mention those were fools enough to do what you told 'em. You'll not be adding any of our names to their list, I can tell you that. If you want to follow us, you'd best learn to keep up. If you want to give the orders, well—'

'South is that way,' said the Dogman, jerking his thumb into the woods. 'Good luck.'

Scant Mercy

To Arch Lector Sult, head of his Majesty's Inquisition.

Your Eminence,

The siege of Dagoska continues. Three days in a row the Gurkish have made assaults against our walls, each one greater in size and determination. They strive to fill in our channel with boulders, to cross it with bridges, to scale our walls and bring rams against our gates. Three times they have attacked and three times we have thrown them back. Their losses have been heavy, but losses they can well afford. The Emperor's soldiers crawl like ants across the peninsula. Still, our men are bold, our defences are strong, our resolve is unshakeable, and Union vessels still ply the bay, keeping us well supplied. Be assured, Dagoska will not fall.

On a subject of lesser importance, you will, no doubt, be pleased to learn that the issue of Magister Eider has been put to rest. I had suspended her sentence while I considered the possibility of using her connection with the Gurkish against them. Unfortunately for her, the chances of such subtle measures bearing fruit have dropped away, leaving us with no further use for her. The sight of a woman's head decorating the battlements might have been detrimental to the morale of our troops. We, after all, are the civilised faction. The one-time Magister of the Guild of Spicers has therefore been dealt with quietly, but, I can assure you, quite finally. Neither one of us need spare her, or her failed conspiracy, any further thought.

As always, your Eminence, I serve and obey.

Sand dan Glokta
Superior of Dagoska.

It was quiet down by the water. Quiet, and dark, and still. The gentle waves slapped at the supports of the wharf, the timbers of the boats creaked softly, a cool breeze washed in off the bay, the dark sea glittered in the moonlight under a sky dusted with stars.

You could never guess that a few short hours ago men were dying in their hundreds less than half a mile away. That the air was split with screams of pain and fury. That even now the ruins of two great siege towers are still smouldering beyond the land walls, corpses scattered round them like leaves fallen in autumn . . .

'Thhhhh.' Glokta felt his neck click as he turned and squinted into the darkness. Practical Frost emerged from the shadows between two dark buildings, peering suspiciously around, herding a prisoner in front of him; someone much smaller, hunched over and wrapped in a cloak with the hood up, arms secured behind them. The two figures crossed the dusty quay and came down the wharf, their footfalls clapping hollow on the wooden planks.

'Alright, Frost,' said Glokta as the albino pulled his prisoner up. 'I don't think we need that any more.' The white fist pulled back the cowl.

In the pale moonlight, Carlot dan Eider's face looked gaunt and wasted, full of sharp edges, with a set of black grazes across her hollow cheek. Her head had been shaved, after the fashion of confessed traitors, and without that weight of hair her skull seemed strangely small, almost child-like, her neck absurdly long and fragile. Especially with a ring of angry bruises round it, the dark after-images left by the links of Vitari's chain. There was hardly any remnant of the sleek and masterful woman who had taken him by the hand in the Lord Governor's audience chamber, it seemed an age ago. *A few weeks in the darkness, sleeping on the rotten floor of a sweltering cell, not knowing if you'll live another hour – that can ruin the looks. I should know.*

She lifted her chin at him, nostrils wide, eyes gleaming in black shadows. *That mixture of fear and defiance that comes on some people when they know they are about to die.* 'Superior Glokta, I hardly dared hope I would see you again.' Her words might have been jaunty, but there was no disguising the edge of fear in her voice. 'What now? A rock tied round the legs and into the bay? Isn't that all a touch dramatic?'

'It would be, but that isn't what I have in mind.' He looked up at Frost and gave the barest of nods. Eider flinched, squeezing her eyes shut and biting on her lip, hunching her shoulders as she felt the hulking Practical loom up behind her. *Waiting for the crushing blow on the back of the skull? The stabbing point between the shoulder blades? The choking wire across the throat? The terrible anticipation. Which shall it be?* Frost raised his hand. There was a flash of metal in the darkness. Then a gentle clicking as the key slid smoothly into Eider's manacles and unlocked them.

She slowly prised open her eyes, slowly brought her hands round in front of her, blinked down as though she had never seen them before. 'What's this?'

'This is exactly what it appears to be.' He nodded his head down the wharf. 'This is a ship leaving for Westport on the next tide. You have contacts in Westport?'

The tendons in her thin neck fluttered as she swallowed. 'I have contacts everywhere.'

'Good. Then this is me setting you free.'

There was a long silence. 'Free?' She lifted one hand to her head and rubbed absently at her stubbly scalp, staring at Glokta for a drawn-out moment. *Not sure whether to believe it, and who can blame her? I'm not sure that I believe it.* 'His Eminence must have mellowed beyond recognition.'

Glokta snorted. 'Not likely. Sult knows nothing about this. If he did, I rather think we both might be swimming with rocks round our ankles.'

Her eyes narrowed. *The merchant Queen judges the bargain.* 'Then what's the price?'

'The price is you're dead. You're forgotten. Put Dagoska from your mind, it's finished. Find some other people to save. The price is you leave the Union and never come back. Not. Ever.'

'That's it?'

'That's it.'

'Why?'

Ah, my favourite question. Why do I do this? He shrugged. 'What does it matter? A woman lost in the desert—'

'Should take such water as she is offered, no matter who it comes from. Don't worry. I won't be saying no.' She reached out suddenly and Glokta half-jerked away, but her fingertips only touched him gently on his cheek. They rested there for a moment, while his skin tingled, and his eye twitched, and his neck ached. 'Perhaps,' she whispered, 'if things had been different . . .'

'If I weren't a cripple and you weren't a traitor? Things are as they are.'

She let her hand drop, half smiling. 'Of course they are. I would say I'll see you again—'

'I'd rather you didn't.'

She nodded slowly. 'Then goodbye.' She pulled the hood over her head, throwing her face back into shadow, then brushed past Glokta and walked quickly towards the end of the wharf. He stood, weight on his cane, and watched her go, scratching his cheek slowly where her fingers had rested. *So. To get women to touch you, you need only spare their lives. I should try it more often.*

He turned away, limped a few painful steps onto the dusty quay, peering up into the dark buildings. *I wonder if Practical Vitari is in there somewhere, watching? I wonder if this little episode will find its way into her next report to the Arch Lector?* He felt a sweaty shiver up his aching back. *I won't be putting it in mine, that's sure, but what does it really matter?* He could smell it, as the wind shifted, the smell that seemed to find its way into every corner of the city now. The sharp smell of burning. Of smoke. Of ash. *Of death. Without a miracle, none of us will leave this place alive.* He looked back. Carlot dan Eider was already crossing the gangway. *Well. Perhaps just one of us will.*

'Things are going well,' sang Cosca in his rich Styrian accent, grinning out over the parapet at the carnage beyond the walls. 'A good day's work, yesterday, considering.'

A good day's work. Below them, on the other side of the ditch, the bare earth was scarred and burned, bristling with spent flatbow bolts like stubble on a brown chin. Everywhere, siege equipment lay wrecked and ruined. Broken ladders, fallen barrows spilling rocks, burned and shattered wicker screens, trampled into the hard dirt. The shell of one of the great siege towers was still half standing, a framework of blackened timbers sticking twisted from a heap of ash, scorched and tattered leather flapping in the salt wind.

'We taught those Gurkish fuckers a lesson they won't soon forget, eh, Superior?'

'What lesson?' muttered Severard. *What lesson indeed? The dead learn nothing.* The corpses were dotted about before the Gurkish front line, two hundred strides or so from the land walls. They were scattered across the no-man's-land between, surrounded by a flotsam of broken weapons and armour. They had dropped so heavily just before the ditch that you could almost have walked from the sea on one side of the peninsula to the sea on the other without once stepping on the earth. In a few places they were crowded together into huddled groups. *Where the wounded crawled to take cover behind the dead, then bled to death themselves.*

Glokta had never seen slaughter like it. Not even after the siege of Ulrioch, when the breach had been choked with Union dead, when Gurkish prisoners had been murdered by the score, when the temple had been burned with hundreds of citizens inside. Corpses sagged and lolled and sprawled, some charred with fire, some bent in attitudes of final prayer, some spread out heedless, heads smashed by rocks flung from above. Some had clothes ripped and rooted through. *Where they tore at their own shirts to check their wounds, hoping they were not fatal. All of them disappointed.*

Flies buzzed in legions around the bodies. Birds of a hundred species hopped and flapped and pecked at the unexpected feast. Even here, high up in the blasting wind, it was starting to reek. *The stuff of nightmares. Of my nightmares for the next few months, I shouldn't wonder. If I last that long.*

Glokta felt his eye twitching, and he blew out a deep breath, stretched his neck from side to side. *Well. We must fight on. It is a little late now for second thoughts.* He peered gingerly over the parapet to take a look down at the ditch, his free hand grasping tight at the pitted stone to keep his balance.

Not good. 'They have nearly filled the channel down below us, and over near the gates.'

'True,' said Cosca cheerfully. 'They drag up their boxes of rocks and try to tip them in. We can only kill them so fast.'

'That channel is our best defence.'

'True again. It was a good idea. But nothing lasts forever.'

'Without it there is nothing to stop the Gurkish mounting ladders, rolling up rams, mining under our walls even. It might be necessary to organise a sortie of some kind, dig it back out.'

Cosca rolled his dark eyes sideways. 'Lowered from the wall by ropes, slaving in the darkness, not two hundred strides from the Gurkish positions? Was that what you had in mind?'

'Something like that.'

'Then I wish you luck with it.'

Glokta snorted. 'I would go, of course.' He tapped his leg with his cane. 'But I'm afraid my days of heroics are far behind me.'

'Lucky for you.'

'Hardly. We should build a barricade behind the gates. That is our weakest point. A half circle, I would guess, some hundred strides across, would make an effective killing ground. If they manage to break through we might still contain them there, long enough to push them back.' *Might . . .*

'Ah, pushing them back.' Cosca scratched at the rash on his neck. 'I'm sure the volunteers will be falling over each other for that duty when the time comes. Still, I'll see it done.'

'You have to admire them.' General Vissbruck strode up to the parapet, his hands clasped tightly behind his impeccably pressed uniform. *I'm surprised he finds the time for presentation, with things as they are. Still, we all cling to what we can.* He shook his head as he peered down at the corpses. 'Some courage, to come at us like this, over and over, against defences so strong and so well manned. I've rarely seen men so willing to give their lives.'

'They have that most strange and dangerous of qualities,' said Cosca. 'They think they're in the right.'

Vissbruck stared sternly out from under his brows. 'It is we who are in the right.'

'If you like.' The mercenary grinned sideways at Glokta. 'But I think the rest of us long ago gave up on the idea that there's any such thing. The plucky Gurkish come on with their barrows . . . and it's my job to shoot them full of arrows!' He barked out a sharp laugh.

'I don't think that's amusing,' snapped Vissbruck. 'A fallen opponent should be treated with respect.'

'Why?'

'Because it could be any one of us rotting in the sun, and probably soon will be.'

Cosca only laughed the louder, and clapped Vissbruck on the arm. 'Now you're getting it! If I've learned one thing from twenty years of warfare, it's that you have to look at the funny side!'

Glokta watched the Styrian chuckling at the battlefield. *Trying to decide when would be the best time to change sides? Trying to work out how good a fight to give the Gurkish before they pay better than I do? There's more than rhymes in that scabby head, but for the moment we cannot do without him.* He glanced at General Vissbruck, who had moved further down the walkway to sulk on his own. *Our plump friend has neither the brains nor the bravery to hold this city for longer than a week.*

He felt a hand on his shoulder, and turned back to Cosca. 'What?' he snapped.

'Uh,' muttered the mercenary, pointing up into the blue sky. Glokta followed his finger. There was a black spot up there, not far above them, but moving upwards. *What is that? A bird?* It had peaked now, and was coming down. Realisation dawned suddenly. *A stone. A stone from a catapult.*

It grew larger as it fell, tumbling over and over, seeming to move with ridiculous slowness, as if sinking through water, its total silence adding to the sense of unreality. Glokta watched it, open-mouthed. They all did. An air of terrible expectancy settled on the walls. It was impossible to tell exactly where the stone was going to fall. Men began to scatter this way and that along the walkway, clattering, scuffling, gasping and squealing, tossing away weapons.

'Fuck,' whispered Severard, throwing himself face down on the stones.

Glokta stayed where he was, his eyes locked on that one dark spot in the bright sky. *Is it coming for me? Several tons of rock, about to splatter my remains across the city? What a ludicrously random way to die.* He felt his mouth twitch up in a faint smile.

There was a deafening crash as a section of parapet was ripped apart nearby, sending out a cloud of dust and flinging chunks of stone into the air. Splinters whizzed around them. A soldier not ten strides away was neatly decapitated by a flying block. His headless body swayed for a moment on its feet before its knees buckled and it toppled backwards off the wall.

The missile crashed down somewhere in the Lower City, smashing through the shacks, bouncing and rolling, flinging shattered timbers up like matchsticks, leaving a trail of destruction in its wake. Glokta blinked and swallowed. His ears were still ringing, but he could hear someone shouting. A strange voice. A Styrian accent. Cosca.

'That the best you can do, you fuckers? I'm still here!'

'The Gurkish are bombarding us!' Vissbruck was squealing pointlessly, squatting down behind the parapet with his hands clasped over his head, a layer of light dust across the shoulders of his uniform. 'Solid shot from their catapults!'

'You don't say,' muttered Glokta. There was another mighty crash as a second rock struck the walls further down and burst apart in a shower of fragments, hurling stones the size of skulls into the water below. The very walkway beneath Glokta's feet seemed to tremble with the force of it.

'They're coming again!' Cosca was roaring at the very top of his voice. 'Man the walls! To the walls!'

Men began to hurry past: natives, mercenaries, Union soldiers, all side by side, cranking their flatbows, handing out bolts, shouting and calling to one another in a confusion of different languages. Cosca moved among them slapping backs, shaking his fist, snarling and laughing with not the slightest sign of fear. *A most inspiring leader, for a half-mad drunkard.*

'Fuck this!' hissed Severard in Glokta's ear. 'I'm no damn soldier!'

'Neither am I, any more, but I can still enjoy a show.' He limped up to the parapet and peered out. This time he saw the catapult's great arm fly up in the distant haze. The distance was poorly judged this time, and it sailed high overhead. Glokta winced at a twinge in his neck as he followed it with his eyes. It crashed down not far short of the Upper City's walls with a deep boom, throwing chunks of stone far into the slums.

A great horn sounded behind the Gurkish lines: a throbbing, rumbling blast. Drums followed behind, thumping together like monstrous footsteps. 'Here they come!' roared Cosca. 'Ready with your bows!' Glokta heard the order echoing across the walls, and a moment later the battlements on the towers bristled with loaded flatbows, the bright points of the bolts glinting in the harsh sun.

The great wicker shields that marked the Gurkish lines began slowly, steadily, to move forwards, edging across the blighted no-man's-land towards them. *And behind, no doubt, Gurkish soldiers crawl like ants.* Glokta's hand clutched the stone of the parapet painfully tight as he watched them come on, his heart beating almost as loud as the Gurkish drums. *Fear, or excitement? Is there a difference? When was the last time I felt such a bittersweet thrill? Speaking before the Open Council? Leading a charge of the King's cavalry? Fighting in the Contest before the roaring crowds?*

The screens were coming steadily closer, still in an even row across the peninsula. *Now a hundred strides, now ninety, now eighty.* He looked sideways at Cosca, still grinning like a madman. *When will he give the order? Sixty, fifty . . .*

'Now!' roared the Styrian. 'Fire!' There was a mighty rattling along the walls as the flatbows were loosed in one great volley, peppering the screens, the ground around them, the corpses, and any Gurkish unlucky enough to be have left some part of their body visible. Men knelt behind the parapet and began to reload, fumbling with bolts, cranking handles, sweating and straining. The drum beats had grown faster, more urgent, the screens passed heedless over the scattered bodies. *Not much fun for the men behind, staring down at the corpses beneath their feet, wondering how long before they join them.*

'Oil!' shouted Cosca.

A bottle with a burning wick was flung spinning from a tower on the left. It smashed against one of the wicker screens and lines of fire shot hungrily out across the surface, turning it brown, then black. It began to wobble, to bend, then gradually started to tip over. A soldier ran out howling from behind it, his arm wreathed in bright flames.

The burning screen fell to the ground, exposing a column of Gurkish troops, some pushing barrows full of boulders, others carrying long ladders, others with bows, armour, weapons. They yelled their war-cries, charging forward with their shields raised, shooting arrows up at the battlements, zig-zagging back and forth between the corpses. Men pitched on their faces, riddled with flatbow bolts. Men howled and clutched at wounds. Men crawled, and gurgled, and swore. They pleaded and bellowed defiance. They ran for the rear and were shot in the back.

Up on the walls bows twanged and clanked. More bottles of oil were lit and hurled down. Some men roared and hissed and spat curses, some cowered behind the parapet as arrows zipped up from below, clattering from stone or shooting overhead, occasionally thudding into flesh. Cosca had one foot up on the battlements, utterly careless, leaning out dangerously far and brandishing a notched sword, bellowing something that Glokta could not hear. Everyone was screaming and shouting, attackers and defenders both. *Battle. Chaos. I remember now. How could I ever have enjoyed this?*

Another of the screens was blazing, filling the air with reeking black smoke. Gurkish soldiers spilled out from behind it like bees from a broken hive, milling around on the far side of the ditch, trying to find a spot to foot their ladder. Defenders further down the walls began to hurl chunks of masonry down at them. Another rock from a catapult crashed down far short and ripped a long hole through a Gurkish column, sending bodies and parts of bodies flying.

A soldier was dragged past with an arrow in his eye. 'Is it bad?' he was wailing, 'is it bad?' A moment later a man just beside Glokta squawked as a shaft hit him in the chest. He was spun half round, his flatbow went off and the bolt thudded into his neighbour's neck, right up to the feathers. The two of them fell together right at Glokta's feet, leaking blood across the walkway.

Down at the foot of the walls, a bottle of oil burst apart in the midst of a crowd of Gurkish soldiers, just as they were trying to raise their ladder. A faint tang of cooking meat joined the stinks of rot and wood smoke. Men burned, scrambling and screaming, charging around madly or flinging themselves into the flooded ditch in full armour. *Death by burning or death by drowning. Some choice.*

'You seen enough yet?' Severard's voice hissed in his ear.

'Yes.' *More than enough.* He left Cosca shouting himself hoarse in Styrian and pushed breathlessly through the press of mercenaries towards the steps. He followed a stretcher down, wincing at every painful step, trying to keep up while a steady stream of men shoved past the other way. *Never thought that I'd be glad to be going down a set of steps again.* His happiness did not last long, however. By the time he reached the bottom his left leg was twitching with the all-too-familiar mixture of agony and numbness.

'Damn it!' he hissed to himself, hopping back against the wall. 'There are casualties more mobile than I am!' He watched the wounded hobbling past, bandaged and bloody.

'This isn't right,' hissed Severard. 'We've done our bit. We found the traitors. What the hell are we still doing here?'

'Fighting for the King's cause beneath you, is it?'

'Dying for it is.'

Glokta snorted. 'You think there's anyone in this whole fucking city enjoying themselves?' He thought he heard the faint sound of Cosca screaming insults floating down over the clamour of the fighting. 'Apart from that crazy Styrian of course. Keep an eye on him, eh, Severard? He betrayed Eider, he'll betray us, especially if things look bleak.'

The Practical stared at him, and for once there was no trace of a smile round his eyes. 'Do things look bleak?'

'You were up there.' Glokta grimaced as he stretched his leg out. 'They've looked better.'

The long, dim hall had once been a temple. When the Gurkish assaults had begun the lightly wounded had been brought here, to be tended to by priests and women. It was an easy place to bring them: down in the Lower City, close to the walls. This part of the slums was mostly empty of civilians now, in any case. *The risks of raging fire and plummeting boulders can quickly render a neighbourhood unpopular.* As the fighting continued the lightly wounded had gone back to the walls, leaving the more serious casualties behind. Those with severed limbs, with deep cuts, with terrible burns, with arrows in the body, lay scattered round the dim arcades on their bloody stretchers. Day by day their numbers had mounted until they choked every part of the floor. The walking wounded were dealt with outside, now. This place was reserved for the ruined, for the maimed. *For the dying.*

Every man had his own special language of agony. Some screamed and howled without end. Some cried out for help, for mercy, for water, for their mothers. Some coughed and gurgled and spat blood. Some wheezed and rattled out their last breaths. *Only the dead are entirely silent.* And there were a lot of them. From time to time you would see them being dragged out, limbs lolling, ready to be wrapped in cheap shrouds and heaped up behind the back wall.

All day, Glokta knew, grim teams of men were busy digging graves for the natives. *According to their firmly-held beliefs. Great pits in the ruins of the slums, good for a dozen corpses at a time.* All night, the same men were busy burning the Union dead. *According to our lack of belief in anything. Up on the bluffs, where the oily smoke will be carried out over the bay. We can only hope it will blow right into the faces of the Gurkish on the other side. One last insult, from us, to them.*

Glokta shuffled slowly through the hall, echoing with the sounds of pain, wiping the sweat from his forehead, peering down at the casualties. Dark-skinned Dagoskans, Styrian mercenaries, pale-skinned Union men, all mixed up together. *People of all nations, all colours, all types, united against the Gurkish, and now dying together, side by side, all equal. My heart would be warmed. If I still had one.* He was vaguely aware of Practical Frost, lurking in the darkness by the wall nearby, eyes moving carefully over the room. *My watchful shadow, here to make sure that no one rewards my efforts on the Arch Lector's behalf with a fatal head wound of my own.*

A small section at the back of the temple had been curtained off for surgery. *Or as close as they can get here. Hack and slash with saw and knife, legs off at the knee, arms at the shoulder.* The loudest screams in the whole place came from behind those dirty curtains. Desperate, slobbering wails. *Hardly any less brutal than what's happening on the other side of the land walls.* Glokta could see Kahdia working through a gap, his white robe spattered, smeared, turned grubby brown with blood. He was squinting down at some glistening meat while he cut away at it with a blade. *The stump of a leg, perhaps?* The screams bubbled to a stop.

'He's dead,' said the Haddish simply, tossing his knife down on the table and wiping his bloody hands on a rag. 'Bring in the next one.' He lifted the curtain and pushed his way through. Then he saw Glokta. 'Ah! The author of our woes! Have you come to feed your guilt, Superior?'

'No. I came to see if I have any.'

'And do you?'

A good question. Do I? He looked down at a young man, lying on dirty straw by the wall, wedged in between two others. His face was waxy pale, eyes glassy, lips moving rapidly as he mumbled some meaningless nonsense to himself. His leg was off just above the knee, the stump bound with a bloody dressing, a belt buckled tight round the thigh. *His chances of survival? Slim to none. A last few hours in agony and squalor, listening to the groans of his fellows. A young life, snuffed out long before his time, and blah, blah, blah.* Glokta raised his eyebrows. He felt nothing but a mild distaste, no more than he might have had the dying man been a heap of rubbish. 'No,' he said.

Kahdia looked down at his own bloody hands. 'Then God has truly blessed you,' he muttered. 'Not everyone has your stomach.'

'I don't know. Your people have been fighting well.'

'Dying well, you mean.'

Glokta's laughter hacked at the heavy air. 'Come now. There's no such thing as dying well.' He glanced round at the endless wounded. 'I'd have thought that you of all people would have learned that by now.'

Kahdia did not laugh. 'How much of this do you think we can stand?'

'Losing heart, eh, Haddish? As with so many things in life, heroic last stands are a great deal more appealing in concept than in reality.' *The dashing young Colonel Glokta could have told us that, dragged away from the bridge with the remains of his leg barely attached, his notions of how the world works radically altered.*

'Your concern is touching, Superior, but I'm used to disappointments. Believe me, I will live with this one. The question remains. How long can we hold out?'

'If the sea lanes stay open and we can be supplied by ship, if the Gurkish cannot find a way round the land walls, if we can stick together and keep our heads, we could hold out here for weeks.'

'Hold out for what?'

Glokta paused. *For what indeed?* 'Perhaps the Gurkish will lose heart.'

'Hah!' snorted Kahdia. 'The Gurkish have no hearts! They did not subdue all Kanta with half measures. No. The Emperor has spoken, and will not be denied.'

'Then we must hope that the war will be quickly settled in the North, and that Union forces will come to our aid.' *An utterly futile hope. It will be months before matters are settled in Angland. Even when they are, the army will be in no state to fight. We are on our own.*

'And when might we expect such help?'

When the stars go out? When the sky falls in? When I run a mile with a smile on my face? 'If I had all the answers I'd hardly have joined the Inquisition!' snapped Glokta. 'Perhaps you should pray for divine help. A mighty wave to wash the Gurkish away would suit nicely. Who was it told me that miracles happen?'

Kahdia nodded slowly. 'Perhaps we should both pray. I fear there is more chance of aid from my god than your masters.' Another stretcher was carried past, a squealing Styrian stretched out on it with an arrow in his stomach. 'I must go.' Kahdia swept away and the curtain dropped back behind him.

Glokta frowned at it. *And so the doubts begin. The Gurkish slowly tighten their grip on the city. Our doom draws nearer, and every man sees it. A strange thing, death. Far away, you can laugh at it, but as it comes closer it looks worse and worse. Close enough to touch, and no one laughs. Dagoska is full of fear, and the doubts can only grow. Sooner or later someone will try to betray the city to the Gurkish, if only to save their lives, or the lives of those they love. They might well begin by disposing of the troublesome Superior who set this madness in motion . . .*

He felt a sudden touch on his shoulder and he caught his breath and spun round. His leg buckled and he stumbled back against a pillar, almost treading on a gasping native with bandages across his face. Vitari was standing behind him, frowning. 'Damn it!' Glokta bit on his lip with his remaining teeth against a searing spasm in his leg. 'Didn't anyone ever teach you not to sneak up on people?'

'They taught me the opposite. I need to talk to you.'

'Then talk. Just don't touch me again.'

She eyed the wounded. 'Not here. Alone.'

'Oh, come now. What can you have to say to me that you can't say in front of a room full of dying heroes?'

'You'll find out when we get outside.'

A chain around the throat, nice and tight, courtesy of his Eminence? Or merely some chat about the weather? Glokta felt himself smiling. *I can hardly wait to find out.* He held one hand up to Frost and the albino faded back into the shadows, then he limped after Vitari, threading their way through the groaning casualties and out through the door at the back, into the open air. The sharp smell of sweat swapped for the sharp smell of burning, and something else . . .

Long, lozenge shapes were stacked up shoulder high against the wall of the temple, swathed in rough grey cloth, some of it spotted and stained with brown blood. A whole heap of them. Corpses, waiting patiently to be buried. *This morning's harvest. What a wonderfully macabre spot for a pleasant little chat. I could hardly have picked a better.*

'So, how are you enjoying the siege? It's a bit noisy for my taste, but your friend Cosca seems to like it—'

'Where's Eider?'

'What?' snapped Glokta, stalling for time while he though about how to answer. *I hardly expected her to find out about that so soon.*

'Eider. You remember? Dressed like an expensive whore? Adornment to the city's ruling council? Tried to betray us to the Gurkish? Her cell's empty. Why?'

'Oh, her. She's at sea.' *True.* 'With fifty strides of good chain round her.' *False.* 'She's adorning the bottom of the bay now, since you ask.'

Vitari's orange brows drew in with suspicion. 'Why wasn't I told?'

'I've got better things to do than keep you informed. We've a war to lose, or hadn't you noticed?' Glokta turned away but her hand shot out in front of him and slapped on to the wall, her long arm barring his path.

'Keeping me informed means keeping Sult informed. If we start telling him different stories—'

'Where have you been the last few weeks?' He chuckled as he gestured at the pile of shrouded shapes beside the wall. 'It's a funny thing. The closer the Gurkish get to breaking through our walls and murdering every living thing in Dagoska, the less I seem to care about his fucking Eminence! Tell him what you please. You're boring me.' He made to push past her arm but found it did not move.

'What if I were to tell him what you please?' she whispered.

Glokta frowned. *Now that isn't boring. Sult's favourite Practical, sent here to make sure I tread the righteous path, offering deals? A trick? A trap?* Their faces were no more than a foot apart, and he stared hard into her eyes, trying to guess what she was thinking. *Is there just the slightest trace of desperation there? Could the motive be nothing more than simple self-preservation? When you lose the instinct yourself, it's hard to remember how powerful it is for everyone else.* He felt himself starting to smile. *Yes, I see it now.* 'You thought you'd be recalled once the traitors had been found, didn't you? You thought Sult would arrange a nice little boat home! But now there are no boats for anyone, and you're worried your kindly uncle's forgotten all about you! That you've been tossed to the Gurkish with the rest of the damn dogmeat!'

Vitari's eyes narrowed. 'Let me tell you a secret. I didn't choose to be here any more than you did, but I learned a long time ago that when Sult tells you to do a thing you'd better look like you did it. All I care about is getting out of here alive.' She moved even closer. 'Can we help each other?'

Can we indeed? I wonder. 'Alright then. I daresay I can squeeze one extra friend into the social whirl that is my life. I'll see what I can do for you.'

'You'll see what you can do?'

'That's the best you'll get. The fact is I'm not much good at helping people. Out of practice, you see.' He leered his toothless grin in her face, lifted her slack arm out of the way with his cane, then hobbled past the heap of bodies and back towards the temple door.

'What shall I tell Sult about Eider?'

'Tell him the truth,' Glokta called over his shoulder. 'Tell him she's dead.'

Tell him we all are.

So This is Pain

'**W**here am I?' asked Jezal, only his jaw would not move.

The cartwheels squealed as they turned, everything blinding bright and blurry, sound and light digging into his aching skull. He tried to swallow, but could not. He tried to raise his head. Pain stabbed through his neck and his stomach heaved.

'Help!' he squealed, but nothing came out beyond a bubbling croak. What had happened? Painful sky above, painful boards underneath. He was lying in a cart, head on a scratchy sack, bouncing and jolting.

There had been a fight, he remembered that. A fight among the stones. Someone had called out. A crunch and blinding light, then nothing but pain. Even trying to think was painful. He lifted his arm to feel his face, but found that he couldn't. He tried to shift his legs, to push himself up, but he couldn't do that either. He worked his mouth, grunting, moaning.

His tongue was unfamiliar, three times its usual size, like a bloody lump of ham that had been shoved between his jaws, filling his mouth so he could hardly breathe. The right side of his face was a mask of agony. With every lurch of the cart his jaws rattled together, sending white-hot stabs of pain from his teeth into his eyes, his neck, the very roots of his hair. There were bandages over his mouth, he had to breathe through the left side, but even the air moving in his throat was painful.

Panic started to claw at him. Every part of his body was screaming. One arm was bound tight across his chest but he clutched weakly at the side of the cart with the other, trying to do something, anything, his eyes bulging, heart hammering, breath snorting in his nose.

'Gugh!' he growled, 'gurrr!' And the more he tried to speak, the more the pain grew, and grew, until it seemed his face would split, until it seemed his skull would fly apart—

'Easy.' A scarred face swam into view above. Ninefingers. Jezal grabbed at him, wildly, and the Northman caught his hand in his own big paw and squeezed it tight. 'Easy, now, and listen to me. It hurts, yes. Seems like more than you can take, but it isn't. You think you're going to die, but you won't. Listen to me, because I've been there, and I know. Each minute. Each hour. Each day, it gets better.'

He felt Ninefingers' other hand on his shoulder, pushing him gently back down into the cart. 'All you got to do is lie there, and it gets better. You understand? You got the light duty, you lucky bastard.'

Jezal let his limbs go heavy. All he had to do was lie there. He squeezed the big hand and the hand squeezed back. The pain seemed less. Awful still, but within his control. His breath slowed. His eyes closed.

The wind cut over the cold plain, plucking at the short grass, tugging at Jezal's tattered coat, at his greasy hair, at his dirty bandages, but he ignored it. What could he do about the wind? What could he do about anything?

He sat, his back against the wheel of the cart, and stared down wide-eyed at his leg. A broken length of spear shaft had been strapped to either side, wrapped round and round with strips of torn-up cloth, held firmly and painfully straight. His arm was no better, sandwiched between two slats from a shield and bound tightly across his chest, the white hand dangling, fingers numb and useless as sausages.

Pitiful, improvised efforts at medicine that Jezal could never see working. They might almost have seemed amusing, had he not been the unfortunate patient. He would surely never recover. He was broken, shattered, ruined. Would he be now a cripple of the kind he avoided on the street corners of Adua? War-wounded, ragged and dirty, shoving their stumps in the faces of passers-by, holding their crabbing palms out for coppers, uncomfortable reminders that there was a dark side to soldiering that one would rather not think about?

Would he be now a cripple like . . . and a horrible coldness crept over him . . . like Sand dan Glokta? He tried to shift his leg and groaned at the pain. Would he walk for the rest of his life with a stick? A shambling horror, shunned and avoided? A salutary lesson, pointed at and whispered of? There goes Jezal dan Luthar! He used to be a promising man, a handsome man, he won a Contest and the crowd cheered for him! Who would believe it? What a waste, what a shame, here he comes, let's move on . . .

And that was before he even thought about what his face might look like. He tried to move his tongue and the stab of agony made him grimace, but he could tell there was a terribly unfamiliar geography to the inside of his mouth. It felt slanted, twisted, nothing fitted together as it used to. There was a gap in his teeth that felt a mile wide. His lips tingled unpleasantly under the bandages. Torn, battered, ripped open. He was a monster.

A shadow fell across Jezal's face and he squinted up into the sun. Ninefingers stood over him, a water-skin hanging from one big fist. 'Water,' he grunted. Jezal shook his head but the Northman squatted down, pulled the stopper from the skin and held it out regardless. 'Got to drink. Keep it clean.'

Jezal snatched the skin bad-temperedly from him, lifted it gingerly to the better side of his mouth and tried to tilt it. It hung bloated and baggy. He struggled for a moment, before realising there was no way of drinking with only one good hand. He fell back, eyes closed, snorting through his nose. He almost ground his teeth with frustration, but quickly thought better of it.

'Here.' He felt a hand slide behind his neck and firmly lift his head.

'Gugh!' he grunted furiously, with half a mind to struggle, but in the end he allowed his body to sag, and submitted to the ignominy of being handled like a baby. What was the point, after all, in pretending he was anything other than utterly helpless? Sour, lukewarm water seeped into his mouth, and he tried to force it down. It was like swallowing broken glass. He coughed and spat the rest out. Or he tried to spit and found the pain far too great. He had to lean forward and let it dribble from his face, most of it running down his neck and into the filthy collar of his shirt. He sat back heavily with a moan and pushed the skin away with his good hand.

Ninefingers shrugged. 'Alright, but you'll have to try again later. Got to keep drinking. You remember what happened?' Jezal shook his head.

'There was a fight. Me and sunshine there,' and he nodded over at Ferro, who scowled back, 'handled most of 'em, but it seems three got around us. You dealt with two, and you did well with that, but you missed one, and he hit you in the mouth with a mace.' He gestured at Jezal's bandaged face. 'Hit you hard, and you're familiar with the outcome. Then you fell, and I'm guessing he hit you when you were down, which is how you got the arm and the leg broke. Could have been a lot worse. If I was you I'd be thanking the dead that Quai was there.'

Jezal blinked over at the apprentice. What did he have to do with anything? But Ninefingers was already answering his question.

'Came up and knocked him on the head with a pan. Well, I say knocked. Smashed his skull to mush, didn't you?' He grinned over at the apprentice, who sat staring out across the plain. 'He hits hard for a thin man, our boy, eh? Shame about that pan, though.'

Quai shrugged as though he stove a man's head in most mornings. Jezal supposed he should be thanking the sickly fool for saving his life, but he didn't feel so very saved. Instead he tried to form the sounds as clearly as he could without hurting himself, making little more than a whisper. 'Ow bad ith it?'

'I've had worse.' Small comfort indeed. 'You'll get through alright. You're young. Arm and leg'll mend quick.' Meaning, Jezal inferred, that his face would not. 'Always tough taking a wound, and never tougher than the first. I cried like a baby at every one of these,' and Ninefingers waved a hand at his battered face. 'Most everyone cries, and that's a fact. If it's any help.'

It was not. 'Ow bad?'

Ninefingers scratched at the thick stubble on the side of his face. 'Your jaw's broke, you lost some teeth, you got your mouth ripped, but we stitched you up pretty good.' Jezal swallowed, hardly able to think. His worst fears seemed to be confirmed. 'It's a hard wound you got there, and a nasty place to get it. In your mouth so you can't eat, can't drink, can't hardly talk without pain. Can't kiss either of course, though that shouldn't be a problem out here, eh?' The Northman grinned but Jezal was in no mood to join him. 'A bad wound, alright. A naming wound they'd call it, where I come from.'

'A wha?' muttered Jezal, immediately regretting it as pain licked at his jaw.

'A naming wound, you know,' and Ninefingers waggled the stump of his finger. 'A wound you could get named after. They'd probably call you Brokejaw, or Bentface or Lackteeth or something.' He smiled again, but Jezal had left his sense of humour on the hill among the stones, along with his broken teeth. He could feel tears stinging at his eyes. He wanted to cry, but that made his mouth stretch, the stitches tug at his bloated lips under the bandages.

Ninefingers made a further effort. 'You got to look at the bright side. It ain't likely to kill you now. If the rot was going to get into it, I reckon it would've already.' Jezal gawped, horrified, eyes going wider and wider as the implications of that last utterance sank in. His jaw would surely have dropped, had it not been shattered and bound tightly to his face. Wasn't *likely* to kill him? The possibility of the wound going bad had never even occurred. Rot? In his *mouth*?

'I'm not helping, am I?' muttered Logen.

Jezal covered his eyes with his one good hand and tried to weep without hurting himself, silent sobs making his shoulders shake.

They had stopped on the shore of a wide lake. Choppy grey water under a dark sky, heavy with bruises. Brooding water, brooding sky, all seeming full of secrets, full of threats. Sullen waves slapped at the cold shingle. Sullen birds croaked to one another above the water. Sullen pain pulsed through every corner of Jezal's body, and would not stop.

Ferro squatted down in front of him, frowning, as always, cutting the bandages away while Bayaz stood behind her, looking down. The First of the Magi had woken from his torpor, it seemed. He had given no explanation of what had caused it, or why he had so suddenly recovered, but he still looked ill. Older than ever, and a lot bonier, his eyes sunken, his skin looking somehow thin, pale, almost transparent. But Jezal had no sympathy to spare, especially not for the architect of this disaster.

'Where are we?' he muttered, through the twinges. It was less painful to talk than it had been, but he still had to speak quietly, carefully, the words thick and stumbling like some village halfwit's.

Bayaz nodded over his shoulder towards the great expanse of water. 'This is the first of the three lakes. We are well on the way to Aulcus. More than half of our journey is behind us, I would say.'

Jezal swallowed. Halfway was hardly the greatest reassurance he could have asked for. 'How long was—'

'I can't work with you flapping your lips, fool,' hissed Ferro. 'Do I leave you like this, or do you shut up?'

Jezal shut up. She peeled the dressing carefully from his face, peered down at the brown blood on the cloth, sniffed it, wrinkled her nose and tossed it away, then stared angrily at his mouth for a moment. He swallowed, watching her dark face for any sign of what she might be thinking. He would have given his teeth for a mirror at that moment, if he had still had a full set. 'How bad is it?' he muttered at her, tasting blood on his tongue.

She scowled up at him. 'You've confused me with someone who cares.'

A sob coughed up from his throat. Tears stung at his eyes, he had to look away and blink to stop himself crying. He was a pitiable specimen, alright. A brave son of the Union, a bold officer of the King's Own, a winner of the Contest, no less, and he could scarcely keep from weeping.

'Hold this,' snapped Ferro's voice.

'Uh,' he whispered, trying to press the sobs down into his chest and stop them cracking his voice. He held one end of the fresh bandage against his face while she wrapped it round his head and under his jaw, round and round, holding his mouth near shut.

'You'll live.'

'Is that supposed to be a comfort?' he mumbled.

She shrugged as she turned away. 'There are plenty who don't.'

Jezal almost envied them as he watched her stalk off through the waving grass. How he wished Ardee was here. He remembered the last sight of her, looking up at him in the soft rain with that crooked smile. She would never have left him like this, helpless and in pain. She would have spoken soft words, and touched his face, and looked at him with her dark eyes, and kissed him gently, and . . . sentimental shit. Probably she had found some other idiot to tease, and confuse, and make miserable, and had never paid him so much as a second thought. He tortured himself with the thought of her laughing at some other man's jokes, smiling into some other man's face, kissing some other man's mouth. She would never want him now, that was sure. No one would want him. He felt his lip trembling again, his eyes tingling.

'All the great heroes of old, you know – the great kings, the great generals – they all faced adversity from time to time.' Jezal looked up. He had almost forgotten that Bayaz was there. 'Suffering is what gives a man strength, my boy, just as the steel most hammered turns out the hardest.'

The old man winced as he squatted down beside Jezal. 'Anyone can face ease and success with confidence. It is the way we face trouble and misfortune that defines us. Self-pity goes with selfishness, and there is nothing more to be deplored in a leader than that. Selfishness belongs to children, and to halfwits. A great leader puts others before himself. You would be surprised how acting so makes it easier to bear ones own troubles. In order to act like a king, one need only treat everyone else like one.' And he placed a hand on Jezal's shoulder. Perhaps it was supposed to be a fatherly and reassuring touch, but he could feel it trembling through his shirt. Bayaz let it rest there for a moment as though he had not the strength to move it, then pushed himself slowly up, stretched his legs, and shuffled off.

Jezal stared vacantly after him. A few weeks ago he would have been left fuming silently by such a lecture. Now he sat limp and absorbed it meekly. He hardly knew who he was any more. It was difficult to maintain any sense of superiority in the face of his utter dependence on other people. And people of whom, until recently, he had held such a very low opinion. He was no longer under any illusions. Without Ferro's savage doctoring, and Ninefingers' clumsy nursing, he would most likely have been dead.

The Northman was walking over, boots crunching in the shingle. Time to go back in the cart. Time for more squeaking and jolting. Time for more pain. Jezal gave a long, ragged, self-pitying sigh, but stopped himself halfway through. Self-pity was for children and halfwits.

'Alright, you know the drill.' Jezal leaned forward and Ninefingers hooked his arm behind his back, the other under his knees, lifted him up over the side of the cart without even breathing hard and dumped him unceremoniously among the supplies. Jezal caught his big, dirty, three-fingered hand as he was moving away, and the Northman turned to look at him, one heavy brow lifted. Jezal swallowed. 'Thank you,' he muttered.

'What, for this?'

'For everything.'

Ninefingers looked at him for a long moment, then shrugged. 'Nothing to it. You treat folk the way you'd want to be treated, and you can't go far wrong. That's what my father told me. Forgot that advice, for a long time, and I done things I can never make up for.' He gave a long sigh. 'Still, it doesn't hurt to try. My experience? You get what you give, in the end.'

Jezal blinked at Ninefingers' broad back as he walked over to his horse. You treat folk the way you'd want to be treated. Could Jezal honestly say that he had ever done that much? He thought about it as the cart set off, axles shrieking, carelessly at first, and then with deepening worry.

He had bullied his juniors, pandered to his seniors. He had often screwed money from friends who could not afford it, had taken advantage of girls, then brushed them off. He had never once thanked his friend West for any of his help, and would happily have bedded his sister behind his back if she had let him. He realised, with increasing horror, that he could scarcely think of a single selfless thing that he had ever done.

He shifted uncomfortably against the sacks of fodder in the cart. You get what you give, in the long run, and manners cost nothing. From now on, he would think of others first. He would treat everyone as if they were his equal. But later, of course. There would be plenty of time to be a better man when he could eat again. He touched one hand to the bandages on his face, scratched absently at them then had to stop himself. Bayaz was riding just behind the cart, looking out across the water.

'You saw it?' Jezal muttered at him.

'Saw what?'

'This.' He jabbed a finger at his face.

'Ah, that. Yes, I saw it.'

'How bad is it?'

Bayaz cocked his head on one side. 'Do you know? All in all, I believe I like it.'

'You like it?'

'Not now, perhaps, but the stitches will come out, the swelling will go down, the bruises will fade, the scabs will heal and drop away. I would guess your jaw will never quite regain its shape, and your teeth, of course, will not grow back, but what you lose in boyish charm you will gain, I have no doubt, in a certain danger, a flair, a rugged mystery. People respect a man who has seen action, and your appearance will be very far from ruined. I daresay girls could still be persuaded to swoon for you, if you were to do anything worth swooning over.' He nodded thoughtfully. 'Yes. All in all, I think it will serve.'

'Serve?' muttered Jezal, one hand pressed against his bandages. 'Serve what?'

But Bayaz' mind had wandered off. 'Harod the Great had a scar, you know, across his cheek, and it never did him any harm. You don't see it on the statues, of course, but people respected him the more for it, in life. Truly a great man, Harod. He had a shining reputation for being fair and trustworthy, and indeed he often was. But he knew how not to be, when the situation demanded it.' The Magus chuckled to himself. 'Did I tell you of the time he invited his two greatest enemies to negotiate with him? He had them feuding one with the other before the day was out, and later they destroyed each other's armies in battle, leaving him to claim victory over both without striking a blow. He knew, you see, that Ardlic had a beautiful wife . . .'

Jezal lay back in the cart. Bayaz had, in fact, told him that story before, but there seemed no purpose in saying so. He was actually enjoying hearing it for a second time, and it was hardly as though there was anything better for him to do. There was something calming in the repetitive droning of the old man's deep voice, especially now the sun was breaking through the clouds. His mouth was barely even hurting, if he kept it still.

So Jezal lay back against a sack of straw, head turned to the side, rocking gently with the movement of the cart, and watched the land slide by. Watched the wind in the grass. Watched the sun on the water.

One Step at a Time

West gritted his teeth as he dragged himself up the freezing slope. His fingers were numb, and weak, and trembling from clawing at the chill earth, the icy tree roots, the freezing snow for handholds. His lips were cracked, his nose was endlessly running, the rims of his nostrils were horribly sore. The very air cut into his throat and nipped at his lungs, smoked back out in tickling wheezes. He wondered if giving his coat to Ladisla had been the worst decision of his life. He decided it probably had been. Except for saving the selfish bastard in the first place, of course.

Even when he had been training for the Contest, five hours a day, he had never imagined that he could be so tired. Next to Threetrees, Lord Marshal Varuz seemed an almost laughably soft taskmaster. West was shaken awake before dawn every morning and scarcely allowed to rest until after the last light faded. The Northmen were machines, every one of them. Men carved from wood who never got tired, who felt no pain. Every one of West's muscles ached from their merciless pace. He was covered in bruises and scratches from a hundred falls and scrambles. His feet were raw and blistered in his wet boots. Then there was the familiar pulsing in the head, throbbing away to the rhythm of his laboured heartbeat, mingling unpleasantly with the burning of the wound on his scalp.

The cold, the pain, and the fatigue were bad enough, but still worse was the overwhelming sense of shame, and guilt, and failure that crushed him down with every step. He had been sent with Ladisla to make sure there were no disasters. The result had been a disaster on a scale almost incomprehensible. An entire division massacred. How many children without fathers? How many wives without husbands? How many parents without sons? If only he could have done more, he told himself for the thousandth time, bunching his bloodless hands into fists. If only he could have convinced the Prince to stay behind the river, all those men might not be dead. So many dead. He hardly knew whether to pity or envy them.

'One step at a time,' he muttered to himself as he clambered up the slope. That was the only way to look at it. If you clenched your teeth hard enough, and took enough strides, you could get anywhere. One painful, weary, freezing, guilty step at a time. What else could you do?

No sooner had they finally made it to the top of the hill than Prince Ladisla flung himself down against the roots of a tree, as he did at least once an hour. 'Colonel West, please!' He gasped for air, breath steaming round his puffy face. He had two lines of glistening snot on his pale top lip, just like a toddler. 'I can go no further! Tell them . . . tell them to stop, for pity's sake!'

West cursed under his breath. The Northmen were annoyed enough as it was, and making less and less effort to disguise the fact, but, like it or not, Ladisla was still his commander. Not to mention the heir to the throne. West could hardly order him to get up. 'Threetrees!' he wheezed.

The old warrior frowned over his shoulder. 'You better not be asking me to stop, lad.'

'We have to.'

'By the dead! Again? You Southerners got no bones in you at all! No wonder Bethod gave you such a kicking. If you bastards don't learn to march he'll be giving you another, I can tell you that!'

'Please. Just for a moment.'

Threetrees glared down at the sprawling Prince and shook his head with disgust. 'Alright, then. You can sit a minute, if that'll get you moving the quicker, but don't get used to it, you hear? We've not covered half the ground we need to today, if we're to keep ahead of Bethod.' And he stalked off to shout at the Dogman.

West sank down onto his haunches, working his numb toes, cupping his icy hands and blowing into them. He wanted to sprawl out like Ladisla, but he knew from harsh experience that if he stopped moving, starting up again would be all the more painful. Pike and his daughter stood over them, scarcely even too far out of breath. It was harsh proof, if any were really needed, that working metal in a penal colony was better preparation for slogging across brutal country than a life of uninterrupted ease.

Ladisla seemed to guess what he was thinking. 'You've no idea how hard this is for me!' he blurted.

'No, of course!' snapped West, his patience worn down to a stub. 'You've got the extra weight of my coat to carry!'

The Prince blinked, then looked down at the wet ground, his jaw muscles working silently. 'You're right. I'm sorry. I realise I owe you my life, of course. Not used to this sort of thing, you see. Not used to it at all.' He plucked at the frayed and filthy lapels of the coat and gave a sorry chuckle. 'My mother always told me that a man should be well presented under all circumstances. I wonder what she'd make of this.' West noticed he didn't offer to give it back, though.

Ladisla hunched his shoulders. 'I suppose I must shoulder a portion of the blame for this whole business.' A portion? West would have liked to serve him a portion of his boot. 'I should have listened to you, Colonel. I knew it all along. Caution is the best policy in war, eh? That's always been my motto. Let that fool Smund talk me into rashness. He always was an idiot!'

'Lord Smund gave his life,' muttered West.

'Shame he didn't give it a day earlier, we might not be in this fix!' The Prince's lip quivered slightly. 'What do you think they'll say about this back home, eh, West? What do you think they'll say about me now?'

'I've no idea, your Highness.' It could hardly be any worse than what they said already. West tried to squash his anger and put himself in Ladisla's position. He was so utterly unprepared for the hardship of this march, so completely without resources, so entirely dependent on others for everything. A man who had never had to make a decision more important than which hat to wear, who now had to come to terms with his responsibility for thousands of deaths. Small wonder he had no idea how to go about it.

'If only they hadn't run.' Ladisla clenched his fist and thumped petulantly at a tree root. 'Why didn't they stand and fight, the cowardly bastards? Why didn't they fight?'

West closed his eyes, did his best to ignore the cold, and the hunger, and the pain, and to push away the fury in his chest. This was always the way of it. Just when Ladisla was finally starting to arouse some sympathy, he would let fall some loathsome utterance which brought West's distaste for the man flooding back. 'I couldn't possibly say, your Highness,' he managed to squeeze through his gritted teeth.

'Right,' grumbled Threetrees, 'that's your lot! On your feet again, and no excuses!'

'Not up again already is it, Colonel?'

'I'm afraid so.'

The Prince sighed and dragged himself wincing to his feet. 'I've no notion of how they can keep this up, West.'

'One stride at a time, your Highness.'

'Of course,' muttered Ladisla, starting to stumble off through the trees after the two convicts. 'One stride at a time.'

West worked his aching ankles for a moment and then bent down to follow, when he felt a shadow fall across him. He looked up to see that Black Dow had stepped into his path, blocking the way with one heavy shoulder, his snarling face no more than a foot away. He nodded towards the Prince's slow moving back. 'You want me to kill him?' he growled in Northern.

'If you touch any one of them!' West had spat out the words before he had any idea of how to finish. 'I'll . . .'

'Yes?'

'I'll kill you.' What else could he say? He felt like a child making ludicrous threats in a schoolyard. An extremely cold and dangerous schoolyard, and to a boy twice his size.

But Dow only grinned. 'That's a big temper you got on you for a skinny man. A lot of killing we're talking about, all of a sudden. You sure you got the bones for it?'

West tried to look as big as he could, which wasn't easy standing down a slope and hunched over with exhaustion. You have to show no fear, if you're to calm a dangerous situation, however much you might be feeling. 'Why don't you try me?' His voice sounded pitifully weak, even in his own ear.

'I might do that.'

'Let me know when it's time. I'd hate to miss it.'

'Oh, don't worry about that,' whispered Dow, turning his head and spitting on the ground. 'You'll know it's time when you wake up with your throat cut.' And he sauntered off up the muddy slope, slow enough to show he wasn't scared. West wished that he could have said the same. His heart was pounding as he pushed on between the trees after the others. He trudged doggedly past Ladisla and caught up to Cathil, falling into step beside her.

'You alright?' he asked.

'I've been worse.' She looked him up and down. 'How about you?'

West suddenly realised what a state he must look. He had an old sack with holes cut in it for his arms pulled over his filthy uniform, his belt buckled tight over the top with the heavy sword pushed through it and knocking against his leg. There was an itchy growth of half beard across his rattling jaw, and he guessed that his face must have been a mixture of angry pink and corpse grey. He wedged his hands under his armpits and gave a sad grin. 'Cold.'

'You look it. Should have kept your coat, maybe.'

He had to nod at that. He peered through the branches of the pines at Dow's back and cleared his throat. 'None of them have been . . . bothering you, have they?'

'Bothering me?'

'Well, you know,' he said awkwardly, 'a woman in amongst all these men, they're not used to it. The way that man Dow stares at you. I don't—'

'That's very noble of you, Colonel, but I wouldn't worry about them. I doubt they'll do anything more than stare, and I've dealt with worse than that.'

'Worse than him?'

'First camp I was in, the commandant took a liking to me. Still had the glow of a good free life on my skin, I suppose. He starved me to get what he wanted. Five days with no food.'

West winced. 'And that was long enough to make him give up?'

241

'They don't give up. Five days was all I could stand. You do what you have to.'

'You mean . . .'

'What you have to.' She shrugged. 'I'm not proud, but I'm not ashamed either. Pride and shame, neither one will feed you. The only thing I regret is those five days of hunger, five days when I could have eaten well. You do what you have to. I don't care who you are. Once you start starving . . .' She shrugged again.

'What about your father?'

'Pike?' She looked up at the burnt-faced convict ahead of them. 'He's a good man, but he's no relative of mine. I've no idea what became of my real family. Split up all over Angland probably, if they're still alive.'

'So he's—'

'Sometimes, if you pretend you're family, people act differently. We've helped each other out. If it wasn't for Pike, I suppose I'd still be hammering metal in the camp.'

'Instead of which you're enjoying this wonderful outing.'

'Huh. You make do with what you're given.' She put her head down and quickened her pace, stalking off through the trees.

West watched her go. She had some bones to her, the Northmen would have said. Ladisla could have learned a thing or two from her tight-lipped determination. West looked over his shoulder at the Prince, stumbling daintily through the mud with a petulant frown on his face. He blew out a smoky sigh. It seemed that it was far too late for Ladisla to learn anything.

A miserable meal of a chunk of old bread and a cup of cold stew. Threetrees wouldn't let them have a fire, for all of Ladisla's begging. Too much risk of being seen. So they sat and spoke quietly in the gathering gloom, a little way from the Northmen. Talking was good, if only to keep one's mind from the cold, and the aches, and the discomfort. If only to stop one's teeth from chattering.

'You said you fought in Kanta, eh, Pike? In the war?'

'That's right. I was a Sergeant there.' Pike nodded slowly, his eyes glittering in the pink mess of his face. 'Hard to believe we were always too hot, eh?'

West gave a sad gurgle. The closest thing to a laugh that he could manage. 'Which was your unit?'

'I was in the first regiment of the King's Own cavalry, under Colonel Glokta.'

'But, that was my regiment!'

'I know.'

'I don't remember you.'

Pike's burns shifted in a way that West thought might have been a smile.

'I looked different, back then. I remember you, though. Lieutenant West. The men liked you. Good man to go to with a problem.'

West swallowed. He wasn't much for fixing problems now. Only for making them. 'So how did you end up in the camp?'

Pike and Cathil exchanged glances. 'In general, among the convicts, you don't ask.'

'Oh.' West looked down, rubbed his hands together. 'I'm sorry. I didn't mean to offend you.'

'No offence.' Pike sniffed, and rubbed at the side of his melted nose. 'I made some mistakes. Let's leave it at that. You got a family waiting for you?'

West winced, folded his arms tight across his chest. 'I have a sister, back home in Adua. She's . . . complicated.' He thought it best to end there. 'You?'

'I had a wife. When I was sent here, she chose to stay behind. I used to hate her for it, but you know what? I can't say I wouldn't have done the same.'

Ladisla emerged from the trees, wiping his hands on the hem of West's coat. 'That's better! Must've been that damn meat this morning.' He sat down between West and Cathil and she scowled as if someone had dropped a shovelful of shit next to her. It was safe to say the two of them were not getting on. 'What were we speaking of?'

West winced. 'Pike was just mentioning his wife—'

'Oh? You know, of course, that I am engaged to be married, to the Princess Terez, daughter of Grand Duke Orso of Talins. She is a famous beauty . . .' Ladisla trailed off, frowning round at the shadowy trees, as if even he was dimly aware of how bizarre talk of such matters seemed in the wilds of Angland. 'Though I am beginning to suspect that she is less than entirely delighted with the match.'

'One can't imagine why,' murmured Cathil, at least the tenth jibe of the evening.

'I am the heir to the throne!' snapped the Prince, 'and will one day be your king! It would not hurt anyone for you to treat me with a measure of respect!'

She laughed in his face. 'I've no country and no king, and certainly no respect for you.'

Ladisla gasped with indignation. 'I will not be spoken to like—'

Black Dow loomed up over them from nowhere. 'Shut his fucking mouth!' he snarled in Northern, stabbing at the air with one thick finger. 'Bethod might have ears anywhere! Stop his tongue flapping or it's coming out!' and he melted away into the shadows.

'He would like us to be quiet, your Highness,' translated West in a whisper.

The Prince swallowed. 'So I gather.' He and Cathil hunched their shoulders and glared at each other in silence.

West lay on his back on the hard ground, the canvas creaking just above his face, watching the snow fall gently down beyond the black lumps of his boots. Cathil was pressed up against him on one side, the Dogman on the other. The rest of the band were all around, squeezed in tight together under a great smelly blanket. All except for Dow, who was out there taking watch. Cold like this was an amazing thing for making people familiar with each other.

There was a rumbling snore coming from the far end of the group. Threetrees or Tul, probably. The Dogman tended to twitch a lot in his sleep, jolting and stretching and twittering meaningless sounds. Ladisla's breath wheezed out on the right, chesty sounding and weak. All sleeping, more or less, as soon as they put their heads down.

But West could not sleep. He was too busy thinking about all the hardships, and the defeats, and the terrible dangers they were in. And not only them. Marshal Burr might be out there in the forests of Angland somewhere, hurrying south to the rescue, not knowing that he was falling into a trap. Not knowing that Bethod was expecting him.

The situation was dire but, against all reason, West's heart felt light. The fact was, out here, things were simple. There were no daily battles to be fought, no prejudices to overcome, no need to think more than an hour ahead. He felt free for the first time in months.

He winced and stretched his aching legs, felt Cathil shift in her sleep beside him, her head falling against his shoulder, her cheek pressing into his dirty uniform. He could feel the warmth of her breath on his face, the warmth of her body through their clothes. A pleasant warmth. The effect was only slightly spoiled by the stink of sweat and wet earth, and the Dogman squeaking and muttering in his other ear. West closed his eyes, the faintest grin on his face. Perhaps things could still be put right. Perhaps he still had the chance to be a hero. If he could just get Ladisla back alive to Lord Marshal Burr.

The Rest is Wasted Breath

Ferro rode, and watched the land. Still they followed the dark water, still the wind blew cold through her clothes, still the looming sky was heavy with chaos, and yet the country was changing. Where it had been flat as a table, now it was full of rises and sudden, hidden troughs. Land that men could hide in, and she did not like that thought. Not that she was fearful, for Ferro Maljinn feared no man. But she had to look and listen all the more carefully, for signs that anyone had passed, for signs that anyone was waiting.

That was simple good sense.

The grass had changed as well. She had grown used to it all around, tall and waving in the wind, but here it was short, and dry, and withered pale like straw. It was getting shorter, too, as they went further. Today there were bald patches scattered round. Bare earth, where nothing grew. Empty earth, like the dust of the Badlands.

Dead earth.

And dead for no reason that she could see. She frowned out across the crinkled plain, out towards far distant hills, a faint and ragged line above the horizon. Nothing moved in all that vast space. Nothing but them and the impatient clouds. And one bird, hovering high, high up, almost still on the air, long feathers on its dark wing tips fluttering.

'First bird I seen in two days,' grunted Ninefingers, peering up at it suspiciously.

'Huh,' she grunted. 'The birds have more sense than us. What are we doing here?'

'Got nowhere better to be.'

Ferro had better places to be. Anywhere there were Gurkish to kill. 'Speak for yourself.'

'What? You got a crowd of friends back in the Badlands, all asking after you? Where did Ferro get to? The laughs all dried up since she went away.' And he snorted as if he had said something funny.

Ferro did not see what. 'We can't all be as well-loved as you, pink.' She gave a snort of her own. 'I'm sure they will have a feast ready for you when you get back to the North.'

'Oh, there'll be a feast alright. Just as soon as they've hung me.'

She thought about that, for a minute, looking sideways at him from the corners of her eyes. Looking without turning her head, so if he glanced over she could flick her eyes away and pretend she never was looking at all. She had to admit, now that she was getting used to him, the big pink was not so bad. They had fought together, more than once, and he had always done his share. They had agreed to bury each other, if need be, and she trusted him to do it. Strange-looking, strange-sounding, but she had yet to hear him say he would do a thing, and see him not do it, which made him one of the better men she had known. Best not to tell him that, of course, or give away the slightest sign that she thought it.

That would be when he let her down.

'You got no one, then?' she asked.

'No one but enemies.'

'Why aren't you fighting them?'

'Fighting? It's got me everything I have.' And he held his big empty hands up to show her. 'Nothing but an evil reputation and an awful lot of men with a burning need to kill me. Fighting? Hah! The better you are at it, the worse off it leaves you. I've settled some scores, and that can feel grand, but the feeling don't last long. Vengeance won't keep you warm nights, and that's a fact. Overrated. Won't do on its own. You need something else.'

Ferro shook her head. 'You expect too much out of life, pink.'

He grinned. 'And here was me thinking you expect too little.'

'Expect nothing and you won't be disappointed.'

'Expect nothing and you'll get nothing.'

Ferro scowled at him. That was the thing about talk. Somehow it always took her where she did not want to go. Lack of practice, maybe. She jerked her reins, and nudged her horse off with her heels, away from Ninefingers and the others, out to the side, on her own.

Silence, then. Silence was dull, but it was honest.

She frowned across at Luthar, sitting up in the cart, and he grinned back like an idiot, as wide as he could with bandages over half his face. He seemed different somehow, and she did not like it. Last time she had changed his dressings he had thanked her, and that seemed odd. Ferro did not like thanks. They usually hid something. It niggled at her to have done something that deserved a thanking. Helping others led to friendships. Friendships led to disappointment, at best.

At worst, betrayal.

Luthar was saying something to Ninefingers now, talking up to him from down in the cart. The Northman tipped back his head and roared with stupid laughter, making his horse startle and nearly dump him to the ground. Bayaz swayed contentedly in his saddle, happy creases round the corners of his eyes as he watched Ninefingers fumble with his reins. Ferro scowled off across the plain.

She had much preferred it when no one had liked each other. That was comfortable, and familiar. That she understood. Trust, and comradeship, and good humour, these things were so far in the past for her that they were almost unknown.

And who likes the unknown?

Ferro had seen a lot of dead men. She had made more than her share. She had buried a good few with her own hands. Death was her trade and her pastime. But she had never seen near so many corpses all at once. The sickly grass was scattered with them. She slid down from her saddle and walked among the bodies. There was nothing to tell who fought who, or one side from the other.

The dead all look alike.

Especially once they have been picked over – their armour, and their weapons, and half their clothes taken. They lay heaped thick and tangled in one spot, in the long shadow of a broken pillar. An ancient-looking thing, split and shattered, crumbling stone sprouting with withered grass and spotted with lichen. A big black bird sat on top of it, wings folded, peering at Ferro with beady, unblinking eyes as she came close.

The corpse of a huge man was lying half-propped against the battered stone below, a broken staff still gripped in his lifeless hand, dark blood and dark dirt crusted under the nails. Most likely the staff had held a flag, Ferro thought. Soldiers seemed to care a great deal for flags. She had never understood that. You could not kill a man with one. You could not protect yourself with one. And yet men would die for flags.

'Foolishness,' she muttered, frowning up at the big bird on the pillar.

'A massacre,' said Ninefingers.

Bayaz grunted and rubbed his chin. 'But of who, by whom?'

Ferro could see Luthar's swollen face peering wide-eyed and worried over the side of the cart. Quai was just in front of him on the driver's seat, the reins dangling loose in his hands, his face expressionless as he looked down at the corpses.

Ferro turned over one of the bodies and sniffed at it. Pale skin, dark lips, no smell yet. 'It did not happen long ago. Two days, maybe?'

'But no flies?' Ninefingers frowned at the bodies. A few birds were perched on them, watching. 'Just birds. And they're not eating. Strange.'

'Not really, friend!' Ferro jerked her head up. A man was striding quickly towards them across the battlefield, a tall pink in a ragged coat, a gnarled length of wood in one hand. He had an unkempt head of greasy hair, a long, matted beard. His eyes bulged bright and wild in a face carved with deep lines. Ferro stared at him, not sure how he could have come so close without her noticing.

The birds rose up from the bodies at the sound of his voice, but they did not scatter from him. They flew towards him, some settling on his shoulders, some flapping about his head and round him in wide circles. Ferro reached for her bow, snatching at an arrow, but Bayaz held out his arm. 'No.'

'Do you see this?' The tall pink pointed at the broken pillar, and the bird flapped from it and across onto his outstretched finger. 'A hundred-mile column! One hundred miles to Aulcus!' He dropped his arm and the bird hopped onto his shoulder, next to the others, and sat there, still and silent. 'You stand on the very borders of the dead land! No animals come here that are not made to come!'

'How now, brother?' called Bayaz, and Ferro shoved her arrow unhappily away. Another Magus. She might have guessed. Whenever you put two of these old fools together there were sure to be a lot of lips flapping, a lot of words made.

And that meant a lot of lies.

'The Great Bayaz!' shouted the new arrival as he came closer. 'The First of the Magi! I heard tell you were coming from the birds of the air, the fish of the water, the beasts of the earth, and now I see with my own eyes, and yet still I scarcely believe. Can it be? That those blessed feet should touch this bloody ground?'

He planted his staff on the earth, and as he did the big black bird scrambled from his shoulder and grasped the tip with its claws, flapping its wings until it was settled. Ferro took a cautious step back, putting one hand on her knife. She did not intend to be shat on by one of those things.

'Zacharus,' said Bayaz, swinging down stiffly from his saddle, although it seemed to Ferro he said the name with little joy. 'You look in good health, brother.'

'I look tired. I look tired, and dirty, and mad, for that is what I am. You are difficult to find, Bayaz. I have been searching all across the plain and back.'

'We have been keeping out of sight. Khalul's allies are seeking for us also.' Bayaz' eyes twitched over the carnage. 'Is this your work?'

'That of my charge, young Goltus. He is fierce as a lion, I tell you, and makes as fine an Emperor as the great men of old! He has captured his greatest rival, his brother Scario, and has shown him mercy.' Zacharus sniffed. 'Not my advice, but the young will have their way. These were the last of Scario's men. Those who would not surrender.' He flapped a careless hand at the corpses, and the birds on his shoulders flapped with him.

'Mercy only goes so far,' observed Bayaz.

'They would not run into the dead land, so here they made their stand, and here they died, in the shadow of the hundred-mile columns. Goltus took the standard of the Third Legion from them. The very standard that

Stolicus himself rode into battle under. A relic of the Old Time! Just as you and I are, brother.'

Bayaz did not seem impressed. 'A piece of old cloth. It did these fellows precious little good. Carrying a stretch of moth-food does not make a man Stolicus.'

'Perhaps not. The thing is much faded, truth be told. Its jewels were all torn out and sold long ago to buy weapons.'

'Jewels are a luxury in these days, but everyone needs weapons. Where is your young Emperor now?'

'Already on his way back eastwards with no time even to burn the dead. He is heading for Darmium, to lay siege to the city and hang this madman Cabrian from the walls. Then perhaps we can have peace.'

Bayaz gave a joyless snort. 'Do you even remember what it feels like, to have peace?'

'You might be surprised at what I remember.' And Zacharus' bulging eyes stared down at Bayaz. 'But how are matters in the wider world? How is Yulwei?'

'Watching, as always.'

'And what of our other brother, the shame of our family, the great Prophet Khalul?'

Bayaz' face grew hard. 'He grows in strength. He begins to move. He senses his moment has come.'

'And you mean to stop him, of course?'

'What else should I do?'

'Hmmm. Khalul was in the South, when last I heard, yet you journey westward. Have you lost your way, brother? There is nothing out here but the ruins of the past.'

'There is power in the past.'

'Power? Hah! You never change. Strange company, you ride with, Bayaz. Young Malacus Quai I know, of course. How goes it, teller of tales?' he called out to the apprentice. 'How goes it, talker? How does my brother treat you?'

Quai stayed hunched on his cart. 'Well enough.'

'Well enough? That's all? You have learned to stay silent, then, at least. How did you teach him that, Bayaz? That I never could make him learn.'

Bayaz frowned up at Quai. 'I hardly had to.'

'So. What did Juvens say? The best lessons one teaches oneself.' Zacharus turned his bulging eyes on Ferro, and the eyes of his birds turned with him, all as one. 'This is a strange one you have here.'

'She has the blood.'

'You still need one who can speak with the spirits.'

'He can.' Bayaz nodded his head at Ninefingers. The big pink had been fiddling with his saddle but now he looked up, bewildered.

'Him?' Zacharus frowned. Much anger, Ferro thought, but some sadness, and some fear. The birds on his shoulders, and his head, and the tip of his staff, stood tall and spread their wings, and flapped and squawked. 'Listen to me, brother, before it is too late. Give up this folly. I will stand with you against Khalul. I will stand with you and Yulwei. The three of us, together, as it was in the Old Time, as it was against the Maker. The Magi united. I will help you.'

There was a long silence, and hard lines spread out across Bayaz' face. 'You will help me? If only you had offered your help long ago, after the Maker fell, when I begged you for it. Then we might have torn up Khalul's madness before it put down roots. Now the whole South swarms with Eaters, making the world their playground, treating the solemn word of our master with open scorn! The three of us will not be enough, I think. What then? Will you lure Cawneil from her books? Will you find Leru, under whatever stone she has crawled beneath in all the wide Circle of the World? Will you bring Karnault back from across the wide ocean, or Anselmi and Brokentooth from the land of the dead? The Magi united, is it?' And Bayaz' lip curled into a sneer. 'That time is done, brother. That ship sailed, long ago, never to return, and we were not on it!'

'I see!' hissed Zacharus, red-streaked eyes bulging wider than ever. 'And if you find what you seek, what then? Do you truly suppose that you can control it? Do you dare to imagine that you can do what Glustrod, and Kanedias, and Juvens himself could not?'

'I am the wiser for their mistakes.'

'I hardly think so! You would punish one crime with a worse!'

Bayaz' thin lips and hollow cheeks turned sharper still. No sadness, no fear, but much anger of his own. 'This war was not of my making, *brother*! Did I break the Second Law? Did I make slaves of half the South for the sake of my vanity?'

'No, but we each had our part in it, and you more than most. Strange, how I remember things that you leave out. How you squabbled with Khalul. How Juvens determined to separate you. How you sought out the Maker, persuaded him to share his secrets.' Zacharus laughed, a harsh cackle, and his birds croaked and squawked along with him. 'I daresay he never intended to share his daughter with you, eh, Bayaz? The Maker's daughter? Tolomei? Is there room in your memory for her?'

Bayaz' eyes glittered cold. 'Perhaps the blame is mine,' he whispered. 'The solution shall be mine also—'

'Do you think Euz spoke the First Law on a whim? Do you think Juvens put this thing at the edge of the World because it was *safe*? It is . . . it is evil!'

'Evil?' Bayaz snorted his contempt. 'A word for children. A word ignorant use for those who disagree with them. I thought we grew out of such notions long centuries ago.'

'But the risks—'

'I am resolved.' And Bayaz' voice was iron, and well sharpened. 'I have thought for long years upon it. You have said your piece, Zacharus, but you have offered me no other choices. Try and stop me, if you must. Otherwise, stand aside.'

'Then nothing has changed.' The old man turned to look at Ferro, his creased face twitching, and the dark eyes of his birds looked with him. 'And what of you, devil-blood? Do you know what he would have you touch? Do you understand what he would have you carry? Do you have an inkling of the dangers?' A small bird hopped from his shoulder and started twittering round and round Ferro's head in circles. 'You would be better to run, and never to stop running! You all would!'

Ferro's lip curled. She slapped the bird out of the air, and it clattered to the ground, hopping and tweeting away between the corpses. The others squawked and hissed and clucked their anger, but she ignored them. 'You do not know me, old fool pink with a dirty beard. Do not pretend to understand me, or to know what I know, or what I have been offered. Why should I prefer the word of one old liar over another? Take your birds and keep your nose to your own business, then we will have no quarrel. The rest is wasted breath.'

Zacharus and his birds blinked. He frowned, opened his mouth, then shut it silently again as Ferro swung herself up into her saddle and jerked her horse round towards the west. She heard the sounds of the others following, hooves thumping, Quai cracking the reins of the cart, then Bayaz' voice. 'Listen to the birds of the air, the fish of the water, the beasts of the earth. Soon you will hear that Khalul has been finished, his Eaters turned to dust, the mistakes of the past buried, as they should have been, long ago.'

'I hope so, but I fear the news will be worse.' Ferro looked over her shoulder, and saw the two old men exchanging one more stare. 'The mistakes of the past are not so easily buried. I earnestly hope that you fail.'

'Look around you, old friend.' And the First of the Magi smiled as he clambered up into his saddle. 'None of your hopes ever come to anything.'

And so they rode away from the corpses in silence, past the broken hundred-mile column and into the dead land. Towards the ruins of the past. Towards Aulcus.

Under a darkening sky.

A Matter of Time

To Arch Lector Sult, head of his Majesty's Inquisition.

Your Eminence,

Six weeks now, we have held the Gurkish back. Each morning they brave our murderous fire to tip earth and stone into our ditch, each night we lower men from the walls to try and dig it out. In spite of all our efforts, they have finally succeeded in filling the channel in two places. Daily, now, scaling parties rush forward from the Gurkish lines and set their ladders, sometimes making it onto the walls themselves, only to be bloodily repulsed.

Meanwhile the bombardment by catapults continues, and several sections of the walls are dangerously weakened. They have been shored up, but it might not be long before the Gurkish have a practicable breach. Barricades have been raised on the inside to contain them should they make it through into the Lower City. Our defences are tested to the limit, but no man entertains a thought of surrender. We will fight on.

As always, your Eminence, I serve and obey.

Sand dan Glokta
Superior of Dagoska.

Glokta held his breath, licking at his gums as he watched the dust clouds settling across the roofs of the slums through his eye-glass. The last crashes and clatters of falling stones faded, and Dagoska, for that one moment, was strangely silent. *The world holds its breath.*

Then the distant screaming reached him on his balcony, thrust out from the wall of the Citadel, high above the city. A screaming he remembered well from battlefields both old and new. *And hardly happy memories. The Gurkish war cry. The enemy are coming.* Now, he knew, they were charging across the open ground before the walls, as they had done so many times these past weeks. *But this time they have a breach.*

He watched the tiny shapes of soldiers moving on the dust-coated walls and towers to either side of the gap. He moved his eye-glass down to take in the wide half-circle of barricades, the triple ranks of men squatting behind them, waiting for the Gurkish to come. Glokta frowned and worked his numb left foot inside his boot. *A meagre-seeming defence, indeed. But all we have.*

Now Gurkish soldiers began to pour through the yawning breach like black ants swarming from a nest; a crowd of jostling men, twinkling steel, waving banners, emerging from the clouds of brown dust, scrambling down the great heap of fallen masonry and straight into a furious hail of flatbow bolts. *First through the breach. An unenviable position.* The front ranks were mown down as they came on, tiny shapes falling and tumbling down the hill of rubble behind the walls. Many fell, but there were always more, pressing in over the bodies of their comrades, struggling forward over the mass of broken stones and shattered timbers, and into the city.

Now another cry floated up, and Glokta saw the defenders charge from behind their barricades. Union soldiers, mercenaries, Dagoskans, all hurled themselves towards the breach. At this distance it all seemed to move with absurd slowness. *A stream of oil and a stream of water dribbling towards one another.* They met, and it became impossible to tell one side from the other. A flowing mass, punctuated by glittering metal, rippling and surging like the sea, a colourful flag or two hanging limp above.

The cries and screams hung over the city, echoing, shifting with the breeze. The far off swell of pain and fury, the clatter and din of combat. Sometimes it sounded like a distant storm, incomprehensible. Sometimes a single cry or word would float to Glokta's ear with surprising clarity. It reminded him of the sound of the crowd at the Contest. *Except the blades are not blunted now. Both sides are in deadly earnest. How many already dead this morning, I wonder?* He turned to General Vissbruck, sweating beside him in his immaculate uniform.

'Have you ever fought in a melée like that, General? A straight fight, toe to toe, at push of pike, as they say?'

Vissbruck did not pause for a moment from squinting eagerly through his own eye-glass. 'No. I have not.'

'I wouldn't recommend it. I have only done it once and I am not keen to repeat the experience.' He shifted the handle of his cane in his sweaty palm. *Not that that's terribly likely now, of course.* 'I fought on horseback often enough. Charged small bodies of infantry, broke and pursued them. A noble business, cutting men down as they run, I earned all kinds of praise for it. I soon discovered a battle on foot is a different matter. The crush is so tight you can hardly take a breath, let alone perform acts of heroism. The heroes are the ones lucky enough to live through it.' He snorted with joyless laughter. 'I remember being pushed up against a Gurkish officer, as close to each other as lovers, neither one of us able to strike, or do anything but snarl at each other. Spear-points digging everywhere, at random. Men pushed onto the weapons of their own side, or crushed underfoot. More killed by mishap than design.' *The whole business is one giant mishap.*

'An ugly affair,' muttered Vissbruck, 'but it has to be done.'

'So it does. So it does.' Glokta could see a Gurkish standard waving around above the boiling throng, silk flapping, tattered and stained. Stones flung from the broken walls above began to crash down amongst them. Men pressed in helpless, shoulder to shoulder, unable to move. A great vat of boiling water was upended into their midst from high above. The Gurkish had lost all semblance of order as they came through the breach, and now the formless mass of men began to waver. The defenders pressed in on them from all sides, relentless, shoving with pike and shield, hacking with sword and axe, trampling the fallen under their boots.

'We're driving them back!' came Vissbruck's voice.

'Yes,' muttered Glokta, peering through his eye-glass at the desperate fighting. 'So it would seem.' *And my joy is limitless.*

The Gurkish assault had been surrounded and men were falling fast, stumbling back up the hill of rubble towards the breach. Gradually the survivors were driven out and down into the no-man's-land behind, flatbows on the walls firing into the mass of men as they fled, spreading panic and murder. The vague sound of the defenders cheering filtered up to them on the walls of the citadel.

One more assault defeated. Scores of Gurkish killed, but there are always more. If they break through the barricades, and into the Lower City, we are finished. They can keep coming as often as they like. We need only lose once, and the game is done.

'It would seem the day is ours. This one, at least.' Glokta limped to the corner of the balcony and peered southwards through his eye-glass, down into the bay and the Southern Sea beyond. There was nothing but calm water, glittering bright to the flat horizon. 'And still no sign of any Gurkish ships.'

Vissbruck cleared his throat. 'With the greatest of respect . . .' *Meaning none, I suppose.* 'The Gurkish have never been sailors. Is there any reason to suppose that they have ships now?'

Only that an old black wizard appeared in my chambers in the dead of night, and told me to watch out for some. 'Simply because we fail to see a thing, it does not mean it is not there. The Emperor has us on the rack as it is. Perhaps he keeps his fleet in reserve, waiting for a better time, refusing to show his whole hand until he needs to.'

'But with ships, he could blockade us, starve us out, get around our defences! He need not have squandered all those soldiers—'

'If the Emperor of Gurkhul has one thing in abundance, General, it is more soldiers. They have made a workable breach.' Glokta scanned along the walls until he came to the other weak spot. He could see the great cracks in the masonry on the inside, shored up with heavy beams, with heaped-up rubble, but still bowing inwards, more each day. 'And they will soon have another. They have filled the ditch in four places. Meanwhile our numbers dwindle, our morale falters. They don't need ships.'

'But we have them.' Glokta was surprised to find the General had stepped up close beside him and was speaking softly and urgently, looking earnestly into his eyes. *Like a man proposing marriage. Or treason. I wonder which we have here?* 'There is still time,' muttered Vissbruck, his eyes swivelling nervously towards the door and back. 'We control the bay. As long as we still hold the Lower City we hold the wharves. We can pull out the Union forces. The civilians at least. There are still some wives and children of officers left in the Citadel, a scattering of merchants and craftsmen who settled in the Upper City and are reluctant to leave. It could be done swiftly.'

Glokta frowned. *True, perhaps, but the Arch Lector's orders were otherwise. The civilians can make their own arrangements, if they so desire. The Union troops will not be going anywhere. Except onto their funeral pyres, of course.* But Vissbruck took his silence for encouragement. 'If you were to give me the word it could be done this very evening, and all away before—'

'And what will become of us all, General, when we step down onto Union soil? A tearful reunion with our masters in the Agriont? Some of us would soon be crying, I do not doubt. Or should we take the ships and sail to far-off Suljuk, do you suppose, to live long lives of ease and plenty?' Glokta slowly shook his head. 'It is a charming fantasy, but that's all it is. Our orders are to hold the city. There can be no surrender. No backing down. No sailing home.'

'No sailing home,' echoed Vissbruck sourly. 'Meanwhile the Gurkish press in closer every day, our losses mount, and the lowest beggar in the city can see that we cannot hold the land walls for much longer. My men are close to mutiny, and the mercenaries are considerably less dependable. What would you have me tell them? That the Closed Council's orders do not include retreat?'

'Tell them that reinforcements will be here any day.'

'I've been telling them that for weeks!'

'Then a few more days should make no difference.'

Vissbruck blinked. 'And might I ask when reinforcements will arrive?'

'Any.' Glokta narrowed his eyes. 'Day. Until then we hold.'

'But why?' Vissbruck's voice had gone high as a girl's. 'What for? The task is impossible! The waste! Why, damn it?'

Why. Always why. I grow bored of asking it. 'If you think I know the Arch Lector's mind you're an even bigger idiot than I supposed.' Glokta sucked slowly at his gums, thinking. 'You are right about one thing, however. The land walls may fall at any moment. We must prepare to withdraw into the Upper City.'

'But . . . if we abandon the Lower City we abandon the docks! There can be no supplies brought in! No reinforcements, even if they do arrive! What of your fine speech to me, Superior? The walls of the Upper City are too long and too weak? If the land walls fall the city is doomed? We must defeat them there or not at all, you told me! If the docks are lost . . . there can be no escape!' *My dear, plump, pudding of a General, do you not see it? Escape has never been an option.*

Glokta grinned, showing Vissbruck the empty holes in his teeth. 'If one plan fails, we must try another. The situation, as you have so cleverly pointed out, is desperate. Believe me, I would prefer it if the Emperor simply gave up and went home, but I hardly think we can count on that, do you? Send word to Cosca and Kahdia, all civilians should be moved out of the Lower City tonight. We may need to pull back at a moment's notice.' *At least I won't have to limp so far to reach the front lines.*

'The Upper City will scarcely hold so many! They will be lining the streets!' *Better than lining a grave pit.* 'They will be sleeping in the squares and the hallways!' *Preferable to sleeping in the ground.* 'There are thousands of them down there!'

'Then the sooner you start the better.'

Glokta half ducked back as he stepped through the doorway. The heat beyond was almost unbearable, the reek of sweat and burnt flesh tickled unpleasantly at his throat.

He wiped his eyes, already running with tears, on the back of his trembling hand and squinted into the darkness. The three Practicals took shape in the gloom. They were gathered round, masked faces lit from underneath by the angry orange of the brazier, all hard bright bone and hard dark shadow. *Devils, in hell.*

Vitari's shirt was soaked right through and stuck to her shoulders, furious creases cut into her face. Severard was stripped to the waist, gasping breath muffled through his mask, lank hair flapping with sweat. Frost was as wet as if he had stood out in the rain, fat drops running down his pale skin, jaw muscles locked and bulging. The only one in the room who showed no sign of discomfort was Shickel. The girl had an ecstatic smile across her face as Vitari ground the sizzling iron into her chest. *Just as if it were the happiest moment of her life.*

Glokta swallowed as he watched, remembering being shown the brand himself. Remembering pleading, begging, blubbering for mercy. Remembering the feeling of the metal pressed into his skin. *So searing hot it feels almost cold.* The mindless din of his own screams. The stink of his own flesh burning. He could smell it now. *First you suffer it yourself, then you inflict it on others, then you order it done. Such is the pattern of life.* He shrugged his aching shoulders and hobbled forwards into the room. 'Progress?' he croaked.

Severard straightened up, grunting and arching his back, wiped his forehead and flicked sweat onto the slimy floor. 'I don't know about her, but I'm more than halfway to breaking.'

'We're getting nowhere!' snapped Vitari, tossing the black iron back in the brazier and sending up a shower of sparks. 'We tried blades, we tried hammers, we tried water, we tried fire. She won't say a word. Fucking bitch is made of stone.'

'Softer than stone,' hissed Severard, 'but she's nothing like us.' He took a knife from the table, the blade briefly flashing orange in the darkness, leaned forward and carved a long gash into Shickel's thin forearm. Her face barely even twitched while he did it. The wound hung open, glistening angry red. Severard dug his finger into it and twisted it round. Shickel showed not the slightest sign of being in pain. He pulled his finger out and held it up, rubbed the tip against his thumb. 'Not even wet. It's like cutting into a week-old corpse.'

Glokta felt his leg trembling, and he winced and slid into the spare seat. 'Plainly, this is not normal.'

'Unnerthatement,' grunted Frost.

'But she's not healing the way she was.' *None of the cuts in her skin were closing. All hanging open, dead and dry as meat in a butcher's shop.* Nor were the burns fading. *Charred black stripes across her skin, like meat fresh from the grill.*

'Just sits there, watching,' said Severard, 'and not a word.'

Glokta frowned. *Can this really be what I had in mind when I joined the Inquisition? The torture of young girls?* He wiped the wet from under his stinging eyes. *But then, this is both much more and much less than a girl.* He remembered the hands clutching at him, the three Practicals straining to pull her back. *Much more and much less than human. We must not make the same mistakes we made with the First of the Magi.*

'We must keep an open mind,' he murmured.

'Do you know what my father would say to that?' The voice croaked out, deep and grinding raw, like an old man's, oddly wrong from that young, smooth face.

Glokta felt his left eye twitching, the sweat trickling under his coat. 'Your father?'

Shickel smiled at him, eyes glinting in the darkness. It almost seemed as if the cuts in her flesh smiled with her. 'My father. The Prophet. Great Khalul. He would say that an open mind is like to an open wound. Vulnerable to poison. Liable to fester. Apt to give its owner only pain.'

'Now you want to talk?'

'Now I choose to.'

'Why?'

'Why not? Now that you know it is my choice, and not yours. Ask your questions, cripple. You should take your chances to learn when you can. God knows you could do with them. A man lost in the desert—'

'I know the rest.' Glokta paused. *So many questions, but what to ask one such as this?* 'You are an Eater?'

'We have other names for ourselves, but yes.' She inclined her head gently, her eyes never leaving his. 'The priests made me eat my mother first. When they found me. It was that or die, and the need to live was so very great, before. I wept afterwards, but that was long ago and there are no tears left in me. I disgust myself, of course. Sometimes I need to kill, sometimes I wish to die. I deserve to. Of that I have no doubts. My only certainty.'

I should have known better than to expect straight answers. One almost feels nostalgic for the Mercers. Their crimes, at least, I could understand. Still, any answers are better than none. 'Why do you eat?'

'Because the bird eats the worm. Because the spider eats the fly. Because Khalul desires it and we are the Prophet's children. Juvens was betrayed, and Khalul swore vengeance, but he stood alone against many. So he made his great sacrifice, and broke the Second Law, and the righteous joined with him, more and more with the passing years. Some joined him willingly. Some not. But none have denied him. My siblings are many, now, and each of us must make our sacrifice.'

Glokta gestured at the brazier. 'You feel no pain?'

'I do not, but plentiful remorse.'

'Strange. It's the other way around for me.'

'You, I think, are the lucky one.'

He snorted. 'Easy to say until you find you can't piss without wanting to scream.'

'I hardly remember what pain feels like, now. All that was long ago. The gifts are different for each of us. Strength, and speed, and endurance beyond the limits of the human. Some of us can take forms, or trick the eye, or even use the Art, the way that Juvens taught his apprentices. The gifts are different for each of us, but the curse is the same.' She stared at Glokta, head cocked over to one side.

Let me guess. 'You can't stop eating.'

'Not ever. And that is why the Gurkish appetite for slaves is never-ending. There is no resisting the Prophet. I know. Great Father Khalul.' And her eyes rolled up reverently towards the ceiling. 'Arch Priest of the Temple of Sarkant. Holiest of all whose feet touch the earth. Humbler of the proud, righter of wrongs, teller of truths. Light shines from him as it shines from the stars. When he speaks it is with the voice of God. When he—'

'No doubt he shits golden turds as well. You believe all that rubbish?'

'What does it matter what I believe? I don't make the choices. When your master gives you a task, you do your best at it. Even if the task is a dark one.'

That much I can understand. 'Some of us are only suited to dark tasks. Once you've chosen your master—'

Shickel croaked dry laughter across the table. 'Few indeed are those who get a choice. We do as we are told. We stand or fall beside those who were born near to us, who look as we do, who speak the same words, and all the while we know as little of the reasons why as does the dust we return to.' Her head sagged sideways and a gash in her shoulder opened up as wide as a mouth. 'Do you think I like what I have become? Do you think I do not dream of being as others are? But once the change has come, you can never go back. Do you understand?'

Oh, yes. Few better. 'Why were you sent here?'

'The work of the righteous is never-ending. I came to see Dagoska returned to the fold. To see its people worship God according to the Prophet's teachings. To see my brothers and sisters fed.'

'It seems you failed.'

'Others will follow. There is no resisting the Prophet. You are doomed.'

That much I know. Let us try another tack. 'What do you know . . . about Bayaz.'

'Ah, Bayaz. He was the Prophet's brother. He is the start of this, and will be the end.' Her voice dropped to a whisper. 'Liar and traitor. He killed his master. He murdered Juvens.'

Glokta frowned. 'That is not the way I heard the story.'

'Everyone has their own way of telling every story, broken man. Have you not learned that yet?' Her lip curled. 'You have no understanding of the war you fight in, of the weapons and the casualties, of the victories and the defeats, every day. You do not guess at the sides, or the causes, or the reasons. The battlefields are everywhere. I pity you. You are a dog, trying to understand the argument of scholars, and hearing nothing but barking. The righteous are coming. Khalul will sweep the earth clean of lies and build a new order. Juvens will be avenged. It is foretold. It is ordained. It is promised.'

'I doubt you'll see it.'

She grinned at him. 'I doubt you will either. My father would rather have taken this city without a fight, but if he must fight for it then he will, and with no mercy, and with the fury of God behind him. That is the first step on the path he has chosen. On the path he has chosen for all of us.'

'What step comes next?'

'Do you think my masters tell me their plans? Do yours? I am a worm. I am nothing. And yet I am more than you are.'

'What comes next?' hissed Glokta. Nothing but silence.

'Answer him!' hissed Vitari. Frost hauled an iron from the brazier, the tip glowing orange, and ground it into Shickel's bare shoulder. Foul-smelling steam hissed up, fat spat and sizzled, but the girl said nothing.

Her lazy eyes watched her own flesh burn, without emotion. *There will be no answers here. Only more questions. Always more questions.*

'I've had enough,' snarled Glokta as he seized hold of his cane and struggled up, squirming in a painful and futile effort to make his shirt come unstuck from his back.

Vitari gestured at Shickel, her gleaming eyes still fixed on Glokta under their drooping lids, a faint smile still clinging to her lips. 'What should we do with this?'

An expendable agent of an uncaring master, sent unwilling to a faraway place, to fight, and kill, for reasons she hardly understands. Sound familiar? Glokta grimaced as he turned his aching back on the stinking chamber.

'Burn it,' he said.

Glokta stood on his balcony in the sharp evening, frowning down towards the Lower City.

It was windy up here on the rock, a cold wind off the dark sea, whipping at Glokta's face, at his fingers on the dry parapet, slapping the tails of his coat against his legs. *The closest thing we'll get to winter in this cursed crucible.* The flames of the torches by the door flapped and flickered in their iron cages, two lights in the gathering darkness. There were more lights out there, many more. Lamps burned on the rigging of the Union ships in the harbour, their reflections flashing and breaking in the water below. Lights glowed in the windows of the dark palaces under the citadel, in the tops of the lofty spires of the Great Temple. Down in the slums, thousands of torches burned. Rivers of tiny points of light, flowing out of the buildings, onto the roads, towards the gates of the Upper City. *Refugees leaving their homes, such as they are. Heading for safety, such as it is. How long can we keep them safe, I wonder, once the land walls fall?* He knew the answer already. *Not long.*

'Superior!'

'Why, Master Cosca. I'm so glad you could join me.'

'Of course! There's nothing like a stroll in the evening air after a skirmish.' The mercenary strutted over. Even in the gloom, Glokta could see the difference in him. He walked with a spring in his step, a glint in his eye, his hair neatly brushed, his moustache waxed stiff. *An inch or two taller and a good ten years younger, all of a sudden.* He pranced to the parapet, closed his eyes and sucked a deep breath through his sharp nose.

'You look remarkably well for someone who has just fought in a battle.'

The Styrian grinned at him. 'I wasn't so much in the battle as just behind it. I've always felt the very front is a poor place to fight from. No one can hear you with all the clatter. That, and the chances of being killed there are really very high.'

'Doubtless. How did it go for us?'

'The Gurkish are still outside, so I'd say, as far as battles go, it went well.

I doubt the dead would agree with me, but who cares a shit for their opinion?' He scratched happily at his neck. 'We did well today. But tomorrow, and the day after, who can say? Still no chance of reinforcement?' Glokta shook his head and the Styrian took in a sharp breath. 'It's all the same to me, of course, but you may want to consider a withdrawal while we still hold the bay.'

Everyone would like to withdraw. Even me. Glokta snorted. 'The Closed Council hold my leash, and they say no. The King's honour will not permit it, they inform me, and apparently his honour is more valuable than our lives.'

Cosca raised his brows. 'Honour, eh? What the hell is that anyway? Every man thinks it's something different. You can't drink it. You can't fuck it. The more of it you have the less good it does you, and if you've got none at all you don't miss it.' He shook his head. 'But some men think it's the best thing in the world.'

'Uh,' muttered Glokta, licking at his empty gums. *Honour is worth less than one's legs, or one's teeth. A lesson I paid dearly for.* He peered towards the shadowy outline of the land walls, studded with burning bonfires. The vague sounds of fighting could still be heard, the odd flaming arrow soared high into the air and fell in the ruined slums. *Even now, the bloody business continues.* He took a deep breath. 'What are our chances of holding out for another week?'

'Another week?' Cosca pursed his lips. 'Reasonable.'

'Two weeks?'

'Two?' Cosca clicked his tongue. 'Less good.'

'Which would make a month a hopeless cause.'

'Hopeless would be the word.'

'You seem almost to revel in the situation.'

'Me? I've made a speciality from hopeless causes.' He grinned at Glokta. 'These days, they're the only ones that will have me.'

I know the feeling. 'Hold the land walls as long as you can, then pull back. The walls of the Upper City must be our next line of defence.'

Cosca's grin could just be seen shining in the darkness. 'Hold as long as we can, and then pull back! I can hardly wait!'

'And perhaps we should prepare some surprises for our Gurkish guests when they finally make it past the walls. You know,' and Glokta waved his hand absently, 'tripwires and hidden pits, spikes daubed with excrement and so on. You've some experience in that type of warfare, I daresay.'

'I am experienced in all types of warfare.' Cosca snapped his heels together and gave an elaborate salute. 'Spikes and excrement! There's honour for you.'

This is war. The only honour is in winning. 'Talking of honour, you'd best let our friend General Vissbruck know where your surprises are. It would be a shame if he were to impale himself by accident.'

'Of course, Superior. A dreadful shame.'

Glokta felt his hand bunching into a fist on the parapet. 'We must make the Gurkish pay for every stride of ground.' *We must make them pay for my ruined leg.* 'For every inch of dirt.' *For my missing teeth.* 'For every meagre shack, and crumbling hut, and worthless stretch of dust.' *For my weeping eye, and my twisted back, and my repulsive shadow of a life.* He licked at his empty gums. 'Make them pay.'

'Excellent! The only good Gurkish are the dead ones!' The mercenary spun and marched through the door into the Citadel, his spurs jingling, leaving Glokta alone on the flat roof.

One week? Yes. Two weeks? Perhaps. Any longer? Hopeless. There may have been no ships, but that old riddler Yulwei was still right. And so was Eider. There never was any chance. For all our efforts, for all our sacrifices, Dagoska must surely fall. It is only a matter of time, now.

He stared out across the darkened city. It was hard to separate the land from the sea in the blackness, the lights on the boats from the lights in the buildings, the torches on the rigging from the torches in the slums. All was a confusion of points of light, flowing around each other, disembodied in the void. There was only one certainty in all of it.

We're finished. Not tonight, but soon. We are surrounded, and the net will only draw tighter. It is a matter of time.

Scars

One by one, Ferro took out the stitches – slitting the thread neatly with the shining point of her knife, working them gently out of Luthar's skin, dark fingertips moving quick and sure, yellow eyes narrowed with concentration. Logen watched her work, shaking his head slowly at the skill of it. He'd seen it done often, but never so well. Luthar barely even looked in pain, and he always looked in pain lately.

'Do we need another bandage on it?'

'No. We let it breathe.' The last stitch slid out, and Ferro tossed the bloody bits of thread away and rocked back on her knees to look at the results.

'That's good,' said Logen, voice hushed. He'd never guessed that it could come out half so well. Luthar's jaw looked slightly bent in the firelight, like he was biting down on one side. There was a ragged notch out of his lip, and a forked scar torn from it down to the point of his chin, pink dots on either side where the stitches had been, the skin around it stretched and twisted. Nothing more, but for some swelling that'd soon go down. 'That's some damn good stitching. I never saw any better. Where d'you learn healing?'

'A man called Aruf taught me.'

'Well he taught you well. Rare skill to have. Happy chance for us that he did it.'

'I had to fuck him first.'

'Ah.' That did shine a bit of a different light on it.

Ferro shrugged. 'I didn't mind. He was a good man, more or less, and he taught me how to kill, into the bargain. I've fucked a lot of worse men for a lot less.' She frowned at Luthar's jaw, pressing it with her thumbs, testing the flesh round the wound. 'A lot less.'

'Right,' muttered Logen. He exchanged a worried glance with Luthar. This conversation hadn't gone at all the way he'd imagined. Maybe he should've expected that with Ferro. He spent half the time trying to prise a word out of her, then when she did give him something, he didn't have a clue where to go with it.

'It's set,' she grunted, after probing Luthar's face for a moment in silence.

'Thank you.' He grabbed hold of her hand as she moved back. 'Truly. I don't know what I'd have—'

She grimaced as if he'd slapped her and snatched her fingers away. 'Fine! But if you get your face smashed again you can stitch it yourself.' And she got up and stalked off, sat down in the shifting shadows in the corner of the ruin, as far away from the others as she could get without going outside. She seemed to like thanks even less than she liked any other kind of talk, but Luthar was too pleased to finally have the dressings off to worry much about it.

'How does it look?' he asked, peering down cross-eyed at his own chin, wincing and prodding at it with one finger.

'It's good,' said Logen. 'You're lucky. You might not be quite so pretty as you were, but you're still a damn sight better-looking than me.'

'Of course,' he said, licking at the notch in his lip, half-smiling. 'It isn't as though they cut my head right off.'

Logen grinned as he knelt down beside the pot and gave it a stir. He was getting on alright with Luthar now. It was a harsh lesson, but a broken face had done that boy a power of good. It had taught him some respect, and a lot quicker than any amount of talk. It had taught him to be realistic, and that had to be a good thing. Small gestures and time. Rarely failed to win folk over. Then he caught sight of Ferro, frowning at him from the shadows, and he felt his grin sag. Some folk take longer than others, and a few never really get there. Black Dow had been like that. Made to walk alone, Logen's father would have said.

He looked back to the pot, but there wasn't much encouragement in it. Just porridge with some shreds of bacon and some chopped-up roots. There was nothing to hunt out here. Dead land meant what it said. The grass on the plain had dwindled to brown tufts and grey dust. He looked round the ruined shell of the house they'd pitched camp in. Firelight flickered on broken stone, crumbled render, ancient splintered wood. No ferns rooted in the cracks, no saplings in the earth floor, not even a shred of moss between the stones. Seemed to Logen as if no one but them had trodden there in centuries. Maybe they hadn't.

Quiet too. Not much wind tonight. Only the soft crackling of the fire, and Bayaz' voice mumbling away, lecturing his apprentice about something or other. Logen was good and glad the First of the Magi was awake again, even if he did look older and seem grimmer than ever. At least now Logen didn't have to decide what to do. That had never worked out too well for anyone concerned.

'A clear night at last!' sang Brother Longfoot as he ducked under the lintel, pointing upwards with huge smugness. 'A perfect sky for Navigation! The stars shine clearly for the first time in ten days and, I do declare, we are not a stride out from our chosen course! Not a foot! I have not led us wrong, my friends. No! That would not have been my way at all! Forty miles to Aulcus, as I reckon it, just as I told you!' No congratulations were forthcoming. Bayaz and Quai were deep in their ill-tempered muttering. Luthar was holding up the blade of his short sword and trying to find an angle where he could see his reflection. Ferro was frowning in her corner. Longfoot sighed and squatted down beside the fire. 'Porridge again?' he muttered, peering into the pot and wrinkling up his nose.

'Afraid so.'

'Ah, well. The tribulations of the road, eh, my friend? There would be no glory in travel without the hardship.'

'Uh,' said Logen. He could have managed with a lot less glory if it meant a decent dinner. He prodded unhappily at the bubbling mush with a spoon.

Longfoot leaned over to mutter under his breath. 'It would seem our illustrious employer is having some further troubles with his apprentice.' Bayaz' lecture was growing steadily louder and more bad-tempered.

'. . . being handy with a pan is all very well, but the practice of magic is still your first vocation. There has been a distinct change in your attitude of late. A certain watchfulness and disobedience. I am beginning to suspect that you may prove a disappointing pupil.'

'And were you always a fine pupil?' There was a trace of a mocking smile on Quai's face. 'Was your own master never disappointed?'

'He was, and the consequences were dire. We all make mistakes. It is a master's place to try to stop his students making the same ones.'

'Then perhaps you should tell me the history of your mistakes. I might learn to be a better student.'

Master and apprentice glared at each other over the fire. Logen did not like the look of Bayaz' frown. He had seen such looks before on the First of the Magi, and the outcome had never been good. He couldn't understand why Quai had shifted from abject obedience to sullen opposition in the space of a few weeks, but it wasn't making anyone's life easier. Logen pretended to be fascinated by the porridge, half-expecting to be suddenly deafened by the roar of searing flame. But when sound came it was only Bayaz' voice, and speaking softly.

'Very well, Master Quai, there is some sense in your request, for once. Let us talk of my mistakes. An expansive subject indeed. Where to start?'

'At the beginning?' ventured his apprentice. 'Where else should a man ever start?'

The Magus gave a sour grunt. 'Huh. Long ago, then, in the Old Time.' He paused for a moment and stared into the flames, the light shifting over his hollow face. 'I was Juvens' first apprentice. But soon after starting my education, my master took a second. A boy from the South. His name was Khalul.' Ferro looked up suddenly, frowning from the shadows. 'From the beginning, the two of us could never agree. We both were far too proud, and jealous of each other's talents, and envious of any mark of favour the other earned from our master. Our rivalry persisted, even as the years passed and Juvens took more apprentices, twelve in all. In the beginning, it drove us to be better pupils: more diligent, more devoted. But after the horror of the war with Glustrod, many things were changed.'

Logen gathered up the bowls and started spooning steaming slop out into them, making sure to keep one ear on Bayaz' talk. 'Our rivalry became a feud, and our feud became a hatred. We fought, with words, then with hands, then with magic. Perhaps, left to ourselves, we would have killed each other. Perhaps the world would be a happier place if we had, but Juvens interposed. He sent me to the far north, and Khalul to the south, to two of the great libraries he had built long years before. He sent us there to study, separately and alone, until our tempers cooled. He thought the high mountains, and the wide sea, and the whole breadth of the Circle of the World would put an end to our feud, but he misjudged us. Rather we each raged in our exile, and blamed the other for it, and plotted our petty revenges.'

Logen shared out the food, such as it was, while Bayaz glared at Quai from under his heavy brows. 'If I had only had the good sense to listen to my master then, but I was young, and headstrong, and full of pride. I burned to make myself more powerful than Khalul. I decided, fool that I was, that if Juvens would not teach me . . . I had to find another master.'

'Slop again, eh, pink?' grunted Ferro as she pulled her bowl from Logen's hand.

'No need to thank me.' He tossed her a spoon and she snatched it out of the air. Logen handed the First of the Magi his bowl. 'Another master? What other master could you find?'

'Only one,' murmured Bayaz. 'Kanedias. The Master Maker.' He turned his spoon over and over thoughtfully in his hand. 'I went to his House, and I knelt before him, and I begged to learn at his feet. He refused me, of course, as he refused everyone . . . at first. But I was stubborn, and in time he relented, and agreed to teach me.'

'And so you lived in the House of the Maker,' murmured Quai. Logen shivered as he hunched down over his own bowl. His one brief visit to the place still gave him nightmares.

'I did,' said Bayaz, 'and I learned its ways. My skill in High Art made me useful to my new master. But Kanedias was far more jealous of his secrets than ever Juvens had been, and he worked me as hard as a slave at his forges, and taught me only such scraps as I needed to serve him. I grew bitter, and when the Maker left to seek out materials for his works, my curiosity, and my ambition, and my thirst for knowledge, drove me to stray into parts of his House where he had forbidden me to tread. And there I found his best-guarded secret.' He paused.

'What was it?' prompted Longfoot, spoon frozen halfway to his mouth.

'His daughter.'

'Tolomei,' whispered Quai, in a hiss barely audible.

Bayaz nodded, and one corner of his mouth curled upwards, as though he remembered something good. 'She was unlike any other. She had never left the Maker's House, had never spoken to anyone besides her father. She helped him with certain tasks, I learned. She handled . . . certain materials . . . that only the Maker's own blood could touch. That, I believe, is why he fathered her in the first place. She was beautiful beyond compare.' Bayaz' face twitched, and he looked down at the ground with a sour smile. 'Or so she seems to me, in memory.'

'That was good,' said Luthar, licking his fingers and setting down his empty bowl. He'd become a great deal less picky with his food lately. Logen reckoned a few weeks of not being able to chew was sure to do that to a man. 'There any more?' he asked hopefully.

'Take mine,' hissed Quai, thrusting his bowl at Luthar. His face was deathly cold, his eyes two points of light in the shadows as he glared across at his master. 'Go on.'

Bayaz looked up. 'Tolomei fascinated me, and I her. It seems strange to say, but I was young then, and full of fire, and still had as fine a head of hair as Captain Luthar.' He ran one hissing palm over his bald scalp, then shrugged his shoulders. 'We fell in love.' He looked at each of them in turn, as though daring them to laugh, but Logen was too busy sucking salty porridge from his teeth, and no one else so much as smiled.

'She told me of the tasks her father gave her, and I began, dimly, to understand. He had gathered from far and wide some fragments of material from the world below, left over from the time when demons still walked our earth. He was trying to tap the power of these splinters, to incorporate them into his machines. He was tampering with those forces forbidden by the First Law, and had already had some success.' Logen shifted uncomfortably. He remembered the thing he had seen in the Maker's House, lying in the wet on a block of white stone, strange and fascinating. The Divider, Bayaz had called it. Two edges – one here, one on the Other Side. He had no appetite now, and he shoved his bowl down by the fire, half-finished.

'I was horrified,' continued Bayaz. 'I had seen the ruin that Glustrod had brought upon the world, and I resolved to go to Juvens and tell him everything. But I feared to leave Tolomei behind, and she would not leave all she knew. So I delayed, and Kanedias returned unexpected, and found us together. His fury was . . .' and Bayaz winced as though the memory alone was painful '. . . impossible to describe. His House shook with it, rang with it, burned with it. I was lucky to escape with my life, and fled to seek sanctuary with my old master.'

Ferro snorted. 'He was the forgiving type, then?'

'Fortunately for me. Juvens would not turn me away, despite my betrayal. Especially once I told him of his brother's attempts to break the First Law. The Maker came in great wrath, demanding justice for the violation of his daughter, the theft of his secrets. Juvens refused. He demanded to know what experiments Kanedias had been undertaking. The brothers fought, and I fled. The sky was lit with the fury of their battle. I returned to find my master dead, his brother gone. I swore vengeance. I gathered the Magi from across the world, and we made war on the Maker. All of us. Except for Khalul.'

'Why not him?' growled Ferro.

'He said that I could not be trusted. That my folly had caused the war.'

'All too true, surely?' muttered Quai.

'Perhaps, in part. But he made far worse accusations also. He and his cursed apprentice, Mamun. Lies,' he hissed at the fire. 'All lies, and the rest of the Magi were not deceived. So Khalul left the order, and returned to the South, and sought for power elsewhere. And he found it. By doing as Glustrod had done, and damning himself. By breaking the Second Law, and eating the flesh of men. Only eleven of us went to fight Kanedias, and only nine of us returned.'

Bayaz took a long breath, and gave a long sigh. 'So, Master Quai. There is the story of my mistakes, laid bare. You could say they were the cause of my master's death, of the schism in the order of Magi. You could say that is why we are now heading westwards, into the ruins of the past. You could say that is why Captain Luthar has suffered a broken jaw.'

'The seeds of the past bear fruit in the present,' muttered Logen to himself.

'So they do,' said Bayaz, 'so they do. And sour fruit indeed. Will you learn from my mistakes, Master Quai, as I have, and pay some attention to your master?'

'Of course,' said the apprentice, though Logen wondered if there was a hint of irony in his voice. 'I will obey in all things.'

'You would be wise to. If I had obeyed Juvens, perhaps I would not have this.' Bayaz undid the top two buttons of his shirt and pulled his collar to one side. The firelight flickered on a faded scar, from the base of the old man's neck down towards his shoulder. 'The Maker himself gave it to me. Another inch and it would have been my death.' He rubbed sourly at it. 'All those years ago, and it still aches, from time to time. The pain it has given me over the slow years . . . so you see, Master Luthar, although you bear a mark, it could be worse.'

Longfoot cleared his throat. 'That is quite an injury, of course, but I believe I can do better.' He took hold of his dirty trouser leg and pulled it right up to his groin, turning his sinewy thigh towards the firelight. There was an ugly mass of puckered grey scar flesh almost all the way round his leg. Even Logen had to admit to being impressed.

'What the hell did that?' asked Luthar, looking slightly queasy.

Longfoot smiled. 'Many years ago, when I was yet a young man, I was shipwrecked in a storm off the coast of Suljuk. Nine times, in all, God has seen fit to dump me into his cold ocean in bad weather. Luckily, I have always been truly blessed as a swimmer. Unluckily, on this occasion, some manner of great fish took me for its next meal.'

'A fish?' muttered Ferro.

'Indeed. A most huge and aggressive fish, with a jaw wide as a doorway and teeth like knives. Fortunately, a sharp blow on the nose,' and he chopped at the air with his hand, 'caused it to release me, and a fortuitous current washed me up on shore. I was doubly blessed to find a sympathetic lady among the natives, who allowed me to recuperate in her abode, for the people of Suljuk are generally most suspicious of outsiders.' He sighed happily. 'That is how I came to learn their language. A highly spiritual people. God has favoured me. Truly.' There was a silence.

'I bet you can do better.' Luthar was grinning across at Logen.

'I got bitten by a mean sheep once, but it didn't leave much of a mark.'

'What about the finger?'

'This?' He stared at the familiar stub, waggling it back and forward. 'What about it?'

'How did you lose it?'

Logen frowned. He wasn't sure he liked the way this conversation was going. Hearing about Bayaz' mistakes was one thing, but he wasn't that keen to delve into his own. The dead knew, he'd made some bad ones. Still, they were all looking now. He had to say something. 'I lost it in a battle. Outside a place called Carleon. I was young back then, and full of fire myself. It was my stupid fashion to go charging into the thick of the fighting. That time, when I came out, the finger was gone.'

'Heat of the moment, eh?' asked Bayaz.

'Something like that.' He frowned and rubbed gently at the stump. 'Strange thing. For a long time after it was gone, I could still feel it, itching, right in the tip. Drove me mad. How can you scratch a finger that's not there?'

'Did it hurt?' asked Luthar.

'Like a bastard, to begin with, but not half as much as some others I've had.'

'Like what?'

That needed some thinking about. Logen scratched at his face and turned over all the hours, and days, and weeks he'd spent injured, and bloody, and screaming. Limping around or trying to cut his meat with his hands all bandaged up. 'I got a good sword cut across my face one time,' he said, feeling the notch Tul Duru had made in his ear, 'bled like anything. Nearly got my eye poked out with an arrow,' rubbing at the crescent scar under his brow. 'Took hours to dig out all the splinters. Then I had a bloody great rock dropped on me at the siege of Uffrith. First day, as well.'

He rubbed the back of his head and felt the lumpy ridges, under his hair. 'Broke my skull, and my shoulder too.'

'Nasty,' said Bayaz.

'My own fault. That's what you get when you try and tear a city wall down with your bare hands.' Luthar stared at him, and he shrugged. 'Didn't work. Like I said, I was hot-headed in my youth.'

'I'm only surprised you didn't try and chew through it.'

'Most likely that would've been my next move. Just as well they dropped a rock on me. At least I've still got my teeth. Spent two months squealing on my back while they laid siege to the city. I only just healed in time for the fight with Threetrees, when I got the whole lot broken again, and more besides.' Logen winced at the memory, curling up the fingers of his right hand and straightening them out, remembering the pain of it, all smashed up. 'Now that really did hurt. Not as much as this, though,' and he dug his hand under his belt and pulled his shirt up. They all peered across the fire to see what he was pointing at. A small scar, really, just under his bottom rib, in the hollow beside his stomach.

'Doesn't look like much,' said Luthar.

Logen shuffled round to show them his back. 'There's the rest of it,' he said, jerking his thumb at what he knew was a much bigger mark beside his backbone. There was a long silence while they took that in.

'Right through?' murmured Longfoot.

'Right through, with a spear. In a duel, with a man called Harding Grim. Damn lucky to live, and that's a fact.'

'If it was in a duel,' murmured Bayaz, 'how did you come out alive?'

Logen licked his lips. His mouth tasted bitter. 'I beat him.'

'With a spear through you?'

'I didn't know about it until afterwards.'

Longfoot and Luthar frowned at each other. 'That would seem a difficult detail to overlook,' said the Navigator.

'You'd think so.' Logen hesitated, trying to think of a good way to put it, but there was no good way. 'There are times . . . well . . . I don't really know what I'm doing.'

A long pause. 'How do you mean?' asked Bayaz, and Logen winced. All the fragile trust he'd built over the last few weeks was in danger of crumbling round his ears, but he didn't see any choice. He'd never been much of a liar.

'When I was fourteen, I think, I argued with a friend. Can't even remember what about. I remember being angry. I remember he hit me. Then I was looking at my hands.' And he looked down at them now, pale in the darkness. 'I'd strangled him. Good and dead. I didn't remember doing it, but there was only me there, and I had his blood under my nails. I dragged him up some rocks, and I threw him off onto his head, and I said he fell out of a tree and died, and everyone believed me. His mother cried, and so on, but what could I do? That was the first time it happened.'

Logen felt the eyes of the group all fixed on him. 'Few years later I nearly killed my father. Stabbed him while we were eating. Don't know why. Don't know why at all. He healed, luckily.'

He felt Longfoot easing nervously away, and he hardly blamed him. 'That was when the Shanka started coming more often. So my father sent me south, over the mountains, to look for help. So I found Bethod, and he offered me help if I'd fight for him. I was happy to do it, fool that I was, but the fighting went on, and on. The things I did in those wars . . . the things they told me I did.' He took a long breath. 'Well. I'd killed friends. You should have seen what I did to enemies. To begin with I enjoyed it. I loved to sit at the top of the fire, to look at men and see their fear, to have no man dare to meet my eye, but it got worse. And worse. There came one winter that I didn't know who I was, or what I was doing most of the time. Sometimes I'd see it happening, but I couldn't change it. No one knew who I'd kill next. They were all shitting themselves, even Bethod, and no one more scared of me than I was.'

They all sat for a while in gaping silence. The ruined building had been seeming like some kind of comfort after all that dead and empty space on the plain, but it didn't any more. The empty windows yawned like wounds. The empty doorways gaped like graves. The silence dragged on, and on, and then Longfoot cleared his throat. 'So, for the sake of argument, do you think it's possible that, perhaps without intending to, you might kill one of us?'

'It's more likely I'd kill all of you than one.'

Bayaz was frowning. 'Forgive me if I feel less than entirely reassured.'

'I wish at least that you had mentioned this earlier!' snapped Longfoot. 'It is the type of information a travelling companion should share! I hardly think that—'

'Leave him be,' growled Ferro.

'But we need to know—'

'Shut your mouth, stargazing fool. You're all a long way from perfect.' She scowled over at Longfoot. 'Some of you make a lot of words and are nowhere near when the trouble starts.' She frowned at Luthar. 'Some of you are a lot less use than you think you are.' She glared at Bayaz. 'And some of you keep a lot of secrets, then fall asleep at bad times and leave the rest of us stranded in the middle of nowhere. So he's a killer. So fucking what? Suited you well enough when the killing needed doing.'

'I only wanted to—'

'Shut your mouth, I said.' Longfoot blinked for a moment, then did as he was told.

Logen stared across the fire at Ferro. The very last place he'd ever have hoped to get a good word. Out of all of them, only she'd seen it happen.

271

Only she knew what he really meant. And still she'd spoken up for him. She saw him looking, and she scowled and shrank back into her corner, but that didn't change anything. He felt himself smile.

'What about you, then?' Bayaz was looking at Ferro as well, touching one finger to his lip as though thinking.

'What about me?'

'You say you don't like secrets. We have all spoken of our scars. I bored the group with my old stories, and the Bloody-Nine thrilled us with his.' The Magus tapped his bony face, full of hard shadows from the fire. 'How did you get yours?'

A pause. 'I bet you made whoever gave you that suffer, eh?' said Luthar, a trace of laughter in his voice.

Longfoot started to chuckle. 'Oh indeed! I daresay he came to a sharp end! I dread to think of the—'

'I did it,' said Ferro.

Such laughter as there was sputtered and died, the smiles faded as they took that in. 'Eh?' said Logen.

'What, pink, you fucking deaf? I did it to myself.'

'Why?'

'Hah!' she barked, glaring at him across the fire. 'You don't know what it is, to be owned! When I was twelve years old I was sold to a man called Susman.' And she spat on the ground and snarled something in her own tongue. Logen didn't reckon it was a compliment. 'He owned a place where girls were trained, then sold on at a profit.'

'Trained to do what?' asked Luthar.

'What do you think, fool? To fuck.'

'Ah,' he squeaked, swallowing and looking at the ground again.

'Two years I was there. Two years, before I stole a knife. I did not know then, how to kill. So I hurt my owner the best way I could. I cut myself, right to the bone. By the time they got the blade away from me I had cut my price down to a quarter.' She grinned fiercely at the fire as if it had been her proudest day. 'You should have heard him squeal, the bastard!'

Logen stared. Longfoot gaped. Even the First of the Magi looked shocked. 'You scarred yourself?'

'What of it?' Silence again. The wind blew up and swirled around inside the ruin, hissing in the chinks between the stones and making the flames flicker and dance. No one had much left to say after that.

Furious

The snow drifted down, white specks swirling in the empty air beyond the cliff's edge, turning the green pines, the black rocks, the brown river below into grey ghosts.

West could hardly believe that as a child he had looked forward to the coming of snow every year. That he had been delighted to wake up and see the world coated in white. That it could have held a mystery, and a wonder, and a joy. Now the sight of the flakes settling on Cathil's hair, on Ladisla's coat, on West's own filthy trouser leg, filled him with horror. More gripping cold, more chafing wet, more crushing effort to move. He rubbed his pale hands together, sniffed and frowned up at the sky, willing himself not to slide into misery.

'Have to make the best of things,' he whispered, the words croaking in his raw throat and smoking thick in the cold. 'Have to.' He thought of warm summer in the Agriont. Blossom blowing from the trees in the squares. Birds twittering on the shoulders of smiling statues. Sunlight pouring through leafy branches in the park. It did not help. He sniffed back runny snot, tried yet again to worm his hands up into his uniform sleeves, but they were never quite long enough. He gripped the frayed hems with his pale fingers. Would he ever be warm again?

He felt Pike's hand on his shoulder. 'Something's up,' murmured the convict. He pointed at the Northmen, squatting in a group, muttering urgently to each other.

West stared wearily over at them. He had only just got nearly comfortable and it was difficult to take an interest in anything beyond his own pain. He slowly unfolded his aching legs, heard his cold knees click as he got up, shook himself, tried to slap the tiredness out of his body. He started shuffling towards the Northmen, bent over like an old man, arms wrapped round himself for warmth. Before he got there the meeting had already broken up. Another decision made without any need for his opinion.

Threetrees strode towards him, utterly unaffected by the falling snow. 'The Dogman's spotted some of Bethod's scouts,' he grunted, pointing through the trees. 'Just down the rise there, right in by the stream, near those falls. Lucky he caught them. They could just as easily have caught us, and we'd most likely all be dead by now.'

'How many?'

'A dozen, he thinks. Getting round 'em could be risky.'

West frowned, rocking his weight from one foot back to the other, trying to keep the blood moving. 'Surely fighting them would be riskier still?'

'Maybe, maybe not. If we can get the jump on 'em, our chances ain't bad. They've got food, weapons,' he looked West up and down, 'and clothes. All kinds o' gear that we could use. We're just past the knuckle o' winter now. We keep heading north, it ain't going to get any warmer. It's decided. We're fighting. A dozen's long odds, so we'll need every man. Your mate Pike there looks like he can swing an axe without worrying too much on the results. You'd best get him ready an' all.' He nodded at Ladisla, hunched up on the ground. 'The girl should stay out but—'

'Not the Prince. It's too dangerous.'

Threetrees narrowed his eyes. 'You're damn right it's dangerous. That's why every man should share the risk.'

West leaned in close, doing his best to sound persuasive with his cracked lips as tough and thick as a pair of overcooked sausages. 'He'd only make the risk greater for everyone. We both know it.' The Prince peered back at them suspiciously, trying to guess what they were talking about. 'He'd be about as much use in a fight as a sack over your head.'

The old Northman snorted. 'Most likely you're right there.' He took a deep breath and frowned, taking some time to think about it. 'Alright. It ain't usual, but alright. He stays, him and the girl. The rest of us fight, and that means you too.'

West nodded. Each man has to do his part, how ever little he might relish the prospect. 'Fair enough. The rest of us fight.' And he stumbled back over to tell the others.

Back home in the bright gardens of the Agriont, Crown Prince Ladisla would never have been recognised. The dandies, the courtiers, the hangers-on who usually clung to his every word would most likely have stepped over him, holding their noses. The coat West had given him was coming apart at the seams, worn through at the elbows, crusted with mud. Beneath it, his spotless white uniform had gradually darkened to the colour of filth. A few tatters of gold braid still hung from it, like a glorious bouquet of flowers rotted down to the greasy stalks. His hair was a tangled thatch, he had developed a patchy growth of ginger beard, and a rash of hair between his brows implied that in happier days he had spent a great deal of time plucking them. The only man within a hundred miles in a sorrier condition was probably West himself.

'What's to do?' mumbled the Prince as West dropped down beside him.

'There are some of Bethod's scouts down near the river, your Highness. We have to fight.'

The Prince nodded. 'I will need a weapon of some—'

'I must ask you to stay behind.'

'Colonel West, I feel that I should be—'

'You would be a great asset, your Highness, but I am afraid it is quite out of the question. You are the heir to the throne. We cannot afford to put you in harm's way.'

Ladisla did his best to look disappointed, but West could almost taste his relief. 'Very well, if you're sure.'

'Absolutely.' West looked at Cathil. 'The two of you should stay here. We'll be back soon. With luck.' He almost winced at the last part. Luck had been decidedly thin on the ground lately. 'Keep out of sight, and keep quiet.'

She grinned back at him. 'Don't worry. I'll make sure he doesn't hurt himself.'

Ladisla glowered sideways, fists clenched with impotent anger. It seemed he was getting no better at dealing with her constant jibes. No doubt being flattered and obeyed your entire life was poor preparation for being made a fool of in awful conditions. West wondered for a moment if he was making a mistake leaving them alone, but it was hardly as though he had any choice. They were well out of the way up here. They should be safe. A lot safer than him, anyway.

They squatted down on their haunches. A ring of scarred and dirty faces, hard expressions, ragged hair. Threetrees, his craggy features creased with deep lines. Black Dow with his missing ear and his savage grin. Tul Duru, his heavy brows drawn in. Grim, looking as careless as a stone. The Dogman, bright eyes narrowed, breath steaming from his sharp nose. Pike, with a deep frown across those few parts of his burned face that were capable of movement. Six of the hardest-looking men in the world, and West.

He swallowed. Every man has to do his part.

Threetrees was scratching a crude map in the hard soil with a stick. 'Alright, lads, they're tucked in down here near the river, a dozen, maybe more. Here's how we'll get it done. Grim, up on the left, Dogman on the right, usual drill.'

'Done, chief,' said the Dogman. Grim nodded.

'Me, Tul, and Pike'll come at 'em from this side, hand to hand. Hope to surprise 'em. Don't shoot any of us, eh, lads?'

The Dogman grinned. 'If you keep well clear of the arrows, you'll be fine.'

'I'll keep that in mind. Dow and West, you'll get across the river and wait by the falls there. Come up behind them.' The stick scratched a hard groove into the earth, and West felt the lump of worry swelling in his throat. 'Noise of the water should keep you out of notice. Go when you see me chuck a stone over into the pool, you hear me? The stone coming over. That's the signal.'

'Course it is, chief,' grunted Dow.

West suddenly realised that Threetrees was glaring right at him. 'You hearing this, boy?'

'Er, yes, of course,' he muttered, tongue clumsy with cold and growing fear. 'When the stone comes over, we go . . . chief.'

'Alright. And the lot of you keep your eyes open. There could be others near. Bethod's got scouts all over the country. Anyone still guessing at what to do?' They all shook their heads. 'Good. Then don't go blaming me if you get yourself killed.'

Threetrees stood up and the others followed him. They made their last few preparations, loosening blades in sheaths, pulling at bowstrings, tightening buckles. There wasn't much for West to prepare. A heavy, stolen sword pushed through a weathered belt, and that was it. He felt an utter fool in amongst this company. He wondered how many people they had killed between them. He would not have been surprised if it had been a whole town full, with enough left over for an outlying village or two. Even Pike looked more than ready to commit careless murder. West had to remind himself that he had not the slightest idea why the man had been convicted to a penal colony in the first place. Looking at him now, running a thoughtful thumb down the edge of his heavy axe, eyes hard in that dead, burned face, it was not difficult to imagine.

West stared at his hands. They were trembling, and not just from the cold. He grabbed one with the other and squeezed them tight. He looked up to see the Dogman grinning at him. 'Got to have fear to have courage,' he said, then turned and followed Threetrees and the others into the trees.

Black Dow's harsh voice hacked at West from behind. 'You're with me, killer. Try and keep up.' He spat on the frozen ground then turned and set off towards the river. West took one last look back towards the others. Cathil nodded to him, once, and he nodded back, then he turned and followed Dow, ducking through the trees in silence, all coated with glittering, dripping ice, while the hissing of the waterfall grew louder and louder in his ears.

Threetrees' plan was starting to seem rather short on details. 'Once we get across the stream, and we get the signal, what do we do?'

'Kill,' grunted Dow over his shoulder.

That answer, useless though it was, sent a sudden stab of panic through West's guts. 'Should I go left or right?'

'Whichever you like, long as you stay out of my way.'

'Where will you be going?'

'Wherever the killing is.'

West wished he had never spoken as he stepped gingerly out onto the bank. He could see the falls just upstream, a wall of dark rock and rushing white water between the black tree trunks, throwing freezing mist and noise into the air.

The river here was no more than four strides across but the water flooded past, quick and dark, frothing round the wet stones at its edges. Dow held his sword and axe up high, waded out steadily, up to his waist in the middle, then crept up onto the far bank, pressing himself dripping against the rocks. He looked round, frowned to see West so far behind, jerked his hand angrily for him to follow.

West fumbled out his own sword and lifted it up, held a deep breath and stepped into the stream. The water flooded into his boot and round his calf. It felt as if his leg had been suddenly clamped in ice. He took a step forward and his other leg vanished up to the thigh. His eyes bulged, his breath came in snorts, but there could be no turning back. He took one more step. His boot slipped on the mossy stones on the bed of the stream and he slid helplessly in up to his armpits. He would have screamed if the freezing water had not hammered the air out of his lungs. He floundered forward, half-stumbling, half-swimming, teeth gritted with panic, sloshed up onto the far bank, breath hissing in shallow, desperate gasps. He staggered up and leaned against the stones behind Dow, his skin numb and prickling.

The Northman smirked at him. 'You look cold, boy.'

'I'm fine,' spluttered West through chattering teeth. He had never been so cold in his life. 'I'll do my puh . . . puh . . . part.'

'You'll do your what? I'll not have you fighting cold boy, you'll get us both killed.'

'Don't worry about—' Dow's open hand slapped him hard across the face. The shock of it was almost worse than the pain. West gawped, dropping his blade in the mud, one hand jerking up instinctively to his stinging cheek. 'What the—'

'Use it!' hissed the Northman at him. 'It belongs to you!'

West was just opening his mouth when Dow's other hand smacked into it and sent him staggering against the rocks, blood dribbling from his lip and onto the wet earth, his head singing.

'It's yours. Own it!'

'You fucking . . .' The rest was nothing more than a mindless growl as West's hands closed round Dow's neck, squeezing, clawing, snarling like an animal, teeth bared and mindless. The blood surged round his body, the hunger, and the pain, and the frustration of the endless freezing march spilling out of him all at once.

But Black Dow was twice as strong as West, however angry he was. 'Use it!' he growled as he peeled West's hands away and crushed him back against the rocks. 'You hot yet?'

Something flashed overhead and splashed into the water beside them.

Dow gave him a parting shove then sprang away, charging up the bank with a roar. West struggled after him, clawing the heavy sword up out of the mud and lifting it high, the blood pulsing in his head, howling meaningless sounds at the top of his lungs.

The muddy ground sped by underneath him. He crashed through bushes and rotten wood into the open. He saw Dow hack a gawping Northman down with his axe. Dark blood leapt into the air, black spots against the tangle of branches and white sky. Trees and rocks and shaggy men jolted and wobbled, his own breath roaring in his ears like a storm. Someone loomed up and he swung the sword at them, felt it bite. Blood spattered into West's face and he reeled, and spat, and blinked, slid onto his side and scrambled up. His head was full of wailing and crying, clashing metal and cracking bone.

Chop. Hack. Snarl.

Someone staggered near him, clutching at an arrow in his chest. West's sword split his skull open down to his mouth. The corpse jerked, twisting the blade from his hand. He stumbled in the dirt, half fell, lashed out at a passing body with his fist. Something crashed into him and flung him back against a tree, knocking the air from his lungs in a breathy wheeze. Someone had him fast around the chest, pinning his arms, trying to crush the life out of him.

West craned forward, and sank his teeth into the man's lip, felt them meet in the middle. He screamed and punched but West hardly felt the blows. He spat out the flap of flesh and butted him in the face. The man squirmed and yelped, blood leaking out of his torn mouth. West clamped his teeth round his nose, growling like a mad dog.

Bite. Bite. Bite.

His mouth filled with blood. He could hear screaming in his ears, but all that mattered was to squeeze his jaws together, tighter and tighter. He twisted his head away and the man reeled back, clutching at his face. An arrow came out of nowhere and thudded into his ribs, he fell to his knees. West dived on him, grabbed hold of his tangled hair with clutching hands and smashed his face into the ground, again and again.

'It's done.'

West's hands jerked back, grasping claws full of blood and ripped-out hair. He struggled up, gasping, eyes bulging.

Everything was still. The world had stopped reeling. Spots of snow filtered gently down into the clearing, settling across the wet earth, the scattered gear, the stretched-out bodies, and the men still standing. Tul was not far away, staring at him. Threetrees was behind, sword in hand. Pike's pink slab of a face had something close to a wince on it, one bloody fist squeezed round his arm. They were all looking. All looking at him. Dow raised his hand, pointing at West. He tipped his head back and started to

278

laugh. 'You bit him! You bit his fucking nose off! I knew you were a mad bastard!'

West stared at them. The thumping in his head was starting to subside. 'What?' he muttered. There was blood all over him. He wiped his mouth. Salty. He looked at the nearest corpse, face down on the earth. Blood was trickling from underneath its head, running down the slope and pooling around West's boot. He remembered . . . something. A sudden cramp in his guts bent him over, spitting pink onto the ground, empty stomach heaving.

'Furious!' shouted Dow. 'That's what y'are!'

Grim had already stepped out of the bushes, bow over his shoulder, and was squatting down, dragging a bloody fur from one of the corpses. 'Good coat,' he muttered to himself.

West watched them all pick over the campsite, bent over and sick and utterly spent. He listened to Dow laughing. 'Furious!' cackled his harsh voice. 'That's what I'll call you!'

'They got arrows over here.' The Dogman pulled something out of one of the packs on the ground, and grinned. 'And cheese. Bit dusty.' He picked some mould off the wedge of yellow with his dirty fingers, bit into it, and grinned. 'Still good though.'

'Lots o' good stuff,' nodded Threetrees, starting to smile himself. 'And we're all still going, more or less. Good day's work, lads.' He slapped Tul on the back. 'We'd best head on north quick before these lot are missed. Let's get what there is fast and pick up those other two.'

West's mind was only just starting to move again. 'The others!'

'Alright,' said Threetrees, 'you and Dow check on them . . . Furious.' He turned away with half a smile.

West lurched off through the trees the way he'd come, slipping and sliding in his haste, blood pulsing again. 'Protect the Prince,' he muttered to himself. He waded across the stream almost without noticing the cold, struggled onto the far bank and back uphill, hurrying towards the cliff where they had left the others.

He heard a woman's scream, quickly cut off, a man's voice growling. Horror crept through every part of his body. Bethod's men had found them. It might already be too late. He urged his burning legs on up the slope, stumbling and sliding in the mud. Had to protect the Prince. The air burned in his throat but he forced himself on, fingers clutching at the tree trunks, scrabbling at the loose twigs and needles on the frosty ground.

He burst out into the open space beside the cliff, breathing hard, the bloody sword gripped tight in his fist.

Two figures struggled on the ground. Cathil was underneath, wriggling on her back, kicking and clawing at someone on top of her. The man had managed to drag her trousers down below her knees and now he was fiddling with his own belt while he struggled to hold his other hand across her mouth. West took a step forward, raising the sword high, and the man's head snapped round. West blinked. The would-be rapist was none other than Crown Prince Ladisla himself.

When he saw West he stumbled up and took a step back. He had a slightly sheepish expression, almost a grin, like a schoolboy caught stealing a pie from the kitchen. 'Sorry,' he said, 'I thought you'd be longer.'

West stared at him, hardly able to understand what was happening. 'Longer?'

'You fucking bastard!' screamed Cathil, scrambling back and dragging her trousers up. 'I'll fucking kill you!'

Ladisla touched his lip. 'She bit me! Look!' He held his bloody finger tips out as though they were proof of an outrage perpetrated against him. West found himself moving forwards. The Prince must have seen something in his face, because he took a step away, holding up one hand while he held up his trousers with the other. 'Now hold on, West, just—'

There was no towering rage. No temporary blindness, no limbs moving by themselves, not the slightest trace of a headache. There was no anger at all. West had never in his life felt so calm, so sober, so sure of himself. He chose to do it.

His right arm jerked out and his open palm thumped against Ladisla's chest. The Crown Prince gave a gentle gasp as he stumbled sharply backwards. His left foot twisted in the mud. He put down his right foot, but there was no ground behind him. His brows went up, his mouth and eyes opened with silent shock. The heir to the throne of the Union fell away from West, his hands clutching vainly, turning slowly to his side in the air . . . and he was gone.

There was a short, breathy cry, a thumping sound, and another, a long clattering of stones.

Then silence.

West stood there, blinking.

He turned to look at Cathil.

She was frozen, a couple of strides away, eyes gawping wide open.

'You . . . you . . .'

'I know.' It hardly sounded like his voice. He edged to the very brink of the cliff, and peered over. Ladisla's corpse lay drooped face down over the rocks far below, West's ragged coat spread out behind him, trousers round his ankles, one knee bent back the wrong way, a ring of dark blood spreading out across the stones around his broken head. Never had anyone looked more dead.

West swallowed. He had done that. Him. He had killed the heir to the throne. He had murdered him in cold blood. He was a criminal. He was a traitor. He was a monster.

And he almost wanted to laugh. The sunny Agriont, where loyalty and deference were given without question, where commoners did what their betters told them, where the killing of other people was simply not the done thing, all this was very far away. Monster he might be, but, out here in the frozen wilderness of Angland, the rules were different. Monsters were in the majority.

He felt a hand clap him heavily on the shoulder. He looked up to see Black Dow's earless head beside him, peering down. The Northman whistled softly through pursed lips. 'Well, that's the end of that, I reckon. You know what, Furious?' And he grinned sideways at West. 'I'm getting to like you, boy.'

To the Last Man

To Sand dan Glokta, Superior of Dagoska, and for his eyes alone.

It is clear that, in spite of your efforts, Dagoska cannot remain in Union hands for much longer. I therefore order you to leave immediately and present yourself to me. The docks may have been lost, but you should have no trouble slipping away by night in a small boat. A ship will be waiting for you down the coast.

You will confer overall command on General Vissbruck, as the only Union member of Dagoska's ruling council left alive in the city. It need hardly be said that the orders of the Closed Council to the defenders of Dagoska remain the same.

To fight to the last man.

Sult

Arch Lector of his Majesty's Inquisition.

General Vissbruck slowly lowered the letter, his jaws locked tight together. 'Are we to understand then, Superior, that you are leaving us?' His voice was cracking slightly. *With panic? With fear? With anger? Who could blame him, for any one of them?*

The room was much the same as it had been the first day Glokta arrived in the city. The superb mosaics, the masterful carvings, the polished table, all shining in the early morning sun streaming through the tall windows. *The ruling council itself, however, is sadly reduced.* Vissbruck, his jowls bulging over the stiff collar of his embroidered jacket, and Haddish Kahdia, slumped tiredly in his chair, were all that remained. Nicomo Cosca stood apart, leaning against the wall near the window and picking his fingernails.

Glokta took a deep breath. 'The Arch Lector wants me to . . . explain myself.'

Vissbruck gave a squeaky chuckle. 'For some reason, the image of rats fleeing a burning house springs to mind.' *An apt metaphor. If the rats are fleeing the flames to fling themselves into a mincing machine.*

'Come now, General.' Cosca let his head roll back against the wall, a faint smile on his lips. 'The Superior didn't have to come to us with this. He could have stolen away in the night, and no one any the wiser. That's what I'd have done.'

'Allow me to have scant regard for what *you* might have done,' sneered Vissbruck. 'Our situation is critical. The land walls are lost, and with them all chance of holding out for long. The slums swarm with Gurkish soldiers. Every night we make sallies from the gates of the Upper City. We burn a ram. We kill some sentries while they sleep. But every day they bring up more equipment. Soon, perhaps, they will have cleared space down among the hovels and assembled their great catapults. Shortly thereafter, one imagines, the Upper City will come under sustained fire from incendiaries!' He stabbed an arm at the window. 'They might even reach the Citadel from there! This very room may sport a boulder the size of a woodshed as a centrepiece!'

'I am well aware of our position,' snapped Glokta. *The stench of panic the last few days has grown strong enough almost for the dead to smell it.* 'But the Arch Lector's orders are most specific. To fight to the last man. No surrender.'

Vissbruck's shoulders slumped. 'Surrender would do no good in any case.' He got up, made a half-hearted attempt to straighten his uniform, then slowly pushed his chair under the table. Glokta almost pitied him at that moment. *Probably he is deserving of pity, but I wasted all I had on Carlot dan Eider, who hardly deserved it at all.*

'Allow me to offer you one piece of advice, from a man who's seen the inside of a Gurkish prison. If the city should fall, I strongly recommend that you take your own life rather than be captured.'

General Vissbruck's eyes widened for a moment, then he looked down at the beautiful mosaic floor, and swallowed. When he lifted his face Glokta was surprised to see a bitter smile. 'This is hardly what I had in mind when I joined the army.'

Glokta tapped his ruined leg with his cane, and gave a twisted grin of his own. 'I could say the same. What did Stolicus write? "The recruiting sergeant sells dreams but delivers nightmares?" '

'That would seem appropriate to the case.'

'If it's any comfort, I doubt that my fate will be even as pleasant as yours.'

'A small one.' And Vissbruck snapped his well-polished heels together and stood to vibrating attention. He remained like that for a moment, frozen, then turned without a word for the door, soles clicking loud against the floor and dying away in the corridor outside.

Glokta looked over at Kahdia. 'Regardless of what I said to the General, I would urge you to surrender the city at the earliest opportunity.'

Kahdia's tired eyes slid up. 'After all this? Now?'

Especially now. 'Perhaps the Emperor will choose to be merciful. In any case, I can see little advantage for you in fighting on. As things stand, there is still something to bargain with. You might be able to get some kind of terms.'

'And that is the comfort you offer? The Emperor's mercy?'

'That's all I have. What did you tell me about a man lost in the desert?'

Kahdia nodded slowly. 'Whatever the outcome, I would like to thank you.'

Thank me, you fool? 'For what? Destroying your city and leaving you to the Emperor's mercy?'

'For treating us with some measure of respect.'

Glokta snorted. 'Respect? I thought I simply told you whatever you wanted to hear, in order to get what I needed.'

'Perhaps so. But thanks cost nothing. God go with you.'

'God will not follow where I am going,' Glokta muttered, as Kahdia shuffled slowly from the room.

Cosca grinned down his long nose. 'Back to Adua, eh, Superior?'

'Back, as you say, to Adua.' *Back to the House of Questions. Back to Arch Lector Sult.* The thought was hardly a happy one.

'Perhaps I'll see you there.'

'You think so?' *More likely you'll be butchered along with all the rest when the city falls. Then you'll miss your opportunity to see me hanged.*

'If I've learned one thing, it's that there's always a chance.' Cosca grinned as he pushed himself away from the wall and strutted towards the door, one hand rested jauntily on the pommel of his sword. 'I hate to lose a good employer.'

'I'd hate to be lost. But prepare yourself for the possibility of disappointment. Life is full of them.' *And the manner of its ending is often the greatest one of all.*

'Well then. If one of us should be disappointed.' And Cosca bowed in the doorway with a theatrical flourish, the flaking gilt on his once magnificent breastplate glinting in a shaft of morning sunlight. 'It has been an honour.'

Glokta sat on the bed, tonguing at his empty gums and rubbing his throbbing leg. He looked around his quarters. *Or Davoust's quarters. That's where an old wizard terrified me in the middle of the night. That's where I watched the city burn. That's where I was nearly eaten by a fourteen-year-old girl. Ah, the happy memories . . .*

He grimaced as he pushed himself up and limped over to the one box he had brought with him. *And this is where I signed a receipt for one million marks, advanced by the banking house of Valint and Balk.* He slid the flat leather case that Mauthis had given him out of his coat pocket. *Half a million marks in polished stones, barely touched.* He felt again the tugging temptation to open it, to dig his hand inside and feel that cool, hard, clicking distillation of wealth between his fingers. He resisted with an effort, bent down with a greater one, pushed some of the folded clothes aside with one hand and dug the case down under them with the other. *Black, black and black. I really should get a more varied wardrobe—*

'Going without saying goodbye?'

Glokta jerked violently up from his stoop and nearly vomited at a searing spasm through his back. He reached out with one arm and slammed the box lid down just in time to flop onto it before his leg buckled. Vitari was standing in the doorway, frowning over at him.

'Damn it!' he hissed, blowing spit through the gaps in his teeth with every heaving breath, left leg numb as wood, right leg cramping up with agony.

She padded into the room, narrowed eyes sliding left and right. *Checking that there's no one else here. A private interview, then.* His heart was starting to beat fast as she slowly shut the door, and not just from the spasms in his leg. The key rattled in the lock. *Just the two of us. How terribly exciting.*

She paced silently across the carpet, her long black shadow stretching out towards him. 'I thought we had a deal,' hissed out from behind her mask.

'So did I,' snapped Glokta, struggling to find a more dignified position. 'Then I got a little note from Sult. He wants me back, and I think we can all guess why.'

'Not because of anything I told him.'

'So you say.'

Her eyes narrowed further, her feet padded closer. 'We had a deal. I kept my end.'

'Good for you! You can console yourself with that thought when I'm floating face down in the docks in Adua and you're stuck here, waiting for the Gurkish to break down the— oof!'

And she was on him, her weight grinding his twisted back into the box, squeezing the air from him in a ragged wheeze. There was a bright flash of metal and the rattle of a chain, her fingers slid round his neck.

'You crippled worm! I should cut your fucking throat right now!' Her knee jabbed painfully into his stomach, cold metal tickled gently at the skin on his neck, her blue eyes glared into his, flickering back and forth, glistening hard as the stones in the box under his back. *My death could be moments away. Easily.* He remembered watching her choke the life out of Eider. *With as little care as I might squash an ant, and I, poor cripple, just as helpless as one.* Perhaps he should have been gibbering with fear, but all he could think was: *when was the last time I had a woman on top of me?*

He snorted with laughter. 'Don't you know me at all?' he blubbered, half chuckling, half sobbing, eyes watering with a sickening mixture of pain and amusement. 'Superior Glokta, pleased to meet you! I don't care a good shit what you do, and you know it. Threats? You'll have to do a sight better than that, you ginger whore!'

Her eyes bulged with fury. Her shoulder came forwards, her elbow went back, ready to apply the greatest possible pressure. *Enough to cut my neck through to my twisted spine, I don't doubt.*

Glokta felt his lips curl back in a sickly grin, wet with spit. *Now.*

He heard Vitari's breath snorting behind her mask. *Do it.*

He felt the blade press against his neck, a chill touch, so sharp that he could hardly feel it. *I'm ready.*

Then she let out a long hiss, lifted the blade high and rammed it into the wood beside his head. She stood up and turned away from him. Glokta closed his eyes and breathed for a moment. *Still alive.* There was an odd feeling in his throat. *Relief, or disappointment? Hard to tell the difference.*

'Please.' It was said so softly that he thought he might have imagined it. Vitari was standing with her back to him, head bent over, fists clenched and trembling.

'What?'

'Please.' *She did say it. And it hurts her to do it, you can tell.*

'Please, eh? You think there's any place here for please? Why the hell should I save you, really? You came here to spy for Sult. You've done nothing but get in my way ever since you got here! It's hard to think of anyone I trust less, and I don't trust anyone!'

She turned back to face him, reached behind her head, took hold of the straps of her mask, and pulled it off. There was a sharp tan line underneath: brown round her eyes, her forehead, her neck, white round her mouth with a pink mark across the bridge of her nose. Her face was far softer, much younger, more ordinary than he had expected. She no longer looked fearsome. She looked scared and desperate. Glokta felt suddenly, ludicrously awkward, as though he had blundered into a room and caught someone naked. He almost had to look away as she kneeled down level with him.

'Please.' Her eyes looked moist, dewy, her lip trembling as if she was on the very point of weeping. *A glimpse at the secret hopes beneath the vicious shell? Or just a good act?* Glokta felt his eyelid fluttering. 'It's not for myself,' she almost whispered. 'Please. I'm begging you.'

He rubbed his hand thoughtfully across his neck. When he took it away there was blood on his fingertip. The faintest brown smear. *A nick. A graze. Just a hair's breadth further, and I'd be pumping blood all over the lovely carpet right now. Only a hair's breadth. Lives turn on such chances. Why should I save her?*

But he knew why. *Because I don't save many.*

He turned painfully round on the box so his back was to her and sat there, kneading at the dead flesh of his left leg. He took a deep breath. 'Alright,' he snapped.

'You won't regret it.'

'I regret it already. Damn but I'm a fool for crying women! And you can carry your own damn luggage!' He looked round, raising a finger, but Vitari already had the mask back on. Her eyes were dry, and narrow, and fierce. *They look like eyes that couldn't shed a tear in a hundred years.*

'Don't worry.' She jerked on the chain round her wrist and the cross-shaped blade sprang from the lid of the box and slapped into her waiting palm. 'I travel light.'

Glokta watched the flames reflected in the calm surface of the bay. Shifting fragments, red, yellow, sparkling white in the black water. Frost pulled at the oars, smoothly, evenly, his pale face half lit by the flickering fires in the city, expressionless. Severard sat behind him, hunched over, glowering out across the water. Vitari was beyond, in the prow, her head no more than a spiky outline. The blades dipped into the sea and feathered the water with barely a sound. It hardly seemed that the boat moved. Rather the dark outline of the peninsula slipped slowly away from them, into the darkness.

What have I done? Consigned a city full of people to death or slavery, for what? For the King's honour? A drooling halfwit who can scarcely control his bowels, let alone a country. For my pride? Hah. I threw it all away long ago, along with my teeth. For Sult's approval? My reward is like to be a rope collar and a long drop.

He could just see the darker outline of the rock against the dark night sky, the craggy form of the citadel perched on top of it. Perhaps even the slender shapes of the spires of the Great Temple. All moving off into the past.

What could I have done differently? I could have thrown in my lot with Eider and the rest. Given the city away to the Gurkish without a fight. Would that have changed anything? Glokta licked sourly at his empty gums. *The Emperor would have set about his purges just the same. Sult would have sent for me, just as he has done. Little differences, hardly worth commenting on. What did Shickel say? Few indeed are those who get a choice.*

A chill breeze blew and Glokta pulled his coat tight around him, folded his arms across his chest, winced as he worked his numb foot back and forward in his boot, trying to make the blood flow. The city was nothing but a dusting of pinprick lights, far away.

It is just as Eider said – all so the Arch Lector and his like can point at a map and say this dot or that is ours. His mouth twitched into a smile. *And after all the efforts, all the sacrifices, all the scheming, and plotting, and killing, we could not even hold the city. All that pain, for what?*

There was no reply, of course. Only the calm waves lapping against the side of the boat, the soft creaking of the rowlocks, the soothing slap, slap of the oars on the water. He wanted to feel disgust at himself. Guilt at what he had done. Pity for all those left behind to Gurkish mercy. *The way other men might. The way I might have, long ago.* But it was hard to feel much of anything beyond the overwhelming tiredness and the endless, nagging ache up his leg, through his back, into his neck. He winced as he sagged back on his wooden seat, searching, as always, for a less painful position. *There is no need to punish myself, after all.*

Punishment will come soon enough.

Jewel of Cities

At least he could ride now. The splints had come off that morning, and Jezal's sore leg knocked painfully against his horse's flank as it moved. His hand was numb and clumsy on the reins, his arm weak and aching without the dressing. His teeth still throbbed dully with every thump of the hooves on the ruined road. But at least he was out of the cart, and that was something. Small things seemed to make him very happy these days.

The others rode in a sombre, silent group, grim as mourners at a funeral, and Jezal hardly blamed them. It was a sombre sort of place. A plain of dirt. Of fissures of bare rock. Of sand and stone, empty of life. The sky was a still white nothing, heavy as pale lead, promising rain but never quite delivering. They rode clustered round the cart as though huddling for warmth, the only warm things in a hundred miles of cold desert, the only moving things in a place frozen in time, the only living things in a dead country.

The road was wide, but the stones were cracked and buckled. In places whole stretches of it had crumbled away, in others flows of mud had covered it entirely. The dead stumps of trees jutted from the bare earth to either side. Bayaz must have seen him looking at them.

'An avenue of proud oaks lined this road for twenty miles from the city gates. In summer their leaves shimmered and shook in the wind over the plain. Juvens planted them with his own hands, in the Old Time, when the Empire was young, long before even I was born.'

The mutilated stumps were grey and dry, splintered edges still showing the marks of saws. 'They look as if they were cut down months ago.'

'Many long years, my boy. When Glustrod seized the city, he had them all felled to feed his furnaces.'

'Then why have they not rotted?'

'Even rot is a kind of life. There is no life here.'

Jezal swallowed and hunched his shoulders, watching the chunks of long dead wood file slowly past like rows of tombstones. 'I don't like this,' he muttered under his breath.

'You think I do?' Bayaz frowned grimly over at him. 'You think any of us do? Men must sometimes do what they do not like if they are to be remembered. It is through struggle, not ease, that fame and honour are won. It is through conflict, not peace, that wealth and power are gained. Do such things no longer interest you?'

'Yes,' muttered Jezal, 'I suppose . . .' But he was far from sure. He looked out across the sea of dead dirt. There was precious little sign of honour out here, let alone wealth, and it was hard to see where fame would come from. He was already well known to the only five people within a hundred miles. Besides, he was starting to wonder if a long, poor life in utter obscurity would really be such a terrible thing.

Perhaps, when he got home, he would ask Ardee to marry him. He amused himself by imagining her smile when he suggested it. No doubt she would make him squirm, waiting for an answer. No doubt she would keep him dangling. No doubt she would say yes. What, after all, was the worst that could happen? Would his father be angry? Would they be forced to live on his officer's pay? Would his shallow friends and his idiot brothers chuckle at his back to see him so reduced in the world? He almost laughed to think that those had seemed weighty reasons.

A life of hard work with the woman he loved beside him? A rented house in an unfashionable part of town, with cheap furniture but a cosy fire? No fame, no power, no wealth, but a warm bed with Ardee in it, waiting for him . . . That hardly seemed like such a terrible fate now that he had looked death in the face, when he was living on a bowl of porridge a day and feeling grateful to get it, when he was sleeping alone out in the wind and the rain.

His grin grew wider, and the feeling of the sore skin stretching across his jaw was almost pleasant. That did not seem like such a bad life at all.

The great walls thrust up sheer, scabbed with broken battlements, blistered with shattered towers, scarred with black cracks and slick with wet. A cliff of dark stone, curving away out of sight into the grey drizzle, the bare earth in front of it pooled with brown water and scattered with toppled blocks as big as coffins.

'Aulcus,' growled Bayaz, jaw set hard. 'Jewel of cities.'

'I don't see it sparkling,' grunted Ferro.

Neither did Logen. The slimy road slunk up to a crumbling archway, gaping open, full of shadows, the doors themselves long gone. He had an awful feeling as he looked at that dark gate. A sick feeling. Like the one he had when he looked into the open door of the Maker's House. As if he was looking into a grave, and possibly his own. All he could think about was turning round and never coming back. His horse nickered softly and took a step away, its breath smoking in the misty rain. The hundreds of long and dangerous miles back to the sea seemed suddenly an easier journey than the few strides to that gate.

'Are you sure about this?' he murmured to Bayaz.

'Am I sure? No, of course not! I brought us weary leagues across the barren plain on a whim! I spent years planning the journey, and gathered this little group from all across the Circle of the World for no reason beyond my own amusement! No harm will be done if we simply toddle back to Calcis. Am I sure?' He shook his head as he urged his horse towards the yawning gateway.

Logen shrugged his shoulders. 'Only asking.' The arch gaped wider, and wider, then swallowed them whole. The sound of the horses' hooves echoed down the long tunnel, clattering around them in the darkness. The weight of stone all around pressed in close and seemed to make it hard to take a breath. Logen put his head down, frowning towards the circle of light at the far end as it grew steadily bigger. He glanced sideways and caught Luthar's eye, licking his lips nervously in the gloom, wet hair plastered to his face.

And then they came out into the open.

'My, my,' breathed Longfoot. 'My, my, my . . .'

Colossal buildings rose up on either side of a vast square. The ghosts of tall pillars and high roofs, of towering columns and great walls, all made for giants, loomed from the haze of rain. Logen gawped. They all did, a tiny huddled group in that outsize space, like scared sheep in a bare valley, waiting for the wolves to come.

Rain hissed on stone high overhead, falling water splattered on the slick cobbles, trickled down the crumbling walls, gurgled in the cracks in the road. The thudding of hooves fell muffled. The cartwheels gently croaked and groaned. No other noise. No bustle, no din, no chatter of crowds. No birds calling, no dogs barking, no clatter of trade and commerce. Nothing lived. Nothing moved. There were only the great black buildings, stretching far away into the rain, and the ripped clouds crawling across the dark sky above.

They rode slowly past the ruins of some fallen temple, a tangled mass of dripping blocks and slabs, sections of its monstrous columns scattered on their sides across the broken paving, fragments from its roof thrown wide, still lying where they fell. Luthar's wet face, apart from the pink stain across his chin, was chalky white as he gazed up at the soaring wreckage to either side. 'Bloody hell,' he muttered.

'It is indeed,' murmured Longfoot under his breath, 'a most impressive sight.'

'The palaces of the wealthy dead,' said Bayaz. 'The temples where they prayed to angry gods. The markets where they bought and sold goods, and animals, and people. Where they bought and sold each other. The theatres, and the baths, and the brothels where they indulged their passions, before Glustrod came.' He pointed across the square and down the valley of dripping stone beyond. 'This is the Caline Way. The greatest road of the city, and where the greatest citizens had their dwellings. It runs straight through, more or less, from the northern gate to the southern. Now listen to me,' he said, turning in his creaking saddle. 'Three miles south of the city there is a high hill, with a temple on its summit. The Saturline Rock, they called it in the Old Time. If we should become separated, that is where we will meet.'

'Why would we be separated?' asked Luthar, his eyes wide.

'The earth in the city is . . . unquiet, and prone to tremble. The buildings are ancient, and unstable. I hope that we will pass through without incident but . . . it would be rash to rely on hope alone. If anything should happen, head south. Toward the Saturline Rock. Until then, stay close together.'

That hardly needed saying. Logen looked over at Ferro as they set off into the city, her black hair spiky, her dark face dewy with wet, frowning up suspiciously at the towering buildings to either side. 'If anything should happen,' he whispered to her, 'help me out, eh?'

She looked at him for a moment, then nodded. 'If I can, pink.'

'Good enough.'

The only thing worse than a city full of people is a city with no people at all.

Ferro rode with her bow in one hand, the reins in the other, staring to both sides, peering down the alleys, into the gaping windows and doorways, straining to see round the crumbling corners and over the broken walls. She did not know what she was looking for.

But she would be ready.

They all felt as she did, she could see it. She watched the fibres of jaw muscle tensing and relaxing, tensing and relaxing, over and over, on the side of Ninefingers' head as he frowned off into the ruins, his hand never far from the grip of his sword, scored cold metal shining with beads of moisture.

Luthar jumped at every noise – at the crack of a stone under the cartwheels, at the splatter of falling water into a pool, at the snort of one of the horses, his head jerking this way and that, the tip of his tongue licking endlessly at the slot in his lip.

Quai sat on the cart, bent over with his wet hair flapping round his gaunt face, pale lips pressed together into a hard line. Ferro watched him snap the reins, saw he was gripping them so tightly that the tendons stood out stark from the backs of his thin hands. Longfoot stared about him at the endless ruins, eyes and mouth hanging slightly open, rivulets of water occasionally streaking through the stubble on his knobbly skull. For once he had nothing to say – the one small advantage of this place abandoned by God.

Bayaz was trying to look confident, but Ferro knew better. She watched his hand tremble when he took it from the reins to rub the water from his thick brows. She watched his mouth work when they stopped at junctions, watched him squinting into the rain, trying to reckon the right course. She saw his worry and his doubt written in his every movement. He knew as well as she did. This place was not safe.

Click-clank.

It came faint through the rain, like the sound of a hammer on a distant anvil. The sound of weapons being made ready. She stood up in her stirrups, straining to listen.

'Do you hear that?' she snapped at Ninefingers.

He paused, squinting off at nothing, listening. Click-clank. He nodded slowly. 'I hear it.' He slid his sword out from its sheath.

'What?' Luthar stared around wild-eyed, fumbling for his own weapons. 'There's nothing out there,' grumbled Bayaz.

She jabbed her palm at them to stop, slid down from her saddle and crept up to the corner of the next building, nocking an arrow to her bow, back sliding across the rough surface of the huge stone blocks. Clank-click. She could feel Ninefingers following, moving carefully, a reassuring presence behind her.

She slid round the corner onto one knee, peering across an empty square, pocked with pools and strewn with rubble. There was a high tower at the far corner, leaning over to one side, wide windows hanging open at its summit under a tarnished dome. Something was moving in there, slowly. Something dark, rocking back and forth. She almost smiled to have something she could point an arrow at.

It was a good feeling, having an enemy.

Then she heard hooves and Bayaz rode past, out into the ruined square. 'Ssss!' she hissed at him, but he ignored her.

'You can put your weapons away,' he called over his shoulder. 'It's nothing but an old bell, clicking in the wind. The city was full of them. You should have heard them pealing out, when an Emperor was born, or crowned, or married, or welcomed back from a victorious campaign.' He started to raise his arms, voice growing louder. 'The air split with their joyous ringing, and birds rose up from every square and street and roof and filled the sky!' He was shouting now, bellowing it out. 'And the people lined the streets! And they leaned from their windows! And they showered the beloved with flower petals! And cheered until their voices were hoarse!' He started to laugh, and he let his arms fall, and high above him the broken bell clicked and clanked in the wind. 'Long ago. Come on.'

Quai snapped the reins and the cart trundled off after the Magus. Ninefingers shrugged at her and sheathed his sword. Ferro stayed a moment, staring up suspiciously at the stark outline of that leaning tower, dark clouds flowing past above it.

Click-clank.

Then she followed the others.

*

The statues swam up out of the angry rain, one pair of frozen giants at a time, their faces all worn down by the long years until every one was the featureless same. Water trickled over smooth marble, dripped from long beards, from armoured skirts, from arms outstretched in threat or blessing, amputated long ago at the wrist, or the elbow, or the shoulder. Some were worked with bronze: huge helmets, swords, sceptres, crowns of leaves, all turned chalky green leaving dirty streaks down the gleaming stone. The statues swam up out of the angry rain, and one pair of giants at a time they vanished into the rain behind, consigned to the mists of history.

'Emperors,' said Bayaz. 'Hundreds of years of them.'

Jezal watched the rulers of antiquity file menacingly past, looming over the broken road, his neck aching from looking up, the rain tickling at his face. The sculptures were twice the height or more of the ones in the Agriont, but there was similarity enough to cause a sudden wave of homesickness.

'Just like to the Kingsway, in Adua.'

'Huh,' grunted Bayaz. 'Where do you think I got the idea?'

Jezal was just absorbing that bizarre comment when he noticed that the statues they were approaching now were the last pair, one tilted over at a worrying angle.

'Hold up the cart!' called Bayaz, raising one wet palm and nudging his horse forward.

Not only were there no more Emperors before them, there was no road at all. A dizzy drop yawned out of the earth, a mighty crack in the fabric of the city. Squinting across, Jezal could just see the far side, a cliff of broken rock and crumbled mud. Beyond were the faint wraiths of walls and pillars, the outline of the wide avenue, melting out of sight and back as the rain swept through the empty air between.

Longfoot cleared his throat. 'I take it we will not be carrying on this way.'

Ever so carefully Jezal leaned from his saddle and peered down. Far below dark water moved, foaming and churning, washing at the tortured ground beneath the foundations of the city, and out of this subterranean sea stuck broken walls, and shattered towers, and the cracked open shells of monstrous buildings. At the top of one tottering column a statue still stood, some hero long dead. His hand must once have been raised in triumph. Now it stuck up in desperation, as if he was pleading for someone to drag him from his watery hell.

Jezal sat back, feeling suddenly dizzy. 'We will not be carrying on this way,' he managed to croak.

Bayaz frowned grimly down at the grinding water. 'Then we must find another, and quickly. The city is full of these cracks. We have miles to go even on a straight course, and a bridge to cross.'

Longfoot frowned. 'Providing it still stands.'

'It still stands! Kanedias built to last.' The First of the Magi peered up into the rain. The sky was already bruising, a dark weight hanging above their heads. 'We cannot afford to linger. We will not make it through the city before dark as it is.'

Jezal looked up at the Magus, horrified. 'We'll be here overnight?'

'Clearly,' snapped Bayaz, turning his horse away from the brink.

The ruins crowded in tighter around them as they left the Caline Way behind and struck out into the thick of the city. Jezal gazed up at the threatening shadows, looming from the murk. The only thing he could imagine worse than being trapped in this place by day was being kept there in the darkness. He would have preferred to spend the night in hell. But what would have been the difference?

The river surged below them through a man-made canyon – tall embankments of smooth, wet stone. The mighty Aos, imprisoned in that narrow space, foamed with infinite, mindless fury, chewing at the polished rock and spitting angry spray high into the air. Ferro could not imagine how anything could have lasted for long above that deluge, but Bayaz had been right.

The Maker's bridge still stood.

'In all my wide travels, in every city and nation under the bountiful sun, I have never seen such a wonder.' Longfoot slowly shook his shaven head. 'How can a bridge be made from metal?'

But metal it was. Dark, smooth, lustreless, gleaming with drops of water. It soared across the dizzy space in one simple arch, impossibly delicate, a spider's web of thin rods criss-crossing the hollow air beneath it, a wide road of slotted metal plates stretching out perfectly level across the top, inviting them to cross. Every edge was sharp, every curve precise, every surface clean. It stood pristine in the midst of all that slow decay. 'As if it was finished yesterday,' muttered Quai.

'And yet it is perhaps the oldest thing in the city.' Bayaz nodded towards the ruins behind them. 'All the achievements of Juvens are laid waste. Fallen, broken, forgotten, almost as though they had never been. But the works of the Master Maker are undiminished. They shine the brighter, if anything, for they shine in a darkened world.' He snorted, and mist blew from his nostrils. 'Who knows? Perhaps they will still stand whole and unmarked at the end of time, long after all of us are in our graves.'

Luthar peered nervously down towards the thundering water, no doubt wondering if his grave might be there. 'You're sure it will carry us?'

'In the Old Time it carried thousands of people a day. Tens of thousands. Horses and carts and citizens and slaves in an endless procession, flowing both ways, day and night. It will carry us.' Ferro watched as the hooves of Bayaz' horse clanged out onto the metal.

'This Maker was plainly a man of . . . quite remarkable talents,' murmured the Navigator, urging his horse after.

Quai snapped his reins. 'He was indeed. All lost to the world.'

Ninefingers went next, then Luthar reluctantly followed. Ferro stayed where she was, sitting in the pattering rain, frowning at the bridge, at the cart, at the four horses and their riders. She did not like this. The river, the bridge, the city, none of it. It had been feeling more and more like a trap with every step, and now she felt sure of it. She should never have listened to Yulwei. She should never have left the South. She had no business here, out in this freezing, wet, deserted wasteland with this gang of godless pinks.

'I am not going over that,' she said.

Bayaz turned to look at her. 'Do you plan to fly across, then? Or simply stay on that side?'

She sat back and crossed her hands before her on the saddle-bow. 'Perhaps I will.'

'It might be better to discuss such matters once we have made it through the city,' murmured Brother Longfoot, looking nervously back into the empty streets.

'He's right,' said Luthar. 'This place has an evil air—'

'Shit on its air,' growled Ferro, 'and shit on you. Why should I cross? What is it exactly, that is so useful to me about that side of a river? You have promised me vengeance, old pink, and given me nothing but lies, and rain, and bad food. Why should I take another stride with you? Tell me that!'

Bayaz frowned. 'My brother Yulwei helped you in the desert. You would have been killed if not for him. You gave him your word—'

'Word? Hah! A word is an easy chain to break, old man.' And she jerked her wrists apart in front of her. 'There. I am free of it. I did not promise to make a slave of myself.'

The Magus gave vent to a long sigh, slumping wearily forward in his saddle. 'As if life were not hard enough without your contributions. Why is it, Ferro, that you would rather make things difficult than easy?'

'Perhaps God had some purpose in mind when he made me so, but I do not know it. What is the Seed?'

Straight to the root of the matter. The old pink's eye seemed to give a sudden twitch as she said the word. 'Seed?' muttered Luthar, baffled.

Bayaz frowned at the puzzled faces of the others. 'It might be better not to know.'

'Not good enough. If you fall asleep for a week again, I want to know what we are doing, and why.'

'I am well recovered now,' snapped Bayaz, but Ferro knew it for a lie. Every part of him seemed shrunken, older and weaker than it had been. He might have been awake, and talking, but he was far from recovered. It would take more than bland assurances to fool her. 'It will not happen again, you can depend on—'

'I will ask you one more time, and hope at last for a simple answer. What is the Seed?'

Bayaz looked at her for a long moment, and she looked back. 'Very well. We will sit in the rain and discuss the nature of things.' And he nudged his horse back off the bridge until it was no more than a stride away. 'The Seed is one name for that thing that Glustrod dug for in the deep earth. It is that thing he used to do all this.'

'This?' grunted Ninefingers.

'All this.' And the First of the Magi swept his arm towards the wreckage that surrounded them. 'The Seed made a ruin of the greatest city in the world, and blighted the land about it from now until eternity.'

'It is a weapon, then?' murmured Ferro.

'It is a stone,' said Quai suddenly, hunched on his cart, looking at no one. 'A rock from the world below. Left behind, buried, when Euz cast the devils from our world. It is the Other Side made flesh. The very stuff of magic.'

'It is indeed,' whispered Bayaz. 'My congratulations, Master Quai. One subject at least of which you are not entirely ignorant. Well? Answers enough for you, Ferro?'

'A rock did all this?' Ninefingers did not look happy. 'What in hell do we want with it?'

'I think some among us can guess.' Bayaz was looking at Ferro, right in the eye, and smiling a sickly grin, as if he knew exactly what she thought. Perhaps he did.

It was no secret.

Stories of devils, and digging, and old wet ruins, none of that mattered to Ferro. She was busy imagining the Empire of Gurkhul made a dead land. Its people vanished. Its Emperor forgotten. Its cities brought to dust. Its power a faded memory. Her mind churned with thoughts of death and vengeance. Then she smiled.

'Good,' she said. 'But why do you need me?'

'Who says I do need you that badly?'

She snorted at him. 'I doubt you would have suffered me this long if you didn't.'

'True enough.'

'Then why?'

'Because the Seed cannot be touched. It is painful even to look upon. We came into the shattered city with the Emperor's army, after the fall of Glustrod, searching for survivors. We found none. Only horrors, and ruins, and bodies. Too many of those to count. Thousands upon thousands we buried, in pits for a hundred each, all through the city. It was long work, and while we were about it a company of soldiers found something strange in the ruins. Their Captain wrapped it in his cloak and brought it to Juvens. By dusk he had withered and died, and his company were not spared. Their hair fell out, their bodies shrivelled. Within a week all hundred men were corpses. But Juvens himself was unharmed.' He nodded at the cart. 'That is why Kanedias made the box, and that is why we have it with us now. To protect us. None of us are safe. Except for you.'

'Why me?'

'Did you never wonder why you are not as others are? Why you see no colours? Why you feel no pain? You are what Juvens was, and Kanedias. You are what Glustrod was. You are what Euz himself was, if it comes to that.'

'Devil-blood,' murmured Quai. 'Blessed and cursed.'

Ferro glowered at him. 'What do you mean?'

'You are descended from demons.' And one corner of the apprentice's mouth curled up in a knowing smile. 'Far back into the Old Time and beyond, perhaps, but still, you are not entirely human. You are a relic. A last weak trace of the blood of the Other Side.'

Ferro opened her mouth to snarl an insult back at him but Bayaz cut her off.

'There can be no denying it, Ferro. I would not have brought you if there were any doubt. But you should not seek to deny it. You should embrace it. It is a rare gift. You can touch the Seed. Perhaps only you in all the wide Circle of the World. Only you can touch it, and only you can carry it to war.' He leaned close and whispered to her. 'But only I can make it burn. Hot enough to turn all Gurkhul to a desert. Hot enough to make bitter ashes of Khalul and all his servants. Hot enough to make such vengeance that even you will have your fill of it, and more. Are you coming now?' And he clicked his tongue, pulling his horse away and back onto the bridge.

Ferro frowned at the old pink's back as she rode after him, chewing hard at her lip. When she licked it, she tasted blood. Blood, but no pain. She did not like to believe anything the Magus said, but there was no denying that she was not as others were. She remembered she had bitten Aruf once, and he had told her that she must have had a snake for a mother. Why not a demon? She watched the water thundering by far below, through the slots in the metal, frowning, and thinking on vengeance.

'Don't hardly matter whose blood you've got.' Ninefingers was riding beside her. Riding badly, as usual, and looking across, voice gentle. 'Man makes his own choices, my father used to tell me. Reckon that goes for women just as much.'

Ferro did not answer. She dragged on her reins and let the others pull ahead. Woman, or demon, or snake, it made no difference. Her concern was hurting the Gurkish. Her hatred was strong, and deep-rooted, warm and familiar. Her oldest friend.

She could trust nothing else.

Ferro was the last one off the bridge. She took a look back over her shoulder as they moved off into the crumbling city, towards the ruins they had come from, half hidden on the far bank by the grey shroud of drizzle.

'Ssss!' She jerked on her reins, glaring over the surging water, eyes flicking over the hundreds of empty windows, the hundreds of empty doorways, the hundreds of cracks and gaps and spaces in the crumbling walls.

'What did you see?' came Ninefingers' worried voice.

'Something.' But she saw nothing now. Along the crumbling embankment the endless shells of buildings squatted, empty and lifeless.

'There is nothing left alive in this place,' said Bayaz. 'Night will find us soon, and I for one could do with a roof to keep the rain off my old bones tonight. Your eyes are playing tricks.'

Ferro scowled. Her eyes played no tricks, devil's eyes or no. There was something out there, in the city. She felt it.

Watching them.

Luck

'**U**p you get, Luthar.'

Jezal's eyes fluttered open. It was so bright that he could hardly make out where he was, and he grunted and blinked, shading his eyes with one hand. Someone had been shaking his shoulder. Ninefingers. 'We need to be on our way.'

Jezal sat up. Sunlight was streaming into the narrow chamber, straight into his face, specks of dust floating in the glare. 'Where is everyone?' he croaked, tongue thick and lazy with sleep.

The Northman jerked his shaggy head towards the tall window. Squinting, Jezal could just see Brother Longfoot standing there, looking out, hands clasped behind him. 'Our Navigator's taking in the view. Rest of the crew are out front, seeing to the horses, reckoning the route. Thought you might use a few minutes more under the blanket.'

'Thanks.' He could have used a few hours more yet. Jezal worked his sour mouth, licking at the aching holes in his teeth, the sore crease in his lip, checking how painful they were this morning. Every day the swelling was a little less. He was almost getting used to it.

'Here.' Jezal looked up to see Ninefingers tossing him a biscuit. He tried to catch it but his bad hand was still clumsy and it dropped in the dirt. The Northman shrugged. 'Bit of dust won't do you any harm.'

'Daresay it won't, at that.' Jezal picked it up, brushed it off with the back of his hand and took a dry bite from it, making sure to use the good side of his mouth. He threw his blanket back, rolled over and pushed himself stiffly from the ground.

Logen watched him take a few trial steps, arms spread out wide for balance, biscuit clutched in one hand. 'How's the leg?'

'It's been worse.' It had been better too. He walked with a fool of a limp, sore leg held straight. The knee and the ankle hurt every time he put his weight on it, but he could walk, and every morning it was improving. When he made it to the rough stone wall he closed his eyes and took a deep breath, half wanting to laugh, half wanting to cry with relief at the simple joy of being able to stand on his own feet again.

'From now on I will be grateful for every moment that I can walk.'

Ninefingers grinned. 'That feeling lasts a day or two, then you'll be moaning about the food again.'

'I will not,' said Jezal firmly.

'Alright. A week then.' He walked towards the window at the far end of the room, casting a stretched-out shadow across the dusty floor. 'In the meantime, you should have a look at this.'

'At what?' Jezal hopped up beside Brother Longfoot, leaned against the pitted column at the side of the window, breathing hard and shaking out his aching leg. Then he looked up, and his mouth fell open.

They must have been high up. At the top of the steep slope of a hill perhaps, looking out over the city. The just-risen sun hung level with Jezal's eyes, watery yellow through the morning haze. The sky was clear and pale above it, a few shreds of white cloud stretched out almost still.

Even in ruins, hundreds of years after its fall, the vista of Aulcus was breathtaking.

Broken roofs stretched away into the far distance, crumbling walls brightly lit or sunk in long shadows. Stately domes, teetering towers, leaping arches and proud columns thrust up above the jumble. He could make out the gaps left by wide squares, by broad avenues, the yawning space cut by the river, curving gently through the forest of stone on his right, light glittering on the shifting water. In every direction, as far as Jezal could see, wet stone glowed in the morning sun.

'And this is why I love to travel,' breathed Longfoot. 'At one stroke, in one moment, this whole journey has been made worthwhile. Has there ever been such another sight? How many men living can have gazed upon it? The three of us stand at a window upon history, at a gate into the long forgotten past. No longer will I dream of fair Talins, glittering on the sea in the red morning, or Ul-Nahb, glowing beneath the azure bowl of the heavens in the bright midday, or Ospria, proud upon her mountain slopes, lights shining like the stars in the soft evening. From this day forth, my heart will forever belong to Aulcus. Truly, the jewel of cities. Sublime beyond words in death, dare one even dream of how she must have looked in life? Who could not be struck with wonder at the magnificence of this sight? Who could not be struck with awe at the—'

'A load of old buildings,' growled Ferro, right behind him. 'And it is past time we were out of them. Get your gear stowed.' And she turned and stalked off towards the entrance.

Jezal frowned back over his shoulder at the gleaming sweep of dark ruins, stretching away into the distant haze. There was no denying that it was magnificent, and yet it was frightening as well. The splendid buildings of Adua, the mighty walls and towers of the Agriont: all that Jezal had thought of as magnificent seemed mean and feeble copies. He felt like a tiny, ignorant boy, from a small and barbaric country, in a petty, insignificant time. He was glad to turn away, and to leave the jewel of cities in the past where it belonged. He would not be dreaming of Aulcus.

Nightmares, maybe.

It must have been late morning when they came upon the only square in the city that was still crowded. A giant space, and thronging from one side to the other. A motionless, silent crowd. A crowd carved from stone.

Statues of every attitude, size, and material. There was black basalt and white marble, green alabaster and red porphyry, grey granite and a hundred other stones of which Jezal could not guess the names. The variety was strange enough, but it was the one thing they all had in common which he found truly worrying. Not one of them had a face.

Colossal features had been picked away leaving formless messes of pock-marked rock. Small ones had been hacked out leaving empty craters of rough stone. Ugly messages in some script that Jezal did not recognise had been chiselled across marble chests, down arms, round necks, into fore-heads. It seemed that everything in Aulcus had been done on an epic scale, and the vandalism was no exception.

There was a path cleared through the middle of this sinister wreckage, wide enough for the cart to pass. So Jezal rode out, at the front of the group, through a forest of faceless shapes, crowded in on either side like the throng at a procession of state.

'What happened here?' he murmured.

Bayaz frowned up at a head that might easily have been ten strides high, its lips still pressed into a powerful frown, its eyes and nose all chopped away, harsh writing cut deep into its cheek. 'When Glustrod seized the city, he gave his cursed army one day to make free with its people. To satisfy their fury, and quench their lust for plunder, rape and murder. As though they could ever be satisfied.' Ninefingers coughed and shifted uncomfort-ably in his saddle. 'Then they were ordered to tear down all the statues of Juvens in the city. From every roof, from every hall, from every frieze and temple. There were many likenesses of my master in Aulcus, for the city was his design. But Glustrod was nothing if not thorough. He sought them all out, and had them gathered here, and defaced them all, and stamped into them terrible curses.'

'Not a happy family.' Jezal had never seen eye to eye with his own brothers, but this seemed to him a little excessive. He ducked away from the outstretched fingers of a giant hand, standing upright on its severed wrist, a ragged symbol chiselled savagely out of the palm.

'What does it say?'

Bayaz frowned. 'Believe me, it is better you do not know.'

A colossal building, even by the standards of this giant's grave-yard, towered over the army of sculptures at one side. Its steps were high as a city wall, the columns of its façade as thick as towers, its monstrous pediment encrusted with faded carvings. Bayaz reined his horse up before it and stared up. Jezal stopped behind him, glancing nervously at the others.

'Let's keep on.' Ninefingers scratched at his face and stared round anxiously. 'Let's leave this place as quickly as we can, and never come back.'

Bayaz chuckled. 'The Bloody-Nine, scared of shadows? I'd never have believed it.'

'Every shadow's cast by something,' growled the Northman, but the First of the Magi was not to be put off.

'We have time enough to stop,' he said as he struggled from the saddle. 'We are close to the edge of the city, now. An hour at the most and we are out and on our way. You might find this interesting, Captain Luthar. As would anyone else who would care to join me.'

Ninefingers cursed under his breath in his own tongue. 'Alright, then. I'd rather walk than wait.'

'You have quite piqued my curiosity,' said Brother Longfoot as he jumped down next to them. 'I must confess that the city does not seem so daunting in the light as it did in the rain of yesterday. Indeed, it is hard now to see why it has such a black reputation. Nowhere in all the Circle of the World can there be such a collection of fascinating relics, and I am a curious man, and unashamed to admit it. Yes indeed, I have always been a—'

'We know what you are,' hissed Ferro. 'I'll wait here.'

'Please yourself.' Bayaz dragged his staff from his saddle. 'As always. You and Master Quai can no doubt each delight the other with comical tales while we are gone. I am almost sorry to miss the banter.' Ferro and the apprentice frowned at each other as the rest of them made their way between the ruined statues and up the wide steps, Jezal limping and wincing on his bad leg. They passed through a doorway as big as a house and into a cool, dim, silent space.

It reminded Jezal of the Lords' Round in Adua, but even bigger. A cavernous, circular chamber, like a great bowl with stepped seating up the sides, carved from stone of many colours, whole sections of it smashed and ruined. The bottom was choked with rubble, no doubt the remnants of a collapsed roof.

'Ah. The great dome fallen.' The Magus squinted up through the ragged space into the bright sky beyond. 'A fitting metaphor.' He sighed, shuffling slowly round the curving aisle between the marble shelves. Jezal frowned up at that vast weight of overhanging stone, wondering what might happen if a chunk of it should fall and hit him on the head. He doubted Ferro would be stitching that up. He had not the slightest idea why Bayaz wanted him here, but then he could have said that for the whole journey, and indeed he often had. So he took a deep breath and limped out after the

Magus, Ninefingers just behind, the noises of their movement echoing around in the great space.

Longfoot picked his way among the broken steps and peered up at the fallen ceiling with a show of great interest. 'What was this place?' he called out, voice bouncing from the curved walls. 'Some manner of theatre?'

'In a sense,' replied Bayaz. 'This was the great chamber of the Imperial Senate. Here the Emperor sat in state, to hear debates between the wisest citizens of Aulcus. Here decisions were made that have set the course of history.' He clambered up a step and shuffled further, pointed excitedly to the floor, voice shrill with excitement.

'It was on this precise spot, as I remember it, that Calica stood to address the senate, urging caution in the Empire's eastern expansion. It was down there that Juvens replied to him, arguing boldness, and carried the day. I watched them, spellbound. Twenty years old, and breathless with excitement. I still recall their arguments, in every detail. Words, my friends. There can be a greater power in words than in all the steel within the Circle of the World.'

'A blade in your ear still hurts more than a word in it, though,' whispered Logen. Jezal spluttered with laughter, but Bayaz did not seem to notice. He was too busy hurrying from one stone bench to another.

'Here Scarpius gave his exhortation on the dangers of decadence, on the true meaning of citizenship. The senate sat, entranced. His voice rang out like . . . like . . .' Bayaz plucked at the air with his hand, as though hoping to find the right word there. 'Bah. What does it matter now? There are no certainties left in the world. That was the age of great men, doing what was right.' He frowned down at the broken rubble choking the floor of the colossal room. 'This is the age of little men, doing what they must. Little men, with little dreams, walking in giant footsteps. Still, you can see it was a grand building once!'

'Er, yes . . .' ventured Jezal, limping away from the others to peer at some friezes carved into the wall at the very back of the seating. Half-naked warriors, awkwardly posed, pushing at each other with spears. All grand, no doubt, but there was an unpleasant smell to the place. Like rot, like damp, like sweating animals. The odour of a badly cleaned stables. He peered into the shadows, wrinkling his nose. 'What is that smell?'

Ninefingers sniffed the air, and his face fell in an instant. A picture of wide-eyed horror. 'By the . . .' He ripped his sword out, taking a step forward. Jezal turned, fumbling for the grips of his steels, a sudden fear pressing on his chest . . .

He took it at first for some manner of beggar: a dark shape, swathed in rags, squatting on all fours in the darkness only a few paces away. Then he saw the hands; twisted and claw-like on the pitted stone. Then he saw the grey face, if you could call it a face; a chunk of hairless brow, a lumpen jaw bursting with outsize teeth, a flat snout like a pig's, tiny black eyes glinting with fury as it glared back at him. Something between a man and an animal, and more hideous by far than either. Jezal's jaw dropped open, and he stood gawping. It scarcely seemed worth telling Ninefingers that he now believed him.

It was clear there were such things as Shanka in the world.

'Get it!' roared the Northman, scrambling up the steps of the great chamber, drawn sword in hand. 'Kill it!'

Jezal shambled uncertainly towards the thing, but his leg was still halfway to useless and the creature was quick as a fox, turning and skittering across the cold stone towards a crack in the curving wall and wriggling through like a cat through a fence before he had got more than a few lurching steps.

'It's gone!'

Bayaz was already shuffling towards the entrance, the tapping of his staff on the marble echoing above them. 'We see that, Master Luthar. We all very clearly see that!'

'There'll be more,' hissed Logen, 'there're always more! We have to go!'

It had been bad luck, Jezal thought as he lurched back towards the entrance, stumbling down the broken steps and wincing at the pain in his knee. Bad luck that Bayaz had decided to stop, right here and now. Bad luck that Jezal's leg had been broken and he couldn't run after that repulsive thing. Bad luck that they had come to Aulcus, instead of being able to cross the river miles downstream.

'How did they get here?' Logen was shouting at Bayaz.

'I can only guess,' grunted the Magus, wincing and breathing hard. 'After the Maker's death we hunted them. We drove them into the dark corners of the world.'

'There are few corners darker than this one.' Longfoot hurried past them for the entrance and down the steps, two at a time, and Jezal hopped after him.

'What is it?' called Ferro, pulling her bow off her shoulder.

'Flatheads!' roared Ninefingers.

She gazed at him blankly and the Northman flapped his free hand at her. 'Just fucking ride!'

Bad luck. That Jezal had beaten Bremer dan Gorst and been chosen by Bayaz for this mad journey. Bad luck that he had ever held a fencing steel. Bad luck that his father had wanted him to join the army instead of doing nothing with his life like his two brothers. Strange how that had always seemed like good luck at the time. Sometimes it was hard to tell the difference.

Jezal stumbled up to his horse, grabbed the saddle-bow and dragged himself clumsily up. Longfoot and Ninefingers were already in their saddles. Bayaz was just shoving his staff back into its place with trembling hands. Somewhere in the city behind them, a bell began to clang.

'Oh dear,' said Longfoot, peering wide-eyed through the multitude of statues. 'Oh dear.'

'Bad luck,' whispered Jezal.

Ferro was staring at him. 'What?'

'Nothing.' Jezal gritted his teeth, and gave his horse the spurs.

There was no such thing as luck. Luck was a word idiots used to explain the consequences of their own rashness, and selfishness, and stupidity. More often than not bad luck meant bad plans.

And here was the proof.

She had warned Bayaz that there was something in the city besides her and five pink fools. She had warned him, but no one had listened. People only believe what they want to. Idiots, anyway.

She watched the others, while she rode. Quai, on the seat of the jolting cart, eyes narrowed and fixed ahead. Luthar, with his lips curled back from his teeth, pressed into the saddle in the crouch of a practised rider. Bayaz, jaw clenched tight, face pale and drawn, clinging on grimly. Longfoot, looking often over his shoulder, eyes wide with fear and alarm. Nine-fingers, jolting in his saddle, breathing hard, spending more time looking at his reins than at the road. Five idiots, and her.

She heard a growl and saw a creature squatting on a low roof. It was like nothing she had seen before – a bent-over ape, twisted and long-limbed. Apes do not throw spears, however. Her eyes followed it as it arced downwards. It thudded into the side of the cart and stuck there, wobbling, then they were past and clattering on down the rutted street.

That one might have missed, but there were more creatures in the ruins ahead. Ferro could see them moving in the shadowy buildings. Scuttling along the roofs, lurking in the crumbling windows, the gaping doorways. She was tempted to try a shaft at one of them, but what would have been the point? There were a lot of them out there. Hundreds, it felt like. What good would killing one of them do, when they were soon left behind? A waste of an arrow.

A rock crashed down suddenly beside her and she felt a fragment from it whiz past and nick the back of her hand. It left a bead of dark blood on her skin. Ferro frowned and put her head down, keeping herself low to the bouncing back of her horse. There was no such thing as luck.

But there was no point being a bigger target.

Logen thought he'd left the Shanka far behind, but after the first shock of seeing one, it came as no surprise. He should've known by now. Only friends get left behind. Enemies are always at your heels.

The bells were all around them, echoing out of the ruins. Logen's skull was full of their clashing, stabbing through the cracking hooves and the shrieking wheels and the rushing air. Clanging, far away, near at hand, ahead and behind. The buildings rushed by, grey shapes full of danger.

He saw something flash by ahead and bounce spinning from the stones. A spear. He heard another twitter behind, then saw one clatter across the road in front. He swallowed, narrowing his eyes against the wind in his face, and tried not to imagine a spear thudding into his back. It wasn't too difficult. Just holding on was taking all his concentration.

Ferro had turned in her saddle to shout something at him over her shoulder, but her words were lost in the noise. He shook his head at her and she stabbed her arm furiously at the road ahead. Now he saw it. A crevasse opened in the road before them, rushing up at a gallop. Logen's mouth gaped just as wide and he gave a breathless squeak of horror.

He dragged on the reins, and his horse's hooves slipped and skittered on the old stones, turning sharply to the right. The saddle lurched and Logen clung on, cobbles flying by underneath in a grey blur, the edge of the great chasm rushing past no more than a few strides away on his left, cracks from it cutting out into the crumbling road. He could feel the others nearby, could hear voices shouting, but he couldn't hear their words. He was too busy rolling and bouncing painfully in the saddle, willing himself to stay on, all the while whispering.

'Still alive, still alive, still alive . . .'

A temple loomed up towards them, straddling the road, its towering pillars still intact, a monstrous triangular weight of stone still standing on top. The cart crashed between two of the columns and Logen's horse found its way between two others, dipping suddenly into shadow and back out, all of them surging into a wide hall, open to the sky. The crack had swallowed the wall to the left, and if there had ever been a roof it had vanished long ago. Logen rode on, breathless, eyes fixed on a wide archway straight ahead, a square of brightness in the dark stone, bouncing and jolting with the movement of his horse. That was safety, Logen told himself. If they could get through there they were away. If they could only get through there . . .

He didn't see the spear coming, but if he had there would've been nothing he could've done. It was lucky, in a way, that it missed his leg. It thudded deep into horseflesh just in front of it. That was less lucky. He heard the horse snort as its legs buckled, as he came free of the saddle, mouth dropping open and no sound coming out, the floor of the hall flashing up to meet him. Hard stone crunched into his chest and snatched his wind away. His jaw smacked against the ground and his head flooded with blinding light. He bounced once, then flopped over and over, the world spinning crazily around him, full of strange sound and blinding sky. He slid to a stop on his side.

He lay in a daze, groaning softly, his head reeling, his ears ringing, not knowing where he was or even who. Then the world came suddenly back together.

He jerked his head up. The chasm was no more than a spear's length from him, he could hear the water rushing far away in its bottom. He rolled over, away from his horse, trickles of dark blood working their way along the grooves in the stones underneath it. He saw Ferro, down on one knee, pulling arrows from her quiver and shooting them towards the pillars they had ridden between a few moments before.

There were Shanka there, a lot of them.

'Shit,' grunted Logen, scrambling back, the heels of his boots scraping at the dusty stones.

'Come on!' shouted Luthar, sliding down from his saddle, half hopping across the dusty floor. 'Come on!'

A Flathead charged towards them, shrieking, a great axe in its hand. It leaped up suddenly and turned over in the air, one of Ferro's arrows stuck through its face, but there were others. There were a lot more, creeping around the pillars, spears ready to throw.

'Too many!' shouted Bayaz. The old man frowned up at the great columns, the huge weight of stone above it, the muscles of his jaw clenching tight. The air around him began to shimmer.

'Shit.' Logen stumbled like a drunkard across to Ferro, his balance all gone, the hall tipping back and forward around him, the sound of his own heart pounding in his ears. He heard a sharp bang and a crack shot up one of the pillars, a cloud of dust flying out from it. There was a grinding rumble as the stone above began to shift. A couple of the Shanka looked up as fragments rained down on them, pointing and gibbering.

Logen grabbed tight hold of Ferro's wrist. 'Fuck!' she hissed, fumbling an arrow as he half fell and dragged her over, scrambled up and started to pull her after him. A spear zipped past them and clattered across the stones, tumbled off over the edge of the crack into empty space. He could hear the Shanka moving, grunting and growling to each other, starting to swarm between the pillars and into the hall.

'Come on!' shouted Luthar again, taking a couple of limping steps forward and beckoning wildly.

Logen saw Bayaz standing, his lips curled back and his eyes bulging from his skull, the air around him rippling and twisting, the dust on the ground lifting slowly and curling up around his boots. There was an almighty crack and Logen looked over his shoulder to see a great lump of carved stone plummet down from above. It hit the ground with a crash that made the floor shake, crushing an unlucky Shanka to flat nothing before it could even scream, a jagged sword clattering across the ground and a long spatter of dark blood the only signs that it had ever existed. But more were coming, he could see the black shapes of them through the flying dust, charging forward, weapons held high.

One of the pillars split in half. It buckled moving with ludicrous slowness, pieces of it flying forward into the hall. The vast mass of stone above began to crack apart, tumbling downwards in chunks as big as houses. Logen turned and flung himself on his face and dragged Ferro down with him, grovelling on the ground, squeezing his eyes shut, throwing his hands over his head.

There was a giant crashing, tearing, splitting such as Logen had never heard in all his life. A roaring and groaning of tortured earth as though the world was falling in. Perhaps it was. The ground bucked and trembled underneath him. There was another deafening crash, a long clattering and scraping, a gentle clicking, then something close to quiet.

Logen unclenched his aching jaw and opened his eyes. The air was full of stinging dust, but it felt as if he was lying on some kind of slope. He coughed and tried to move. There was a sharp grinding sound beneath his chest and the stone underneath him began to shift, the slope getting steeper. He gasped and pressed himself back flat against it, clinging to it with his fingertips. He still had his hand clenched round Ferro's arm, and he felt her fingers squeeze tight into his wrist. He turned his head slowly to look around him, and froze.

The pillars were gone. The hall was gone. The floor was gone. The vast crack had swallowed them all up, and now yawned underneath him. Angry water slapped and hissed at the shattered ruins far below. Logen gaped, hardly able to believe his eyes. He was lying sideways on a huge slab of stone, until a moment ago part of the floor of the hall, now teetering at an angle on the very edge of a plunging cliff.

Ferro's dark fingers were clamped round his wrist, her ripped sleeve gathered up round her elbow, sinews standing out stark from her brown forearm with the effort. Beyond that he could see her shoulder, beyond that her rigid face. The rest of her was invisible – dangling over the edge of the slab and into the yawning air.

'Ssss,' she hissed, yellow eyes wide, fingers scrabbling desperately for a hand hold on the smooth slope. A chunk of stone cracked suddenly from the ragged edge and Logen heard it fall, pinging and bouncing from the ruptured earth.

'Shit,' he whispered, hardly daring even to breathe. What the hell were the chances of this? Say one thing for Logen Ninefingers, say that he has poor luck.

He crawled his free hand up the pitted stone until he found a shallow ridge to cling to. He lifted himself inch by inch towards the edge of the block above. He flexed his arm and started to drag at Ferro's wrist.

There was a horrifying scraping and the stone underneath him jolted and tipped slowly upwards. He whimpered and pressed himself back against it, willing it to stop. There was a sickening jolt and some dust filtered down into his face. Stone squealed as the block swung ever so slowly back the other way. He lay there, gasping. No way up, no way down.

'Ssss!' Ferro's eyes flicked down to their hands, gripped tight round each other's wrists. She jerked her head up towards the edge of the block, then down towards the gaping crack behind.

'Have to be realistic,' she whispered. Her fingers uncurled, letting him go.

Logen remembered hanging from a building, far above a circle of yellow grass. He remembered sliding back, whispering for help. He remembered Ferro's hand closing round his, pulling him up. He slowly shook his head, and gripped her wrist tighter than ever.

She rolled her yellow eyes at him. 'Stupid fucking pink!'

Jezal coughed, turned over, and spat out dust. He blinked around him. Something was different. It seemed much brighter than it had been, and the edge of the crack was much nearer. Not far away at all, in fact.

'Uh,' he breathed, words failing him. Half the building had collapsed. The rear wall was still standing, and one of the pillars at the far end, broken off halfway up. All the rest was gone, vanished into the yawning chasm. He staggered up, wincing as his weight went onto his bad leg. He saw Bayaz lying propped against the wall nearby.

The Magus' withered face was streaked with sweat, bright eyes glittering in black circles, bones of his face poking through stretched skin. He looked like nothing so much as a week-old corpse. It was a surprise to see him move at all, but Jezal watched him raise one palsied hand to point towards the crack. 'Get them,' he croaked.

The others.

'Over here!' Ninefingers' voice came strangled-sounding from beyond the edge of the crevasse. So he was alive, at least. One great slab was sticking up at an angle and Jezal shuffled gingerly towards it, worried that the floor might suddenly give way beneath him. He peered over into the chasm.

The Northman was lying spread out on his front, left hand up near the top edge of the tilting block, right fist near the bottom clutched tight round Ferro's wrist. Her body was out of sight, her scarred face just visible. They both looked equally horrified. Several tons of stone, rocking, ever so gently, balanced on the finest of margins. It was plain that it might easily slide into the abyss at any moment.

'Do something . . .' whispered Ferro, not even daring to raise her voice. Jezal noticed that she did not suggest any specifics, however.

He licked at the slot in his lip. Perhaps if he were to put his weight on this end it would tilt back level and they could simply crawl off? Could it possibly be so straightforward? He reached out carefully, thumbs rubbing nervously against fingertips, all suddenly weak and sweaty-feeling. He laid his hand gently on the ragged edge while Ninefingers and Ferro stared, holding their breath.

He applied the very slightest pressure, and the slab began to swing smoothly downwards. He put a little more weight on it. There was a loud grating sound and the whole block gave a horrifying lurch.

'Don't fucking push it!' screamed Ninefingers, clinging to the smooth rock with his fingernails.

'What then?' squealed Jezal.

'Get something!'

'Get anything!' hissed Ferro.

Jezal stared around wildly, saw no source of help. Of Longfoot and Quai there was no sign. Either they were dead somewhere at the bottom of the chasm, or they had made a timely bid for freedom. Neither one would have much surprised him. If anyone was going to be saved, Jezal would have to do it by himself.

He dragged his coat off, started to twist it round to make a kind of rope. He weighed it in his hand, shaking his head. Surely this would never work, but what were the choices? He stretched it out, then swung one end over. It slapped against the stone a few inches short of Logen's clutching fingers, sending up a puff of grit.

'Alright, alright, try again!'

Jezal lifted the coat up high, leaning out over the slab as far as he dared, and swung it down again. The arm flopped out just far enough for Logen to seize hold of.

'Yes!' He wound it round his wrist, the material dragging out tight over the edge of the slab.

'Yes! Now pull it!'

Jezal gritted his teeth and hauled, his boots slipping in the dust, his sore arm and his sore leg aching with the effort. The coat came towards him, slowly, slowly, sliding over the stone, inch by torturous inch.

'Yes!' grunted Ninefingers working his shoulders up the slab.

'Pull it!' growled Ferro, wriggling her hips up over the edge and onto the slope.

Jezal hauled for all he was worth, eyes squeezed almost shut, breath hissing between his teeth. A spear clattered down beside him and he looked up to see a score or more Flatheads gathered on the far side of the great crack, waving their misshapen arms. He swallowed and looked away from them. He could not allow himself to think of the danger. All that mattered was to pull. To pull and pull and not let go, however much it hurt. And it was working. Slowly, slowly, they were coming up. Jezal dan Luthar, the hero at last. He would finally have earned his place on this cursed expedition.

There was a sharp ripping sound. 'Shit,' squeaked Logen. 'Shit!' The sleeve was coming slowly away from the body of the coat, the stitches stretching, ripping, coming undone. Jezal whimpered with horror, his hands burning. Should he pull or not? Another stitch pinged open. How hard to pull? One more stitch went.

'What do I do?' he squealed.

'Pull, you fucker!'

Jezal dragged at the coat as hard as he could, muscles burning. Ferro was up on the stone, scrabbling at the smooth surface with her nails. Logen's clutching hand was almost at the edge, almost there, his three fingers stretching, stretching out for it. Jezal hauled again—

And he stumbled backwards, holding nothing but a limp rag. The slab shuddered, and groaned, and tipped up. There was a squawk, and Logen slid away, the ripped-off sleeve flapping useless in his hand. There were no screams. Just a clatter of tumbling stones, then nothing. They both were gone, over the edge. The great slab rocked slowly back and lay there, flat and empty, at the edge of the crack. Jezal stood and stared, his mouth open, the sleeveless coat still dangling from his throbbing hand.

'No,' he whispered. That was not how it happened in the stories.

Beneath the Ruins

'**Y**ou alive, pink?'

Logen groaned as he shifted his weight, felt a lurch of horror as stones moved underneath him. Then he realised he was lying in a heap of rubble, the corner of a slab digging hard into a sore spot in his back. He saw a stone wall, blurry, a hard line across it between light and shadow. He blinked, wincing, pain creeping up his arm as he tried to rub the dust out of his eyes.

Ferro was kneeling just beside him, her dark face streaked with blood from a cut on her forehead, her black hair full of brown dust. Behind her a wide vaulted chamber stretched into the shadows. The ceiling was broken away above her head, a ragged line with the pale blue sky beyond it. Logen turned his head painfully, baffled. No more than a stride from him the stone slabs he was lying on were sheared off, jutting out into the empty air. A long way away he could see the far side of the crack, a cliff of crumbling rock and earth, the outlines of half-fallen buildings jutting from the top.

He began to understand. They were underneath the floor of the temple. When the crack opened up it must have torn this place open, leaving just enough of a ledge for them to fall onto. Them and a lot of broken rock. They couldn't have fallen far. He almost felt himself grinning. He was still alive.

'What ab—'

Ferro's hand slapped down hard over his mouth, her nose not a foot from his. 'Ssss,' she hissed softly, yellow eyes rolling upward, one long finger pointing towards the vaulted ceiling.

Logen felt his skin go prickling cold. He heard them now. Shanka. Scuffling and clattering, gibbering and squeaking to each other, up above their heads. He nodded, and slowly Ferro lifted her dirty hand away from his face.

He eased himself up out of the rubble, slow and stiff, trying to stay as quiet as possible, wincing all the while at the effort, dust running off his coat as he came up to his feet He tested his limbs, waiting for the searing pain that would tell him he had broken his shoulder, or his leg, or his skull.

His coat was ripped and his elbow was skinned and throbbing, streaks of blood all down his forearm to his fingertips. When he put his fingers to his aching head he felt blood there, and underneath his jaw, where he cracked it on the ground. His mouth was salty with it. Must have bitten his tongue, yet again. It was a wonder the damn thing was still attached. One knee was painful, his neck was stiff, his ribs were a mass of bruises, but everything still moved. If he forced it to.

There was something wrapped round his hand. The torn sleeve of Luthar's coat. He shook it off and let it drop in the rubble beside him. No use now. Not much use then. Ferro was at the far end of the hall, peering into an archway. Logen shambled up beside her, doing his grimacing best to keep silent.

'What about the others?' he whispered. Ferro shrugged her shoulders. 'Maybe they got away?' he tried, hopefully. Ferro gave him a long, slow look, one black eyebrow raised, and Logen winced and squeezed his aching arm. She was right. The two of them were alive, for now. That was about as much luck as they could hope for, and it might be a while before they got any more.

'This way,' whispered Ferro, pointing into the darkness.

Logen peered into that black opening and his heart sank. He hated being underground. All that weight of stone and earth, pressing above, ready to fall. And they had no torch. Inky black, with hardly air to breathe, no notion of how far to go, or in what direction. He peered up nervously towards the vaulted stones above his head, and swallowed. Tunnels were places for Shanka or for the dead. Logen was neither one, and he didn't much fancy meeting either down there. 'You sure?'

'What, scared of the dark?'

'I'd rather be able to see, if I had the choice.'

'You see any choices?' sneered Ferro at him. 'You can stay here, if you want. Maybe another pack of idiots will come wandering through in a hundred years. You'll fit right in!'

Logen nodded, sucking sourly at his bloody gums. It seemed like a long time since the two of them had last been in a fix like this one, sliding across the dizzy rooftops of the Agriont, hunted by men in black masks. It seemed a long, hard time, but nothing much had changed. For all their riding together, and eating together, and facing death together, Ferro was still as bitter, and as angry, and as sore a pain in his arse as she had been when they first set out. He tried to be patient, really he did, but it was getting to be tiring.

'Do you have to?' he muttered, looking her right in one yellow eye.

'Have to what?'

'Be a cunt. Do you have to?'

She frowned at him for a moment, opened her mouth, paused, then shrugged her shoulders. 'You should have let me fall.'

'Eh?' He'd been expecting some furious insult from her. Some stabbing at him with a finger, certainly, and possibly with a blade. That had sounded almost like regret. But if it had been, it didn't last long.

'You should have let me fall, then I'd be on my own down here without you to get in my way!'

Logen snorted with disgust. There was no helping some people. 'Let go of you? Don't worry! Next time I will!'

'Good!' spat Ferro, stalking off into the tunnel, shadows quickly swallowing her. Logen felt a sudden stab of panic at the idea of being left alone.

'Wait!' he hissed, and hurried after.

The passageway sloped downwards, Ferro's feet padding noiseless, Logen's scraping in the dust, the last shreds of light gleaming on wet stone. He kept the fingertips of his left hand trailing along the wall, trying not to groan with each step at the pain in his bruised ribs, and his torn elbow, and his bloody jaw.

It grew darker, and darker yet. The walls and the floor became nothing but hints, then nothing at all. Ferro's dirty shirt was a grey ghost, hovering in the dead air before him. A few weak-kneed steps further and it was gone. He waved his hand in front of his face. Not so much as a trace. Just inky, fizzing blackness.

He was buried. Buried in the darkness, alone. 'Ferro, wait!'

'What?' He blundered into her in the dark, felt something shove him in the chest and nearly fell over backwards, staggering against the damp wall. 'What the hell—'

'I can't see anything!' he hissed, hearing his own voice full of panic. 'I can't . . . where are you?' He flailed at the air with his open hands, all sense of direction gone, his heart pounding, his stomach sick and heaving. What if she'd left him down there, the evil bitch? What if—

'Here.' He felt her hand catch hold of his and close round it, cool and reassuring. He heard her voice not far from his ear. 'You think you can follow me without falling on your face, fool?'

'I . . . I think so.'

'Just try to keep quiet!' And he felt her move off, pulling him impatiently after her.

If only the old crew could've seen him now. Logen Ninefingers, the most feared man in the North, piss-wet frightened of the dark, clinging tight to the hand of a woman who hated him, like a child clinging to his mother's tit. He might almost have laughed out loud. But he was scared the Shanka would hear.

Ninefingers' big paw felt hot, clammy with fear. An unpleasant sensation, his sticky skin pressed tight against hers. Sickening, almost, but Ferro made herself hold on. She could hear his breathing, quick and snatched in the tight space, his clumsy footsteps stumbling after her.

It felt like only yesterday that the two of them were last in a fix like this one, hurtling down the lanes of the Agriont, sneaking through its darkened buildings, chased all the way. It felt like yesterday, but everything had changed.

Back then, he had seemed nothing but a threat. One more pink that she would have to keep her eye on. Ugly and strange, stupid and dangerous. Back then, he might easily have been the last man in the world she would have trusted. Now he might easily have been the only one. He had not let her fall, even though she had told him to. He had chosen to fall with her rather than let her go. Out there on the plain, he had said he would stick if she did.

Now he had proved it.

She looked over her shoulder, saw his pale face gawping in the dark, eyes wide but unseeing, free hand stretched out and feeling for the walls. She should have thanked him, maybe, for not letting her fall, but that would have been as good as admitting she needed the help. Help was for the weak, and the weak die, or are made slaves. Never hope for help and you can never be disappointed when it does not come. And Ferro had been disappointed often.

So instead of thanking him she dragged at his hand and nearly made him fall.

A glimmer of cold light was starting to creep back into the tunnel, the slightest glow at the edges of the rough stone blocks. 'Can you see now?' she hissed over her shoulder.

'Yes.' She could hear the relief in his voice.

'Then you can let go,' she snapped, snatching her hand away and wiping it on the front of her shirt. She pressed on through the half-light, working her fingers and frowning down at them. It was an odd feeling.

Now that his hand was gone she almost missed it.

The light was growing brighter now, leaking into the passage from a narrow archway up ahead. She crept towards it, padding on the balls of her feet and peered round the corner. A great cavern opened out below them, its walls partly of smooth carved blocks, partly of natural stone, soaring up and bulging out in strange, melted formations, its ceiling lost in shadows. A shaft of light came down from high above, casting a long patch of brightness on the dusty stone floor. Three Shanka were gathered there in a clump, muttering and scratching over something on the floor, and all around them, piled in great heaps, as high as a man and higher to the very walls of the cave, were thousands, upon thousands, upon thousands, of bones.

'Shit,' breathed Logen, from just behind her. A skull grinned up at them from the corner of the arch. Human bones, without a doubt.

'They eat the dead,' she whispered.

'They what? But—'

'Nothing rots.' Bayaz had said the city was full of graves. Countless corpses, flung in pits for a hundred each. And there they must have lain down the long years, tangled up together in a cold embrace.

Until the Shanka came and dragged them out.

'We'll have to get around them,' whispered Ninefingers.

Ferro stared into the shadows, looking for a route into the cavern. There was no way to climb down that hill of bones without making noise. She shrugged her bow off her shoulder.

'You sure?' asked Ninefingers, touching her on the elbow.

She nudged him back. 'Give me some room, pink.' She would have to work quickly. She wiped the blood out of her eyebrow. She slid three arrows out of her quiver and between the fingers of her right hand, where she could get at them fast. She took a fourth in her left and levelled her bow, drawing back the string, aiming at the furthest Flathead. When the arrow struck it through the body she was already aiming at the second. It took the shaft in the shoulder and fell down with a strange squawk just as the last one was turning. Her arrow caught it clean through its neck before it got all the way round and it pitched on its face. Ferro nocked the last arrow, waiting. The second Flathead tried to scramble up, but it had not got half a stride before she nailed it through the back and sent it sprawling.

She lowered the bow, frowning towards the Shanka. None of them moved.

'Shit,' breathed Logen. 'Bayaz is right. You are a devil.'

'Was right,' grunted Ferro. The chances were good that those creatures had him by now, and it was abundantly clear that they ate men. Luthar, and Longfoot, and Quai as well, she guessed. A shame.

But not a big one.

She shouldered her bow and crept cautiously into the cavern, keeping low, her boot crunching down in the hill of bones. She wobbled out further, arms spread wide for balance, half-walking, half-wading, up to her knees in places, bones cracking and scraping around her legs. She made it down onto the cavern floor and knelt there, staring round and licking her lips.

Nothing moved. The three Shanka lay still, dark blood pooling on the stone underneath their bodies.

'Gah!' Ninefingers tumbled down the slope, clattering splinters flying up around him, rolling over and over. He crashed down on his face in the midst of a rattling slide of bones and scrambled up. 'Shit! Ugh!' He shook half a dusty rib-cage off his arm and flung it away.

'Quiet, fool!' hissed Ferro, dragging him down beside her, staring across the cavern towards a rough archway in the far wall, expecting hordes of those things to come pouring in at any moment, keen to add their bones to the rest. But nothing came. She gave him a dark look but he was too busy nursing his bruises, so she left him be and crept over to the three corpses.

They had been gathered round a leg. A woman's leg, Ferro guessed, from the lack of hair on it. A stub of bone poked out of dry, withered flesh round the severed thigh. One of them had been going at it with a knife and it still lay nearby, the bright blade shining in the shaft of light from high above. Ninefingers stooped and picked it up.

'You can never have too many knives.'

'No? What if you fall in a river and can't swim for all that iron?'

He looked puzzled for a moment, then he shrugged and put it carefully back down on the ground. 'Fair point.'

She slipped her own blade out from her belt. 'One knife will do well enough. If you know where to stick it.' She dug the blade into one of the Flatheads' backs and started to cut out her arrow. 'What are these things anyway?' She worked the shaft out, intact, and rolled the Flathead over with her boot. It stared up at her, piggy black eyes unseeing under a low, flat forehead, lips curled back from a wide maw full of bloody teeth. 'They're even uglier than you, pink.'

'Very good. They're Shanka. Flatheads. Kanedias made them.'

'Made them?' The next arrow snapped off as she tried to twist it out.

'So Bayaz said. As a weapon, to use in a war.'

'I thought he died.'

'Seems his weapons lived on.'

The one she shot through the neck had fallen on the shaft and broken it near the head. Useless, now. 'How does a man make one of these things?'

'You think I've got the answers? They'd come across the sea, every summer, when the ice melted, and there'd always be work fighting 'em. Lots of work.' She hacked out the last shaft, bloody but sound. 'When I was young they started coming more and more often. My father sent me south, over the mountains, to get help with the fighting of 'em . . .' He trailed off. 'Well. That's a long story. The High Valleys are swarming with Flatheads now.'

'It hardly matters,' she grunted, standing up and sliding the two good arrows carefully back into her quiver, 'as long as they die.'

'Oh, they die. Trouble is there's always more to kill.' He was frowning down at the three dead things, frowning down hard with a cold look in his eye. 'There's nothing left now, north of the mountains. Nothing and no one.'

Ferro did not much care about that. 'We need to move.'

'All back to the mud,' he growled, as though she had not spoken, his frown growing harder all the time.

She stepped up in front of his face. 'You hear me? We need to move, I said.'

'Eh?' He blinked at her for a moment, then he scowled. The muscles round his jaw tightened rigid under his skin, the scars stretching and shifting, face tipped forward, eyes lost in hard shadow from the light overhead. 'Alright. We move.'

Ferro frowned at him as a trickle of blood crept down from his hair and across the greasy, stubbly side of his face. He no longer looked like anyone she would trust.

'Not planning to go strange on me, are you, pink? I need you to stay cold.'

'I am cold,' he whispered.

Logen was hot. His skin prickled under his dirty clothes. He felt strange, dizzy, his head full of the stink of Shanka. He could hardly breathe for their smell. The hallway seemed to move under his feet, shifting before his eyes. He winced and hunched over, sweat running down his face, dripping onto the tipping stone below.

Ferro whispered something at him, but he couldn't make sense of the words – they echoed from the walls and round his face, but wouldn't go in. He nodded and flapped one hand at her, struggled on behind. The hallway was growing hotter and hotter, the blurry stone had taken on an orange glow. He blundered into Ferro's back and nearly fell, crawled forwards on his sore knees, gasping hard.

There was a huge cavern beyond. Four slender columns rose up in the centre, up and up into the shifting darkness far above. Beneath them fires burned. Many fires, printing white images into Logen's stinging eyes. Coals crackled and cracked and spat out smoke. Sparks came up in stinging showers, steam came up in hissing gouts. Globs of melted iron dripped from crucibles, spattering the ground with glowing embers. Molten metal ran through channels in the floor, striking lines of red and yellow and searing white into the black stone.

The yawning space was full of Shanka, ragged shapes moving through the boiling darkness. They worked at the fires, and the bellows, and the crucibles like men, a score of them, or more. There was a furious din. Hammers clanged, anvils rang, metal clattered, Flatheads squawked and shrieked to each other. Racks stood against the distant walls, dark racks stacked with bright weapons, steel glittering in all the colours of fire and fury.

Logen blinked and stared, head pounding, arm throbbing, the heat pressing onto his face, wondering if he could believe his eyes. Perhaps they had walked into the forge of hell. Perhaps Glustrod had opened a gate beneath the city after all. A gate to the Other Side, and they had passed through it without ever guessing.

He was breathing fast, in ragged gasps, and couldn't make them slow, and every breath he took was full of the sting of smoke and the stink of Shanka. His eyes were bulging, his throat was burning, he could not swallow. He wasn't sure when he had drawn the Maker's sword, but now the orange light flashed and flickered on the bare dark metal, his right hand bunched into a fist around the grip, painful tight. He couldn't make the fingers open. He stared at them, glowing orange and black, pulsing as if they were on fire, veins and tendons starting from the taut skin, knuckles pale with furious pressure.

Not his hand.

'We'll have to go back,' Ferro was saying, pulling at his arm, 'find another way.'

'No.' The voice was harsh as a hammer falling, rough as a whetstone turning, sharp as a drawn blade in his throat.

Not his voice.

'Get behind me,' he managed to whisper, grabbing hold of Ferro's shoulder and dragging himself past her.

There could be no going back now . . .

. . . and he could smell them. He tipped his head up and sucked in hot air through his nose. His head was full of the reek of them and that was good. Hatred was a powerful weapon, in the right hands. The Bloody-Nine hated everything. But his oldest-buried, and his deepest-rooted, and his hottest-burning hatred, that was for the Shanka.

He slid into the cavern, a shadow between the fires, the noise of angry steel echoing around him. A beautiful and familiar song. He swam in it, revelled in it, drank it in. He felt the heavy blade in his hand, power flowing from the cold metal into his hot flesh, from his hot flesh into the cold metal, building and swelling and growing in waves with his surging breath.

The Flatheads had not seen him yet. They were working. Busy with their meaningless tasks. They could not have expected vengeance to find them where they lived, and breathed, and toiled, but they would learn.

The Bloody-Nine loomed up behind one, lifting the Maker's sword high. He smiled as he watched the long shadow stretch out across the bald skull – a promise, soon to be fulfilled. The long blade whispered its secret and the Shanka split apart, clean down the middle like a flower opening, blood spraying out warm and comforting, spattering the anvil, and the stone floor, and the Bloody-Nine's face with wet little gifts.

Another saw him now and he came for it, faster and angrier than the boiling steam. It lifted an arm, lurching backwards. Not nearly far enough. The Maker's sword sheared through its elbow, the severed forearm spinning over and over in the air. Before it hit the ground the Bloody-Nine had struck the Shanka's head off on the backswing. Blood sizzled on molten iron, glowed orange on the dull metal of the blade, on the pale skin of his hand, on the harsh stone under his feet, and he beckoned to the others.

'Come,' he whispered. They all were welcome.

They scattered for the racks, seizing their spiked swords, and their sharp axes, and the Bloody-Nine laughed to watch them. Armed or not, their death was a thing already decided. It was written into the cavern in lines of fire and lines of shadow. Now he would write it in lines of blood. They were animals, and less than animals. Their weapons stabbed and cut at him, but the Bloody-Nine was made of fire and darkness and he drifted and slithered between their crude blows, around their fumbling spears, under and over their worthless screams and their useless fury.

Easier to stab the flickering flame. Easier to cut the shifting shadows. Their weakness was an insult to his strength.

'Die!' he roared, and the blade made circles, savage and beautiful, the letter on the metal burning red and leaving bright trails behind. And where the circles passed everything would be made right. The Shanka would scream and gibber, and the pieces of them would scatter, and they would be sliced and divided as neatly as meat on the butcher's block, as dough on the baker's block, as the corn stubble left by the farmer's scythe, all according to a perfect design.

The Bloody-Nine showed his teeth, and smiled to be free, and to see the good work done so well. He saw the flash of a blade and jerked away, felt it leave him a lingering kiss across his side. He knocked a barbed sword from a Flathead's hand, seized it by the scruff of the neck and forced its face down into the channel where the molten steel flowed, furious yellow, and its head hissed and bubbled, shooting out stinking steam.

'Burn!' laughed the Bloody-Nine, and the ruined corpses, and their gaping wounds, and their fallen weapons, and the boiling bright iron laughed with him.

Only the Shanka did not laugh. They knew their hour was come.

The Bloody-Nine watched one jump, springing over an anvil, a club raised to crush his skull. Before he could slash it from the air an arrow slipped into its open mouth and snatched it backwards, dead as mud. The Bloody-Nine frowned. He saw other arrows now, among the corpses. Someone else was spoiling his good work. He would make them pay, later, but something was coming at him from between the four columns.

It was cased all in bright armour sealed with heavy rivets, a round helmet clamped over the top half of its skull, eyes glinting beyond a thin slot. It grunted and snorted, sounds loud as a bull, iron-booted feet thudding on the stone as it thundered forwards, a massive axe in its iron-gloved fists. A giant among Shanka. Or some new thing, made from iron and flesh, down here in the darkness.

Its axe curved in a shining arc and the Bloody-Nine rolled away from it, the heavy blade crashing into the ground and sending out a shower of fragments. It roared at him again, maw opening wide under its slotted visor, a cloud of spit hissing from its hanging mouth. The Bloody-Nine faded back, shifting and dancing with the shifting shadows and the dancing flames.

He fell away, and away, and he let the blows miss him on one side and the other, miss him above his head and beneath his feet. Let them clang into the metal and the stone around him and fill the air with a fury of dust and splinters. He fell back, until the creature began to tire under all that weight of iron.

The Bloody-Nine saw it stumble, and he felt the touch of his moment upon him, and he surged forward, raising the sword above his head, opening his mouth and making a scream that pressed on his arm, and his hand, and the blade and the very walls of the cavern. The great Shanka brought the shaft of its axe up in both fists to block the blow. Good bright steel, born in these hot fires, hard and strong and tough as the Flatheads could forge it.

But the work of the Master Maker would not be denied. The dull blade cleaved through the shaft with a sound like a child screaming and scored a gash a hand deep through the Shanka's heavy armour from its neck down to its groin. Blood splattered out onto the bright metal, onto the dark stone. The Bloody-Nine laughed and dug his fist into the wound, ripping out a handful of the Shanka's guts as it toppled away and crashed onto its back, the neatly severed halves of its axe clattering from its twitching claws.

He smiled upon the others. They lurked there, three of them, weapons in hand, but they would not come on. They lurked in the shadows, but the darkness was no friend to them. It belonged to him, and him alone. The Bloody-Nine took a step forward, and one more, sword hanging from one hand, a length of bloody gut from the other, winding slowly from the slaughtered Flathead's corpse. The creatures shuffled back before him, squeaking and clicking to each other, and the Bloody-Nine laughed in their faces.

The Shanka might be ever so full of mad fury, but even they had to fear him. Everything did. Even the dead, who felt no pain. Even the cold stone, which did not dream. Even the molten iron feared the Bloody-Nine. Even the darkness.

He roared and sprang forward, flinging his handful of entrails away. The point of his sword raked across a Shanka's chest and spun it round, squealing. A moment later and the blade thudded into its shoulder and split it to its breastbone.

The last two turned to run, scrambling across the stone, but fight or run, where was the difference? Another arrow slid into the back of one before it got three strides and it sprawled on its face. The Bloody-Nine darted out and his fingers closed round the ankle of the last, tight as a vice, dragging it towards him, its claws scrabbling at the soot-caked stone.

His fist was the hammer, the floor was the anvil, and the Shanka's head was the metal to be worked. One blow and its nose split open, broken teeth falling. Two and he smashed its cheekbone in. Three and its jaw burst apart under his knuckles. His fist was made of stone, of steel, of adamant.

It was heavy as a falling mountain and blow after blow it crushed the Shanka's thick skull to formless mush.

'Flat . . . head,' hissed the Bloody-Nine, and he laughed, hauling up the ruined body and flinging it away, turning in the air, to crash down into the broken racks. He reeled around, weaving across the chamber, the Maker's sword dangling from his hand, the point striking sparks from the stone as it clattered after him. He glared into the darkness, turning and shifting, but only the fires moved, and the shadows moving around them. The chamber was empty.

'No!' he snarled. 'Where are you?' His legs were weak, they would hardly hold him up any longer. 'Where are you, you fuckers . . .' He stumbled and fell on one knee on the hot stone, gasping in air. There had to be more work. The Bloody-Nine could never do enough. But his strength was fickle, and now it was flowing out of him.

He saw something move, blinked at it. A streak of darkness, sliding slow and quiet between the pulsing fires and the tipping bodies. Not a Shanka. Some other kind of enemy. More subtle and more dangerous. Sooty dark skin in the shade, soft steps padding around the smears of blood his work had left. She had a bow in her hard hands, string pulled back halfway and the bright head of the arrow glinting sharp. Her yellow eyes shone like melted metal, like hot gold, mocking him. 'You safe, pink?' Her voice boomed and whispered in his ringing skull. 'I don't want to kill you, but I will.'

Threats? 'Cunt bitch,' he hissed at her, but his lips were stupid clumsy and nothing came out but a long dribble of spit. He wobbled forward, leaning on the sword, straining to get up, fury burning in him hotter than ever. She would learn. The Bloody-Nine would give her such a lesson that she would never need another. He would cut her in pieces, and grind the pieces under his heels. If he could just get up . . .

He swayed, blinking, breath rasping in and out, slow, slow. The flames dimmed and guttered, the shadows lengthened, blurred, swallowed him up and pushed him down.

One more, just one more. Always one more . . .

But his time was up . . .

. . . Logen coughed, and trembled, shivering weak. His hands took shape in the murk, curled into fists on the dirty stone, bloody as a careless slaughterman's. He guessed what must have happened, and he groaned and felt tears stinging his eyes. Ferro's scarred face loomed at him out of the hot darkness. So he hadn't killed her, at least.

'You hurt?'

He couldn't answer. He didn't know. It felt like there might be a cut on his side, but there was so much blood it was hard to tell. He tried to stand, lurched against an anvil and nearly put his hand in a glowing furnace. He blinked and spat, knees trembling. Searing fires swam before his eyes. There were corpses everywhere, sprawled out shapes on the sooty ground. He looked around, dull-witted, for something to wipe his hands on, but everything was spattered with gore. His stomach heaved, and he stumbled on wobbly legs between the forges towards an archway in the far wall, one bloody hand clamped to his mouth.

He leaned there, against the warm stone, dribbling sour blood and spit onto the ground, pain licking at his side, at his face, at his torn knuckles. But if he'd been hoping for pity, he'd chosen the wrong companion.

'Let's go,' snapped Ferro. 'Come on, pink, up.'

He couldn't have said how long he shambled through the darkness, gasping after Ferro's heels, the sound of his own breath echoing in his skull. They crept through the guts of the earth. Through ancient halls filled with dust and shadows, stone walls riddled with cracks. Through archways into winding tunnels, ceilings of mud propped with rickety beams.

Once they came to a junction and Ferro pressed him back into the darkness by the wall, both of them holding their breath as ragged shapes scraped and shuffled down a hallway that crossed theirs. On and on – corridor, cavern, burrow. He could only follow, dragging after her until he knew he would fall on his face at any moment from simple tiredness. Until he was sure that he would never see daylight again . . .

'Wait,' hissed Ferro, putting her hand against his chest to stop him and nearly pushing him over his legs were so weak. A sluggish stream joined the hallway, slow-moving water flapping and rippling in the shadows. Ferro knelt down beside it, peering into the dark tunnel it flowed out of.

'If it joins the river downstream, it must come from outside the city.'

Logen was not so sure. 'What if it . . . comes up from . . . underground?'

'Then we find another way. Or we drown.' Ferro shouldered her bow and slid in, up to her chest, her thin lips pressed tight together. Logen watched her wade out, arms held up above the dark water. Did she never tire? He was so sore and weary he wanted only to lie down and never get up. For a moment he considered doing it. Then Ferro turned and saw him squatting on the bank. 'Come on, pink!' she hissed at him.

Logen sighed. There was never any changing her mind. He heaved one reluctant, trembling leg into the cold water. 'Right behind you,' he muttered. 'Right behind.'

No Good for Each Other

Ferro waded on against the current, up to her waist in fast-flowing water, teeth gritted against the gripping cold, Ninefingers sloshing and gasping behind her. She could just see an archway up ahead, faint light from beyond glinting on the water. It was blocked with iron bars, but as she forced her way close she could see they were rusted through, thin and flaking. She pressed herself up against them. Beyond she could see the stream flowing down towards her between banks of rock and bare mud. Above was the evening sky, stars just starting to show themselves.

Freedom.

Ferro fumbled at the old iron, air hissing between her teeth, fingers slow and weak from the cold. Ninefingers came up beside her and planted his hands next to hers – four hands in a row, two dark and two pale, clamped tight and straining. They were pressed against each other in the narrow space and she heard him grunting with effort, heard the rushing of her own breath, felt the ancient metal beginning to bend, squealing softly.

Far enough for her to slither between.

She pushed her bow, and quiver, and sword through first, holding them up in one hand. She hooked her head between the bars, turning sideways, sucking in her stomach and holding her breath, wriggling her shoulders, then her chest, then her hips through the narrow gap, feeling the rough metal scraping at her skin through her wet clothes.

She dragged herself onto the other side, tossing her weapons onto the bank. She braced her shoulders in the archway and planted her boots against the next bar, every muscle straining while Ninefingers dragged on it from the other side. It gave all of a sudden, snapping in half and showering flakes of rust into the stream, dumping her on her back, over her head in the freezing water.

Ninefingers started to haul himself through, face twisted with effort. Ferro floundered up, gasping with the cold, grabbed him under the arms and started pulling, felt his hands grip round her back. She grunted and wrestled and finally dragged him out. They flopped together onto the muddy bank and lay there, side by side. Ferro stared up at the crumbling walls of the ruined city rising sheer above her in the grey dusk, breathing hard and listening to Ninefingers do the same. She had not expected to get out of that place alive.

But they were not away quite yet.

She rolled and clambered up, dripping wet and trying to stop herself shivering. She wondered if she had ever been so cold in her whole life.

'That's it,' she heard Ninefingers muttering. 'By the fucking dead, that's it. I'm done. I'm not moving another stride.'

Ferro shook her head. 'We need to make some distance while we still have light.' She snatched up her weapons from the dirt.

'You call this light? Are you fucking crazy, woman?'

'You know I am. Let's go, pink.' And she poked him in the ribs with her wet boot.

'Alright, damn it! Alright!' He stumbled reluctantly up, swaying, and she turned, started to walk up the bank through the twilight, away from the walls.

'What did I do?' She turned and looked at him, standing there, wet hair dripping round his face. 'What did I do, back there?'

'You got us through.'

'I meant—'

'You got us through. That's all.' And she slogged off up the bank. After a moment she heard Ninefingers following.

It was so dark, and Logen was so tired, that he barely even saw the ruin until they were almost inside it. It must have been a mill, he reckoned. It was built out right next to the stream, though he guessed the wheel had been missing for a few hundred years or more.

'We'll stop here,' hissed Ferro, ducking through the crumbling doorway. Logen was too tired to do anything but nod and shamble after her. Thin moonlight washed down into the empty shell, picking out the edges of stones, the shapes of old windows, the hard-packed dirt of the ground. He stumbled to the nearest wall and sagged against it, sliding slowly down until his arse hit the mud.

'Still alive,' he mouthed silently, and grinned to himself. A hundred cuts and scrapes and bruises clamoured for attention, but he was still alive. He sat motionless – damp and aching and utterly spent, let his eyes close, and enjoyed the feeling of not having to move.

He frowned. There was a strange sound in the darkness, over the trickling of the stream. A tapping, clicking sound. It took him a moment to realise what it was. Ferro's teeth. He dragged his coat off, wincing as he pulled it over his torn elbow, and held it out to her in the dark.

'What's this?'

'A coat.'

'I see it's a coat. What for?'

Damn it but she was stubborn. Logen almost laughed out loud. 'I may not have your eyes, but I can still hear your teeth rattling.' He held the coat out again. 'Wish I had more to offer you, but this is all I've got. You need it more 'n me, and there it is. No shame in that. Take it.'

There was a pause, then he felt it pulled out of his hand, heard her wrapping it round herself. 'Thanks,' she grunted.

He raised his eyebrows, wondering if he could have heard that right. Seemed there was a first time for everything. 'Alright. And to you.'

'Uh?'

'For the help. Under the city, and on the hill with the stones, and up on the roofs, and all the rest.' He thought about it for a moment. 'That's a lot of help. More than I deserve, most likely, but, well, I'm still good and grateful for it.' He waited for her to say something, but nothing came. Only the sound of the stream gurgling under the walls of the building, the sound of the wind hissing through the empty windows, the sound of his own rough breathing. 'You're alright,' he said. 'That's all I'm saying. Whatever you try to make out, you're alright.'

More silence. He could see her outline in the moonlight, sitting near the wall, his coat wrapped round her shoulders, damp hair sticking spiky from her head, perhaps the slightest gleam of a yellow eye, watching him. He cursed to himself under his breath. He was no good at talking, never had been. Probably none of that meant anything to her. Still, at least he'd tried.

'You want to fuck?'

He looked up, mouth hanging open, not sure if he could've heard right. 'Eh?'

'What, pink, you gone deaf on me?'

'Have I what?'

'Alright! Forget it!' She turned away from him, pulling the coat angrily round her hunched shoulders.

'Hold on, though.' He was starting to catch up. 'I mean . . . I just wasn't expecting you to ask is all. I'm not saying no . . . I reckon . . . if you're asking.' He swallowed, his mouth dry. 'Are you asking?'

He saw her head turn back towards him. 'You're not saying no, or you're saying yes?'

'Well, er . . .' He puffed his cheeks out in the dark, tried to make his head work. He'd never thought to be asked that question again in all his days, and least of all by her. Now it had been asked, he was scared to answer. He couldn't deny it was somewhat of a daunting prospect, but it was better to do it, than to live in fear of it. A lot better. 'Yes, then. I think. I mean, of course I am. Why wouldn't I? I'm saying yes.'

'Uh.' He saw the outline of her face frowning down at the ground, thin lips pressed angrily together, like she'd been hoping for a different answer and wasn't quite sure what to do with the one he'd given. He wasn't either, if it came to that. 'How do you want to get it done?' Matter of fact, as if it was a job they had to get through, like cutting a tree down or digging a hole.

'Er . . . well, you'll have to get a bit closer, I reckon. I mean, I hope my cock ain't that disappointing, but it won't reach you over there.' He half smiled, then cursed to himself when she didn't. He knew she wasn't much for jokes.

'Right then.' She came at him so quick and businesslike he half backed off, and that made her falter.

'Sorry,' he said. 'Haven't done this in a while.'

'No.' She squatted down next to him, lifted her arm, paused as if she was wondering what to do with it. 'Nor me.' He felt her fingertips on the back of his hand – gentle, cautious. It almost tickled, her touch was so light. Her thumb rubbed at the stump of his middle finger, and he watched her do it, grey shapes moving in the shadows, awkward as a pair who'd never touched another person in their lives. Strange feeling, having a woman so close to him. Brought back all kind of memories.

Logen reached up slowly, feeling like he was about to put his hand in the fire, and touched Ferro's face. It didn't burn. Her skin was smooth and cool, just like anyone's would have been. He pushed his hand into her hair, felt it tickling the webs between his fingers. He found the scar on her forehead with the very tip of his thumb, traced the line of it down her cheek to the corner of her mouth, tugging at her lip, his skin brushing rough against hers.

There was a strange set to her face, he could tell it even in the dark. It was one he wasn't used to seeing on her, but there was no mistaking it. He could feel the muscles tense under her skin, see the moonlight on the cords standing from her scrawny neck. She was scared. She could laugh while she kicked a man in the face, smile at cuts and punches, treat an arrow through her flesh like it was nothing, but it seemed a gentle touch could put the fear in her. Would've seemed pretty strange to Logen, if he hadn't been so damn frightened himself. Frightened and excited all at once.

They started pulling at each other's clothes together, as if someone had given the signal for the charge and they were keen to get it over with. He struggled with the buttons on her shirt in the darkness, hands trembling, chewing at his lip, as clumsy as if he'd had gauntlets on. She had his open before he'd even done one of hers.

'Shit!' he hissed. She slapped his hands away and undid the buttons herself, pulled her shirt off and dropped it beside her. He couldn't see much in the moonlight, only the gleaming of her eyes, the dark outline of her bony shoulders and her bony waist, splashes of faint light between her ribs and the curve underneath one tit, a bit of rough skin round a nipple, maybe.

He felt her pull his belt open, felt her cool fingers sliding into his trousers, felt her—

'Ah! Shit! You don't have to lift me up by it!'

'Alright . . .'

'Ah.'

'Better?'

'Ah.' He dragged at her belt and fumbled it open, dug his hand down inside. Hardly subtle, maybe, but then he'd never been known for subtlety. His fingertips made it more or less into hair before he got his wrist stuck tight. It wouldn't go any further, for all his straining.

'Shit,' he muttered, heard Ferro suck her teeth, felt her shift and grab her trousers with her free hand, dragging them down over her arse. That was better. He slid his hand up her bare thigh. Good thing he still had one middle finger. They have their uses.

They stayed like that for a while, the pair of them kneeling in the dirt, nothing much moving apart from their two hands working back and forward, up and down, in and out, starting slow and gentle and getting quicker, silent except for Ferro's breath hissing through her teeth, Logen's rasping in his throat, the quiet suck and squelch of damp skin moving.

She pushed herself up against him, wriggling out of her trousers, shoving him back up against the wall. He cleared his throat, suddenly hoarse. 'Should I—'

'Ssss.' She got up on one foot and one knee, squatting over him with her legs wide open, spat in one cupped hand and took hold of his cock with it. She muttered something, shifting her weight, easing herself down onto him, grunting softly. 'Urrrr.'

'Ah.' He reached out and pulled her closer, one hand squeezing at the back of her thigh, feeling the muscles bunch and shift as she moved, the other tangled tight in her greasy hair, dragging her head down against his face. His trousers were screwed up tight round his ankles. He tried to kick them off and only got them tangled worse than ever, but he was damned if he was going to ask her to stop just for that.

'Urrrr,' she whispered at him, mouth open, lips sliding warm and soft against his cheek, breath hot and sour in his mouth, her skin rubbing against his, and sticking to it, and peeling away again.

'Ah,' he grunted back at her, and she rocked her hips against him, back and forward, back and forward, back and forward.

'Urrrr.' One of her hands was clamped round his jaw, her thumb in his mouth, the other was between her legs, sliding up and down, he could feel her wet fingers curling round his fruits, more than a bit painful, more than a bit pleasant.

'Ah.'

'Urrrr.'

'Ah.'

'Urrrr.'

'Ah—'

'What?'

'Er . . .'

'You're joking!'

'Well . . .'

'I was just getting started!'

'I did say it'd been a long time—'

'Must've been years!' She slid off his wilting cock, wiped herself with one hand and smeared it angrily on the wall, dropped down on her side with her back to him, grabbed his coat and dragged it over her.

So that was an embarrassment, and no mistake.

Logen cursed silently to himself. All that time waiting and he hadn't been able to keep the milk in the bucket. He scratched his face sadly, picked at his scabby chin. Say one thing for Logen Ninefingers, say he's a lover.

He looked sideways at Ferro, at her faint outline in the darkness. Spiky hair, long neck stretched out, sharp shoulder, long arm pressed down against her side. Even with the coat over her he could see the rise of her hip, he could guess her shape underneath. He looked at her skin, knowing what it felt like – smooth, and sleek, and cool. He could hear her breathing. Soft, slow, warm breathing . . .

Hold on.

There was something stirring down below again, now. Sore, but definitely stiffening. The one advantage of having a long time without – the bucket fills up again quick. Logen licked his lips. It would be a shame to let the chance pass, just for a lack of nerve. He slid down beside her, shuffled up close, and cleared his throat.

'What?' Her voice was sharp, but not quite sharp enough to warn him off.

'Well, you know, give me a minute, and maybe . . .' He lifted the coat up and ran his hand up her side, skin hissing quietly against skin, nice and slow, so she had plenty of time to shove him off. It wouldn't have surprised him any if she'd turned over and kneed him in the fruits. But she didn't.

She shifted back against him, her bare arse pressing into his stomach, lifting one knee up. 'Why should I be giving you another chance?'

'I don't know . . .' he muttered, starting to grin. He slid his hand gently over her chest, across her belly, down between her legs. 'Same reason you gave me the first one?'

Ferro woke with a sudden jolt, not knowing where she was, only that she was trapped. She snarled and thrashed and flailed out with her elbow, fought her way free and scrambled away, teeth gritted, fists clenched to fight. But there were no enemies. Only bare dirt and bleak rock in the pale grey morning.

That and the big pink.

Ninefingers stumbled up, grunting and spitting, staring wildly around. When he saw no Flatheads poised to kill him he turned slowly to look at Ferro, eyes blinking bleary with sleep. 'Ah . . .' He winced and touched his fingertips to his bloody mouth. They glared at each other for a moment, both stark naked and silent in the cold shell of the ruined mill, the coat they had been lying under crumpled on the damp earth between them.

And that was when Ferro realised that she had made three serious mistakes.

She had let herself fall asleep, and nothing good ever happened when she did that. Then she had elbowed Ninefingers in the face. And what was much, much worse, so stupid she almost grimaced to think of it: she had fucked him the night before. Staring at him now in the harsh light of day, hair plastered against one side of his scarred and bloody face, a great smear of dirt down his pale side where he had been lying in the mud, she was not sure why. For some reason, cold and tired in the dark, she had wanted to touch someone, and be warm for just a moment, and she had let herself think – who would be worse off for it?

Madness.

They both were worse off, that was clear enough. Where things had been simple, now they were sure to be complicated. Where they had been getting an understanding, now there would be only confusion. She was confused already, and he was starting to look hurt, and angry, and what was the surprise? No one enjoys an elbow in the face while they sleep. She opened her mouth to say sorry, and it was then she realised. She did not even know the word. All she could do was say it in Kantic, but she was so angry with herself she growled it at him like an insult.

He certainly took it as one. His eyes narrowed and he snapped something at her in his own tongue, snatched his trousers up and shoved one leg in, muttering angrily under his breath.

'Fucking pink,' she hissed back, fists bunched with a surge of fury. She snatched up her torn shirt and turned her back on him. She must have left it in a wet patch. The ragged cloth stuck tight to her crawling skin like a layer of cold mud as she yanked it on.

Damn shirt. Damn pink.

She ground her teeth with frustration as she dragged her belt closed. Damn belt. If only she could have kept it closed. It was always the same. Nothing was easy with people, but she could always count on herself to make things more difficult than they had to be. She paused for a moment, with her head down, then she half turned towards him.

She was about to try and explain that she had not meant to smash his mouth, but that nothing good ever happened when she slept. She was about to try and tell him that she had made a mistake, that she had only wanted to be warm. She was about to ask him to wait.

But he was already stomping out of the broken doorway with the rest of his clothes clutched in one hand.

'Fuck him then,' she hissed as she sat down to pull her boots on.

But then that was the whole problem.

Jezal sat on the broken steps of the temple, picking sadly at the frayed stitches on the torn-off shoulder of his coat, and staring out across the limitless expanse of mud towards the ruins of Aulcus. Looking for nothing.

Bayaz lay propped up in the back of the cart, face bony and corpse-pale with veins bulging round his sunken eyes, a hard frown chiselled into his colourless lips. 'How long do we wait?' asked Jezal, once again.

'As long as it takes,' snapped the Magus, without even looking at him. 'We need them.'

Jezal saw Brother Longfoot, standing higher up on the steps with his arms folded, give him a worried glance. 'You are, of course, my employer, and it is scarcely my place to disagree—'

'Don't then,' growled Bayaz.

'But Ninefingers and the woman Maljinn,' persisted the Navigator, 'are most decidedly dead. Master Luthar quite specifically saw them slide into a chasm. A chasm of very great depth. My grief is immeasurable, and I am a patient man, few more, it is one among my many admirable qualities but . . . well . . . were we to wait until the end of time, I fear that it would make no—'

'As long . . .' snarled the First of the Magi, 'as it takes.'

Jezal took a deep breath and frowned into the wind, looking down from the hill towards the city, eyes scanning over the expanse of flat nothing, pocked with tiny creases where streams ran, the grey stripe of a ruined road creeping out towards them from the far-off walls, between the streaky outlines of ruined buildings: inns, farms, villages, all long fallen.

'They're down there,' came Quai's emotionless voice.

Jezal stood up, weight on his good leg, shading his hand and staring at where the apprentice was pointing. He saw them suddenly, two tiny brown figures in a brown wasteland, down near the base of the rock.

'What did I tell you?' croaked Bayaz.

Longfoot shook his head in amazement. 'How in God's name could they have survived?'

'They're a resourceful pair, alright.' Jezal was already starting to grin. A month before he could not have dreamed that he would ever be glad to see Logen again, let alone Ferro, but here he was, smiling from ear to ear almost to see them still alive. Somehow, a bond was formed out here in the wilderness, facing death and adversity together. A bond that strengthened quickly, regardless of all the great differences between them. A bond that left his old friendships weak, and pale, and passionless by comparison.

Jezal watched the figures come closer, trudging along the crumbling track that led up through the steep rocks to the temple, a great deal of space between the two of them, almost as if they were walking separately. Closer still, and they began to look like two prisoners that had escaped from hell. Their clothes were ripped, and torn, and utterly filthy, their dirty faces were hard as a pair of stones. Ferro had a scabbed-over gash across her forehead. Logen's jaw was a mass of grazes, the skin round his eyes stained with dark bruising.

Jezal took a hopping step towards them. 'What happened? How did—'

'Nothing happened,' barked Ferro.

'Nothing at all,' growled Ninefingers, and the two of them scowled angrily at each other. Plainly, they had both gone through some awful ordeal that neither one wished to discuss. Ferro stalked straight to the cart without the slightest greeting and started rooting through the back. Logen stood, hands on his hips, frowning grimly after her.

'So . . .' mumbled Jezal, not quite sure what to say, 'are you alright?'

Logen's eyes swivelled to his. 'Oh, I'm grand,' he said, with heavy irony. 'Never better. How the hell did you get that cart out of there?'

The apprentice shrugged. 'The horses pulled it out.'

'Master Quai has a gift for understatement,' chuckled Longfoot nervously. 'It was a most exhilarating ride to the city's South Gate—'

'Fight your way out, did you?'

'Well, not I, of course, fighting is not my—'

'Didn't think so.' Logen leaned over and spat sourly onto the mud.

'We should at least consider being grateful,' croaked Bayaz, the air sighing and crackling in his throat as he breathed in. 'There is much to be grateful for, after all. We are all still alive.'

'You sure?' snapped Ferro. 'You don't look it.' Jezal found himself in silent agreement there. The Magus could not have looked worse if he had actually died in Aulcus. Died, and already begun to decompose.

She ripped off her rag of a shirt and flung it savagely on the ground, sinews shifting across her scrawny back. 'Fuck are you looking at?' she snarled at Jezal.

'Nothing,' he muttered, staring down at the dirt. When he dared to look up she was buttoning a fresh one up the front. Well, not entirely fresh. He had been wearing it himself a few days ago.

'That's one of mine . . .' Ferro looked up at him with a glare so murderous that Jezal found himself taking a hesitant step back. 'But you're welcome to it . . . of course . . .'

'Ssss,' she hissed, jamming the hem violently down behind her belt, frowning all the while as if she was stabbing a man to death. Probably him.

All in all, it was hardly the tearful reunion that Jezal might have hoped for, even if he did now feel somewhat like crying.

'I hope I never see this place again,' he muttered wistfully.

'I'm with you there,' said Logen. 'Not quite so empty as we thought, eh? Do you think you could dream up a different way back?'

Bayaz frowned. 'That would seem prudent. We will return to Calcis down the river. There are woods on this side of the water, further downstream. A few sturdy tree trunks lashed together, and the Aos will carry us straight to the sea.'

'Or to a watery grave.' Jezal remembered with some clarity the surging water in the canyon of the great river.

'My hope is better. In any case, there are still long miles to cover westward before we think about the return journey.'

Longfoot nodded. 'Indeed there are, including a pass through a most forbidding range of mountains.'

'Lovely,' said Logen. 'I can hardly wait.'

'Nor I. Unfortunately, not all the horses survived.' The Navigator raised his eyebrows. 'We have two to pull the cart, two to ride . . . that leaves us two short.'

'I hate those fucking things anyway.' Logen strode to the cart and clambered up opposite Bayaz in the back.

There was a long pause as they all considered the situation. Two horses, three riders. Never a happy position. Longfoot was the first to speak. 'I will need, of course, to scout forward as we come close to the mountains. Scouting, alas, is an essential part of any successful journey. One for which, unfortunately, I will require one of the horses . . .'

'I should probably ride,' murmured Jezal, shifting painfully, 'what with my leg . . .'

Ferro looked at the cart, and Jezal saw her eyes meet Logen's for a brief and intensely hostile moment.

'I'll walk,' she barked.

The Hero's Welcome

It was raining as Superior Glokta hobbled back into Adua. A mean, thin, ugly sort of rain on a hard wind off the sea, that rendered the treacherous wood of the gangplank, the squealing timbers of the wharf, the slick stones of the quay, all slippery as liars. He licked at his sore gums, rubbed at his sore thigh, swept his grimace up and down the grey shoreline. A pair of surly-looking guardsmen were leaning against a rotten warehouse ten paces away. Further on a party of dockers were involved in a bitter dispute over a heap of crates. A shivering beggar nearby took a couple of paces towards Glokta, thought better of it, and slunk away.

No crowds of cheering commoners? No carpet of flower petals? No archway of drawn swords? No bevy of swooning maidens? It was hardly too great a surprise. There had been none the last time he returned from the South. *Crowds rarely cheer too loudly for the defeated, no matter how hard they fought, how great their sacrifices, how long the odds. Maidens might wet themselves over cheap and worthless victories, but they don't so much as blush for 'I did my best'. Nor will the Arch Lector, I fear.*

A particularly vicious wave slapped at the sea wall and threw a cloud of sullen spray all over Glokta's back. He stumbled forward, cold water dripping from his cold hands, slipped and almost fell, tottered gasping across the quay and clung to the slimy wall of a crumbling shed at the far side. He looked up and saw the two guards staring at him.

'Is there something?' he snarled, and they turned their backs, muttering and pulling up their collars against the weather. Glokta fumbled his coat tight around him, felt the tails snatching at his wet legs. *A few months in the sun and you feel as though you'll never be cold again. How soon we forget.* He frowned up and down the empty wharves. *How soon we all forget.*

'Ome ageh.' Frost looked pleased as he stepped off the gangplank with Glokta's box under his arm.

'You don't much like hot weather, do you?'

The Practical shook his heavy head, half-grinning into the winter drizzle, white hair spiky with wet. Severard followed behind him, squinting up at the grey clouds. He paused for a moment at the end of the plank, then he stepped off onto the stones of the quay.

'Good to be back,' he said.

I only wish I could share your enthusiasm, but I cannot relax quite yet. 'His Eminence has sent for me, and judging by the way we left things in Dagoska, I think it more than likely that the meeting will . . . not go well.'

A spectacular understatement. 'You had better stay out of sight for a couple of days.'

'Out of sight? I don't plan to see outside of a whorehouse for a week.'

'Very wise. And Severard. In case we don't see each other again. Good luck.'

The Practical's eyes glinted. 'Always.' Glokta watched him stroll off through the rain towards the seedier parts of town. *Just another day for Practical Severard. Never thinking more than an hour ahead. What a gift.*

'Damn your miserable country and damn its bloody weather,' Vitari grumbled in her sing-song accent. 'I have to go and speak to Sult.'

'Why so do I!' cried Glokta with exaggerated glee. 'What a charming coincidence!' He offered her his bent elbow. 'We can make a couple, and visit his Eminence together!'

She stared back at him. 'Alright.'

But the pair of you will have to wait another hour for my head. 'There's just one call I need to make first.'

The tip of his stick cracked against the door. No answer. *Damn it.* Glokta's back was hurting like hell and he needed to sit down. He rapped again with his cane, harder this time. The hinges creaked, the door swung open a crack. *Unlocked.* He frowned, pushed it all the way. The door frame was split inside, the lock shattered. *Broken open.* He limped across the threshold, into the hall. Empty and frosty cold. Not a stick of furniture anywhere. *Almost as if she moved out. But why?* Glokta's eyelid gave a twitch. He had scarcely once thought about Ardee his whole time in the South. *Other matters seemed so much more pressing. My one friend gave me this one task. If anything has happened to her . . .*

Glokta pointed to the stairs, and Vitari nodded and crept up them silently, bending and sliding a glinting knife out from her boot. He pointed down the hall and Frost padded off deeper into the house, pressed up into the shadows by the wall. The living room door stood ajar, and Glokta shuffled to it and pushed it open.

Ardee was sitting in the window with her back to him: white dress, dark hair, just as he remembered her. He saw her head move slightly as the door's hinges creaked. *Alive, then.* But the room was strangely altered. Aside from the one chair she sat in, it was entirely empty. Bare whitewashed walls, bare wooden boards, windows without curtains.

'There's nothing fucking left!' she barked, voice cracked and throaty.

Clearly. Glokta frowned, and stepped through the door into the room. 'Nothing left, I said!' She stood up, still with her back to him. 'Or did you decide you'd take the chair after all?' She spun round, grabbing hold of the back, lifted it over her head and flung it at him with a shriek. It crashed into the wall beside the door, sending fragments of wood and plaster flying. One leg whizzed past Glokta's face and clattered into the corner, the rest tumbled to the floor in a mass of dust and splintered sticks.

'Most kind,' murmured Glokta, 'but I prefer to stand.'

'You!' He could see her eyes wide with surprise through her tangled hair. There was a gauntness and a paleness to her face that he did not remember. Her dress was rumpled, and far too thin for the chilly room. She tried to smooth it with shivering hands, plucked ineffectually at her greasy hair. She gave a snort of laughter. 'I'm afraid I'm not really prepared for visitors.'

Glokta heard Frost thumping down the hall, saw him looming up at the doorway, fists clenched. He held up a finger. 'It's alright. Wait outside.' The albino faded back into the shadows, and Glokta hobbled across the creaking boards into the empty sitting room. 'What happened?'

Ardee's mouth twisted. 'It seems my father was not nearly so well off as everyone imagined. He had debts. Soon after my brother left for Angland, they came to collect.'

'Who came?'

'A man called Fallow. He took all the money I had, but it wasn't enough. They took the plate, my mother's jewels, such as they were. They gave me six weeks to find the rest. I let my maid go. I sold everything I could, but they wanted more. Then they came again. Three days ago. They took everything. Fallow said I was lucky he was leaving me the dress I was wearing.'

'I see.'

She took a deep, shuddering breath. 'Since then, I have been sitting here, and thinking on how a friendless young woman can come by some money.' She fixed him with her eye. 'I have thought of only one way. I daresay, if I had the courage, I would have done it already.'

Glokta sucked at his gums. 'Lucky for us both that you're a coward, then.' He shrugged one shoulder out of his coat, then had to wriggle and flail to get his arm out. Once he finally did, he had to fumble his cane across into his other hand so he could finally throw it off. *Damn it. I can't even make a generous gesture gracefully.* Finally he held it out to her, tottering slightly on his weak leg.

'You sure you don't need it more than me?'

'Take it. At least then I won't have to get the bloody thing back on.'

That brought half a smile from her. 'Thank you,' she muttered as she pulled it round her shoulders. 'I tried to find you, but I didn't know . . . where you were . . .'

'I am sorry for that, but I am here now. You need not worry about anything. You will have to come and stay with me tonight. My quarters are not spacious, but we'll find a way.' *There will be plenty of room once I am face down in the docks, after all.*

'What about after that?'

'After that you will come here. Tomorrow this house will be just as it was.'

She stared at him. 'How?'

'Oh, I will see to it. First of all we get you in the warm.' *Superior Glokta, friend to the friendless.*

She closed her eyes as he spoke, and he heard breath snorting fast through her nose. She swayed slightly, as if she hardly had the strength to stand any longer. *Strange how, as long as the hardship lasts, we can stand it. As soon as the crisis is over, the strength all leeches away in an instant.* Glokta reached out, almost touched her shoulder to steady her, but at the last moment her eyes flickered open, and she straightened up again, and he pulled his hand away.

Superior Glokta, rescuer of young women in distress. He guided her into the hallway and towards the broken front door. 'If you could give me one moment with my Practicals.'

'Of course.' Ardee looked up at him, big, dark eyes rimmed with worried pink. 'And thank you. Whatever they say, you're a good man.'

Glokta had to stifle a sudden urge to giggle. *A good man? I doubt that Salem Rews would agree. Or Gofred Hornlach, or Magister Kault, or Korsten dan Vurms, General Vissbruck, Ambassador Islik, Inquisitor Harker, or any of a hundred others scattered through the penal colonies of Angland or squatting in Dagoska, waiting to die. And yet Ardee West thinks me a good man.* A strange feeling, and not an unpleasant one. *It feels almost like being human again. What a shame that it comes so late in the day.*

He beckoned to Frost as Ardee shuffled out in his black coat. 'I have a task for you, my old friend. One last task.' Glokta slapped his hand down on the albino's heavy shoulder and squeezed it. 'Do you know a money-lender called Fallow?'

Frost nodded slowly.

'Find him and hurt him. Bring him here and make him understand who he has offended. Everything must be restored, better than it was, tell him that. Give him one day. One day, and then you find him, wherever he is, and you start cutting. You hear me? Do me that one favour.'

Frost nodded again, his pink eyes glinting in the dim hallway.

'Sult will be expecting us,' murmured Vitari, peering down at them from the stairs, arms crossed, gloved hands hanging limp over the rail.

'Of course he will.' Glokta winced as he hobbled to the open door. *And we wouldn't want to keep his Eminence waiting.*

Click, tap, pain, that was the rhythm of Glokta's walking. The confident click of his right heel, the tap of his cane on the echoing tiles of the hallway, then the long scrape of his left foot with the familiar pain in the knee, arse and back. Click, tap, pain.

He had walked from the docks to Ardee's house, to the Agriont, to the House of Questions, and all the way up here. *Limped. On my own. Without help.* Now every step was agony. He grimaced with each movement. He grunted and sweated and cursed. *But I'm damned if I'm slowing down.*

'You don't like to make things easy, do you?' muttered Vitari.

'Why should they be?' he snapped. 'You can console yourself with the thought that this conversation will most likely be our last.'

'Then why even come? Why not run?'

Glokta snorted. 'In case you hadn't noticed, I am an exceptionally poor runner. That and I'm curious.' *Curious to know why his Eminence didn't leave me there to rot along with all the rest.*

'Your curiosity might be the death of you.'

'If the Arch Lector wants me dead, limping the other way will do me little good. I'd rather take it standing up.' He winced at a sudden spasm through his leg. 'Or maybe sitting down. Either way, face to face, with my eyes open.'

'Your choice, I suppose.'

'That's right.' *My last one.*

They came into Sult's ante-room. He had to admit to being somewhat surprised to have come this far. He had been expecting every black-masked Practical they had passed in the building to seize hold of him. He had been expecting every black-clothed Inquisitor to point and scream for his immediate arrest. *And yet here I am again.* The heavy desk, the heavy chairs, the two towering Practicals flanking the heavy doors, were all the same.

'I am—'

'Superior Glokta, of course.' The Arch Lector's secretary bowed his head respectfully. 'You may go in at once. His Eminence is expecting you.' Light spilled out of the Arch Lector's office and into the narrow chamber.

'I'll wait here.' Vitari slid into one of the chairs and swung her damp boots up on an other.

'Don't bother waiting too long.' *My last words, perhaps?* Glokta cursed inwardly as he shuffled towards the doorway. *I really should have thought of something more memorable.* He paused for just a moment at the threshold, took a deep breath, and hobbled through.

The same airy, round room. The same dark furniture, the same dark pictures on the bright walls, the same great window with the same view of the University, and the House of the Maker beyond. *No assassins loitering under the table, no axemen waiting behind the door.* Only Sult himself, sitting at his desk with a pen in hand, the nib scratching calmly and evenly across some papers spread out before him.

'Superior Glokta!' Sult started up and swept gracefully across the polished floor towards him, white coat flapping. 'I'm so glad you are safely returned!' The Arch Lector gave every impression of being pleased to see him, and Glokta frowned. He had been prepared for almost anything but this.

Sult held out his hand, the stone on his ring of office flashing purple sparks. Glokta grimaced as he bent slowly to kiss it. 'I serve and obey, your Eminence.' He straightened up with an effort. *No knife in the back of the neck?* But Sult was already flowing across to the cabinet, grinning broadly.

'Sit, please sit! You need not wait to be asked!'

Since when? Glokta grunted his way into one of the chairs, taking only the briefest moment to check for poisoned spikes on the seat. The Arch Lector, meanwhile, had plucked open the cabinet and was rummaging inside. *Will he pull out a loaded flatbow, and shoot me through the throat?* But all that emerged were two glasses. 'It would seem congratulations are in order,' he threw over his shoulder.

Glokta blinked. 'What?'

'Congratulations. Excellent work.' Sult grinned down at him as he slid the glasses gracefully onto the round table, eased the stopper, clinking, from the decanter. *What to say? What to say?*

'Your Eminence . . . Dagoska . . . I must be candid. It was on the point of falling when I left. Very soon now, the city will be overrun—'

'Of course it will.' Sult dismissed it all with a wave of his white-gloved hand. 'There was never the slightest chance of holding it. The best I was hoping for was that you'd make the Gurkish pay! And how you did that, eh, Glokta? How you did that!'

'Then . . . you are . . . pleased?' He hardly dared say the word.

'I am delighted! If I had written the tale myself, it could not have worked out better! The incompetence of the Lord Governor, the treachery of his son, it all showed how little the regular authorities can be relied upon in a crisis. Eider's treason exposed the duplicity of the merchants, their dubious connections, their rotten morality! The Spicers have been dissolved alongside the Mercers: their trade rights are in our hands. The pair of them, consigned to the latrine of history and the power of the merchants broken! Only his Majesty's Inquisition remained staunch in the face of the Union's most implacable enemy. You should have seen Marovia's face when I presented the confessions to the Open Council!' Sult filled Glokta's glass all the way to the top.

'Most kind, your Eminence,' he muttered as he took a sip from it. *Excellent wine, as always.*

'And then he got up in the Closed Council, before the King himself, mark you, and declared to everyone that you wouldn't last a week once the Gurkish attacked!' The Arch Lector spluttered with laughter. 'I wish you could have been there. I'm confident he'll do better than that, I said. Confident he'll do better.' *A ringing endorsement indeed.*

Sult slapped the table with his white-gloved palm. 'Two months, Glokta! Two months! With every day that passed he looked more of a fool, and I looked more of a hero . . . we, that is,' he corrected himself, 'we looked like heroes, and all I had to do was smile! You could almost see them, each day, shuffling their chairs away from Marovia and down towards me! Last week they voted extra powers to the Inquisition. Nine votes to three. Nine to three! Next week we'll go further! How the hell did you manage it?' And he gazed at Glokta expectantly.

I sold myself to the bank that funded the Mercers, then used the proceeds to bribe the world's least reliable mercenary. Then I murdered a defenceless emissary under flag of parley and tortured a serving girl until her body was mincemeat. Oh, and I let the biggest traitor of the lot go free. It was, without doubt, a heroic business. How did I manage it? 'Rising early,' he murmured.

Sult's eye flickered, and Glokta caught it. *A trace of annoyance, perhaps? A trace of mistrust?* But it was quickly extinguished. 'Rising early. Of course.' He raised his glass. 'The second greatest virtue. It comes just behind ruthlessness. I like your style, Glokta, I've always said so.'

Have you indeed? But Glokta humbly inclined his head.

'Practical Vitari's despatches were filled with admiration. I particularly enjoyed the way you dealt with the Gurkish emissary. That must have wiped the smile from the Emperor's face, if only for a moment, the arrogant swine.' *So she kept her end of the bargain, then? Interesting.* 'Yes, things proceed smoothly. Except for the damn peasants making a nuisance of themselves, and Angland of course. Shame about Ladisla.'

'About Ladisla?' asked Glokta, baffled.

Sult looked sour. 'You didn't hear? Another of Chief Justice Marovia's brilliant notions. He had it in mind to lift the Crown Prince's popularity by giving him a command in the North. Something out of the way, where he'd be in no danger and we could heap him with glory. It wasn't a bad scheme, really, except that out of the way became in the way, and he commanded himself straight into his grave.'

'His army with him?'

'A few thousand of them, but mostly that rubbish the nobles sent as levies. Nothing of much significance. Ostenhorm is still in our hands, and it wasn't my idea so, all in all, no harm done. Between you and me it's probably for the best, Ladisla was insufferable. I had to dig him out of more than one scandal. Never could keep his trousers closed, the damn halfwit. Raynault seems to be a different kind of a man. Sober, sensible. Do as he's bloody told. Better all round. Providing he doesn't go and get himself killed, of course, we'd be in a pickle then.' Sult took another swig from his glass and worked it round his mouth with some satisfaction.

Glokta cleared his throat. *While he is in a good mood . . .* 'There was one issue I wished to discuss with you, your Eminence. The Gurkish agent we found within the city. She was . . .' *How to describe this without sounding like a madman?*

But Sult was ahead of him once again. 'I know. An Eater.' *You know? Even about this?* The Arch Lector sat back and shook his head. 'An occult abomination. A tale straight from a story book. Eating the flesh of men. Apparently it is a practice well established down in the barbaric South. But don't concern yourself about it. I am already taking advice.'

'Who gives advice about such things as these?'

The Arch Lector only flashed his silky smile. 'You must be tired. The weather over there can be so very draining. All that heat and dust, even in the winter. Take a rest. You deserve it. I'll send for you if anything comes up.' And Sult took up his pen and looked back to his papers, leaving Glokta with nothing to do but shuffle for the door, a look of profound puzzlement on his face.

'You almost look like you're still alive,' muttered Vitari as he hobbled out into the anteroom.

True. Or about as close as I come to it. 'Sult was . . . pleased.' He still could hardly believe it. The very words sounded strange together.

'He damn well should be, after the talking-up I gave you.'

'Huh.' Glokta frowned. 'It seems I owe you an apology.'

'Keep it. It isn't worth shit to me. Just trust me next time.'

'A fair demand,' he conceded, glancing sideways at her. *But you have to be joking.*

The chamber was filled with fine furniture. *Almost overfilled.* Richly upholstered chairs, an antique table, a polished cabinet, all lavish for the small sitting-room. A huge old painting of the Lords of the Union paying homage to Harod the Great entirely filled one wall. A thick Kantic carpet had been rolled out across the boards, almost too big for the floor. A healthy fire crackled in the grate between two antique vases, and the room was homely, and pleasant, and warm. *What a difference a day can make, with the right encouragement.*

'Good,' said Glokta as he looked round. 'Very good.'

'Of course,' muttered Fallow, head bowed respectfully, hat halfway to being crushed in his hands. 'Of course, Superior, I have done everything possible. Most of the furniture I had . . . I had sold already, and so I replaced with better, the best I could find. The rest of the house is just the same. I hope that . . . I hope that it's adequate?'

'I hope so too. Is it adequate?'

Ardee was scowling at Fallow. 'It will serve.'

'Excellent,' said the moneylender nervously, glancing briefly at Frost and then down at his boots. 'Excellent! Please accept my very deepest apologies! I had no idea, of course, absolutely no idea, Superior, that you were involved in any way. Of course, I would never . . . I am so very sorry.'

'It really isn't me you should be apologising to, is it?'

'No, no, of course.' He turned slowly to Ardee. 'My lady, please accept my deepest apologies.'

Ardee glared at him, lip curled, and said nothing.

'Perhaps if you were to beg,' suggested Glokta. 'On your knees. That might do it.'

Fallow dropped to his knees without hesitation. He wrung his hands 'My lady, please—'

'Lower,' said Glokta.

'Of course,' he muttered as he fell to all fours. 'I do apologise, my lady. Most humbly. If you could only find it in your heart, I beg you—' He reached out gingerly to touch the hem of her dress and she jerked back, then swung her foot and kicked him savagely in the face.

'Gah!' squawked the moneylender, rolling onto his side, dark blood bubbling out of his nose and all over the new carpet. Glokta felt his brows go up. *That was unexpected.*

'That's for you, fucker!' The next kick caught him in the mouth and his head snapped back, spots of blood spattering onto the far wall. Ardee's shoe thudded into his gut and folded him up tight.

'You,' she snarled, 'you . . .' She kicked him again and again and Fallow shuddered and grunted and sighed, curling up in a ball. Frost moved away from the wall a step, and Glokta held up his finger.

'That's alright,' he murmured, 'I think she has it covered.'

The kicks began to slow. Glokta could hear Ardee gasping for air. Her heel dug into Fallow's ribs, her toe cracked into his nose again. *If she ever gets bored, she might have a bright future as a Practical.* She worked her mouth, leaned over and spat onto the side of his face. She kicked him again, weakly, then stumbled back against the cabinet and leaned on the polished wood, bent over and breathing hard.

'Happy?' asked Glokta.

She stared up at him through her tangled hair. 'Not really.'

'Will kicking him some more make you happier?'

Her brows wrinkled as she looked down at Fallow, wheezing on his side on the carpet. She took a step forward and booted him hard in the chest one more time, rocked away, wiping some snot from under her nose. She pushed her hair out of her face. 'I'm done.'

'Fine. Get out,' hissed Glokta. 'Out, worm!'

'Of course,' Fallow drooled through his bloody lips, crawling for the door, Frost looming over him the whole way. 'Of course! Thank you! Thank you all so much!' The front door banged shut.

Ardee sat down heavily in one of the chairs, elbows resting on her knees, forehead resting on her palms. Glokta could see her hands trembling slightly. *It can really be very tiring, hurting someone. I should know. Especially if you aren't used to it.* 'I wouldn't feel too badly,' he said. 'I'm sure he deserved it.'

She looked up, and her eyes were hard. 'I don't. He deserves worse.'

That was unexpected too. 'Do you want him to have worse?'

She swallowed, slowly sat back. 'No.'

'Up to you.' *But it's nice to have the option.* 'You may want to change your clothes.'

She looked down. 'Oh.' Spots of Fallow's blood were spattered as far as her knees. 'I don't have anything—'

'There's a room full of new ones, upstairs. I made sure of it. I'll arrange for some dependable servants as well.'

'I don't need them.'

'Yes, you do. I won't hear of you here alone.'

She shrugged her shoulders hopelessly. 'I have nothing to pay them with.'

'Don't worry. I'll take care of it.' *All compliments of the hugely generous Valint and Balk, after all.* 'Don't worry about anything. I made a promise to your brother, and I mean to see it through. I'm very sorry that things came this far. I had a great deal to take care of . . . in the South. Have you heard from him, by the way?'

Ardee looked up sharply, her mouth slightly open. 'You don't know?'

'Know what?'

She swallowed, and stared down at the floor. 'Collem was with Prince Ladisla, at this battle that everyone is talking of. Some prisoners were taken, have been ransomed – he wasn't among them. They presume . . .' She paused for a moment, staring at the blood on her dress. 'They presume he was killed.'

'Killed?' Glokta's eyelid fluttered. His knees felt suddenly weak. He took a lurching step back and sank into a chair. His own hands were trembling now, and he clasped them together. *Deaths. They happen every day. I caused thousands of them not long ago, with hardly a thought. I looked at heaps of corpses and shrugged. What makes this one so hard to take?* And yet it was.

'Killed?' he whispered.

She nodded slowly, and put her face in her hands.

Cold Comfort

West peered out of the bushes, through the drifting flakes of snow, down the slope toward the Union picket. The sentries were sat in a rough circle, hunched round a steaming pan over a miserable tongue of fire on the far side of the stream. They wore thick coats, breath smoking, weapons almost forgotten in the snow around them. West knew how they felt. Bethod might come this week, he might come next week, but the cold they had to fight every minute of every day.

'Right then,' whispered Threetrees. 'You'd best go down there on your own. They might not like the looks of me and the rest of the boys, all rushing down on 'em from the trees.'

The Dogman grinned. 'Might shoot one of us.'

'And that'd be some kind o' shame,' hissed Dow, 'after we come so far.'

'Give us the shout when they're good and ready for a crew of Northmen to come wandering out the woods, eh?'

'I will,' said West. He dragged the heavy sword out of his belt and handed it to Threetrees. 'You'd better hold on to this for me.'

'Good luck,' said the Dogman.

'Good luck,' said Dow, lips curling back into his savage grin. 'Furious.'

West walked out slowly from the trees and down the gentle slope towards the stream, his stolen boots crunching in the snow, his hands held up above his head, to show he was unarmed. Even so, he could hardly have blamed the sentries if they shot him on sight. No one could have looked more like a dangerous savage than he did now, he knew. The last tatters of his uniform were hidden beneath a bundle of furs and torn scraps, tied around his body with twine, a stained coat stolen from a dead Northman over the top. He had a few weeks' growth of scraggy beard across his scabby face, his eyes were sore and watering, sunken with hunger and exhaustion. He looked like a desperate man, and what was more, he knew, he was one. A killer. The man who murdered Crown Prince Ladisla. The very worst of traitors.

One of the sentries looked up and saw him, started clumsily from his place, knocking the pan hissing into the fire, snatching his spear out of the snow. 'Stop!' he shouted, in slurred Northern. The others jumped up after him, grabbing at their weapons, one fumbling at the string on his flatbow with mittened fingers.

West stopped, flecks of snow settling gently on his tangled hair and across his shoulders. 'Don't worry,' he shouted back in common. 'I'm on your side.'

They stared at him for a moment. 'We'll see!' shouted one. 'Come on across the water, but do it slow!'

He crunched on down the slope and sloshed out into the stream, gritted his teeth as the freezing water soaked him up to his thighs. He struggled up the far bank and the four sentries shuffled into a nervous half circle around him, weapons raised.

'Watch him!'

'It could be a trick!'

'It's no trick,' said West slowly, keeping his eyes on the various hovering blades and trying to stay calm. It was vitally important to stay calm. 'I'm one of you.'

'Where the hell have you come from?'

'I was with Prince Ladisla's division.'

'With Ladisla? You walked up here?'

West nodded. 'I walked.' The bodies of the sentries started to relax, the spear-points started to waver and drift upwards. They were on the point of believing him. After all, he spoke the common tongue like a native, and certainly looked as if he had slogged a hundred leagues across country. 'What's your name, then?' asked the one with the flatbow.

'Colonel West,' he muttered, voice cracking. He felt like a liar even though it was true. He was a different man from the one who set out for Angland.

The sentries exchanged worried glances. 'I thought he was dead,' mumbled the one with the spear.

'Not quite, lad,' said West. 'Not quite.'

Lord Marshal Burr was poring over a table covered in crumpled maps as West pushed through the flap into his tent. It seemed in the lamplight that the pressures of command had taken their toll on him. He looked older, paler, weaker, his hair and beard wild and straggling. He had lost weight and his creased uniform hung loose, but he started up with all his old vigour.

'Colonel West, as I live and breathe! I never thought to see you again!' He seized West's hand and squeezed it hard. 'I'm glad you made it. Damn glad! I've missed your cool head around here, I don't mind telling you.' He stared searchingly into West's eyes. 'You look tired, though, my friend.'

There was no denying it. West had never been the prettiest fellow in the Agriont, that he knew, but he had always prided himself on having an honest, friendly, pleasant look. He had scarcely recognised the face in the mirror once he had taken his first bath in weeks, dragged on a borrowed uniform, and finally shaved. Everything was changed, sharpened, leached of colour. The prominent cheekbones had grown craggy, the thinning hair and brows were full of iron grey, the jaw was lean and wolf-like. Angry lines were cut deep into the skin down the pale cheeks, across the narrow bridge of the sharp nose, out from the corners of the eyes. The eyes were worst of all. Narrow. Hungry. Icy grey, as though the bitter cold had eaten into his skull and still lurked there, even in the warmth. He had tried to think of old times, to smile and laugh, and use the expressions he had used to use, but it all looked foolish on that stone wall of a face. A hard man had glared back at him from the glass, and would not go away.

'It was a difficult journey, sir.'

Burr nodded. 'Of course it was, of course. A bastard of a journey and the wrong time of year for it. A good thing I sent those Northmen with you, eh, as it turned out?'

'A very good thing, sir. A most courageous and resourceful group. They saved my life, more than once.' He glanced sideways at Pike, loitering behind him in the shadows at a respectful distance. 'All our lives.'

Burr peered over at the convict's melted face. 'And who is this?'

'This is Pike, sir, a Sergeant with the Stariksa levies, cut off from his company in the battle.' The lies spilled out of West's mouth with a surprising ease. 'He and a girl, I believe a cook's daughter who was with the baggage, joined us on the way north. He has been a great help, sir, a good man in a tight spot. Wouldn't have made it without him.'

'Excellent!' said Burr, walking over to the convict and seizing his hand. 'Well done. Your regiment is gone, Pike. Not many survivors, I'm sorry to say. Damn few survivors, but I can always use trustworthy men here at my headquarters. Especially ones who are good in a tight spot.' He gave a long sigh. 'I have few enough of 'em to hand. I hope that you'll agree to stay with us.'

The convict swallowed. 'Of course, Lord Marshal, it would be an honour.'

'What about Prince Ladisla?' murmured Burr.

West took a deep breath and looked down at the ground. 'Prince Ladisla . . .' He trailed off and slowly shook his head. 'Horsemen surprised us, and overran the headquarters. It happened so fast . . . I looked for him afterwards, but . . .'

'I see. Well. There it is. He should never have been in command, but what could I do? I'm only in charge of the damn army!' He laid a fatherly hand on West's shoulder. 'Don't blame yourself. I know you did everything you could.'

West dared not look up. He wondered what Burr would have said had he known what really happened, out there in the cold wilderness. 'Have there been any other survivors?'

'A handful. No more than a handful, and a sorry one at that.' Burr burped, grimaced and rubbed at his gut. 'I must apologise. Damn indigestion simply will not go away. Food up here and all . . . ugh.' He burped again.

'Forgive me, sir, but what is our situation?'

'Right to business, eh, West? I always liked that about you. Right to business. Well, I'll be honest. When I received your letter we planned to head back south to cover Ostenhorm, but the weather has been dire and we've scarcely been able to move. The Northmen seem to be everywhere! Bethod may have had the bulk of his army near the Cumnur but he left enough up here to make things damned difficult for us. We've had constant raids against our lines of supply, more than one pointless and bloody skirmish, and a chaotic night-time action which almost caused full-scale panic in Kroy's division.'

Poulder and Kroy. Unpleasant memories began to crowd back into West's mind, and the simple physical discomforts of the journey north began to seem rather appealing. 'How are the Generals?'

Burr glared up from under his heavy eyebrows. 'Could you believe me if I said they were worse than ever? You can scarcely put the two in the same room without them starting to bicker. I have to have briefings with each on alternate days, so as to avoid fisticuffs in my headquarters. A ludicrous state of affairs!' He gripped his hands behind him as he strode grimly round the tent. 'But the damage they're doing pales compared to the damn cold. There are men down with frostbite, with fever, with scurvy, the sick tents are brimming. For every man the enemy have killed we've lost twenty to the winter, and those still walking have got precious little stomach left for a fight. As for scouting, hah! Don't get me started!' He slapped angrily at the maps on the table. 'Charts of the land up here are all works of imagination. Useless, and we've barely any skilled scouts at all. Mist every day, and snow, and we can't see from one side of the camp to the other! Honestly, West, we've not the slightest idea where Bethod's main body is right now—'

'He's to the south, sir, perhaps two days' march behind us.'

Burr's brows went up. 'He is?'

'He is. Threetrees and his Northmen kept them under close watch as we moved, and even arranged a few unpleasant surprises for some of their outriders.'

'Like the one that they gave us, eh, West? Rope across the road and all that?' He chuckled to himself. 'Two days' march behind, you say? This is useful information. This is damn useful!' Burr winced and put one hand on his gut as he moved back to his table, picking up a ruler and starting to measure out distances. 'Two days' march. That would put him somewhere here. You're sure?'

'I'm sure, Lord Marshal.'

'If he's heading for Dunbrec, he'll pass near General Poulder's position. It might be that we can bring him to battle before he gets round us, perhaps even give him a surprise he won't forget. Well done, West, well done!' He tossed his ruler down. 'Now you should get some rest.'

'I'd rather get straight back into it, sir—'

'I know, and I could use you, but take a day or two in any case, the world won't end. You've come through quite an ordeal.'

West swallowed. He did feel terribly tired all of a sudden. 'Of course. I should write a letter . . . to my sister.' It was strange saying it. He had not thought about her for weeks. 'I should let her know that I'm . . . alive.'

'Good idea. I'll send for you, Colonel, when I need you.' And Burr turned away and hunched back over his charts.

'I won't forget that,' whispered Pike in West's ear as he lurched back through the flap into the cold.

'It's nothing. They won't miss either one of you at that camp. It's Sergeant Pike again, is all. You can put your mistakes behind you.'

'I won't forget it. I'm your man, now, Colonel, whatever happens. Your man!' West nodded as he made off, frowning, through the snow. War killed a lot of men, it seemed. But it gave a few a second chance.

West paused on the threshold. He could hear voices inside, chuckling. Old, familiar voices. They should have made him feel safe, warm, welcomed, but they did not. They worried him. Scared him, even. They, surely, would know. They would point and scream. 'Murderer! Traitor! Villain!' He turned back towards the cold. Snow was settling gently over the camp. The closest tents were black on the white ground, the ones behind grey. Further back they were soft ghosts, then only dim suggestions through the flurry of tiny flakes. No one moved. All was quiet. He took a deep breath and pushed through the flap.

The three officers were sat around a flimsy folding table inside, pushed close up to a glowing stove. Jalenhorm's beard had grown to shovel-like proportions. Kaspa had a red scarf wrapped round his head. Brint was swaddled in a dark greatcoat, dealing cards out to the other two.

'Close that flap damn it, it's freezing out—' Jalenhorm's jaw dropped. 'No! It can't be! Colonel West!'

Brint leaped up as though he had been bitten on the arse. 'Shit!'

'I told you!' shouted Kaspa, flinging down his cards and grinning madly. 'I told you he'd be back!'

They surrounded him, clapping his back, squeezing his hands, pulling him into the tent. No manacles, no drawn swords, no accusations of treason. Jalenhorm conducted him to the best chair, meaning the one furthest from imminent collapse, while Kaspa breathed into a glass and wiped it clean with his finger and Brint pulled the cork from the bottle with a gentle thwop.

'When did you get here?'

'How did you get here?'

'Were you with Ladisla?'

'Were you at the battle?'

'Hold on,' said Jalenhorm, 'give him a minute!'

West waved him down. 'I got here this morning, and would have come to you at once apart from a crucial meeting with a bath and a razor, and then one with Marshal Burr. I was with Ladisla, at the battle, and I got here by walking across country, with the help of five Northmen, a girl, and a man with no face.' He took the glass and gulped down the contents in one go, winced and sucked his teeth as the spirit burned its way down into his stomach, already starting to feel glad that he decided to come in. 'Don't be shy,' he said as he held the empty glass out.

'Walking across country,' whispered Brint, shaking his head as he poured, 'with five Northmen. A girl, you say?'

'That's right.' West frowned, wondering what Cathil was doing right now. Wondering whether she needed help . . . foolishness, she could look after herself. 'You made it with my letter, then, Lieutenant?' he asked Jalenhorm.

'Some cold and nervous nights on the road,' grinned the big man, 'but I did.'

'Except that it's Captain now,' said Kaspa, sitting back on his stool.

'Is it indeed?'

Jalenhorm shrugged modestly. 'Thanks to you, really. The Lord Marshal put me on his staff when I got back.'

'Though *Captain* Jalenhorm still finds time to spend with us little people, bless him.' Brint licked his fingertips and started dealing four hands.

'I've no stake, I'm afraid,' muttered West.

Kaspa grinned. 'Don't worry, Colonel, we don't play for money any more. Without Luthar to make poor men of us all, it hardly seemed worth it.'

'He never turned up?'

'They just came and pulled him off the boat. Hoff sent for him. We've heard nothing since.'

'Friends in high places,' said Brint sourly. 'Probably swanning about in Adua on some easy detail, making free with the women while the rest of us are freezing our arses off.'

'Though let's be honest,' threw in Jalenhorm, 'he made free enough with the women even when we were there.'

West frowned. That was all too unfortunately true.

Kaspa scraped his hand up off the table. 'So anyway, we're just playing for honour.'

'Though you'll not find much of that here,' quipped Brint. The other two burst out laughing and Kaspa dribbled booze into his beard. West raised his eyebrows. Clearly they were drunk, and the sooner he joined them the better. He swilled down the next glass and reached for the bottle.

'Well, I'll tell you one thing,' Jalenhorm was saying, sorting his cards with fumbling fingers, 'I'm glad as all hell that I won't have to tell your sister anything for you. I've scarcely slept in weeks for thinking through how I'd go about it, and I still haven't got a thought in my head.'

'You've never yet had a thought in your head,' said Brint, and the other two chortled away again. Even West managed a smile this time, but it didn't last long.

'How was the battle?' asked Jalenhorm.

West stared at his glass for a long moment. 'It was bad. The Northmen set a trap for Ladisla and he fell right into it, squandered his cavalry. Then a mist came up, all of a sudden, and you couldn't see the hand before your face. Their horse were on us before we knew what was happening. I took a knock on the head, I think. Next I remember I was in the mud on my back and there was a Northman bearing down on me. With this.' He slid the heavy sword out of his belt and laid it down on the table.

The three officers stared at it, spellbound. 'Bloody hell,' muttered Kaspa.

Brint's eyes were wide. 'How did you get the better of him?'

'I didn't. This girl I was telling you about . . .'

'Yes?'

'She smashed his brains out with a hammer. Saved my life.'

'Bloody hell,' muttered Kaspa.

'Phew,' Brint sat back heavily in his chair. 'Sounds like quite a woman!'

West was frowning, staring down at the glass in his hand. 'You could say that.' He remembered the feeling of Cathil sleeping beside him, her breath against his cheek. Quite a woman. 'You really could say that.' He drained his glass and stood up, stuck the Northman's sword back through his belt.

'You're going?' asked Brint.

'There's something I need to take care of.'

Jalenhorm stood up with him. 'I should thank you, Colonel. For sending me off with the letter. It sounds like you were right. There was nothing I could have done.'

'No.' West took a deep breath, and blew it out. 'There was nothing anyone could have done.'

The night was still, and crisp, and cold, and West's boots slipped and squelched in the half-frozen mud. Fires burned here and there and men clustered round them in the darkness, swaddled in all the clothes they possessed, breath smoking, pinched faces lit in flickering yellow. One fire burned brighter than the others, up on a slope above the camp, and West made for that now, feet weaving from the drink. He saw two dark figures sitting near it, taking shape as he came closer.

Black Dow was having a pipe, chagga smoke curling out from his fierce grin, an open bottle wedged between his crossed legs, several empty ones scattered in the snow nearby. Somewhere away to the right, off in the darkness, West could hear someone singing in Northern. A huge, deep voice, and singing very badly. 'He cut him to the boooones. No. To the boooones. To the . . . wait on.'

'You alright?' asked West, holding his gloved hands out to the crackling flames.

Threetrees grinned happily up at him, wobbling slightly back and forward. West wondered if it was the first time he had seen the old warrior smile. He jerked a thumb down the hill. 'Tul's having a piss. And singing. I'm drunk as fucking shit.' He fell slowly backwards and crunched down into the snow, arms and legs spread out wide. 'And I been smoking. I'm soaked. I'm wet as the fucking Crinna. Where are we, Dow?'

Dow squinted across the fire, mouth wide open, like he was looking at something far away. 'Middle o' fucking nowhere,' he said, waving the pipe around. He started cackling, grabbed hold of Threetrees' boot and shook it. 'Where else would we be? You want this, Furious?' He thrust the pipe up at West.

'Alright.' He sucked on the stem, felt the smoke biting in his lungs. He coughed brown steam out into the frosty air, and sucked again.

'Give me that,' said Threetrees, sitting up and snatching the pipe off him.

Tul's great rumbling voice came floating up out of the darkness, horribly out of tune. 'He swung his axe like . . . what is it? He swung his axe like . . . shit. No. Hold on . . .'

'Do you know where Cathil is?' asked West.

Dow leered up at him. 'Oh, she's around.' He waved his hand toward a cluster of tents higher up the slope. 'Up that way, I reckon.'

'Around,' echoed Threetrees, chuckling softly. 'Around.'

'He was . . . the Bloody . . . Niiiiine!' came gurgling from the trees.

West followed footprints off up the slope, towards the tents. The smoke was already having an effect on him. His head felt light, his feet moved easily. His nose didn't feel cold any more, just pleasantly tingling. He heard a woman's voice, laughing softly. He grinned, took a few more crunching steps through the snow towards the tents. Warm light spilled out from one, through a narrow gap in the cloth. The laughter grew louder.

'Uh . . . uh . . . uh . . .'

West frowned. That didn't sound like laughter. He came closer, doing his best to be quiet. Another sound wandered into his fuzzy mind. An intermittent growling, like some kind of animal. He edged closer still, bending down to peer through the gap, hardly daring even to breathe.

'Uh . . . uh . . . uh . . .'

He saw a woman's bare back, squirming up and down. A thin back, he could see the sinews bunching as she moved, the knobbles of her backbone shifting under her skin. Closer still, and he could see her hair, shaggy brown and messy. Cathil. A pair of sinewy legs stuck out from under her towards West, one foot almost close enough for him to touch, its thick toes wriggling.

'Uh . . . uh . . . uh . . .'

A hand slid up under her armpit, another round behind one knee. There was a low growl and the lovers, if you could call them that, rolled smoothly over so she was underneath. West's mouth dropped open. He could see the side of the man's head, and he stared at it. There was no mistaking the sharp, stubbly jaw line. The Dogman. His arse was sticking up towards West, moving in and out. Cathil's hand clutched at one hairy buttock, squeezing at it in time to the movement.

'Uh . . . Uh . . . Uh!'

West clamped one hand over his mouth, eyes bulging, half-horrified, half strangely aroused. He was caught hopelessly between wanting to watch, and wanting to run, and came down on the latter without thinking. He took a step back, his heel caught a tent peg and he went sprawling over with a stifled cry.

'What the fuck?' he heard from inside the tent. He scrambled up and turned away, started to flounder through the snow in the darkness as he heard the flap thrown back. 'Which of you is it, you bastards?' came Dogman's voice from above, bellowing in Northern. 'That you, Dow? I'll fucking kill you!'

The High Places

'The Broken Mountains,' breathed Brother Longfoot, his voice hushed with awe. 'Truly, a magnificent sight.'

'I think I'd like it better if I didn't have to climb 'em,' grunted Logen.

Jezal by no means disagreed. The character of the land they rode through had been changing day by day, from softly sloping grassland, to gently rolling plains, to buckled hills spattered with bare rocks and sullen groups of stunted trees. Always in the distance had been the dim grey rumours of the mountain peaks, growing larger and more distinct with each morning until they seemed to pierce the brooding clouds themselves.

Now they sat in their very shadow. The long valley they had been following with its waving trees and winding stream ended at a maze of broken walls. Beyond it lay a steep rise into the rugged foothills, beyond them the first true outlier of the mountains rose, a stark outline of jagged rock, proud and magnificent, smeared at the distant top with white snow. A child's vertiginous notion of what a mountain should be.

Bayaz swept the ruined foundations with his hard green eyes. 'There was a strong fortress here. It marked the western limits of the Empire, before pioneers crossed the pass and settled the valleys on the far side.' The place was nothing more now than a home for stinging weeds and scratching brambles. The Magus clambered from the cart and squatted down, stretching out his back and working his legs, grimacing all the while. He still looked old and ill, but a great deal of both flesh and colour had returned to his face since they left Aulcus behind. 'Here ends my rest,' he sighed. 'This cart has served us well, and the beasts too, but the pass will be too steep for horses.'

Jezal saw the track now, switching back and forth as it climbed, a faint line through the piles of wild grass and steep rock, lost over a ridge high above. 'It looks a long way.'

Bayaz snorted. 'But the first ascent of many we will make today, and there will be many more beyond them. We will be a week at least in the mountains, my boy, if all goes well.' Jezal hardly dared ask what might happen if things went badly. 'We must travel light. We have a long, steep road to follow. Water and all the food we have left. Warm clothes, for it will be bitter cold among the peaks.'

'The birth of spring is perhaps not the best time to cross a mountain range,' observed Longfoot under his breath.

Bayaz looked sharply sideways. 'Some would say the best time to cross an obstacle is when one finds oneself on the wrong side of it! Or do you suggest we wait for summer?' The Navigator chose, wisely in Jezal's opinion, not to reply. 'The pass is well-sheltered in the main, the weather should be far from our most pressing worry. We will need ropes, though. The road was good, in the Old Time, if narrow, but that was long ago. It might have been washed away in places, or tumbled into deep valleys, who knows? We may have some tough climbing ahead of us.'

'I can hardly wait,' muttered Jezal.

'Then there is this.' The Magus pulled one of the nearly empty fodder sacks open, pushed the hay out of the way with his bony hands. The box they had taken from the House of the Maker lay in its bottom, a block of darkness among the pale, dry grass.

'And who gets the joy of carrying that bastard?' Logen looked up from under his brows. 'How about we draw lots? No?' No one said anything. The Northman grunted as he hooked his hands under it and dragged it off the cart towards him, its edge squealing against the wood. 'Reckon it's me, then,' he said, thick veins standing out from his neck as he hauled the weighty thing onto a blanket.

Jezal did not at all enjoy looking at it. It reminded him too much of the suffocating hallways of the Maker's House. Of Bayaz' dark stories about magic, and demons, and the Other Side. Of the fact that there was a purpose to this journey that he did not understand, but definitely did not like the sound of. He was glad when Logen finally had it wrapped up in blankets and stowed in a pack. Out of sight, at least, if not entirely out of mind.

They all had plenty to carry. Jezal took his steels, of course, sheathed at his belt. The clothes he wore: the least stained, torn and reeking he possessed, his ripped and battered, one-armed coat over the top. He had a spare shirt in his pack, a coil of rope above it, and half their stock of food on top of that. He almost wished that were heavier: they were down to their last box of biscuits, half a sack of oatmeal and a packet of salted fish that disgusted everyone except Quai. He rolled up a pair of blankets and belted them to the top of his pack, hung a full canteen at his waist, and was ready to go. As ready as he was going to get, anyway.

Quai unhitched the carthorses while Jezal stripped the saddles and harness from the other two. It seemed hardly fair, leaving them in the middle of nowhere after they had carried them all the way from Calcis. It felt like years ago to Jezal, thinking back. He was a different man now from the one who had set out from that city across the plain. He almost winced to remember his arrogance, and his ignorance, and his selfishness.

'Yah!' he shouted. His horse looked at him sadly without moving, then put its head down and began to nibble at the grass near his feet. He rubbed its back fondly. 'Well. I suppose they will find their way in time.'

'Or not,' grunted Ferro, drawing her sword.

'What are you—'

The curved blade chopped halfway through the neck of Jezal's horse, spattering warm, wet specks in his stricken face. Its front legs crumpled and it slid to the ground, toppled onto its side, blood gushing out into the grass.

Ferro grabbed hold of one of its hooves, hauled it towards her with one hand and started hacking the leg from the carcass with short, efficient blows while Jezal stared, his mouth open. She scowled up at him.

'I am not leaving all this meat for the birds. It will not keep long, but we will eat well enough tonight, at least. Get that sack.'

Logen flung one of the empty feed bags to her, and shrugged. 'You can't get attached to things, Jezal. Not out here in the wild.'

No one spoke as they began to climb. They all were bent over and concentrating on the crumbling track beneath their shuffling feet. The path rose and turned back, rose and turned back time after time and soon Jezal's legs were aching, his shoulders were sore, his face was damp with sweat. One step at a time. That was what West used to tell him, when he was flagging on the long runs round the Agriont. One step at a time, and he had been right. Left foot, right foot, and up they went.

After a spell of this repetitive effort he stopped and looked down. It was amazing, how high they had climbed in so short a time. He could see the foundations of the ruined fortress, grey outlines in the green turf at the foot of the pass. Beyond it the rutted track led back through the crumpled hills towards Aulcus. Jezal gave a sudden shudder and turned back towards the mountains. Better to leave all that behind him.

Logen slogged up the steep path, his worn boots scraping and crunching in the gravel and the dirt, the metal box in his pack a dead weight that dragged on his shoulders and seemed to get heavier with each step, that dug into his flesh like a bag of nails even though it was wrapped in blankets. But Logen was not so very bothered by it. He was too busy watching Ferro's arse move as she walked ahead of him, lean muscles squeezing with every step under the stained canvas of her trousers.

It was an odd thing. Before he'd fucked her he hadn't thought about her that way at all. He'd been too concerned with trying to stop her running off, or shooting him, or stabbing one of the others. So busy watching her scowl that he hadn't seen her face. So busy watching her hands that he'd never noticed the rest of her. Now he couldn't think about anything else.

Every movement of hers seemed fascinating. He'd catch himself watching her all the time. While they were on the move. While they were sitting down. While she was eating, or drinking, or talking, or spitting. While she was pulling her boots on in the morning or pulling them off at night. To make matters worse, his cock was halfway hard the whole time from watching her out of the corners of his eyes, and imagining her naked. It was getting to be quite an embarrassment.

'What are you looking at?' Logen stopped and gazed up into the sun. Ferro was frowning down at him. He stood and shifted the pack on his back, rubbing at his sore shoulders, wiping a sheen of sweat from his forehead. He could've thought up a lie, easily enough. He'd been watching the magnificent mountain peaks. He'd been watching where he put his feet. He'd been checking that her pack was on right. But what would've been the point? They both knew well enough what he'd been looking at, and the others had pushed on well out of earshot.

'I'm looking at your arse,' he said, shrugging his shoulders. 'Sorry, but it's a good one. No harm looking, is there?'

She opened her mouth angrily but he put his head down and trudged round her before she had the chance to speak, his thumbs hooked under the straps of his pack. When he'd got ten paces or so he looked over his shoulder. She was still standing there, hands on her hips, frowning up at him. He grinned back.

'What are you looking at?' he said.

They stopped for water in the cold fresh morning, on a ledge above a plunging valley. Through spreading trees heavy with red berries growing sideways from the bare rock, Jezal could see white water surging in its narrow bottom. Dizzying cliffs rose on the far side, sheets of grey stone not far from sheer, ending in towering crags high above, where dark birds flapped and crowed to each other, while swirls of white cloud turned in the pale sky beyond. A spectacular setting, if somewhat unsettling.

'Beautiful,' murmured Jezal, but taking care not to get too close to the edge.

Logen nodded. 'Reminds me of home. When I was a lad, I used to spend weeks at a time up in the High Places, testing myself against the mountains.' He took a swallow from the flask then handed it to Jezal, staring up through narrowed eyes at the dark peaks. 'They always win, though. This Empire's come and gone, and here they still are, looking down on it all. Here they'll still be, long after all of us have gone back to the mud. They looked down on my home.' He gave a long snort, then spat phlegm over the edge of the valley. 'Now they look down on nothing.'

Jezal took a swallow of water himself. 'Will you go back to the North, after this?'

'Maybe. I've some scores to settle. Some deep, hard scores.' The Northman shrugged his shoulders. 'But if I let 'em lie I daresay no one would be the worse off. I reckon they all think I'm dead, and no one's anything but relieved about it.'

'Nothing to go back to?'

Logen winced. 'Nothing but more blood. My family's long dead and rotted, and those friends I didn't turn on and kill myself, I got killed with my pride and my stupidity. So much for my achievements. But you've still got time, eh, Jezal? A good chance at a nice, peaceful life. What will you do?'

'Well . . . I've been thinking . . .' he cleared his throat, suddenly nervous, as though giving voice to his plans made them far closer to reality. 'There's a girl back home . . . well, a woman, I suppose. My friend's sister, in fact . . . her name is Ardee. I think that, perhaps, I love her . . .' It was strange, that he was discussing his innermost feelings with this man he had thought a savage. With this man who could understand nothing of the delicate rules of life in the Union, of the sacrifice that Jezal was considering. But somehow it was easy to say. 'I've been thinking . . . well . . . if she'll have me, perhaps . . . we might marry.'

'That sounds like a good plan.' Logen grinned and nodded. 'Marry her, and sow some seeds.'

Jezal raised his eyebrows. 'I don't know much about farming.'

The Northman spluttered with laughter. 'Not those kind of seeds, boy!' He clapped him on the arm. 'One piece of advice, though, if you'll take one from the likes of me, find something to do with your life that don't involve killing.' He bent and swung up his pack, shoved his arms through the straps. 'Leave the fighting to those with less sense.' And he turned and struggled up the track.

Jezal nodded slowly to himself. He touched one hand to the scar on his chin, his tongue finding the hole in his teeth. Logen was right. Fighting was not the life for him. He already had one scar too many.

It was a bright day. The first time Ferro had been warm in a long while and the sun felt good, hot and angry on her face, on her bare forearms, on the backs of her hands. The shadows of rock and branch were laid out sharp on the stony ground, the spray from the falling water that flowed beside the old track flashed as it fell through the air.

The others had fallen behind. Longfoot, taking his time, smiling up at anything and everything, blathering on about the majesty of the views. Quai hunched up and dogged under the weight of his pack. Bayaz wincing and sweating, puffing as though he might fall dead at any minute. Luthar moaning about his blisters to anyone who would listen, which was no one. So it was only her and Ninefingers, striding up ahead in stony silence.

Just the way she liked it.

She scrambled over a lip of crumbling rock and came upon a dark pool, lapping at a crescent of flat stones, water hissing and splattering down into it over piled up rocks bearded with wet moss. A pair of twisted trees spread their branches out above, thin, fresh-budded leaves shimmering and rustling in the breeze. The sunlight sparkled, and insects skated and buzzed lazily on the rippling water.

A beautiful place, most likely, if you thought that way.

Ferro did not. 'Fish in there,' she murmured, licking her lips. A fish would be nice, stuck on a twig over a fire. The bits of horse they had carried with them were all gone, and she was hungry. She watched the vague shapes flicker under the shimmering water as she squatted down to fill up her canteen. Lots of fish. Ninefingers dumped his heavy pack and sat down on the rocks beside it, dragging his boots off. He rolled his trousers up above his knees. 'What are you doing, pink?'

He grinned at her. 'I'm going to tickle me some fish out of that pool.'

'With your hands? You got clever enough fingers for that?'

'I reckon you'd know.' She frowned at him but he only smiled the wider, skin creasing up round the corners of his eyes. 'Watch and learn, woman.' And he paddled out, bent over, lips pressed tight together with concentration, feeling gently around in the water.

'What's he up to?' Luthar dumped his pack down beside Ferro's and wiped his glistening face with the back of his hand.

'Fool thinks he can catch a fish.'

'What, with his hands?'

'Watch and learn, boy,' muttered Ninefingers. 'Aaaah . . .' His face broke out into a smile. 'And here she is.' The muscles in his forearm shifted as he worked his fingers under the water. 'Got it!' And he snatched his hand up in a shower of spray. Something flashed in the bright sun and he tossed it onto the bank beside them leaving a trail of dark wet spots on the dry stones. A fish, flipping and jumping.

'Hah hah!' cried Longfoot, stepping up beside them. 'Tricking fish out of the pool, is he? A most impressive and remarkable skill. I once met a man of the Thousand Isles who was reckoned the greatest fisherman in the Circle of the World. I do declare, he could sit upon the bank and sing, and the fish would jump into his lap. They would indeed!' He frowned to find no one delighted by his tale, but now Bayaz was dragging himself over the lip, almost on hands and knees. His apprentice appeared behind him, face set hard.

The First of the Magi tottered down, leaning heavily on his staff, and fell back against a rock. 'Perhaps . . . we should camp here.' He gasped for breath, sweat running down his gaunt face. 'You would never guess I once ran through this pass. I made it in two days.' He let his staff drop from his trembling fingers and it clattered down amongst the dry grey driftwood near the water's edge. 'Long ago . . .'

'I've been thinking . . .' muttered Luthar.

Bayaz' tired eyes swivelled sideways, as though even turning his head might prove too much of an effort. 'Thinking *and* walking? Pray do not strain yourself, Captain Luthar.'

'Why the edge of the World?'

The Magus frowned. 'Not for the exercise, I assure you. What we seek is there.'

'Yes, but why is it there?'

'Uh,' grunted Ferro in agreement. A good question.

Bayaz took a long breath and puffed out his cheeks. 'Never any rest, eh? After the destruction of Aulcus, the fall of Glustrod, the three remaining sons of Euz met. Juvens, Bedesh, and Kanedias. They discussed what should be done . . . with the Seed.'

'Have that!' shouted Ninefingers, pulling another fish from the water and flinging it onto the stones beside the first. Bayaz watched it, expressionless, as it squirmed and flopped, mouth and gills gulping desperately at the suffocating air.

'Kanedias desired to study it. He claimed he could turn it to righteous purposes. Juvens feared the stone, but knew of no way to destroy it, so he gave it into his brother's keeping. Over long years though, as the wounds of the Empire failed to heal, he came to regret his decision. He worried that Kanedias, hungry for power, might break the First Law as Glustrod had done. He demanded the stone be put beyond use. At first the Maker refused, and the trust between the brothers dwindled. I know this, for I was the one who carried the messages between them. Even then, I learned since, they were preparing the weapons that they would one day use against each other. Juvens begged, then pleaded, then threatened, and eventually Kanedias relented. So the three sons of Euz journeyed to Shabulyan.'

'No place more remote in the whole Circle of the World,' muttered Longfoot.

'That is why it was chosen. They gave up the Seed to the spirit of the island, to keep safe until the end of time.'

'They commanded the spirit never to release it,' murmured Quai.

'My apprentice shows his ignorance again,' returned Bayaz, glaring from under his bushy brows. 'Not never, Master Quai. Juvens was wise enough to know that he could not guess all outcomes. He realised that a desperate time might come, in some future age, when the power of . . . this thing might be needed. So Bedesh commanded the spirit to release it only to a man who carried Juvens' staff.'

Longfoot frowned. 'Then where is it?'

Bayaz pointed to the length of wood he used for a stick, lying on the ground beside him, rough and unadorned. 'That's it?' muttered Luthar, sounding more than a little disappointed.

'What did you expect, Captain?' Bayaz grinned sideways at him. 'Ten feet of polished gold, inlaid with runes of crystal, topped by a diamond the size of your head?' The Magus snorted. 'Even I have never seen a gem *that* big. A simple stick was good enough for my master. He needed nothing more. A length of wood does not by itself make a man wise, or noble, or powerful, any more than a length of steel does. Power comes from the flesh, my boy, and from the heart, and from the head. From the head most of all.'

'I love this pool!' cackled Ninefingers, tossing another fish out onto the rocks.

'Juvens,' murmured Longfoot softly, 'and his brothers, powerful beyond guessing, between men and gods. Even they feared this thing. They went to such pains to put it beyond use. Should we not fear it, as they did?'

Bayaz stared at Ferro, his eyes glittering, and she stared back. Beads of sweat stood from his wrinkled skin, darkened the hairs of his beard, but his face was flat as a closed door. 'Weapons are dangerous, to those who do not understand them. With Ferro Maljinn's bow I might shoot myself in the foot, if I did not know how to use it. With Captain Luthar's steel I might cut my ally, had I not the skill. The greater the weapon, the greater the danger. I have the proper respect for this thing, believe me, but to fight our enemies we need a powerful weapon indeed.'

Ferro frowned. She was yet to be convinced that her enemies and his were quite the same, but she would let it sleep, for now. She had come too far, and got too close, not to see this business through. She glanced over at Ninefingers and caught him staring at her. His eyes flicked away, back to the water. She frowned deeper. He was always looking at her lately. Staring, and grinning, and making bad jokes. And now she found herself looking at him more often than there was any need for. Patterns of light flowed across his face, reflected from the rippling water. He looked up again, and their eyes met, and he grinned at her, just for an instant.

Ferro's frown grew deeper yet. She pulled her knife out, snatched up one of the fish and took its head off, slit it open and flicked its slimy guts out, plopping down into the water next to Ninefingers' leg. It had been a mistake to fuck him, of course, but things had not turned out so very badly after all.

'Hah!' Ninefingers sent up another glittering spray of water, then he stumbled, clutching at the air. 'Ah!' The fish flapped from his hands, a streak of flipping brightness, and the Northman crashed into the water on his face. He came up spitting and shaking his head, hair plastered to his skull. 'Bastard!'

'Every man has, somewhere in the world, an adversary cleverer than himself.' Bayaz stretched out his legs in front of him. 'Could it be, Master Ninefingers, that you have finally found yours?'

Jezal woke with a start. It was the middle of the night. It took him a dizzy moment to remember where he was, for he had been dreaming of home, of the Agriont, of sunny days and barmy evenings. Of Ardee, or someone like her, smiling lop-sided at him in his cosy living room. Now the stars were scattered bright and stark across the black sky, and the chill, sharp air of the High Places nipped at Jezal's lips, and his nostrils, and the tips of his ears.

He was back up in the Broken Mountains, half the width of the world from Adua, and he felt a pang of loss. At least his stomach was full. Fish and biscuit, the first proper meal he'd eaten since the horse ran out. There was still warmth from the fire on the side of his face and he turned towards it, grinning at the glowing embers and dragging his blankets up under his chin. Happiness was nothing more than a fresh fish and a fire still alight.

He frowned. The blankets beside him, where Logen had been sleeping, were moving around. At first he took it for the Northman turning in his sleep, but they carried on moving, and did not stop. A slow, regular shifting, accompanied, Jezal now realised, by a soft grunting sound. He had taken it at first for Bayaz' snoring, but now he saw otherwise. Straining into the darkness he made out Ninefingers' pale shoulder and arm, thick muscles straining. Under his arm, squeezing hard at his side, there was a dark-skinned hand.

Jezal's mouth hung open. Logen and Ferro, and from the sound of it there could be no doubt that they were coupling! What was more, not a stride from his head! He stared, watching the blankets bucking and shifting in the dim light from the fire. When had they . . . Why were they . . . How had they . . . It was a damned imposition is what it was! His old distaste for them flooded back in a moment and his scarred lip curled. A pair of savages, rutting in full view! He had half a mind to get up and kick them as you might kick a pair of dogs who had, to the general embarrassment of all, unexpectedly taken to each other at a garden party.

'Shit,' whispered a voice. Jezal froze, wondering if one of them had seen him.

'Hold on.' There was a brief pause.

'Ah . . . ah, that's it.' The repetitive movement started up again, the blankets flapping back and forward, slowly to begin with, then faster. How could they possibly have expected him to sleep through this? He scowled and rolled away, pulling his own covers over his head, and lay there in the darkness, listening to Ninefingers' throaty grunting and Ferro's urgent hissing growing steadily louder. He squeezed his eyes shut, and felt a sting of tears underneath his lids.

Damn it but he was lonely.

Coming Over

The road curved down from the west, down the bare white valley between two long ridges, all covered in dark pines. It met the river at the ford, the Whiteflow running high with meltwater, fast flowing over the rocks and full of spit and froth – earning its name alright.

'So that's it then,' muttered Tul, lying on his belly and peering through the bushes.

'I reckon,' said Dogman, 'less there's another giant fortress anywhere on the river.'

From up here on the ridge the Dogman could see its shape clear, towering great walls of sheer dark stones, perfectly six sided, twelve strides high at the least, a massive round tower at each corner, the grey slate roofs of buildings round a courtyard in the midst. Just outside that there was a smaller wall, six sides again, half as high but still high enough, studded with a dozen smaller towers. One side backed to the river, the other five had a wide moat dug round them, so the whole thing was made an island of sharp stone. One bridge out to it, and one bridge only, stretching to a gatehouse the size of a hill.

'Shit on that,' said Dow. 'You ever seen walls the like of those? How the hell did Bethod get in there?'

Dogman shook his head. 'Don't hardly matter how. He won't fit his whole army in it.'

'He won't want to,' said Threetrees. 'Not Bethod. That's not his way. He'd rather be outside, where he can move, waiting for his chance to catch 'em off guard.'

'Uh,' grunted Grim, nodding.

'Fucking Union!' cursed Dow. 'They're never on guard! All that time we followed Bethod up from the south and they bloody let him past without a fight! Now he's all walled up here, close to food and water, nice and happy, waiting for us!'

Threetrees clicked his tongue. 'No point crying 'bout it now, is there? Bethod got round you once or twice before, as I recall.'

'Huh. Bastard's got one hell of a knack for turning up where he ain't wanted.'

Dogman looked down at the fortress, and the river behind, and the long valley, and the high ground on the other side, covered with trees. 'He'll have men up on the ridge opposite, and down there in those woods round the moat too, I shouldn't wonder.'

'Well you got it all figured, don't you?' said Dow, looking sideways. 'There's just one thing we still need to know. She suck your cock yet?'

'What?' said the Dogman, caught not knowing what to say. Tul spluttered with laughter. Threetrees started chuckling to himself. Even Grim made a kind of sound, like breath, but louder.

'Simple question ain't it?' asked Dow. 'Has she, or has she not, sucked it?'

Dogman frowned and hunched his shoulders. 'Shit on that.'

Tul could barely hold his giggling back. 'She did what to it? She shit on it? You was right, Dow, they don't do it the same down there in the Union!' Now they were all laughing, apart from the Dogman of course.

'Piss on the lot o' you,' he grunted. 'Maybe you should suck each other's. At least it might shut you up.'

Dow slapped him on the shoulder. 'Don't think so. You know how Tul is for talking with his mouth full!' Tul clamped his hand over his face and blew snot out of his nose, he was laughing so hard. Dogman gave him a look but that was like hoping a look would stop a rock falling. It didn't.

'Alright now, best be quiet,' muttered Threetrees, but still grinning. 'Someone better take a closer look. See if we can work out where Bethod's boys are all at before the Union come fumbling up that road like a pack o' fools.'

Dogman felt his heart sinking. 'One of us better? Which of you bastards is it going to be then?'

Black Dow grinned as he slapped him on the shoulder. 'I reckon whoever got to stick his twig in the fire last night should be the one to face the cold this morning, eh, lads?'

Dogman crept down through the trees, bow in one hand with a shaft nocked to it but the string not pulled back, for fear of letting it go by accident and shooting himself in the leg or some foolishness. He'd seen that happen before, and he'd no wish to be hopping back to the camp, trying to explain to the others how he got one of his own arrows through his foot. He'd never hear the end of it.

He knelt and peered through the trees, looked down at the ground – bare brown earth, and patches of white snow, and piles of wet pine needles, and . . . he stopped breathing. There was a footprint near him. Half in mud and half in snow. The snow was melting and falling, melting and falling off and on. A print wouldn't have lasted long today. That meant it was made recent. The Dogman sniffed the air. Not much to smell, but it was harder to smell anything in the cold – nose all pink and numb and full of cold snot. He crept the way the footprint was pointing, looking all round. He saw another, and another. Someone had come this way, no doubt, and not long ago.

'You're the Dogman, ain't you.'

He froze, heart thumping like big boots upstairs all of a sudden. He turned round, to look where the voice came from. There was a man sitting on a fallen tree ten strides away, lying back against a thick branch, hands clasped behind his head, stretched out like he was near asleep. He had long black hair hanging in his face, but one eye peered out at the Dogman, watchful. He sat forward, slowly.

'Now I'll leave these here,' he said, pointing at a heavy axe half-buried in the rotten trunk, and a round shield leaning near it. 'So you know I'm looking to talk, and I'll come on over. How's that sound to you?'

Dogman raised his bow and drew the string back. 'Come on over if you must, but if you try more 'n talk I'll put an arrow through your neck.'

'Fair enough.' Long Hair rocked himself forward and slithered off the trunk, leaving his weapons behind, and came on through the trees. He walked with his head stooped over but he was a tall bastard still, holding his hands up in the air, palms out. All peaceful looking, no doubt, but the Dogman wasn't taking no chances. Peaceful-looking and peaceful are two different things.

'Might I say,' said the man as he came closer, 'in the interests of working up some trust between us, that you never saw me. If I'd had a bow I could've shot you where you stood.' It was a fair point, but the Dogman didn't like it any.

'You got a bow?'

'No I don't, as it goes.'

'There's your mistake, then,' he snapped. 'You can stop there.'

'I believe I will,' he said, standing a few strides distant.

'So I'm the Dogman, and you know it. Who might you be?'

'You remember Rattleneck, aye?'

'Of course, but you ain't him.'

'No. I'm his son.'

Dogman frowned, and drew his bowstring back a touch tighter. 'You'd best make your next answer a damn good one. Ninefingers killed Rattleneck's son.'

'That's true. I'm his other son.'

'But he was hardly more 'n a boy . . .' Dogman paused, counting the winters in his head. 'Shit. It's that long ago?'

'That long ago.'

'You've grown some.'

'That's what boys do.'

'You got a name now?'

'Shivers, they call me.'

'How come?'

He grinned. 'Because my enemies shiver with fear when they face me.'

'That so?'

'Not entirely.' He sighed. 'Might as well know now. First time I went out raiding, I got drunk and fell in the river having a piss. Current sucked my trousers off and dumped me half a mile downstream. I got back to the camp shivering worse than anyone had ever seen, fruits sucked right up into my belly and everything.' He scratched at his face. 'Bloody embarrassment all round. Made up for it in the fighting, though.'

'Really?'

'I got some blood on my fingers, over the years. Not compared to you, I daresay, but enough for men to follow me.'

'That so? How many?'

'Two score Carls, or thereabouts. They're not far away, but don't get nervous. Some o' my father's people, from way back, and a few newer. Good hands, each man.'

'Well, that's nice for you, to have a little crew. Been fighting for Bethod, have you?'

'Man needs some kind o' work. Don't mean we wouldn't take better. Can I put my hands down yet?'

'No, I like 'em there. What you doing out here in the woods alone, anyhow?'

Shivers pursed his lips, thoughtful. 'Don't take me for a madman, but I heard a rumour you got Rudd Threetrees over here.'

'That's a fact.'

'Is it now?'

'And Tul Duru Thunderhead, and Harding Grim, and Black Dow an' all.'

Shivers raised his brows, leaned back against a tree, hands still up, while Dogman watched him careful. 'Well that's some weighty company you got there, alright. There's twice the blood on you five than on my two score. Those are some names and no mistake. The sort of names men might want to follow.'

'You looking to follow?'

'Might be that I am.'

'And your Carls too?'

'Them too.'

It was tempting, the Dogman had to admit. Two score Carls, and they'd know where Bethod was at, maybe something of what he'd got planned. That'd save him some skulking around in the cold woods, and he was getting good and tired of wet trees. But he was a long way off trusting this tall bastard yet. He'd take him back to the camp, and Threetrees could weigh up what to do. 'Alright,' he said, 'we'll see. Why don't you step off up the hill there, and I'll follow on a few paces behind.'

'Alright,' said Shivers, turning and trudging up the slope, hands still up in the air, 'but watch what you do with that shaft, eh? I don't want to get stuck for you not looking where you're stepping.'

'Don't worry about me, big lad, the Dogman don't miss no— gah!'

His foot caught on a root and he lurched a step and fumbled his string. The arrow shot past Shivers' head and thudded wobbling into a tree just beyond. Dogman ended up on his knees in the dirt, looking up at him looming over, clutching an empty bow in one hand. 'Piss,' he muttered. If the man had wanted to, Dogman had no doubt he could have swung one of those big fists down and knocked his head off.

'Lucky you missed me,' said Shivers. 'Can I put my hands down now?'

Dow started as soon as they walked into the camp, of course. 'Who the hell's this bastard?' he snarled, striding straight up to Shivers and staring him out, bristling up to him with his axe clutched in his hand. It might have looked a touch comical, Dow being half a head shorter, but Shivers didn't seem much amused. Nor should he have.

'He's—' the Dogman started, but he didn't get any further.

'He's a tall bastard, eh? I ain't talking up to a bastard like him! Sit down, big lad!' and he threw his arm out and shoved Shivers over on his arse.

The Dogman thought he took it well, considering. He grunted when he hit the dirt, of course, then he blinked, then he propped himself on his elbows, grinning up at them. 'I reckon I'll just stay down here. Don't hold it against me though, eh? I didn't choose to be tall, any more than you chose to be an arsehole.'

Dogman winced at that, expecting Shivers to get a boot in the fruits for his trouble, but Dow started to grin instead. 'Chose to be an arsehole, I like that. I like him. Who is he?'

'His name's Shivers,' said the Dogman. 'He's Rattleneck's son.'

Dow frowned. 'But didn't Ninefingers—'

'His other son.'

'But he'd be no more 'n a—'

'Work it out.'

Dow frowned, then shook his head. 'Shit. That long, eh?'

'He looks like Rattleneck,' came Tul's voice, his shadow falling across them.

'Bloody hell!' said Shivers. 'I thought you didn't like tall folk? It's two of you standing on top of each other ain't it?'

'Just the one.' Tul reached down and pulled him up by one arm like he was a child fell over. 'Sorry 'bout that greeting, friend. Those visitors we get we usually end up killing.'

'I'll hope to be the exception,' said Shivers, still gawping up at the Thunderhead. 'So that must be Harding Grim.'

'Uh,' said Grim, scarcely looking up from checking his shafts.

'And you're Threetrees?'

'That I am,' said the old boy, hands on his hips.

'Well,' muttered Shivers, rubbing at the back of his head. 'I feel like I'm in deep water now, and no mistake. Deep water. Tul Duru, and Black Dow, and . . . bloody hell. You're Threetrees, eh?'

'I'm him.'

'Well then. Shit. My father always said you was the best man left in all the North. That if he ever had to pick a man to follow, you'd be the one. 'Til you lost to the Bloody-Nine, o' course, but some things you can't help. Rudd Threetrees, right before me now . . .'

'Why've you come here, boy?'

Shivers seemed to have run out of words, so the Dogman spoke for him. 'He says he's got two score Carls following him, and they all want to come over.'

Threetrees looked Shivers in the eye for a while. 'Is that a fact?'

Shivers nodded. 'You knew my father. He thought the way you did, and I'm cut from his cloth. Serving Bethod sticks in my neck.'

'Might be I think a man should pick his chief and stick to him.'

'I always thought so,' said Shivers, 'but that blade cuts both ways, no? A chief should look out for his people too, shouldn't he?' Dogman nodded to himself. A fair point to his mind. 'Bethod don't care a shit for none of us no more, if he ever did. He don't listen to no one now but that witch of his.'

'Witch?' said Tul.

'Aye, this sorceress, this Caurib, or whatever. The witch. The one who makes the mist. Bethod's dabbling with some dark company. And this war, there's no purpose to it. Angland? Who wants it anyway, we got land aplenty. He'll lead us all back to the mud. Long as there was no one else to follow we stuck with it, but when we heard Rudd Threetrees might still be alive, and with the Union, well . . .'

'You decided to have a look, eh?'

'We've had enough. Bethod's got some strange boys along. These easterners, from out past the Crinna, bones and hides men, you know, hardly men at all. Got no code, no mercy, don't hardly speak the same language we do. Fucking savages, the lot of 'em. Bethod's got some down in the Union fortress there, and they got all the bodies hung up on the walls, all cut with the bloody cross, guts hanging out, rotting. It ain't right. Then there's Calder and Scale tossing out orders like they know shit from porridge, like they got some names o' their own besides their father's.'

'Fucking Calder,' growled Tul, shaking his head.

'Fucking Scale,' hissed Dow, spitting on the wet ground.

'No bigger pair o' bastards in all the north,' said Shivers. 'And now I hear tell that Bethod's made a deal.'

'What kind of a deal?' asked Threetrees.

Shivers turned and spat over his shoulder. 'A deal with the fucking Shanka, that's what.'

Dogman stared. They all did. That was some evil kind of a rumour. 'With the Flatheads? How?'

'Who knows? Might be that witch found some way to talk to 'em. Times are changing, fast, and it ain't right, any of it. There's a lot of boys over there ain't happy. That's without getting started on that Feared.'

Dow frowned. 'Feared? I never heard of him.'

'Where you lot been? Under the ice?'

They all looked at each other. 'Pretty much,' said the Dogman. 'Pretty much.'

Cheap at the Price

'You have a visitor, sir,' muttered Barnam. His face, for some reason, was pale as death.

'Clearly,' snapped Glokta. 'That was them knocking at the door, I assume.' He dropped his spoon into his barely touched bowl of soup and licked sourly at his gums. *A particularly disgusting excuse for a meal, this evening. I miss Shickel's cooking, if not her attempts to kill me.* 'Well, who is it, man?'

'It's . . . er . . . it's . . .'

Arch Lector Sult ducked through the low doorway so as not to disturb his flawless white hair on the frame. *Ah. I see.* He swept the cramped dining room with a scowl, lip wrinkled as though he had stumbled into an open sewer. 'Don't get up,' he spat at Glokta. *I wasn't planning to.*

Barnam swallowed. 'Can I get your Eminence any—'

'Get out!' sneered Sult, and the old servant nearly fell over in his haste to make it to the door. The Arch Lector watched him go with withering scorn. *The good humour of our previous meeting seems a vaguely remembered dream.*

'Damn peasants,' he hissed as he slid in behind Glokta's narrow dining table. 'There's been another uprising near Keln, and this bastard the Tanner was in the midst of it again. An unpopular eviction turned into a bloody riot. Lord Finster entirely misjudged the mood, got three of his guards killed and himself besieged in his manor by an angry mob, the halfwit. They couldn't get in, fortunately, so they satisfied themselves with burning down half the village.' He snorted. 'Their own damn village! That's what an idiot does when he gets angry. He destroys whatever's nearest, even if it's his own house! The Open Council are screaming for blood of course. Peasant blood, and lots of it. Now we have to get the Inquisition going down there, root out some ringleaders, or some fools who can be made to look like them. It should be Finster himself we're hanging, the dolt, but that's hardly an option.'

Glokta cleared his throat. 'I will pack for Keln immediately.' *Tickling the peasantry. Hardly my choice of task, but—*

'No. I need you for something else. Dagoska has fallen.'

Glokta raised an eyebrow. *Not so great a surprise, though. Hardly enough of a shock, one would have thought, to squeeze such a figure as his Eminence into my narrow quarters.*

'It seems the Gurkish were let in by a prior arrangement. Treason, of course, but at a time like that . . . hardly surprising. The Union forces were massacred, such as they were, but many of the mercenaries were merely enslaved, and the natives, by and large, were spared.' *Gurkish mercy, who could have thought it? Miracles do happen, then.*

Sult flicked angrily at a speck of dust on one immaculate glove. 'I hear that, when the Gurkish had broken into the citadel, General Vissbruck killed himself rather than be captured.' *Well I never. I didn't think he had it in him.* 'He ordered his body burned, so as not to give the enemy any remains to defile, then he cut his own throat. A brave man. A courageous statement. He will be honoured in Open Council tomorrow.'

How wonderful for him. A horrible death with honour is far preferable to a long life in obscurity, of course. 'Of course,' said Glokta quietly. 'A brave man.'

'That is not all. An envoy has arrived on the very heels of this news. An envoy from the Emperor of Gurkhul.'

'An envoy?'

'Indeed. Apparently seeking . . . peace.' The Arch Lector said the word with a sneer of contempt.

'Peace?'

'This room seems rather small for an echo.'

'Of course, your Eminence, but—'

'Why not? They have what they want. They have Dagoska, and there is nowhere further for them to go.'

'No, Arch Lector.' *Except, perhaps, across the sea . . .*

'Peace. It sticks in the craw to give anything away, but Dagoska was never worth much to us. Cost us more than we made from it, if anything. Nothing more than a trophy for the King. I daresay we're better off without it, the worthless rock.'

Glokta bowed his head. 'Absolutely, your Eminence.' *Although it makes one wonder why we bothered fighting for it.*

'Unfortunately, the loss of the place leaves you with nothing to be Superior of.' The Arch Lector looked almost pleased. *So it's back to plain old Inquisitor, eh? I suppose I'll no longer be welcome at the best social gatherings—* 'But I have decided to let you keep the title. As Superior of Adua.'

Glokta paused. *A considerable promotion, except that . . .* 'Surely, your Eminence, that is Superior Goyle's role.'

'It is. And will continue to be.'

'Then—'

'You will share the responsibilities. Goyle is the more experienced man, so he will be the senior partner, and continue running the department. For you I will find some tasks suited to your particular talents. I'm hoping that a little healthy competition will bring out the best in you both.'

More than likely it will end with one of us dead, and we can all guess who the favourite is. Sult gave a thin smile, as though he knew precisely what Glokta was thinking. 'Or perhaps it will simply demonstrate that one of you is *superior* to the other.' He barked a joyless laugh at his own joke, and Glokta gave a watery, toothless grin of his own.

'In the meantime, I need you to deal with this envoy. You seem to have a way of handling these Kantics, though you might avoid beheading this one, at least for the time being.' The Arch Lector allowed himself another minuscule smile. 'If he's after anything more than peace, I want you to sniff it out. If we can get anything more than peace from him, then of course, sniff that out too. It would do no harm if we could avoid looking like we got our backs whipped.'

He stood awkwardly and manoeuvred himself out from behind the table, all the while frowning as though the tightness of the room was an intentional affront to his dignity. 'And please, Glokta, find yourself some better quarters. A Superior of Adua, living like this? It's an embarrassment!'

Glokta humbly bowed his head, causing an unpleasant stinging right down to his tailbone. 'Of course, your Eminence.'

The Emperor's envoy was a thickset man with a heavy, black beard, a white skull-cap, and a white robe worked with golden thread. He rose and bowed humbly as Glokta hobbled over the threshold. *As earthy and humble-seeming as the last emissary I dealt with was airy and arrogant. A different kind of man, I suppose, for a different purpose.*

'Ah. Superior Glokta, I should have guessed.' His voice was deep and rich, his mastery of the common tongue predictably excellent. 'Many people on our side of the sea were very disappointed when your corpse was not among those found in the citadel of Dagoska.'

'I hope you will convey my sincere apologies to them.'

'I will do so. My name is Tulkis, and I am a councillor to Uthman-ul-Dosht, the Emperor of Gurkhul.' The envoy grinned, a crescent of strong white teeth in his black beard. 'I hope I fare better at your hands than the last emissary my people sent to you.'

Glokta paused. *A sense of humour? Most unexpected.* 'I suppose that would depend on the tone you take.'

'Of course. Shabbed al Islik Burai always was . . . confrontational. That, and his loyalties were . . . mixed.' Tulkis' grin grew wider. 'He was a passionate believer. A very religious man. A man closer perhaps to church, than to state? I honour God, of course.' And he touched his fingertips to his forehead. 'I honour the great and holy Prophet Khalul.' He touched his head again. 'But I serve . . .' And his eyes slid up to Glokta's. 'I serve only the Emperor.'

Interesting. 'I thought that in your nation, church and state spoke with one voice.'

'It has often been so, but there are those among us who believe that priests should concern themselves with prayer, and leave the governing to the Emperor and his advisors.'

'I see. And what might the Emperor wish to communicate to us?'

'The difficulty of capturing Dagoska has shocked the people. The priests had convinced them that the campaign would be easy, for God was with us, our cause was righteous, and so forth. God is great, of course,' and he looked up to the ceiling, 'but he is no substitute for good planning. The Emperor desires peace.'

Glokta sat silent for a moment. 'The great Uthman-ul-Dosht? The mighty? The merciless? Desires peace?'

The envoy took no offence. 'I am sure you understand that a reputation for ruthlessness can be useful. A great ruler, especially one of as wide and various a country as Gurkhul, must first be feared. He would desire to be loved also, but that is a luxury. Fear is essential. Whatever you may have heard, Uthman is neither a man of peace, nor of war. He is a man of . . . what would be your word? Necessity. He is a man of the right tool at the right time.'

'Very prudent,' muttered Glokta.

'Peace, now. Mercy. Compromise. These are the tools that suit his purposes, even if they do not suit the purposes of . . . others,' and he touched his fingers to his forehead. 'And so he sends me, to find out if they suit you also.'

'Well, well, well. The mighty Uthman-ul-Dosht comes with mercy, and offers peace. These are strange times we live in, eh, Tulkis? Have the Gurkish learned to love their enemies? Or simply fear them?'

'One need not love one's enemy, or even fear him, to desire peace. One need only love oneself.'

'Is that so?'

'It is. I lost two sons in the wars between our peoples. One at Ulrioch in the last war. He was a priest, and burned in the temple there. The other died not long ago, at the siege of Dagoska. He led the charge when the first breach was made.'

Glokta frowned and stretched out his neck. *A hail of flatbow bolts. Tiny figures, falling in the rubble.* 'That was a brave charge.'

'War is harshest on the brave.'

'True. I am sorry for your losses.' *Though I feel no sorrow, in particular.*

'I thank you for your heartfelt condolences. God has seen fit to bless me with three more sons, but the spaces left by those two children lost will never close. It is almost like losing your own flesh. That is why I feel I understand something of what you have lost, in these same wars. I am sorry for those losses also.'

'Most kind.'

'We are leaders. War is what happens when we fail. Or are pushed into failure by the rash and the foolish. Victory is better than defeat, but . . . not by much. Therefore, the Emperor offers peace, in the hope that this may be a permanent end to the hostilities between our great nations. We have no true interest in crossing the seas to make war, and you have no true interest in toeholds on the Kantic continent. So we offer peace.'

'And is that all your offer?'

'All?'

'What will our people make of it, if we surrender Dagoska up to you, so dearly bought in the last war?'

'Let us be realistic. Your entanglements in the North put you at a considerable disadvantage. Dagoska is lost, I would put it from your mind.' Tulkis seemed to think about it for a moment. 'However, I could arrange for a dozen chests to be delivered, as reparations from my Emperor to your King. Chests of fragrant ebony wood, worked with golden leaf, carried by bowing slaves, preceded by humble officials of the Emperor's government.'

'And what would these chests contain?'

'Nothing.' They stared at each other across the room. 'Except pride. You could say they contained whatever you wished. A fortune in Gurkish gold, in Kantic jewels, in incense from beyond the desert. More than the value of Dagoska itself. Perhaps that would mollify your people.'

Glokta breathed in sharply, and let it out. 'Peace. And empty boxes.' His left leg had gone numb under the table and he grimaced as he moved it, hissed through his gums as he forced himself out of his chair. 'I will convey your offer to my superiors.'

He was just turning away when Tulkis held out his hand. Glokta looked at it for a moment. *Well, where's the harm?* He reached out and squeezed it.

'I hope you will be able to persuade them,' said the Gurkish envoy.

So do I.

To the Edge of the World

On the morning of their ninth day in the mountains, Logen saw the sea. He dragged himself to the top of yet another painful scramble, and there it was. The track dropped steeply away into a stretch of low, flat country, and beyond was the shining line on the horizon. He could almost smell it, a salty tang on the air with each breath. He would have grinned if it hadn't reminded him of home so much.

'The sea,' he whispered.

'The ocean,' said Bayaz.

'We have crossed the western continent from shore to shore,' said Longfoot, grinning all the way across his face. 'We are close now.'

By afternoon they were closer still. The trail had widened to a muddy lane between fields, split up with ragged hedges. Mostly brown squares of turned earth, but some green with fresh grass, or with the sprouts of vegetables, some waving tall with a grey, tasteless-looking winter crop. Logen had never known much about farming, but it was plain enough that someone had been working this ground, and recently.

'What kind of people live all the way out here?' murmured Luthar, looking suspiciously out across the ill-tended fields.

'Descendants of the pioneers of long ago. When the Empire collapsed, they were left out here alone. Alone they have flourished, after a fashion.'

'You hear that?' hissed Ferro, her eyes narrowed, already fishing an arrow from her quiver. Logen put his head up, listening. A thumping sound, echoing from some distance, then a voice, thin on the wind. He put his hand on the grip of his sword and crouched down. He crept to an unruly stretch of hedge and peered over, Ferro beside him.

Two men were struggling with a tree stump in the midst of a turned field, one chopping at it with an axe, the other watching, hands on hips. Logen swallowed, uneasy. These two hardly looked much of a threat, but looks could lie. It had been a long time since they met a living thing that hadn't tried to kill them.

'Calm now,' muttered Bayaz. 'There is no danger here.'

Ferro frowned across at him. 'You've told us that before.'

'Kill no one until I tell you!' hissed the Magus, then called out in a language Logen didn't know, waving one arm over his head in a gesture of greeting. The two men jerked round, staring open-mouthed. Bayaz shouted again. The farmers looked at each other, then set down their tools and walked slowly over.

They stopped a few strides away. An ugly-looking pair, even to Logen's eye – short, stocky, rough-featured, dressed in colourless work clothes, patched and stained. They stared nervously at the six strangers, and at their weapons in particular, as though they'd never seen such people or such things before.

Bayaz spoke to them warmly, smiling and waving his arms, pointing out towards the ocean. One nodded, answered, shrugged and pointed down the track. He stepped through a gap in the hedge, off the field and into the road. Or from soft mud to hard mud, at least. He beckoned at them to follow while his companion watched suspiciously from the other side of the bushes.

'He will take us to Cawneil,' said Bayaz.

'To who?' muttered Logen, but the Magus did not answer. He was already striding westward after the farmer.

Heavy dusk under a grim sky, and they trudged through an empty town after their sullen guide. A singularly ill-favoured fellow, Jezal rather thought, but then peasants were rarely beauties in his experience, and he supposed that they were much the same the world over. The streets were dusty and deserted, weedy and scattered with refuse. Many houses were derelict, furry with moss and tangled with creeper. Those few that did show signs of occupation were, in the main, in a slovenly condition.

'It would seem the glory of the past is faded here also,' said Longfoot with some disappointment, 'if indeed there ever was any.'

Bayaz nodded. 'Glory is in short supply these days.'

A wide square opened out from the neglected houses. Ornamental gardens had been planted round the edge by some forgotten gardener, but the lawns were threadbare, the flowerbeds turned to briar-patches, the trees no more than withered claws. Out of this slow decay rose a huge and striking building, or more accurately a jumble of buildings of various confused shapes and styles. Three tall, round, tapering towers sprouted from their midst, joined at their bases but separating higher up. One was broken off before the summit, its roof long fallen in, leaving naked rafters exposed.

'A library . . .' whispered Logen under his breath.

It scarcely looked like one to Jezal. 'It is?'

'The Great Western Library,' said Bayaz, as they crossed the dilapidated square in the looming shadow of those three crumbling towers. 'Here I took my first hesitant steps along the path of Art. Here my master taught me the First Law. Taught it to me again and again until I could recite it flawlessly in every language known. This was a place of learning, and wonder, and great beauty.'

Longfoot sucked his teeth. 'Time has not been kind to the place.'

'Time is never kind.'

Their guide said a few short words and indicated a tall door covered in flaking green paint. Then he shuffled away, eyeing them all with the deepest suspicion.

'You simply cannot get the help,' observed the First of the Magi as he watched the farmer hurry off, then he raised his staff and struck the door three good knocks. There was a long silence.

'Library?' Jezal heard Ferro asking, evidently unfamiliar with the word.

'For books,' came Logen's voice.

'Books,' she snorted. 'Waste of fucking time.'

Vague sounds echoed from beyond the gate: someone approaching inside, accompanied by an irritated muttering. Now locks clicked and grated and the weathered door squealed open. A man of an advanced age and a pronounced stoop gazed at them in wonder, an unintelligible curse frozen on his lips, a lighted taper casting a faint glow over one side of his wrinkled face.

'I am Bayaz, the First of the Magi, and I have business with Cawneil.' The servant continued to gawp. Jezal half expected a string of drool to escape from his toothless mouth it was hanging open so wide. Plainly, they did not receive large numbers of visitors.

The one flickering taper was pitifully inadequate to light the lofty hall beyond. Weighty tables sagged under tottering piles of books. Shelves rose up high on every wall, lost in the fusty darkness overhead. Shadows shifted over leather-bound spines of every size and colour, on bundles of loose parchments, on scrolls rolled and carelessly stacked in leaning pyramids. Light sparked and flashed on silver gilt, and gold ornamentation, and dull jewels set into tomes of daunting size. A long staircase, banister highly polished by the passage of countless hands, steps worn down in the centres by the passage of countless feet, curved gracefully down into the midst of this accumulation of ancient knowledge. Dust sat thickly on every surface. One particularly monstrous cobweb became stickily tangled in Jezal's hair as he passed over the threshold, and he flicked and wrestled at it, face wrinkled in distaste.

'The lady of the house,' wheezed the doorman in a strange accent, 'has already taken to her couch.'

'Then wake her,' snapped Bayaz. 'The hour grows dark and I am in haste. We have no time to—'

'Well. Well. Well.' A woman stood upon the steps. 'The hour grows dark indeed, when old lovers come calling at my door.' A deep voice, smooth as syrup. She sauntered down the stairs with exaggerated slowness, one set of long nails trailing on the curving banister. She seemed perhaps of middle age: tall, thin, graceful, a curtain of long black hair falling over half her face.

'Sister. We have urgent matters to discuss.'

'Ah, do we indeed?' The one eye that Jezal could see was large, dark and heavy-lidded, rimmed faintly with sore, tearful pink. Languorously, lazily, almost sleepily it flowed over the group. 'How atrociously tiresome.'

'I am weary, Cawneil, I need none of your games.'

'We all are weary, Bayaz. We all are terribly weary.' She gave a long, theatrical sigh as she finally glided to the foot of the steps and across the uneven floor towards them. 'There was a time when you were willing to play. You would play my games for days at a time, as I recall.'

'That was long ago. Things change.'

Her face twisted with a sudden and unsettling anger. 'Things rot, you mean! But still,' and her voice softened again to a deep whisper, 'we last remnants of the great order of Magi should at least try to remain civil. Come now, my brother, my friend, my sweet, there is no need for undue haste. The day grows late, and there is time for you all to wash away the dirt of the road, discard those stinking rags and dress for dinner. Then we can talk over food, as civilised persons are wont to do. I so rarely have guests to entertain.' She swept past Logen, looking him admiringly up and down. 'And you have brought me such rugged guests.' She lingered on Ferro with her eyes. 'Such exotic guests.' Now she reached up and let a long finger trail across Jezal's cheek. 'Such comely guests!'

Jezal stood, rigid with embarrassment, entirely at a loss as to how to respond to this liberty. At close quarters her black hair was grey at the roots, no doubt heavily dyed. Her smooth skin seemed wrinkled and a touch yellow, no doubt heavily powdered. Her white gown was dirty round the hem, had a noticeable stain on one sleeve. She seemed as old as Bayaz looked, or perhaps older yet.

She peered into the corner where Quai was standing, and frowned. 'What manner of guest this is, I am not sure . . . but you are welcome all at the Great Western Library. Welcome all . . .'

Jezal blinked at the looking-glass, his razor hanging from one nerveless hand.

Only a few moments before he had been reflecting on the journey, now that it was finally approaching its end, and congratulating himself on how much he had learned. Tolerance and understanding, courage and self-sacrifice. How he had grown as a man. How much he had changed. Congratulations no longer seemed appropriate. The looking-glass might have been an antique, his reflection in it dark and distorted, but there could be no doubt that his face was a ruin.

The pleasing symmetry was gone forever. His perfect jaw was skewed round sharply to the left, heavier on one side than the other, his noble chin was twisted at a slovenly angle. The scar began on his top lip as no more than a faint line, but it split in two and gouged brutally into the bottom one, dragging it down and giving him the appearance of having a permanent and unsightly leer.

No effort on his part helped. Smiling made it far worse yet, exposing the ugly gaps in his teeth, more suited to a prize-fighter or a bandit than to an officer of the King's Own. The one mercy was that he would very likely die on the return journey, and no one of his old acquaintance would ever see him so horribly disfigured. A meagre consolation indeed.

A single tear plopped down into the basin under his face.

Then he swallowed, and he took a shuddering breath, and he wiped his wet cheek with the back of his forearm. He set his jaw, in its strange new configuration, and he gripped the razor tightly. The damage was done now, and there could be no going back. Perhaps he was an uglier man, but he was a better man too, and at least, as Logen would have said, he was still alive. He gave the razor a flourish and scraped the patchy, straggling hair from his cheeks, from before his ears, from his throat. On his lip, his chin, and around his mouth he left it be. The beard looked well on him, he rather thought, as he rubbed the razor dry. Or it went a meagre way towards hiding his disfigurement, at least.

He pulled on the clothes that had been left for him. A fusty-smelling shirt and breeches of an ancient and absurdly unfashionable design. He almost laughed at his ill-formed reflection when he was finally prepared for dinner. The carefree denizens of the Agriont would hardly have recognised him. He hardly recognised himself.

The evening repast was not all that Jezal might have hoped for at the table of an important historical figure. The silverware was tarnished in the extreme, the plate worn and cracked, the table itself slanted to the point that Jezal was constantly expecting the entire meal to slide off onto the dirty floor. Food was served by the shambling doorman, at no faster pace than he had answered the gate, each dish arriving colder and more congealed than the last. First came a sticky soup of surpassing tastelessness. Next was a piece of fish so overcooked it was little more than ashes, then most recently a slab of meat so undercooked as to be virtually still alive.

Bayaz and Cawneil ate in stony silence, staring at each other down the length of the table in a way which seemed calculated to make everyone uncomfortable. Quai did nothing more than pick at his food, his dark eyes flicking intently between the two elderly Magi. Longfoot stuck into every course with relish, smiling round at the company as though they were all enjoying themselves equally. Logen was holding his fork in his fist, frowning and stabbing clumsily at his plate as if it were a troublesome Shanka, the ballooning sleeves of his ill-fitting doublet trailing occasionally in his food. Jezal had little doubt that Ferro could have used the cutlery with great dexterity had she wished, but she chose instead to eat with her hands, staring aggressively at anyone who met her gaze as if daring them to tell her not to. She had on the same travel-stained clothes she had worn for the past week, and Jezal wondered for a moment if she had been provided with a dress to wear. He nearly choked on his dinner at the notion.

Neither the meal, nor the company, nor the surroundings were quite what Jezal would have chosen, but the fact was that they had largely run out of food a few days before. Rations in that space of time had included a handful of chalky roots dug from the mountainside by Logen, six tiny eggs stolen by Ferro from a high nest, and some berries of indescribable bitterness which Longfoot had plucked from a tree, apparently at random. Jezal would happily have eaten his plate. He frowned as he hacked at the gristly meat on it, wondering if the plate might indeed be a tastier option.

'Is the ship still seaworthy?' growled Bayaz. Everyone looked up. The first words to have been said in quite some time.

Cawneil's dark eye regarded him coldly. 'Do you mean that ship on which Juvens and his brothers sailed to Shabulyan?'

'What other?'

'Then no. It is not seaworthy. It is rotted to green mulch in its old dock. But do not fear. Another was built, and when that rotted also, another after it. The latest rocks on the tides, tethered to the shore, well-coated with weed and barnacle but kept always crewed and victualled. I have not forgotten my promise to our master. I marked well my obligations.'

Bayaz' brows drew angrily down. 'Meaning, I suppose, that I did not?'

'I did not say so. If you hear a reproach it is your own guilt that goads you, not my accusation. I take no sides, you know that. I never have.'

'You speak as though sloth were the greatest of virtues,' muttered the First of the Magi.

'Sometimes it is, if acting means taking part in your squabbles. You forget, Bayaz, that I have seen all this before, more than once, and a wearisome pattern it seems to me. History repeats itself. Brother fights brother. As Juvens fought Glustrod, as Kanedias fought Juvens, so Bayaz struggles with Khalul. Smaller men in a bigger world, but with no less hatred, and no more mercy. Will this sordid rivalry end even as well as the others? Or will it be worse?'

Bayaz snorted. 'Let us not pretend you care, or would drag yourself ten strides from your couch if you did.'

'I do not care. I freely admit it. I was never like you or Khalul, or even like Zacharus or Yulwei. I have no endless ambition, no bottomless arrogance.'

'No, indeed, not you.' Bayaz sucked disgustedly at his gums and tossed his fork clattering down onto his plate. 'Only endless vanity and bottomless idleness.'

'Mine are small vices and small virtues. To see the world recast according to my own great designs has never interested me. I have always been content with the world as it is, and so I am a dwarf among giants.' Her heavy-lidded eyes swept slowly over her guests, one by one. 'And yet dwarves crush no one underfoot.' Jezal coughed as her searching stare fell on him and gave careful attention to his rubbery meat. 'Long is the list of those you have trodden over in pursuit of your ambitions, is it not, my love?'

Bayaz' displeasure began to weigh on Jezal as heavily as a great stone. 'You need not speak in riddles, sister,' growled the old man. 'I would have your meaning.'

'Ah, I forgot. You are a straight talker, and cannot abide deception of any kind. You told me so just after you told me you would never leave me, and just before you left me to find another.'

'That was not my choice. You wrong me, Cawneil.'

'*I* wrong *you*?' she hissed, and now her anger pressed hard at Jezal from the other side. 'How, brother? Did you not leave? Did you not find another? Did you not steal from the Maker, first his secrets, then his daughter?' Jezal squirmed and hunched his shoulders, feeling as squeezed as a nut in a vice. 'Tolomei, do you remember her?'

Bayaz' frown grew frostier yet. 'I have made my mistakes, and still pay for them. Not a day passes that I do not think of her.'

'How outrageously noble of you!' sneered Cawneil. 'No doubt she would swoon with gratitude, if she could hear you now! I think on that day too, now and then. The day the Old Time ended. How we gathered outside the House of the Maker, thirsty for vengeance. How we put forth all of our Art and all of our anger, and could not make a scratch upon the gates. How you whispered to Tolomei in the night, begging her to let you in.' She pressed her withered hands to her chest. 'Such tender words you used. Words I never dreamed were in you. Even an old cynic like me was moved. How could an innocent like Tolomei deny you, whether it was her father's gates or her own legs she was opening? And what was her reward, eh, brother, for her sacrifices? For helping you, for trusting you, for loving you? It must have been quite the dramatic scene! The three of you, up on the roof. A foolish young woman, her jealous father, and her secret lover.' She snorted bitter laughter. 'Never a happy formula, but it can rarely have ended quite so badly. Father and daughter both. The long drop to the bridge!'

'Kanedias had no mercy in him,' growled Bayaz, 'even for his own child. Before my eyes he threw his daughter from the roof. We fought, and I cast him down in flames. So was our master avenged.'

'Oh, well done!' Cawneil clapped her hands in mock delight. 'Everyone loves a happy ending! Tell me only one thing more. What was it that made you weep so long for Tolomei, when I could never make you shed a tear? Did you decide you like your women pure, eh, brother?' And she fluttered her eyelashes in an ironical show, one strangely unsettling on that ancient face. 'Innocence? That most fleeting and worthless of virtues. One to which I have never laid claim.'

'Perhaps then, sister, the one thing you have never laid?'

'Oh, very good, my old love, very fine. It was always your ready wit that I enjoyed, above all else. Khalul was the more skilful lover, of course, but he never had your passion, nor your daring.' She speared a chunk of meat viciously with her fork. 'Travelling to the edge of the World, at your age? To steal that thing our master forbade? Courage indeed.'

Bayaz sneered his contempt down the table. 'What would you know of courage? You, who have loved no one in all these long years but yourself? Who have risked nothing, and given nothing, and made nothing? You, who have let all the gifts our master gave you rot! Keep your stories in the dust, sister. No one cares, and me least of all.'

The two Magi glared at each other in icy silence, the atmosphere heavy with their seething fury. The feet of Ninefingers' chair squealed gently as he edged it cautiously away from the table. Ferro sat opposite, her face locked in a frown of the deepest suspicion. Malacus Quai had his teeth bared, his fierce eyes fixed on his master. Jezal could only sit and hold his breath, hoping that the incomprehensible argument did not end with anyone on fire. Especially not him.

'Well,' ventured Brother Longfoot, 'I for one would like to thank our host for this excellent meal . . .' The two old Magi locked him simultaneously with their pitiless gazes. 'Now that we are close . . . to our final . . . destination . . . er . . .' And the Navigator swallowed and stared down at his plate. 'Never mind.'

Ferro sat naked, one leg drawn up against her chest, picking at a scab on her knee, and frowning.

She frowned at the heavy walls of the room, imagining the great weight of old stone all round her. She remembered frowning at the walls of her cell in Uthman's palace, pulling herself up to look through the tiny window, feeling the sun on her face and dreaming of being free. She remembered the chafing iron on her ankle, and the long thin chain, so much stronger than it had looked. She remembered struggling with it, and chewing on it, and dragging at her foot until the blood ran from her torn skin. She hated walls. For her, they had always been the jaws of a trap.

Ferro frowned at the bed. She hated beds, and couches, and cushions. Soft things make you soft, and she did not need them. She remembered lying in the darkness on a soft bed when she was first made a slave. When she was still a child, and small, and weak. Lying in the darkness and weeping to be alone. Ferro dug savagely at the scab and felt blood seep from underneath. She hated that weak, foolish, child who had allowed herself to be trapped. She despised the memory of her.

Ferro frowned most of all at Ninefingers, lying on his back with the blankets rucked and rumpled round him, his head tipped back and his mouth hanging open, eyes closed, breath hissing soft in his nose, one pale arm flung out wide at an uncomfortable-looking angle. Sleeping like a child. Why had she fucked him? And why did she keep doing it? She should never have touched him. She should never have spoken to him. She did not need him, the ugly, big pink fool.

She needed no one.

Ferro told herself she hated all these things, and that her hatred could never fade. But however she curled her lip, and frowned, and picked her scabs, it was hard to feel the same. She looked at the bed, at the dark wood shining in the glow from the embers in the fireplace, at the shifting blobs of shadow in the wrinkled sheet. What difference would it really make to anyone, if she lay there rather than on the cold, wide mattress in her own room? The bed was not her enemy. So she got up from the chair, and padded over and slid down into it with her back to Ninefingers, taking care not to wake him. Not for his sake, of course.

But she had no wish to explain herself.

She wriggled her shoulders, moving backwards towards him where it was warmer. She heard him grunt in his sleep, felt him roll. She tensed to spring out of the bed, holding her breath. His arm slid over her side and he muttered something in her ear, meaningless sleep sounds, breath hot on her neck.

His big warm body pressed up tight against her back no longer made her feel so trapped. The weight of his pale hand resting gently against her ribs, his heavy arm around her felt almost . . . good. That made her frown.

Nothing good ever lasts for long.

And so she slid her hand over the back of his and felt his fingers, and the stump of the one that was missing, pressing into the spaces between hers, and she pretended that she was safe, and whole. Where was the harm? She held on to the hand tightly, and pressed it to her chest.

Because she knew it would not be for long.

Before the Storm

'**W**elcome, gentlemen. General Poulder, General Kroy. Bethod has retreated as far as the Whiteflow, and it does not seem likely that he will find any more favourable ground on which to face us.' Burr took a sharp breath, sweeping the gathering with a grave expression. 'I think it very likely that there will be a battle tomorrow.'

'Good show!' shouted Poulder, slapping his thigh with great aplomb.

'My men are ready,' murmured Kroy, lifting his chin one regulation inch. The two generals, and the many members of their respective staffs, glowered at each other across the wide space of Burr's tent, every man trying to outdo his opposite number with his boundless enthusiasm for combat. West felt his lip curling as he watched them. Two gangs of children in a schoolyard could scarcely have behaved with less maturity.

Burr raised his eyebrows and turned to his maps. 'Luckily for us, the architects who built the fortress at Dunbrec also surveyed the surrounding land in some detail. We are blessed with highly accurate charts. Furthermore, a group of Northmen have recently defected to our cause, bringing with them detailed information on Bethod's forces, position, and intentions.'

'Why should we believe the word of a pack of Northern dogs,' sneered General Kroy, 'who have no loyalty even to their own king?'

'Had Prince Ladisla been more willing to listen to them, sir,' intoned West, 'he might still be with us. As might his division.' General Poulder chuckled heartily to himself and his staff joined him. Kroy, predictably, was less amused. He shot a deadly glare across the tent, one which West returned with an icy blankness.

Burr cleared his throat, and soldiered on. 'Bethod holds the fortress of Dunbrec.' The point of his stick tapped at the black hexagon. 'Positioned to cover the only significant road out of Angland, where it fords the river Whiteflow, our border with the North. The road approaches the fortress from the west, cutting eastwards down a wide valley between two wooded ridges. The body of Bethod's forces are encamped near the fortress, but he means to mount an attack, eastward up the road, as soon as we show our faces.' And Burr's stick slashed along the dark line, swishing against the heavy paper. 'The valley through which the road passes is bare, open grass with some gorse and rocky outcroppings, and will give him ample room for manoeuvre.' He turned back to the assembled officers, stick clenched tight, and placed his fists firmly on the table before him. 'I mean to fall into his trap. Or at least . . . to seem to. General Kroy?'

Kroy finally broke off glowering at West to reply with a sullen, 'Yes, Lord Marshal?'

'Your division is to deploy astride the road and push steadily eastwards towards the fortress, encouraging Bethod to launch his attack. Slowly and steadily, with no heroics. General Poulder's division, meanwhile, will have worked its way through the trees on top of the northern ridge, here,' and his stick tapped at the green blocks of the wooded high ground, 'just forward of General Kroy's position.'

'Just *forward* of General Kroy's position,' grinned Poulder, as though he was being shown special favour. Kroy scowled with disgust.

'*Just* forward, yes,' continued Burr. 'When Bethod's forces are entirely occupied in the valley, it shall be your task to attack them from above, and take them in the flank. It is important that you wait until the Northmen have been fully engaged, General Poulder, so that we can surround them, overwhelm them, and hope to bag the majority at one throw. If they are allowed to retire to the fords the fortress will cover their retreat, and we will be unable to pursue. Reducing Dunbrec might take us months.'

'Of course, my Lord Marshal,' exclaimed Poulder, 'my division will wait until the last moment, you may depend upon it!'

Kroy snorted. 'That should present no difficulty. Arriving late is a specialty of yours, I understand. There would be no need for a battle if you had intercepted the Northmen last week, rather than allowing them to get around you!'

Poulder bristled. 'Easy for you to say, while you were sitting on the right wing doing nothing! It's fortunate they didn't pass by in the night! You might have taken their retreat for an assault and fled with your entire division!'

'Gentlemen, please!' roared Burr, smashing the table with his stick. 'There will be fighting enough for every man in the army, that I promise you, and if each man does his part there will be ample glory too! We must work together if this plan is to bear fruit!' He burped and grimaced and licked his lips sourly, while the two Generals and their staffs glowered at one another. West would almost have laughed, had men's lives not hung in the balance, his own among them.

'General Kroy,' said Burr, in the tone of a parent addressing a wayward child. 'I wish to make sure that you understand your orders.'

'To deploy my division in line astride the road,' hissed Kroy, 'and to advance slowly and in good order, eastwards down the valley towards Dunbrec, drawing Bethod and his savages into an engagement.'

'Indeed. General Poulder?'

'To move my division out of sight through the trees, *just ahead* of General Kroy's regiments, so that at the last moment I can charge down on the Northern scum and take them in the flank.'

Burr managed a smile. 'Correct.'

'An excellent plan, Lord Marshal, if I may!' Poulder tugged happily at his moustaches. 'You can depend upon it that my horse will cut them to pieces. To! Pieces!'

'I am afraid you will not have any cavalry, General,' said West in an emotionless monotone. 'The woods are dense and horse will be useless to you there. They might even alert the Northmen to your presence. A risk we cannot take.'

'But . . . my cavalry,' muttered Poulder, stricken with woe. 'My best regiments!'

'They will be kept here, sir,' droned West, 'near Marshal Burr's head-quarters, and under his direct control, as a reserve. They will be deployed if they are needed.' Now it was Poulder's fury he met with a stonewall stare, while the faces of Kroy and his staff broke out in broad, neat, utterly joyless smiles.

'I hardly think—' hissed Poulder.

Burr cut him off. 'That is my decision. There is one last point that you should all bear in mind. There are some reports that Bethod has called on reinforcements. Some manner of wild men, savages from across the mountains to the north. Keep your eyes open and your flanks well screened. You will receive word from me tomorrow when it is time to move, most likely before first light. That is all.'

'Can we really rely on them to do what they are told?' muttered West as he watched the two surly groups file from the tent.

'What choice do we have?' The Marshal threw himself into a chair with a grimace and rested his hands on his belly, frowning up at the great map. 'I wouldn't worry. Kroy has no option but to move down the valley and fight.'

'What about Poulder? I wouldn't put it past him to find some excuse to stay sitting in the woods.'

The Lord Marshal grinned as he shook his head. 'And leave Kroy to do all the fighting? What if he were to beat the Northmen on his own, and take all the glory for himself? No. Poulder could never risk that. This plan gives them no choice but to work together.' He paused, looking up at West. 'You might want to treat the pair of them with a touch more respect.'

'Do you think they deserve it, sir?'

'Of course not. But if, for instance, we should lose tomorrow, one of them will most likely step into my boots. Then where will you be?'

West grinned. 'I'll be finished, sir. But my being polite now won't change that. They hate me for what I am, not what I say. I might as well say what I please while I can.'

'I suppose you might at that. They're a damn nuisance, but their folly can be predicted. It's Bethod that worries me. Will he do what we want him to?' Burr burped, and swallowed, and burped again. 'Damn this damn indigestion!'

Threetrees and the Dogman were sprawled on a bench outside the tent flap, an odd pair in amongst the well-starched press of officers and guards.

'Smells like battle to me,' said Threetrees as West strode up to them.

'Indeed.' West pointed after Kroy's black-uniformed staff. 'Half the army are going down the valley tomorrow morning, hoping to draw Bethod into a fight.' He pointed to Poulder's crimson entourage. 'The other half are going up into the trees, and hope to surprise them before they can get away.'

Threetrees nodded slowly to himself. 'Sounds like a good plan.'

'Nice and simple,' said the Dogman. West winced. He could hardly bear to look at the man.

'We'd have no plan at all if you hadn't brought us that information,' he managed to say through gritted teeth. 'Are you sure we can trust it?'

'Sure as we can be,' said Threetrees.

Dogman grinned. 'Shivers is alright, and from what I've scouted up, I reckon it's true. No promises, course.'

'Of course not. You deserve a rest.'

'We wouldn't say no.'

'I've arranged a position for you up at the far left of the line, at the end of General Poulder's division, up in the trees, on the high ground. You should be well out of the action there. The safest place in the whole army tomorrow, I shouldn't wonder. Dig in and make yourself a fire, and if things go right, we'll talk again over Bethod's dead body.' And he held out his hand.

Threetrees grinned as he took it. 'Now that's our kind of language, Furious. You take care, now.' He and the Dogman started to trudge away up the slope towards the tree line.

'Colonel West?'

He knew who it was before he turned. There weren't many women in the camp that would have had much to say to him. Cathil, standing in the slush, a borrowed coat wrapped round her. She looked somewhat furtive, somewhat shamefaced, but the sight of her still somehow brought up a sudden surge of anger and embarrassment.

It was unfair, he knew. He had no rights over her. It was unfair, but that only made it worse. All he could think of was the side of the Dogman's face and her grunting, uh . . . uh . . . uh. So horribly surprising. So horribly disappointing. 'You'd better go with them,' said West with an icy formality, scarcely able to bring himself to say anything at all. 'Safest place.' He turned away but she brought him up short.

'It was you, wasn't it, outside the tent . . . the other night?'

'Yes, I'm afraid it was. I simply came to check if there was anything you needed,' he lied. 'I really had no idea . . . who you would be with.'

'I certainly never meant for you to—'

'The Dogman?' he muttered, face suddenly crunching up with incomprehension. 'Him? I mean . . . why?' Why him instead of me, was what he wanted to say, but he managed to stop himself.

'I know . . . I know you must think—'

'You've no need to explain yourself to me!' he hissed, though he knew he'd just asked her to. 'Who cares what I think?' He spat it out with a deal more venom than he had intended, but his own loss of control only made him angrier, and he lost more. 'I don't care what you choose to fuck!'

She winced and stared down at the ground beside his feet. 'I didn't mean to . . . well. I owe you a lot, I know. It's just that . . . you're too angry for me. That's all.'

West stared at her as she trudged off up the hill after the Northmen, hardly able to believe his ears. She was happy to bed that stinking savage, but *he* was too angry? It was so unfair he almost choked on his rage.

Questions

Colonel Glokta charged into his dining room in a tremendous hurry, wrestling manfully with the buckle on his sword belt.

'Damn it!' he fumed. He was all thumbs. Couldn't get the thing closed. 'Damn it, damn it!'

'You need some help with that?' asked Shickel, sitting wedged in behind the table, black burns across her shoulders, cuts hanging open, dry as meat in the butcher's shop.

'No I do not need bloody help!' he shrieked, flinging his belt onto the floor. 'What I need is for someone to explain what the hell is going on here! This is a disgrace! I will not have members of my regiment sitting around naked! Especially with such unsightly wounds! Where is your uniform, girl?'

'I thought you were more worried about the Prophet.'

'Never mind about him!' snapped Glokta, worming his way onto the bench opposite her. 'What about Bayaz? What about the First of the Magi? Who is he? What's he really after, the old bastard?'

Shickel smiled a sweet smile. 'Oh, that. I thought everyone knew that. The answer is . . .'

'Yes!' muttered the Colonel, mouth dry, eager as a schoolboy, 'The answer is?'

She laughed, and slapped at the bench beside her. *Thump, thump, thump.*

'The answer is . . .'

The answer is . . .

Thump, thump, thump. Glokta's eyes snapped open. It was still half dark outside. Only a faint glow was coming through the curtains. *Who comes belting at the door at this hour? Good news comes in the daylight.*

Thump, thump, thump. 'Yes, yes!' he screeched. 'I'm crippled, not deaf! I damn well hear you!'

'Then open the bloody door!' The voice came muffled from the corridor, but there was no mistaking the Styrian note. *Vitari, the bitch.*

Just what one needs in the middle of the night. Glokta did his best to stifle his groans as he carefully disentangled his numb limbs from his sweaty blanket, rolling his head gently from side to side, trying to stretch some movement into his twisted neck, and failing.

Thump, thump. *I wonder, when was the last time I had a woman beating down my bedroom door?* He snatched his cane from its place, resting against the mattress, then pressed one of his few teeth hard into his lip, grunting softly to himself as he wormed his way down the bed and let one leg flop off onto the boards. He threw himself forward, eyes squeezed shut at a withering pain through his back, and finally reached sitting, gasping as though he had run ten miles. *Fear me, fear me, all must fear me! If I can just get out of bed, that is.*

Thump. 'I'm coming, damn it!' He footed his cane on the floor and rocked himself up to standing. *Careful, careful.* The muscles in his mutilated left leg were shaking violently, making his toeless foot twitch and flop like a dying fish. *Damn this hideous appendage! It would feel like someone else's, if it didn't hurt so much. But calm, calm, we must be gentle.*

'Shhh,' he hissed, like a parent trying to sooth a wailing child, kneading softly at his ruined flesh and trying to breathe slow. 'Shhh.' The convulsions slowly calmed to a more manageable trembling. *About the best that we can hope for, I fear.* He was able to pull his nightshirt down and shuffle to the door, flip the key angrily round in the lock, and pull it open. Vitari stood outside in the corridor, draped against the wall, a darker shape in the shadows.

'You,' he grunted, hopping to the chair. 'You just can't stay away, can you? What is your fascination with my bedchamber?'

She sauntered through the door, peering around scornfully at the miserable room. 'Perhaps I just like seeing you in pain.'

Glokta snorted, rubbing gingerly at his burning knee. 'Then you must be wet between the legs right now.'

'Surprisingly, no. You look like death.'

'When don't I? Did you come to mock my looks, or have we some business?'

Vitari folded her long arms and leaned against the wall. 'You need to get dressed.'

'More excuses to see me naked?'

'Sult wants you.'

'Now?'

She rolled her eyes. 'Oh no, we can take our time. You know how he is.'

'Where are we going?'

'You'll see when we get there.' And she upped her pace, making him gasp and wince, snorting his aching way through the dim archways, down the shadowy lanes and the grey courtyards of the Agriont, colourless in the thin light of early morning.

His clumsy boots crunched and scraped in the gravel of the park. The grass was heavy with cold dew, the air thick with dull mist. Trees loomed up, black and leafless claws in the murk, and then a towering, sheer wall. Vitari led him towards a high gate, flanked by two guards. Their heavy armour was worked with gold, their heavy halberds were studded with gold, the golden sun of the Union was stitched into their surcoats. *Knights of the Body. The King's personal guard.*

'The palace?' muttered Glokta.

'No, the slums, genius.'

'Halt.' One of the two knights raised his gauntleted hand, voice echoing slightly from the grill in his tall helmet. 'State your names and business.'

'Superior Glokta.' He hobbled to the wall and leaned against the damp stones, pressing his tongue into his empty gums against the pain in his leg. 'As for the business, ask her. This wasn't my idea, I can damn well tell you that.'

'Practical Vitari. And the Arch Lector is expecting us. You know that already, fool, I told you on the way out.'

If it were possible for a man in full armour to appear hurt, this one did. 'It is a matter of protocol that I ask everyone—'

'Just get it open!' barked Glokta, pressing his fist into his trembling thigh, 'while I can still lurch through on my own!'

The man thumped angrily on the gate and a small door opened inside it. Vitari ducked through and Glokta limped after her, along a path of carefully-cut stones through a shadowy garden. Drops of cold water clung to the budding branches, dripped from the towering statuary. The cawing of a crow somewhere out of sight seemed ridiculously loud in the morning stillness. The palace loomed up ahead of them, a confusion of roofs, towers, sculptures, ornamental stonework outlined against the first pale glow of morning.

'What are we doing here?' hissed Glokta.

'You'll find out.'

He limped up a step, between towering columns and two more Knights of the Body, still and silent enough to have been empty suits of armour. His cane clicked on the polished marble floor of an echoing hallway, half lit by flickering candles, the high walls covered entirely with dim friezes. Scenes of forgotten victories and achievements, one king after another pointing, brandishing weapons, reading proclamations, standing with their chests puffed out in pride. He struggled up a flight of steps, ceiling and walls carved entirely in a glorious pattern of golden flowers, flashing and glittering in the candlelight, while Vitari waited impatiently for him at the top. *Their being priceless doesn't make them any easier to climb, damn it.*

'Down there,' she muttered at him.

A worried-looking group were gathered round a door twenty strides away. A Knight of the Body sat bent over on a chair, his helmet on the floor beside him, his head in his hands, fingers pushed through curly hair. Three other men stood, huddled together, their urgent whispering rebounding from the walls and echoing down the hallway.

'Aren't you coming?'

Vitari shook her head. 'He didn't ask for me.'

The three men looked up at Glokta as he limped towards them. *And what a group to find muttering in a palace corridor before daybreak.* Lord Chamberlain Hoff was wearing a quickly flung on nightgown, his puffy face stricken as though by a nightmare. Lord Marshal Varuz had one collar of his rumpled shirt sticking up, the other down, his iron grey hair shooting off his skull at all angles. High Justice Marovia's cheeks were gaunt, his eyes were rimmed with red, and there was a slight tremble to his liverish hand as he raised it to point at the door.

'In there,' he whispered. 'A terrible business. Terrible. Whatever shall be done?'

Glokta frowned, stepped past the sobbing guard and limped over the threshold.

It was a bedchamber. *And a magnificent one. This is a palace, after all.* The walls were papered with vivid silk, hung with dark canvases in old gilt frames. An enormous fireplace was carved from brown and red stone to look like a miniature Kantic temple. The bed was a monstrous four-posted creation whose curtains probably enclosed more space than Glokta's entire bedroom. The covers were flung back and rumpled, but there was no sign of the former occupant. One tall window was standing ajar, and a chill breeze washed in from the grey world outside, making the flames on the candles dance and flutter.

Arch Lector Sult was standing near the centre of the room, frowning thoughtfully down at the floor on the other side of the bed. If Glokta had expected him to be as dishevelled as his three colleagues outside the door, he was disappointed. His white gown was spotless, his white hair neatly brushed, his white gloved hands clasped carefully before him.

'Your Eminence . . .' Glokta was saying as he shuffled up. Then he noticed something on the floor. Dark fluid, glistening black in the candle-light. *Blood. How very unsurprising.*

He hobbled a little further. The corpse lay on its back on the far side of the bed. Blood was spattered on the white sheets, smeared over the boards and across the wall behind, had soaked up into the hem of the opulent drapes by the window. The ripped nightshirt was soaked through with it. One hand was curled up, the other was torn off, ragged, just beyond the thumb. There was a gaping wound on one arm, a chunk of flesh missing.

As though it were bitten away. One leg was broken and bent back on itself, a snapped off length of bone poking through split flesh. The throat had been so badly mauled that the head was barely attached, but there was no mistaking the face, seeming to grin up at the fine stucco work on the ceiling, teeth bared, eyes wide, bulging open.

'Crown Prince Raynault has been murdered,' muttered Glokta.

The Arch Lector raised his gloved hands and slowly, softly clapped two fingertips against his palm. 'Oh, very good. It is for just such insights that I sent for you. Yes, Prince Raynault has been murdered. A tragedy. An outrage. A terrible crime that strikes at the very heart of our nation, and at every one of its people. But that is far from the worst of it.' The Arch Lector took a long breath. 'The King has no siblings, Glokta, do you understand? Now he has no heirs. When the king dies, where do you suppose our next illustrious ruler will come from?'

Glokta swallowed. *I see. What a towering inconvenience.* 'From the Open Council.'

'An election,' sneered Sult. 'The Open Council, voting for our next king. A few hundred self-serving halfwits who can't be trusted to vote for their own lunch without guidance.'

Glokta swallowed. *I would almost be enjoying his Eminence's discomfort, were my neck not on the block beside his.* 'We are not popular with the Open Council.'

'We are reviled by them. Few more so. Our actions against the Mercers, against the Spicers, against Lord Governor Vurms, and more besides. None of the nobles trust us.'

Then if the king dies . . . 'How is the king's health?'

'Not. Good.' Sult frowned down at the bloody remains. 'All our work could be undone at this one stroke. Unless we can make friends in the Open Council, Glokta, while the king yet lives. Unless we can curry enough favour to choose his successor, or at least to influence the choice.' He stared at Glokta, blue eyes glittering in the candlelight. 'Votes must be bought, and blackmailed, coaxed and threatened our way. And you can depend upon it that those three old bastards outside are thinking just the same thing. How will I stay in power? With which candidate should I align myself? Whose votes can I control? When we announce the murder, we must assure the Open Council that the killer is already in our hands. Then swift, and brutal, and highly visible justice must be done. If the vote does not go our way, who knows what we could end up with? Brock on the throne, or Isher, or Heugen?' Sult gave a horrified shudder. 'We will be out of our jobs, at best. At worst . . .' *Several bodies found floating by the docks . . .* 'That is why I need you to find me the Prince's murderer. Now.'

Glokta looked down at the body. *Or what remains of it.* He poked at the gouge out of Raynault's arm with the tip of his cane. *We have seen wounds like these before, on that corpse in the park, months ago. An Eater did this, or at least, we are meant to think so.* The window tapped gently against its frame on a sudden cold draft. *An Eater who climbed in through the window? Unlike one of the Prophet's agents to leave such clues behind. Why not simply vanished, like Davoust? A sudden loss of appetite, are we meant to suppose?*

'Have you spoken to the guard?'

Sult waved his hand dismissively. 'He says he stood outside the door all night as usual. He heard a noise, entered the room, found the Prince as you see him, still bleeding, the window open. He sent immediately for Hoff. Hoff sent for me, and I for you.'

'The guard should be properly questioned, nonetheless . . .' Glokta peered down at Raynault's curled-up hand. There was something in it. He bent with an effort, his cane wobbling under his weight, and snatched it up between two fingers. *Interesting.* A piece of cloth. White cloth, it seemed, though mostly stained dark red now. He flattened it out and held it up. Gold thread glittered faintly in the dim candlelight. *I have seen cloth like this before.*

'What is that?' snapped Sult. 'Have you found something?'

Glokta stayed silent. *Perhaps, but it was very easy. Almost too easy.*

Glokta nodded to Frost, and the albino reached forward and pulled the bag from the head of the Emperor's envoy. Tulkis blinked in the harsh light, took a deep breath, and squinted round at the room. A dirty white box, too brightly lit. He took in Frost, looming at his shoulder. He took in Glokta, seated opposite. He took in the rickety chairs, and the stained table, and the polished case sitting on top of it. He did not seem to notice the small black hole in the very corner opposite him, behind Glokta's head. He was not meant to. That was the hole through which the Arch Lector watched the proceedings. *The one through which he hears every word that is said.*

Glokta watched the envoy closely. *It is in these early moments that a man often gives away his guilt. I wonder what his first words will be? An innocent man would ask what crime he is accused of—*

'Of what crime am I accused?' asked Tulkis. Glokta felt his eyelid twitch. *Of course, a clever guilty man might easily ask the same question.*

'Of the murder of Crown Prince Raynault.'

The envoy blinked, and sagged back in his chair. 'My deepest condolences to the Royal Family, and to all the people of the Union on this black day. But is all this really necessary?' He nodded down at the yards of heavy chain wrapped round his naked body.

'It is. If you are what we suspect you might be.'

'I see. Might I ask if it will make any difference that I am innocent of any part in this heinous crime?'

I doubt it will. Even if you are. Glokta tossed the bloodstained fragment of white cloth onto the table. 'This was found clasped in the Prince's hand.' Tulkis frowned at it, puzzled. *Just as if he never saw it before.* 'It matches exactly with a tear in a garment found in your chambers. A garment also stained liberally with blood.' Tulkis looked up at Glokta, eyes wide. *Just as though he has no idea how it got there.* 'How would you explain this?'

The envoy leaned forwards across the table, as far as he could with his hands chained behind him, and spoke swift and low. 'Please attend to me, Superior. If the Prophet's agents have discovered my mission – and they discover everything sooner or later – they will stop at nothing to make it fail. You know what they are capable of. If you punish me for this crime, it will be an insult to the Emperor. You will slap away his hand of friendship, and slap him in the face besides. He will swear vengeance, and when Uthman-ul-Dosht has sworn . . . my life means nothing, but my mission cannot fail. The consequences . . . for both our nations . . . please, Superior, I beg of you . . . I know you for an open-minded man—'

'An open mind is like to an open wound,' growled Glokta. 'Vulnerable to poison. Liable to fester. Apt to give its owner only pain.' He nodded to Frost and the albino placed the paper of confession carefully on the table top and slid it towards Tulkis with his white fingertips. He put the bottle of ink beside it and flipped open the brass lid. He placed the pen nearby. *All neat and crisp as a Sergeant-Major could wish for.*

'This is your confession.' Glokta waved his hand at the paper. 'In case you were wondering.'

'I am not guilty,' muttered Tulkis, his voice hardly more than a whisper.

Glokta twitched his face in annoyance. 'Have you ever been tortured?'

'No.'

'Have you ever seen torture carried out?'

The envoy swallowed. 'I have.'

'Then you have some inkling of what to expect.' Frost lifted the lid on Glokta's case. The trays inside lifted and fanned out like a huge and spectacular butterfly unfurling its wings for the first time, exposing Glokta's instruments in all their glittering, hypnotic, horrible beauty. He watched Tulkis' eyes fill with fear and fascination.

'I am the very best there is at this.' Glokta gave a long sigh and clasped his hands before him. 'It is not a matter for pride. It is a matter of fact. You would not be with me now if it were otherwise. I tell you so you can have no doubts. So you can answer my next question with no illusions. Look at me.' He waited for Tulkis' dark eyes to meet his. 'Will you confess?'

There was a pause. 'I am innocent,' whispered the ambassador.

'That was not my question. I will ask it again. Will you confess?'

'I cannot.'

They stared at each other for a long moment, and Glokta was left in no doubt. *He is innocent. If he could steal over the wall of the palace and in through the Prince's window without being noticed, surely he could have stolen out of the Agriont and away before we were any the wiser? Why stay, and sleep, leaving his bloodstained garment hanging in the cupboard, waiting for us to discover it? A trail of clues so blatant a blind man could follow them. We are being duped, and not even subtly. To punish the wrong man, that is one thing. But to allow myself to be made a fool of? That is another.*

'One moment,' murmured Glokta. He struggled out of his chair to the door, shut it carefully behind him, hobbled wincing up the steps to the next room and went in.

'What the hell are you up to in there?' the Arch Lector snarled at him.

Glokta kept his head bowed in a position of deep respect. 'I am trying to establish the truth, your Eminence—'

'You are trying to establish *what*? The Closed Council are waiting for a confession, and you're blathering about *what*?'

Glokta met the Arch Lector's glare. 'What if he is not lying? What if the Emperor does desire peace? What if he is innocent?'

Sult stared back at him, cold blue eyes wide open with disbelief. 'Did you lose your teeth in Gurkhul or your fucking mind? Who cares a shit for innocent? What concerns us now is what must be done! What concerns us now is what is necessary! What concerns us now is ink on paper you . . . you . . .' he was near frothing at the mouth, fists clenching and unclenching with fury, '. . . you crippled shred of a man! Make him sign, then we can be done with this and get to licking arses in the Open Council!'

Glokta bowed his head still lower. 'Of course, your Eminence.'

'Now is your perverse obsession with the *truth* going to cause me any more trouble tonight? I'd rather use a needle than a spade, but I'll dig a confession out of this bastard either way! Must I send for Goyle?'

'Of course not, your Eminence.'

'Just get in there, damn you, and make . . . him . . . sign!'

Glokta shuffled out of his room, grumbling, stretching his neck to either side, rubbing his sore palms, working his aching shoulders round his ears and hearing the joints click. *A difficult interrogation.* Severard was sitting cross-legged on the floor opposite, his head resting against the dirty wall. 'Has he signed?'

'Of course.'

'Lovely. Another mystery solved, eh, chief?'

'I doubt it. He's no Eater. Not like Shickel was, anyway. He feels pain, believe me.'

Severard shrugged. 'She said the talents were different for each of them.'

'She did. She did.' *But still.* Glokta wiped at his runny eye, thinking. *Someone murdered the Prince. Someone had something to gain from his death. I would like to know who, even if no one else cares.* 'There are some questions

I still need to ask. The guard at the Prince's chambers last night. I want to speak to him.'

The Practical raised his brows. 'Why? We've got the paper haven't we?'

'Just bring him in.'

Severard unfolded his legs and sprang up. 'Alright, then, you're the boss.' He pushed himself away from the greasy wall and sauntered off down the corridor. 'One Knight of the Body, coming right up.'

Holding the Line

'**D**id you sleep?' asked Pike, scratching at the less burned side of his ruined face.

'No. You?'

The convict turned Sergeant shook his head.

'Not for days,' murmured Jalenhorm, wistfully. He shaded his eyes with a hand and squinted up towards the northern ridge, a ragged outline of trees under the iron grey sky. 'Poulder's division already set off through the woods?'

'Before first light,' said West. 'We should hear that he's in position soon. And now it looks as if Kroy's ready to go. You have to respect his punctuality, at least.'

Below Burr's command post, down in the valley, General Kroy's division was moving into battle order. Three regiments of the King's Own foot formed the centre, with a regiment of levies on the higher ground on either wing and the cavalry just behind. It was an entirely different spectacle from the ragged deployment of Ladisla's makeshift army. The battalions flowed smoothly forwards in tightly ordered columns: tramping through the mud, the tall grass, the patches of snow in the hollows. They halted at their allotted positions and began to spread out into carefully dressed lines, a net of men stretching right across the valley. The chill air echoed with the distant thumping of their feet, the beating of their drums, the clipped calls of their commanders. Everything clean and crisp and according to procedure.

Lord Marshal Burr thrust aside his tent flap and strode out into the open air, acknowledging the salutes of the various guards and officers scattered about the space in front with sharp waves of his hand.

'Colonel,' he growled, frowning up at the heavens. 'Still dry, then?'

The sun was a watery smudge on the horizon, the sky thick white with streaks of heavy grey, darker bruises hanging over the northern ridge. 'For the moment, sir,' said West.

'No word from Poulder yet?'

'No, sir. But it might be hard-going, the woods are dense.' Not as dense as Poulder himself, West thought, but that hardly seemed the most professional thing to say.

'Did you eat yet?'

'Yes, sir, thank you.' West had not eaten since last night, and even then not much. The very idea of food made him feel sick.

'Well at least one of us did.' Burr placed a hand sourly on his stomach. 'Damned indigestion, I can't touch a thing.' He winced and gave a long burp. 'Pardon me. And there they go.'

General Kroy must finally have declared himself satisfied with the precise positioning of every man in his division, because the soldiers in the valley had begun to move forward. A chilly breeze blew up and set the regimental standards, the flags of the battalions, the company ensigns snapping and fluttering. The watery sun twinkled on sharpened blades and burnished armour, shone on gold braid and polished wood, glittered on buckles and harness. All advanced smoothly together, as proud a display of military might as could ever have been seen. Beyond them, down the valley to the east, a great black tower loomed up behind the trees. The nearest tower of the fortress of Dunbrec.

'Quite the spectacle,' muttered Burr. 'Fifteen thousand fighting men, perhaps, all told, and almost as many more up on the ridge.' He nodded his head at the reserve, two regiments of cavalry, dismounted and restless down below the command post. 'Another two thousand there, waiting for orders.' He glanced back towards the sprawling camp: a city of canvas, of carts, of stacked up boxes and barrels, spread out in the snowy valley, black figures crawling around inside. 'And that's without counting all the thousands back there – cooks and grooms, smiths and drivers, servants and surgeons.' He shook his head. 'Some responsibility, all that, eh? You wouldn't want to be the fool who had to take care of all that lot.'

West gave a weak smile. 'No, sir.'

'It looks like . . .' murmured Jalenhorm, shading his eyes and squinting down the valley into the sun. 'Are those . . . ?'

'Eye-glass!' snapped Burr, and a nearby officer produced one with a flourish. The Marshal flicked it open. 'Well, well. Who's this now?'

A rhetorical question, without a doubt. There was no one else it could be. 'Bethod's Northmen,' said Jalenhorm, ever willing to state the obvious.

West watched them rush across the open ground through the wobbling round window of his own eye-glass. They flowed out from the trees at the far end of the valley, near to the river, spreading out across the open ground like the dark stain creeping from a slit wrist. Dirty grey and brown masses congealed on the wings. Thralls, lightly armed. In the centre better ordered ranks took shape, dull metal gleaming, mail and blade. Bethod's Carls.

'No sign of any horse.' That made West more nervous than ever. He had already had one near-fatal encounter with Bethod's cavalry, and he did not care to renew the acquaintance.

'Feels good to actually see the enemy, at last,' said Burr, voicing the exact opposite of West's own feelings. 'They move smartly enough, that's sure.' His mouth curved up into a rare grin. 'But they're moving right where we want them to. The trap's baited and ready to spring, eh, Captain?' He passed the eye-glass to Jalenhorm, who peered through it and grinned himself.

'Right where we want them,' he echoed. West felt a good deal less confident. He could clearly remember the thin line of Northmen on the ridge, right where Ladisla had thought he wanted them.

Kroy's men halted and the units shuffled into perfect position once again, just as calmly as if they stood on a vast parade ground: lines four ranks deep, reserve companies drawn up neatly behind, a thin row of flatbowmen in front. West just made out the shouted orders to fire, saw the first volley float up from Kroy's line, shower down in amongst the enemy. He felt his nails digging painfully into his palm as he watched, fists clenched tight, willing the Northmen to die. Instead they sent back a well organised volley of their own, and then began to surge forward.

Their battle cry floated up to the officers outside the tent, that unearthly shriek, carrying on the cold air. West chewed at his lip, remembering the last time he heard it, echoing through the mist. Hard to believe it had only been a few weeks ago. Again he was guiltily glad to be well behind the lines, though a shiver down his back reminded him that it had done little good on that occasion.

'Bloody hell,' said Jalenhorm.

No one else spoke. West stood, teeth gritted, heart thumping, trying desperately to hold his eye-glass steady as the Northmen charged full-blooded down the valley. Kroy's flatbows gave them one more volley, then pulled back through the carefully prepared gaps in the carefully dressed ranks, forming up again behind the lines. Spears were lowered, shields were raised, and in virtual silence, it seemed, the Union line prepared to meet the howling Northmen.

'Contact,' growled Lord Marshal Burr. The Union ranks seemed to wave and shift somewhat, the watery sunlight seemed to flash more rapidly on the mass of men, a vague rattling drifted on the air. Not a word was said in the command post. Each man was squinting through his eye-glass, or peering into the sun, craning to see what was happening down in the valley, hardly daring even to breathe.

After what seemed a horribly long time, Burr lowered his eye-glass. 'Good. They're holding. It seems your Northmen were right, West, we have the advantage in numbers, even without Poulder. When he gets here, it should be a rout—'

'Up there,' muttered West, 'on the southern ridge.' Something glinted in the treeline, and again. Metal. 'Cavalry, sir, I'd bet my life on it. It seems Bethod had the same idea as us, but on the other wing.'

'Damn it!' hissed Burr. 'Send word to General Kroy that the enemy has horse on the southern ridge! Tell him to refuse that flank and prepare to be attacked from the right!' One of the adjutants leaped smoothly into his saddle and galloped off in the direction of Kroy's headquarters, cold mud flying from his horse's hooves.

'More tricks, and this may not be the last of 'em.' Burr snapped the eye-glass closed and thumped it into his open palm. 'This must not be allowed to fail, Colonel West. Nothing must get in the way. Not Poulder's arrogance, not Kroy's pride, not the enemy's cunning, none of it. We must have victory here today. It *must* not be allowed to fail!'

'No, sir.' But West was far from sure what he could do about it.

The Union soldiers were trying to be quiet, which meant they made about as much racket as a great herd of sheep being shoved indoors for shearing. Moaning and grunting, slithering on the wet ground, armour rattling, weapons knocking on low branches. Dogman shook his head as he watched 'em.

'Lucky thing there's no one out here, or we'd have been heard long ago,' hissed Dow. 'These fools couldn't creep up on a corpse.'

'No need for you to be making noise,' hissed Threetrees, up ahead, then beckoned them all forward.

It was a strange feeling, marching with such a big crew again. There were two score of Shivers' Carls along with 'em, and quite an assortment. Tall men and short, young and old, all manner of different weapons and armour, but all pretty well seasoned, from what the Dogman could tell.

'Halt!' And the Union soldiers clattered and grumbled to a stop, started sorting themselves out into a line, spread across the highest part of the ridge. A great long line, the Dogman reckoned, judging from the number of men he'd watched going up into the woods, and they were right at the far end of it. He peered off into the empty trees on their left, and frowned. Lonely place to be, the end of a line.

'But the safest,' he muttered to himself.

'What's that?' asked Cathil, sitting down on a great fallen tree trunk.

'Safe here,' he said in her tongue, managing a grin. He still didn't have half an idea how to behave around her. There was a hell of a gap between them in the daylight, a yawning great gap of race, and age, and language that he wasn't sure could ever be bridged. Strange, how the gap dwindled down to nothing at night. They understood each other well enough in the dark. Maybe they'd work it out, in time, or maybe they wouldn't, and that'd be that. Still, he was glad she was there. Made him feel like a proper human man again, instead of just an animal slinking in the woods, trying to scratch his way from one mess to another.

He watched a Union officer break off from his men and walk towards them, strut up to Threetrees, some kind of a polished stick wedged under his arm. 'General Poulder asks that you remain here on the left wing, to secure the far flank.' He spoke slow and very loud, as though that'd make him understood if they didn't talk the language.

'Alright,' said Threetrees.

'The division will be deploying along the high ground to your right!' And he flicked his stick thing towards the trees where his men were slowly and noisily getting ready. 'We will be waiting until Bethod's forces are well engaged with General Kroy's division, and then we will attack, and drive them from the field!'

Threetrees nodded. 'You need our help with any of that?'

'Frankly I doubt it, but we will send word if matters change.' And he strutted off to join his men, slipping a few paces away and nearly going down on his arse in the muck.

'He's confident,' said the Dogman.

Threetrees raised his brows. 'Bit too much, if you're asking me, but if it means he leaves us out I reckon I can live with it. Right then!' he shouted, turning round to the Carls. 'Get hold o' that tree trunk and drag it up along the brow here!'

'Why?' asked one of 'em, sitting rubbing at one knee and looking sullen.

'So you got something to hide behind if Bethod turns up,' barked Dow at him. 'Get to it, fool!'

The Carls downed their weapons and set to work, grumbling. Seemed that joining up with the legendary Rudd Threetrees was less of a laugh than they'd hoped. Dogman had to smile. They should've known. Leaders don't get to be legendary by handing out light duty. The old boy himself was stood frowning into the woods as Dogman walked up beside him. 'You worried, chief?'

'It's a good spot up here for hiding some men. A good spot for waiting 'til the battles joined, then charging down.'

'It is,' grinned the Dogman. 'That's why we're here.'

'And what? Bethod won't have thought of that?' Dogman's grin started to fade. 'If he's got men to spare he might think they'd be well used up here, waiting for the right moment, just like we are. He might send 'em through these trees here and up this hill to right where we're sitting. What'd happen then, d'you reckon?'

'We'd set to killing each other, I daresay, but Bethod don't have men to spare, according to Shivers and his boys. He's outnumbered worse'n two to one as it is.'

'Maybe, but he likes to cook up surprises.'

'Alright,' said Dogman, watching the Carls heaving the fallen tree trunk around so it blocked off the top of the slope. 'Alright. So we drag a tree across here and we hope for the best.'

'Hope for the best?' grunted Threetrees. 'Just when did that ever work?' He strode off to mutter to Grim, and Dogman shrugged his shoulders. If a few hundred Carls did turn up all of a sudden, they'd be in a fix, but there weren't much he could do about it now. So he knelt down beside his pack, pulled out his flint and some dry twigs, stacked it all up careful and started striking sparks.

Shivers squatted down near him, palms resting on his axe-handle. 'What're you at?'

'What does it look like?' Dogman blew into the kindling, watched the flame spreading out. 'I'm making me a fire.'

'Ain't we waiting for a battle to start?'

Dogman sat back, pushed some of the dry twigs closer in and watched 'em take light. 'Aye, we're waiting, and that's the best time for a fire, I reckon. War's all waiting, lad. Weeks of your life, maybe, if you're in our line o' work. You could spend that time being cold, or you could try to get comfortable.'

He slid his pan out from his pack and onto the fire. New pan, and a good one, he'd got it off the Southerners. He unwrapped the packet inside. Five eggs there, still whole. Nice, brown, speckled eggs. He cracked one on the edge of the pan, poured it in, heard it hiss, grinning all the while. Things were looking up, alright. Hadn't had eggs in a good long time. It was as he was cracking the last one that he smelled something, just as the breeze turned. Something more than eggs cooking. He jerked his head up, frowning.

'What?' asked Cathil.

'Nothing, most likely.' But it was best not to take chances. 'You wait here a moment and watch these, eh?'

'Alright.'

Dogman clambered over the fallen trunk, made for the nearest tree and leaned against it, squatting on his haunches, peering down the slope. Nothing to smell, that he could tell. Nothing to see in the trees either – just the wet earth patched with snow, the dripping pine branches and the still shadows. Nothing. Just Threetrees got him nervous with his talk about surprises.

He was turning back when he caught a whiff again. He stood up, took a few paces downhill, away from the fire and the fallen tree, staring into the woods. Threetrees came up beside him, shield on his arm, sword drawn and clutched in his big fist.

'What is it, Dogman, you smell something?'

'Could be.' He sniffed again, long and slow, sucking the air through his nose, sifting at it. 'Most likely nothing.'

'Don't nothing me, Dogman, your nose has got us out of a scrape or two before now. What d'you smell?'

The breeze shifted, and this time he caught it full. Hadn't smelled it in a while, but there was no mistaking it. 'Shit,' he breathed. 'Shanka.'

'Oy!' And the Dogman looked round, mouth open. Cathil was just climbing over the fallen tree, the pan in her hand. 'Eggs are done,' she said, grinning at the two of them.

Threetrees flailed his arm at her and bellowed at the top of his lungs. 'Everyone get back behind the—'

A bowstring went, down in the brush. Dogman heard the arrow, felt it hiss past in the air. They're not the best of archers, on the whole, the Flatheads, and it missed him by a stride or two. It was just piss-poor luck it found another mark.

'Ah,' said Cathil, blinking down at the shaft in her side. 'Ah . . .' and she fell down, just like that, dropping the pan in the snow. Then Dogman was running up the hill towards her, his breath scraping cold in his throat. Then he was scrabbling for her arms, saw Threetrees take a hold round her knees. It was a lucky thing she weren't heavy. Not heavy at all. An arrow or two shot past. One stuck wobbling in the tree trunk, and they bundled her over and took cover on the other side.

'There's Shanka down there!' Threetrees was shouting, 'They shot the girl!'

'Safest place in the battle?' growled Dow, crouching down behind the tree, spinning his axe round and round in his hand. 'Fucking bastards!'

'Shanka? This far south?' someone was saying.

Dogman took Cathil under the arms and pulled her groaning back to the hollow by the fire, her heels kicking at the mud. 'They shot me,' she muttered, staring down at the arrow, blood spreading out from it into her shirt. She coughed, looked up at the Dogman, eyes wide.

'They're coming!' Shivers was shouting. 'Ready, boys!' Men were drawing their weapons, tightening their belts and their shield straps, gritting their teeth and thumping each other on the backs, making ready to fight. Grim was up behind the tree, shooting arrows down the hill, calm as you like.

'I got to go,' said the Dogman, squeezing at Cathil's hand, 'but I'll be back, alright? You just sit tight, you hear? I'll be back.'

'What? No!' He had to pry her fingers away from his. He didn't like doing it, but what choice did he have? 'No,' she croaked at his back as he scrambled towards the tree and the thin line of Carls hunching down behind it, a couple kneeling up to shoot their own bows. An ugly spear came over the trunk and thudded into the earth just beside him. Dogman stared at it, then slithered past, up onto his knees not far from Grim, looking down the slope.

'Fucking shit!' The trees were alive with Flatheads. The trees below, the trees to their left, the trees to their right. Dark shapes moving, flapping shadows, swarming up the hill. Hundreds of them, it seemed like. Off to their right the Union soldiers were shouting and clattering, confused, armour clanking as they set their spears. Arrows hissed angry up out of the woods, flitted down into 'em. 'Fucking shit!'

'Maybe start shooting, aye?' Grim loosed a shaft, pulled another out of his quiver. Dogman snatched out an arrow himself, but there were so many targets he could hardly bring himself to pick one, and he shot too high, cursing all the while. They were getting close now, close enough for him to see their faces, if you could call 'em faces. Open flapping jaws, snarling and full of teeth, hard little eyes, full of hate. Clumsy weapons – clubs with nails in, axes made from chipped stone, rust-spotted swords stolen from the dead. Up they came, seeming fast as wolves through the trees.

Dogman got one in the chest, saw it drop back. He hit another through the leg, but the rest weren't slowing. 'Ready!' he heard Threetrees roaring, felt men standing up around him, lifting their blades, their spears, their shields, to meet the charge. He wondered how a man was meant to get ready for this.

A Flathead came springing through the air over the tree, mouth wide open and snarling. Dogman saw it there, black in the air, heard a great roar in his ear, then Tul's sword ripped into it and flung it back, blood spraying out of it like water from a smashed bottle.

Another came scrambling up and Threetrees took its arm clean off with his sword, smashed it back down the slope with his shield. More of 'em were coming now, and still more, swarming over the fallen trunk in a crowd. Dogman shot one in the face at no more than a stride away, pulled his knife out and stabbed it in the gut, screaming as loud as he could, blood leaking warm over his hand. He tore its club from its claw as it fell and swung it at another, missed and reeled away. Men were shouting and stabbing and hacking all over.

He saw Shivers wedge a Shanka's head against the tree with his boot, lift his shield high above his head and ram the metal rim deep into its face. He knocked another sprawling with his axe, spraying blood into Dogman's eyes, then caught a third in his arms as it sprang over the tree and they rolled onto the wet dirt together, flopping over and over. The Shanka came out on top and Dogman smashed it in the back with the club, once, twice, three times and Shivers shoved it off and scrambled up, stomped on the back of its head. He charged past, hacking another Flathead down just as it spitted a squealing Carl through the side with a spear.

Dogman blinked, trying to wipe the blood from his eyes on the back of his sleeve. He saw Grim lift his knife and stab it through a Flathead's skull, the blade sliding out its mouth and nailing it tight to a tree trunk. He saw Tul smashing his great fist into a Shanka's face, again and again until its skull was nothing but red pulp. A Flathead sprang up onto the tree above him, spear raised, but before it could stab him Dow leaped up and chopped its legs out from under it. It spun in the air, screaming.

Dogman saw a Shanka on top of a Carl, taking a great bite out of his neck. He snatched the spear out of the ground behind him and flung it square into the Flathead's back. It fell, gibbering and clawing over its own shoulders, trying to get to the thing, but it was stuck clean through.

Another Carl was thrashing around, roaring, a Shanka's teeth sunk into his arm, punching at it with his other hand. Dogman took a step to help him but before he got there a Flathead came at him with a spear. He saw it in good time and dodged round it, slashed it across the eyes with his knife as it came past, then cracked the club down on the back of its skull, felt it crunch like a breaking egg. He turned to face another. A damn big one. It opened its jaws at him and snarled, drool running out from its teeth, a great axe in its claws.

'Come on!' he screamed at it, raising the club and the knife. Before it could come at him Threetrees had stepped up behind it and split it open from shoulder to chest. Blood spattered out and it grovelled in the mud. It managed to get up a ways, somehow, but all that did was put its face in the best place for Dogman to stab his knife into.

Now the Shanka were falling back and the Carls were shouting and hacking them down as they turned. The last one squawked and went for the tree, trying to scramble over. It gibbered as Dow's sword hacked a bloody gash across its back, all red meat and splinters of white bone. It fell tangled over a branch, twitched and lay still, its legs dangling.

'They're done!' roared Shivers, his face spotted with blood under his long hair. 'We did 'em!'

The Carls cheered and shouted and shook their weapons. Leastways most of 'em did. There were a couple lying still and a few more laid out wounded, groaning, gurgling through clenched teeth. The Dogman didn't reckon they felt much like celebrating. Neither did Threetrees.

'Shut up, you fools! They're gone for now but there'll be more. That's the thing with Flatheads, there's always more! Get them bodies out of the way! Salvage all the arrows we can get! We'll need 'em before today's through!'

The Dogman was already limping back towards the smouldering fire. Cathil was lying where he'd left her, breathing fast and shallow, one hand pressed against her ribs around the shaft. She watched him coming with wide, wet eyes and said nothing. He said nothing either. What was there to say? He took his knife and slit her bloody shirt, from the arrow down to the hem, peeled it away from her until he could see the shaft. It was stuck between two ribs on the right hand side, just under her tit. Not a good place to get shot, if there was such a thing.

'Is it alright?' she mumbled, teeth rattling. Her face was white as snow, eyes feverish bright. 'Is it alright?'

'It's alright,' he said, rubbing the dirt off her wet cheek with his thumb. 'Don't you fret now, eh? We'll get it sorted.' And all the time he was thinking, you fucking liar, Dogman, you fucking coward. She's got an arrow in her ribs.

Threetrees squatted down beside them. 'It'll have to come out,' he said, frowning hard. 'I'll hold her, you pull it.'

'Do what?'

'What's he saying?' hissed Cathil, blood on her teeth. 'What's he . . .' Dogman took hold of the shaft in both hands while Threetrees took her wrists. 'What're you—'

Dogman pulled, and it wouldn't come. He pulled, and blood ran out from the wound round the shaft and slid down her pale side in two dark lines. He pulled, and her body thrashed and her legs kicked and she screamed like he was killing her. He pulled, and it wouldn't come, and it wouldn't even shift a finger's breadth.

'Pull it!' hissed Threetrees.

'It won't fucking come!' snarled the Dogman in his face.

'Alright! Alright.' Dogman let go the arrow and Cathil coughed and gurgled, shuddering and shaking, gasping in air and dribbling out pink spit.

Threetrees rubbed at his jaw, leaving a bloody smear across his face. 'If you can't pull it out, you'll have to push it on through.'

'What?'

'What's he . . . saying?' gurgled Cathil, her teeth chattering.

Dogman swallowed. 'We got to push it through.'

'No,' she muttered, eyes going wide. 'No.'

'We got to.' She snorted as he took hold of the shaft and snapped it off halfway down, cupped his palms over the broken end.

'No,' she whimpered.

'Just hold on, girl,' muttered Threetrees in common, gripping hold of her arms again. 'Just hold on, now. Do it, Dogman.'

'No . . .'

Dogman gritted his teeth and shoved down hard on the broken shaft. Cathil jerked and made a kind of sigh, then her eyes rolled back, passed out clean. Dogman half rolled her, body limp as a rag, saw the arrow head sticking out her back.

'Alright,' he muttered, 'alright, it's through.' He took hold of it just below the blade, twisted it gently as he slid it out. A splatter of blood came with it, but not too much.

'That's good,' said Threetrees. 'Don't reckon it got a lung, then.'

Dogman chewed at his lip. 'That's good.' He grabbed up a roll of bandage, put it against the leaking hole in her back, started winding it round her chest, Threetrees lifting her up while he passed it underneath her. 'That's good, that's good.' He said it over and over, winding the bandage round, fumbling fast as he could with cold fingers until it was done up tight, as good as he knew how. His hands were bloody, the bandage was bloody, her stomach and her back were covered in his pink finger marks, in streaks of dark dirt and dark blood. He pulled her shirt back down over her, rolled her gently onto her back. He touched her face – warm, eyes closed, her chest moving softly, her breath smoking round her mouth.

'Need to get a blanket.' He started up, fumbled through his pack, pulled out his blanket, scattering gear around the fire. He dragged it back, shook it out and laid it over her. 'Keep you warm, eh? Nice and warm.' He pushed it in around her, keep the cold out. He tugged it down over her feet. 'Keep warm.'

'Dogman.'

Threetrees was bending over, listening to her breath. He straightened up, and slowly shook his head. 'She's dead.'

'What?'

White specks drifted down round them. It was starting to snow again.

'Where the hell is Poulder?' snarled Marshal Burr, staring down the valley, his fists clenching and unclenching with frustration. 'I said wait until we're engaged, not damn well overrun!'

West could think of no reply. Where, indeed, was Poulder? The snow was thickening now, coming down softly in swirls and eddies, letting fall a grey curtain across the battlefield, lending to everything an air of unreality. The sounds came up as though from impossibly far away, muffled and echoing. Messengers rode back and forth behind the lines, black dots moving swiftly over the white ground with urgent calls for reinforcement. The wounded were building up, dragged groaning in stretchers, gasping in carts, or trudging, silent and bloody down the road below the headquarters.

Even through the snow it was clear that Kroy's men were hard pressed. The carefully drawn lines now bulged alarmingly in the centre, units dissolved into a single straining mass, merged with one another in the chaos and confusion of combat. West had lost track of the number of staff officers General Kroy had sent to the command post demanding support or permission to withdraw, all of them sent back with the same message. To hold, and to wait. From Poulder, meanwhile, came nothing but an ominous and unexpected silence.

'Where the hell is he?' Burr stomped back to his tent leaving dark footprints in the fresh crust of white. 'You!' he shouted at an adjutant, beckoning him impatiently. West followed at a respectful distance and pushed through the tent flap after him, Jalenhorm just behind.

Marshal Burr leaned over his table and snatched a pen from an ink-bottle, spattering black drops on the wood. 'Get up into those woods and find General Poulder! Establish what the hell he is doing and return to me at once!'

'Yes, sir!' squawked the officer, standing to vibrating attention.

Burr's pen scrawled orders across the paper. 'Inform him that he is commanded to begin his attack *immediately*!' He signed his name with an angry slash of the wrist and jerked the paper out to the adjutant.

'Of course, sir!' The young officer strode purposefully from the tent.

Burr turned back to his maps, wincing as he glared down, one hand tugging on his beard, the other pressed to his belly. 'Where the hell is Poulder?'

'Perhaps, sir, he has himself come under attack—'

Burr burped, and grimaced, burped again and thumped the table making the ink bottle rattle. 'Curse this fucking indigestion!' His thick finger stabbed at the map. 'If Poulder doesn't arrive soon we'll have to commit the reserve, West, you hear me? Commit the cavalry.'

'Yes, sir, of course.'

'This cannot be allowed to fail.' The Marshal frowned, swallowed. It seemed to West he had gone suddenly very pale. 'This cannot . . . cannot . . .' He swayed slightly, blinking.

'Sir, are you—'

'Bwaaaah!' And Marshal Burr jerked forwards and sprayed black vomit over the table top. It splattered against the maps and turned the paper angry red. West stood frozen, his jaw gradually dropping open. Burr gurgled, fists clenched on the table in front of him, his body shaking, then he hunched over and poured out puke again. 'Guuurgh!' And he lurched away, red drool dangling from his lip, eyes starting from his white face, gave a strangled groan and toppled back, dragging one bloody chart with him.

West finally understood what was happening just in time to dive forwards and catch the Lord Marshal's limp body before he fell. He staggered across the tent, struggling to hold him up.

'Shit!' gasped Jalenhorm.

'Help me, damn it!' snarled West. The big man started over and took Burr's other arm, and together they half lifted, half dragged him to his bed. West undid the Marshal's top button, loosened his collar. 'Some sickness of the stomach,' he muttered through clenched teeth. 'He's been complaining for weeks . . .'

'I'll get the surgeon!' squealed Jalenhorm.

He started up but West caught hold of his arm. 'No.'

The big man stared back. 'What?'

'If it becomes known that he's ill, there'll be panic. Poulder and Kroy will do as they please. The army might fall apart. No one can know until after the battle.'

'But—'

West got up and put his hand on Jalenhorm's shoulder, looking him straight in the eye. He knew already what had to be done. He would not be a spectator at another disaster. 'Listen to me. We must follow through with the plan. We must.'

'Who must?' Jalenhorm stared wildly round the tent. 'Me and you, alone?'

'If that's what it takes.'

'But this is a man's life!'

'This is thousands of men's lives,' hissed West. 'It cannot be allowed to fail, you heard him say it.'

Jalenhorm had turned almost as pale as Burr. 'I hardly think he meant that—'

'Don't forget you owe me.' West leaned still closer. 'Without me you'd be one in a pile of corpses rotting nicely north of the Cumnur.' He didn't like doing it, but it had to be done, and there was no time for niceties. 'Do we understand each other, Captain?'

Jalenhorm swallowed. 'Yes, sir, I think so.'

'Good. You watch Marshal Burr, I'll take care of things outside.' West got up and made for the tent flap.

'What if he—'

'Improvise!' he snapped, over his shoulder. There were bigger things to worry about now than any one man. He ducked out into the cold air. At least a score of officers and guards were scattered around the command post before the tent, pointing down into the white valley, peering through eye-glasses and muttering to one another. 'Sergeant Pike!' West beckoned to the convict and he strode over through the falling snow. 'I need you to stand guard here, do you understand?'

'Of course, sir.'

'I need you to stand guard here, and admit no one but me or Captain Jalenhorm. No one.' He dropped his voice lower. 'Under any circumstances.'

Pike nodded, his eyes glittering in the pink mass of his face. 'I understand.' And he moved to the tent flap and stood beside it, almost carelessly, his thumbs tucked into his sword belt.

A moment later a horse plunged down the slope and into the headquarters, smoke snorting from its nostrils. Its rider slid down from his saddle, stumbled a couple of steps before West managed to get in his way.

'An urgent message for Marshal Burr from General Poulder!' blathered the man in a rush. He tried to take a stride towards the tent but West did not move.

'Marshal Burr is busy. You can deliver your message to me.'

'I was explicitly told to—'

'To me, Captain!'

The man blinked. 'General Poulder's division is engaged, sir, in the woods.'

'Engaged?'

'Hotly engaged. There have been several savage attacks on the left wing and we're hard pressed to hold our own. General Poulder requests permission to withdraw and regroup, sir, we're all out of position!'

West swallowed. The plan was already coming unravelled, and in imminent danger of falling apart completely. 'Withdraw? No! Impossible. If he pulls back, Kroy's division will be left exposed. Tell General Poulder to hold his ground, and to go through with the attack if he possibly can. Tell him he must not withdraw under any circumstances! Every man must do his part!'

'But, sir, I should—'

'Go!' shouted West. 'At once!'

The man saluted and clambered back onto his horse. Even as he was spurring up the slope another visitor was pulling up his mount not far from the tent. West cursed under his breath. It was Colonel Felnigg, Kroy's chief of staff. He would not be so easily put off.

'Colonel West,' he snapped as he swung down from the saddle. 'Our division is fiercely engaged all across the line, and now cavalry has appeared on our right wing! A charge by cavalry against a regiment of levies!' He was already making for the tent, pulling off his gloves. 'Without support they won't hold long, and if they break, our flank will be up in the air! It could be the end! Where the hell is Poulder?'

West attempted unsuccessfully to slow Felnigg down. 'General Poulder has come under attack himself. However, I will order the reserves released immediately and—'

'Not good enough,' growled Felnigg, brushing past him and striding towards the tent flap. 'I must speak to Marshal Burr at—'

Pike stepped out in front of him, one hand resting on the hilt of his sword. 'The Marshal . . . is busy,' he whispered. His eyes bulged from his burned face in a manner so horribly threatening that even West felt slightly unnerved. There was a tense silence for a moment as the staff officer and the faceless convict stared at one another.

Then Felnigg took a hesitant step back. He blinked, licked his lips nervously. 'Busy. I see. Well.' He took another step away. 'The reserves will be committed, you say?'

'Immediately.'

'Well then, well then . . . I will tell General Kroy to expect reinforcements.' Felnigg shoved one toe into his stirrup. 'This is highly irregular, though.' He frowned down at the tent, at Pike, at West. 'Highly irregular.' And he gave his horse the spurs and charged back down into the valley. West watched him go, thinking that Felnigg had no idea just how irregular. He turned to an adjutant.

'Marshal Burr has ordered the reserve into action on the right wing. They must charge Bethod's cavalry and drive them off. If that flank weakens, it will mean disaster. Do you understand?'

'I should have written orders from the Marshal—'

'There is no time for written orders!' roared West. 'Get down there and do your duty, man!'

The adjutant hurried obediently away through the snow, down the slope towards the two regiments of reserves, waiting patiently in the snow. West watched him go, his fingers working nervously. The men began to mount up, began to trot into position for a charge. West was chewing at his lip as he turned around. The officers and guards of Burr's staff were all looking at him with expressions ranging from mildly curious to downright suspicious.

He nodded to a couple of them as he walked back, trying to give the impression that everything was routine. He wondered how long it would be before someone refused to simply take his word, before someone forced their way into the tent, before someone discovered that Lord Marshal Burr was halfway to the land of the dead, and had been for some time. He wondered if it would happen before the lines broke in the valley, and the command post was overrun by Northmen. If it was after, he supposed it would hardly matter.

Pike was looking over at him with an expression that might have been something like a grin. West would have liked to grin back, but he didn't have it in him.

The Dogman sat, and breathed. His back was to the fallen tree, his bow was hanging loose in his fist. A sword was stuck into the wet earth beside him. He'd taken it from a dead Carl, and put it to use, and he reckoned he'd have more use for it before the day was out. There was blood on him – on his hands, on his clothes, all over. Cathil's, Flatheads', his own. Wiping it off hardly seemed worth the effort – there'd be plenty more soon enough.

Three times the Shanka had come up the hill now, and three times they'd fought them off, each fight harder than the one before. Dogman wondered if they'd fight them off when they came again. He never doubted that they were coming. Not for a minute. When and how many were the questions that bothered him.

Through the trees he could hear the Union wounded screeching and squealing. Lots of wounded. One of the Carls had lost his hand the last time they came. Lost was the wrong word, maybe, since it got cut off with an axe. He'd been screaming loud just after, but now he was quiet, breathing soft and wheezy. They'd strapped the stump up with a rag and a belt, and now he was staring at it, with that look the wounded get sometimes. White and big-eyed, looking at his hacked-off wrist as if he couldn't understand what he was seeing. As if it was a constant surprise to him.

Dogman eased himself up slow, peering over the top of the fallen tree trunk. He could see the Flatheads, down in the woods. Sat there in the shadows. Waiting. He didn't like seeing 'em lurking down there. Shanka come at you until they're finished, or they run.

'What are they waiting for?' he hissed. 'When did bloody Flatheads learn to wait?'

'When did they learn to fight for Bethod?' growled Tul, wiping his sword clean. 'There's a lot that's changing, and none of it for the better.'

'When did anything change for the better?' snarled Dow from further down the line.

Dogman frowned. There was a new smell in his nose, like damp. There was something pale, down in the trees, getting paler while he watched. 'What is that? That mist?'

'Mist? Up here?' Dow chuckled harsh as a crow calling. 'This time of day? Hah! Hold on, though . . .' They could all see it now – a trace of white, clinging to the wet slope. Dogman swallowed. His mouth was dry. He was feeling uneasy, all of a sudden, and not just from the Shanka waiting down there. Something else. The mist was creeping up through the trees, curling round the trunks, rising while they watched. The Flatheads were starting to move, dim shapes shifting in the grey murk.

'Don't like this,' he heard Dow saying. 'This ain't natural.'

'Steady, lads!' Threetrees' deep voice. 'Steady, now!' Dogman took heart from that, but his heart didn't last long. He rocked back and forth, feeling sick.

'No, no,' whispered Shivers, his eyes sliding around like he was looking for a way out. Dogman could feel the hairs on his own arms rising, his skin prickling, his throat closing up tight. A nameless sort of a fear was taking him, flowing up the hillside along with the mist – creeping through the forest, swirling round the trees, sliding under the trunk they were using as cover.

'It's him,' whispered Shivers, his eyes open wide as a pair of boot-tops, squashing himself down like he was scared of being heard. 'It's him!'

'Who?' croaked Dogman.

Shivers just shook his head and pressed himself to the cold earth. The Dogman felt a powerful need to do the same, but he forced himself to rise up, forced himself to take a look over the tree. A Named Man, scared as a child in the dark, and not knowing why? Better to face it, he thought. Big mistake.

There was a shadow in the mist, too tall and too straight for a Shanka. A great, huge man, big as Tul. Bigger even. A giant. Dogman rubbed his sore eyes, thinking it must be some trick of the light in all that gloom, but it wasn't. He came on closer, this shadow, and he took on more shape, and more, and the clearer he got, the worse grew the fear.

He'd been long and far, the Dogman, all over the North, but he'd never seen so strange and unnatural a thing as this giant. One half of him was covered in great plates of black armour – studded and bolted, beaten and pointed, spiked and hammered and twisted metal. The other half was mostly bare, apart from the straps and belts and buckles that held the armour on. Bare foot, bare arm, bare chest, all bulging out with ugly slabs and cords of muscle. A mask was on his face, a mask of scarred black iron.

He came on closer, and he rose from the mist, and the Dogman saw the giant's skin was painted. Marked blue with tiny letters. Scrawled across with writing, every inch of him. No weapon, but he was no less terrible for that. He was more, if anything. He scorned to carry one, even on a battlefield.

'By the fucking dead,' breathed the Dogman, and his mouth hung wide with horror.

'Steady, lads,' growled Threetrees. 'Steady.' The old boy's voice was the only thing stopping the Dogman from running for it, and never coming back.

'It's him!' squealed one of the Carls, voice shrill as a girl's. 'It's the Feared!'

'Shut your fucking hole!' came Shivers' voice, 'We know what it is!'

'Arrows!' shouted Threetrees.

Dogman's hands were trembling as he took an aim on the giant. It was hard somehow, to do it, even from this distance. He had to make his hand let go the string, and then the arrow pinged off the armour and away into the trees, harmless. Grim's shot was better. His shaft sank clean into the giant's side, buried deep in his painted flesh. He seemed not even to notice. More arrows shot over from the Carls' bows. One hit him in the shoulder, another stuck right through his huge calf. The giant made not a sound. He came on, steady as the grass growing, and the mist, and the Flatheads, and the fear came with him.

'Fuck,' muttered Grim.

'It's a devil!' one of the Carls screeched. 'A devil from hell!' Dogman was starting to think the same thing. He felt the fear growing up all round him, felt the men starting to waver. He felt himself edging backwards, almost without thinking about it.

'Alright, now!' bellowed Threetrees, voice deep and steady as if he felt no fear at all. 'On the count of three! On the count of three, we charge!'

Dogman stared over as if the old boy had lost his reason. At least they had a tree to hide behind up here. He heard a couple of the Carls muttering, no doubt thinking much the same. They didn't much like the sound of this for a plan, charging down a hill into a great crowd of Shanka, some unnatural giant at the heart of 'em.

'You sure about this?' Dogman hissed.

Threetrees didn't even look at him. 'Best thing for a man to do when he's afeared is charge! Get the blood up, and turn the fear to fury. The ground's on our side, and we ain't waiting here for 'em!'

'You sure?'

'We're going,' said Threetrees, turning away.

'We're going,' growled Dow, glaring round at the Carls, daring 'em to back down.

'On three!' rumbled the Thunderhead.

'Uh,' said Grim. Dogman swallowed, still not sure whether he'd be going or not. Threetrees peered over the trunk, his mouth a hard, flat line, watching the figures in the mist, and the great big one in the midst of 'em, his hand down flat behind him to say wait. Waiting for the right distance. Waiting for the right time.

'Do I go on three?' whispered Shivers, 'or after three?'

Dogman shook his head. 'Don't hardly matter, as long as you go.' But his feet felt like they were two great stones.

'One!'

One already? Dogman looked over his shoulder, saw Cathil's body lying stretched out under his blanket near the dead fire. Should have made him feel angry maybe, but it only made him feel more scared. Fact was, he'd no wish to end up like her. He swallowed and turned away, clutched tight to the handle of his knife, to the grip of the sword he'd borrowed off the dead. Iron felt no fear. Good weapons, ready to do bloody work. He wished he was halfway as ready himself, but he'd done this before, and he knew no one was ever really ready. You don't have to be ready. You just have to go.

'Two!'

Almost time. He felt his eyes opening wide, his nose sucking in cold air, his skin tingling cold. He smelled men and sharp pine trees, Shanka and damp mist. He heard quick breath behind, slow footsteps down below, shouts from along the line, his own blood thumping in his veins. He saw every bit of everything, all going slow as dripping honey. Men moved around him, hard men with hard faces, shifting their weight, pushing forward against the fear and the mist, making ready. They were going to go, he'd no doubt left of it. They were all going to go. He felt the muscles in his legs begin to squeeze, pushing him up.

'Three!'

Threetrees was first over the trunk and the Dogman was just behind, men all round him charging, and the air full of their shouts and their fury and their fear, and he was running, and screaming, feet pounding and shaking his bones, breath and wind rushing, black trees and white sky crashing and wobbling, mist flying up at him and dark shapes inside the mist, waiting.

He swung his sword at one as he roared past and the blade chopped deep into it and threw it back, turned the Dogman half round and he went along, spinning, falling, shouting. The blade hacked deep into a Shanka's leg and snatched it off its feet, and Dogman spilled down the slope, slithering around in the slush, trying to right himself. The sounds of fighting were all round, muffled and strange. Men bellowing curses, and Shanka snarling, and the rattles and thuds of iron on iron and iron in flesh.

He spun about, sliding between the trees, not knowing where the next Flathead might come from, not knowing whether he might get a spear in his back any minute. He saw a shape in the murk and sprang forward at it, shouting as hard as he could. The mist seemed to lift away in front of him, and he slithered to a horrified stop, the sound rattling out in his throat, nearly falling over backwards in his hurry to get away.

The Feared was no more than five strides from him, bigger and more terrible than ever, broken arrows sticking from his tattooed flesh all over. Didn't help that he had a Carl round the neck, out at arm's length, kicking and struggling. The painted sinews in his forearm twisted and squirmed and the huge fingers tightened, and the Carl's eyes bulged, and his mouth opened and no sound came out. There was a crunch, and the giant tossed the corpse away like a rag and it turned over and over in the snow and the mud, head flopping about, and lay still.

The Feared stood, mist flowing round him, looking down at the Dogman from behind his black mask, and the Dogman looked back, halfway to pissing himself.

But some things have to be done. Better to do 'em, than to live with the fear of 'em. That's what Logen would have said. So the Dogman opened his mouth, and screamed as loud as he could, and he charged, swinging the borrowed sword over his head.

The giant lifted his great iron-plated arm and caught the blade. Metal clanged on metal and rattled the Dogman's teeth, tore the sword away and sent it spinning, but he stabbed with his knife at the same moment and slipped it under the giant's arm, ramming it right to the hilt in his tattooed side.

'Hah!' shouted the Dogman, but he didn't get long to celebrate. The Feared's huge arm flashed through the mist, caught him a backhand across the chest and flung him gurgling through the air. The woods reeled and a tree came out of nowhere, crashed into his back and sent him sprawling in the mud. He tried to get a breath and couldn't. Tried to roll over and couldn't. Pain crushed his ribs, like a great rock pressing on his chest.

He looked up, hands clutching at the mud, hardly enough breath in him even to groan. The Feared was walking to him, no rush. He reached down and pulled the knife out of his side. It looked like a toy between his huge finger and thumb. Like a tooth-pick. He flicked it away into the trees, a long drip of blood going with it. He lifted his great armoured foot, ready to stomp down on the Dogman's head and crush his skull like a nut on an anvil, and Dogman could only lie there, helpless with pain and fear as the great shadow fell across his face.

'You bastard!' And Threetrees came flying out of the trees, crashed into the giant's armoured hip with his shield and knocked him sideways, the huge metal boot squelching into the dirt just beside the Dogman's face and spattering him with mud. The old boy pressed in, hacking away at the Feared's bare side while he was off balance, snarling and cursing at him while the Dogman gasped and squirmed, trying to get up and only making it as far as sitting, back to the tree.

The giant threw his armoured fist hard enough to bring a house down, but Threetrees got round it and turned it off his shield, brought his sword up and over and knocked a fearsome dent in the Feared's mask, snapping his great head back and making him stagger, blood splattering from the mouth hole. The old boy pressed in quick and slashed hard across the plates on the giant's chest, blade striking sparks from the black iron and carving a great gash into the bare blue flesh beside it. A killing blow, no doubt, but only a few specks of blood flew off the swinging blade, and it left no wound at all.

The giant found his balance now, and he gave a great bellow that left Dogman trembling with fear. He set his huge foot behind him, lifted his massive arm and hurled it forward. It crashed into Threetrees' shield and ripped a chunk out of the edge, split the timbers and went on through, thudded into the old boy's shoulder and flung him groaning onto his back. The Feared pressed in on top of him, lifting his big blue fist up high. Threetrees snarled and stabbed his sword clean through his tattooed thigh right to the hilt. Dogman saw the point slide bloody out the back of his leg, but it didn't even slow him. That great hand dropped down and crunched into Threetrees' ribs with a sound like dry sticks breaking.

Dogman groaned, clawing at the dirt, but his chest was on fire and he couldn't get up, and he couldn't do anything but watch. The Feared lifted up his other fist now, covered in black iron. He lifted it up slow and careful, waited up high, then brought it whistling down, smashed it into Threetrees' other side and crushed him sighing into the dirt. The great arm went up again, red blood on blue knuckles.

And a black line came out of the mist and stabbed into the Feared's armpit, shoving him over sideways. Shivers, with a spear, jabbing at the giant and shouting, pushing him across the slope. The Feared rolled and slithered up, faked a step back and flicked out his hand quick as a massive snake, slapped Shivers away like a man might swat a fly, squawking and kicking into the mist.

Before the giant could follow him there was a roar like thunder and Tul's sword crashed into his armoured shoulder and flung him down on one knee. Now Dow came out of the mist, slashed a great chunk out of his leg from behind. Shivers was up again, snarling and jabbing with his spear, and the three of 'em seemed to have the giant penned in.

He should've been dead, however big he was. The wounds Threetrees, and Shivers, and Dow had given him, he should have been mud. Instead he rose up again, six arrows and Threetrees' sword stuck through his flesh, and he let go a roar from behind his iron mask that made Dogman tremble to his toes. Shivers fell back on his arse, going white as milk. Tul blinked and faltered and let his sword drop. Even Black Dow took a step away.

The Feared reached down and took hold of the hilt of Threetrees' sword. He slid it out from his leg and let it drop bloody in the dirt at his feet. It left no wound behind. No wound at all. Then he turned and sprang away into the gloom, and the mist closed in behind him, and the Dogman heard the sounds of him crashing away through the trees, and he was never so glad to see the back of anything.

'Come 'ere!' Dow screamed, making ready to tear down the slope after him, but Tul got in his way with one big hand held up.

'You're going nowhere. We don't know how many Shanka there are down there. We can kill that thing another day.'

'Out o' my way, big lad!'

'No.'

Dogman rolled forward, wincing all the way at the pain in his chest, started clawing his way up the slope. The mist was already spilling back, leaving the cold clear air behind. Grim was coming down the other way, bow string drawn back with an arrow nocked. There were a lot of corpses in the mud and the snow. Shanka mostly, and a couple of Carls.

Seemed to take the Dogman an age to drag himself up to Threetrees. The old boy was lying on his back in the mud, one arm lying still with his broken shield strapped to it. Air was snorting in shallow through his nose, bubbling back out bloody from his mouth. His eyes rolled down to Dogman as he crawled up next to him, and he reached out and grabbed a hold of his shirt, pulled him down, hissing in his ear through clenched tight, bloody teeth.

'Listen to me, Dogman! Listen!'

'What, chief?' croaked Dogman, hardly able to talk for the pain in his chest. He waited, and he listened, and nothing came. Threetrees' eyes were wide open, staring up at the branches. A drop of water splattered on his cheek, ran down into his bloody beard. Nothing else.

'Back to the mud,' said Grim, face hanging slack as old cobwebs.

West chewed at his fingernails as he watched General Kroy and his staff riding up the road, a group of dark-dressed men on dark horses, solemn as a procession of undertakers. The snow had stopped, for now, but the sky was angry black, the light so bad it felt like evening, and an icy wind was blowing through the command post making the fabric of the tent snap and rustle. West's borrowed time was almost done.

He felt a sudden impulse, almost overpowering, to turn and run. An impulse so ludicrous that he immediately had another, equally inappropriate, to burst out laughing. Luckily, he was able to stop himself from doing either. Lucky to stop himself laughing, at least. This was far from a laughing matter. As the clattering hooves came closer, he was left wondering whether the idea of running was such a foolish one after all.

Kroy pulled his black charger up savagely and climbed down, jerked his uniform smooth, adjusted his sword belt, turned sharply and came on towards the tent. West intercepted him, hoping to get the first word in and buy a few more moments. 'General Kroy, well done, sir, your division fought with great tenacity!'

'Of course they did, *Colonel West*.' Kroy sneered the name as though he were delivering a mortal insult, his staff gathering into a menacing half circle behind him.

'And might I ask our situation?'

'Our *situation*?' snarled the General. 'Our situation is that the Northmen are driven off, but not routed. We gave them a mauling, in the end, but my units were fought out, every man. Too weary to pursue. The enemy have been able to withdraw across the fords, thanks to Poulder's cowardice! I mean to see him cashiered in disgrace! I mean to see him hanged for treason! I will see it done, on my honour!' He glowered around the headquarters while his men muttered angrily amongst themselves. 'Where is Lord Marshal Burr? I demand to see the Lord Marshal!'

'Of course, if you could just give me . . .' West's words were smothered by the mounting noise of more rushing hooves, and a second group of riders careered around the side of the Marshal's tent. Who else but General Poulder, accompanied by his own enormous staff. A cart pulled into the headquarters along with them, crowding the narrow space with beasts and men. Poulder vaulted down from his saddle and hastened through the dirt. His hair was in disarray, his jaw was locked tight, there was a long scratch down his cheek. His crimson entourage followed behind him: steels rattling, gold braid flapping, faces flushed.

'Poulder!' hissed Kroy. 'You've some nerve showing your face in front of me! Some nerve! The only damn nerve you've shown all day!'

'How dare you!' screeched Poulder. 'I demand an apology! Apologise at once!'

'Apologise? Me, apologise? Hah! You'll be the one saying sorry, I'll see to it! The plan was for you to come in from the left wing! We were hard pressed for more than two hours!'

'Almost three hours, sir,' chipped in one of Kroy's staff, unhelpfully.

'Three hours, damn it! If that is not cowardice I fumble for the definition!'

'*Cowardice?*' shrieked Poulder. A couple of his staff went as far as to place their hands on their steels. 'You will apologise to me immediately! My division came under a brutal and sustained attack upon our flank! I was obliged to lead a charge myself! On foot!' And he thrust forward his cheek and indicated the scratch with one gloved finger. 'It was *we* who did all the fighting! *We* who won the victory here today!'

'Damn you, Poulder, you did nothing! The victory belongs to *my* men alone! An attack? An attack from what? From animals of the forest?'

'Ah-ha! Exactly so! Show him!'

One of Poulder's staff ripped back the oilskin on the cart, displaying what seemed at first to be a heap of bloody rags. He wrinkled up his nose and shoved it forward. The thing flopped off onto the ground, rolled onto its back and stared up at the sky with beetling black eyes. A huge, misshapen jaw hung open, long, sharp teeth sticking every which way. Its skin was a greyish brown colour, rough and calloused, its nose was an ill-formed stub. Its skull was flattened and hairless with a heavy ridge of brow and a small, receding forehead. One of its arms was short and muscular, the other much longer and slightly bent, both ending in claw-like hands. The whole creature seemed lumpen, twisted, primitive. West gawped down at it, open-mouthed.

Plainly, it was not human.

'There!' squealed Poulder in triumph. 'Now tell us my division didn't fight! There were hundreds of these . . . these creatures out there! Thousands, and they fight like mad things! We only just managed to hold our ground, and it's damn lucky for you that we did! I demand!' he frothed, 'I demand!' he ranted, '*I demand*!' he shrieked, face turning purple, 'an apology!'

Kroy's eyes twitched with incomprehension, with anger, with frustration. His lips twisted, his jaw worked, his fists clenched. Clearly there was no entry in the rule book for a situation such as this. He rounded on West.

'I demand to see Marshal Burr!' he snarled.

'As do I!' screeched Poulder shrilly, not to be outdone.

'The Lord Marshal is . . .' West's lips moved silently. He had no ideas left. No strategies, no ruses, no schemes. 'He is . . .' There would be no retreat across the fords for him. He was finished. More than likely he would end up in a penal colony himself. 'He is—'

'I am here.'

And to West's profound amazement, Burr was standing in the entrance to his tent. Even in the half-light, it seemed obvious that he was terribly ill. His face was ashen pale and there was a sheen of sweat across his forehead. His eyes were sunken and ringed with black. His lip quivered, his legs were unsteady, he clutched at the tent-pole beside him for support. West could see a dark stain down the front of his uniform that looked very much like blood.

'I am afraid I have been . . . somewhat unwell during the battle,' he croaked. 'Something I ate, perhaps.' His hand trembled on the pole and Jalenhorm lurked near his shoulder, ready to catch him if he fell, but by some superhuman effort of will the Lord Marshal stayed on his feet. West glanced nervously at the angry gathering, wondering what they might make of this walking corpse. But the two Generals were far too caught up in their own feud to pay any attention to that.

'Lord Marshal, I must protest about General Poulder—'

'Sir, I demand that General Kroy apologise—'

The best form of defence seemed to West to be an immediate attack. 'It would be traditional!' he cut in at the top of his voice, 'for us first to congratulate our commanding officer on his victory!' He began to clap, slowly and deliberately. Pike and Jalenhorm joined him without delay. Poulder and Kroy exchanged an icy glance, then they too raised their hands.

'May I be the first to—'

'The *very* first to congratulate you, Lord Marshal!'

Their staffs joined in, and others around the tent, and then more further away, and soon a rousing cheer was going up.

'A cheer for Lord Marshal Burr!'

'The Lord Marshal!'

'Victory!'

Burr himself twitched and quivered, one hand clutched to his stomach, his face a mask of anguish. West slunk backwards, away from the attention, away from the glory. He had not the slightest interest in it. That had been close, he knew, impossibly close. His hands were trembling, his mouth tasted sour, his vision was swimming. He could still hear Poulder and Kroy, already arguing again, like a pair of furious ducks quacking.

'We must move on Dunbrec immediately, a swift assault while they are unwary and—'

'Pah! Foolishness! The defences are too strong. We must surround the walls and prepare for a lengthy—'

'Nonsense! My division could carry the place tomorrow!'

'Rubbish! We must dig in! Siegecraft is my particular area of expertise!'

And on, and on. West rubbed his fingertips in his ears, trying to block out the voices as he stumbled through the churned-up mud. A few paces further on and he clambered around a rocky outcrop, pressed his back to it and slowly slid down. Slid down until he was sitting hunched in the snow, hugging his knees, the way he used to do when he was a child, and his father was angry.

Down in the valley, in the gathering gloom, he could see men moving over the battlefield. Already starting to dig the graves.

A Fitting Punishment

It had been raining, not long ago, but it had stopped. The paving of the Square of Marshals was starting to dry, the flagstones light round the edges, dark with damp in the centres. A ray of watery sun had finally broken through the clouds and was glinting on the bright metal of the chains hanging from the frame, on the blades, and hooks, and pincers of the instruments on their rack. *Fine weather for it, I suppose. It should be quite the event. Unless your name is Tulkis, of course, then it might be one you'd rather miss.*

The crowd were certainly anticipating a thrill. The wide square was full of their chattering, a heady mixture of excitement and anger, happiness and hate. The public area was packed shoulder to shoulder, and still filling, but there was ample room here in the government enclosure, fenced in and well guarded right in front of the scaffold. *The great and the good must have the best view, after all.* Over the shoulders of the row in front he could see the chairs where the members of the Closed Council were sitting. If he went up on his toes, an operation he dared not try too often, he could just see the Arch Lector's shock of white hair, stirred gracefully by the breeze.

He glanced sideways at Ardee. She was frowning grimly up at the scaffold, chewing slowly at her lower lip. *To think. The time was I would take young women to the finest establishments in the city, to the pleasure gardens on the hill, to concerts at the Hall of Whispers, or straight to my quarters, of course, if I thought I could manage it. Now I take them to executions.* He felt the tiniest of smiles at the corner of his mouth. *Ah well, things change.*

'How will it be done?' she asked him.

'He'll be hung and emptied.'

'What?'

'He will be lifted up by chains around his wrists and neck, not quite tight enough to kill him through strangulation. Then he will be opened with a blade, and gradually disembowelled. His entrails will be displayed to the crowd.'

She swallowed. 'He'll be alive?'

'Possibly. Hard to say. Depends whether the executioners do their job properly. Anyway, he won't live long.' *Not without his guts.*

'Seems . . . extreme.'

'It is meant to be. It was the most savage punishment our savage forebears could dream up. Reserved for those who attempt harm to the royal person. Not carried out, I understand, for some eighty years.'

'Hence the crowd.'

Glokta shrugged. 'It's a curiosity, but you always get a good showing for an execution. People love to see death. It reminds them that however mean, however low, however horrible their lives become . . . at least they have one.'

Glokta felt a tap on his shoulder and looked round, with some pain, to see Severard's masked face hovering just behind him. 'I dealt with that thing. That thing about Vitari.'

'Huh. And?'

Severard's eyes slid suspiciously sideways to Ardee, then he leaned forward to whisper in Glokta's ear. 'I followed her to a house, down below Galt's Green, near the market there.'

'I know it. And?'

'I took a peek in through a window.'

Glokta raised an eyebrow. 'You're enjoying this, aren't you? What was in there?'

'Children.'

'Children?' muttered Glokta.

'Three little children. Two girls and a boy. And what colour do you suppose their hair was?'

You don't say. 'Not flaming red, by any chance?'

'Just like their mother.'

'She's got children?' Glokta licked thoughtfully at his gums. 'Who'd have thought it?'

'I know. I thought that bitch had a block of ice for a cunt.'

That explains why she was so keen to get back from the South. All that time, she had three little ones waiting. The mothering instinct. How terribly touching. He wiped some wet from beneath his stinging left eye. 'Well done, Severard, this could be useful. What about that other thing? The Prince's guard?'

Severard lifted his mask for a moment and scratched underneath it, eyes darting nervously around. 'That's a strange one. I tried but . . . it seems he's gone missing.'

'Missing?'

'I spoke to his family. They haven't seen him since the day before the Prince died.'

Glokta frowned. 'The day before?' *But he was there . . . I saw him.* 'Get Frost, and Vitari too. Get me a list of everyone who was in the palace that night. Every lord, every servant, every soldier. I am getting to the truth of this.' *One way or another.*

'Did Sult tell you to?'

Glokta looked round sharply. 'He didn't tell me not to. Just get it done.'

Severard muttered something, but his words were lost as the noise of the crowd suddenly swelled in a wave of angry jeering. Tulkis was being led out onto the scaffold. He shuffled forwards, chains rattling round his ankles. He did not cry or wail, nor did he yell in defiance. He simply looked drawn, and sad, and in some pain. There were light bruises round his face, tracks of angry red spots down his arms and legs, across his chest. *Impossible to use hot needles without leaving some marks, but he looks well, considering.* He was naked aside from a cloth tied round his waist. *To spare the delicate sensibilities of the ladies present. Watching a man's entrails spilling out is excellent entertainment, but the sight of his cock, well, that would be obscene.*

A clerk stepped to the front of the scaffold and started reading out the prisoner's name, the nature of the charge, the terms of his confession and his punishment, but even at this distance he could hardly be heard for the sullen muttering of the crowd, punctuated by an occasional furious scream. Glokta grimaced and worked his leg slowly back and forth, trying to loosen the cramping muscles.

The masked executioners stepped forward and took hold of the prisoner, moving with careful skill. They pulled a black bag over the envoy's head, snapped manacles shut around his neck, his wrists, his ankles. Glokta could see the canvas moving in and out in front of his mouth. *The desperate last breaths. Does he pray, now? Does he curse and rage? Who can know, and what difference can it make?*

They hoisted him up into the air, spreadeagled on the frame. Most of his weight was on his arms. Enough on the collar round his neck to choke him, not quite enough to kill. He struggled somewhat, of course. *Entirely natural. An animal instinct to climb, to writhe, to wriggle out and breathe free. An instinct that cannot be resisted.* One of the executioners went to the rack, pulled out a heavy blade, displayed it to the crowd with a flourish, the thin sun flashing briefly on its edge. He turned his back on the audience, and began to cut.

The crowd went silent. Almost deathly still, aside from the odd hushed whisper. It was a punishment that brooked no calling out. A punishment which demanded awestruck silence. A punishment to which there could be no response other than a horrified, fascinated staring. *That is its design.* So there was only silence, and perhaps the wet gurgling of the prisoner's breath. *Since the collar makes screaming impossible.*

'A fitting punishment, I suppose,' whispered Ardee as she watched the envoy's bloody gut slithering out of his body, 'for the murderer of the Crown Prince.'

Glokta bowed his head to whisper in her ear. 'I'm reasonably sure that he did not kill anyone. I suspect he is guilty of nothing more than being a courageous man, who came to us speaking truth and holding out the hand of peace.'

Her eyes widened. 'Then why hang him?'

'Because the Crown Prince has been murdered. Someone has to hang.'

'But . . . who really killed Raynault?'

'Someone who wants no peace between Gurkhul and the Union. Someone who wants the war between us to grow, and spread, and never end.'

'Who could want that?'

Glokta said nothing. *Who indeed?*

You don't have to admire that Fallow character, but he can certainly pick a good chair. Glokta settled back into the soft upholstery with a sigh, stretching his feet out towards the fire, working his aching ankles round and round in clicking circles.

Ardee did not seem quite so comfortable. *But then this morning's diversion was hardly a comforting spectacle.* She stood frowning out of the window, thoughtful, one hand pulling nervously at a strand of hair. 'I need a drink.' She went to the cabinet and opened it, took out a bottle and a glass. She paused, and looked round. 'Aren't you going to tell me it's a little early in the day?'

Glokta shrugged. 'You know what the time is.'

'I need something, after that . . .'

'Then have something. You don't need to explain yourself to me. I'm not your brother.'

She jerked her head round and gave him a hard look, opened her mouth as though about to speak, then she shoved the bottle angrily away and the glass after it, snapped the doors of the cabinet shut. 'Happy?'

He shrugged. 'About as close as I get, since you ask.'

Ardee dumped herself into a chair opposite, staring sourly down at one shoe. 'What happens now?'

'Now? Now we will delight each other with humorous observations for a lazy hour, then a stroll into town?' He winced. 'Slowly, of course. Then a late lunch, perhaps, I was thinking of—'

'I meant about the succession.'

'Oh,' muttered Glokta. 'That.' He reached round and dragged a cushion into a better position, then stretched out further with a satisfied grunt. *One could almost pretend, sitting in this warm and comfortable room, in such attractive and agreeable company, that one still had some kind of life.* He nearly had a smile on his face as he continued. 'There will be a vote in Open Council. Meaning, I have no doubt, that there will be an orgy of blackmail, bribery, corruption and betrayal. A carnival of deal-making, alliance-breaking, intrigue and murder. A merry dance of fixing, of rigging, of threats and of promises. It will go on until the king dies. *Then* there will be a vote in Open Council.'

Ardee gave her crooked smile. 'Even commoners' daughters are saying the king cannot live long.'

'Well, well,' and Glokta raised his eyebrows. 'Once the commoners' daughters start saying a thing, you know it must be true.'

'Who are the favourites?'

'Why don't you tell me who the favourites are?'

'Alright, then, I will.' She sat back, one fingertip rubbing thoughtfully at her jaw. 'Brock, of course.'

'Of course.'

'Then Barezin, I suppose, Heugen, and Isher.'

Glokta nodded. *She's no fool.* 'They're the big four. Who else, do we think?'

'I suppose Meed sunk his chances when he lost to the Northmen. What about Skald, the Lord Governor of Starikland?'

'Very good. You could get long odds for him, but he'd be on the sheet—'

'And if the Midderland candidates split the vote enough—'

'Who knows what could happen?' They grinned at each other for a moment. 'At this point it really could be anyone,' he said. 'And then any illegitimate children of the king might also be considered . . .'

'Bastards? Are there any?'

Glokta raised an eyebrow. 'I believe I could point out a couple.' She laughed, and he congratulated himself on it. 'There are rumours, of course, as there always are. Carmee dan Roth, have you heard of her? A lady-at-court, and reckoned an exceptional beauty. She was quite a favourite with the king at one point, years ago. She disappeared suddenly and was later said to have died, perhaps in childbirth, but who can say? People love to gossip, and beautiful young women will die from time to time, without ever bearing a royal bastard.'

'Oh, it's true, it's true!' Ardee fluttered her eyelashes and pretended to swoon. 'We certainly are a sickly breed.'

'You are, my dear, you are. Looks are a curse. I thank my stars every day to have been cured of that.' And he leered his toothless grin at her. 'Members of the Open Council are flooding to the city in their scores, and I daresay many of them have never set foot in the Lords' Round in their lives. They smell power, and they want to be a part of it. They want to get something out of it, while there's something to be had. It might well be the only time in ten generations that the nobles get to make a real decision.'

'But what a decision,' muttered Ardee, shaking her head.

'Indeed. The race could be lengthy and the competition near the front will be savage.' *If not to say lethal.* 'I would not like to discount the possibility of some outsider coming up at the last moment. Someone without enemies. A compromise candidate.'

'What about the Closed Council?'

'They're forbidden from standing, of course, to ensure impartiality.' He snorted. 'Impartiality! What they passionately want is to foist some nobody on the nation. Someone they can dominate and manipulate, so they can continue their private feuds uninterrupted.'

'Is there such a candidate?'

'Anyone with a vote is an option, so in theory there are hundreds, but of course the Closed Council cannot agree on one, and so they scramble with scant dignity behind the stronger candidates, changing their loyalties day by day, hoping to insure their futures, doing their best to stay in office. Power has shifted so quickly from them to the nobles their heads are spinning. And some of them will roll one way or another, you may depend on that.'

'Will yours roll, do you think?' asked Ardee, looking up at him from under her dark brows.

Glokta licked slowly at his gums. 'If Sult's does, it may well be that mine will follow.'

'I hope not. You've been kind to me. Kinder than anyone else. Kinder than I deserve.' It was a trick of utter frankness that he had seen her use before, but still an oddly disarming one.

'Nonsense,' mumbled Glokta, wriggling his shoulders in the chair, suddenly awkward. *Kindness, honesty, comfortable living rooms . . . Colonel Glokta would have known what to say, but I am a stranger here.* He was still groping for a reply when a sharp knocking echoed in the hallway. 'Are you expecting anyone?'

'Who would I be expecting? My entire acquaintance is here in the room.'

Glokta strained to listen as the front door opened, but could hear nothing more than vague muttering. The door handle turned and the maid poked her head into the room.

'Begging your pardon, but there is a visitor for the Superior.'

'Who?' snapped Glokta. *Severard, with news of Prince Raynault's guard? Vitari, with some message from the Arch Lector? Some new problem that needs solving? Some new set of questions to ask?*

'He says his name is Mauthis.'

Glokta felt the whole left side of his face twitching. *Mauthis?* He had not thought about him for some time, but an image of the gaunt banker sprang instantly into his mind now, holding out the receipt, neatly and precisely, for Glokta to sign. *A receipt for a gift of one million marks. It may be that in the future, a representative of the banking house of Valint and Balk will come to you requesting . . . favours.*

Ardee was frowning over at him. 'Something wrong?'

'No, nothing,' he croaked, striving to keep his voice from sounding strangled. 'An old associate. Could you give me the room for a moment? I need to talk with this gentleman.'

'Of course.' She got up and started to walk to the door, her dress swishing on the carpet behind her. She paused halfway, looked over her shoulder, biting her lip. She went to the cabinet and opened it, pulled out the bottle and the glass. She shrugged her shoulders. 'I need something.'

'Don't we all,' whispered Glokta at her back as she went out.

Mauthis stepped through the door a moment later. The same sharp bones in his face, the same cold eyes in deep sockets. There was something changed in his demeanour, however. *A certain nervousness. A certain anxiety, perhaps?*

'Why, Master Mauthis, what an almost unbearable honour it is to—'

'You may dispense with the pleasantries, Superior.' His voice was shrill and grating as rusty hinges. 'I have no ego to bruise. I prefer to speak plainly.'

'Very well, what can I—'

'My employers, the banking house of Valint and Balk, are not pleased with your line of investigation.'

Glokta's mind raced. 'My line of investigation into what?'

'Into the murder of Crown Prince Raynault.'

'That investigation is concluded. I assure you that I have no—'

'Speaking plainly, Superior, they know. It would be easier for you to assume that they know everything. They usually will. The murder has been solved, with impressive speed and competence, I may say. My employers are delighted with the results. The guilty man has been brought to justice. No one will benefit from your delving any deeper into this unfortunate business.'

That is speaking very plainly indeed. But why would Valint and Balk mind my questions? They gave me money to frustrate the Gurkish, now they seem to object to my investigating a Gurkish plot? It makes no sense . . . unless the killer did not come from the South at all. Unless Prince Raynault's murderers are much closer to home . . .

'There are some loose ends that need to be tied,' Glokta managed to mumble. 'There is no need for your employers to be angry—'

Mauthis took a step forward. His forehead was glistening with sweat, though the room was not hot. 'They are not angry, Superior. You could not have known that they would be displeased. Now you know. Were you to continue with this line of investigation, knowing that they are displeased . . . then they would be angry.' He leaned down towards Glokta and almost whispered. 'Please allow me to tell you, Superior, as one piece on the board to another. We do not want them angry.' There was a strange note in his voice. *He does not threaten me. He pleads.*

'Are you implying,' Glokta murmured, scarcely moving his lips, 'that they would inform Arch Lector Sult of their little gift to the defence of Dagoska?'

'That is the very least of what they would do.' Mauthis' expression was unmistakable. *Fear.* Fear, in that emotionless mask of a face. Something about it left a certain bitterness on Glokta's tongue, a certain coldness down his back, a certain tightness in his throat. It was a feeling he remembered, from long ago. It was the closest he had come to being afraid, himself, in a long time. *They have me. Utterly and completely. I knew it when I signed. That was the price, and I had no choice but to pay.*

Glokta swallowed. 'You may tell your employers that there will be no further enquiries.'

Mauthis closed his eyes for a moment and blew out with evident relief. 'I am delighted to carry that message back to them. Good day.' And he turned and left Glokta alone in Ardee's living room, staring at the door, and wondering what had just happened.

The Abode of Stones

The prow of the boat crunched hard into the rocky beach and stones groaned and scraped along the underside. Two of the oarsmen floundered out into the washing surf and dragged the boat a few steps further. Once it was firmly grounded they hurried back in as though the water caused intense pain. Jezal could not entirely blame them. The island at the edge of the World, the ultimate destination of their journey, the place called Shabulyan, had indeed a most forbidding appearance.

A vast mound of stark and barren rock, the cold waves clutching at its sharp promontories and clawing at its bare beaches. Above rose jagged cliffs and slopes of treacherous scree, piled steeply upwards into a menacing mountain, looming black against the dark sky.

'Care to come ashore?' asked Bayaz of the sailors.

The four oarsmen showed no sign of moving, and their Captain slowly shook his head. 'We have heard bad things of this island,' he grunted in common so heavily accented it was barely intelligible. 'They say it is cursed. We will wait for you here.'

'We may be some time.'

'We will wait.'

Bayaz shrugged. 'Wait, then.' He stepped from the boat and waded through knee-high breakers. Slowly and somewhat reluctantly the rest of the party followed him through the icy sea and up onto the beach.

It was a bleak and blasted place, a place fit only for stones and cold water. Waves foamed greedily up the shore and sucked jealously back out through the shingle. A pitiless wind cut across this wasteland and straight through Jezal's wet trousers, whipping his hair in his eyes and chilling him to the marrow. It snatched away any trace of excitement he might have felt at reaching the end of their journey. It found chinks and holes in the boulders and made them sing, and sigh, and wail in a mournful choir.

There was precious little vegetation. Some colourless grass, ill with salt, some thorny bushes more dead than alive. A few clumps of withered trees, higher up away from the sea, clung desperately to the unyielding stone, curved and bent over in the direction of the wind as though they might be torn away at any moment. Jezal felt their pain.

'A charming spot!' he shouted, his words flying off into the gale as soon as they left his lips. 'If you are an enthusiast for rocks!'

'Where does the wise man hide a stone?' Bayaz hurled back at him. 'Among a thousand stones! Among a million!'

There certainly was no shortage of stones here. Boulders, rocks, pebbles and gravel also were in abundant supply. It was the profound lack of anything else that rendered the place so singularly unpleasant. Jezal glanced back over his shoulder, feeling a sudden stab of panic at the notion of the four oarsmen shoving the boat back out to sea and leaving them marooned.

But they were still where they had been, their skiff rocking gently near the beach. Beyond them, on the churning ocean, Cawneil's ill-made tub of a ship sat at anchor, its sails lowered, its mast a black line against the troubled sky, moving slowly back and forward with the stirring of the uneasy waves.

'We need to find somewhere out of the wind!' Logen bellowed.

'Is there anywhere out of the wind in this bloody place?' Jezal shouted back.

'There'll have to be! We need a fire!'

Longfoot pointed up towards the cliffs. 'Perhaps up there we might find a cave, or a sheltered spot. I will lead you!'

They clambered up the beach, first sliding in the shingle, then hopping from teetering rock to rock. The edge of the World hardly seemed worth all the effort, as far as final destinations went. They could have found cold stone and cold water in plenty without ever leaving the North. Logen had a bad feeling about this barren place, but there was no point in saying so. He'd had a bad feeling for the last ten years. Call on this spirit, find this Seed, and then away, and quickly. What then, though? Back to the North? Back to Bethod, and his sons, racks full of scores and rivers of bad blood? Logen winced. None of that held much appeal. Better to do it, than to live in fear of it, his father would have said, but then his father said all kinds of things, and a lot of them weren't much use.

He looked over at Ferro, and she looked back. She didn't frown, she didn't smile. He'd never been much at understanding women, of course, or anyone else, but Ferro was some new kind of riddle. She acted just as cold and angry by day as she ever had, but most nights now she still seemed to find her way under his blanket. He didn't understand it and he didn't dare ask. The sad fact was, she was about the best thing he'd had in his life for a long time. He puffed his cheeks out and scratched his head. That didn't say much for his life, now he thought about it.

They found a kind of cave at the base of the cliffs. More of a hollow really, in the lee of two great boulders, where the wind didn't blast quite so strongly. Not much of a place for a conversation, but the island was a wasteland and Logen saw little chance of finding a better. You have to be realistic, after all.

Ferro took her sword to a stunted tree nearby and soon they had enough sticks to make an effort at a flame. Logen hunched over and fumbled the tinderbox out with numb fingers. Draughts blew in around the rocks and the wood was damp, but after much cursing and fumbling with the flint he finally managed to light a fire fit for the purpose. They huddled in around it.

'Bring out the box,' said Bayaz, and Logen hauled the heavy thing out from his pack and set it down next to Ferro with a grunt. Bayaz felt around its edge with his fingertips, found some hidden catch and the lid lifted silently. There were a set of metal coils underneath, pointing in from all sides to leave a space the size of Logen's fist.

'What are they for?' he asked.

'To keep what is inside still and well-cushioned.'

'It needs to be cushioned?'

'Kanedias thought so.' That answer did not make Logen feel any better. 'Place it inside as soon as you are able,' said the Magus, turning to Ferro. 'We do not wish to be exposed to it for longer than we must. It is best that you all keep your distance.' And he ushered the others back with his palms. Luthar and Longfoot nearly scrambled over each other in their eagerness to get away, but Quai's eyes were fixed on the preparations and he scarcely moved.

Logen sat cross-legged in front of the flickering fire, feeling the weight of worry in his stomach growing steadily heavier. He was starting to regret ever getting involved with this business, but it was a bit late now for second thoughts. 'Something to offer them will help,' he said, looking round, and found Bayaz already holding a metal flask out. Logen unscrewed the cap and took a sniff. The smell of strong spirits greeted his nostrils like a sorely missed lover. 'You had this all the time?'

Bayaz nodded. 'For this very purpose.'

'Wish I'd known. I could've put it to good use more than once.'

'You can put it to good use now.'

'Not quite the same thing.' Logen tipped the flask up and took a mouthful, resisted a powerful urge to swallow, puffed out his cheeks and blew it out in a mist over the fire, sending up a gout of flame.

'And now?' asked Bayaz.

'Now we wait. We wait until—'

'I am here, Ninefingers.' A voice like the wind through the rocks, like the stones falling from the cliffs, like the sea draining through the gravel. The spirit loomed over them in their shallow cave among the stones, a moving pile of grey rock as tall as two men, casting no shadow.

Logen raised his eyebrows. The spirits never answered promptly, if they bothered to answer at all. 'That was quick.'

'I have been waiting.'

'A long time, I reckon.' The spirit nodded. 'Well, er, we've come for—'

'For that thing that the sons of Euz entrusted to me. There must be desperate business in the world of men for you to seek it out.'

Logen swallowed. 'When isn't there?'

'Do you see anything?' Jezal whispered behind him.

'Nothing,' replied Longfoot. 'It is indeed a most remarkable—'

'Shut your mouths!' snarled Bayaz over his shoulder.

The spirit loomed down close over him. 'This is the First of the Magi?'

'It is,' said Logen, keeping the talk to the point.

'He is shorter than Juvens. I do not like his look.'

'What does it say?' snapped Bayaz impatiently, staring into the air well to the left of the spirit.

Logen scratched his face. 'It says that Juvens was tall.'

'Tall? What of it? Get what we came for and let us be gone!'

'He is impatient,' rumbled the spirit.

'We've come a long way. He has Juvens' staff.'

The spirit nodded. 'The dead branch is familiar to me. I am glad. I have held this thing for long winters, and it has been a heavy weight to carry. Now I will sleep.'

'Good idea. If you could—'

'I will give it to the woman.'

The spirit dug its hand into its stony stomach and Logen shuffled back warily. The fist emerged, and something was clutched inside, and he felt himself shiver as he saw it.

'Hold your hands out,' he muttered to Ferro.

Jezal gave an involuntary gasp and scrambled away as the thing dropped down into Ferro's waiting palms, raising an arm to shield his face, his mouth hanging open with horror. Bayaz stared, eyes wide. Quai craned eagerly forward. Logen grimaced and rocked back. Longfoot scrambled almost all the way out of the hollow. For a long moment all six of them stared at the dark object in Ferro's hands, no one moving, no one speaking, no sound except for the keening wind. There it was, before them. That thing which they had come so far, and braved so many dangers to find. That thing which Glustrod dug from the deep earth long years ago. That thing which had made a blasted ruin of the greatest city in the world.

The Seed. The Other Side, made flesh. The very stuff of magic.

Then Ferro slowly began to frown. 'This is it?' she asked doubtfully. 'This is the thing that will turn Shaffa to dust?'

It did, in fact, now that Jezal was overcoming the shock of its sudden appearance, look like nothing more than a stone. A chunk of unremarkable grey rock the size of a big fist. No sense of unearthly danger washed from it. No deadly power was evident. No withering rays or stabs of lightning shot forth. It did, in fact, look like nothing more than a stone.

Bayaz blinked. He shuffled closer, on his hands and knees. He peered down at the object in Ferro's palms. He licked his lips, lifting his hand ever so slowly while Jezal watched, his heart pounding in his ears. Bayaz touched the rock with his little finger tip then jerked it instantly back. He did not suddenly wither and expire. He probed it once more with his finger. There was no thunderous detonation. He pressed his palm upon it. He closed his thick fingers round it. He lifted it up. And still, it looked like nothing more than a stone.

The First of the Magi stared down at the thing in his hand, his eyes growing wider and wider. 'This is not it,' he whispered, his lip trembling. 'This is just a stone!'

There was a stunned silence. Jezal stared at Logen, and the Northman gazed back, scarred face slack with confusion. Jezal stared at Longfoot, and the Navigator could only shrug his bony shoulders. Jezal stared at Ferro, and he watched her frown grow harder and harder. 'Just a stone?' she muttered.

'Not it?' hissed Quai.

'Then . . .' The meaning of Bayaz' words was only just starting to sink into Jezal's mind. 'I came all this way . . . for nothing?' A sudden gust blew up, snuffing out the miserable tongue of flame and blowing grit in his face.

'Perhaps there is some mistake,' ventured Longfoot. 'Perhaps there is another spirit, perhaps there is another—'

'No mistake,' said Logen, firmly shaking his head.

'But . . .' Quai's eyes were bulging from his ashen face. 'But . . . how?'

Bayaz ignored him, muscles working on the side of his head. 'Kanedias. His hand is in this. He found some way to trick his brothers, and switch this lump of nothing for the Seed, and keep it for himself. Even in death, the Maker denies me!'

'Just a stone?' growled Ferro.

'I gave up my chance to fight for my country,' murmured Jezal, indignation starting to flicker up in his chest, 'and I slogged hundreds of miles across the wasteland, and I was beaten, and broken, and left scarred . . . for nothing?'

'The Seed.' Quai's pale lips were curling back from his teeth, his breath snorting fast through his nose. 'Where is it? Where?'

'If I knew that,' barked his master, 'do you suppose we would be sitting here on this forsaken island, bantering with spirits for a chunk of worthless rock?' And he lifted his arm and dashed the stone furiously onto the ground. It cracked open and split into fragments, and they bounced, and tumbled, and clattered down among a hundred others, a thousand others, a million others the same.

'It's not here.' Logen shook his head sadly. 'Say one thing for—'

'Just a stone?' snarled Ferro, her eyes swivelling from the fallen chunks of rock to Bayaz' face. 'You fucking old liar!' She sprang up, fists clenched tight by her sides. 'You promised me vengeance!'

Bayaz rounded on her, his face twisted with rage. 'You think I have no greater worries than your *vengeance*?' he roared, flecks of spit flying from his lips and out into the rushing gale. 'Or your *disappointment*?' he screamed in Quai's face, veins bulging in his neck. 'Or your fucking *looks*?' Jezal swallowed and faded back into the hollow, trying to seem as small as he possibly could, his own anger extinguished by Bayaz' towering rage as sharply as the meagre fire had been by the blasting wind a moment before. 'Tricked!' snarled the First of the Magi, his hands opening and closing with aimless fury. 'With what now will I fight Khalul?'

Jezal winced and cowered, sure at any moment that one of the party would be ripped apart, or be flung through the air and dashed on the rocks, or would burst into brilliant flames, quite possibly him. Brother Longfoot chose a poor moment to try and calm matters. 'We should not be downhearted, my comrades! The journey is its own reward—'

'Say that once more, you shaven dolt!' hissed Bayaz. 'Only once more, and I'll make ashes of you!' The Navigator shrank trembling away, and the Magus snatched up his staff and stalked off, down from the hollow towards the beach, his coat flailing around him in the bitter wind. So terrible had his fury been that, for a brief moment, the idea of staying on the island seemed preferable to getting back into a boat with him.

It was with that ill-tempered outburst, Jezal supposed, that their quest was declared an utter failure.

'Well then,' murmured Logen, after they had all sat in the wind for a while longer. 'I reckon that's it.' He snapped the lid of the Maker's empty box shut. 'No point crying about it. You have to be—'

'Shut your fucking mouth, fool!' snarled Ferro at him. 'Don't tell me what I have to be!' And she strode out of the hollow and down towards the hissing sea.

Logen winced as he pushed the box back into his pack, sighed as he swung it up onto his shoulder. 'Realistic,' he muttered, then set off after her. Longfoot and Quai came next, all sullen anger and silent disappointment. Jezal came up the rear, stepping from one jagged stone to another, eyes nearly shut against the wind, turning the whole business over in his mind. The mood might have been deathly sombre, but as he picked his way back towards the boat, he found to his surprise that he was almost unable to keep the smile from his face. After all, success or failure in this mad venture had never really meant anything to him. All that mattered was that he was on his way home.

*

The water slapped against the prow, throwing up cold white spray. The sailcloth bulged and snapped, the beams and the ropes creaked. The wind whipped at Ferro's face but she narrowed her eyes and ignored it. Bayaz had gone below decks in a fury and one by one the others had followed him out of the cold. Only she and Ninefingers stayed there, looking down at the sea.

'What will you do now?' he asked her.

'Go wherever I can kill the Gurkish.' She snapped it without thinking. 'I will find other weapons and fight them wherever I can.' She hardly even knew if it was true. It was hard to feel the hatred as she had done. It no longer seemed so important a matter if the Gurkish were left to their business, and she to hers, but her doubts and her disappointment only made her bark it the more fiercely. 'Nothing has changed. I still need vengeance.'

Silence.

She glanced sideways, and she saw Ninefingers frowning down at the pale foam on the dark water, as if her answer had not been the one he had been hoping for. It would have been easy to change it. 'I'll go where you go,' she could have said, and who would have been worse off? No one. Certainly not her. But Ferro did not have it in her to put herself in his power like that. Now it came to the test there was an invisible wall between them. One that there was no crossing.

There always had been.

All she could say was, 'You?' He seemed to think about it a while, angry-looking, chewing at his lip. 'I should go back to the North.' He said it unhappily, without even looking at her. 'There's work there I should never have left. Dark work, that needs doing. That's where I'll go, I reckon. Back to the North, and settle me some scores.'

She frowned. Scores? Who was it told her you had to have more than vengeance. Now scores was all he wanted? Lying bastard. 'Scores,' she hissed. 'Good.'

And the word was sour as sand on her tongue.

He looked her in the eye for a long moment. He opened his mouth, as if he was about to speak, and he stayed there, his lips formed into a word, one hand part-way lifted towards her.

Then he seemed suddenly to slump, and he set his jaw, and he turned his shoulder to her and leaned back on the rail. 'Good.'

And that easily it was all done between them.

Ferro scowled as she turned away. She curled up her fists and felt her nails digging into her palms, furious hard. She cursed to herself, and bitterly. Why could she not have said different words? Some breath, and a shape of the mouth, and everything is changed. It would have been easy.

Except that Ferro did not have it in her, and she knew she never would have. The Gurkish had killed that part of her, far away, and long ago, and left her dead inside. She had been a fool to hope, and in her bones she had known it all along.

Hope is for the weak.

Back to the Mud

Dogman and Dow, Tul and Grim, West and Pike. Six of them, stood in a circle and looking down at two piles of cold earth. Below in the valley, the Union were busy burying their own dead, Dogman had seen it. Hundreds of 'em, in pits for a dozen each. It was a bad day for men, all in all, and a good one for the ground. Always the way, after a battle. Only the ground wins.

Shivers and his Carls were just through the trees, heads bowed, burying their own. Twelve in the earth already, three more wounded bad enough they'd most likely follow before the week was out, and another that'd lost his hand – might live, might not, depending on his luck. Luck hadn't been good lately. Near half their number dead in one day's work. Brave of 'em to stick after that. Dogman could hear their words. Sad words and proud, for the fallen. How they'd been good men, how they'd fought well, how bad they'd be missed and all the rest. Always the way, after a battle. Words for the dead.

Dogman swallowed and looked back to the fresh turned dirt at his feet. Tough work digging, in the cold, ground frozen hard. Still, you're better off digging than getting buried, Logen would've said, and the Dogman reckoned that was right enough. Two people he'd just finished burying, and two parts of himself along with 'em. Cathil deep down under the piled-up dirt, stretched out white and cold and would never be warm again. Threetrees not far from her, his broken shield across his knees and his sword in his fist. Two sets of hopes Dogman had put in the mud – some hopes for the future, and some hopes from the past. All done now, and would never come to nothing, and they left an aching hole in him. Always the way, after a battle. Hopes in the mud.

'Buried where they died,' said Tul softly. 'That's fitting. That's good.'

'Good?' barked Dow, glaring over at West. 'Good, is it? Safest place in the whole battle? Safest place, did you tell 'em?' West swallowed and looked down, guilty seeming.

'Alright, Dow,' said Tul. 'You know better than to blame him for this, or anyone else. It's a battle. Folk die. Threetrees knew that well enough, none better.'

438

'We could've been somewhere else,' growled Dow.

'We could've been,' said Dogman, 'but we weren't, and there it is. No changing it, is there? Threetrees is dead, and the girl's dead, and that's hard enough for everyone. Don't need you adding to the burden.'

Dow's fists bunched up and he took a deep breath in like he was about to shout something. Then he let it out, and his shoulders sagged, and his head fell. 'You're right. Nothing to be done, now.'

Dogman reached out and touched Pike on his arm. 'You want to say something for her?' The burned man looked at him, then shook his head. He wasn't much for speaking, the Dogman reckoned, and he hardly blamed him. Didn't look like West was about to say nothing either, so Dogman cleared his throat, wincing at the pain across his ribs, and tried it himself. Someone had to.

'This girl we buried here, Cathil was her name. Can't say I knew her too long, or nothing, but what I knew I liked . . . for what that's worth. Not much I reckon. Not much. But she had some bones to her, I guess we all saw that on the way north. Took the cold and the hunger and the rest and never grumbled. Wish I'd known her better. Hoped to, but, well, don't often get what you hope for. She weren't one of us, really, but she died with us, so I reckon we're proud to have her in the ground with ours.'

'Aye,' said Dow. 'Proud to have her.'

'That's right,' said Tul. 'Ground takes everyone the same.'

Dogman nodded, took a long ragged breath and blew it out. 'Anyone want to speak for Threetrees?'

Dow flinched and looked down at his boots, shifting 'em in the dirt. Tul blinked up at the sky, looking like he had a bit of damp in his eye. Dogman himself was only a stride away from weeping as it was. If he had to speak another word he knew he'd set to bawling like a child. Threetrees would have known what to say, but there was the trouble, he was gone. Seemed like no one had any words. Then Grim took a step forward.

'Rudd Threetrees,' he said, looking round at 'em one by one. 'Rock of Uffrith, they called him. No bigger name in all the North. Great fighter. Great leader. Great friend. Lifetime o' battles. Stood face to face with the Bloody-Nine, then shoulder to shoulder with him. Never took an easy path, if he thought it was the wrong one. Never stepped back from a fight, if he thought it had to be done. I stood with him, walked with him, fought with him, ten years, all over the North.' His face broke out in a smile. 'I've no complaints.'

'Good words, Grim,' said Dow, looking down at the cold earth. 'Good words.'

'There'll be no more like Threetrees,' muttered Tul, wiping his eye like he'd got something in it.

'Aye,' said the Dogman. That was all he could manage.

West turned and trudged off through the trees, his shoulders hunched up, not a word said. Dogman could see the muscles clenching in the side of his head. Blaming himself, most likely. Men liked to do that a lot when folk died, in the Dogman's experience, and West seemed the type for it. Pike followed him, and the two of them passed Shivers, coming up the other way.

He stopped beside the graves, frowning down, hair hanging round his face, then he looked up at them. 'Don't mean no disrespect. None at all. But we need a new chief.'

'The earth's only just turned on him,' hissed Dow, giving him the eye.

Shivers held up his hands. 'Best time to discuss it, then, I reckon. So there's no confusion. My boys are jumpy, being honest. They've lost friends, and they've lost Threetrees, and they need someone to look to, that's a fact. Who's it going to be?'

Dogman rubbed his face. He hadn't even thought about it yet, and now that he did he didn't know what to think. Tul Duru Thunderhead and Black Dow were two big, hard names, both led men before, and well. Dogman looked at them, standing there, frowning at each other. 'I don't care which o' you it is,' he said. 'I'll follow either one. But it's clear as clear, it has to be one of you two.'

Tul glared down at Dow, and Dow glowered back up at him. 'I can't follow him,' rumbled Tul, 'and he won't follow me.'

'That's a fact,' hissed Dow. 'We talked it out already. Never work.'

Tul shook his head. 'That's why it can't be either one of us.'

'No,' said Dow. 'It can't be one of us.' He sucked at his teeth, snorted some snot into his face and spat it out onto the dirt. 'That's why it has to be you, Dogman.'

'That's why what now?' said Dogman, his eyes wide open and staring.

Tul nodded. 'You're the chief. We've all agreed it.'

'Uh,' said Grim, not even looking up.

'Ninefingers gone,' said Dow, 'and Threetrees gone, and that leaves you.'

Dogman winced. He was waiting for Shivers to say, 'You what? Him? Chief?' He was waiting for them all to start laughing, and tell him it was a joke. Black Dow, and Tul Duru Thunderhead, and Harding Grim, not to mention two dozen Carls besides, all taking his say-so. Stupidest idea he ever heard. But Shivers didn't laugh.

'That's a good choice, I reckon. Speaking for my lads, that's what I was going to suggest. I'll let 'em know.' And he turned and made off through the trees, with the Dogman gawping after him.

'But what about them others?' he hissed once Shivers was well out of hearing, wincing at a stab of pain in his ribs. 'There's twenty fucking Carls down there, and jumpy! They need a name to follow!'

'You got the name,' said Tul. 'You came across the mountains with Ninefingers, fought all those years with Bethod. There ain't no bigger names than yours left standing. You seen more battles than any of us.'

440

'Seen 'em, maybe—'

'You're the one,' said Dow, 'and that's all. So you ain't the hardest killer since Skarling, so what? Your hands are bloody enough for me to follow, and there's no better scout alive. You know how to lead. You've seen the best at it. Ninefingers, and Bethod, and Threetrees, you've watched 'em all, close as can be.'

'But I can't . . . I mean . . . I couldn't make no one charge, not the way Threetrees did—'

'No one could,' said Tul, nodding down at the earth. 'But Threetrees ain't an option no more, sorry to say. You're the chief, now, and we'll stand behind you. Any man don't care to do as you tell 'em can speak to us.'

'And that'll be one short-arsed conversation,' growled Dow.

'You're the chief.' Tul turned and strode off through the trees.

'It's decided.' And Black Dow followed him.

'Uh,' said Grim, shrugging his shoulders and making off with the other two.

'But,' muttered the Dogman. 'Hold on . . .'

They'd gone. So he guessed that made him chief.

He stood there for a moment, blinking, not knowing what to think. He was never leader before. He didn't feel no different. He didn't have any ideas, all of a sudden. No notions of what to tell men to do. He felt like an idiot. Even more of one than usual.

He knelt down, between the graves, and he stuck his hand in the soil, and he felt it cold and wet around his fingers. 'Sorry, girl,' he muttered. 'Didn't deserve this.' He gripped the ground tight, and he squeezed it in his palm. 'Fare you well, Threetrees. I'll try and do what you'd have done. Back to the mud, old man.'

And he stood up, and he wiped his hand on his shirt, and he walked away, back to the living, and left the two of them behind him in the earth.

Acknowledgments

Four people without whom . . .

Bren Abercrombie, whose eyes are
sore from reading it

Nick Abercrombie, whose ears are
sore from hearing about it

Rob Abercrombie, whose fingers are
sore from turning the pages

Lou Abercrombie, whose arms are
sore from holding me up

Also . . .

Jon Weir, for putting the word out

Simon Spanton, for not
putting the boot in

And who could forget . . .

Gillian Redfearn, who not only
made it happen, but made it better